Pushing Boundaries

THE COLLECTION

LAUREN LANDISH

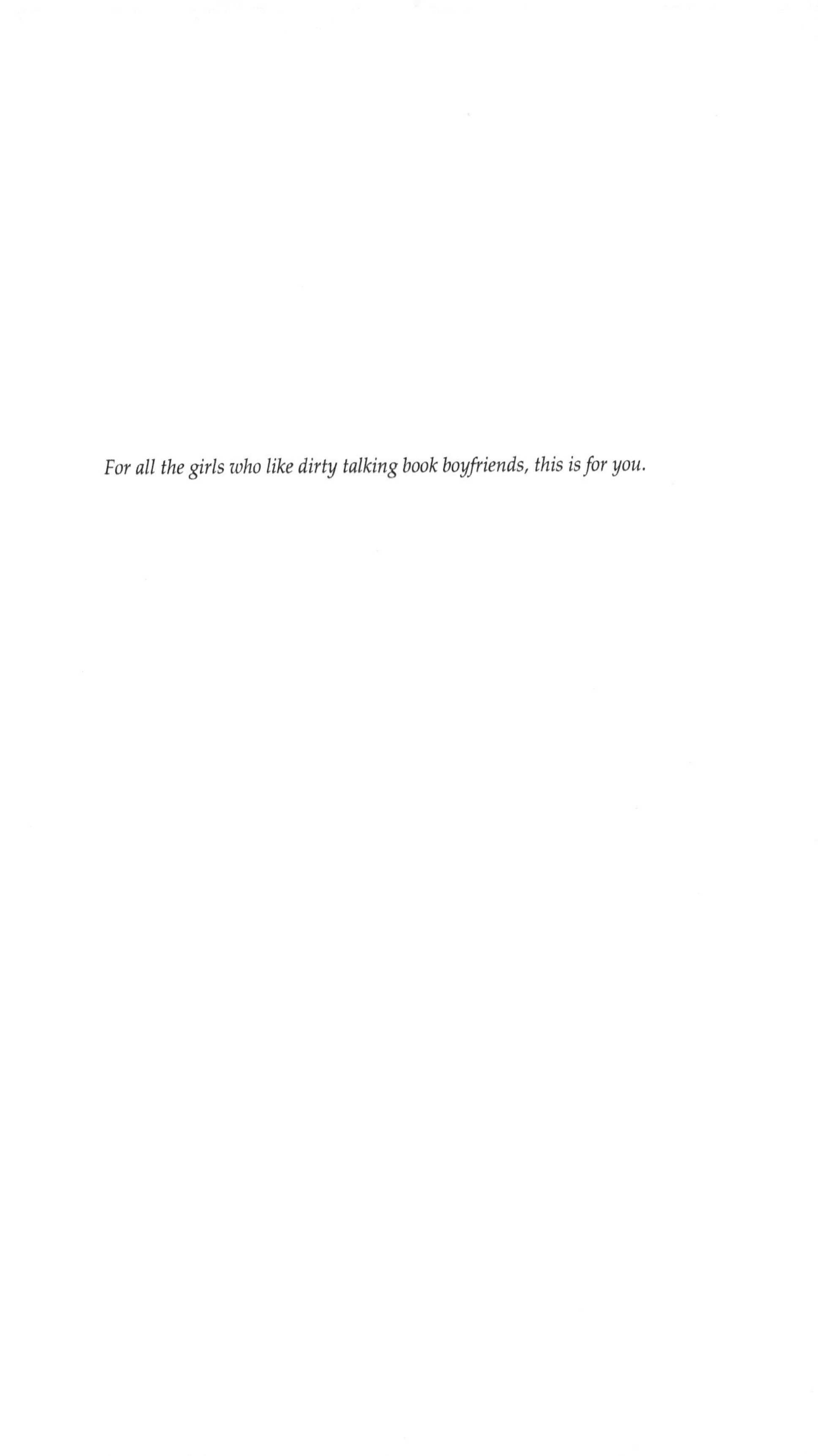

For all the girls who like dirty talking book boyfriends, this is for you.

Also by Lauren Landish

Truth or Dare Series:
The Dare | | The Truth

Big Fat Fake Series:
My Big Fat Fake Wedding | | My Big Fat Fake Engagement | | My Big Fat Fake Honeymoon

Standalones:
One Day Fiance | | Drop Dead Gorgeous | | The Blind Date

Bennett Boys Ranch:
Buck Wild | | Riding Hard | | Racing Hearts

The Tannen Boys:
Rough Love | | Rough Edge | | Rough Country

Dirty Fairy Tales:
Beauty and the Billionaire | | Not So Prince Charming | | Happily Never After

Dirty Talk

CHAPTER

One

KATRINA

"CHECKMATE, BITCH," I exclaim as I do a victory dance that's comprised of fist pumps and ass wiggles in my chair while my best friend Elise laughs at me. I turn in my seat and start doing a little half-stepping Rockettes dance. "Can-can, I just kicked some can-can, I so am the wo-man, and I rule this place!"

Elise does a little finger dance herself, cheering along with me.

"You go, girl. Winner, winner, chicken dinner. Now let's eat!"

I laugh with her, joyful in celebrating my new promotion at work, regardless of the dirty looks the snooty ladies at the next table are shooting our way.

I get their looks. I mean, we are in the best restaurant in the city. While East Robinsville isn't New York or Miami, we're more of a Northeastern suburb of . . . well, everything in between. This just isn't the sort of restaurant where five-foot-two-inch women in work clothes go shaking their ass while chanting something akin to a high school cheer.

But right now, I give exactly zero fucks.

"Damn right, we can eat! I'm the youngest person in the company to ever be promoted to Senior Developer and the first woman at that level. Glass ceiling? Boom, busting through! Boys' club? Infiltrated."

I mime like I'm sneaking in, shoulders hunched and hands pressed tightly in front of me before splaying my arms wide with a huge grin.

"Before they know it, I'm gonna have that boys' club watching chick flicks and the whole damn office is going to be painted pink!"

Elise snorts, shaking her head again. "I still don't have a fucking clue what you actually do, but even I understand the words *promotion* and *raise*. So huge congrats, honey."

She's right, no one really understands when I talk about my job. My brain has a tendency to talk in streams of binary zeroes and ones that make perfect sense to me, but not so much to the average person. When I was in high school, I even dreamed in Java.

And even I don't really understand what my promotion means. Senior Developer? Other than the fact that I get updated business cards with my fancy new title next week, I'm not sure what's changed. I'm still doing my own coding and my own work, just with a slightly higher pay grade. And when I say slightly, I mean barely a bump after taxes. Just enough for a bonus cocktail at a swanky club on Friday maybe. *Maybe* more at year end, they'd said. Ah, well, I'm excited anyway. It's a first step and an acknowledgement of my work.

The part people do get is when my company turns my strings of code into apps that go viral. After my last app went number one, they were forced to give me a promotion or risk losing my skills to another development company. They might not understand the zeroes and ones, but everyone can grasp dollars and cents, and that's what my apps bring in.

I might be young at only twenty-six, and female, as evidenced by my long honey-blonde hair and curvy figure, but as much as I don't fit the stereotypical profile of a computer nerd, they had to respect that my brain creates things that no one else does.

I think it's my female point of view that really helps. While a chunk of the other people in the programming field fit the stereotype of being slightly repressed geeks who are more comfortable watching animated 'girlfriends' than talking to an actual woman, I'm different. I understand that merely slapping a pink font on things or adding sparkly shit and giving more pre-loaded shopping options doesn't make technology more 'female-friendly.'

It's insulting, honestly. But it gives me an edge in that I know how to actually create apps that women like and want to use. Not just women, either, based on sales. I'm getting a lot of men downloading my apps too, especially men who aren't into tech-geeking out every damn thing they own.

And so I celebrate with Elise, holding up our glasses of wine and clinking them together in a toast. Elise sips her wine and nods in appreciation, making me glad we went with the waiter's recommendation.

"So you're killing it on the job front. What else is going on? How are things with you and Kevin?"

Elise has been my best friend since we met at a college recruiting event. She's all knockout looks and sass, and I'm short, nervous, and shy in professional situations, but we clicked. She knows I've been through the wringer with some previous boyfriends, and even though Kevin is fine—well-mannered, ambitious, and treats me right—she just doesn't care for him for some reason. So my joyful buzz is instantly dulled, knowing that she doesn't like Kevin.

"He's fine," I reply, knowing it's not a great answer, but I also know she's going to roast me anyway. "He's been working a lot of hours so I haven't even seen him in a few days, but he texts me every morning and night. We're supposed to go out for dinner this weekend to celebrate."

Elise sighs, giving me that look that makes her normally very cute face look sort of like a sarcastic basset hound.

"I'm glad, I guess. Not to beat a dead horse," —*too late*— "but you really can do better. Kevin is just so . . . meh. There's no spark, no fire between you two. It's like you're friends who fuck."

I duck my chin, not wanting her to read on my face the woeful lack of fucking that has been happening, but I'm too transparent.

"Wait . . . you two *do* fuck, right?" Elise asks, flabbergasted. "I figured that was why you were staying with him. I was sure he must be great in the sack or you'd have dumped his boring ass a long time ago."

I bite my lip, not wanting to get into this with her . . . again. But one of Elise's greatest strengths is also one of her most annoying traits as well. She's like a dog with a bone and isn't going to let this go.

"Look, he's fine," I finally reply, trying to figure out how much I need to feed Elise before she gives me a measure of peace. "He's handsome, treats me well, and when we have sex, it's good . . . I guess. I don't believe in some Prince Charming who is going to sweep me off my feet to a castle where we'll have romantic candlelit dinners, brilliant conversation, and bed-breaking sexcapades. I just want someone to share the good and bad times with, some companionship."

Elise holds back as long as she can before she explodes, her snort and guffaw of derision getting even more looks in our direction.

"Then get a fucking Golden Retriever and a rabbit. The buzzing kind that uses rechargeable batteries."

One of the ladies at the next table huffs, seemingly aghast at Elise's outburst, and they stand to move toward the bar on the other side of the restaurant, far away from us.

"Well, if this is the sort of trash that passes for dinner conversation," the older one says as she sticks her nose far enough into the air I wonder if it's going to be clipped by the ceiling fans, "no wonder the country's going to hell under these Millennials!"

She storms off before Elise or I can respond, but the second lady pauses slightly and talks out of the side of her mouth. "Sweetie, you do deserve more than *fine*."

With a wink, she scurries off after her friend, leaving behind a grinning Elise. "See? Even snooty old biddies know that you deserve more than *meh*."

"I know. We've had this conversation on more than one occasion, so can we drop it?" I plead between clenched teeth before calming slightly. "I want to celebrate and catch up, not argue about my love life."

Always needing the last word, Elise drops her voice, muttering under her breath. "What love life?"

"That's low."

Elise holds her hands up, and I know I've at least gotten a temporary reprieve. "Okay then, if we're sticking to work, I got a new scoop that I'm running with. I'm writing a piece about a certain famous someone who got caught sending dick pics to a social media princess. Don't ask me who because I can't divulge that yet. But it'll be all there in black and white by next week's column."

Elise is an investigative journalist, a rather fantastic one whose talents are largely being wasted on celebrity news gossip for the tabloid paper she writes for. I can't even call it a paper, really. With the downfall of actual print news, most of her stuff ends up in cyberspace, where it's digested, Tweeted, hashtagged, and churned out for the two-minute attention span types to gloat over for a moment before they move on to . . . well, whatever the next sound bite happens to be.

Every once in awhile, she'll get to do something much more newsworthy, but mostly it's fact-checking and ass-covering before the paper publishes stories celebrities would rather see disappear. I know what burns her ass even more is when she has to cover the stories where some downward-trending celebrity manufactures a scandal just to get some social media buzz going before their latest attempt at rejuvenating a career that peaked about five years ago.

This one at least sounds halfway interesting, and frankly, better than my love life, so I laugh. "Why would he send a dick pic to someone on social media? Wouldn't he assume she'd post it? What a dumbass!"

"No, it's usually close-ups and they're posted anonymously," Elise says with a snort. "Of course, she knows because she sees the user name on their direct message, but she cuts it out so that it's posted to her page as an anonymous flash of flesh. Look."

She pulls out her phone, clicking around to open an app, one I didn't design but damn sure wish I had. It's got one hell of a sweet interface, and Elise is using it to organize her web pages better than anything the normal apps have. It takes Elise only a moment to find the page she wants.

"See?" she says, showing me her phone. "People send her messages with dick pics, tit pics, whatever. If she deems them sexy enough, she posts them with little blurbs and people can comment. She also does Q-and-As with followers, shows faceless pics of herself, and gives little shows sometimes. Kinda like porn but more 'real people' instead of silicone-stuffed, pump-sucked, fake moan scenes."

She scrolls through, showing me one image after another of body part close-ups. Some of them . . . well damn, I gotta say that while they might not be professionals or anything, it's a hell of a lot hotter than anything I'm getting right now.

"Wow. That's uhh . . . quite something. I don't get it, but I guess lots of folks are into it. Wait."

She stops scrolling at my near-shout, smirking. "What? See something you like?"

My mouth feels dry and my voice papery. "Go back up a couple."

She scrolls back up and I read the blurb above a collage of pics. *Little titty fuck with my new boy toy today. Look at my hungry tits and his thick cock. After this, things got a little deeper, if you know what I mean. Sorry, no pics of that, but I'll just say that he was insatiable and I definitely had a very good morning. ;)*

The pictures show a close-up of her full cleavage, a guy's dick from above, and then a few pictures of him stroking in and out of her pressed-together breasts. I'm not afraid to say the girl's got a nice rack that would probably have most of my co-workers drooling and the blood rushing from their brains to their dicks, but that's not what's causing my stomach to drop through the floor.

I know that dick.

It's the same, thick with a little curve to the right, and I can even see a sort of donut-shaped mole high on the man's thigh, right above the shaved area above the base of his cock.

Yes, that mole seals it.

That's Kevin.

His cock with another woman, fucking her for social media, thinking I'd probably never even know. He has barely touched me lately, but he's willing to do it almost publicly with some social media slut?

I realize Elise is staring at me, her previous good-natured look long gone to be replaced by an expression of concern. "Kat, are you okay? You look pale."

I point at her phone, trying my best to keep my voice level. "That post? The one right there?"

"Oh, Titty Fuck Girl?" Elise asks. "She's on here at least once a month with a new set of pics. Apparently, she loves her rack. I still think they're fake. Why?"

"She's talking about Kevin. That's him."

She gasps, turning the phone to look closer. "Holy shit, honey. Are you sure?"

I nod, tears already pooling in my eyes. "I'm sure."

She puts her phone down on the table and comes around the table to hug me. "Shit. Shit. Shit. I am so sorry. I told you that douchebag doesn't deserve someone like you. You're too fucking good for him."

I sniffle, nodding, but deep inside, I know that this is always how it goes. Every single boyfriend I've ever had ended up cheating on me. I've tried playing hard to get. I've tried being the good little go-along girlfriend. I've even tried being myself, which seems to be somewhere in between, once I figured out who I actually was.

It's even worse in bed, where I've tried being vanilla, being aggressive, and being submissive. And again, being myself, somewhere in the middle, when I figured out what I enjoyed from the experimentation.

But honestly, I've never been satisfied. No matter what, I just can't seem to find that 'sweet spot' that makes me happy and fulfilled in a relationship. And while I've tried everything, depending on the guy, it never works out. The boyfriends I've had, while few in number considering I can count them on one hand, all eventually cheated, saying that they just wanted something different. Something that's *not* me.

Apparently, Kevin's no different. My mood shifts wildly from self-pity to anger to finally, a numb acceptance.

"What a fucking jerk. I hope he likes being a boy toy for a social media slut, because he's damn sure not my boyfriend anymore."

"That's the spirit," Elise says, refilling my wine glass. "Now, how about you and I finish off this bottle, get another, and by the time you're done, you'll have forgotten all about that loser while we take a cab back to your place?"

"Maybe I will just get a dog, and I sure as hell already have a buzzing rabbit. Several of them, in fact," I mutter. "You know what? They're better than he ever was by a damn country mile."

"Rabbits . . . they just keep going and going and going," Elise jokes, trying to keep me in good spirits. She twirls her hands in the air like the famous commercial bunny and signals for another bottle of wine.

She's right. Fuck Kevin.

CHAPTER

Two

DERRICK

MY BLACK LEATHER office chair creaks, an annoying little trend it's developed over the past six months that's the primary reason I don't use it in the studio. Admittedly, that's probably for the better because if I had a chair this comfortable in the studio, I'd be too relaxed to really be on point for my shows.

Still, it's helpful to have something nice like this office since it's a hell of a big step up from the days when my office was also the station's break room.

"All right, hit me. What's on the agenda for today's show?"

My co-star, Susannah, checks her papers, making little checkmarks as she goes through each item.

She's an incessant checkmarker, and I have no idea how the fuck she can read her sheets by the end of the day.

"The overall theme for today is cheaters, and I've got several emails pulled for that so we can stay on track. We'll field calls, of course, and some will be on topic and some off, like always. I'll try and screen them as best I can, and we should be all set."

I nod, trying to mentally prep myself for another three-hour stint behind the mic, offering music, advice, hope, and sometimes a swift kick in the pants to our listeners. Two years ago, I never would've believed that I'd be known as the 'Love Whisperer' on a radio talk segment called the same thing. Part Howard Stern, part Dr. Phil, part DJ Love Below, I've found a niche that's just . . . unique.

I started out many years ago as a jock, playing football on my high school team with dreams of college ball. A seemingly short derailment after an injury led me to do sports reporting for my high school's news and I fell in love.

After that, my scholarships to play football never came, but it didn't bother me as much as I thought it would. I decided to chase after a sports broadcast degree instead, marrying my passion for football and my love of reporting.

I spent four years after graduation doing daily sports talks from three to six as the afternoon drive-home DJ. It wasn't a big station, just one of the half-dozen stations that existed as an alternative for people who didn't want to listen to corporate pop, hip-hop, or country. It was there I received that fateful call.

Looking back, it's kind of crazy, but a guy had called in bitching and moaning about his wife not understanding his need to follow all these wild superstitions to help his team win.

"I'm telling you D, I went to church and asked God himself. I said, if you can bless the Bandits with a win, I'll show myself true and wear those ugly ass socks my pastor gave me for Christmas the year before and never wash them again. You know what happened?"

Of course, everyone could figure out what happened. Still, I respectfully told him that I didn't think his unwashed socks were doing a damn thing for his beloved team on the basketball court, but if he didn't put those fuckers in the washing machine, they were sure going to land him in divorce court.

He sighed and eventually gave in when I told him to wash the socks, thank his wife for putting up with his shit, and full-out romance her to bed and do his damndest to make up for his selfish ways.

And that was that. A new show and a new me were born. After a few marketing tweaks, I've been the so-called 'Love Whisperer' for almost a year now, helping people who ask for advice to get the happily ever after they want.

Ironically, I'm single. Funny how that works out, but all the good advice I try to give stems from my parents who were happily married for over forty years before my mom passed. I won't settle for less than the real thing, and I try to advise my listeners to do the same.

And then there's the sex aspect of my job.

Talking about relationships obviously involves discussing sex with people, as that's one of the major areas that cause problems for folks. At first, talking about all the crazy shit people want to do even made me blush a little, but eventually, it's just gotten to be second nature.

Want to talk about how to get your wife to massage your prostate? Can do. Want to talk about how your girlfriend wants you to wear Underoos and call her Mommy? Can do. Want to talk about your husband never washing the dishes, and how you can get him to help? I can do that too.

All-in-one, real relationships at your service. Live from six to nine, five days a week, or available for download on various podcast sites and clip shows on the weekends. Hell of a lot for a guy who figured *making it* would involve becoming the voice of some college football team.

So I want to do a good job. And that means working well with Susannah, who is the control-freak yin to my laissez-faire yang.

"Thanks. I know this week's topics from our show planning meeting, but I spaced on tonight's focus."

Susannah nods, unflappable. "No problem. Do you want to scan the emails or just do your thing?"

I smile at her. She already knows the answer. "Same as always, spontaneous. You know that even though I was a Boy Scout, being prepared for this doesn't do us any favors. I sound robotic when I read ahead. First read, real reactions work better and give the listeners knee-jerk common sense."

She shrugs, scribbling on her papers. "I know, just checking."

It's probably one of the reasons we work so well together, our totally different approaches to the show. Joining me from day one, she's the one who keeps our show running behind the scenes and keeps me on track on-air, serving as both producer and co-host. Luckily, her almost anal-retentive penchant for prep totally doesn't come across on the air, where she's the playful, comedic counter to my gruff, tell-it-like-it-is style.

"Then let's rock," I tell her. "Got your drinks ready?"

Susannah nods as we head toward the studio. Settling into my broadcast chair, a much less comfortable but totally silent one, I survey my normal spread of one water, one coffee, and one green tea, one for every hour we're gonna be on the air. With the top of the hour news breaks and spaced out music jams, I've gotten used to using the exactly four minute and thirty second breaks to run next door and drain my bladder if I need to.

Everything ready, we smile and settle in for another show. "Gooooood evening! It's your favorite 'Love Whisperer,' Derrick King here with my lovely assistant, Miss Susannah Jameson. We're ready for an evening of love, sex, betrayal, and lust, if you're willing to share. Our focus tonight is on cheaters and cheating. Are you being cheated on? Maybe *you* are the cheater? Call in and we'll talk."

The red glow from the holding calls is instant, but I traditionally go to an email first so that I can roll right in.

"While Susannah is grabbing our first caller, I'll start with an email. Here's one from P. 'Dear Love Whisperer,' it says, 'my husband travels extensively for work, leaving me home and so lonely. I don't know if he's cheating while he's gone, but I always wonder. I've started to develop feelings for my personal trainer, and I think I'm falling in love with him. What should I do?' "

I *tsk-tsk* into the microphone, making my displeasure clear. "Well, P, first things first. Your marriage is your priority because you made a vow. For better or worse, remember? It's simple. Talk to your husband. Maybe he's cheating, maybe he isn't. Maybe he's working his ass off so his bored wife can even *have* a trainer and you're looking for excuses to justify your own bad behavior. But talking to him is your first step. You need to explain your feelings and that you need him more than perhaps you need the money. Second, you need to get a life beyond your husband and trainer. I get the sense you need some attention and your trainer is giving it to you, so you think you're in love with him. Newsflash—he's being paid to give you attention. By your husband, it sounds like. That's not a healthy foundation for a relationship even if he is your soulmate, which I doubt."

I sigh and lower my voice a little. I don't want to cut this woman's guts out. I want to help her. "P, let's be honest. A good trainer is going to be personable. They're in a sales profession. They're not going to make it in the industry without either being the best in the world at what they do or having a good personality. And a lot of them have good bodies. Their bodies are their business cards. So it's natural to feel some attraction to your trainer. But that doesn't mean he's going to stick by you. Here's a challenge—tell your trainer you can't pay him for the next three months and see how available he is to just give you his time."

Susannah snickers and hits her mic button. "That's why I do group yoga classes. Only thing that happens there is sweaty tantric orgies. Ohmm . . . my . . ." Her initial yoga-esque ohm dissolves into a pleasure-induced moan that she fakes exceedingly well.

I roll my eyes, knowing that she does nothing of the sort. "To the point, though, fire your trainer because of your weakness and tell him why. He's a pro. He needs to know that his services were not the reason you're leaving. Next, get a hobby that fulfills you beyond a man and talk to your husband."

I click a button and a sound effect of a cheering audience plays through my headset. It goes on like this for a while, call after call, email after email of helping people.

Well, I hope I'm helping them. They seem to think I am, and I'm certainly giving it my best shot. In between, I mix in music and a hodgepodge of stuff that fits the daily themes. Tonight I've got some Taylor Swift, a little Carrie Underwood, some old-school TLC. I even, as a joke, worked in Bobby Brown at Susannah's insistence.

Coming back from that last one, I see Susannah gesture from her mini-booth and give the airspace over to her, letting her introduce the next caller.

"Okay, Susannah's giving me the big foam finger, so what've we got?"

"You wish I had a big finger for you," Susannah teases like she always does on air—it's part of our act. "The next caller would like to discuss some rather incriminating photos she's come across. Apparently, Mr. Right was Mr. Everybody?"

I click the button, taking the call live on-air. "This is the 'Love Whisperer', who am I speaking with?"

The caller stutters, obviously nervous, and in my mind I know I have to treat this one gently. Some of the callers just want to laugh, maybe have their fifteen seconds of fame or get their pound of proverbial flesh by exposing their partner's misdeeds. But there are also callers like this, who I suspect really needs help.

"This is Katrina . . . Kat."

Whoa, a first name. And from the sound of it, a real one. She's not making a thing up. I need to lighten the mood a little, or else she's gonna clam up and freak out on me.

"Hello, Kitty Kat. What seems to be the problem today?"

I hear her sigh, and it touches me for some reason. "Well . . . I can't believe I actually got through, first of all. I worked up the nerve to dial the numbers but didn't expect an answer. I'm just . . . I don't even know what I am. I'm just a little lost and in need of some advice, I guess." She huffs out a humorless laugh.

I can hear the pain in her voice, mixed with nerves. "Advice? That I can do. That's what I'm here for, in fact. What's going on, Kat?"

"It's my boyfriend, or my soon-to-be ex-boyfriend, I guess. I found out today that he slept with someone else." She sounds like she's found a bit of steel as she speaks this time, and it makes her previous vulnerability all the more touching.

"Ouch," I say, truly wincing at the fresh wound. A day of cheat call? I'm sure the advertisers are rubbing their hands in glee, but I'm feeling for this girl. "I'm so sorry. I know that hurts and it's wrong no matter what. I heard something about compromising pics. Please tell me he didn't send you pics of him screwing someone else?"

She laughs but it's not in humor. "No, I guess that would've been worse, but he had sex with someone kind of Internet famous and she posted face-less pics of them together. But I recognized his . . . uhm . . . his . . ."

Let's just get the schlong out in the open, why don't we? "You recognized his penis? Is that the word you're looking for?"

"Yeah, I guess so," Kat says, her voice cutting through the gap created by the phone line. "He has a mole, so I know it's him."

There's something about her voice, all sweet and breathy that stirs me inside like I rarely have happen. It's not just her tone, either. She's in pain, but she's mad as fuck too, and I want to help her, protect her. She seems innocent, and something deep inside me wants to make her a little bit dirty.

"Okay, first, repeat after me. Penis, dick, cock." I wait, unsure if she'll do it but holding my breath in the hopes that she will.

"Uh, what?"

I feel a small smile come to my lips, and it's my turn to be a little playful. "Penis, dick, cock. Trust me, this is important for you. You can do it, Kitty Kat."

I hear her intake of breath, but she does what I demanded, more clearly than the shyness I expected. "Penis, dick, cock."

"Good girl," I growl into the mic, and through the window connecting our booths, I can see Susannah giving me a raised eyebrow. "Now say . . . I recognized his cock fucking her."

I say a silent prayer of thanks that my radio show is on satellite. I can say whatever I want and the FCC doesn't care.

I can tell Kat is with me now, and her voice is stronger, still sexy as fuck but without the lost kitten loneliness to it.

"I recognized his cock fucking her tits."

My own cock twitches a little, and I lean in, smirking. "Ah, so the plot thickens. So Kat, how does it feel to say that?"

She sighs, pulling me back a little. "The words don't bother me. I'm just not used to being on the radio. But saying that about my boyfriend pisses me off. I can't believe he'd do that."

"So, what do you think you should do about it?" I ask, leaning back in my chair and pulling my mic toward me. "Is this a 'talk it through and our relationship will be stronger on the other side of this' type situation, or is this a 'hit the road, motherfucker, and take Miss Slippy-Grippy Tits with you?' Do you want my opinion or do you already know?"

"You're right," Kat says, chuckling and sounding stronger again. "I already know I'm done. He's been a wham-bam-doesn't even say thank you, ma'am guy all along, and I've been hanging on because I didn't think I deserved better. But I don't deserve this. I'm better off alone."

Whoa, now, only half right there, Kat with the sexy voice. "You don't deserve this. You should have someone who treats you so well you never question their love, their commitment to you. Everyone deserves that. Hey, Kitty Kat? One more thing. Can you say 'cock' for me one more time? Just for . . . entertainment."

I'm pushing the line here, both for her and for the show, but I ask her to do it anyway because I want, no need, to hear her say it.

She laughs, her voice lighter even as I know the serious conversation had to hurt. "Of course, Love Whisperer. Anything for you. You ready? Cock." She draws the word out, the k a bit harsher, and I can hear the sass, almost an invitation, as she speaks.

"Ooh, thanks so much, Kitty Kat. Hold on the line just a second." My cock is now fully hard in my pants, and I'm not sure if my upcoming bathroom break is going to be to piss or to take care of that.

I click some buttons, sending the show to a song, Shaggy's *It Wasn't Me* coming over the airwaves to keep the cheating theme rolling. "Susannah?"

"Yeah?"

"Handle the next call or so after the commercial break," I tell her. "Pick something . . . funny after that one."

"Gotcha," Susannah says, and I'm glad she's able to handle things like that. It's part of our system too that when I get a call that needs more than on-air can handle, she fills the gap. Usually with less serious questions or listener stories that always make for great laughs.

Checking my board, I click the line back, glad that Susannah can't hear me now. "Kat? You still there?"

"Yes?" she says, and I feel another little thrill go down my cock just at her word. God, this woman's got a sexy voice, soft and sweet with a little undercurrent of sassiness . . . or maybe I really, really need to get laid.

"Hey, it's Derrick. I just wanted to say thanks for being such a good sport with all of that."

"No problem," she says as I make a picture in my head of her. I can't fill in the details, but I definitely want to. "Thanks for helping me realize I need to walk away. I already knew it, but some inspiration never hurts."

"I really would like to hear the rest of the story if you don't mind calling me back. I want to hear how he grovels when he finds out what he's lost. Would you call me?"

I don't know what I'm doing. This is so not like me. I never talk to the callers after they're on air unless I think they're going to hurt themselves or others, and I certainly never invite them to call back. But something about her voice calls to me like a siren. I just hope she's not pulling me into the rocky shore to crash.

"You mean the show?" Kat asks, uncertain and confused. "Like . . . I dunno, like a guest or something?"

"Well, probably not, to be honest," I reply, crossing my fingers even as my cock says I need to take this risk. "We'll be done with the cheating theme tonight and it probably won't come back up for a couple of weeks. I meant . . . call me. I want to make sure you're okay afterward and standing strong."

"Okay."

Before she can take it back, I rattle off my personal cell number to her, half of my brain telling me this is brilliant and the other half saying it's the stupidest thing I've ever done. I might not have the FCC looking over my shoulder, but the satellite network is and my advertisers for damn sure are. Still . . .

"Got it?"

"I've got it," Kat says. "I'll get back to you after I break up with Kevin. It's been a weird night and I guess it's going to get even weirder. Guess I gotta go tell Kevin his dick busted him on the internet and he can get fucked elsewhere . . . permanently. I can do this."

"Damn right, you can," I tell her. "You can do this, Kitty Kat. Remember, you deserve better. I'll be waiting for your report."

Kat laughs and we hang up. I don't know what just happened but my body feels light, bubbly inside as I take a big breath to get ready for the next segment of tonight's show.

CHAPTER
Three

KAT

I KNOCK on the door to Kevin's apartment, the voice of Derrick the Love Whisperer still running around in my head. I deserve better than to be cheated on.

"Hey, babe," Kevin says when he opens his door. He's still wearing his 'work clothes,' a black tank top with *KH Nutrition* emblazoned on it along with track pants that are just a little tight and normally worn just a little low on his hips when he works out. I've never really understood why he does it, but it's part of his 'thang.' Every Instagram pic and video he does, he whips off the tank, adjusts his track pants in a way that highlights the Adonis belt V-cut of his abs, then flexes and sort of makes a hooting grunt before finishing the show with "KH, Bay-bay!"

I used to think it was sexy, in a musclehead, caveman-ish sort of way. No longer. "Don't 'hey, babe' me," I growl, looking up into his eyes. I'm not in work clothes, so I'm missing the extra inches of height my heels normally give me. But I'm a legit five-two of fury right now, so I don't care if he's nearly a foot taller. "How long have you been fucking her behind my back?"

"Huh?" Kevin asks, but in his eyes I can see he has a damn good idea what I'm talking about.

"Don't act stupid, you son of a bitch!" I hiss, poking him in the chest. "You know exactly what I'm talking about. Titty Fuck Girl. Where'd you meet her, the gym? When you went out shopping for a new smartphone with the money I gave you because you swore you needed the better camera for your Instagram page? How long has it been going on, Kevin?"

Kevin looks up and down the hallway. For a guy whose Internet presence makes him look like a big baller, he's living in a cracker box POS apartment building, and I know he's worried about his neighbors hearing me blab his private business.

"Come on inside. We can talk—"

"If you don't tell me how long it's been going on, I'm going to put my knee right in your nuts," I growl. "This isn't a negotiation, Kevin." It really doesn't matter at this point. It's most likely just going to make me angrier, but I can't stop myself.

He looks like he's about to run but sighs. "Fine. I met her a couple of months ago when she came into the gym. I was filming a squat."

"What? So she just walked up behind you to compliment your form and suddenly, you're in bed?" I laugh, realizing just how short I sold myself. He's fake—the tan, the persona, the entire image. Just to get more followers.

Kevin looks sheepish but nods. "She said she'd promote my supps, do some spots on her Instagram feed, and let me shoot some selfies with her wearing a KH tank top."

"So you titty fucked her?" I hiss, shaking my head. Seriously, what the fuck? I can hardly take it as I stare at his chiseled face, wanting so badly to slap him. "Do you realize how ridiculous you sound right now? How stupid do you think I am?"

Kevin looks pouty, the same look he used when he hit me up for four hundred bucks for his new smartphone.

"You never believe in me, never think I can be successful even though I work so hard."

It's in this moment that I see it. Though his face is schooled into a puppy dog look, his eyes are alight as he turns the blame back on me, thinking he's pulled one over on me once again. And all the fire leaves me. I'm mad he cheated, but I don't even really like him right now, and honestly, I haven't for a long time but was too afraid to do anything about it.

My voice takes a parental, lecturing tone. "You're not working. You're a lazy ass who spends hours at the gym bullshitting with the bros and thinking some scam is going to magically make you money without your having to actually do anything. But you know what? I looked the other way for too long even though everyone told me you were no good. None of that even matters now. You cheated on me. Done. Game over."

Kevin inhales, trying to stand at his tallest, most imposing. His forearms clench and his biceps start to strain as he puffs up. It strikes me that once upon a time, he'd stand over me like this and I'd find it so damn sexy I'd be instantly wet, but now, his attempt at intimidating me is just ridiculous.

"You'll be sorry. You'll never find someone who treats you like I do, who satisfies you like I do."

God, how could I have been so blind? "Like you do? You know, I hope you're right because you treat me like an afterthought, using me as an ATM when you're a little short, screwing around, and blaming me for your lack of success when it's your own fault," I reply, keeping my voice calm but firm, not letting him get an inch on me. I'm not going to raise my voice, to yell or let him think that he's gotten to me, because for some reason, honestly, he hasn't. "And as for satisfied in bed, I have literally never had a single orgasm with you. Ever. I'm not gonna lie, your dick is nice to look at and photographs well, apparently, but you don't even know what to do with it. Sticking it in and out for two minutes before blowing into a condom and then rolling over to gasp while staring at the ceiling doesn't quite cut it, Kev. So yeah, I hope I never find someone who treats me like you do. I thought I could settle for content, just float along and not rock the boat, but I deserve so much more."

Before Kevin can reply, I turn and walk toward the stairs, not wanting to lose my nerve in front of him. It's not until I'm halfway down that the shakes start as the adrenaline leaves me, but I keep it cool until I get to my car.

———

One Week Later

A week since the blow-up with Kevin and I'm surprisingly not upset. Disappointed, sure, but if you end a one-year relationship with someone, shouldn't you feel sad? I've felt a lot of other emotions, anger mostly, but they've faded too. Instead, I'm just left with this . . . I guess more than anything, lack of things to do. I've got more free time on my hands, but I'm not sad or upset.

I guess the lack of depression goes to show how far apart we'd drifted and how unattached I was from him without even realizing it.

Really, the most annoying part of this whole thing has been that I've had to change my gym membership because I didn't want drama or to limit myself to when I could or couldn't go based on his haunting the place.

Maybe I never really was in love with him. We'd met at the gym, and he'd been charming and admittedly hot, so when he asked me out, I said yes. Our dating just naturally progressed, and somewhere along the way, we started calling it a relationship, but who knows if he was ever really committed? I was faithful, but that was more out of habit and the fact that I would never cheat than any obvious commitment we had. It's not like he ever put a ring on it.

Even though it had been over a month since we'd been intimate, I'd gone to the doctor for a checkup just to be safe, and luckily, everything was clear. I can't believe he'd put me at risk, but I guess I should've seen it coming considering guys always cheat.

Taking the opportunity to do a purge on everything in my life, I've got the radio turned up and I'm cleaning my apartment like a mad woman when I hear the voice. *His* voice.

It's like velvet-covered gravel, and just a few words make me breathless and hot. "Good evening, listeners. Derrick King here, aka the 'Love Whisperer'. What's happening in your love life? Our focus tonight is on pushing boundaries in the bedroom. What's encouraging and fun? What's demanding and over the line? Call in if you've got something to discuss."

I've gone stock-still, my cleaning completely forgotten as his voice washes over me. I turn it up a little more as I finish sweeping, deciding everything else can wait as I listen.

Over the next few hours, Derrick is surprisingly simple in his answers to callers, who want to try a variety of things sexually but for whatever reason haven't discussed it with their partners. It's almost comical how every call gets into a groove, and it sort of goes like this:

I want to do this crazy thing.

Have you asked your partner?

No.

Talk to them. Maybe they're into it.

But I'm not sure they want to.

How could you know if you don't talk with them? If they are, great. If not, decide if it's a deal breaker and move forward according to your answer. Chances are it's not a deal-breaker if you're not doing it now.

It's funny and spiced up with plenty of little anecdotes and witticisms that leave me grinning, while his voice turns me on even as I'm comforted. I listen to his no-nonsense approach as he advocates conversation and honesty at every turn, and I only wish I had a man like that who'd actually talk and be honest with me.

As the show wraps up, I remember his request for me to call him back and tell him what happened with Kevin. He was probably just being nice and doesn't actually expect me to call, but something about it felt real.

I wait for a bit after the show ends to give him time to get out of the studio and wherever it is he goes after work, and then I call. I'm heading out anyway. I've got a late-night rumbling tummy that can only be satisfied by something cheesy and takeout.

The phone rings several times and I'm about to hang up, mad at myself for being stupidly excited about talking to *The Love Whisperer* again, when he answers.

"Talk to me."

It's the same purring growl. That panty-melting voice of his isn't an act.

"Hey, Love Whisperer. It's your Kitty Kat."

There's a throaty chuckle on the other end, but there's concern in it too, which helps me feel better. "*My* Kitty Kat now?" he asks, and I can hear the smile in his voice. "After a week went by, I wasn't sure if I was going to get that return call. I was starting to doubt whether I had an effect at all."

"You set me straight. Hold on. Let me put you on speaker. I've got this technogeek wonder phone that I love to use speaker on."

"Well, I'm in my office, so this isn't private . . . but tell me, how'd it go?"

I plug my phone into the charging dock in my dash and slip my Bluetooth earpiece in as I fire up my car. "First off, I can't believe I didn't listen to anyone."

Derrick

"I can't believe you're the type to settle for anyone," I reply, relaxing back in my office chair. It's late. Almost nobody is around the studio right now. It's one of the benefits of satellite radio, I guess. You can run a lot more shows pre-recorded. "So he fessed up?"

"He gave me the most ridiculous line of shit ever," Kat says, her breathy voice causing a stir in my pants. What the fuck is wrong with me? "He said that he did it because she was willing to pimp his line of supplements on her Instagram page."

"You're shitting me," I say, rolling my eyes. "What a stupid asshole."

"You're right there. Honestly, I waited a week to call because I wanted to get a clear head."

"I can understand that. So he fed you a line of bullshit, and you chucked his ass out on the street. That's what I wanted to hear."

"Not quite," Kat says. "I went to his apartment to give him the news. No waiting around."

"Good for you," I tell her. "So, that's it? I mean, I like it, but sounds a bit easy, don't you think?"

"Well, he did try to puff his chest out and tell me no man would ever treat me like he did or satisfy me like him. I took a little delight in telling him that I sure as hell hoped not since he's a cheater whom I had to fake it with because he'd never even made me . . . ." Kat says with spunkiness before stopping herself short. "Uhm, I mean—"

"Wait, seriously?" I ask in a sputtering laugh. "Is that true? You weren't just busting his balls? Damn, Kat . . . for how long?"

"It's okay," she says, seemingly comfortable talking to me. "My best friend told me to get a dog or a new rabbit. Or both. She's probably right."

"A rabbit?" I ask, my brain half-buzzed from her voice. Fuck me, I need to get laid.

"Well, um, not a bunny rabbit," she replies, her voice becoming even a little breathier. "You know . . . a rabbit."

She makes a buzzing sound, and all of a sudden, it hits me. She's making me seem like an amateur. I talk about sex for a living. I shouldn't be caught off guard like this. Trying to maintain at least a veneer of professionalism, I clear my throat.

"Yeah, I can see where that'd come in handy. Take matters into your own hands, so to speak. I've done that myself more than a few times."

What I just said sinks in for both of us, and the tension between us can be felt even over the phone lines. If I could see her right now, I'd swear we'd just crossed a line. And I'd probably see how far I could push to make a move.

Kat can feel it too. "So, uh, yeah, anyway. That was probably an over-share on my part. Sorry about that."

Fuck it. I don't know why I'm doing this, but I'm just gonna go for it. Her sweet voice is doing something magically delicious to me, something about her intriguing me in a way I haven't felt in a long while. Time to jump in the pool and see if she's willing to swim with me. I look around the studio, not seeing Susannah.

"Not an overshare at all. I'm just in the middle of picturing you with your new pet bunny, what you would look like spread wide open with your tits pearled up, pussy pulsing around a little toy that can't fill it, and what you'd sound like when you come."

I know my voice has gotten deeper, lust making it even rougher than my usual smooth radio sound, but I can't stop it. I adjust myself in my jeans, glad she can't see the effect she's having on me right now.

There's a slight hitch in her voice as she adjusts to what I just said. "Derrick, wow. I don't know what to say to that. Fuck."

She's all but whispering by the end of her sentence and I wonder if she's touching herself to let out some tension. I don't even know what she looks like, but I don't care. I want to see her just like I said, maybe in a little skirt that's hiked up so she can show me as I inhale her scent. "You don't have to say anything unless you want me to stop."

I pause, hoping she doesn't say stop because I damn sure don't want to. I barely know this woman, this voice coming through my phone, but she's got me rock hard and on the edge with barely a word. I reach down and undo the button on my jeans, giving myself at least a little room to breathe.

"I think I need to—"

I interrupt, hoping to give her what she wants and needing my own release as well. "What do you need, Kitty Kat? I'll give it to you."

Kat pauses, and I can feel her trembling on the edge before she lets out another deep breath, half moan, half sigh of regret.

"I think I need to go. I'm sorry. This is all new to me and I wasn't expecting this tonight. And . . . well, I'm driving. Gotta stay safe. Good night, Derrick."

Before I can say a single thing to stop her, she hangs up. *Damn it, Derrick! You pushed her too far, too fast.* I literally just did a show about listening, not going beyond your partner's limits, and I just blasted past Kat's, lost in my own desire.

My brain is yelling at me, disappointed that she hung up, but my cock is still at full attention, begging for release. I let the image of Kat take over my mind, not even knowing what she actually looks like, but imagining her pink pussy dripping as she rubs a vibrator across her clit.

I reach into my briefs, taking my cock out and grabbing it in one fist, then stroke up and down my shaft, giving me instant relief as I groan. To hell with it. As hot as I am, this will be fast, so the odds of anyone catching me are slim. And if they do, well, they're in for a sight because I can't stop.

I imagine Kat holding the vibe to herself as she slips two fingers into her pussy, thrusting them in and out in time to my own strokes, her eyes hooded with lust and watching my every breath.

In my head, I talk to her, telling her to fuck herself with her fingers. To show me how much she wishes it were my cock filling her tight pussy, how she wants to squeeze and milk me until I fill her up with so much cum that it spills out of her, too much for her little cunt to hold.

The combination of memories of her voice and my own mind filling the gaps and imagining dirty talking to Kat sends me over the edge. I explode, my come coating my hand as I jerk, getting every last shudder from the orgasm as I picture Kat screaming my name as she's lost in her own pleasure.

I glance around my office again, seeing the box of tissues on the corner of my desk. I grab a handful, glad there's something to help clean up this particular spill . . . and damn glad nobody's around to see the mess I've made.

CHAPTER

Four

KAT

"YO, KAT!"

"You already spent that new bonus check?"

I huff, wishing I got a bonus check, but I play along anyway. I give a wave to Harry and Larry, two of my co-workers. "You'll see when the pizzas come in at lunch!" I joke back.

Harry rubs his Monday shirt, a stretched and faded *Pizza The Hut* custom job he got off the Internet. "Just remember, no sausage!"

"That's not what I've heard," I tease, and Harry snorts. He claims to be a ladies-man love machine, but I have more than a sneaking suspicion that's all talk and some serious next-level self-aggrandizing. He's a good guy, though, and he doesn't take anything too seriously.

"Yeah, well, hope you've got another doozy cooked up," Larry says. "My latest game's gonna have me taking your shine soon enough."

I laugh and head to my cubicle. I've finally gotten it exactly the way I want, with triple screens that allow me to code, visualize, and debug all at the same time.

I immediately pull up my next project, an ambitious attempt at totally integrating calendars, social media, and office apps that could turn the whole damn system on its head.

I need to focus because the coding on this is going to be tricky. Integrating all these systems is easy. Doing it without turning someone's smartphone into a brick that works at the speed of a turtle? That's tricky.

As I work, I know I should be focusing on code. Every line has to be correct and every phrase has to be perfect. I can't have any mistakes or any clogs. But instead, my mind keeps wandering back to my phone conversation with Derrick.

The conversation had been nice until it got a little too heated. I mean, he had me half moaning even before he said what he did. I can't believe I just bailed like that.

Sure, I know I was a total coward, but I truly wasn't expecting it and I didn't know what to say. Especially since all of my blood was rushing to my neglected pussy, making me squirm around in my seat and tempting me to pull over right then to take matters into my own hands once again. I was this close to telling him exactly what I needed.

Face it, Kat, you wanted to, my mind tells me. *In fact, you wanted him to be there, his silky voice telling you what to do, talking you through every action as his eyes watched you with rapt attention.*

Shaking my head, I try to get back to work, putting in hour after hour of work and making little progress. Coding is a lot like speaking a foreign language. For some people, those folks who get paid big bucks, they can translate on the fly, able to listen in one language and talk in another almost instantaneously.

Others, like me, might be just as fluent in both languages but can't operate in both at the same time. So for me, coding means I have to put my brain in 'code mode' to really get in the groove.

Just as my left-hand monitor flashes me a signal that it's noon and time for lunch, my phone rings. It's my sister Jessie, who's learned to never, ever call me during my work hours unless someone important is dying.

Jessie's always been like a second mom to me. Eight years older, we never really had that period when she was a teen where she thought taking care of her little sister was a pain in the ass. Instead, she looked out for me, making sure I got my schoolwork done and never letting me veer too far off the path into crazy.

She's not some stick in the mud though. Actually, the first time I ever got drunk was with Jessie, and we both have had plenty of good laughs along the way. With hair two shades darker than mine and another three inches on me, she's beautiful and a stellar wife and mom, all the while holding down a full-time job as a risk management specialist for an insurance company.

She's truly Super Woman and everything I want to be when I grow up, whenever that'll be. With my new promotion, I'm at least *halfway* there, the professional success coming more readily than the personal.

"What's up in the land of vehicle recall calculations?" I ask her. "Got anything that'll blow up in my face?"

"Very funny," Jess says with a laugh. "Actually, I called to say congrats on work and your promotion. Good job, Sis. I knew you could do it. Acing it at work, and on the home front too? How's Kevin?"

I wonder for a split second if she can read my mind, the professional-personal discrepancy coming out of her mouth just a beat after it crossed my mind. I can tell she doesn't care but feels like she should ask.

"What about Kevin?" I ask, trying to not sound snippy. Hell, maybe I should listen to her more because she was spot-on with him and has been right before about boyfriends too. "There *is* no more Kevin."

"What do you mean?" she asks, and I tell her about our breakup, leaving out the issues with our sex life and focusing on his cheating and my not putting up with it.

When I finish, Jess gives me a little cheer. "Good for you, girl. You're beautiful *and* smart, and there's no reason you should have to put up with any man who can't see that."

"Well, I don't want to be a downer, but not everyone finds a fairytale Prince Charming who loves you like Liam does you. Gonna be honest here. He's the only thing giving me hope that such a man exists in the real world, because all the ones I run into are cheaters, liars, and users looking for a booty call and nothing else."

Jess knows my experience with men so she gives me a pass. "He's out there," she tells me reassuringly. "You'll find him soon. Probably when you least expect it."

Unbidden, my mind jumps to Derrick and how that was so unexpected. But I don't even know him. Not really, just his radio persona, although he did seem genuine and real when he was listening to my drama about breaking up with Kevin.

Of course, he seems to have a bad boy side too. Good guys don't start talking about how they want to watch me toy my pussy on a second conversation unless they've got at least a decent naughty streak running through them.

There's a part of me that wants to get my own bad girl vibe going . . . kind of. I mean, I want to, but my wild child streak is sadly narrow, but maybe I could learn a few things from Derrick.

"Yeah, well," I finally say, not wanting to go down that particular rabbit hole at the moment, pun intended, "either way, I'm single now."

"Sexy and single," Jess replies. "Whatcha gonna do with all that ass inside them jeans?"

"I'm wearing a skirt today, actually," I retort. "But I do need to get some lunch."

"I gotcha," Jess says, letting it drop. "Listen, don't let any of those cretins you work with have a heart attack because your beautiful ass goes walking by, okay? And if anyone tries to grab anything, you break their wrist with one hand and slap a sexual harassment lawsuit on them with the other."

"I will," I promise her, smiling. "See you later, Jess."

"Will do. Call me tonight. We can catch up on Mom," Jess says. "Love ya, Kat."

"Love you too. Bye."

———

Getting home tonight, I can't help it. I find myself listening to Derrick's radio show.

"Good evening, listeners, your Love Whisperer Derrick King here, and tonight, our topic is something that seems mysterious to most men. Some men say it doesn't even exist."

"The stupid bastards," Susannah says with an exaggeratedly venomous tone of disdain, making me chuckle.

"I wouldn't say stupid, just . . . uneducated and in need of some enlightenment," Derrick purrs, making the muscles on the insides of my thighs tremble. Oh, what this man could educate me on.

"So tonight, our topic is The Female Orgasm. We're going to start off with an email. This is from . . . H. H writes that she and her girlfriend have sex often, but she is frustrated that her girlfriend can only climax from a dildo or a strap-on. H feels like that's off limits. What can she do?"

I lift an eyebrow. Derrick's chosen a doozy to start the night. "Sounds like someone needs some dick," I murmur to myself before my body whispers back that yes, it does need some dick.

"H," Derrick says, his voice sure and slightly stern, making my mouth go dry, "first, penetration has nothing to do with sexual orientation. What your girlfriend needs is what she needs. There's nothing wrong with her body saying that's what it likes best. It has nothing to do with how she feels about you as a person or her attraction to you. I'm just going to be straight with you. What your email tells me is that you might need to deal with your own insecurities. Talk to your girlfriend. I'm sure you two will be just fine."

I'm hanging on to his every word, and I idly wonder if perhaps my confession to him last week inspired this topic.

"Susannah's got us another caller, Z. Z, go ahead."

"Yeah, D, listen . . . I'm trying my best with my lady, but it seems like no matter what I do, she just doesn't get there. Like, we have sex and stuff, and she says she enjoys it, but she rarely has an orgasm. It's messing with my head and I really want to please her."

In his velvety voice, Derrick tells the caller to take his time and he's gotta build up to the main event with foreplay, not just dive in and pound her and think that'll do it.

"It starts in the mind, talking to her and telling her how sexy she is, what you want to do to her," he purrs. I can't take it anymore. I can feel my nipples tightening in my t-shirt and I cup my left breast, imagining Derrick telling me this face-to-face.

"Cup her face in your hands and kiss her gently at first, then devour her. Move down her neck, maybe tease a little nibble to see if she's into that, and lick along her collarbone. Make it down to her breasts which by now should be full and heavy," he says, and I echo him, massaging both of my breasts. It feels so good I have to sit down on my couch, leaning back and my legs spreading slowly.

"Tease her nipples, palm them and circle your hands, cradle her breasts and lick the nipples until they tighten up, then suck them deeply. If she liked the neck nibbles, maybe light bites or easy pinches here too. Your mileage may vary with that because everyone is different. Make your way down her body, layering kisses with licks and sucks along the way."

"Fuck," I moan, my eyes rolling up as my pussy quivers in anticipation. I let my left hand slide down, cupping myself through my shorts, the heat making me gasp at the first touch. The whole world swims away and all I can hear is Derrick's sexy growling.

"Compliment her pussy and let your hot breath warm her as you let the anticipation build. Then lick her with a flat tongue from slit to clit several times before focusing on her clit for circles. I've heard writing the alphabet with your tongue can be good, and when you find a letter that makes her moan, do that one over and over, but if that's too much, just trace patterns and rhythms. Flat tongue, pointed tongue, fast, slow to see what she responds to best. The answer's easy really, just pay attention to her. Take your time. Take as much time as you need to help her get into it. You'll be able to tell. She's not gonna be shy about it and you'll know. She'll open up like a flower."

I can't take this anymore. I slide a hand inside my panties, rubbing at my lips and wishing it were Derrick. I bet he's got strong fingers that could leave me dripping with desire and a tongue that could write poetry on my clit.

"Eventually," Derrick continues, "slip a finger inside slowly and pull it out, teasing her opening and stretching her. Hell, who knows, maybe two or three fingers or more. Like I said, just pay attention. Curl them toward her front wall to slide across her G-spot if you can find hers."

I follow his words, slipping two fingers inside my soaking pussy and pumping them slowly before finding my G-spot. Derrick's got me so turned on that finding the spot is easy, and each intense stroke leaves my toes curling on the carpet.

"All the while, you finger bang her and you lick and suck her clit like a starving man. It might take a few minutes, it might take a lot longer, but you do what she likes and stick with it until she comes. It'll be the best reward ever, trust me. After that, well, you see what it takes. She'll be open to you. Just listen to her body and be creative. No wham-bam, thank you, ma'am. Most women are more complex than that, all right?"

Susannah interrupts, and I can hear it in her voice that she's turned on too. "Wow, Derrick. That was rather . . . descriptive. Fellas, from a female perspective, let me tell you . . . hell yes to all of that. Hell. Yes."

They laugh, sending the show over to a song, and Mazzy Star's *Fade Into You* comes grooving out of my radio. I keep my fingers going, pumping them in and out and finding all the ways that my body likes it, grinding the heel of my hand against my clit before easing up and brushing it with my thumb.

The whole time, I can only imagine that Derrick's there doing it.

I don't even know what he looks like, but holy fuck, I don't know if it matters when a man knows what he knows.

My pussy clenches around my two fingers as I strum my clit with my thumb, and I cry out, pushing myself over the edge and coating my hand in my sweet slickness. The orgasm's intense, and I bite my lip hard, moaning his name.

"Derrick."

Fuck me. God, I want him to fuck me so badly. When I come back to reality again, I realize the commercial break's over, and I take my hand out of my soaked panties, panting shakily.

Holy Shit, Derrick's cohost is right. Hell yes to all of that. Listening to his voice describe how he gets a woman to come, giving but always in control . . . it's worshipful mastery and I want it.

I want it so badly.

I definitely should not have hung up last night. Kicking myself for my cowardice and the missed opportunity, I click off the radio as Derrick moves on to another caller who apparently wants to know why his girlfriend can't come from anal.

I can't take another answer from Derrick. Not if I want to get any sleep.

CHAPTER

Five

DERRICK

THE RESTAURANT IS FULL, but not too busy as I scan the tables. It doesn't take long to find my target. After all, there aren't too many six-foot-five, two hundred and eighty-five pound men who have a build like my best friend.

"Jacob!" I call, seeing my friend turn. He's so massive, I didn't even see that he was talking to someone, a petite blonde girl who's looking up at him with one purpose in her eyes. Jacob gives me a nod and turns back, scribbling a signature along with something else on the piece of paper the girl's holding before sending her on her way.

"Good to see you, Derrick!" Jacob says as we embrace like we did back when we were roommates in college. It was a pure chance pairing, two jocks, one on the football team and one moving away from the sport, but it clicked.

"You too. How's the shoulder treating you?" I ask.

"Not as bad as the sportswriters made it out to be. Mostly it was just one hell of a bruise. I've been resting it for two weeks now since we've got a bye week. I'm good heading into the rest of the season. Then, of course, contract talks."

Contract talks. Big money. Jacob's coming off two All-Pro years, and if he's going to stay with his current team, they're going to have to pony up some top-flight money this offseason to do it. Everyone's saying the team would be smart to try and sign him to an extension before crunch time.

"Big contract so you can pay for all of your groupies," I joke. "What is it, thirty-two girls for thirty-two cities now?"

"Don't hate the player, hate the game," Jacob jokes. "Green ain't your color, bro. You ain't a Notre Dame fan. Besides, I know that when I find the right girl, I'll settle down. Until then, fuck it. What about you?"

"Not my thing," I admit, sitting down at the table across from him. The waitress comes over, taking our orders, and then I continue. "I'm not gonna hate on you, but that's just not what I'm looking for right now."

"You never were," Jacob admits. "No matter how many times I tried to bring you to the dark side."

"What can I say? I saw the real thing with my parents, and I've never been able to settle for less. Besides, it's not like I don't get out there at all."

"We all heard that. Lookin' for that perfect freak in the sheets, lady in the streets, I guess. Anyway, I won't bust your balls. How's work?"

"Fine. Been busy, more folks calling in and we can't even get to them all in a three-hour show. But the show seems to be helping people and the ratings are through the roof."

Jacob laughs, sipping his sparkling water. "Yeah, I'm not surprised. I heard last night's show. You probably caused every woman listening to come right then and there. Shit, I'm good, never get complaints for damn sure, but hell, even I was taking notes. Never hurts to up your game a little bit."

We laugh, and I remember what Jacob told me last time we got together.

Apparently, more and more of his teammates are listening in to my show as well. It seems odd that celebs and people I know would be listening to the show, but I do majorly appreciate the support.

Somehow, when I'm on the mic, it feels more anonymous. The 'Love Whisperer' is just more of an amped-up facet of my personality, not exactly the real everyday version of me.

"You ever miss ball?" he asks me after we finish our food. "I mean, you helped me train during the offseasons. I know you still had the skills back in college."

I shake my head, leaning back.

I remember those days, sweating it out in the winter weight room, the summers running wind sprints with Jacob up and down the steps of the stadium. Even though I'm ninety pounds lighter than him, there were too many times I was a step behind or busting my ass just to keep pace. I had the love of the game, but not that one in ten thousand talent like him.

"No, not really. I miss the teamwork, the brotherhood. But it wasn't meant for me. I'm happy where I landed. You?"

He nods, rolling his shoulder unconsciously, and I wonder how much of what he told me about his injury being just a bruise was bullshit. If it is an injury, his season's going to be a lot harder than he's letting on.

"Definitely happy. It's a crazy amount of work and I already feel like an old man on some days, but it's all I ever dreamed of."

"I'm glad," I reply honestly. "You think you'll make All-Pro again?"

"Pretty sure," Jacob says with a smile. "You coming to the game tomorrow? Season kick-off."

I nod, grinning. "It's a hell of a drive, but no way I'm missing it. Already pre-recorded my show for tomorrow. It'll be an all-write-in show so that I can watch my boy get his ass whooped."

Jacob laughs. "Fuck you, man. You know I'm going to be having a party in the backfield."

"I hope you party all fucking night long. I'll be partying right with you if you do."

———

One of the benefits of being a radio celebrity is that my face isn't as well-known as my name.

So as I sit in prime seats, fifty yard line, two rows up, right behind the players, I'm pretty anonymous. If I yelled, Jacob could probably hear me, but I won't distract him like that because he's at work.

The game is close coming out of halftime, and the tension strums through the stadium. I can see Jacob stretching his shoulder subtly as he leans low to keep his hamstrings warm and loose. He'll be going out with the defense to start the second half and there's a bounce in his step that reminds me how much I loved playing ball.

It started when I was only four years old, throwing a miniball around with my dad, watching games, or at least highlights, since what four year old can sit through a three-hour football game when there were cartoons around, but I loved pretending I was one of the guys on the big TV in our living room.

When I was six, Dad started me with peewee flag ball, the ball damn-near the size of my head.

In some ways, I was lucky. Spending four years playing flag allowed me to learn and understand the movements of the game without taking hits. Not that it started that way.

For my first year, it seemed every snap the play turned into everyone being directionless ants, running around the field and sometimes generally toward someone who had the ball.

Once I got into sixth grade, he let me play a year of Pop Warner ball before junior high started, and the games got more serious.

I learned to appreciate the smell of sweaty plastic and to listen for the sound of my parents in the stands, cheering for me. They never, ever missed a game.

It was during the last game of my junior year that I jacked up my knee. I was playing fullback and linebacker for my team—we were that sort of small school. A chop block on my blind side, two pops, and I was down on the grass with a lot of my dreams strained but not yet shattered.

The surgery wasn't much, a quick repair to my meniscus, some therapy, and I would've been good to go for my senior year. But while it healed, I reported on the playoffs for the little in-school TV program, and I was gone, hook, line, and sinker.

Sure, I played my senior year. I'd put too much into the team and too much time with my boys to just let it go like that.

But I didn't eat, sleep, and breathe football like I did before. Dad was disappointed at first, but I'd shown him how serious I was, even interning the summer after I graduated with our local news station as a gopher guy, running for coffees and making copies just so I could be in the excitement of the whole process.

Sitting in my seat, enjoying the late summer breeze and sunshine, watching Jacob and his team fight for victory, pushing their bodies to the limits . . . there's a part of me that wants to be out there. But knowing that they'll be traveling in a few days just to do it all again doesn't make me miss playing.

Maybe I miss reporting sports, but not the actual playing. It was fun to be able to get to know and to watch the athletes, and hell, it was a lot of fun to be paid to watch.

Then again, I had a lot of late nights trying to cram a story in to meet a deadline. The job I've got now is a pretty sweet gig, and I can always watch the game without playing or reporting on them. I can be casual and have fun with it now.

The second half kickoff soars through the air, and I sit forward, cheering as Jacob snugs his chinstrap tight. He jogs out onto the field, ready to defend his house.

In this instance, better him than me.

CHAPTER

Six

KAT

I **PICK** up my phone for what feels like the hundredth time, my thumb hovering over Derrick's name in my contacts.

Since last night's show, all I can do is think about how much I want all the things he described, want to experience them with his silky voice making me putty in his arms.

But even as I'm about to call, I know deep down that although it felt like he was speaking directly to me, that's just his shtick.

It's his *job* to answer the relationship and sex questions, use his sexy voice to get all the female listeners hot and bothered, and maybe add a little shock factor to keep folks tuning in day after day, week after week.

I was able to hold out for hours simply because of the announcement at the top of his show that he wasn't taking calls. It's a recorded show, so he may not even be around.

But as the evening's worn on, I can't help but think that maybe he'd *want* to take a call from me.

Even as I admit it's a stupid move, sure to end in disappointment, I just have to find out. I'm curious if he used our conversation as inspiration for his show, if he was talking to me, maybe even just a little bit subconsciously.

It rings a few times and I'm on the edge of losing my nerve and hanging up when he picks up the line, his smooth voice instantly putting me at ease.

"Kitty Kat. I was hoping I'd hear from you again."

I notice that he knew who I was before I even said anything. That must mean he programmed my number into his phone, right?

I take a second to calm myself so I can sound casual and cool, even as my brain keeps jumping to conclusions that he must have really wanted to hear from me. I clear my throat before answering.

"Hey, Derrick. I wanted to apologize for freaking out on you the other night. I wasn't expecting that and I handled it like a jumpy virgin instead of the smooth, mature seductress I am."

I hope he hears the sarcasm in my voice because I'm so far from smooth and mature, it's actually laughable.

Despite having a sex drive that I think is pretty respectable, I'm no queen of the bedroom either, even if I have desires to the contrary. Hell, the last time I gave Kevin a blowjob was months ago, and he nearly put my eye out when I jumped back because he came without warning me first.

I'm good with swallowing, but it's considered polite to give a girl a little head tap as a warning so she can catch a breath first. Instead, I ended up sputtering, my left eye burning from a blast right in the eyeball and a rug burn on my ass that stuck around for a week.

So yeah, I'm totally smooth and mature. Not. I mentally sigh at my lack of game.

Derrick's chuckle is deep and rumbly, and it makes me feel like not only does he see through my sarcasm, but he's ready to have fun with it.

"I feel like you're making fun of yourself here, but I'd be willing to bet that's more true than you realize. You just need a partner you feel safe with to explore how smooth . . . or rough . . . you'd like to be."

Two sentences. Just two sentences, and hearing the implied challenge, my body's instant response is a resounding 'yes, yes, yes.' I decide to be coy, adding a flirty tone to my voice.

"Perhaps you're right. Maybe I do just need the right guy. Do you happen to know anyone?"

There's flirty and then there's jumping in the deep end, and I'm definitely jackknifing about two inches above the surface as I wait with bated breath to see if this really is as deep as he's letting on or if I'm going to crack my head open and have to back out in total shame.

I hear him swallow, the gulp audible through the line in the prolonged moment before he growls in my ear, turning my knees to jelly and my nipples to diamonds.

"Where are you right now, Kitty Kat?"

I stammer, shocked that I'm brave enough, horny enough, or stupid enough to be doing this. But fuck, I need him like I need air right now, even if all I really know is his voice.

"At home. I–I worked from home today."

I have a flash of a thought that maybe he's going to demand to come over, and that seems a little too real even as my pussy flutters in excitement at the idea. Still, my nerves are screaming, waiting for his response.

"Good, good," he says, making me lick my lips. "I just got home too. Go to your bedroom for me."

With a tinge of regret mixed with excitement, I realize that I've never told him my address. He *can't* come over unless I tell him. This is something different, something I've never done before, but as much as I want him and need him, I'm completely on board even if I am feeling in over my head a bit already.

I try to reassure myself. I'm a grown ass woman and this isn't all that unusual, if Elise can be believed.

I can do this.

Worst-case scenario, I make a fool of myself, hang up, and never talk to him again. Best-case, this could be just what I need.

There's no worries about a relationship here. Intimate, but totally secure because it's casual. There's no concerns of whether he's going to cheat on me because there's no commitment to be more than just this. Faceless, no strings, just his velvet voice softening all the anger and disappointment from the last few weeks, getting me off and making my pussy throb in the best of ways.

Resolving myself to go through with this, I feel a thrill of excitement rush through me.

Walking quickly down the hall to my room, I sink into the fluffiness of my soft white comforter, perching on the edge of the bed.

"I'm here. What about you? Where are you?"

There's a sound in the background of someone walking, then a settling sound before Derrick replies. "I'm in my bedroom. I'm lying back on my bed, propped up on the pillows. What are you wearing?"

I look down at my dowdy work-from-home outfit of a tank top and Winnie the Pooh pajama pants that's decidedly unsexy, and I decide to lie. I don't want to kill the mood.

"I'm wearing a sexy pajama set with little boy shorts and a crop top. The boy shorts keep riding up, showing more and more of my ass."

Derrick laughs a bit, and I can hear the grin in his voice. "Kitty Kat, I don't want you to create some fake story about what you think is sexy. Right here in this moment, all I'm thinking about is you and what's real. What do you *really* have on?"

I smirk, knowing I'm busted but somehow, the fact that he wants the truth puts me at ease and sends another little flutter through my belly.

"Loose pajama pants and a black tank top. But . . ." I bite my lip, letting the tease build for a split second before continuing, "I don't have a bra on. The girls are free, perky under my favorite black tank."

"Mmm, that's more like it. A natural woman is always better than some fantasy," Derrick says, making my breath catch. Does he understand that he's a fantasy himself right now? If he does, he's not letting on. "How big are your tits? Small little handfuls, medium ripe melons, or large mouthfuls I can bury my face in and feast upon until my lips ache? Be real."

I look down, knowing that I'm curvy in all the right places, but I want to do this right, whatever the hell that means.

"They're definitely more than a handful. I wouldn't say they're huge, but I'd love for you to take in a mouthful and suck and lick them."

I can hear the tension in Derrick's voice at my little secret, and he hums for a moment. I can imagine him adjusting himself, picturing me in his head.

"Take your shirt off and tease your nipples so they're stiff and achy for me."

As I do what he asks, a small sigh escapes my mouth, and I know he heard it. "That's it, Kitty Kat. Imagine your hands are mine, running through your cleavage and pinching those needy nipples." I whimper, rolling my left nipple between my fingers and watching the dark pink nub turn almost red. "Soothe the shock of pain away. You're not gonna hurt yourself. Just enough to let the sensations mix."

I keep rubbing, arching my back into my own hands as I flip it on him. I love feeling the warm touch of fingers on my skin, but I want more.

"Your turn. Take your shirt off."

He chuckles, adjusting himself by the sound of it. "Already done, Kitty Kat. I took my shirt off when I told you to."

Feeling bold, I follow up, my knees parting on their own as I undo the bow tie at the waistband of my pants. "All right, move your hands down your chest and belly to your waist. What kind of pants do you have on?"

There's the sound of a belt buckle being released, and in my mind's eye, I can see it, black leather and shiny as it dangles from the belt loops.

"Black denim Levi's."

Black denim? Holy shit, he knows just what to say. "Slip them down and off."

There's a rustle on his end of the line, then his voice comes back strong. "Kat, I'd ask if I should take my underwear off too, but it seems that the same way you were letting your tits free, I'm commando over here too."

The thought of him lying naked in his bed is doing crazy things to my head and especially to my body. I smile to myself, knowing I want to push him the way he pushed me with his questions about my breasts. My pussy flutters in my panties as I mewl like a kitten, hungry for him.

"Is your cock just enough to fill me up, maybe more than I can handle, or a monster I'm gonna choke on?"

I know I hit my mark when he groans, and I can almost imagine him reaching down, holding himself and trying not to stroke.

"I bet you could handle me. I'd stuff you so full of cock you'd feel places touched that you never even knew existed . . . but something tells me you could handle everything I could dish out. Am I right?"

"I'm no extra-small, teeny tiny thing," I admit. "Is that a problem?"

Derrick purrs, and when he speaks up, his voice is raspy, thick with desire. "No, I like a woman with some curves, hips I can dig in and hold on to. I'm stroking it for you now, up and down my shaft, spreading out my precum and thinking about your pink pussy, imagining how wet you are right now. Slide those pajama pants off for me, Kat."

I do as he says, settling back against the pillows as he tells me to spread my legs wide and trace my fingers across my heated pussy.

"God, Derrick, I'm already so wet. My panties are . . . fuck, you've got me soaked. Your words, your voice . . ." I trail off as the pleasure gets too intense for my brain to multitask, my focus gathering on the slide of my fingers across the drenched cotton.

"Slide your panties to the side. Let me help you make that beautiful pussy feel good. That's the way your whole body should feel, Kitty Kat. So good and ready . . . ready for more. Rub from top to bottom. Let your fingers spread your honey all over your lips and up to your clit. Tell me how that feels, Kat."

When my fingers find the bundle of nerves, I can't hold back the moan, which rises until I can barely breathe. "Mmm, right there. Derrick, what are you doing to me? How does it feel so good with your voice washing over me, telling me what to do? Are you touching yourself still? I want you to feel this with me. Stroke your cock slow and tight."

Derrick's moan is deep, rumbling and making my fingers speed up a little. "Fuck, yes, I'm touching myself. Your breathy sighs and moans are so damn sexy. I'm imagining it's your hand stroking me. I don't know how much longer I can hold out when I know your needy pussy wants me to fill it up. Is that what you want? You want me to fill you up?"

Incoherent, I moan, but he hears my meaning loud and clear, and I can hear his breath quicken. "Slip your fingers inside for me. Imagine it's my cock thrusting into you, every thick inch stretching you and taking you right to the edge."

I do as instructed, my palm grinding on my clit with every press of my fingers inside. "Fuck, Derrick . . . yes, fuck me just like that."

My hips are bucking, helping my hand, and I ride so close to the edge. I know the sounds I'm making are guttural, but they're out of my control and Derrick is echoing them back in my ear, taking his pleasure as I find mine.

"Faster, Derrick. Fuck your hand like you'd fuck my pussy, pounding into me hard, bottoming out deep inside me." I pant, barely holding on. "I'm about to come, and I want you to come with me."

I can hear the smile in his voice and the tension in his breathing. "Kitty Kat, I've been holding back as much as I can, letting you get there. As soon as I hear the sounds of you coming, I'm a fuckin' goner. I'm gonna nut all over my hand an instant after you come on yours. Together."

In my mind, I picture him pumping his hard cock, his eyes squeezed tight and tension through every muscle as he holds onto the edge for me. I can see him shiny with precum dripping down his shaft and wanting me, and his stomach muscles are tensed, ridged under his skin with the repressed power inside him.

I hear him growl at me. "Kat . . ." And it feels like a warning that he's reached his threshold. When I imagine his come coating his hand as it rushes out of his cock, it's all I can take. The orgasm crashes over me in waves, the cries loud even to my own ears.

Faintly in the background of my climax, I hear Derrick's grunts and know he's coming with me. I tease it out as long as I can, eventually forced into taking a big breath to settle my body from the intense release.

"Wow," I half whisper in total wonder. That was the most intense orgasm of my life, to the point I can almost feel a cramp developing somewhere in my hips because I was bucking so hard and squeezing so tightly. "That was . . . you're fucking amazing."

Derrick laughs, and I'd feel bad except . . . he's out of breath just like me, and I know he's just as shaken as I am. "Mmm, yes it was. You sound surprised. Have you ever had phone sex before?"

I shake my head before remembering that he can't see me, and I giggle lightly. "No. Never. But definitely checking that off my bucket list now."

"How about you don't mark it off, and maybe we can do that again?" Derrick asks.

"I might take you up on that," I reply, biting my lip. Late-night sessions with the Love Whisperer? Lucky me.

There's a moment of comfortable silence before my brain kicks in and I remember why I called in the first place. Well, I remember the excuse I used to justify calling.

"Hey, can I ask you something?"

"Shoot," Derrick replies easily, and I feel another notch of comfort with him. He's not trying to cut the call short now that he's gotten a little action. No wham-bam, thank you, ma'am here. Vaguely, I wonder if he's the rare type that actually likes to cuddle. He might be an actual freaking unicorn . . . sexy, sweet, and dare I say it, nice. "What's up?"

"This is silly, but . . . I listened to the shows this week. The female orgasm topic seemed rather on point."

Derrick laughs softly, and another little tremble goes through my belly. I could listen to that throaty rumble all fucking day.

"Yeah, you got me. You mentioned that in our conversation, and it made me think about how many women are not getting what they need. If I can help one guy be a better, more considerate lover and one woman have the orgasm she deserves, I'm calling that a successful show. Thank you for the inspiration. And I'm sure that somewhere out there in the city, there's at least one woman thanking you too."

Me, an inspiration and a muse? He knows how to make me feel even sexier. "See, and here I was thinking you just wanted to get all of us ladies turned on. I bet power companies all over had to fire up an extra reactor for the electrical surge from all the vibrators turned on as soon as you finished that bit. Hell, it sounded like your cohost had to run to the bathroom to rub one out before continuing the next call."

He laughs in that way that tells me something else. Whoever his coworker may be, he's not interested in her. He's not calling her up late at night and causing her to come her brains out.

"Susannah? Definitely not. Most of the time, she barely puts up with me, but she does a great job of keeping the show on track. She's the real backbone. I'm just the pretty voice. As for the rest of the listeners, I don't know. I just hope to help, I guess."

I smile, realizing he does seem like a truly nice guy, with a sexy voice and an unabashed sex drive. I feel a shot of warmth through my cynical heart, a drop of hope for mankind taking hold before I remember that Kevin was like that once too. Actually, several of my boyfriends were.

Too many men in my life start off charming and kind, on their best behavior to get you to relax around them. They made me laugh, they were warm and built trust until I let my guard down, and they found purchase in my heart. I didn't mind, of course. I thought everything was cool until they used that foothold to rip my life to shreds, leaving me spinning, wondering what happened.

My mood darkens, even as my body still hums with satisfaction. Trying not to let the change show in my voice, I try to lighten the vibe.

"Ah, noble Sir Sex-a-Lot, riding in on his steed to save the citizens from a woeful lack of romance."

He laughs at my comment, and I can tell at least this one time, I fooled him. "Well, maybe not quite that dramatic, but something like that. Hey, you asked a question. You mind if I ask you one?"

"Sounds fair. I keep the bodies in the attic."

Derrick laughs, sending another thrill through me. "I'll be sure to remember that. But . . . would you mind if I texted you during the days too? I mean, I've got your number, after all."

I smile, lying back on my pillows. "I'd like that."

CHAPTER

Seven

DERRICK

I'M FLOATING, trying not to get too far ahead of myself. But the mere fact that Kat called me back and was equally engaged in our phone proclivities makes me smile.

Part of me can't believe it really. It's been so long since I found a woman interesting, and I was beginning to wonder if my work had made me jaded. I've certainly had several serious relationships, in college and after, but for one reason or another, they weren't the one.

All except one were good women. I tend to be a decent judge of character, but things never really clicked. I couldn't picture myself with them decades from now, happily hanging out and still chasing each other around the room to get frisky.

I don't even really know Kat yet, but something tells me that she's worth getting to know to see if she has potential to be the one.

There's a shy sweetness to her, even as she stands strong against a shitty boyfriend and says dirty things to me. It's an intoxicating combination. It's been a few days since our late-night session, but even with our conflicting schedules that have her working days and me working well into the evening, we've found time to text. A lot.

There's an anonymity to sitting behind a small screen, a disconnect that somehow lets you feel like you really know someone while simultaneously making it easier to spill your guts because there's no eye contact. There's always that built-in safety net of stopping the texting.

But we've never stopped, and sitting at my desk now, I've got my phone out, tapping away.

Hey KK, I text, my shorthand for Kitty Kat. *What are you doing?*

It's only moments before the reply pops up, making me feel good. *Work stuff. Nothing fun like you.*

I smirk, dipping into the naughtiness that's become a regular for us. *Oh, you want to do me?*

Funny . . . I meant your work is fun. She sends back after a moment. *Mine's dry & I'm rushing to my latest deadline.*

Dry, huh? Well . . . I bet I can change that. *I could distract u. Maybe make things a little less . . . dry. Maybe even slick and wet.*

So tempting . . . so very tempting, but I need to get this done. What's tonight's topic? Should I tune in?

Message received. You want to talk but can't afford to get naughty. That's okay, there's later. *Always. I like knowing you're listening. I don't remember what the show is about tonight. We do the whole week's schedule at once & I forget. Languages of love? BDSM kink? One of those.*

LOL . . . those are very different topics.

Almost as if she were here, I shrug as I type out my reply. *Not really. Both about open communication & respecting ur partner's wishes.*

If you say so, Kat sends back. *I guess I'll have to listen.*

I glance up and see the clock, hissing at the time. *Gotta go. Pre-show meeting has probably started without me.*

I see her kissy face emoji as I slip my phone into my pocket, smiling as I enter the conference room. Susannah raises an eyebrow as I sit down.

She's always one to dress nice, especially nicer than my usual jeans and t-shirt, but she's dressed even better than usual in a creamy silk blouse with understated gold jewelry at her neck and ears. Wonder what's up with that, who she's trying to impress? This is radio, after all. We could do this in our pjs and listeners would be none the wiser since they can't see us.

"Nice of you to join us, Mr. Love Whisperer. Something more pressing than tonight's show?"

She's scolding me like she's my boss. There's even a thinly veiled trace of anger in her voice, and I wonder why she's so upset and behaving like a snarky child. Shit, I'm less than five minutes late for the meeting, and beyond a refresher on the topic, I don't need any more prep. I'm ready to roll like I always am. I attempt to defuse, showing I'm on board.

"Nope. Here and ready. What's tonight . . . love language or BDSM?"

She clucks, obviously surprised I knew what was on the agenda and disappointed that she doesn't get to ream me out. Looking down at her checklist, she makes a mark with her pen.

"Technically, it's called *Languages of Love* tonight. Remember, we're doing an on-air interview with the psychologist who wrote the book. She's hot shit on the Amazon market and there's talk she might end up on New York Time's Bestselling list by year end. So we're basically a big commercial block for the book without sounding like an infomercial. Here's the monologue for the top of the show explaining it all, along with a background on her so you don't stumble into any issues. I picked emails to highlight each of the points she wants to cover so we need to hit those as a priority over phone calls."

I take her typed notes, skimming the psycho-babble descriptions contained in each section. Boring as fuck, honestly. It takes me fewer than ten seconds to realize that whatever this lady has to say, it could be summed up in two paragraphs written in really little words. Ah well, guess my job's the same.

"Emails are the priority. Got it. Hey, Susannah?"

She looks at me, her eyes still flinty. "Yes?"

"Thanks for this. There's more here than usual. I can see you pulled a lot together for tonight's show, and I'll try to do all of your hard work justice," I say, but not just to assuage her hurt feelings. She's a good co-worker and does do a great job of keeping me on track, especially with a fancy topic like this. I'm more of a 'love her well and treat her right' kinda guy, but obviously, some folks need a bit more guidance, and I'm glad Susannah is here to make sure I don't do something stupid like contradict the author.

She really is the glue that keeps the show successful, even if her work is more behind-the-scenes. There've been several times she's had to feed me good advice for a caller when the questions got a little beyond dark and into *whoa* territory. I have a pretty broad 'book knowledge' at least on most things, including some of the darker sides of sexual relationships, but I've always been sort of the 'good guy with an edge.' Nobody's ever accused me of being the bad boy.

That's one of the ways Susannah balances me. She's dabbled in a lot of things I haven't, or at least she comes off as familiar with them in a way I'm not, and she's always focused on making the show the best it can be while I focus on helping the most folks. Without her driving us and scheduling topics, I'd have run out of shit to say months ago.

I see her soften, and I know despite the hard-edged bitch persona she likes to project, she's got a real side to her too. "Sure thing, Derrick. We've got this. C'mon, Love Whisperer."

There's a teasing note back in her voice, and I know whatever made her mad about my being late is settled, or at least pushed to the back burner. Susannah is an utmost professional, and she's ready to rock this show with me like always.

"Good. Now, what's the schedule for the other upcoming shows?"

"Like you ever remember?" Susannah says, and I smirk. She's right.

"Amuse me," I retort. "Imagine that I actually am a professional at this, and forget to remind me that I'm an idiot tomorrow and the rest of the week."

"Don't I always?"

CHAPTER

Eight

KAT

"AND THAT, ladies, is why you should always tell your man where exactly you want him to bury his tongue. That's what I call 'quality time.' Am I right?"

I was just getting my dinner ready and missed the opening segment of Derrick's show, but now, as he gives advice to a woman who wrote in about her partner's oral skills, I have to set my fork down before I drop it on the floor. The deep intensity in his voice sends a shiver through my body even as he talks to the whole city. It feels like he's talking just to me.

Setting the bowl of pasta down, I hold my breath, not sure if I'm listening to *Languages of Love* so I can get to know Derrick's heart a bit better, or *BDSM* to get to know his sexual leanings better. I've never been into hardcore BDSM, but the way Derrick speaks . . . maybe a little spanking wouldn't be too bad at all.

Of course, there's always a degree of fakeness for the airwaves. Derrick's careful. He's not going to divulge too much personal information, but he always manages to weave enough of himself into the advice he gives that you can't help but get to know him. So I keep listening, mixing in the little tidbits he tosses the listeners with the information he's shared only with me . . . and liking what I'm finding more and more.

"Okay, here's an email from Lexus," Derrick says. "Now, I'd like everyone's opinion on this one. It says, 'Dear Love Whisperer, I've been with my boyfriend for three years now, and I've got a problem. You see, I only really feel like he loves me or gives me attention when he buys me things. For the first two and half years of our relationship, he bought me diamonds, pearls, even a new car for my birthday. Recently, though, he lost his job and he's tried to make up for it with what he calls 'little things' like cooking me breakfast in bed or drawing me pictures, but it doesn't feel the same. What should I do?' "

"I have no idea what *she* should do," Susannah says, "but if I were Lexus's boyfriend, I'd be thinking it's time to trade her in and see if there's a better ride that doesn't cost so much."

"Hold on," Derrick says, barely holding back his laughter.

I snort, thinking Susannah's right. But the special guest tonight butts in. "I disagree," she says in a haughty voice.

"It's obvious that Lexus has felt a lack of dialogue with her partner as their situation has changed, and she must take the initiative to make sure both of their needs are being met on a level they agree on—"

Derrick interrupts, his tell-it-like-it-is self not wanting to wait his turn. "Let me put it to Miss Lexus straight. I get that some people feel loved with gifts, surprises that let you know your partner was thinking of you and wanted to give you something to make your day a little brighter. But hell, honey, it sounds like you're venturing into gold digger territory here. It seems like you don't want a boyfriend. That's a relationship of partners, of equal give and take across all areas of your life. That's what it sounds like your boyfriend's tried to do. I'm curious how many late bills he's accumulated to buy you those diamonds and pearls. Unless he happens to play second base for the Red Sox, I would think quite a few."

"Now, hold on—" the guest says, but Derrick is on a roll and wants to finish.

"Sorry, just one second. Lexus, what you want is a sugar daddy, someone who will just take care of you and spoil you. And just so it's clear, there's nothing wrong with that. Just recognize what you really want and set out for that. Find someone who gets his joy from buying you things."

It's surprisingly good advice for a listener who sounded rather unlikeable from the whiny tone of her email. Maybe they were a little harsh, but with an email like that, it's hard not to get a little snappy.

With that, the show goes into a song break, the recognizable beats of Iggy Azalea's "Fancy" blasting out of my speakers. Feeling light and happy, I dance around my apartment a little bit, the song is infectious and making me laugh at how decidedly *not* fancy I am.

I'm mid-twerk, dropping it down at the start of the second verse when my phone dings on the table, signaling a text message. I'm surprised to see it's from Derrick.

U listening? Just had a doozy.

Always listening, I text back, smiling. *U kno I'm ur #1 fan. Btw, can you buy me a Benz, Daddy?*

Stop it. I'm on air. Can't laugh yet. Suz is still pissed at me.

Then y r u texting me?

Song break. Was thinking of you.

I smile, the simple idea of him thinking of me while he's supposed to be focused and attentive at work somehow making me feel good.

He's all I think about too, playing and replaying the phone conversations and texts over in my mind. I bite my lip, knowing I shouldn't do what I'm considering. This is going to take things to a whole new level, but it's not too serious.

U want something to really think about?

There's a bit of a delay, and in the back of my mind, I hear the song change over from "Fancy" to "Yeah!" by Usher. Nice transition.

Song says it all.

Fuck it, if a man is willing to send me messages through the radio, I'm doing this. I slip into the kitchen where there's better light and pull my V-neck tee down, revealing the deep line of my cleavage and the pretty floral bra I selected this morning because I was feeling extra sassy.

I snap a pic from above, being smart while doing something totally crazy and making sure nothing else is in the shot. No face, no room, nothing identifiable. Ensuring it's flattering and anonymous, I click *Send*, along with the note, *think about these.*

I've never done this before, but he makes me feel so wanted even though I've never met him face-to-face. And something about the whole thing with Kevin makes me feel like taking this risk, like it's a common cultural phenomenon I've somehow never participated in and am maybe missing out on.

This is a fuck you to Kevin, an invitation to Derrick, and a shout from my spirit that I am the head bitch in charge of my destiny. Seems like a lot to ask from one spontaneous shot of my breasts, but I have to admit, they do look great from this angle.

The response comes back so quickly that I know he's watching his phone like a hawk. *Holy shit, KK. So fucking hot. Look at that, they're begging me to taste them and mark them as my own. Bad girl, gonna make it hard for me to focus on the next segment because all my blood is rushing to my cock.*

I smile, glad that it worked. This is a big step for me. And a big step in whatever this is I'm doing with Derrick. Phone calls and texts are not the same as real-life pics, and I'm well aware how quickly a simple pic can send things into a tailspin.

But I'm not cheating like Kevin was, and I'm not trying to get more out of Derrick. I'm just having a bit of fun. I'm single, he's single, and it's all good.

Right?

Give me a call later. Maybe you can see . . . more.

CHAPTER
Nine

DERRICK

MY PULSE IS RACING in my veins as I set my phone aside, my throat suddenly dry at the thought of what Kat just said.

Holy fuck, did she just invite me to see her? I'm going to be hard-pressed . . . wait, I'm already hard. But more to point, after the beautiful set of breasts that I just saw, I'm going to have to do my best to be semi-gentlemanly. Gotta at least see what color her eyes are before I dive into those puppies for a suckle.

I look up and Susannah is giving me the evil eye, obviously annoyed that I'm texting during the show. It's not against the rules. We don't have too many rules that we actually have to follow, but it is something I rarely do since my focus is supposed to be work. And during the songs, Susannah and I usually chat about the last caller or sometimes the next segment.

Tonight especially, I should be schmoozing with the guest author, not pushing that off to Susannah to handle alone. Still, this fucking pic . . . I smile at Susannah sheepishly, hoping the silent recognition will be enough apology to move on as I hit *Send* on one last text to Kat, promising to get her back later.

Susannah's not buying it, it seems. "Who's so important that you're texting them mid-show, Derrick? We've got a lot of information to cover tonight and I need you here with me. You could've at least said bye to our guest, especially after cutting her off."

Something in her tone of voice makes me think the first question was what she really wanted to ask and the last bit about the show or guest was an afterthought.

I shake my head, trying to clear my thoughts. "Just a friend," I lie through my teeth. "She's listening in and we're chatting about the show."

Susannah snorts, shaking her head and making her brown hair bounce. "Lovely. Perhaps you'd like to discuss the show with me too, considering we're still in the middle of it?"

Damn, what's up with her tonight? First the pre-show meeting and then busting my balls about texting Kat. For the first time ever, I'm ready to get off the air and out of here.

"My bad," I reply, trying to keep it light. "Let's keep it rolling for the rest of the show."

"Of course. Just keep your head in the game. We've still got two hours of show left, several more emails to read, and callers too. You can't just drift off whenever you want." She's back to chastising me, not responding to my semi-apology.

She's riled up now, almost ranting. "We have to stay focused so the show doesn't bomb tonight. The bigwigs will be listening to see how we handle a guest that's a paying advertiser, and so far, it wasn't stellar. She's gone, but we still have to do a few plugs for her. Pull it together, Derrick, so that we represent the book effectively." She rolls her eyes. "In case you didn't know, or care, advertisers are how we actually make money for the station."

"Fine," I snip as I move back into position for the next bit. Maybe I was off my game tonight, but I don't need her bitching me out. "Let's get this done."

———

It's a lot later than normal when I get home, but it's all I can do to get inside before I'm texting Kat again to see if she's still up. I've been thinking about this all fucking night, and after the night I've had, I need this.

I want to see more of her, but I don't want to scare her off either.

As soon as she responds, I hit dial, calling her. Her voice is like a shot straight to my dick, breathy and low and purring like the sex kitten I know she has buried deep inside her.

"Hello."

"Kitty Kat, you don't know what you've done," I growl, yanking my shoes off and sitting on the couch.

I'm so heated that I realize I made her worry when I hear the apprehension in her voice. "What? Did I get you in trouble at work?"

I know the pic had to be a big leap for her, and I appreciate that she did that with me, *for* me. Quickly, I reassure her.

"No, Kitty Kat, I'm not the one in trouble. *You* are. Because all I have been able to think about are those tits."

Kat's voice is lighter now, playful as she realizes everything's more than okay, and she's been waiting for this too. "Oh, really? Seems I did get promised a little something in return that I haven't gotten yet. I have to tell you, Derrick. You're my first. I have never done something like this, so go easy on me."

I growl, something about her teasing about my being her first making my cock grow to full hardness in the blink of an eye.

"Hang on, then. I have something for you."

I lean back on the couch, pulling my shirt up and my pants down to grab my throbbing cock in my hand and snap a pic. I check to make sure it's showing just how thick and hard I am for her and hit *Send*.

"There you go, Kitty Kat. That's what you do to me."

I hear her breathe in as the pic comes through on her end and she sees what she does to me. "Damn, Derrick," she gasps, her voice quavering, "Is all of that for me?"

We're starting to slip into this with ease, the buildup from multiple get-to-know-you texts and flirty jokes making the initial awkwardness a thing of the past.

"All yours, Kitty Kat. I need you to do something for me tonight."

"Anything," she replies immediately. The lack of hesitation makes me shake, knowing that she's with me, whatever I say next. "I want to see you. I want to see you come for me. Can you FaceTime or Skype me, Kat? Let me see you."

There's a long, silent pause on her end, and I wonder if I scared her. "Derrick, I don't know. I've never done anything like that and I'm not done up. What if . . ."

She trails off, and I'm eager to put any concerns she may have at ease. "What if what? It's just you and me like it was before, turning each other on."

Kat sighs in my ear, her voice quiet and insecure. "What if you don't like what you see?"

I laugh. This woman is crazy in a good way. "Kat, I already know I'll like what I see because it's you. I've pictured you a million times already, in all different shapes and sizes, and they're all sexy as fuck because they're you. I just want to see you for real. Are you saying that if I'm old and fat and hairy, you'll never want to talk to me again?"

I wait a split second before I continue, "By the way, I'm none of those things, in case I just scared you." When she chuckles a little, I know she's relaxing and I can tell she's thinking about it.

I hear her take a big breath, and I'm already prepping for the no I know is coming when my phone beeps.

Oh, yeah, this what I know we both need. She's changed our phone call to a video call. My pulse pounds in anticipation, palms sweaty. I know it's intense, but I'm so ready to show her just how intense I can be and still keep her within her comfort limits.

A huge smile breaks across my face as I accept the call, and a split second later, I see her.

Kat's eyes are huge, the brown orbs wide with nerves, but she's stunning. Her honey blonde hair falls in messy waves down around her bare face like she just pulled it out of a bun, and she's wearing the same V-neck t-shirt from the picture earlier.

There's no way to describe her except to say that she's an angelic dream. So fucking beautiful.

She waves shyly, and I realize neither of us has said anything yet. Finally, she finds the nerve, even if her voice is small, worried that perhaps I wouldn't accept her.

"Hi, Derrick."

I smile widely, both at having a face to match to the pure eroticism of her voice and also in surprise that this gorgeous woman would ever doubt that she is the epitome of sexiness.

"Hello, Kitty Kat. I don't want to sound trite, but . . . you are stunning."

I watch as she bites her lip, obviously not really believing me but pleased with the compliment nonetheless. Her eyes race across my face, taking in my wavy dark hair, blue eyes, and my trimmed beard. I have a moment of uncertainty, hoping she likes what she sees too.

"You too," she finally manages. "Well, not stunning. I mean . . . you're handsome. Hot."

The last bit comes out quieter, like she meant to only think it but it slipped out anyway. It makes me smile, but it's softer, and I lean forward, setting my phone on my coffee table. "You okay? We good?"

Kat nods her head, her smoldering eyes on me through the screen driving me insane. It's like her body knows what she wants, and most of her mind knows it too . . . but she's got something that's pulling her back.

"Yes. I'm okay."

I grin, planting my elbows on my knees and watching my screen like a hawk. I smile before continuing. "Take your shirt off, just like before. Show me those tits I've been dreaming about all evening."

There's a jostle on her end as she props the phone up and steps back, letting me see more of her curves. I swallow as I take her in.

She's about average size but has a thickness to her in all the right places. I don't even realize that I haven't said anything yet so she speaks up instead.

"Derrick?"

I hear the uncertainty in her voice and finally drag my eyes back up her body slowly to meet hers, "Damn, Kitty Kat. You are so fucking sexy."

I see her chest rise and fall as she takes in a breath, for courage, I think. I consider encouraging her more, but I back off slightly, wanting this to be her choice. I want her to want to do it for me as much as I want her to do it, so I stay quiet, my eyes rapt on her, telling her everything that I want.

After what seems like an eternity but is probably really just a few seconds, she pulls the t-shirt hem up and over her head, revealing that she doesn't have on a bra anymore.

Her breasts are full and ripe with deep pink areolas surrounding her hard nipples. I pull my eyes away from the mesmerizing force of her nipples to scan down her body, across her nipped-in waist, soft tummy, and curvy hips to her pussy covered in black bikini panties.

They're functional and basic, not designed for seduction but oh, so sexy anyway. The high straps curve up and over the swell of her hips, making the whole visual even sexier. My cock throbs with hunger to feel what she'd feel like against me, under me.

Somewhere deep inside, I like that she's not *done up*, as she called it, not some fake version of herself that only highlights the good stuff. This is really her, just hanging out at home in comfy clothes and no makeup, and she's letting me into her life for a moment, vulnerable and real. For that, I can only say one thing.

"You're absolutely stunning. I know I said that already, but this is better than I've imagined."

She blushes but smiles. "Thank you."

"Can you touch yourself for me?" I ask, transfixed by the image on my screen. "I need to see you . . ."

I watch as she traces her hands up her hips, across her waist, and up to cup her breasts, lifting them up and together. As she does, the uncertainty and shyness vanish in increments as she gets more aroused and comfortable with what we're doing.

My eyes lock on the image before me, my mouth watering as I fantasize about licking her luscious mounds. I hear her make a noise, a soft moan of desire mixed with an admonition. My eyes shoot up to meet hers, and she's smiling at me.

"Nuh-uh, Derrick," she says, *tsk*ing me. "This isn't one-sided. I want to see you too. Take your shirt off."

I don't even think. I reach back to grab my shirt and rip it over my head and off. The cotton stretches but holds enough that I don't embarrass myself by just Hulking out of the shirt. I slide my fingers across my chest and down my stomach, letting her see where I'm put together.

"You have tattoos," Kat mentions, looking at the ink work I had done in college. "I wasn't expecting that, for some reason."

I nod, looking at my left arm and ribs, the intertwining designs still something I like. "Do you like them?"

Kat's eyes gleam and I recognize that she's turned on. Not necessarily by my tatts, but my questions. "I guess I've never really thought about them before, one way or another, but right now, I want to trace them with my fingers and tease and tickle you as I draw every line across your arms and chest."

I do what she suggests, tracing the lines I have memorized from seeing them in the mirror every day, closing my eyes and imagining it's her soft touch. I hear her breathing hitch, and I open my eyes to see her drawing circles around her breasts, getting closer with each round to her stiff nipples, her back arching to chase her own fingers.

"Fuck, Kitty Kat. Are you ready? I need more." She nods, giving me permission. "Can you sit down somewhere? Prop the phone up so I can see you spread wide for me."

"Yeah, hang on . . ." There's a bit of shuffling, and the phone swirls wildly around her room, but I'm too busy ripping my pants off to get a good look at her apartment.

In a moment, we're both settled back down on our couches, the phones propped on the tables in front of us, and we're both flushed with anticipation. Kat looks nervous again, excited but definitely a bit anxious. It makes her even more beautiful, the light flush of her skin letting her feel real to me. I lean forward, taking her in.

"Kat, you okay?"

Her breasts shudder as she takes a deep breath, causing my cock to throb but also something else to move inside me. This woman, she's one of a kind.

"I am now," she finally says. "Just . . . this is so hot. Crazy. And hot."

I grin, letting her see just a hint of the bulge in my shorts. "Rub your tits for me again. Show me exactly what you want me to do. Get back in the moment, here with me."

She does as I say, the tension leaving her body as she responds. "You too. Lean back. I want . . . I want to see."

I smirk, knowing she's with me now even as she stumbles a bit in her demand. I lean back on the couch, easing my underpants down until my dick comes into her view through the screen. Her breath catches, and I wrap my hand around my shaft.

"This? Is this what you want to see? My cock hard for you? Because fuck, I'm rock hard for you right now."

I give myself a few strokes, spreading the precum across the head and down my shaft as she watches. I see her pinch her nipple a bit, and the sound she makes forces me to squeeze myself tight to stop from coming right then.

"Fuck, Kat," I gasp, trying to hold on. "More . . . I want to see your pussy."

She bites her lip, pausing for a second before adding a pillow behind her back and adjusting to lift her feet to the table edge out of my view. She's laid back, her pussy close to the screen and her body rising up in perspective from her wide hips to her small waist, to her lush tits, and to her flushed face. She smiles dreamily, her hooded eyes looking down her body at me.

"How's this? Can you see?"

"Oh, I can definitely see," I reply, my hand moving slowly up and down my cock again, totally of its own volition. "I can see everything a man could ever want. I can see your pretty pink pussy, so wet for me it's leaving honey on your thighs where you were pressing them together. Touch yourself, Kat. Tell me how wet you are."

Her fingers move down, running up her inner thighs to brush lightly across her lips. "Mmm, I'm soaked, Derrick. I need more. Fuck, I need . . ."

Without my telling her to, she starts to trace her fingers through her lips, slipping up to coat her clit with moisture as she swirls a circle around and then begins the pattern over again. Something about her knowing her own pleasure and confidently taking it without me is so fucking hot. She's in control right now, and I love being the lucky fucker who gets to see her in this moment of strength. I'm still slowly stroking my length, enjoying the sight before me, and I decide to let her stay in charge for now.

"What do you want me to do, Kitty Kat?"

Her eyes pop open to meet mine, and she grins naughtily. "Jack yourself off, Derrick. Fast. I need it now."

Just her words are almost my undoing, so I give my head another squeeze, and with a breath, the moment passes so I can do as she said. I watch her fingers beginning to blur across her clit, and damn, the limits of digital technology because I want to see every detail of her hard nub pulsing as she rubs.

"That's it, Kat. Imagine those are my fingers strumming across your slick clit, spreading your juices everywhere I want to touch and taste you. Hold yourself open for me. Show me your sweet little cunt."

I lift my hips, thrusting into my fist in time with her strokes, and I start to groan. Looking up, I realize that as closely as I've been watching her hand, she's been watching me too. Knowing that she's turned on by my body, my hand sliding up and down my shaft does it and I can't hold back.

"Kat, fuck, baby. I'm gonna come. Come with me."

She cries out, her head falling back and her eyes rolling as her orgasm overtakes her. Seeing her so gone like that is all I can take, and I come too, the thick ropes slicking the way for the last few strokes.

We catch our breaths, our pants slowing as we come back to awareness. Kat's eyes are wide as she sits forward, robbing me of the beautiful sight of her pulsating pussy but at the same time gifting me with the flushed, smiling face of this angel I just came with.

"Fuck, Derrick. I don't think I've come that hard in . . . well, maybe never. I thought you tore me apart last time, but this time was even more intense."

She's done, already satisfied and settling, but I'm roaring inside. That orgasm was probably the hardest I've ever come too, but it's not enough. I need more. I need her. I know my voice is full of gravel, every touch of my trademark velvet gone as I'm filled with lust.

"Kitty Kat," I rasp, staring into her eyes. "I know I said it earlier, but I need you. Let me come over. Fuck, I need your sweet pussy."

She blinks, then grins. "Here's my address. Hurry."

CHAPTER

Ten

KAT

I SIT BACK, my still-damp thighs trembling, whether in fear of what the fuck I just did or in anticipation of what the fuck is about to happen, I'm not sure.

Oh, my God, I told him yes. Derrick "The Love Whisperer" King, the sexiest man on radio and the sexiest man I've ever laid eyes on, is on his way to my apartment right now.

What am I doing?

I need to . . . something. When I told him my address, he said it would take him fewer than twenty minutes to get here. He told me not to get dressed, to stay just like I am, but sitting here is killing me.

I know. I'll call Elise. Probably a good idea for someone to know that I have a stranger coming to my house anyway, but she'll tell me if this is crazy or not because it feels crazy. Making sure I've turned off my camera, I dial her number, running my fingers through my hair as it rings.

"Kat," she greets me, not surprised at all that I'm calling her this late at night. "What's shaking, baby?"

"Elise, this is urgent. I need your advice."

Elise's voice immediately sobers, and I can hear her sit up. She's probably been binge-watching TV again. "What's wrong? Need something?"

I run my fingers through my hair again and decide that staying ready for Derrick doesn't mean I can't brush my hair and teeth. I head toward my bathroom, talking all the while.

"Okay, so I'll try to make this long story really short because time is of the essence here. You know the radio guy, Derrick King?"

Elise chuckles. She was the one who turned me on to his show to begin with. "Oh yeah, the Love Whisperer. Let's get it oooonnnnnn."

She says it with the full effect of Marvin Gaye singing the ultimate sex song, but I'm not in the mood to laugh. "Yes, *him*. So I called in a couple of weeks ago about Kevin."

"You did what?" she says, shocked. "I know it's hard, Kat, but you have to let him go. Kevin is a total douchewaffle and you deserve so much better. I can fix you up with someone if you want. Maybe we could even double-date?"

I roll my eyes, loving this girl, but sometimes, she needs to be quiet and let me finish. If not, she's going to snowball the whole time Derrick's driving and I won't get any advice.

"Elise. Stop talking for a second and lemme finish. This isn't about Kevin. It's about Derrick."

Elise stops mid-word when she realizes what I just said, and when she speaks again, her voice is rapt with attention. "Sorry. Continue."

"So I called, and he told me to dump Kevin and then told me to call him back personally because he was interested in how it turned out."

"I didn't know he did that," Elise says, surprised. "That's surprisingly nice for a radio semi-celebrity."

I find my hairbrush and start running it through my hair, smoothing out the tangles. "He *doesn't* do that. He did that . . . with me."

Elise hums knowingly, already deciding she knows where this is going now. "We-he-hell, now, you just made my night interesting."

Great, I made her night interesting. Meanwhile, my previously semi-behaving waves are now a knot of tangles where I thrashed my head against the couch. Definitely some freshly-fucked hair going on here. I grab my spritzer bottle and lightly spray the back, detangling the mess gently so it doesn't frizz out like an electrified poodle.

"So I called him back, and we got to talking, texting, and other stuff."

"Oh, and what 'other stuff' is my oh-so-shy but oh-so-beautiful friend talking about?" She knows what I mean, and I don't know if I can say it out loud, but I need advice, so I try to charge ahead like this is normal, no big deal for me.

"Fine, we've been having phone sex, texting dirty innuendos, and tonight . . . tonight, we had sex on FaceTime."

Elise is clapping, cheering in my ear like I just won an Olympic medal or something. "That's awesome, Kat! Welcome to the 21st century. Everyone does this, you know. How was it?"

I'm blushing. Apparently, I'm behind the times if this is supposedly common. Maybe I'm reading too much into it? At least my damn hair is starting to look decent again.

"Well, it's been great, really great. But tonight was different. It was . . . wow. I don't even know what to say, but that's why I'm calling. I've never, ever come so fucking hard, and at the end . . . it was like epic or something, and now he's coming over! What do I do?"

"Uh, wait a minute," Elise says, stuttering a bit at the end. "You had phone sex and *now* he's coming over? Have you ever met him face-to-face?"

I hear the tone change in her voice, and I know she's worried about something. "No, is that weird? You know I have no idea what I'm doing here. I've barely dated, just one semi-long relationship after another. And I certainly never had phone sex before. Is it not common for him to come over afterward?"

Elise sighs, but like the supportive friend she is, she gives the truth as she sees it. "Uhm, honey, that's definitely not the norm. Usually, it's just an awkward bye after you're both done with business. But if it was *that* good, and you like him, hell, this could be a good thing."

I set my hairbrush down, picking up my toothbrush and stopping just as the drop of green gel is a fraction of an inch about the bristles, listening.

"A good thing?"

Elise chuckles, but it's not derisive. "Yes, a good thing. You need this, Kat. It's not serious, you're not jumping into some fairytale here. But some wallbanging sex with a hot man to get over the last douchcanoe is just what you need. Oh, wait. He is hot, right?"

I feel something icky on my thumb and realize my drop of toothpaste has become a veritable splooge of minty freshness, and I quickly put the tube aside, flicking the majority of the junk into the sink.

"He is so fucking hot, Elise. I couldn't have programmed a hotter man."

"Now I'm jelly," Elise replies with a chuckle. "Not too jelly, but jelly."

"I was nervous he wouldn't like me after he saw me."

"Honey, I'm not gonna listen to a word of that," Elise growls as I start to brush my teeth quickly. "You're a fucking gorgeous woman, not some twiggy pre-pubescent little girl. And any man worth your time will not just accept your curves, but he will drool for them with appreciation."

I laugh, feeling a little better, and spit into the sink before answering. "So you think this is okay? I'm not being stupid?"

"Yeah, babe. You're good. Just don't get too tangled up," Elise advises. "Use this for what it is . . . some hot sex to rebound, a nice casual hookup. Not some Disney shit where he's going to sweep you off your feet."

I know what she's saying, but she doesn't have to worry. "You know I don't believe in that fairytale crap anyway. The last thing I need is some guy playing me for a fool again. I think I've finally learned my lesson."

I hang up with Elise, feeling more confident in the whole thing but nervous because I'm about to have sex for real for the first time in months, and I don't exactly have a good track record with guys satisfying me.

I look at myself in the mirror, hoping I'm not playing myself. I'm hoping Derrick will be different because somehow, this feels different. I may not believe in getting swept off my feet romantically, but something tells me Derrick might be able to knock my socks off.

Well, if I were *wearing* socks.

The knock on the door comes almost too quickly. I barely feel like I've finished rinsing my sink out. Padding in my bare feet to the door, I take a big breath, still deciding whether I'm going to go through with this. Maybe I just don't answer and I'll never have to face the reality of this.

But I know I'll fucking regret that for the rest of my life. I'll never know just how good Derrick can make me feel. There's this nagging feeling inside me that for the first time in my life, I've got a chance to meet a man who will satisfy my every carnal desire, to take my body places that I've never imagined it could go.

Forget the humor and sweet conversations we've had that make my spirit lighter and my heart clench in my chest. Forget the fact that every time I talk with him, I'm left smiling for hours or that even a short text from him can bring a little twitch to my lips. I focus on the need deep in my core and make my decision.

Just sex. That's all we're doing and all I need. If we can be friendly too . . . that's great. I can't expect more as I stand here naked, not getting dressed like he instructed, and I open the door to find Derrick standing there, his breath coming in fast pants and his eyes bright with lust.

He presses a hand to either side of the door frame, not coming in yet, but if I wanted to leave, I'd have to go through him to do so.

"I thought you weren't going to answer for a second. Are you not as sure about this as I am?" He seems like he's on the edge of control, ready to burst into my apartment and take me. It's a heady sight to see him so close to the edge . . . over me.

I shake my head, biting my lip to keep my nerves and insecurities inside. "You don't see any clothes, do you?"

He smiles. "The whole way here, I've been picturing you under me as I pound into you, you straddling me to ride, the taste of your sweet pussy, and you on your knees, sucking me down. God, I want you every way you'll let me. I want to know you inside and out. If you don't want that, tell me right now and I'll go. But if you let me in, neither of us is going to be the same again."

Every word from his mouth is like he's weaving a spell around me, his voice dripping with sex and turning me on as I picture all the things he describes.

I lower my hands away from their protective stance, showing off my naked body to him and anybody else who happens down the hallway.

Fortunately, it's late and the hallway is empty. I'm somehow more upset that someone might see the thick tent Derrick has going on in his pants than I am about someone possibly seeing me nude in my doorway.

His cock is mine, just for me. And that's what does it for me. I want this. I want him. I dip my head once, and it's all the affirmation he needs to rush me, slamming the door behind him as he grabs my ass, lifting me to straddle his waist.

His lips meet mine in a desperate kiss, nothing soft and sweet. This is instant fire spreading through me as our bodies meet for the first time. His touch is electric, his lips devouring mine as he carries me deeper into my apartment, so worked up that we don't even make it to my couch but instead, he presses me against the wall.

Our tongues tangle, fighting to lessen the heat but only serving to intensify the need pulsing through me. He kisses to my neck, sucking and licking at my ear, jolts going through me with every stroke.

"Where?" he growls, my lust-overloaded brain lost for a moment before I realize he's asking where I want him to fuck me.

"On the left, end of the hallway," I groan, tugging on his hair and looking him in the eye, any uncertainty blasted away by his presence. "Fuck me, Derrick."

"God, yes," he says, striding with me in his arms. His grip never loosens, and I feel secure in his arms as I lick down his neck, nibbling on the thick cord of muscles connecting to his shoulder. He groans, squeezing my ass and grinding my pussy against the hard ridge in his pants. "Fuck, Kat. I don't think I can wait. I need to be inside you. I swear I'll take care of you, but I need to feel you surrounding my cock."

God, I want that too, and I mewl out my agreement as we reach my bedroom. He lays me down on my bed, moving down to taste my neck with licks and sucks and then to my nipples, hard with desire.

He swirls his tongue around before sucking my breast in deep, pulling draws. Shit, that's new and awesome. He moans, the vibrations deep in his chest rumbling against me.

My body writhes in waves, my tits lifting for him to suck at me more, before I shudder and my pussy lifts, begging silently to be filled. It's beyond my control as the surge of desire flows through me. I don't know how much longer I can wait to have him inside me.

"Derrick . . . I can't wait any longer. Fuck me."

Too soon, or maybe not soon enough, he lifts away, standing up to grab a condom from his back pocket before stripping naked. He's even sexier standing in front of me, his skin tanned golden and his tattoos rippling over top of his muscles.

Suddenly, he freezes, both of us fully able to take the other's body in for the first time.

"My God, Kitty Kat. You're even better in real life. I can't wait to feel you."

I spread my legs, letting him see, using my fingers to open up my labia just for him. "Derrick, fill me, please."

I hear the begging plea in my voice, but I can't even care right now because if he wanted me to, I'd damn sure get on my knees at his feet to beg and not feel a bit of guilt about it. He doesn't seem to need it as he strokes his shaft a few times, opening the condom with his teeth and then rolling it on.

I watch, mesmerized, and slip my fingers down to play through my folds, relishing the way his eyes widen and lock onto my now-wet fingers.

Climbing onto my bed, Derrick grabs my hand. "That's my job now, Kitty Kat. I've got you, but fuck, I need your taste on my tongue when I fuck you." He lifts my coated fingers, inhaling my scent before licking and sucking them into his mouth. I moan, the thought of him tasting me on my own fingers doing strange things to my suddenly dirty mind. "That's it, taste me."

For a good minute, he savors me, his eyes never leaving mine until we're both gasping with need. Reaching down, he takes his cock in his hand, rubbing it along the length of my slit and coating himself, teasing my clit and preparing me for him.

"That's it, cover me, baby, mark me with your honey. I could come just rubbing my cock against your little clit, Kat. Does that feel good?"

The circles he's drawing on my pussy with his cockhead are driving me wild, and I chase him, moving my hips to get him where I need him. "Ready, Kat?"

I nod, and he thrusts inside me in one deep stroke, filling me completely. Inside, he pauses to let me adjust as I cry out, the stretch both sharp and so good all at once.

I begin to move, rolling my hips as my fingers dig into his forearms, pulling him down. I need more. I need to feel him pressing me into the mattress and dominating me with his strength, his masculine essence that nobody's ever been able to bring enough of before.

Derrick takes the cue, beginning to press in and pull out slowly but powerfully, bottoming out deep inside me on every stroke. His body presses into mine, my breasts flattening against the hard muscles of his chest, and I wrap my arms and legs around him, drawing him in tighter.

"You're so tight, Kat," Derrick rasps in my ear. "It's like you can barely take me. Please tell me I'm not hurting you."

I'm barely able to string a coherent thought together, so I use my feet to urge his hips closer to mine, rambling, "Not hurting, just so good. Fuck, Derrick . . . I don't think I've ever been this full." My rambles die out into breathy hitches with every thrust of his cock into me.

I see him smile and know I said the right thing. He keeps pressing inside me, and I tighten my grip, letting my fingers roam over the muscles that stretch across his back. He covers my mouth in a kiss, holding my hips still as he stays deep, grinding into me.

"You can take me, Kitty Kat. You're squeezing my cock just right. You're fucking milking me every time you fuck me back."

I tense my inner muscles, lifting my hips to meet his, the rhythm becoming frantic and my movements becoming wild. Derrick pulls back slightly, slipping a hand between us to strum across my clit, and I cry out.

"Yes!"

"Keep telling me what you want, Kat," he growls as he strokes my clit. "Do you want me to tease your needy clit, barely brush across it, or do you want it slow and steady? Maybe fast and hard?"

As he says each option, he demonstrates, progressing from a feathering touch to soft circles and finally to a blurring stroke. It doesn't matter. My orgasm is building with every thrust, every caress of my clit, and I squeeze him, loving it.

"Yes! I'm coming," I cry out, and he pinches my clit firmly, the sharp sting mixing with pleasure as he pounds into me. It shatters me, my body flying apart, and I buck wildly beneath him, my hands grabbing for the blanket to keep me grounded. Somehow, I'm floating away, white sparks flashing across the blackness of my closed eyelids.

From far away, I hear Derrick panting, his voice growling and wondrous at the same time. "Goddamn, Kitty Kat. You're damn-near choking my cock. Keep squeezing me like that and I'm gonna fill you up. Your pretty little pussy, so full of my come until you can't even hold it."

The idea must trigger something for him, and his whole body tightens as he holds himself deep inside me.

He roars as the orgasm takes him, and he loses the rhythm, his body jerking as he comes. I lift against him, taking over the rhythm to help him ride out the pleasure as long as possible until he collapses onto me, our gasping breaths mixing as we smile at each other.

He lifts up to kiss me gently but thoroughly before he pulls out slowly, both of us groaning. I feel the immediate loss of fullness and already wish he were inside me again. He steps out to the bathroom to handle the condom and I take a big breath. It's late, and after the two best orgasms of my life, both of which shockingly happened in one night, I can't keep my eyes open.

He walks back into the bedroom, and there's no need to ask, and even if he did, I think my open arms answer the question well enough. Snuggling up, we drift off together, and it's probably less than ten seconds later before I'm fast asleep.

CHAPTER

Eleven

DERRICK

IT FEELS a little weird to be getting dressed up for a first date with a woman I've already seen naked and had sex with, but that's what I'm doing. Weirder still, we're getting ready for our 'first date' while the sun is still up. With my job making me a consistent night worker and Kat's job leaving her with a lot of flexibility as to when she does her work, it just seemed natural to have our date now.

There's a cool early fall wind ruffling the collar of my leather jacket as I get out of my car and head toward Kat's building. It's not the fanciest apartment building in the city, but it's cozy. It suits her, not flashy but somehow just right when you pay attention and really see its charm.

I walk up the stairs to the third floor, nervous for some reason. It's not like we don't kinda know each other. After all, we've talked and sent messages back and forth for weeks . . . and we've rocked each other's bodies to the point that I'm aching while still wanting more.

But this is different. This isn't a late-night video chat and booty call. This is a *real* date, and there are *real* consequences to this.

In the days since our little impromptu sleepover, we've been almost mentally inseparable. Text messages have led to phone calls. Phone calls have led to flirting and even one more late-night rush over here to tear our clothes off for hot, pulse-pounding, brain-rattling sex that has shaken me to the very core.

So here we are. We're both off work tonight and I'm picking her up for our first real date. Maybe we're going at this whole thing backward, sex first and getting to know each other after, but I'm determined to play on the attraction we've had from the beginning because no one has intrigued me quite like Kat has in a very long time.

She deserves—hell, *we* deserve—a proper date with fancy clothes, dinner, and a walk around the park. A date where we're going to talk face to face, where all the nuances and details can't be hidden behind emojis and blurry screens that lag at the most inopportune moments.

Knocking on her door, it feels strange to have her open up and see that she's not half-naked or more, her full breasts heaving with desire and her eyes sparkling with need.

Instead, when the door opens, she looks . . . almost shy. Her beautiful hair is pulled back in a ponytail and her eyes are guarded, like she realizes something is different, special about tonight too. "Hi."

"Hi," I reply, nervous as well. I look her over and realize one of the biggest differences. Every other time I've seen Kat, she's been barefoot. No idea why that's what I notice first, but I do.

She's wearing sky-high heels, at least six inches tall, her poor toes nearly bent ninety degrees in them. Her jeans hug her thighs and hips, showing off her curves in delicious relief. Her left shoulder peeks out of an off-center sweater that looks soft and inviting, making my palms itch to pet it.

"Would you like to come in?" Kat asks after a moment, and I understand. I've been standing in her doorway like an idiot, ogling her. "Uhm, if there's time."

"No rush," I reply, giving her my most reassuring smile. "Actually, the place I picked out was in the park. You might want to change shoes."

Kat looks down, blushing. "But then I'll be short. I thought these heels were . . .sexy, and I didn't want to look so short next to you."

I blink, surprised, and say the first thing that comes to mind. "I haven't minded your height when your ankles have been wrapped around my head."

Kat blushes more deeply, then laughs. "Good point. Okay, well, fill me in on the plans and I can adjust."

"I thought we could go down to Jordan Park. There's a restaurant that gets great views of the pond over there and has some of the best crab soup in the entire city. Other good stuff too, if you're not up for crab."

"No . . . I love crab," Kat replies, smiling. "Did I tell you that before?"

"No, but you mentioned something about seafood once, so I ran with it."

Kat smiles and goes to change into some more appropriate shoes, wedge-heeled boots that still bring her up a few inches but aren't going to have her walking a tightrope down the sidewalk. We head downstairs, and I do a slight double-take when she reaches into her small purse and pulls out her wallet.

"Wow . . . what is that thing?"

She looks at the device, which has carbon fiber sides and a couple of other high-tech looking things on it.

"Nerd moment. It looks a little intimidating, but I'm just techy. My wallet is RFID scanner secure, waterproof, and holds my IDs, cards, and work access behind an access code. You can never be too safe these days, especially in my industry." She uses a swipe card to let us out of a side door and slips the contraption back into her purse.

I chuckle. "Wow. Talk nerdy to me some more. I think I like it."

She smiles as we start driving, and I feel like we're off to a good start. There's a slight tension between us, but it's casual, not uncomfortable. This is just a new milestone for us. My mind clicking through our interactions like a slideshow, a thought occurs to me.

"Hey, can I ask," I say as we pull up to a stop light, "how'd you meet Kevin? I mean, you describe him as this meathead, but you don't seem the type to be into meatheads."

Kat smirks, looking down at her lap and blushing a little. "I guess it's because of my background. I've always been the girl who was more comfortable with tech than people, but even in my area of expertise, I'm an anomaly. Somehow, I'm both an outsider of the boys' club and intimidating because I'm damn good at my job, so I guess when Kevin approached me, it just seemed easy to go along with it. Until it wasn't. Every guy I've let in has been like that, charming but on some level, just meh."

"Well, I promise you one thing," I reply as we start moving again, "I'm nothing like Kevin."

"I would never think otherwise," Kat says. "My past relationships, even with Kevin, were pleasant at first, but there was never any fiery passion. Not like how we seem to be."

For some reason, that gives me a buzz of pride. "If you don't mind me saying, I know what you mean. This isn't how I usually feel either, especially on a first date."

I turn into the parking lot at Jordan Park, and we take in the view in front of us. Set aside by a wealthy businessman who wanted to have a little bit of immortality, the park's built on his old estate grounds, complete with a pond, a small river, miles of walking paths, and lots of other stuff.

As she scans, I look at her profile, long lashes brushing her cheeks as she blinks, the corners of her lips turned up in a bare hint of a smile. I want that smile, full-watt and focused on me. My voice is quiet, soft as a cashmere whisper.

"I'm glad you realized you deserve more, Kat."

She blushes and looks over at me. "I've never really had this before. You make me feel so sexy."

Inwardly, I shake my head. I don't know how that's possible, but it makes me want to show Kat just how sexy she really is. I lean across the seat, cupping her cheek in my palm and tracing her cheekbone with my thumb before meeting her lips with my own. She sighs, our lips parting as we kiss, stoking the fire that's always burning just below the surface with her. With a groan, I pull back, trying to lighten the mood before I pull her into my lap right here in the parking lot.

"Date. We need to . . ." I swallow, looking up at her from below the flop of hair that's fallen in my face. Continuing, "We need to walk. The nerd herd does exercise, right?" I give her a saucy wink, and she takes the hint.

Kat mimes pushing up a set of glasses on her nose and snorts. "Uhh . . . is that where we get all sweaty? My heart rate is rising already."

We get out of the car, and I have to give my cock a thump to get it to calm down so we can start walking. As we move along the sun-dappled path, I can't help but keep looking over at her. Her bare shoulder is close to me, and all I want to do is kiss it, maybe lick the line of her collarbone. My cock starts to harden in my jeans again, and I have to look away before I start perving on her in public.

"Derrick?"

I blink and look at Kat, who's giving me another shy look. "Yeah?" I ask, confused.

"I just wondered why you looked away," she says.

Heat creeps up my neck, and I lean in to whisper in her ear. "This is supposed to be a first date, all polite and maybe a little romantic, right?"

"Right," she whispers back. "Why?"

"Because I've spent the last two minutes thinking that you look hot as fuck in those painted-on jeans and pettable sweater, but I know you'll look even hotter in those fuck-me pumps we left back at your place. Those heels and nothing else . . . maybe pinned back next to your ears as I watch you take all of me." Kat blushes and grins, and I move my hand to her lower back.

"I've been checking out your ass in those jeans too, so I guess we're both guilty."

We move closer to each other, and I can feel her hands sliding inside my jacket when music fills the air. I place the tune quickly, *She Blinded Me With Science*. "What's that?"

Kat reaches into her purse and pulls out her phone, holding up a finger while mouthing a *friend*. I step back, inhaling the cool air and letting it chill my burning blood while she talks.

"Uh huh? Oh, no, I'm so sorry. I understand. I'll be right there. No, it's okay, babe. Yeah, I am, but he'll understand. Besides, you're my bestie, right? Okay, see you soon."

She hangs up and turns to me, sighing. "You're not gonna believe this."

"There's an emergency," I say, making little air quotes with my fingers, "and you have to go? Is this a fake friend call to get you out of our date?"

We both laugh, and Kat shakes her head. "No, I swear. But my bestie, Elise . . . she's having a man crisis."

"You seem like you've done that before."

Kat looks surprised and snorts. "No, just been the girl on the other end of the line with Elise a few times. Somehow, this time, I'm the rescuer, not the rescuee. This is a little different, which makes it important. It's time to return the favor."

"A woman with her head on straight, taking care of her friends when they need it. I like it," I reply, resisting the urge to ask the obvious question of whether Kat's talked to Elise about me.

She laughs, and I find myself more enchanted with her even as my desire to take her back to bed doesn't diminish at all.

"Elise has a wild and crazy side, but most of the time, she doesn't need saving, just uses me to be polite on occasion if the situation calls for more finesse than bridge-burning. She's fun, the yin to my yang, and would burn the world to ashes, no questions asked, to protect me. That's more than even my sister would do."

"What's with your sister?" I ask, tucking every detail away for later. If Kat's trusting me enough to let me know about her background and her family, it's a start, even if we're not getting our early dinner.

"Oh, that came out wrong. She's awesome, just *too* perfect," Kat admits with a laugh. "Jessie's happily married to a great guy. He's the rare one-in-a-million, but she thinks there are carbon copies of him on every street corner just waiting to be picked up. She forgets sometimes about the reality the rest of us live in. Even my mom. She was married to my dad for years, but he stepped out on her all the time. We just didn't know it for a long time. When she found out, she kicked him out, and Jessie and I supported her through the divorce, even when her friends told her she should've looked the other way and made do. I was still a teenager, but I did what I could. Jessie and Mom are really the powerhouses though. I'm just the little sister still figuring things out. Sometimes, I wish life could be like one of my programs . . . organized, predictable, and when an issue comes up, you troubleshoot and resolve it logically, no facades or ulterior motives. Just data."

She looks up a bit, and I feel like of everything she just said, the last part was probably the most insightful thing about her true self.

After a beat, she finishes, "Mom's remarrying in a few months. He seems like a great guy, but we'll see. Odds are not in her favor."

Ouch, that's harsh. Then again, with what she's gone through, I guess Kat's earned a few harshness points, and maybe even some cynicism. "I hope for the best. May the odds forever be in her favor."

"Me too," Kat admits, then shakes her head, smiling. "Come on, nice nerd moment there. Now tell me your story while you walk me back to the car. You know, being a gentleman and all, maybe I can bum a ride to Elise's place while you go grab us some caffeine since it's too early for the wine I'm betting Elise will want?"

"Sure," I reply. I'm quiet for a few while I try and figure out how I'm going to answer Kat's question, then I just decide to jump in. Fuck it, I can't help I've had a pretty ideal childhood. "I know it's a little boring, but my parents did well together. They loved each other fiercely until Mom died a few years back, and Dad has said he'll never remarry because he's already had the great love of his life."

Kat smiles, shaking her head in disbelief. "Really? That's old-school romantic. What's he doing now?"

"He's doing okay now, still works hard and has friends to keep him busy," I answer. "He sold the old house—totally understand that—but stayed in town, moving into a little starter home. I go see him a few times a month, more during football season so we can watch the games together. I wish I could go more because he's getting older, but it's a ways out to see him, and he's staying busy and happy."

Kat looks down, looking sad. "I'm sorry to hear about your mom. If anything, she seems to have raised a good son."

I swallow, thinking that Mom would be happy to hear a girl like Kat say that. "It's okay. It was a sudden aneurysm. She didn't suffer, and she left behind a lot of friends, a lot of good memories. I don't think there are too many bad feelings in the world about her."

Kat hums. "That's really sweet, a testament to how she lived. You said your dad is *'getting older'*. How old is he?"

"They had me when they were almost forty—tried for years and years. She thought she was going through menopause, but . . . surprise. It was me. They were thrilled, and I always knew how much they loved me. I was a lucky kid, their little plot twist in life."

"Damn . . . your parents were like one in ten million," Kat says. "Does that mean you're the same?"

"I'd like that happily ever after sort of thing," I admit. "Wouldn't you?"

"I've never thought that was meant for people like me," Kat finally says. "It's like catching lightning in a bottle. For most of us, that just doesn't happen."

We get back to the car and I don't really know what to say. I mean, if we're not in this for trying to find something more than a short-lived flash of fun, then what the hell is this all for?

———

Kat and Elise take forever to handle the man crisis, but they seemed appreciative when I returned with Chinese takeout and wine instead of the requested coffees.

I sat by quietly, not sure if my input would be welcome but mostly because Elise didn't need advice, just some support as she bitched about finding out that her slimy boss, who's married, is sleeping with one of the other reporters. Kat had given me a look like, *See? Always happens.* It felt like another nail in the coffin of her perception of reality.

Elise hadn't even paused in her rant, going on about nepotism in the workplace and that maybe she should report him to HR, even if the reporter had been doggedly pursuing the boss in a flawed attempt to get better stories. It was draining and lasted until later than I'd thought. The moon is high in the sky and the stars are twinkling as I pull up in front of Kat's place. I'm thinking the day, and date, are pretty well done.

Kat seems to think so too and looks exhausted as I walk her to her door. "Thanks," she says, smiling softly. "Maybe next time, we can have an actual first date."

"Oh, I don't know," I joke. "I mean, I know all about what's happening in Hollyweird now from flipping through Elise's coffee table magazines. That's not too bad, right? Did you hear about the pregnant Kardashian?"

Kat chuckles. "Which one? I guess I could say that I've had worse dates, but I'm not sure if that's particularly flattering to say." She smirks, and I smile back, happy to find some humor after this decidedly unusual first date.

There's a moment where we just look at each other, and I lean in, breathing in the scent of her floral perfume. "So . . . think I might be able to come inside?"

Kat bites her lip, looking up into my eyes where I see desire building inside her. "That sounds like a loaded question. We're switching gears here, from whatever we were . . . to actually dating. And I don't fuck on the first date, and that's what you said this was. Even if it wasn't epic."

"True, I did say that, but sometimes, first dates end with a little more than a kiss at the door."

Kat blushes, mocking outrage. "What kind of woman do you think I am?"

I pull her into my arms, pressing her voluptuous curves against me and lowering my voice to growl in her ear.

"Apparently, a lot more proper than I thought. I like it, but I also appreciate the naughty side of you that likes it when I talk dirty in your ear and loves to moan my name when I make you come."

Kat's hands wrap around my neck, pulling me down closer. "Well, as long as you can respect me in the morning, you can have a good kiss."

"That," I say as I bring my lips closer for a searing kiss, "is a given."

Our lips touch, and moments later, I'm pressing her up against the door and staking my claim on her mouth. She kisses me back just as hard, clutching at my ass until she feels my cock pressing against her belly. We don't stop until our moans become too loud for the public hallway, and I pull away, leaving her gasping for breath.

"Well, Miss Snow, that was a very fine and proper kiss," I say in a mocking formal accent. "It was such a delight to spend the afternoon and evening with you. I hope you'll do me the honor of escorting me again. Soon."

Kat catches her breath, smirking as she leans in close again. "I'd be delighted, Mr. King. Don't get any ideas though. I'm a lady, and even if you've got a world class cock, I don't *fuck* on the second date either."

She breathily draws out the word *fuck*, intentionally emphasizing it to drive me out of my mind. I pull her close again, groaning as I admit . . . she wins this time. There's a demand, an order in my steely voice.

"Say it again, Kitty Kat."

Her eyes are wide, innocent as she looks up at me, her lip quivering and her nipples hard against my chest. "What? *Fuck.* Is that what you want me to say? How about . . . no matter how much I want you to fill me up with that thick *cock* of yours, *fuck* me hard, and maybe even bend me over the arm of my sofa to smack my *ass* . . . I don't do that on the second date."

She's killing me as she accentuates the dirty words, knowing that I love it when she lets loose on those triggers, already so much easier than our first conversation when I had to force her to say 'cock' on the radio.

I grin at her, playing even as desire courses through my veins. "Yeah, *that*. You're playing with fire here. You know . . . you never said anything about my licking your pussy until you soak my face. Maybe that can be an acceptable second date activity?" She giggles a bit and hope soars in my chest. "Maybe I can call you when I get home?"

I kiss her neck, hopeful that somehow, she'll relent, our phone calls being somehow separate from our first date, that she wants me so much she'll give in to a phone call at least. But she's loving this game, and as she runs her fingernails down my neck, she chuckles under her breath.

"Oh, no, that definitely wouldn't be proper after a first date. I guess I'll just have to take care of things myself tonight. When did you say our next date will be?"

My brain zeroes in on the image of her pleasuring herself like I've seen so many times already, and my cock jerks in my pants.

"Tomorrow night. It'll have to be late because I've got a meeting with a sponsor as well as the show . . . but fuck, I need it to be tomorrow."

She's driving me wild, this almost dual nature of Kat as she reaches down, cupping my cock. "I can do tomorrow. I'll be listening in after work. Call me around ten or so?"

I nod, reaching up and rubbing a thumb across her stiff nipple. "Ten. Be ready."

Kat smiles mysteriously and gives my cock a final caress through my jeans. "Have a good night, Derrick. I know I will." She says it with a raised eyebrow, obviously teasing me further about just what she'll be doing tonight.

She steps back, closing her door and leaving me stunned. It's not until the brass knocker presses against my chin that I realize I never said goodnight.

I lean close, whispering loudly through the door, trusting that she's just on the other side.

"Goodnight, Kitty Kat."

CHAPTER
Twelve

KAT

"KAT? EARTH TO KAT?"

The fog of my daydreams lifts as I realize my sister is calling me, and by the look on her face, she's been saying my name for a while. We're taking a long lunch for a family errand. I'm going to work late tonight to make up for it.

"Sorry, what?"

Jessie smirks at me, tilting her voice salaciously. "And what, pray tell, are you fantasizing about, dear little sister?"

Blushing, embarrassed at being caught red-handed, I try to divert the attention away from me in any way I can. "Not fantasizing, you horny bitch. Get your mind out of the gutter. I'm just daydreaming, thinking about work and a new project I'm developing."

She nods wisely before rolling her eyes hard enough to let me hear the thunks as they hit the backs of her eye sockets. "A project you're developing? Is that what the kids are calling it these days? Take a hint from an old lady. If he's a project model, move on. Guys that need work aren't worth the time. Find a grown up." She freezes, a look of horror shooting across her face. "Oh, God, you're not talking about Kevin, are you? Please say you're not trying to *fix* him. Girl, tell me I'm wrong."

I flinch back, wondering if Elise and Jessie have been sharing a brain or something. "God, no, definitely not Kevin. He's long gone and I've moved on . . . way on."

She smiles triumphantly, and I realize I walked right into her trap. Dammit, that's what I get for being the little sister. "So moved on to . . . whom? What's his name?"

I give in. Besides, I kind of want to tell her anyway. "His name is Derrick, and he's a radio personality. That's actually how we met, but it's not serious. We've just . . . chatted a bunch, and we had our first official date yesterday. So it's all super-new."

I'm relieved when she gloms on to the date part and doesn't question my stutter as I described our late-night phone proclivities as 'chatting,' or to Derrick's job. I mean, how do I explain to my sister that her nerdy, seemingly straight-laced little sister is dating a sex advice expert?

"First date?" Jessie asks, leaning far enough forward that she's invading my personal bubble. "Oh, my gosh, so how was it? Are you going to see him again? When?"

She's almost jumping up and down in her chair as she lobs questions at me faster than I can answer them. It's joyful to watch, and I laugh at her excitement, forgetting my nervousness a little.

"It was great, yes, and tonight."

She squeals, making a sound I haven't heard since . . . well, since about the time she got that fan form-letter from Justin Timberlake back when she was in high school.

"Tonight! Oh, my gawd!"

As she's still buzzing, our mom steps out of the dressing room behind Jessie. I'm breathless as I take her in, stunning in a soft ivory floor-length gown covered with lace and beading. Jessie sees my face and whirls around, her jaw dropping in shock too.

"Well, girls?" Mom asks. "What's the verdict?"

"Mom, you look gorgeous," I tell her truthfully, stepping forward and taking her hands. "Truly. Bob is going to forget his vows when he sees you walking toward him." I mime a fish mouth opening and closing. "The whole church is going to see him rendered speechless."

She laughs lightly, smoothing invisible wrinkles in the dress. "Really? You think it's all right?"

Jessie and I look at each other and then back at her, shaking our heads before Jess speaks up. "No, Mom. It's not *all right*. It's amazing."

We walk around her, taking in all the little details of the dress while Jessie, who's always been the fashionista of our little duo, gives a rundown.

"It hugs your hips just right, not so tight you can't sit down, but tight enough to show your curves."

I have to chime in something, so I blurt the first thing that comes out of my mouth. "And the girls look va-voom! Thanks for the good genetics there, Mom."

Probably not the smoothest line that's ever been said, but Mom laughs, posing and visibly more confident in her dress.

"Thanks, girls. I don't know what I'd do without you two here for this."

Her eyes fill with tears as she pulls us in for a tight three-way hug. After a moment, she giggles, letting go. "Okay, enough of that. You two are going to get makeup on my dress, and I can't have that."

We step back, standing behind her as she looks in the mirror at herself, but she seems to be talking to us.

"I never thought I'd do this again. Your father . . . well, he really did a number on me. You know I don't like to talk bad about him because he's your father, and we did have a lot of good years together. But there at the end, it wasn't pretty. I hope I protected you from most of that."

We nod, knowing that she'd done her best, but Jessie and I spent many evenings curled up in the same bed as they'd fought, our mother's screams and our father's booming yells the soundtrack more than once. We hugged each other to sleep on too many occasions to be completely fooled by her comfortable lie.

She never told us, but we knew he'd been cheating, had heard her accusations, his denials, and his eventual admissions, but always with some justifying reason why it was Mom's fault that he'd had to resort to that.

Even when she would take him back, we didn't understand why, but in some ways, it was nice . . . at least we had peace and quiet again, and a comfortable normality to things. But it tore us apart.

It's why when she'd finally had enough and divorced him, we supported her and cut him out of our lives. Dad didn't understand at first, thinking we didn't know about his affairs and that Mom had poisoned us against him. The letters and even calls from his lawyer as they dealt with the divorce lasted for months, until Jessie had been the mature one to tell him that we knew, we didn't approve, and to never contact us again.

I just avoided the whole confrontation and didn't return his calls until eventually, he stopped calling altogether, much to my relief.

If I learned anything from my father, it's that whatever happiness you get . . . it's just an island in the sea of misery. It can be a big island the size of Antarctica for some . . . for others, it's like a Styrofoam cup floating in the Pacific. And sometimes, you don't know when you're getting too close to the shoreline, and the wave will just crash suddenly and pull you back out with the tide.

"Mom, you deserve this. For as long you can have it with Bob, enjoy every moment."

I mean it to sound loving and supportive. It's not her fault or mine that we tend to be Styrofoam cups, but she hears the bitterness. She turns around and comes over to hug me.

"Kat, I know you don't understand this . . . but I would happily take one blissful day with Bob over a lifetime alone. It's not a risk to love him and let him love me. It's a gift, one that I am blessed to have for as many days as we get. Sure, maybe one day, it'll explode and I'll cry in devastation. But even then, the days of joy will be worth the pain. Even as bad as it got with your father, we had a lovely life for a long time and he gave me the two best gifts of my life, you girls. So yeah, I'll take this happiness for as long as I can have it, without bitterness or cynicism."

I'm taken aback, my mom's words hitting rather close to home. I *am* bitter and cynical. And she's right, because Bob really is a good guy who wants to make her happy.

He didn't have to ask her to marry him, I know. After his first wife died of cancer, he could have just been a rather well-to-do older bachelor. Mom would have been happy just dating him exclusively, I know it. She never asked for his support and didn't need it after she made her way successfully after the divorce. Neither of them needed the other. They just wanted to be together, forever.

So when he dropped to a knee on Valentine's Day and asked her to marry him . . . it was totally legit and love-filled. Ever since then, he's been great while they plan their second weddings as if they were kids doing it for the first time. There's no reason I should doubt him.

Unfortunately, it's not just my dad's influence. I've had a run-in or two myself.

The good memories with them definitely don't outweigh the bad endings. Kevin was, if anything, one of the longer 'islands' in my history. Some of us just aren't destined for happily ever afters. Or even happy for nows.

Jessie pipes up, ever the optimist. "Maybe this new guy, Derrick, will be the one . . . tonight!"

I turn to Jess, ready to go claws and hissing on her, but Mom smiles. "Tonight? Do you have a date? Is that what Jessie's caterwauling about?"

I try to smile back, but the thought of having a bad ending with Derrick is already pressing on my heart. The fact is, despite whatever guards I've put up about Derrick, I like him already. A lot. We've barely begun whatever this is, but I already know it's gonna hurt like a son of a bitch when it ends.

It's not just the sex, or the fact that he pushes me just enough that I feel like I'm stepping outside my comfort zone without feeling like I just got chucked out of an airplane with no parachute.

It's in the way he looks at me, the way he talks with me when we're not being dirty . . . even the fact that he spent hours last night hanging out while I helped Elise through her latest drama and did so without a single complaint.

Derrick . . . God, he's everything I could ask for, so hot I find myself thinking of him and wondering if I could run to the bathroom at work to send him a quick naughty video. And he's intelligent and perceptive, and even gentlemanly in a lot of ways. If telling a woman you want to fuck her until she passes out from so many orgasms can be called gentlemanly, Derrick's figured out how.

But that's what's scaring the shit out of me . . . every high has to be met with an equal low. Locking a forced excitement to my face, I tell my mom the same thing I told Jessie about it being our second date but we've been talking for a few weeks.

"Really, it's no big deal."

Mom rolls her eyes, refusing to be put off. "No big deal? This is so exciting! New potential, new stories, the anticipation of liking each other and falling in love."

She hugs me, forgetting her earlier concerns about getting makeup on her wedding gown, and I just smile and nod back. Maybe Mom is getting her big island of happiness again, but I'm still last week's floating Styrofoam cup.

"Yeah, we'll see."

Thirteen

DERRICK

"I REALLY THINK tonight's sponsor should be ChapStick or something," I joke, glancing again at the pre-show sheet. "I mean . . . blowjobs? They actually approved that one?"

"Well, there were a few requirements," Susannah says, smiling. She's been a lot nicer today than the past couple of days. I dunno, maybe whatever was biting her ass has worked itself out, or maybe she just realized that being pissed wasn't doing us any favors.

"What's that?" I ask, sipping my water and already thinking to tonight. Kat . . . blowjobs . . . Kat's blowjobs . . . fuck, I'm hard again. "Sorry, one more time?"

"I said, they want us to do a series of shows on oral sex," Susannah says, looking at her clipboard.

I groan. "Sounds like we're going to be fielding a lot of callers to fill all that time."

"We'll make it work like usual," she replies. "You ready?"

"Five minutes," I reply. "Just want to make sure . . . well, no early bathroom breaks."

I rush to the bathroom, pulling my phone out of my pocket as soon as I'm in the stall. *Thinking of u.*

Oh? What's tonight's show?

I smirk, wondering if I should tell the truth or not. *You'll just have to listen and find out. See you tonight.*

I do try to force out whatever's inside, but no dice. Still, I flush and get to the studio just in time to plop down in my chair. The entry music starts, and I lean into my mic just as Suz gives me a thumbs-up.

"Good evening, listeners! This is Derrick King, the Love Whisperer, welcoming you to the next three hours of advice, music, and a little bit of fun. With me, of course, is my right-hand woman, Susannah 'Don't Call Her Jenna' Jameson."

"Tonight's show is about a subject that, well, let's just say it's near and dear to my heart."

"I didn't know your heart was next to your balls," Susannah jokes, and I have to grin. That was a good one.

"Well, let's just say I've thought about this subject a lot. You want the honor of telling our audience what we'll be discussing?"

"Sure, D. Tonight, let's talk fellatio. Blowjobs, knob slobbing, or sucking cock. Take your pick. If it involves dicks and lips, we're gonna talk about it tonight."

"Hell of an intro. I always liked the term *blowjob* myself," I admit. "By the way, if blowjobs aren't your thing, don't worry, folks, we're having a show on licking pussy too. But for now, you know the deal. Give us a call, drop us an email. The lines are open. First, let's go to an email. Suz, will you start us off?"

"Love to," Susannah says, lowering her voice to a sultry purr to set the tone. She's got a great range of voices, from shrill to sexy. I guess that's why she's working in this business. "Dear Love Whisperer, I've got a problem. You see, my boyfriend wants me to blow him, but I struggle with it. Am I doing it right? Is he gonna choke me? What about when he comes . . . what do I do? His birthday is coming up, and I'd love to give him this gift. See if I can make it happen for him. Advice? From Kitty."

Kitty? Great, just fucking awesome. I'm trying to work, and all I can think of is Kat crawling across the floor like a kitten, her lips stretched wide around my cock, balls-deep in her mouth. Shit. Focus. I gotta be a pro here.

"Well, Kitty," I husk, licking my lips before I can continue, "first, I'd like to say you're quite the girlfriend if you're worried about this. For a lot of guys, blowjobs tend to consist of a little begging, some half-hearted licks, and then it's time to move on."

"Not me," Susannah teases, and I give her a raised eyebrow. She normally doesn't get this expressive. Maybe she's just really into it tonight. "I love feeling my man slide over my tongue."

"That's the thing," I add. "Kitty, there are two main ingredients to a good blowjob. One, you have to really devote yourself to it. Don't just do it because you think he'll like it. You have to suck him off because you *want* to. Show some excitement about it because it's supposed to be sexy and fun! Second, pay attention to what he likes. Does he want it hard, lots of tongue action, deep-throating, hands involved, or not involved? Maybe some ball play or even a little bit of anal play. Pay attention to what he likes, and then when you find out, give it to him and don't hold back."

"So, Derrick, what do you like?" Susannah asks, a gossipy tone to her voice. "I'm sure our listeners would love to know your hottest desires . . .

fast and rough, teasing little sucks, maybe the grapefruit trick I've been hearing about?"

I purse my lips, thinking, and all I can see is Kat. My cock throbs in my pants, and I smirk before answering. "I'm gonna be honest, I'm not sure there's such a thing as a bad blowjob. Unless there's teeth," I say, a shudder of fear snaking through my body. "But I'm sure some guys are into that too. But I'd advise a Q-and-A before going that route, ladies. But let's just say that I'm loving what I'm getting."

"Oh, *he* must be good then," Susannah shoots back, a little cattier than I expected, but before I can say anything, she gives a big laugh. "All right, let's try a caller. Go ahead, Eric."

I don't have time to ask Suz what the fuck was up with that crack because I've gotta help this caller. *"Yeah, uh, first thing, big fan, Derrick. You've helped me a lot with my girl. Big props to you."*

"Thanks, Eric. What can I help you with tonight?"

"Well, how can I convince my girl that swallowing isn't deadly? I swear, every time she goes down on me it's either she pulls off in time for me to blow on her face or she starts spitting like a garden sprinkler. But I really, really want to see her take a mouthful and swallow it down, know what I mean?"

"I do. It's a pretty common thing for a lot of guys," I reply, trying to pull my thoughts together. "At the same time, a lot of women don't like it. Some of it is cultural or demographic. They've been taught that cum is somehow dirty or gross. Spitting can feel like they're rejecting you on some level, and swallowing seems sexy, like they're taking a part of you into themselves." I pause. Susannah raises a hand at me, and I segue to include her. "Susannah, what's your take?"

She smiles, her eyes glinting with naughtiness. "So many thoughts. From the woman's perspective, there's a point of gag where nothing's going to stop your body's natural reaction. The trick is to get behind the gag or in front of it. She needs to take you deeper down her throat so that when you come, it goes down easier. Or, maybe compromise and stay in front of the gag, come into her open mouth, get the visual of her with a mouthful and then she swallows like a good girl without the pressure of you continuing to fuck her face at the same time."

"Good advice. Thanks for the female point of view. Also, Eric . . . man-to-man here, this might not be about her. Are you making it attractive for her to want to put her face in your crotch? I mean, what's your lifestyle like?"

"Uhm, I'm pretty busy. I work long hours but do my best to stay healthy. I take vitamins, stuff like that."

"All good, but before you want to get down with your lady, make sure you're showered and fresh, and stay hydrated," I reply. "And lay off alcohol and caffeine, and if you do smoke . . . well, this is another reason to quit. Eat right too. All of these things have been shown to affect the taste of your cum. Keep it clean, keep it healthy, and hopefully, tasty."

We continue, and I give Eric a few pointers. Once we're done, it's time for a music break, so I turn it over to Susannah, who spins Madonna's 'Like a Prayer.'

"Little old-school, isn't it?" I ask once the mics are off. She gives me a look, and there's something different about the way she's looking at me. Back to that upset look, I don't know.

"Best song about blowjobs ever made," Susannah says before singing along with some of the lyrics. I raise my eyebrow. She's got a point, but I've got other things on my mind.

Leaving the booth, I pull out my phone, texting Kat. *You listening?*

Of course. And no, I'm not Kitty, just in case you were wondering. I know just how to make you come in my mouth. And don't worry, it's delicious.

I moan, thinking of the sight of her and text back. *I wish I could see you naked and with my dick in your mouth right now.*

Well, we'll see if I can make that happen later.

I hear the song wrapping up, so I hop back in the booth while Susannah grumbles, "We've got work to do."

"Chill, Suz, we've got this," I reply. Madonna finishes up her ode to the sacrilegious blowjob, and we go to an email about a woman who gets off most when she's got her head tilted back off the edge of the bed. The idea's hot, though I've never tried it. I toss it to Susannah. "I dunno, Suz, sounds like a good way to get a head rush for the sucker, not the suckee."

She laughs a little. "Maybe some people like a little head rush? For real, don't hang upside down too long. This is a finishing move that will get you past your gag reflex like we talked about earlier with Eric. But don't go falling off the bed and blaming your concussion on us."

We bounce back and forth, taking calls and doing music breaks for the next hour. I try to stay focused on my job, but about halfway through, I get another buzz on my cellphone. Dad.

How is the show going tonight, Derrick?

That's Dad, never uses a single text contraction or emoji or anything. *Not bad. Hey, Jacob will be at home to play in a few weeks and got us box tickets. Can you go?*

Of course I can go. It's football so I'll be watching either way, there or at the house.

Growing up, that was what he and I bonded over first. Not that he didn't let me explore other things, but where some fathers would tell their son about the baseball greats or take their sons camping, with us, it was football. Oh, we'd still go fishing or hiking, but his 'old man stories' weren't about fish that got away but about watching Dwight Clark make 'The Catch,' or Doug Flutie's miracle throw while at Boston College. We bonded over the somehow fated Super Bowl win of the Patriots after 9/11, and now that my former college roommate is a pro and relatively local . . . well, Dad's got a reason to closely follow the team.

I know he felt like it was the end of an era when I quit playing, but ultimately, I think he's glad I did reporting. Especially with all the medical data these days about players getting their heads smacked on the field.

Now, I think he's still trying to understand just what this whole Love Whisperer thing is about. Personally, I'm glad he's probably not listening in tonight. Better for him to think I talk about love and relationships than blowjobs and swallowing.

OK, I text him. *I'll send you details tomorrow. Jacob should have them to me by then.*

"Yo, Derrick!" Susannah growls, and I look up guiltily. "We've got a show to do!"

"My bad," I reply, setting my phone down on the table. The light comes on saying we're live. "We're back, and I hope you've been drinking plenty of water, because it's getting warm in here. What do we have next, Susannah?"

"A little offshoot from the norm," she says, grinning wickedly. "We've got Jamie, who has one of my personal fantasies happening in real life."

"Go ahead, Jamie, I'm listening."

"Hi, Derrick," a woman says. *"I've just started a new relationship with a guy from France, and he's had a lot more experience than me. Last Friday night, I came home and he . . . well, he was on his knees with another man. They invited me to join in, and while the sex was mind-blowing, I'm a little worried in that my boyfriend seems to be more into sucking cock himself than into me. He's asked if he could invite his friend over again this weekend, and I'm not sure what to say."*

Well, now, that's awkward. I get through the call with the same advice I normally give, communicate and be honest with each other, because what the fuck else can I really say to that? But by the time we're done, it's time for another commercial break. As soon as the clear light goes on, I reach for my phone, tapping out a message to Kat.

1 hr left.

U can do it!

I smirk, naughty thoughts running through my head. *Got anything to motivate me?*

I seriously don't expect her to reply, and at first I think maybe she's busy. With about thirty seconds left in the commercial break, my phone buzzes again and I pick it up to see it's a pic.

"Oh, Jesus," I whisper as I see Kat, naked from the waist up, her hair framing her face as she shows me a mouthful of what's obviously milk or something, but the image gets through, especially as she's let a little dribble from the side of her mouth.

Motivated enough?

I gulp, my cock surging in my pants until I'm nearly desperate to have some relief. With shaking thumbs, I text back. *Don't plan on sleeping alone. And no panties 4 our date.*

She sends back an evil smiley emoji, and I've got a very horny and very worried feeling that I've unleashed a long-repressed . . . perfection.

So what is a second date to you?

Kat's quick with her reply. *It's late, so pick me up. We can have drinks at a bar around the corner.*

I'm aware enough to see Susannah giving me the signal, and I go back to the show, faking my way through another email. As soon as I can, I'm back on my phone with Kat.

Still listening?

Always. Getting some new ideas too. If you're good . . . maybe I'll show you. Not second date tho. Gotta wait a little longer.

My balls are aching, but her message is clear. No sex tonight. Fuck. Okay, I guess I'll survive. I try to go back to the show, but I'm distracted by thoughts of Kat and I know I'm fumbling my way through some of the calls. Hopefully, no one's noticing.

During the next song break, Fifty's *Candy Shop*, I duck out to not only take a piss but to get my head right.

Honestly, Suz does have a reason to be upset with me. I realize I've phoned it in tonight, on exactly the type of show I shouldn't be. God, just the idea of three hours of talk about blowjobs has me rolling my eyes while at the same time, my cock pulses in my pants, thinking of Kat and her pic.

But that's the problem, I should be focusing, I should be able to for three hours. I shouldn't be focusing on Kat but instead on each of my callers. If I get bored, I crack jokes with Susannah about the calls or emails. I deliver on the mic, not on text.

"Tomorrow," I promise myself as I head back down the hallway. I open the door to see Susannah not in her mini-booth but in mine. Surprised, I stop to see her set my phone down on my desk. "Somethin' wrong?"

"Sorry," she says, seemingly all smiles. "Your phone was buzzing around again. I turned it off for now, if you don't mind. We really need to focus and finish tonight out right."

"I agree," I reply a little sheepishly. "I'm sorry about tonight's show. I know it's been a clusterfuck sometimes, and you've saved my ass. I'll do better tomorrow."

"I get it, I really do," Susannah says. "Derrick, we've all got shows that are tough and lives outside this place. But we've got the potential to do really great things here, bigger and better than ever, but that will never happen if you're fucking around, barely dialing it in for the shows. I'm happy to do the prep, research, and planning. All you've got to do is show up and speak, but tonight, you've barely done that. I need you to be a fucking pro like usual, okay?"

The venom in her last sentence irks me and I'm about to shoot back about her own cattiness, but Fifty's ending and we've got to get back on the air.

Somehow, we get through the rest of the show and ironically, things go well enough that as the outro music plays, Susannah's in a lot better mood.

"Hey, D?"

I'm in a hurry to see Kat, but still, I look over, leaning back in my chair. "Yeah?"

"Sorry about the bitch act before. I'm just worried about you, that's all. Is everything okay? You keep texting and calling and that's not you. This isn't the first time that's happened lately either. You seem distracted. Anything I can do to help?"

I shake my head, getting out of my chair. "No, I'll get it together. I'm sorry too. Do me a favor though—let's just keep this between us, but I met someone and it's a little all-consuming. I got this, promise."

"Fresh relationships are like that," Susannah agrees. "Lucky girl. Is that all?"

"No, I was talking to my dad but he's fine. Just been awhile since I really spent time with him, so I gave him some more text time than I should have. All good, sorry if I wasn't pulling my weight. I'll do better."

"Okay," Susannah says, giving me her trademark smile. "Keep it up though, and I'll make sure that we do a whole slew of topics that you hate. Should I go crazy romantic until you vomit pink roses, or some seriously kinky fetish that makes your ass pucker? I got it . . . baby talk. Does Derrick-werrick need a little powder-poofy?" She laughs maniacally, and I can't help but grin at her. This is why we work together.

"Okay, okay . . . I promise to get it together as long as you never, ever call me *that* again! You mind wrapping up the studio? I kinda have a date." I smile, knowing it's a big ask after the night we've had but hopeful she'll cut me some slack because I need to get to Kat.

"Go party, Don Juan de Radio," Suz says. "But I demand perfection tomorrow. We're poised for great things!"

I'm already walking toward the door, thankful for the reprieve, but I answer her. "We *are* doing great things, Suz. We're actually helping people here."

She says it softly, but I hear it anyway. "But we could help more if we had a bigger platform. Syndication, Derrick. We're so close."

"It'll happen or it won't, Suz. I'm happy either way. Don't worry about chickens that aren't even eggs yet. Anyway, gotta run. Thanks! You're the best. Tomorrow . . . I promise. I'm back on track and ready to rock." And before the door even closes behind me, all thoughts of work whoosh out of my head to be replaced with Kat and how she's waiting for me.

CHAPTER
Fourteen

KAT

"WELL, well, this isn't too bad," Derrick says as he closes the door to the bar behind me, cutting off the icy wind. The holiday season isn't that far off, and honestly, I'm making a few early Christmas wishes even if I know they won't come true.

"It's no dive, but it's not so fancy that nobody can afford a mineral water," I admit. "As long as you don't mind not having a coat check girl."

"Never had a need for that," Derrick growls, looking me over. "I've got everything I want right here."

Heat creeps up my neck as he consumes me with his gaze, and I know that I made the right choice in clothes. Sure, my calves are cold, but this hip hugging skirt and tight blouse look sexy as hell. Or at least it seems to tick all the boxes that Derrick likes.

"Should we sit?" I ask, and Derrick nods, his hand warm on my lower back as he leads me over to a corner table. The lights are low. It's that time of night where people are here to either quietly drink their sorrows away or find someone.

"You know," Derrick says as he takes my jacket to hang it over one of the spare chairs, "you didn't have to."

"Didn't have to what?" I ask, waiting while the waitress comes over. I order a glass of white wine while Derrick orders a beer on tap, and we decide on some tapas to give us something to nibble on besides each other.

"You didn't have to get dressed up," Derrick says. "You don't need to show off for me. I feel like you've never been more comfortable than when we hung out over breakfast and you were wearing yoga pants and an old white t-shirt."

"I'm trying to be more comfortable," I admit. "But no way am I going out with you wearing *that*."

Derrick smiles and nods. "Just so you know. You're sexy, beautiful, *and* you've got brains. What's there not to like?"

"Good question," I reply. "What about you? You've gotta have a few bad tendencies."

"Sure," Derrick says, pausing when our drinks are brought and we toast each other. "For one, I'm terrible at laundry. In fact, I've got a single method. I pick up everything on the floor and chuck it all in the washer at once. Main reason I have all dark clothes . . . black, grey, charcoal, navy."

"You what?" I ask, sipping my wine. It's good and warm as it flows down my throat.

"Let's just say . . . pink football practice pants," Derrick says with a chuckle. "Take one pair of football pants, two brand-new red cotton t-shirts, throw in hot water with cheap detergent, and magic happens. So yeah, all darks and that doesn't happen."

I laugh, imagining Derrick wearing pink football pants. "Okay, that'll teach you. Thankfully for me, wearing pink pants isn't a problem."

"Nope, never had a problem with you and anything pink," Derrick purrs, heat blooming between my legs. "So . . . how was your day? Miss me?"

I giggle, thinking of all that we've done so far today. "How could I have? You were texting me all day."

"When I get motivation like you sent me, I have to."

"I admit, that was pretty dirty. I hope you didn't get in trouble."

"Not too much. Susannah did almost kill me today between texting you and my dad, but that's not your fault."

"Is he okay?" I ask, worried, and Derrick waves me off.

"Yeah, he was just checking in. I think he didn't realize the time at first. He knows I work in the studio, even if he doesn't listen in often . . . thankfully."

"Oh, I'm sure," I tease. "I mean, what father would want to listen to their son talk all about how to please a man with your mouth? Speaking of which . . . you never answered some questions tonight about what you like best."

Derrick leans in, smiling. "I think you know the answer to that one. You know exactly what I like. And for a woman who said that she wasn't going to do it anyway, you're waving a red flag at a bull that's about to charge you."

"Don't let me taunt you at work. I know how serious you take helping your listeners. After all, look where we are," I joke back, my pussy tingling underneath my skirt. "You've helped me a lot so far."

Derrick nods, reaching across the table to place his warm fingers on top of my hand, sparks radiating up my arm from the contact.

"I take it very seriously. What can I do to keep helping you, Kitty Kat?"

There's a thousand things Derrick could do, but as we've moved into something more fragile here with actually dating, I know the most important thing he can do.

"Maybe just show me a good time and that not all guys are after one thing?"

"And what one thing is that?"

"You know . . ." I whisper back, heat creeping up my neck again. "Fucking."

Derrick leans in closer, his voice low and seductive. "But what if I do want to fuck you? Right now, as much as I know I should be, I don't want to be a gentleman. I want to bend you over this table and slip your skirt over your ass. I could make you come right here."

I'd let you and come like a freight train, I think, but I have to keep control somehow, so I flirt back instead. "Rather public, don't you think?"

Derrick glances around, then comes back to me, his eyes burning. "Would you rather disappear to the back? We could do that if you want? Kat, I respect you and if you say no, I'll accept that. But . . . I think you want to say yes."

My breath catches in my chest. He's got me. Sure, I don't want to be easy to get, but the way he makes me feel, I want him inside me every fucking moment we're together.

Derrick leans in, his thumb drawing circles on my hand, making my nipples tighten in my bra and my pussy clench.

"There's nothing wrong with wanting it. I want you just as much. We could sneak back there and find a dark corner, maybe you sink down to your knees and suck my cock right there. I'd stand in front of you so no one could see. No one would be the wiser but us. Only we would know how much you drive me crazy."

"I drive *you* crazy?" I murmur, feeling a little bit of control return. He's right, we both want it . . . we just have to figure out where. "Little ol' me?"

Derrick leans in closer, and our lips are this close to touching when there's a harsh harrumph next to us and a sneering laugh. I'm horrified to see Kevin standing there, smirking like he's busting me doing something wrong.

He looks a little extra swollen, obviously using his free time in the gym the last few weeks. And like super tan . . . orange fake-bake tan. Eww. I sit back, my elbow bumping my wine glass, but I catch it before it crashes to the floor. I definitely don't need any more attention in this moment.

"Kevin? What the fuck?"

Kevin chuckles. "Seriously, Kat, this is sad. I mean this guy? He looks like a total douchebag."

"Fuck you!" I hiss, feeling the flush paint my cheeks. Deep down, I don't really care what Kevin thinks or says, but in the moment, with him sneering at me, it's hard not to react or to fall into old habits. "You don't get a say in whom I see. You cheated on me, remember?"

"Didn't take you long to find some new dick," Kevin replies, not taking the obvious hint to leave. He looks at Derrick, who's coiled tight, ready to get up if need be, but he's also letting me handle this myself for now. I appreciate that he knows I need to do this. He talks to Derrick, but Kevin's eyes are on me, watching his barbs hit home. "Can I give you a tip, man? You don't need to go through that much effort. She's an easy fuck. Not that good, but easy." He leans back, the pride at seeing the insecurities he's brought up in me obvious in his eyes.

Derrick's heard enough and gets to his feet. For the first time, I see that he actually towers over Kevin by a couple of inches.

"Okay, that's it," Derrick rumbles. "I've heard enough of this."

"Oh, I'm shaking in my boots," Kevin drawls, wiggling his fingers. "Why don't you sit back down, buddy? You don't know who you're talking to."

"Sure I do," Derrick says, his voice dropping to a threatening whisper. "You're the two-pump chump piece of shit who couldn't give Kat what she deserved. You took advantage of her, fucked around on her, and lost her. Now, you've probably figured out that she was the best damn woman to walk into your life and you blew it. She figured out you're worthless, and she deserves better."

"And you think *you're* better?" Kevin says. He laughs, half turning away, but it's a feint. His left hand flashes out, catching Derrick just above the eyebrow, and the fight's on.

It's the first fight I've seen since a little push-shove thing in high school, and it's nothing like the movies. Nobody gets involved to peel them apart, but at the same time, it doesn't last long. Kevin tries to follow up his punch with another, but Derrick grabs his arm and somehow pushes it across his body. Kevin's thrown off-balance, and as he stumbles past, Derrick picks him up in a massive bear hug before slamming him to the floor of the bar.

"That's enough!" the bartender yells. "Don't make me call the cops!"

"Call them. I'm pressing charges," Kevin whines from underneath Derrick. "He assaulted me."

"Boy, from where I'm sittin', you threw the first punch and he defended himself from your shenanigans. Where I come from, you put money in the register, you gon' get a receipt more often than not," one of the bar patrons drawls. "Figure at least four more of us saw the same thing."

Kevin looks like he's about to whine, but he slumps down. Derrick gets up, and I notice he's bleeding. I go to touch the wound as Kevin gets up, grabbing a tumbler off a nearby table, but one hard look from Derrick is all it takes, and he lets go of the weapon to leave the bar.

"Are you okay?" Derrick asks, turning to look at me for the first time. "I'm sorry. I would have let you handle that, but he was being a bit too much of an asshole."

I feel oddly excited. I mean, Derrick just went Neanderthal. Why not clunk me on the head and drag me back to his cave by the hair? But I'm turned on, power coursing through me not only in that I stood up to Kevin, but that Derrick had my back.

I grab his head and pull him down into a deep kiss, our tongues swirling as I reward him for being there for me.

"Let's get out of here and get that cut looked at," I whisper.

———

I usher Derrick onto the couch, where I strip off my jacket. "Okay, let me get the alcohol," I say, going to grab my kit.

I come back, soaking a few cotton balls in alcohol. I dab at his cut, which is a lot deeper than I expected. "Damn," Derrick says, inspecting it. "Got any tape?"

"Uh . . . probably," I say, looking in my kit. "Why?"

"Learned from a friend," Derrick says, taking the roll. He tears strips and carefully covers the cut with a narrow piece of gauze before taping his eyebrow back together. "Damn . . . could have done without this, but there was no way I was throwing the first punch."

"You let him hit you," I whisper, running my finger through his hair just above his eyebrow. "Why?"

"Because you deserve to have someone take a punch for you," Derrick says, his hand closing over mine and pulling me closer. "Besides, I heard somewhere that chicks dig scars."

I chuckle and gently trace my fingertips along his forehead and down around his eye to his cheek. I'm checking for any tender spots but mostly just marking him with my touch, appreciating that he was willing to sacrifice himself for me. I dip down, finding his lips with mine, hoping he feels the *thank you* I'm trying to communicate with my kisses. The fire we've been stoking for the last few days rages at my center, and I need to . . . worship him.

This man isn't showing me who I am but is helping me actually discover who I am for myself, which feels even more important. I lower to my knees, my face level with the hardness already pressing against his jeans.

"Kat, you don't have to. What about our second date?" There's a plea to his voice, and I know he's trying his damndest to do the right thing. But I know that *this* is the right thing. It's not some guidebook dating rule, arbitrary so everyone thinks you're a 'good girl'. This is just real and what I want. Using all the tips from the show today, and maybe a few tricks of my own, I take Derrick to the edge in minutes.

"Damn it, Kat. Just like that . . . suck that cock, take me all in. Are you gonna swallow for me? Because I'm about to fill you up. Where do you want it?" I feel his balls pull tight, and I suck him in deep, leaving no doubt to my answer. I swallow down every drop, satisfaction humming through me.

I lay my head on his thigh, tracing lines along his softening cock as he pants above me. I realize that I'm really falling for him, despite my misgivings and fears, and that's both exciting and terrifying. He's not just healing my heart like the casual rebound I thought this might be, but he's filling my heart with new hopes and dreams, which feels dangerous.

CHAPTER

Fifteen

DERRICK

I WAKE up in an increasingly familiar, comfortable tangle of arms and legs, opening my eyes to see again the increasingly familiar poster of Einstein with his tongue poking out that's next to the closet. I stretch, feeling Kat's breast shift to press warmly against my ribs.

"Mmm, good morning."

"Mid-morning." Kat yawns sleepily. "You better be glad that my job lets me do flex time, stud. Let's get brunch."

I hum happily, turning over and kissing her forehead. "I don't know about brunch, but I've got a nice sausage for you if you're interested."

Kat chuckles but reaches down and gives my cock a good morning stroke. "I've never thought of myself as sexually insatiable before meeting you. Now it's like sex is as necessary as oxygen or high-speed Wi-Fi."

I laugh and give her a kiss. After the passionate heat of last night, both of our bodies are taken care of for now, and we roll out of bed, getting ready for the day.

"How's the eye?" Kat asks as she quickly showers. "Oh, and if you don't mind pink, I've got some disposable razors in the medicine cabinet. Gonna have to use soap though."

"Conditioner will do the trick," I reply, finding a bottle and squeezing it out. "Did a show on grooming for lovemaking once and found out that conditioner is better for softening the hair and the skin than soap. As for the eye, not too bad. The tape held it together."

We swap places, and I wash carefully, avoiding my eye. When I get out, Kat's already in her bedroom getting dressed. What I see stirs both my loins and something else as she pulls on a pair of her ever-present jeans, but instead of one of her normal shirts, she has on one of mine.

"Where'd you get that?"

"You left it the second night you came over," Kat says, blushing. It's adorable. My shirt practically swallows her to the point she could wear it like a dress if she wants. "Mind if I wear it?"

"Looks better on you than it ever did on me," I say, pulling her in close. "You're beautiful, Katrina Snow. And you make me feel lucky to be part of your life."

We kiss tenderly while I pick her up, amazed at how far things have gone and glad at the same time. I set her down, looking at the way my shirt covers her, wrapping her up the way I'd like to but knowing we need to get some food . . . fuel, whatever.

She steps back, putzing with the oversized shirt, rolling the sleeves and tying it at the waist in an almost country-girl fashion, but when she's done, I whistle.

"Woman, you definitely make that shirt look better than I ever did. As far as I'm concerned, it's yours. And I want to see you in that and nothing else very soon."

Kat looks at herself in the mirror and gives me a grin. Reaching down, she unbuttons one more button, giving me a hint of her cleavage.

"You make me feel sexy, and I want the world to know it. Now . . . pancakes!"

We drive to a nearby restaurant, ordering complete brunch specials, and chat innocently while sipping our orange juice. Just after our plates arrive, I hear a voice call out my name.

"Hey, D!"

I turn, grinning as Jacob dominates the room, his massive presence almost making the tightly packed tables and booths melt away.

"Jacob, I didn't even know you were in town."

"Yeah, well, team's got a long week with the Monday night game, so Coach gave us an extra day off. Who's your friend?" Jacob asks, giving Kat his Sports Illustrated megawatt smile. "Jacob Knight. Pleased to meet you."

"Jacob, this is my girlfriend, Katrina Snow. Kat, Jacob's my old college roommate."

His eyes widen a little at my calling Kat my girlfriend, and I didn't even mean to say it at first—it just sort of came out. But it feels right, and as the surprise melts away, I can see that Kat's pleased as punch with the designation.

"It's nice to meet you," Kat says. "Join us for brunch?"

"That little snack? We're in the middle of the season. I need protein, so excuse me . . ." He motions to the waitress, who buzzes to the table, seemingly overjoyed to be asked to come over judging by the way she's been eyeing Jacob. "Can I get a half-dozen eggs, scrambled, four slices of bacon, extra crispy, and a bowl of oatmeal with a touch of brown sugar?" The waitress nods absently in a trance as she stares at Jacob's mouth before she snaps out of it and scurries off. Jacob laughs, looking back at us. "What do you think the chances are she's going to get that right?"

He settles in, and under the table, I can feel Kat's hand rest on my thigh. She gives me a squeeze, and when I look in her eyes, they're full of emotion that I know we'll talk about soon.

For now, though, Jacob's full of energy and questions. "So, where'd you get the shiner, man? Didn't I teach you enough to avoid a beating?"

"It's not a shiner. It's a cut. And that deflection move that you and I drilled for two summers came in handy," I tell him. I fill him in on the incident with Kevin, Jacob's face clouding at first before clearing.

"So, he did you right?" Jacob asks Kat, who smiles and nods. "Good. Because if he doesn't, give me a call. I'll show him a few moves that I haven't taught him yet. I wouldn't worry, though. D's a good man."

I watch as Jacob and Kat get to know each other, and I'm glad to see that they get along well. They're total and complete opposites, the towering physical gladiator who makes his millions by terrorizing quarterbacks while she makes apps for smartphones and tablets, but it seems to be working. He's gregarious and rarely stops talking, asking questions and giving her quieter approach a direction to keep the conversation rolling.

"So, you listen to Derrick's show?" Kat asks in surprise. "Just didn't think that'd happen. You're sort of . . ."

"Big?" Jacob asks ironically, making Kat laugh. "Yeah, well, if anything, that helps guys like me. I ain't ashamed to admit it—I've used a few tips D's said to help things along. Haven't found the right girl yet, but that's okay. I gotta say, though," he says as he stares Derrick down. "You've never called me up after a breakup to see if I was doing okay." He fakes a sniffle, tracing a dry fingertip down his cheek like it's a tear before grinning madly.

I see Kat blush, and I know just what she's thinking about. "You're a big boy. I figure you know to pick up the phone if that's what you need. No offense."

"None taken," Jacob says. Kat gets up, and he rises like a gentleman. "You okay?"

"Yeah." Kat giggles, charmed. "Just two cups of coffee and then OJ . . . ladies' room is calling. Excuse me a moment."

Kat walks away, and Jacob turns back to me. "Seems like a good girl. She gets the stamp of approval."

I laugh. "Didn't know I needed one, but thanks. Why's that?"

"Just seems like the girl for you, that's all. Listen, D, I've known you for almost a decade now. Everyone has a type that's meant for them. Me . . . I need some kick-ass chick who's going to take no prisoners and probably butt heads with me right up until the point we're tearing each other's clothes off. You though, you're the kind that needs someone you just gel with. And while you two aren't peas and carrots, you gel."

"Peas and carrots?" I ask, smirking. "Let me guess, *Forrest Gump* on the last cross-country flight?"

"Besides," Jacob continues, not getting thrown off at all, "you like her too. I can see it in your eyes and not just that cut over your eyebrow. She's doing something to you, man. And in my opinion, it's a *good* something."

"Yeah, well, I gotta take my time. The asshole ex we told you about isn't the only guy who's treated her like shit in the past. So I plan to just treat her right, go slow, and treat her with the respect that I don't think any other man has ever given her, and we'll see what happens."

Jacob nods sagely. "Well said, brother. Might not be a complex game plan, but it's a solid one. Hey, I can get you another ticket for the game if you want to bring her with your dad."

"Fuck, yeah!" I reply, grinning. "You're the best, man."

"I can get you one of the cheerleader outfits for her too . . . if the Love Whisperer is into that."

I close my eyes, imagining Kat in a cheerleader outfit. Not a bad idea, but maybe later. "Probably not a safe idea for now. But thanks for the offer."

CHAPTER
Sixteen

KAT

I FEEL GIGGLY and light as I wrap up my coding for the evening, knowing that I'm rocking this new app and am right on target for my deadline. I kick back in my cubicle, pulling out my phone.

"I can miss Derrick's show for *one* night," I say to myself. "Besides, I can get the real deal any time I want now. So . . ."

I hit speed dial, glad that I have most of the office to myself.

After just two rings, the call's picked up. "Hey, babe, how's life in the silicon world?"

I smile. Sounds like Elise is doing better. "Not bad, how's life in the dirt sheets?"

"Same as always, dirty, and I can only tell half of it," Elise says. "Gimme some good news. I can use some after the shit I listened to today."

"Well . . ." I say, drawing it out, "you won't believe what happened last night."

I tell Elise about my night out that turned into a night of passion with Derrick, leaving out my nude 'swallow' pic, glossing over most of my day and really starting the story after Derrick picked me up and we went to the bar.

"That local place we've been to?" Elise asks. "Fancy."

I chuckle at the sarcasm and continue. "Derrick didn't mind. Actually, it was going great. We'd gotten our tapas order in and were sharing more about ourselves. Derrick was flirting with me pretty hardcore, but I liked it."

"You seem to like everything he does," Elise says, but there's not too much jealousy there. "At least tell me he's hung like a peanut so I don't have to kill you."

"Sorry, you're just gonna have to kill me," I joke back. "But, you'll love him too when you hear what happened next. Kevin showed up."

"That son of a bitch," Elise growls. "Bastard better be glad I wasn't there. I'd have castrated him with a broken beer bottle."

I don't doubt it, and that's why I love her so damn much. "Derrick wasn't too happy either. But he was so fucking awesome. First, he let me handle it, just having my back. But when Kevin crossed the line . . . Derrick handed him his ass."

"Is that so?" Elise comments, impressed. "Well then, babe, I'm starting to like Derrick more and more. Anyone who stands up for my girl is worth a thank you grope."

"Uh-huh, hands off my man. This morning, we went to brunch and he introduced me to Jacob Knight . . . as his girlfriend."

"Jacob Knight, the football stud?" Elise says, whistling. "Phew, that's a lot of man there. I've heard rumors about him too. Let's just say the man knows his way around the field, in football and with women."

"Maybe, but he was a total gentleman with me. As we were leaving, he even said he'd get me a ticket to join Derrick and his father for an upcoming game. I'm . . .I can't believe I'm saying this, but I'm excited to go to a football game!"

"Sounds like you'd be excited to go to a demolition derby if it was with Derrick," Elise says. "Maybe he can use that sexy radio voice to tell you all the plays step by detailed step." She mimics a sultry seductress tone. "The tight end grabs the ball, tugging it close to his body and letting loose a burst of speed as he thrusts toward the end zone. Touchdown. Oh, my . . . the celebratory champagne seems to have spilled all over his sweaty body. Bubbles popping . . . everywhere."

I erupt into giggles at her silly antics. "Holy shit, Elise. That's some upper-level imagination there, and I didn't know you had that voice. You never told me you were a phone-sex operator, but I'd believe it now. Were you undercover for a story or just needing a bit of extra cash?"

She laughs back, taking my teasing in stride. "Whatever. You try that voice on Derrick and he'll be eating out of your hand . . . or whatever orifice you want him to eat out." We're both quiet for a moment, the laughter giving way but the smile still stretching my face. "But seriously, babe, if I didn't know any better . . ."

"What?" I ask, curious where she's going now after her little tangent.

"Nothing, it's just . . . what do you feel for him? What's happening with you two?"

I bite my lip, chewing thoughtfully as I try to figure out the words. "Elise, since getting together with Derrick, I feel like a little bit of that darkness inside me is starting to fade. He's a gentleman with a naughty streak a mile wide that he still respects me with. He's protective, he's kind, he listens when I bore the shit out of him talking about work . . . I think I'm falling for him. Hard."

"Whoa. You sure, babe? I mean, I'm happy as fuck for you, but . . . you're you. And no offense, but this sounds awfully fast. I mean, considering what you've been through."

"I know, which is part of what scares the hell out of me. There's no logic in this, and I need a balanced pro/con sheet to feel like life makes sense. He's a radio personality with a sports background. I'm going to be reading *Football For Dummies* so I can understand the damn game I'm invited to. He's tall and built like a Greek statue. I'm . . . well, like you said, I'm me."

"So you're scared," Elise says. "You're going by your guts and not your brains."

"And you know what happens when I let my heart get involved," I reply. "What if D's just like every other man I've let inside?"

"He could be, but he could also be the guy who might give you what you most deserve," Elise says. "A happily ever after."

"A happily ever after? Those are for cheesy romance books and fairy tales."

Elise snickers and raises her voice, singing, *"When you wish upon a star . . ."*

"Yeah, yeah," I snort. "You're a horrible Jiminy Cricket. No offense, but your conscience is not much better than mine, and you're a hell of a lot hotter."

"Why, thank you. I do say I'm a lot more fuckable than an insect," Elise retorts. "Listen, I gotta ask up front after your Kevin bombshell, or lack of bombshelling, I should say. Does Derrick knock your socks off?"

I giggle, feeling warmth between my thighs as I think of Derrick last night. "My socks, my panties, my bra . . . he's the best *ever*. If he were a computer program, he'd be the Big Oh-S-E-X."

"Apple's so going to love that you're making fun of their operating system." Elise snickers. "Nerd dirty talk, gotta love it. So, what's his style? Pound you into submissive bliss, or do you like to take charge?"

"That's the thing," I admit, my heart beating a little faster, "he's so good at listening, reading my body language. Like last night, I started off saying I wanted to be all prim and proper, no sex on the second date. But he read me so well and pushed his flirting to delicious naughtiness. My God, Elise, I was so ready to go to a dark corner and get it on in public. Me! In public! Can you imagine? But this morning, after we woke up, he totally saw that I wasn't really feeling it for sex, and we just talked as I showered. We even broke the toilet barrier."

"You're fucking shitting me," Elise says wonderingly. She's the one who introduced me to the various barriers, with the toilet barrier, or feeling comfortable enough to use the toilet in front of the other person, being one of the greatest. "You aren't *maybe* falling for him. You're head over heels for this guy. Is there any limit you won't cross with him?"

"I don't know. Sometimes, I feel like if that man asks me anything, I'd do it," I admit. "God, I can't believe it. I am so head over heels for this man. Okay, pause button pressed or I'm gonna get too worked up and have to call him back for a repeat performance." I shake my head a bit, rattling the sexy thoughts of Derrick out, and hear Elise laughing at me across the line. "What about you? Tell me about your day. Any better news about your boss? Are you still dating that same guy? The chef."

"Trevor?" Elise asks, snorting. "Nah, he was a tumbling, bumbling dick-weed. Today's mostly sucked because I'm chasing some stupid celeb rumors. Fuck, why couldn't I have been on the Prince Harry and Meghan Markle beat?"

"Because you're barred from the UK after that little incident five years ago?" I tease, making Elise give me a long, loud raspberry in my ear.

"I wasn't banned from the whole country, just the Defence Ministry," Elise says. "And besides, the reporter's not going to England. It's all state-side reporting. I didn't get the assignment though because I'm not willing to fuck my way into plum assignments, unlike some people in my office," she says with a snotty tone. "Really, though, I'm cool. Standard stuff, nothing too exciting right now . . . usual celeb sightings, gossip mongering, ass-kissing, and covering to prevent lawsuits. Hey, what do you think of money shots?"

"Money shots?" I ask.

"Oh, come on, Kat. You know what a money shot is. When a guy blows his load all over—"

"I know what a money shot is. That was just so random I figured you meant something else."

Elise laughs. "Sorry, I'm chasing a rumor that there's a TV star whose specialty is getting money shots with some pretty A-list celebs. Can't name names yet, you know how that shit is, but what do you think?"

"I guess it depends on the couple? I mean, if they're both into it, who am I to say no?"

"Yup, you've been Love Whispered," Elise jokes. "So sweet, yet sexy, and no smut to you at all."

"You mean, too high-class," I tease. "Like you, babe. Elise, you're a legit journalist. I've read your real work. Why are you chasing down who blows a load in who's face?"

"Pays the bills for now. You know that. Just like your work on that never-to-be mentioned again adult dating sim. Not saying I always like it, but it does pay well."

"Yeah, but . . ." I reply, then sigh, not wanting to make her feel bad about her job, even if she really is too good for the drivel she reports on. "Okay, I get it. So, now that Trevor's out of the way, anything interesting for you?"

"Not really, but I am hitting a club tonight with a few coworkers. It's *mostly* a work outing though. I won't be there looking to get my freak on," Elise admits. "Wanna join us? I got a new skirt that would make your ass look like a million bucks."

I think about it, then hum. "No can do. I got a man."

"What's your man got to do with me?" Elise asks, joking right along with me. "Come on, be my wing girl. I'm not going to get my freak on, but I didn't say I'm not gonna flirt. Drinks are on me."

I shake my head, leaning back. "No, that's okay, Elise. Not saying I'm not interested in hanging with my best friend . . . I'm just sort of hoping to see or talk to Derrick after his show, know what I mean?"

"I know exactly what you mean. Four letter word, starts with L, ends with E. You know, I . . ." Elise says, her words failing her for a moment. "I'm happy for you, Kat. I really am. Listen, I need to maintain my saucy bitchiness, so I'm gonna get ready to go. This weekend or something, girl time though, okay?"

"Only if you bring chocolate chip cookies to my place. And you can teach me about football. You dated a quarterback in college, right?"

Elise laughs. "I caught more balls from him than anyone on the team, but that doesn't mean I know a damn thing about football. But we'll figure it out together. Talk to you later."

CHAPTER
Seventeen

DERRICK

MY PHONE IS out of my pocket as soon as my front door's closed, and I flop down in my favorite chair, the line ringing in my ear.

"Hey, sexy man," Kat purrs, making my cock twitch. "I thought I heard a little tension in your voice tonight. What, behaving while you talked about how to go down on a woman for three hours has you worked up?"

I reach down, massaging my already hardening cock. "Fuck, Kitty Kat, you know I was thinking of you all show long. You were right to have your phone turned off. But . . . goddamn, I couldn't stop thinking of how good you taste."

"Mmm, I was thinking of you too. Especially when you talked about doing that figure-eight with your tongue, you naughty man, giving away your special move on me. Millions of women will thank you later."

"Just need one," I rasp, my cock hard and tenting my pants. "Fuck, I miss you. Remind me again why we couldn't get together tonight?"

Kat chuckles, lowering her voice just the way she knows I like it. "Because *I* have to put in a *very* long, *hard* day behind my keyboard tomorrow," she teases. "*Someone's* been keeping me so distracted with thoughts of his big cock pumping in and out of me that I've got a lot to catch up on."

"You know I'm sorry about that," I half tease. "I thought I was inspiring you."

"Oh, you are, but if we saw each other tonight, we both know we're not going to get any sleep. I'd spend all night with my legs wrapped around your hips, pulling you into me and holding you deep inside."

"And that's a problem why?" I tease, reaching for the button on my jeans.

"Because I have to put the finishing touches on this app for the presentation at the end of the week. You know how hard I've been working on this.

Other than being with you, I've put nearly every minute of every day for the last few months into this and it's all coming down to the presentation. I've got to prove myself as more than a one-hit wonder and the graphics are giving the team a hard time to integrate with the gesture-sensing technology . . . oops, sorry, I get a little excited and fall down the rabbit hole sometimes. It's just a few days apart and then we can have our next date at the football game."

I run my hand through my hair, knowing she's right but also knowing that I have to have her. "I know, I just miss you. Your business doesn't mean we can't go back to our roots a bit though, does it?"

There's a throaty, sexy chuckle that makes my throat go dry, and Kat comes back on. "Definitely not. But promise me one thing . . . one and done. This can't be an all-nighter."

One and done? The way I'm feeling right now, it might be five minutes and goodnight, but I'll do my best. "I promise."

My phone dings, and I see she's sending me a FaceTime call. I quickly hit the *Accept* button, and what I see makes my jaw drop.

Kat's grinning at me, already changed into a set of not trashy but definitely sexy lingerie, a sheer teddy and lacy boy shorts that give me quite a view of her ass cheeks as she poses, twirling for me before sitting down on her couch.

"Whatcha think, boyfriend?"

"You little cock tease!" I growl even as I grin. "You had this planned all along."

"Maybe," Kat says with a naughty smirk. "Are you complaining?"

"Definitely not, just wish I were there with you to take that sexy top off with my teeth."

Kat giggles naughtily, running a thumb under the strap on her teddy. "Oh, this thing?" She plays with the straps on her shoulders, dipping them down in turn before pulling it back up and cupping her breasts, lifting them up for my inspection. "I just figured it showed off the feature you like best about me."

"You know I love your tits," I growl, leaning forward. "But I love every single thing about you. That's why I love you."

Kat stops, her eyes wide with emotion. We've said it to each other before, but it still hits with a lot of feeling every time.

"And I love you. But . . ." she says, slipping back into her playful flirtiness, "I can't just pull my heart out of my chest. Things don't work that way. I can, however . . ."

Kat lifts her breasts up again, sliding the teddy down to reveal the beautiful half globes to me. Pressing them together, she jiggles them a little.

"You do like these too, right?"

Reaching down off camera, I open my jeans, letting my cock jut out tall and stiff. "Yes, Kitty Kat, just like that. Show those perfect tits to me. Rub your thumb across your nipples until they're all pearled up for me."

Kat moans, doing just as I ask while lifting them. She tweaks and rubs her nipples, and I can't stop myself from reaching down to slowly stroke my cock.

"Mmm, baby, I know you're amazing in person. But I won't lie, I've missed this. It's been awhile since we've had to do this long-distance, and it's . . ."

Her voice drifts off, and I add a bit of steel to my gravelly voice. "Tell me, Kat. Tell me what you're thinking, what you're feeling."

She lets out a sigh. "You make me feel clean and dirty at the same time. I love imagining it's your hands squeezing me."

Kat tells me exactly how she feels, her hands massaging as she throws her head back, and my cock throbs in my grip. "Fuck you've got me so hard."

"Show me," Kat rasps, picking her phone up. "Show me that thick, beautiful cock that I love to feel stroking in and out of my soaked pussy."

I tilt my camera, showing her. I wrap my hand around my shaft, pumping it slowly until a drop of precum oozes out the top. "Is that what you like? You want that little raindrop, a bit of sweetness? I want to trace it along your lips like lipstick until you're glossy with it. And then have you lick it all off before you suck my cock to get more."

"Mmm," Kat moans. "You know I do. I love the taste of you. God, you make me feel so naughty."

"You're my naughty little slut now, aren't you?" I ask as I pump my cock for her, letting her see how the head swells with each stroke. "You dream of having my cock fucking you anywhere and everywhere you are."

"Oh, shit," Kat gasps. Her screen shifts, and I see that she's got two fingers buried inside her pussy already, pumping them in and out. "I love being your little plaything. Nothing boring about me now."

"Never was, you just needed to feel safe to explore." I moan, watching her fingers. "That's it, baby. Watch me, pace yourself with me. Slide those slick fingers into your tight little cunt as I fuck my fist for you." I time my strokes with her hand, both of us rising.

Kat cries out, needing more, and uses her other hand to tug her boy shorts the rest of the way down, lewdly spreading her legs and showing every sexy inch of herself to me.

"Mmm . . . so, are you going to show me your pretty little asshole after the anal show?"

"Oh, God . . ." Kat whines, her fingers smearing her wetness around her clit before she plunges in again, her thumb stroking her clit. "I . . . I'd let you be my first. Fuck . . . oh, fuck, I'm gonna come soon."

"Do it, baby, I'm gonna come for you too," I reply, my hand speeding up. My cock throbs as I pump myself quickly, squeezing and relaxing. "My hand's not nearly as good as your hot, tight pussy, or even your little hands, but I could watch you tighten around your fingers, your thighs shaking forever. Squeeze your pussy tight, Kitty Kat. Choke those fingers the way I like it when you milk my cock." We both moan louder and louder, and it's enough. "Oh, fuck . . . Katrina!"

"Derrick . . ." Kat gasps as we both climax at the same time. I come hard, my cock erupting in thick spurts. Kat's hips shake and buck up and down on her couch, and it's a long time before either of us can move. When she does, she turns her phone to show me her smiling face. "Damn, baby . . . God, I love how you know just what to say."

"Just saying how you make me feel," I tell her. "And Kat . . . I love you."

She smiles, then giggles. "You love me all the way up to your chest from the way it looks. Glad I make you wear a condom, or else you'd have come shooting out my nose."

I grab my discarded t-shirt, wiping off the mess a bit. We chat for about another thirty minutes until Kat yawns. "Ready to turn in?"

"I'm beat," Kat admits. "I just hate getting up to an alarm. You wake me up so much better."

"After your presentation Friday, I can wake you up just the way you like more and more often," I assure her. "Uhm . . . maybe this is too quick, but if you'd like, you can move some things over here. I've got space in my closet for you."

"The closet barrier, huh?" Kat says, giggling when I give her a confused look. "I'll explain later. Let me think on it, and I'll call you after work tomorrow. I love you, Derrick. G'night."

"G'night, Kat. I love you too."

Eighteen

KAT

IT SEEMS ALMOST prophetic as I walk into the office, chugging what's already my second coffee of the day. It's Wednesday, and of course, the local radio station is cranking it loud. *I don't wanna work, I want to bang on the drum all day . . .*

"How nearly appropriate," I mutter to myself, half slinging my backpack onto my desk. Looking up, I see Tyler, one of the other coders. "Hey, Tyler, you mind turning that down?"

"Oh, lighten up, Kat, it's Hump Day!" Tyler, who isn't facing a deadline and certainly isn't worried about proving himself in this industry, calls back. "If you want, I can change it. Maybe some Rihanna on repeat? Work, work, work!"

I give him a glare that says I'm ready to work, not joke around. "As soon as the ode to Wednesday ends, can you turn it down though? I gotta focus and get this done."

"Will do," Tyler says. "Hey, Kat?"

"Yeah?"

"Kick some ass Friday. You know . . . because you're awesome."

I smile, feeling good that the guys around here support me. "Thanks, Tyler."

I sit down, reviewing the results of my last bug check. With a hundred thousand lines of code, it's a bitch to wrap my head around. Until now, it's been a matter of sending the app to various beta testers who put it through its paces, and then tracking down the errors they find.

But no amount of beta testing is going to be able to catch everything, so I hunker down, obsessively looking at my notes and trying to hunt down which lines need to be adjusted. It's hard, stressful work, and I'm running out of time.

Part of me knows I shouldn't stress. Lots of programs are released without being perfect. That's what updates and patches are for. But I really want to make sure this is good right off the bat so it doesn't get a bad rap.

Still, it's slow, dull work, and my mind keeps going to thoughts of Derrick. Since my talk with Elise where I realized how hard I was falling, and our subsequent confessions of 'I love you', we've texted constantly, even as he's given me time to do work. Pic exchanges helped some, but damn, there's no substitute for being in his arms.

The day wears on, lunch scarfed while I try to focus, but by the time six o'clock rolls around, my eyes are half-crossed and I'm needing a break. Firing up my browser, I go to the website that lets me listen in to Derrick, ready for my own Love Whispering on my headphones.

"Good evening, it's my personal second favorite day of the week, Hump Day Wednesday," Derrick says, making me grin. At least someone enjoys Wednesdays, even if it's just for a corny opening joke.

"What's your favorite day of the week?" Susannah asks. "Friday?"

"Nope," Derrick replies. "Saturday. Get to sleep in, watch cartoons in my PJs, and have the whole day and night to do whatever, or whomever, I want."

You mean you have all evening to spend with me, if the last month or so has been any indication, I think. *I like Saturdays too.*

Susannah gives a grade-school-worthy "Ooh!" and her delight at Derrick's joke is palpable.

"Tonight's show is about something that could even be more important than actual bedroom performance," Derrick says.

"Wait, there's something more important?"

"Yep. What's the point of having all the best tricks in the toolbox if you never get a chance to show them off?" Derrick asks. "What I mean, of course, is flirting and the art of meeting someone. Now, unless you get all your dates off Craigslist, you gotta actually talk to someone and meet them. That takes guts and sometimes reading signals. Not everyone has a blinking sign on their chest that says 'take me to bed, you big stud.'"

"You and I must go to very different parties then," Susannah quips. "Personally, I just have to say one word . . . yes."

I giggle. Susannah's funny sometimes. Normally, she's not, but recently, she's been a lot more playful as Derrick's been more straight-talking, less flirty.

"Maybe that works for you," Derrick says, chuckling, "but for a lot of us, we need some help. I sure did."

"You?" I ask in stereo with Susannah. "How?"

"Way back when, I developed a crush on one of the girls in my school. She was pretty, a social leader, played on the girls' volleyball team, all that. I was a sophomore and basically ate, slept, and breathed football. Didn't have much practice talking to the opposite sex. Needless to say, she left me tongue-tied."

"Oh, really? Mr. Love Whisperer didn't know what to say?"

"Nope. Every time I had a chance to talk to her, I found myself acting stupid or posing awkwardly like I was Mr. Chill. In the end, I lost my chance. She started dating a guy, and they stayed together until they both graduated. That's okay. I've moved on and things are great, but lesson learned. Take the shot! I never even knew if she liked me back because I didn't know how to read her signs or if I was giving out any signs myself other than a Wyle E. Coyote 'Help!' sign. Anyway, let's get to some callers. Who's up first, Suz?"

"First up, we've got Rich."

"How're you doing, Rich?"

The voice that comes on has to be partly played up. This guy sounds like he just came out of a *Dukes of Hazzard* re-run. *"Well D, I done got me an issue. You see, there's this lady that I see quite often. Actually, she's my hair stylist."*

"So you see her how often?" Derrick asks, and I lean forward, forgetting my work.

"About twice a month, but every time, I swear she's lookin' at me like she's interested. I mean, I know she's single, a little older than me but not too much, and she's as purty as they come. But I don't want to make it awkward if I approach her and she says no, know what I mean? I mean, I've got one of those heads of hair that just needs a good touch, and she's about the only one who can keep me from just saying fuck it and shaving the whole thing off."

The call continues, with Susannah taking most of the lead on that one. "A lot of how women flirt can be almost subtle, and it's a combination of things," she says. "For example . . . Derrick, describe what I'm doing."

"You just tossed your hair over your shoulder," Derrick says, and inside, I feel a little jealous.

"And now?"

"You did the same thing."

"Right, but this time, I smiled and kept eye contact for longer. You see, when a woman is interested in a man, we usually play it like . . . well, Rich, do you fish?"

"Who doesn't like to fish?"

"That's up for another debate," Derrick says. "But go ahead, Suz."

"Sometimes, we try to play it like a fisherman trying to get that big bass to latch onto the hook. If we just throw ourselves out there, the fish knows either the bait's bad or it's just a trap to get them on a big fucking hook, right? But if you play it too hard, the fish will lose interest and move on to something easier. So sometimes, teasing a man along to see if they're really interested is the best way. But Rich, you'll never know if you don't try."

"And if there's a big fucking hook in the middle of the bait?"

"Some people call that marriage," Derrick jokes, and even I have to laugh at that one. "Seriously, though, sounds like good advice. If you think she's interested, and you're obviously interested, go for it. Not saying you have to show up next time singing Alan Jackson for her, but hell, man, call her up and ask if she wants to get a cup of coffee or go to dinner. Worst thing that could happen is she says no. Best thing . . . well, there's a lot of great things that can happen too. Even with big hooks."

The calls continue, and as I listen, I notice a trend. I realize the show is about flirting and how to ask the opposite sex out, but I can't shake the idea of Susannah flirting with Derrick, even if it's for the radio. Normally, I'm not the jealous, possessive type, but damn . . . I'm ready to kick some ass when the song break comes on and I fire off a text to Derrick.

How's the show coming along?

Fun, but I can't wait until it's over. Getting awkward.

Relief. He's upfront about what's happening, which means he's just doing this professionally. I can deal with that.

Me2. OK, gonna try and work. Call U after show.

Reassured a little, I turn back to my code as the show comes back on. "Okay, everyone, after spending the last hour or so talking about how ladies show attraction, let's talk about how men do it."

"Besides popping a stiffy, you mean."

"Obviously," Derrick says.

"Well, if that's the case, since I did you, you have to do me now," Susannah says. "I mean . . . well, that certainly didn't come out how I meant it."

I can hear bullshit in someone's voice . . . and I'd say right now, Derrick's studio stinks like a dairy farm.

Derrick laughs a little awkwardly. "You know, Suz, I think a list might be better, since our fans listen and don't watch. Quit pouting, Suz, we've only got a three-hour show."

Pouting? What the fuck, Derrick, are you blind? She's flirting with you right now! All that shit she's been doing for the past hour hasn't been for the show!

Derrick is trying to get back on topic while Susannah tries to play it off. Finally, he gets around to listing how guys like to flirt. There's nothing all that groundbreaking from my point of view. Eye contact, compliments, smiles, brushing hair behind her ear, touching the small of her back.

Actually, listening to him makes me smile and forget the anger at Susannah. Derrick's done all those things to me, plus some. I blush, knowing that Derrick's little flirts fill my belly with warmth, and that he still does them makes me feel . . . I dunno, safe? Appreciated?

"Okay, time for another caller," Derrick says. "Now, we've been covering a lot of classical flirting, but our next caller's got a slightly more twenty-first-century problem. We've got Kim. Go ahead, Kim."

"Hi, Derrick," a slightly nervous girl says. *"I've been talking to this guy online. How do I know if he's flirting with me? A lot of guys just send me pickup lines, or after the bare minimum of back and forth conversation, they send dick pics. But what about the ones that aren't perverts?"*

Derrick hums. "Sounds like you've learned to avoid the sketchy ones. That's fishing . . . just looking for a hole to put a hook in. Some are just looking for some attention, maybe seeing if they can get some nudie pics without having to actually work for it. Now, maybe you want that—nothing wrong with casual hookups if that's what you both want. But if you want more, it's hard to get to really know someone through words on a tiny screen. Eventually, you need to talk and spend some time together. You need those physical clues."

Susannah speaks up in agreement. "You gotta look into their eyes for real. And be on the lookout everywhere. You might find the one person you've been looking for somewhere you go all the time, like the coffee shop, the gym, or work. Be open and friendly with everyone, and see who's receptive and then flirt away."

"That's kinda hard. I don't really have a lot of guys around."

Derrick chuckles. "Kim, roughly half of the population is male. They're around. I promise. Just stay open to finding them."

He ends the call and hums into the mic. "One other area of flirting we haven't addressed yet is the flirting you do after you've already snagged someone." His usual velvet radio voice has a hint of gravel, and I know it's for me, a signal that he's thinking of me with this topic. Warmth builds in my tummy.

"Even after you're in a relationship, flirting is still important. Send good morning and goodnight texts or calls. Get them little presents if something reminded you of them. It doesn't have to be anything big, just a sign you thought of them and what they'd like. Maybe get him a coffee cup from his favorite team to keep at your place, or buy her favorite lotion to keep at yours. Speak to each other, and more importantly, listen. Compliment them, their body, their brain, their talents. Your partner should always know what attracted you to them in the first place and what attracts you to them today, whether it's the same things or new things."

I smile, thinking that this is nearly a blueprint of how we get along. He's right. Every day, he does something to remind me how I make him feel, and he helps me feel beautiful every day. He helps me feel like maybe, just maybe, there's a silver lining to the clouds in life.

Maybe my little Styrofoam cup isn't so small after all and I can have a bigger slice of 'happily ever after' like the one Jessie has and the one my mom is finally getting.

It also reminds me that he needs to get that too. Reaching for my phone, I send him another text. *Just to let you know . . . you're the sexiest, kindest man I've ever met. Just thinking of you. Call me later.*

Count on it.

They take two more calls, nothing major, although one is cute as he says this is his chance to tell the girl he's interested in, and then they go to another song break, old-school Sophie B. Hawkins with *Damn, Wish I Was Your Lover.*

I jam out for a bit. This was a song Mom loved to sing along to before Carpool Karaoke was around, but after a moment, my phone rings. Derrick.

"I've only got a minute while the song plays," he says, his voice low, "but I was missing you. And thanks for the text."

"I miss you too, not just sex but actually being with you. In your arms, hearing your voice turn to gravel just for me. Just hanging out and spending time together."

Derrick growls lightly, and I know exactly how he feels. "Damn, Kitty Kat. I know you're busy and I don't want to take away from your work, but I need to be with you tonight. I need to touch you, feel you."

Just his words already have me simmering and I need him just as much. "How soon can you get home after work?"

"As soon as this song ends, we're wrapping up for the night," Derrick says. "Leave the office. I'll be home in less than an hour. Hey, Kat . . . wear that teddy and boy short set from the other night. I believe I promised to take them off with my teeth."

I whimper at the thought and remind myself that I need to start packing a backpack for nights like this. "Fuck, Derrick. Yes, you did. I'm gonna hold you to that promise. Oh, one other thing."

"What's that?"

"I'm dropping off my toothbrush too."

"Damn right, you are."

CHAPTER
Nineteen

DERRICK

IT'S ONLY thirty minutes later that I'm opening my front door, rushing to pick up my coffee cup from the table. Usually, there's a post-show meeting, but I bailed tonight with an excuse about having plans.

Susannah gave me the stink eye, but that seems to be her status quo lately. And it wasn't a lie, I do have plans. Specifically, to slip that sexy lace right off Kat's body, slow and easy with my teeth, licking all along her skin as I do so.

I rush to the bathroom and give my teeth a quick brush. Making love after spicy enchiladas for dinner is *not* a good idea, and I just get my mouth rinsed when there's a knock on the door, and I grin, looking at myself in the mirror. The man who looks back is overjoyed, not just horny, and I know I've found a woman who could really be for me like Mom was for Dad.

Opening the front door, my stomach leaps as I see Kat standing there. There's none of the elevated heels, none of the little pretentious pieces of armor she used at first to hide her worry and insecurity. Instead, there's just a five-foot-two-inch, honey blonde beautiful woman in sweatpants and a zipped-up jacket, her eyes sparkling as she looks up at me.

"Well, hello there, lover. Wondered if you might have space to put me up for the night?"

"I can think of a space I can fill," I joke, tugging her inside. She's got a backpack over her shoulder. She did just like I asked and brought clothes for tomorrow too, it looks like. "God, I missed you."

"I can tell," Kat says, setting her bag down and half jumping into my arms. "I missed you too. How was work?"

"Susannah's being kind of a tyrant, but I get it. I'm not exactly putting a hundred and ten percent into each show recently," I admit, hugging her tightly and nuzzling her neck. "I need a bit more practice at work-life balance, because I've found someone more important than my work."

"Mmm . . .anyone I know?" she teases, her eyes glinting with delight.

I look up at her, deviling her back. "Oh, just my new pet . . . Kitty Kat." I move back to her neck, nibbling at the soft skin, hoping I leave tiny marks to show she's mine.

Kat purrs. "God, that feels good. Really, Derrick. You make me feel special, worthy." Her words light me up, knowing that she's finally letting go of the chinks her life has left in her armor. She's developed her own self-confidence. She's always been worth so much more than she's received. I didn't change that. I just offered her what I could . . . all of me, and I'm proud that she's giving herself back to me. I trace along her jawline with my tongue, finding her lips in a breathy kiss. Our kiss deepens as I carry her through my living room, but she pulls back, her eyes alight with naughty heat. "Not the bedroom . . . not yet. I want you to have dessert first. Take me to the kitchen."

I nod, my brain swirling with excitement and anticipation for what Kat might have in her mind. Along with her blooming self-confidence, she's definitely unleashed her inner sex kitten. She said she was quiet, even repressed, but as we've explored together, she's relaxed and has shown that she has a deep well of passion inside her that I feel damn lucky to swim in.

I set her on the countertop and step back, watching as Kat unslings her backpack and opens it. The first thing she pulls out is a set of black heels, which she sets aside. "Tomorrow's work outfit. The rest is downstairs in the car."

"You have something for dessert in there for me?" I ask, and she nods, pulling out a jar of maraschino cherries. "Cherries?"

"Uh-huh," Kat says, unzipping her jacket. Underneath, she's only wearing the same see-through teddy she wore for our hot phone chat the other night. I can see her pink nipples already pulled tight, poking out the thin, silky fabric, inviting me to taste. "Just have to choose the right bowl." She opens the jar, plucking a single cherry out and holding it up, her tongue peeking out to swipe the small drop of juice off the fruit. "Here? Here . . .?" She asks as she traces the sweet fruit along her cleavage before pulling down her sweatpants to reveal panties that match her top. "Or maybe here?" She dangles the cherry right over her bare mound, visible through the sheer fabric.

Kat spreads her legs, and I can't help but lick my lips at the almost see-through window of her panties and I watch her puffy lips spread slightly.

"I'm feeling a little gluttonous—might want more than one cherry," I tease, pulling my shirt off and stepping between her creamy thighs to snap my teeth around the cherry, pulling it roughly off the stem before swallowing it almost whole. I kiss her, the sweet tang of the cherries blending with our breaths as she sets the jar down on the counter to tangle her hands in the belt loops of my jeans, pulling me close as she wraps her feet around my legs, locking me in place as if there's anywhere else I'd rather be.

The cherries momentarily forgotten, like promised, I take the strap of her teddy in my teeth and slide it off, kissing down the exposed swell of her breast until I find the stiff, crinkled tip of her nipple. I run my tongue around the edge and then bite it gently, pulling her into my mouth and stretching her breast until she gasps.

"Oh, fuck, Derrick . . . God, you're making my pussy so wet."

"Let's find out," I growl, reaching down and slipping my fingers inside her panties. She's more than wet. She's nearly dripping, and I let my fingers slide through her slick folds, teasing her lips and clit as I look in her eyes. "Who does this belong to?"

"You. Only you," Kat mewls, wiggling her hips as my thumb rubs over her clit. "I can't imagine anyone but you."

"Good, because all I am, all I have, belongs to you too," I promise. I dip two fingers deep inside her, brushing along her velvet walls as she squeezes me tightly. Pulling out my coated fingers, I smear her wetness over her other nipple before pulling back to lock my eyes on her perfect tits. "And sometimes, it's fun to mix your desserts."

I devour her coated breast, sucking and feasting upon her warm, sweet flesh until I can't wait any longer. I kiss my way down her body, tracing designs with my tongue around her belly button and making her giggle.

"I thought you were going to make me come, not laugh."

"Why not both?" I reply, grinning up at her. I see the jar of cherries and reach over as I lay her back, her petite frame and wide hips perfect for keeping her balance on the countertop. Uncapping the cherries, I peel her panties off before letting a drizzle of the bright red syrup flow over her glistening lips. Kat watches, her breasts heaving as she breathes deeply in anticipation. "Mmm, looks tasty."

"I hope I can have a big banana split later," Kat teases, licking her lips. I nod and kiss up the inside of her thigh, letting my warm breath play over her wet folds until she's squirming in need.

"Be still or you'll spill it all. Tell me, Kat. Tell me what you need." I can feel the tension in her thighs as she tries to fight the urge to lift her hips toward my mouth.

"Oh, Derrick . . . don't tease me. Lick my pussy. Taste me. Please."

"I can never deny you, especially when that's exactly what I want too," I growl, looking up her body into her beautiful eyes. Keeping my eyes locked on her, I drag my tongue through the sweet juice and syrup-covered folds of her pussy, tasting every nerve ending crackling along my tongue as Kat shivers, moaning from deep in her chest.

"Yes . . . that's it, make me come," Kat says, grinding her pussy against my lips. I dive in, taking turns using my tongue to lick up and down her silky lips and nibbling on her soft flesh, the sweet sugar of the cherries mixing with Kat's natural taste and making my head whirl. I cup her ass, pulling her close as I feast on her.

Kat's naturally spicy and tangy and sweet. Irresistible, and I know that half of my daydreams of Kat are filled with memories of how she tastes.

I nip lightly at her inner thigh and she bucks, begging, "Derrick . . .more." I understand. She needs something intense, something that will ground her and let her soar. I could happily lick and suck her for hours, but after all the teasing we've given each other tonight, she needs something now. I bite each inner thigh harder as I thumb her clit, leaving a round imprint of my teeth, praying that the outline stays. Some dark place inside me likes that she'll have that reminder of my claim on her.

Satisfied with the visual, I nibble at her clit, biting, not hard, but just enough to set her body shaking, her ass rising off the countertop as she cries out, coming hard. I keep sucking and biting her clit as she pulses, loving every quiver of her body as she unleashes on me.

When she sags to the countertop, I pull back, standing up to gather her in my arms. "You're fucking delicious. I want your taste on my tongue all the fucking time."

"Your turn," Kat says, wiggling. "You can fuck me later . . . but I've got a few tips from the Love Whisperer I've been wanting to try."

I set Kat down, and she gets on her knees, reaching for the waistband of my jeans. She doesn't have to do much. I'm so fucking hard by everything I've just done that my cock nearly bursts my zipper, and Kat chuckles, watching it bob in time with my racing heartbeat.

"You look like you're about three seconds from coming down my throat."

"You know I'm better than that," I boast, but she's pretty much right. Still, I spread my legs a little, watching as Kat reaches up, fondling my balls in her soft hands before rolling them gently, tugging them down and relieving a little bit of the pressure that's building inside me. I moan, reaching down to stroke a hand through her hair as she reaches up with her other hand, barely wrapping her fingers around the base of my cock as she brings her face closer, rubbing the head with her cheeks, moaning and closing her eyes. "Fuck me, Kitty Kat. You're good."

"One of the lessons that I've been taught," she says, her eyes gleaming as she gives me feather-light butterfly kisses up and down my shaft. I moan. She's amazing. "And I can see you love it."

"I love everything you do," I tell her, groaning as she licks my cock from base to tip before spreading her lips and sucking just the head of my cock like a lollipop. "But damn, you have talent."

I can't form any more words as Kat continues. From running her tongue just around the head and then down the bottom and around the spot that she knows makes my toes curl, she uses every hint that I've ever talked about on my show to tease out my pleasure. I'm brought to new heights, my cock throbbing nearly painfully as my brain swims in pulses of light. I can't stand the teasing anymore, my voice gone as I growl.

"Suck me, Kat. Suck that cock down like my good girl." Kat slowly bobs up and down on my cock, her cheeks hollow as she swallows my entire shaft before pulling back.

I wish it could go on forever, this feeling that she's creating in me. Never before have I felt so powerful, this honey-blonde angel lovingly worshipping my cock. Kat closes her eyes, pinching her nipples with her right hand before slipping it between her legs, rubbing her pussy in time with her head.

"That's it," I rasp, watching her fingers speed up. "Touch yourself for me. Rub your needy little clit so you come when I do. Swallow me all down, baby."

Kat mumbles something that sounds like 'yes' around my cock and sucks faster, her tongue caressing and stroking every inch of my shaft. She reaches up, grabbing my left hand and guiding it to the back of her head. Gathering her hair in my fist, I use it to hold her still as I start pumping my cock in and out of her eager mouth. Her moans increase in pitch and volume until we're both groaning and gasping while Kat takes me all the way, burying the head of my cock in her throat and swallowing.

"Oh shit, babe . . . is this what you want? You want me to fuck your face like you're my dirty little slut? God damn, you are so fucking sexy. I'm gonna come, Kat. You ready?"

I pull back just as Kat starts shaking, her fingers pumping in and out of her pussy so fast that her hips jerk, and we both go over the edge. I cry out, my cock filling her mouth with my cream as Kat's groans vibrate to the very depths of my soul. I think I say her name, but if I do it's so swallowed up in the heat of my orgasm that all that comes out is something primal, animal.

This is the woman I love. This is the woman I need for as long as I live. "Holy shit, babe . . . you didn't miss a single bit."

"Good," Kat says, getting up and kissing me softly. "Now, how about some real dessert to get our strength up, and then you can have one last round before we hit the bed? And this one, cowboy, is going to be very special."

"Why's that?" I ask, kissing the tip of her nose. I've gotta have some ice cream or something around here somewhere. I eat right, but not perfectly.

"Because if you want, how about you do a little research and practice for that anal episode you're going to do?" she asks. "I figure I'm ready. If you want to."

I look into her eyes and see the mix of desire, excitement, love, and yes, a big helping of fear in there, and it fills my heart with an intense need to do this right. "Of course. On one condition. You say stop, I stop. No judgement, no worries. Agreed?"

Kat's eyes sparkle in tears and she kisses my chest. "Agreed." Her voice tickles across me as she lays her cheek against my chest, wrapping her arms around my waist. "Derrick, I'm . . . a little scared."

I lean down to kiss the top of her head, hugging her back. "Hey, no pressure. We don't have to do anything you don't want to."

I feel her smile against me, "Not about that—well, not really. Just this, *us*. I've really never felt like this before, and it's scary. It feels big, and you've got me dreaming of things I never thought I'd be dreaming about. Like a future. Like forever."

I take a big breath, knowing that this is a turning point for her and for us. We've said 'I love you' and meant it and have woven ourselves together into a routine that's become the focal point of my life, and those things are easy for me, both because of who I am and more importantly, who *she* is. But it's more difficult for her to trust, to believe and hope. I want to be worthy of her heart, even if I have to earn it every day for the rest of our lives.

"Kat, I've got you and I won't hurt you. I love you."

She leans back, looking up at me. "Thank you. For everything." And with a bearhug-tight squeeze, she shifts the mood. "All right, let's get some damn cookies!"

CHAPTER

Twenty

KAT

THE FACES around the table look slightly less than convinced, and there's a little bit of sweat trickling down the small of my back as the twin projectors pump heat through the room.

"So how is this supposed to be targeted to the female audience?" one of them asks. "There's not a lot of real on-the-surface differences between your app and the competitors already on the market."

"On the surface, you're right," I reply. "It's when you get into the guts and the way the app seamlessly and uniquely integrates various systems within the architecture of the pre-existing operating system and apps that makes it a winner."

"But what's the marketing angle? Your user interface is rather plain. Nothing really screams feminine."

I squirm, feeling the heat. They're really coming at me.

"If by feminine you mean frilly laces and a lot of pink fonts and motifs, you're right, this isn't feminine," I reply. "This is meant for the modern powerful female, the post- *#MeToo*er who's kicking ass and taking names at work and in her personal life. Because she's making a name for herself in the office, she's gotta look professional. So the interface does look professional . . . except that it's going to have that perspective that's going to give her the edge she needs in her life."

"So twenty-first-century Boss Bitch?" someone else, part of the marketing group, asks. "I like the sound of it and I think I can work with that. How's the guts of it?"

"As good as any other app in the category, and better in a lot of ways," I say. "It's lean. There's no bloat, so it runs faster. Let me give you a test drive."

The meeting continues, and while there are a few times I have to really drive my point home hard, I feel like it went easier than my last app presentation.

Maybe it's that I've earned at least a little cred with these people . . . but more than anything, I think it's the newfound strength and confidence I've had since meeting Derrick. I've always felt pretty confident in myself when it came to work, but I can't help but feel that his giving me more personal confidence has given me that extra leg up when talking to these guys.

It's not only that Derrick makes me feel sexy. I just feel like I'm starting to truly understand the strength and power that come from my own femininity, and that's a huge plus considering I create apps for the modern female demographic.

"You know, Katrina," one of the company vice-presidents says after playing with the app for almost an hour, "this app of yours, while I guess it's got a feminine touch, is just a good app for everyone. Can we consider just marketing it to the general public or giving it a slightly different skin and releasing it again as a partner app for men?"

"We will whip up presentations for both ideas," the marketing guru says. "Either way, with the muscle behind this hustle . . . congrats, Kat. I think you've got your next number one on your hands."

The congratulations go around the table, and I feel like I'm floating, damn-near seven feet tall as I walk out. Reaching my cubicle, I flop down, kicking off my high heels and rubbing my toes. Another sign that I'm getting comfortable with myself is that these stripper heels aren't daily wear anymore. I still like wearing something that elevates me, but only because it makes it easier to kiss Derrick.

"Tomorrow, I'm wearing stacked heel boots," I promise myself as I pull out my phone. I hit the speed dial, knowing I might not reach him but I promised him I'd give him a call as soon as my meeting was over.

Before the call can connect, one of the company Vice Presidents, a forty-three-year-old tech geek named Edgar, knocks on the edge of my wall. "Katrina?"

"Hi, Edgar," I reply, setting my phone down. "How can I help you?"

"I think you can help the company in a lot of ways, actually," he says. "Because your app is streamlined and clean. What would you think about being a team leader for the new game app we're developing?"

"Team leader? Game app?" I ask, surprised. "I'd love the opportunity, but are you sure? Games haven't really been my experience, and most of those guys have been at it for a long time."

"That's exactly why you're the man—woman—for the job. Bring in some new blood, different perspective than what they're used to. Maybe find a way to bring the conciseness of your coding style to the game side because they're always working to balance the functionality with the size and speed of the game. You've proven yourself, and I'm confident you'll whip them into shape."

"I . . . of course! Can we discuss the details Monday?"

Edgar nods, flashing me a grin. "Enjoy your successful presentation. We'll talk about the future Monday morning."

He leaves, and I blink before a small sound from my desk makes me realize . . . "Derrick?"

"Hey, Kitty Kat, I got to hear the good news," Derrick says in my ear. "Always knew you were as smart as you are beautiful." He's switched to his deeper, richer voice and it fills me with heat.

"Yeah, well, right now, I'm wearing lined granny panties and squirming in my chair because of you," I tease back. "Thanks."

"Anytime, love. So, you nailed me . . . I mean, you nailed the presentation, I take it?" Derrick asks, making me chuckle.

"Honey, as good as I feel right now, I'm feeling like a million bucks," I purr, dropping my voice. "I've got the sexiest man in the world, and I feel like I can do any damn thing I want."

"That's because you can," Derrick says. "Listen, can we get together tonight then? My place, your place, I don't care. I just want one of us to come to the other, then we'll both come together. Guaranteed."

I shake my head and look up to wave off another congrats from one of the other coders in the cubicle crew. "Sorry, babe. I was already told before the meeting that the whole Geek Patrol is going out to celebrate, and it'll be late. I think someone's already got their Jedi robes ready."

"Jedi robes?" Derrick asks, and I laugh.

"I'm just kidding. We're not that far gone. How about tomorrow afternoon, I come over to your place and we spend the whole rest of the weekend together?"

I can hear his smile even through the phone, and the naughty lilt to his voice. "Twenty-four-hour wait . . . by then, I'm going to be ready to pound you into total submission, my little Kitty Kat. I've got a confession. You've got me addicted to your sweet taste, your tight pussy. I need you every day, at least once a day."

"Don't worry, you've got me the same way. If I'm not getting a big, throbbing Vitamin D injection at least daily, I feel empty . . . speaking of which, I'm feeling a little empty now."

"Oh, don't tease me," Derrick growls. "I'm already keeping Susannah waiting for our pre-show meeting . . . and I want to give you the time you deserve. And let's be honest, you're not in a place to turn on your video either."

"Nah," I admit. "The cubicle's a little . . . lacking in soundproofing. But later, maybe I can find some privacy to show you something."

"Mmm . . . you know you always knock my socks off," Derrick replies. "Listen, babe, I'm thinking, if you want to stay the weekend, bring some more stuff over. You know, just in case you want to stay longer or something."

I smile. "Careful there, love. You're going to regret it when I bring in a hundred pairs of shoes and take over your closet."

"You don't have a hundred pairs of shoes."

I laugh, mockingly evil. "Bwahaha, after this app hits number one and I get gamer coding bankroll, I might go shoe shopping!"

Derrick laughs. "Add in a couple more pairs of fuck-me pumps, and I'm happy. You can wear them while I make you scream my name in ecstasy."

"You mean like this?" I ask, lowering my voice to my breathiest whisper. "Oh, Derrick . . . yes, baby, please. God, I need you to fuck me."

The answering moan on the other end of the line is all I need, and I smile. "I love you."

"I love you too, Kat." There's a holler on the other end of the line, and Derrick growls. "I'll be there in a minute!"

He comes back on, slightly abashed. "Okay, babe, if I don't go now, Susannah's going to be doing a special show tonight on castration with a pair of office scissors."

"Can't lose those. I need them too much." I laugh. "Go do your meeting. I love you."

"I love you too. Bye. And congrats."

The line goes dead, and I lean back, smiling to myself. A great presentation, a huge opportunity, and I think a backdoor invitation to move in if I want with the man of my dreams?

How'd this happen? For so long, I thought this sort of life wasn't possible. That I'd never have a chance to have it all, a good man, a good job, and best of all, some actual inner peace. I thought I'd always be hustling, worried about what others would say about me, that I'd never be able to get on top . . . and suddenly, I feel like I am. And the view up here is fucking awesome.

The old me would be looking for the other shoe to drop any time now, but that was the old me. The new me, she's going to celebrate with her co-workers. And tomorrow, I'm going lingerie shopping before going over to Derrick's so we can do our own kind of celebrating.

"Like the man said, it don't get much better than this."

"SO ANYWAY, we're going to spend the last hour doing an interview with a woman who's making a series of videos . . ."

I let Susannah's words just descend into a sort of buzz in the background. Hell, I can't even pretend to focus on what she's saying in the pre-show meeting because my head is in the clouds with thoughts of Kat and how well she's doing.

Hey, babe, I read, looking down at my phone, *just leaving work now. Wish you were here, but I'll try and catch your show later. Love you.*

I smile, earning a growl from Susannah. "For fuck's sake, Derrick, you said you were done with that."

"I'm listening. You know I'm always impromptu," I lamely defend myself. "I got it. Guest coming in, makes videos, blah, blah."

"That blah, blah is what's going to make up the last hour of the show," she shoots back. "Or do you plan on pissing this one off like you did the last?"

"Hey, I can't help we didn't agree," I reply. Before I can continue, my phone buzzes again. I don't even have a chance to look down before Susannah erupts.

"Dammit, Derrick, it won't hurt you to turn that thing off for a while! You didn't even hear what I said about her, did you?

I feel a bit bad. She's right in that I have no idea what the hell this guest is about, but hoping to salve her temper tantrum, I set my phone aside and focus my full attention on her. "Let's start over. What's this guest's deal?"

Susannah shakes her head, tossing her clipboard aside. Rubbing at her temples, she looks up, taking a big breath before answering.

"You've been completely off your game for over a month now. After I found out why, I've cut you some slack. But things haven't gotten better. If anything, they've gotten worse. You're distracted during the shows, barely talking to me before or after, and just generally being an asshole. We've got a good thing here, I think, and you're ruining it for some chick of the week. You need to ditch the needy bitch."

I slam my hand down on the table, pissed off. "She's not a chick of the week, and don't you dare call her a bitch. What the fuck, Susannah? You know I don't fuck around like that. Kat and I have something serious going on here. I'm sorry if I've been distracted during the show, but we're doing fine other than your trying to dictate my every word and action. You're not my boss, Susannah. We have a good thing going with the show, but let's keep it there. Stay out of my personal life."

"That's it?" Susannah shoots back. "That's it, like all we've done is do shows about gardening or some lame ass Top 40 countdown. In case you haven't noticed, I know more about your sex life than even your avid listeners do. Hell, I've been able to see when you're talking book talk, and when you're talking fantasies, and when you're talking real-life experiences. You've seen the same from me."

"We work together. That's the nature of the show. Of course you know a lot about me. I don't get what your point is."

"I'm just fucking pissed, Derrick. I've poured my guts into this show and I thought you were too. It works because we bounce off each other and balance each other's style. Now you're just phoning it in? That's bullshit and it's only a matter of time before it costs us."

Her little speech puts me on my heels, and I look down, wondering if she's right. I've checked our ratings. They're still holding strong, even if Susannah is freaking out.

"Suz, I've never been a prepper. The show's doing okay, and we're fine on-air. I'm sorry if you feel like I'm not giving you as much focus, but I'm as committed as I've always been. You need to chill out."

Susannah sighs. "I wasn't going to say anything until we got something harder on the plate, but there's been a few feelers by a production company. They're talking national syndication plus maybe TV or Internet video broadcasting our shows too."

"What?" I ask, shocked. I've heard nothing about this. "Why haven't I been told?"

"Well, you *would* have, but you haven't stuck around. It'd be a lot like how Stern and some of the other talk radio people have their shows broadcast. They'll set up a couple of hard cameras in a new studio that they'll pay for, and then we do our show like normal. But none of that can happen unless these guys see you at the top of your game. I'm doing everything I can to hold this shit together and grow the show, but I can't do it by myself."

I blink, stunned. "Okay . . . okay, you've got a point. But Suz, and this is serious, if you're mad at me, leave it work-related. It's not Kat's fault, so leave her out of it. I think I may have found *the one*, and I'm not going to listen to that."

I see something glimmer in Susannah's eyes, but she nods. "Okay then, agreed. Now, about tonight's show."

"Yeah," I say, putting aside the bad feelings. We aired them out and it's over. Kinda like when I was in football and two guys on the team had beef. We'd hash it out, sometimes a punch or two was thrown, but after that, it was time to play the game and turn that anger against our opponents. "I get the feeling there's something unique about her. You said videos. What's the deal?"

Before Susannah can speak, my phone rings again. "For fuck's sake!"

"Sorry," I reply, looking down.

She's right back pissed again, muttering under her breath. "Of course you're going to answer it, regardless of what you just said. Her little lap dog, running whenever she calls or texts a damn thing." She stomps out of the room, venomous contempt dripping from every word.

Knowing we'll definitely have to revisit that since apparently, our truce from mere moments ago didn't last, I growl and answer the call.

"Dad?"

Dad's breathing is heavy and labored, and inside, I immediately start to worry. "Derrick, I'm so sorry."

"Dad, what's wrong?" I ask, standing up. "What's happening?"

"I was outside, moving stuff around in the shed, and . . ." he says, gasping for air and groaning. "My heart. I think I'm having a heart attack."

"Dad, I'm calling 9-1-1." I go to grab a desk phone, but he stops me.

"Already called. They're on their way. Derrick, I love you, son. I'm damn proud of you." There's a tone to his voice that sounds like he's trying to say goodbye.

Choking back a sob, I growl at the phone, "I know, Dad. I love you too, but don't do that. You're gonna be okay. I'm gonna meet you at the hospital."

I keep talking, but I'm running out of the office to my car. The show never even crosses my mind as I peel out of the lot and head toward the hospital.

"Dad, I met someone. She's the one and I'm going to marry her. I want you to meet her, so you gotta fight. Just like you always taught me when football got tough. You gotta keep fighting, okay?"

"Okay, son . . . they're here." There's a jostling sound on the phone and a woman's voice comes on the line.

"Hello? We're taking him to City Center Hospital. You can meet us there."

I think I say okay, but then it's just dead air. There's not much traffic, and I'm admittedly driving way too fast, but it still feels like forever and a day to get there.

Rushing inside, I get help from the first nurse I see. "I'm here to see Daniel King. He was just brought in. I'm his son."

She leads me over, but other than looking in through a glass window to see a man who has my father's face but I swear looks about twenty years older, there's nothing I can do.

I pace back and forth in the hallway, doing my best not to get in the way as nurses and doctors come in and out. Occasionally, I hear some medical jargon that scares me, but before I can even ask them what the hell 'hs-CRP' or 'Troponins test' means, they're gone. I'm left to sit in a chair by the door, staring down at the tile and hoping that the next time a doctor comes out, it's not to tell me it's time to say goodbye to my father.

"Mr. King?"

I look up. It's nearly eight o'clock now, but the doctor who's looking down at me has a relieved look on his face. "Is he . . .?"

"I think we've gotten him out of the woods," the doctor says as he holds out a hand. "Glen Stoker. I'm the on-call cardiologist. When your father was brought in, it was for a suspected myocardial infarction . . . a heart attack. We've confirmed that he did, in fact, have a pretty severe MI. We've stabilized him for now, and I think he's out of the woods. He looks like he's normally a pretty active guy, so that's in his favor."

"He is," I confirm, standing up to look at Dad. He's sleeping, but I can see the heart monitor next to his head, and the little wiggly line reassures me. "He's been on blood pressure and cholesterol meds for a few years, but nothing like this has ever happened."

"We'll have to keep him here a few more days and talk with his primary care doctor. Do you have that information?"

"I think he's still going to Dr. Jack Reynolds. I don't have his number though. That's at home."

"That's okay, I know Jack," Dr. Stoker says. "Listen, it'll be a few minutes before we can have a room ready for him. For now, though, he'd do better if his son was with him. And Mr. King?"

"Yeah?" I ask, not looking at the doctor at all.

"He's in good hands here. For now, just make sure he stays calm."

I go inside the exam room, where the beeping of the various machines still reassures me that my father is still alive. Looking down at him, he looks so old, so frail . . . my vision doubles, then blurs, and before I know, it tears are running down my face as I reach down, blindly taking his hand.

"I never told you how much you mean to me," I whisper, afraid to wake him. "But I promise you, you're going to find out. You think you never understood why I do what I do . . . but I'm just trying to tell the world that love, real love, like what you and Mom had . . . it does exist. And I want to do everything in my power to make sure that type of love doesn't die. I love you, Dad."

In the movies, he'd wake up right now, maybe whisper a few words, either sarcastic or loving, depending on the type of movie. But this isn't a movie. This is real life, and all I can do is sit down in another chair and rest my forehead against the bars on the side of his bed.

I want to call Kat. I need to hear her voice telling me it'll be okay, but in my haste of rushing into the hospital, I left my phone in the car and I can't leave right now.

It'll be all right, for now. She's out with friends, happy and celebrating. I don't want to ruin her celebration. I know how hard she worked for this. I'll let her enjoy the evening and when dad gets transferred up to his room, I'll slip out and grab my phone.

It'll be late, but I need to hear her voice.

THE BAR, one of those weird little spots that could only exist in a city near a university with a large computer science department and plenty of techies like me, is rockin' for the type of customers it collects. On one side of the place, three of the interns from the company are engaged in a sick *StarCraft* battle royale, while around my table are a gaggle of people tossing back European microbrews, trying to look hipster and utterly failing. But we're having a blast, and that's all that matters.

"So, what's next?" my co-worker asks as he looks over at me. "Plan to take over the world?"

I shake my head, sipping at my wine. "Nope, team lead for the new game app. Apparently, they need a healer."

It's a cheesy as fuck joke, but I've already downed a few glasses, and we're all at that point where we can set aside our worries and just be silly. Thankfully, everyone else is maybe drunker than I am, and they all laugh even if it wasn't that funny.

Cheers go up, each of them congratulating me. I finish off the glass of Merlot I'm drinking, and just as I set my glass down, my phone rings. I grin, figuring it's Derrick on a song break on his show.

I hate that I'm missing it tonight. Listening in has gotten to be such a daily dirty habit. His voice coming through my stereo, or even my earbuds, all sex and silk, just warms me up for when he whispers dirty things in my ear later, that softness turning to sex just for me. Sure, it's meant a few nights of working different hours . . . but then again, I'd say the benefits have been more than worth it.

I look at my phone and see that it's not Derrick.

It's Elise. Getting up, I head out into the chilly night air, where it's not quite so insane and the cool helps me clear my head. Still, the music is easily heard. "Hey Elise! What's up?"

"Kat? Where are you? It's loud on your end. Can you hear me?"

"Sorry, I'm out with people from work. They loved my new app. We're sort of celebrating. Why, what's up?"

"So you're not listening to the show right now?"

There's something in Elise's voice that does more than the cool air to pierce through my wine-induced haze. "No, why? Should I be?"

"Honey," Elise says in that voice that she uses whenever shit's hit the fan somewhere and she knows I'm going to need her to be strong, "I need you to come to my place right now. Wherever you are, whatever you're doing, just stop and come here now."

The fact that Elise isn't telling me what's going on scares me, and I rub at my face, another part of me already in emergency procedure mode. I need to settle tonight's bar tab, get a ride, get to Elise, and . . . well, I don't know from there. Ugh, I hate being buzzed and adult at the same time.

"Elise, what's wrong? What aren't you telling me?"

"Just come," Elise says. "Now. Get over here."

That settles it. I trust her with my life. "I'm on my way."

I head back into the bar, prepared to make half-hearted excuses, but as soon as he sees me, Tyler sets his drink aside. "You okay?"

"A friend called. Something important came up," I tell him. "Listen, can you cover the tab? I mean, I don't want to . . ." I look at the door, the urgency live in my chest.

"You can PayPal me the tab on Monday," Tyler says, waving me off before hooking a thumb at the assembled crew. "As long as these fuckers don't drink five thousand dollars of cheap beer and wine, I think we're okay."

"Deal. Thanks, Tyler."

I gather my purse and head out the door, flagging down the first taxi I see to head to Elise's place. "Hey," I ask as I settle in, "you got satellite radio?"

"Sure do, this baby's almost brand-new," the driver says. "Whatcha want me to put on?"

"Think you can put on The Love Whisperer?" I ask. "Channel fifty-seven I think."

"No problem," the cabbie says. He turns his dial a few times, and soon enough, *The Love Whisperer* pops up. "You ain't the first lady who's asked to listen to that guy. He's got a voice that could talk the panties off a mannequin."

They're in a song break, and when they come back, my heart skips a beat.

"We're back, everyone," Susannah says, and I give the radio a raised eyebrow. What the hell? *"I'm Susannah Jameson, and welcome back to The Love Whisperer. We're continuing our evening chat on technology in dating before*

getting to our special guest tonight. More specifically, how to use technology to spice up your love life and get you to the bedroom, since some folks need a little help even getting there for some real-time action."

"Ain't that the damn truth," the cabbie mutters.

"So let's continue our discussion of phone sex and video chat sex and how it can spice things up for long-distance relationships and new hook-ups. Or even for regular Joes-and-Bettys who want to try something a little more . . . dirty, raunchy, or dare I say . . . naughty. Whether its Skype, FaceTime, or whatever new app you like, technology can lend a lot of fun to your nighttime activities. Hell, maybe your daytime ones too. But really, once you decide to try a little verbal foreplay beyond just flirting, what do you actually say? Any suggestions, oh Love Whisperer?"

There's a pause and Derrick's satin voice comes across the radio, *"Just keep it hot, hot, hot, and it'll do the trick. Guaranteed."*

There's a hint to Susannah's voice that I don't like, an edge that makes me think things aren't right with her. She sounds . . . angry.

And I wonder what's happening in the studio to cause that. Maybe something happened on air? Did she and Derrick have an argument? Maybe that's what Elise is calling about?

"Now, we've played a few clips already, as shared by our generous Love Whisperer from his personal collection, but we saved this one for last, the crème de la crème of some crazy-hot phone sex. Make sure you've got a pen to take notes, listeners. Maybe a towel too . . . for the drool." She giggles throatily. *"Let's take a listen, and we'll open up the lines for you after this."*

Derrick chuckles, saying, *"Let's hear it."* And there's a split second before the recording starts.

From the first grunt, all the blood rushes from my face as I recognize who it is. *"You know I love your tits,"* Derrick growls. *"Show those perfect tits to me. Rub your thumb across your nipples until they're pearled up for me."*

It's edited, but not for content. Instead, every mention of emotion, every dimming of anything except lewd, nasty fucking sex is stripped out. I listen as my voice comes through the radio, mewling that yes, I'm Derrick's dirty little slut, my breath audibly quickening and the squelching noises obvious even over the radio as I finger fucked myself for him.

Just as I call out his name, the cabbie reaches over, switching it off. The taxi driver looks at me in the rearview mirror, "Sorry, Miss, that's a bit much for me. The wife would skin me alive for listening to something like that with a lady in the car."

I nod absently, the ice in my gut rushing through my entire body. Why is there a recording of our conversations? What's this shit about a personal collection?

I thought those were private, just Derrick and me. I guess he never said that, but obviously, I assumed. Why *wouldn't* they be? And why would he play them on the air?

Oh, God, I've been getting played this entire time. The thought hits me like a grenade in the stomach, and the shakes start. I'm barely keeping it together when the taxi pulls up to Elise's apartment and she's outside waiting for me.

"I can tell by the look on your face that you already know. What the fuck is happening, Kat?"

Her matter-of-fact tone gives me some stability, and I hug myself, shaking my head. "I don't know. That's us, our private conversations. Why?"

Elise gives the cab driver his fare and leads me into her place. "I don't know what's going on, but that shit's not okay."

"Why would he even record them in the first place?" I ask softly, hurt and confused. "I . . . they weren't meant for the public. They were me, baring my heart to him."

Elise looks at me with pity, then sighs. "Well, I could see why he would. They're pretty fucking hot. Maybe he was just recording them for later . . . spank bank type deal?"

I snort. If Derrick needed spank bank material, all he had to do was give me a call, the way we've gotten it on over the past few weeks. "He never told me he was recording me . . . us. Oh, God, Elise! He played it on the air, and everyone heard me have an orgasm and tell how hungry for his cock I am. He said my name!"

The last fact saps the last of my reserve and I dissolve into tears. Elise does what she can as she gathers me up, pulling me into a hug. I collapse on the couch and she covers me with a blanket, mistaking my shivers of heartbreak as cold. "It'll be okay, Kat. I listened to the first couple before calling you. He said your name, but there's gotta be what, a million 'Kats'? Nobody can prove it was you."

She rushes into the kitchen, making me a cup of coffee, but I just hold it, not able to take a sip with my heart in my throat.

"People will know," I whisper. "God, he's been to my place. I've been to his. Kevin knows I've been with him . . . it'll get out, Elise. If Kevin knows, he'll make sure of it. It'll get out, and I'll be ruined."

Elise slips an arm around my shoulders, hugging me from the side. "You need to call him. Figure out what the hell is going on!"

I sigh, looking into the black mirror that is the surface of my coffee. "You're right. Maybe there's some reason . . ." I look up at Elise again, but the truth is clearly written on her face. "Guess not, huh?"

Elise shakes her head. "Damn it, Kat. I'm so sorry. I pushed you into this. I really thought he was a good guy with all the things you said about him."

"I felt like I had a good feel of him from our dates and his show too, but I guess that's all façade. Love Whisperer, my ass. God, I should've known better. Hell, I do know better! Guys are always out for themselves and a piece of ass. But he made me believe, and I played right into his hands. This hurts so much worse than before because he made me . . . hope." The tears come, hot and burning as they roll down my face, and I cry my heartbreak out for Elise, who strokes my hair and kisses my forehead.

"I promise you, Kat, I don't care if the whole gender of men is going to hell. I'm right here with you."

"I guess I need to get this over with," I whisper. I reach into my bag, grabbing my phone. It hurts to see his name in my recent contacts, surrounded with little heart-eyed face emojis, but I need to get this over with before I lose my nerve. And I need answers.

The call rings . . . and rings . . . and rings. "Hey, you've reached Derrick King. Leave me a message. Or, as this is the twenty-first century, send me a text. Bye."

The phone beeps, and I clear my throat before speaking, but my voice is still wavering. "Derrick, it's Kat. You need to call me."

As I hang up, I look at the time and I realize the show is over. He should be able to pick up his phone if he wanted to, just like he has countless times before. He's avoiding my call. Ignoring me after what he's done. He doesn't have the balls to face me.

The ice in my veins freezes. He'd systematically broken down all my defenses from the beginning, one by one, pecking away at them to get me to open up to him, and he makes me think he was one of the good guys.

But he lied. This is so much worse than Kevin or my other boyfriends cheating on me. This is a public betrayal at a foundational level. I loved him, truly and deeply, and I thought he loved me. But obviously not if he can air our private life without even asking me. Fuck, he even joked and laughed about it, like it was no big deal.

I don't know why he'd do this, but fuck him if he thinks I'm some fuck toy he can screw around with.

I'm done with him, done with men.

Forever.

I turn my phone off and hug Elise as the tears roll down my face. I'll cry out every last tear so that there's nothing left and then I'll turn my heart off and never risk loving some backstabbing asshole again.

I'm done, my heart shattered into unfixable shards in my chest.

CHAPTER
Twenty~Three
DERRICK

THE SUN IS JUST CREEPING over the horizon when I can sneak out of the hospital and down to my car to grab my phone.

It was a long night. Once Dad was transferred, he'd woken up a little but was disoriented. I was uncomfortable leaving him alone, even with nurses twenty feet away and watching the monitors.

I stayed by his bedside until he fell into a fitful sleep. I drifted off soon after, uncomfortably perched in a chair beside him until the shift-change nurse woke us both to take his vitals.

Turning on my phone, I see it's been blowing up all night. I've got several missed calls from Jacob, one from Kat . . . but more worrisome, at least two dozen calls from Susannah and the station number.

I rub the back of my neck, not sure what I'm going to do. I knew I'd likely get shit for bailing on the show with no notice, but what the hell did they want me to do? My dad was having a heart attack.

If Susannah couldn't handle things, there are plenty of archived shows they could air if need be. We already do that on our two nights off each week, and listeners seem to like the classics. If Suz was in a lurch, she could've just punched play on one of those.

Yeah, shitty on my part to duck like I did, but a necessary deal when there's a medical emergency. I decide to give Jacob a call first. He doesn't call often so it must have been important for him to call multiple times. Kat was probably just checking in to tell me everything was going okay and she was being safe. I won't wake her up with the bad news just yet.

Besides, Jacob will want to know. He and Dad got pretty friendly back in my college days, and Jacob really took a liking to my father, often hanging out at the house when the lifestyle of being a superstar student-athlete with a professional future got to be a bit too much to deal with.

I hit *Dial* and lean against my car, yawning as the cold morning air wakes me up.

As soon as Jacob picks up the line, however, all sleepiness is driven from me when he yells, "What the fuck, man?!"

"Hey, bro, I know it's early as fuck. You just don't normally call multiple times like that. Besides, aren't you usually up at this hour?"

"What the hell are you doing? The show last night? How could you do that to that girl?"

Oh, hell, what happened on the show? Did the guest go apeshit or something? "Do what? I'm at the hospital with dad. He had a heart attack, man. He's gonna be okay, but if you're in town or close, I'm sure he'd love it if you could come see him."

Jacob quiets, and when he speaks up, he sounds more like his normal self. "Holy shit, man, is he okay?"

I sigh, purging some of the fear that's been roiling in my gut all night. "Yeah, it was some scary shit there for a bit, but he called in time. He knew right away something was wrong, so he got help within minutes. It was serious, but he's gonna be okay."

"I get that, and I don't mean to be insensitive, but I gotta ask. What about the show last night? You didn't air the recordings?"

"Recordings?" I ask, confused. "What recordings? I ran out the door as soon as Dad called. Figured Susannah would handle it."

I'm getting an ugly feeling in the pit of my stomach as the silence on the other end of the line stretches out, and I'm nervous as hell waiting for an answer.

"Fuck, Derrick. Susannah, she played . . ."

"What?" I ask, nearly panic-stricken at this point. I don't need this shit. I so don't need this shit right now. "Just say it."

"She spent most of the first two hours playing recordings of you and Kat for the audience to comment on. It sounded like you were in the studio, talking with her, answering her questions, and you even laughed and said 'let's hear it.' Then, after that, it was you and Kat . . . uh, getting down and dirty."

"What are you talking about? Are you sure? Did you hear it yourself? How in the fuck are there even recordings of that?"

"You didn't record them? I mean, that doesn't sound like something you'd do, but how else?"

I feel the world start to spin, and I lean against my car, planting my hand on the roof to make sure I don't pass out. "No, I didn't record them. How bad was it?"

"It was bad. I'm not gonna repeat it all to you, but you should know, it was bad. I mean, I've seen pornos that had less explicit dialogue."

Oh, dear God. "What? How do those even exist? I didn't record them. I have to go, Jacob. I have to find Kat, find out what the fuck happened. Can you come to the hospital and sit with Dad for a little bit?"

"I'll be there this afternoon. The team's doing okay. I can take a day off for personal time. Hell, training staff keeps telling me to rest my shoulder anyway. I'm on my way, brother. Go get your woman and fix this. From what it sounds like, you might want a lawyer. If you do, I know a guy."

"Uh, right. We'll figure that out later though. Thanks, I appreciate it."

I hang up and run back upstairs to Dad's room, trying to figure out what to do as my mind races. Susannah could totally use sound bites of me on-air to make it sound like I was in the studio. We do that all the time for popular jokes so we can replay them and laugh at ourselves.

But this is wholly different. She made it sound like I agreed with airing my own sex tapes, for fuck's sake. She might have ruined everything . . . with work, and more importantly, with Kat.

"Derrick?"

I stop, realizing I've been pacing the floor, and turn to see Dad. He's woken up, looking better than he did last night, but he's worried. "Everything okay?" I ask him.

He reaches over and uses the buttons on his bed to elevate himself to a near-seated position. "Son, you look worse than me, like the world just came crashing down on your head. What's going on? Besides the obvious."

I come over to his bed, feeling like I really shouldn't be burdening him. But looking in his eyes, I realize that maybe that's exactly what he needs right now. To not feel like a burden himself, but to be able to be that strong man who helped me so many times before in my life.

"I don't know what happened, but I think my entire relationship with Kat just got really messed up last night."

"Kat's the young woman you told me about," Dad says, nodding. "The one you say you want to marry?"

I nod, swallowing. "And work, but I don't care about work . . . just Kat." I give him the fast and dirty of what I know, which admittedly, isn't much. I try to leave out some of the graphic details, as if it were just a little dirty talk. "And then last night, Susannah apparently aired some recordings of my chats with Kat. What the hell am I supposed to do?"

Dad nods, speaking slowly in that way he does when he's handing out his wisdom and wants to make sure you hear his best advice in your heart, not just your ears. "You love her?"

I nod. "Yes, of course. I love her so much."

"I know I raised you better than to disrespect any woman like that, so I won't even ask if you had anything to do with it."

It's a statement, but there's a threat in his tone and I can tell he's fishing for me to put his mind at ease. "Stay in bed, old man. I swear I had nothing to do with this. I'm just as horrified and pissed as she probably is. I never recorded any of it. How it got recorded, I have no idea."

He nods, his eyes flinty with furious anger and righteous determination. "Then you need to go fix this. I'll be fine right here in this bed. I ain't going nowhere. Make your mom and me proud, Son, just like you always have."

"Thanks, Dad. Jacob said he'd stop by this afternoon though. He's going to take a personal day and sit with you as long as you want."

I lean in and give him another hug, knowing that I could've lost him yesterday, and I'm so damn thankful for the man he is and the man he taught me to be. Whatever the hell just happened, I'm going full-throttle to fix this shit.

CHAPTER

Twenty~Four

KAT

THE KNOCK on the door comes at a time when the last thing I want is more people around, but Elise is having nothing of it. "I already called them. Jess heard the show anyway, so she's not going to take no for an answer."

She's right. My mother and sister come into Elise's apartment like a pair of Tasmanian devils, whirling around and searching for me.

"Kat?" Jess says before seeing me curled up on the couch underneath Elise's comforter. "There you are. Good. I've got that ginger beer you like, those flannel pajamas from your third drawer down in your dresser, and my samurai sword."

"You've got a samurai sword?" Elise asks.

"Not really, but I do have a big ass chef's knife back at home if I need to go get it. Just as good," Jess replies.

"That won't be necessary," I grumble, smiling some at her being so protective. "But thanks for the PJs."

"Of course," she says, handing me the threadbare but much-loved Elmo pajamas.

"Sis, if I give one of my clients a call, he knows some guys who could pay him a little visit and rough him up."

"No," I mumble around a mouthful of ice cream. "Please, no."

"Yeah, you're probably right," she says, sipping at the ginger beer, "but if you don't rip him a new one, I'm doing it for you!"

Mom butts in, getting down to business. "Katrina, I don't want to put you down, but have you thought that maybe there's an explanation for this?" she asks. "I mean, I've never talked to Derrick, but from everything you said, he seems like a good man. While his show's not *Mr. Roger's Neigh-*

borhood, why would he do it? Seems like he'd be just as embarrassed as you. I can't imagine his employers liked that going on the air either."

"Wait, you listen to *The Love Whisperer*?" Elise asks. "Oh, my God, I'm so glad my parents don't have satellite radio."

"Mom," Jess says, shaking her head. "Mom, I love you, but even I've got to say you're being a little too naive here. Come on, the recordings were phone calls and video chats, not police wiretapping or some spy cam action."

"But Derrick broke the law if he recorded them, right?" Mom asks. "I mean, you can't just broadcast someone's sex life without their consent, can you?"

Elise shrugs. "Gray area right now. Recording a call one-sided is legal in this state. Trust me, I know all about that one with my job. Beats me if the content matters."

"Besides," Elise says, "he gave his permission to broadcast. Kat, I know you missed that part, but I heard it."

I sniffle, tears threatening again. "Can we just change the subject, please?"

Mom nods, hugging me again. "I'm so sorry, baby."

I lean against her, drawing scant comfort from her presence, but at least there's something. "Remember when you said that even with the pain of it ending with Dad, you wouldn't trade the good days?"

"Yeah."

"Well, I would," I declare miserably. "It's not just the good days. It was the hope that maybe I was wrong, that I could have what you and Jess have. This isn't about our being over. This is about my hope being dashed beyond recognition. I'm not doing this anymore, ever again."

Before anyone can say anything, I get up, wrapping up in Elise's comforter and shuffling off to the bedroom. She's got a big bed, and between the comforter I've already got and her fluffy blanket she's got here, I quickly get a good misery nest wormed up and snuggle in deep, hiding in my cocoon.

I have a half-formed thought that instead of eventually emerging a beautiful butterfly, I'm going to come out of this a hardened bitch. But maybe that's safer in the end.

There's no way I'm going to sleep, even if I couldn't still hear them talking.

"Has she even talked to him yet?" Jess asks Elise quietly. "I mean, all jokes aside, I'd like to hear this excuse."

"Maybe screaming and cussing him out would help?" Elise asks. "I mean, it couldn't hurt, right? Sorry, she hasn't even turned her phone back on after that call to him when she realized that he ignored her."

Mom sounds bleakly hopeful. "Maybe he's called by now?"

Elise lowers her voice, but I can still hear her. "No. I turned it back on when I forced her into the shower this morning. He still hadn't called and I deleted a bunch of texts from people at work who heard about it. Oh, and Kevin sent her stupid shit that makes me want to slap his fucking face. I'm planning on dealing with his ass soon enough."

I hear my Mom's gasp, and while I'm pissed that Elise screwed with my phone, she's got a good heart. She's right. I should have checked for Derrick to call back.

"I never liked that weasel," Mom says.

I groan and roll over. Everyone knows I'll never be able to show my face at work again. Fuckstick Kevin even thinks he's worthy of my time now. I may be embarrassed as hell, but I'm never falling that far off the scale again.

Nope, just gonna stay alone, me and my lines of code that are predictable and reliable, unlike men. Maybe get that dog after all.

There's a buzzing sound, and then Elise's voice. "Ugh . . . They're not being completely rude like Kevin, but I'm going to have to teach some of her co-workers a lesson too. I'm gonna turn this back off for now. She doesn't need any of this shit right now."

I bury my head underneath the dual comforters, hoping to drown out the noise. Maybe eventually, I'll get to sleep and wake up to find out this was all just a nightmare.

"**HEY**, *this is Kat. I'm busy so leave a message at the beep.*"

I slam my fist down on the passenger seat of my car, growling. Each time I call, it goes straight to voicemail.

I went to her apartment, banging on her door loudly enough for one of the neighbors to stick their head out and tell me to shut the fuck up or else they'd call the cops. Yeah, that's the last fucking thing I need.

Knowing I've got at least one more shitstorm I've got to deal with, I head into work. Walking through the small reception area, I know I've got laser beams shooting from my eyes and fire drifting from my nostrils as two of the front staff cower from my glare. They normally are pretty nice. I've shot the shit with them plenty of times. Not today.

"What the fuck was that last night?" I explode as I storm into my office to see Susannah seated at the work table, her little clipboard arranged perfectly in front of her. "What was going through your fucking head?"

She taps her clipboard with a pen, looking up with an expression on her face of total and complete calm. "Nice to see you too. I covered for you when you bailed and didn't answer your phone the dozens of times I called to find out where the fuck you went. You've been mentally absent for weeks now, Derrick. I saved your ass and the show, just like I always do. You're welcome, by the way."

I stop in my tracks, dumbfounded. Not sure what excuse I was expecting, but it damn sure wasn't that. "Covered for me? You should've just played an old show. How the hell did you get those recordings?"

My yelling is attracting an audience, people poking their heads out and freezing in the hallway to watch the show through the glass door, but I'm way beyond caring.

Susannah, on the other hand, is playing it cool as a cucumber. "You're the one having phone sex in the middle of the studio. I just aired them. I could've filed suit for creating a hostile work environment, you know. I did you a favor."

The door to my office opens and the station manager, Quincy Kilborne, comes in. A long-time veteran of the radio game, Quincy's been a strong supporter of my show from the beginning. Today, though, he looks pissed.

"What the hell's going on in here? Why are you two yelling at each other when the show starts in an hour?" He crosses his arms over his chest, looking at us like we're misbehaving children.

I swallow back an eruption of rage and stifle my voice. "Susannah played recordings of my private conversations on air. Last night's show . . . I didn't make those recordings, and I damn sure didn't give my permission to air them."

"Is that true?" Quincy asks, raising an eyebrow. "Let's be clear—we're talking about a possible felony accusation here. What happened yesterday?"

"He . . ." Susannah says, her mask of self-control faltering as she stutters slightly. "You heard it. I played it. He gave permission to play those recordings. Go back and listen. You'll see."

Quincy looks at me, but before he can even ask, I'm all over it. "Bullshit. That was an edited soundbite. The whole damn thing was edited. I left during the pre-show meeting yesterday in a hurry."

"Yeah," Susannah scoffs. "Running off to go see your fuck buddy instead of working, just like you have every day for weeks. So typical of you these days. I've been covering for you every damn day."

Quincy looks between us, and I can see it in his eyes that he doesn't believe Susannah either. Who would? I fucking hope Kat doesn't.

"I went to the hospital to see my dad," I explain. "He had a heart attack. He called during the pre-show and I ran to meet the ambulance at the hospital. I didn't have time to explain. I was in a panic. Call the damn hospital. I spent the whole night there. Fire me if you need to for bailing, but the bigger problem here is how Susannah got the recordings. Those were private."

Susannah starts to fidget in her seat for a few moments. "Well?" Quincy asks. "How did you get those conversations?"

"I recorded them!" Susannah finally explodes after seeing the silent act isn't going to work. "You're sitting there in the studio every night, just winging the whole damn thing by the seat of your Jockeys while I'm prepping the music, the emails, the next caller. Meanwhile, you're fucking off talking to your latest and greatest. Fuck that. We had something good going when you were single, or at least you were focused on the show and helping me make it great."

"Wait . . . but how's that possible?" I fume back. "And yeah, I admitted to you that I wasn't giving a hundred percent. I apologized for that. But I was still pulling my weight. The show's been doing fine and that's no fucking excuse!"

"Because I'm picking up your slack!" Susannah screams. "I'm the one who sets up the callers. I'm the one who does the music. I'm the one who chooses the emails. I'm the one who does every *fucking* thing this show needs except, of course, milk your fucking cock when you want it milked! And for that, what do I get? You texting your goddamn girlfriend while I'm busting my ass!"

"Susannah, I already apologized—"

"Stick your apology up your ass!" Susannah screams. "I do all the work, and somehow, you get to waltz in, drop some Barry White smooth tones and lame advice, and you get all the credit. The damn show's even named after you. I'm not even a fucking side note. I'm the one carrying the whole show on my shoulders, working to get us into syndication and studio deals, and I barely get anything! ANYTHING!"

"What you do get is invading my privacy," I seethe, my voice dropping to an enraged calmness. "I talked it over with a friend and pulled the archives of the show. That wasn't just phone calls, and it wasn't stuff I did in the studio. At least three of the clips you played were things I did in my apartment, on *my* time. How the fuck did you do that?"

Susannah says nothing, crossing her arms over her chest. "I want a lawyer. This is sexual harassment."

Quincy speaks up. "If anyone has a case for harassment, it's Derrick. Can I see your phone?" he says, nodding to me.

I'm hesitant for a second, considering what's just happened with my phone, but I hand it over and he starts tapping at the screen. He hands it to me, showing me the task manager with something running in the background I've never installed.

"Uh-huh . . . thought so. Wouldn't have had a damn clue how to check this, but I saw it on TV the other day. She must've installed this on your phone somehow."

"What—" I start, taking the phone in trembling fingers before remembering. "That time you were screwing with my phone, when I stepped out to take a piss."

Susannah shrugs, finally deciding that offense is the best defense. "I had to do it. I just wanted to see what I was up against. I needed you here with me, and knowledge is power. If I knew what you were doing, I could cover for you, work with you, maybe get you to see the light that you don't need her and she's screwing everything up. We're on the cusp of greatness here, and it's everything I've worked so hard for. And you're not only letting it slip away, you're walking away for some damn pussy. After I listened to a few of the conversations, I thought it would be good for the show. Hell, it got me hot and I don't even think of you that way. If she got mad and dumped you, then you'd re-focus on the show and we could go back to how it was before. Win-win."

"Win-win? Like before?" I ask, staring at my phone. My hands are shaking so hard I can barely control myself, and the world narrows to a single black tunnel as I stare at the welcome screen for the spyware. My fist clenches, squeezing the sides of my phone until there's a cracking sound, and suddenly, my phone's screen goes black. I drop the wreck on the table and look up at Susannah. "How on earth could it be like before after what you did?"

Quincy doesn't let her respond. "Susannah, you're fired. Gather your shit and get out."

"You'll be hearing from my lawyer," Susannah growls. "You hear me? I'm gonna own this station by the time I'm done with you."

"Ms. Jameson, you're going to be lucky if you don't serve time. I'm reporting your actions to the police even if Mr. King here doesn't. You're not walking away from this. Your actions have risked the station and the show. I'll call security to escort you out."

Instead of waiting, Susannah storms out, kicking my office door open before screaming in rage as she heads down the hallway. In the strange silence that follows, I turn to Quincy, who's watching my office door close on its pneumatic hinge. "I'm sorry about all—" I attempt.

"Forget it," Quincy says. "I actually listen to the show, Derrick. Not as a boss, but just as a listener. Maybe she was carrying more load behind the scenes, but the success of the show on-air is about you, and there *has* been something different lately. You seem *happier* on-air, like you believe the happily ever after shit you peddle, and it gives us all hope, even my crusty old soul. Maybe we need to get you an assistant for the prep and a co-host for on-air, but regardless, what Susannah did is about as wrong as it gets."

I let out a relieved sigh, realizing I'm not fired too. "What about the show? We *had* to be breaking some rules last night."

Quincy shrugs. "We'll probably catch some shit, but as long as we don't pull anything like that again, we'll be fine."

"And the show tonight?" I ask, looking at my cracked phone. "I really shouldn't have done that . . . how the hell am I going to call Kat now?"

"Go get a new phone. If she meant that much to you, you have to know her number," Quincy says. "As for your show, we'll cue up one of the recorded ones. Take a few days, get yourself together, and we'll line up some help for you. I know we've got some producers in-house who would give anything to work with the Love Whisperer, and I'll put out some feelers for a co-host. Think of it this way, you've got a hell of an opening monologue to do if you want."

"Yeah . . ." I mumble, not sure what else to say. "Quincy, I know I should start helping with everything now, but—"

"Go handle your business," he says, patting me on the shoulder. "We got this."

I think. How am I supposed to reach out to Kat when she isn't answering me and I don't know where she is? Suddenly, it hits me, and I look Quincy in the eye. "Actually, I need to get on the radio tonight. At least that first half hour or so. Think Phil would mind being my producer tonight?"

He gives me a small, tight smile. "Hell, if he can't, I think I can still run a basic board. Just don't ask me to do any digital magic."

CHAPTER
Twenty-Six

KAT

I'M LYING on the couch, trying to ignore the pain inside me by shooting balloons with monkeys on Elise's laptop when she comes in, carrying her phone. "Kat!"

"What?" I mutter, watching as a giant black blimp appears on screen. How appropriate. It fits my mood.

"Kat, you gotta listen to this," Elise says, dropping her phone into her stereo system. "Derrick's on!"

"You know I don't want to hear—" I start to shoot back, but before I can, Derrick's voice fills the room. It's raw, different from anything I've ever heard on the radio before. No, I've heard this voice . . . but only when he's just talking to me. I close my mouth, listening to every word.

"*Okay, that was our opening break . . . Toni Braxton's* Another Sad Love Song," Derrick says. "*Now normally, I'd start off the show with an introduction, a few laughs, maybe a little innuendo to get things rolling. But right now . . . well, this isn't The Love Whisperer talking. For those of you who are looking for some advice, maybe something closer to what we normally do here, tune in next hour. This hour, this is just me . . . plain ol' Derrick King trying to fix something that happened last night.*"

"*You see,*" Derrick continues, "*last night was something that I never planned. Those of you who tuned in heard me give permission for certain racy recordings to be played on the air. Let me be clear. At no time did I authorize that. Folks, I didn't even know I was being recorded. What you heard last night were the highly edited versions of private conversations between me and the woman I love more deeply than I can ever say.*"

"Do you believe him?" Elise asks.

"Shh!"

I turn my attention back as Derrick keeps going. *"I was betrayed by a now former coworker who put spyware on my phone when I wasn't looking. This person, and I'm not naming names due to pending legal action, but this person then took intimate private phone calls and video chats and spliced them together to create what she wanted. Fuck it, let's be plain. Who knows how many people heard it live? No need to beat around the bush. Kat, I didn't know about the recordings. I left the studio yesterday because my dad's in the hospital. What happened last night, I had no part in. Last night, I missed your phone call because I left my phone in my car when I rushed into the ER. I damn-near puked when I talked to Jacob this morning and he told me what had happened. I . . . I'm sorry."*

I stand up, walking toward the radio. "Derrick . . ."

I can hear the honesty in his voice, the raspiness as he speaks. *"Kat, I never wanted to hurt you. You've been through so much, and all I wanted in our lives was to keep making you happy. You've told me so many things, and I'd never do what happened last night even to an enemy . . . let alone to the woman I love. Please, I know you're angry. I'm angry too. Call me. I sorta broke my phone when I found out about the software, but they got me a new one and it's clean, I promise. Same number. It's sitting here in front of me. If you don't want to do that, call the show. I'll put the whole damn rest of the show on a mixtape if I need to. I love you, Kat. Call me."*

"I need to go to him," I say, turning to Elise. "I don't want to do this over the phone. I have to look him in the eye."

"Not like that, you aren't," Elise says with a tiny smile. "No offense, babe, but you smell like stale wine, along with a shitload of sweat and other general yuckiness. And you're still in your pajamas."

I look down and pull my pajama top off. Elmo drops to the floor, and I rush to the shower. "Lend me some clothes!"

"Got some sweats . . . not much else for this weather. You're too damn short!" Elise calls from her bedroom. "Good enough?"

"Good enough!" I say, scrubbing quickly. I hit the major areas and am jogging out the door exactly six minutes later, Elise's phone still broadcasting Derrick's voice.

"Folks, to everyone listening, I have this advice for you. Check your computers. Check your phones. What happened to me . . . well, I didn't even know spyware like that existed. It's invisible and they don't even need your phone password to install it, just your number. But you see, even knowing that, I don't regret having phone sex with a woman I care deeply for. I don't regret the video chats either. I do regret that what was loving and private between us was broadcast by someone jealous of my position on this show. I do regret that my sweet Kat, who is one of the kindest, most precious people in the world, was made to sound like something she's not through the magic of sound editing. Guys, you never heard the important parts of our calls. You didn't get to hear that, in between the sexy playful talk, we exchanged words of love, of commitment. You never got to listen as she joked with me about our breaking the closet barrier right after that last sound clip where she called out my

name. So protect yourselves. If you want to have phone sex, that's fine. You want to naughty chat, that's fine too. But protect yourself."

We peel ass through the city, heading toward the studio. When I get there, Elise struggles to keep up with me as I rush in the front door.

"Where's Derrick?"

"I'm sorry," the receptionist says, "but Mr. King—"

"Goddammit, I'm Kat!" I yell. "His Kitty Kat!"

The receptionist's eyes flash in recognition, and without another word, she leads me down a short hallway to a studio, where she knocks on the door. "Derrick? You have a visitor."

I step into the studio, where Derrick cuts off his most recent monologue mid-sentence. "Excuse me, everyone, we're going to cut to some music. Uh . . . Kat's here. Wish me luck."

In another connecting booth, an older, slightly balding man in a suit throws some switches, and Nirvana's *All Apologies* starts playing.

"Kat," Derrick says, but before he can say anything more, I collapse into his arms, holding him close. "I'm so sorry."

"I'm so sorry too." I cry, burying my nose in his shirt. He smells a little funky too and is going on a couple of days' growth of untrimmed beard for sure. Somehow, those two little details tell me that everything he's said is the truth.

Derrick holds me close, "Kat, I know I hurt you—"

"No . . . *she* did," I reply, looking up at him. "Yeah, I was furious at you last night, but I should've trusted that something wasn't right. It wasn't like you to do that, but it was hard to trust my heart over my own ears. It brought up old issues and insecurities, and I just fell back into that dark place so fast, but it was so much worse because it was you and I love you so damn much. But I heard you just now. It wasn't your fault and we were both hurt by her actions. It wasn't our fault. Where is she?"

"I love you too, Kat. She's been fired, and both me and the station have retained lawyers," Derrick says. "Illegal wiretapping, invasion of privacy, I don't fucking know what you call it but it's damn sure illegal. She'll never work in radio again and might do jail time. Quincy, the station manager, says he'll back me in whatever I want to do."

I nod and settle deeper into Derrick's arms. "Okay, we'll deal with that. But I've got more important things to worry about now that I know it wasn't you."

"Like what?" Derrick asks, and I reach up, cupping his face.

"Tell me what happened with your dad." my eyes are imploring here, the concern shining genuinely.

Derrick nods. "He's gonna be okay, but he had a major heart attack and it was pretty serious for a while last night at the hospital. It was scary." He shrugs as if even saying he was scared isn't okay, but it's obviously the truth. "He's my dad, and I thought I was gonna lose him."

I wrap both arms around his waist, hugging him tight. "I'm so sorry, Derrick. I know that must have been terrifying. I'm glad he's gonna be okay though."

He smiles a bit, his eyes crinkling at the corners. "I told him about you, by the way."

The fact that he was thinking about me at all with everything going on with his dad warms my heart. He was lost last night, unaware of the storm raging on the radio and in my heart, but even in his dark moment, he thought to tell his dad about me. "Really?"

He kisses the top of my head, "He can't wait to meet you."

He turns to the producer, who gives him a single finger. "One minute, then let's get out of here."

I wait as Derrick slides behind the mic, leaning forward and looking at me, his eyes gleaming. As soon as the little red light on his board lights up, he speaks.

"Love Whisperer fans, there are times when I don't know if I'm reaching anyone with my show. But tonight, I know the most important person was listening, and I reached her, and she reached right back out to me. So, we're going to flip the show over to one of our *Best of the Love Whisperer* shows, because I'm taking the love of my life to meet my father. Until next time."

Derrick tosses the producer a wave as another song starts up. I have to laugh as Smashmouth's version of *I'm A Believer* starts playing. As we walk out, I see the receptionist give a little fist pump. "You know all of your fans are going to want to find out the details now."

"They're going to have to wait," Derrick says. "Our business is our business."

"Actually, I was thinking . . . It might do us both some good to get in front of the gossip and address it, maybe do a bit of damage control on air with a special guest . . . chick named Katrina. Might help your reputations, the show, and the station. Just a thought."

"I'll think about it," Derrick growls, pulling me close. I wrap my arms around his neck as he lifts me in his powerful arms. Our lips touch, and in the first tender caress of his lips, I know all I need to know.

His tongue strokes over my bottom lip and I open up to him, moaning softly as his hands pull me against his body. I'm exhausted. I barely slept last night, but it doesn't matter as I press my body against his. I feel a tingle deep inside, but it's more than just desire . . . it's my heart.

"I love you," Derrick whispers when we part to breathe.

"I know, and me too," I reply. "Come on, take me to see your dad."

As soon as we make it to the car, Derrick roughly pulls me into his lap, his warm kiss taking the breath out of my lungs in the chilly night air. I moan as he brings a hand up to cup my breast, squeezing gently as he kisses and nibbles down the line of my neck. I reach between us to trace the line of his growing cock in his jeans. Panting, Derrick breaks our kiss, pulling back to rest his forehead against mine.

"Make no mistake, you are mine, Kat. Now and always."

I nod, biting my lip. "Yours forever. And you're mine too."

He presses one more quick kiss to my lips in agreement. "Yours too."

It seems to be the reassurance we both need, and he works to calm the heated tension sparking in the confined space of the car. "Can't wait to finish this. But first, I've got an old man for you to meet."

———

It's a normal-looking hospital room, but the giant of a man sitting in the chair next to the bed certainly isn't. "Well, now, we weren't expecting you two to stop by," Jacob says as he gets up. "I figured you'd be at home."

"Yeah, well," Derrick says, scratching at his head, "Dad, this is Katrina Snow, my girlfriend. Kat, this is my father, Daniel King."

Daniel sits up, smiling a little, and I see he's wearing a t-shirt from Jacob's team. "Check out the new swag," he says with a grin before looking at me. "So you're the one who's making my boy see stars?"

I know I'm blushing, but I step forward, shaking his hand. "Maybe so, sir, but he's the one making me believe in fairy tales, that sometimes they do come true, even if they're a bit messy."

"Not messy," Jacob says, grinning. "Just sometimes a little . . . dirty. And there ain't a thing wrong with that."

I smile a bit uncomfortably. It's more than a little weird to know that my boyfriend's father and friends have probably heard me say things I wouldn't want a soul on Earth to hear. I guess I'll have to get used to it for a bit until all of this dies down.

"That's true. So, are we still on for the game?"

"Actually, I had to turn in the box tickets to get the day off," Jacob admits, "but we've got one more home game before the playoffs. It's going to be chilly, and I'll be honest, you'll have to share the box with some other player's guests, but it's a big box. What do you say?"

"I say this old man will be ready for it, but only if you quit hovering about. Go on, you all get out of here," Daniel says, chuckling. "Leave me to heal and rest. And Jacob? Make damn sure you get into the playoffs."

"You heard the man," Derrick says, taking my hand. "Dad, we'll come by sometime tomorrow."

We leave, and at the elevator, Jacob wraps his arms around me, nearly crushing me in a bear hug. "I'm happy for you. Take care of him, okay?"

"I will," I groan, trying to hug him back but nowhere able to get my arms around his enormous torso. Still, I pound him on the back as best I can, touched that for such a fearsome football gladiator, he's a big teddy bear inside.

CHAPTER

Twenty-Seven

DERRICK

MY HANDS ARE TREMBLING with excitement as I turn my key in the lock to my place, letting me lead Kat inside. "Kat . . ."

She turns to me, placing a finger over my lips and looking at me saucily. "Derrick, fuck me. Make love to me. That's all I need." And she walks inside, heading for my bedroom. "Make me feel like the woman that you've reminded me I am."

I can't really argue, so I just watch in utter fascination as she sways her way across my living room, an utter sex goddess in oversized sweatpants.

But it's not the clothes. It's the aura of sensuality that just seems to exude from every pore in her body. She's the total package, the one I've always known was out there for me somewhere—sexy, intelligent, sweet, and overall, an amazing woman. Maybe I sensed all that way back on our first phone conversation on the air somehow, and I just didn't realize what it meant yet.

But I do now.

"Wait," I say, locking my door behind me. "Not the bedroom."

"Oh?" Kat asks, turning to me. "Why not?"

"Because I'm pretty funky . . . I was thinking the shower?" I ask in reply. "That is . . . if you don't mind my washing you down so I can dirty you up?"

"Well, I had a shower just before coming to the studio," she teases lightly before continuing with a bit of promise, "but my hair could use a good washing. By your hands, of course."

The idea of running my fingers through Kat's honey tresses suddenly has my cock aching, and I hurry to follow her into the bathroom. It's one of the benefits of my not being a sports reporter anymore. I've been able to upgrade to an apartment with one sweet bathroom that has a large glass shower stall lined in black marble. Kat's been here before, of course, but she takes a moment to admire the room as she reaches for the hem of her shirt.

"Nice choice."

"For what?" I ask, regaining some of my control and pulling her toward me.

Kat teases, reaching down and cupping my cock through my jeans again, and the response is immediate, my body already warmed up from before.

"I was thinking this is a nice choice for the first place I want you to really fuck me. Fill me with that big cock and come inside me."

I swallow, looking into her eyes. "Kat, before this all happened, I was thinking about—"

"The same thing I was thinking about. And when the time's right, we'll get there. My answer's going to be the same as before all of this. Yes."

Her words are all I need as I crush her lips in a searing kiss, tearing at her clothes as we undress each other. I say a silent prayer of thanks for sweatpants. They're so easy to peel off as I kneel in front of her, kissing at the soft skin of her belly just above the line of her panties, then tugging them down to look at her beautiful pussy.

I see her sweet clit start to pulse in time with her heartbeat, needy for attention. "Tell me, Kat."

She eases her legs a little farther apart, giving me more of a peek at her sexy center but still not saying what I need to hear.

Kat runs her fingers through my hair, pulling the strands back and making me growl. I inhale her, memorizing every nuance to her natural perfume before lifting my eyes toward her without moving away from her sexy cunt. There's a warning in my voice.

"Kat . . ."

She smirks, but the quiver in her thighs under my hands belies her flirty tone. "I think I like being in charge a little."

"And you can be, from time to time," I joke, kissing lower, deciding that if she wants to tease me by not letting me have my way with her dripping pussy, I can torment her right back and make it impossible for her to deny me.

I nip at her stomach, and she gasps, relenting with a moan. "Eat my pussy, Derrick. Do it for me."

Permission granted, I stroke my tongue between her slick pussy lips, the soft and silky folds parting under my tongue. I shiver as I eat her slowly, relishing every sweet drop of her arousal.

"Oh, fuck, Derrick, that's it. You make me feel so good, don't stop, please. Suck my clit. Hard."

I want to give her everything—what she asks for, what she needs, and what she doesn't even know she needs. I'll give her all that I am, all that I have, knowing that she'll do the same for me. So I cup her ass, bringing her in close to lick up and down her slit, circling her clit slowly before drawing it in. I suck her hard nub and thrash my tongue across it at the same time, giving her no mercy. Kat's hips shiver and her thighs clench under my hands.

"Derrick, fuck, I'm gonna—"

"Come for me, my love," I rasp, looking up at her with devotion. "Come all over my face."

I dive back in, hungry to taste her orgasm. She cries out as a gush of wetness covers my face and chin, and I feel reborn, connected in a way that we've never been before. Kat pulls on my hair, pushing me in deeper and deeper until her orgasm finally ebbs.

"That's the warm-up?" Kat asks shakily as she steps back, stepping the rest of the way out of her clothes. She pulls her shirt off while I quickly strip out of my clothes, getting into the shower and starting the water. Kat watches, her naked body glowing under the lights, smirking. "Warm enough?"

"I'll make sure it is," I promise her, holding open the glass door for her. As soon as she's in, I consume her, kissing her hard and pressing her lush body against the cool glass. My cock is throbbing, mashed between our bodies as the steamy air fills the shower.

Nibbling down Kat's neck, I bring my hand up, massaging and pinching her nipple as she moans in my ear. "Mmm, your turn to be in charge now?"

"You know damn well it is," I growl, loving the look in her eyes. It's the look of the future, the rest of my life, and I can't wait for it. Love, intense and overflowing . . . taking turns 'being in charge' while the whole time, things are really a team effort. "You're my woman. Forever."

"Forever," Kat repeats, reaching down and grasping my rock-hard cock in her soft hand. The water sprays over my back and shoulders as we kiss, her hand slowly stroking my shaft while I run my thumb over her nipple, teasing and pinching it until it's diamond hard. Kat's whimpers tell me how good it feels, and I turn her around, massaging her breasts while lavishing her neck with kisses. "Mmm . . . that's wonderful."

"Just getting started," I rasp in her ear, running my hand down to cup her pussy. She's already recovered, her pussy clenching around my two fingers as I slide them in, pumping them in and out slowly. Finally, I withdraw them and line myself up. "You ready?"

"Make me yours forever," Kat moans. I spread my legs, lowering myself enough that I can slide the head of my cock between her legs. With one long, slow thrust, I slide inside her, both of us groaning as every inch of my cock stretches her. Once I'm balls-deep, I still to let her adjust, enjoying the sensation of her wet heat wrapped around my bare cock, nothing coming between the love and trust we share. Kat's deep gasp comes from the depths of her soul, and I feel the same way as I join with her . . . the last woman I'll ever join with.

I push in deeper, bottoming out inside her, both of us gasping again as her pussy squeezes me tightly, massaging my shaft. Kat turns her head to look into my eyes, her open mouth trembling.

"I love you."

"I love you, too," I answer. The pleasure is too much and instinct takes over. I pull back and thrust deep into her again, grinning. "Forever."

Kat nods, and we let our bodies tell us what to do. My cock strokes in and out as my hands roam her body, memorizing every inch of her soft skin. "Your sweet pussy feels so good around me. God, Kat, I want to be inside you all the time." Her soft mewls echo in the shower, encouraging me.

I can't go too fast, the open-legged stance I have to take keeping me from jackhammering her, but that's okay. I pound into her, watching her ass shake from the force of each driving plunge. "You like that, Kat?"

She nods, and I do it again and again, grabbing handfuls of her hips for leverage. "Me too. I'm gonna pound your pussy and remind you that you're mine." The warm water cascades down our bodies, the slap of my hips against Kat's ass beating in time with our rising heartrates as we caress each other.

Kat presses her hands against the glass wall, urging me on, and I lift her onto her tiptoes, my fingers digging into the soft flesh of her hips to keep her there.

"Yes, fuck me, Derrick. Give it all to me. Fill me up."

I speed up, her voice sending me into overdrive. My pulse hammers in my veins, and my eyes fix at the beautiful, sexy sight of my cock pumping in and out of Kat's pussy, squeezed and caressed. My nerves are on fire, and her pussy's clenching around me with every hard stroke, begging me to stay inside while at the same time begging for release. I go faster, as hard as I dare until I feel it.

"Take it all!"

My orgasm hits me like an uppercut to the chin. Stars shoot across my vision, and I explode, filling Kat with everything that I have.

My arms tremble, and in the dim recesses of my mind, I hear Kat cry out too, her pussy clamping down on me as we stay frozen. I think we'd be there forever if it wasn't for the sudden cramp in my hamstring that pulls me back from this eternity, and I pull out, panting and laughing at the same time.

"What is it?" Kat asks, turning around to see me bending over, stretching my leg.

"Cramp," I hiss, my cock slowly wilting as the now cool water splashes down my back and ass to drip off my balls. "We need to put a step in here if this is going to be a regular thing."

Kat blinks, then chuckles as she raises an eyebrow. "Is that your way of saying I'm short?"

I laugh lightly, pulling her into me, our bodies slippery and slick against each other. "Of course not. You're not short, just fun-sized. You just need a little lift so I can *really* give it to you like I want."

"Is that your way of inviting me to move in?" She's smiling, but I can see the smallest hint of uncertainty in the depths of her eyes.

"As soon as you can break your lease," I reply. "I want to go to sleep with you in my arms, wake up with you in our bed, and spend every day together. I'm ready when you are."

CHAPTER

Twenty-Eight

KAT

THE BOX IS BUSY, but Jacob had warned us of that. The team's facing their last home game, and it's a must-win situation, according to Derrick, so a lot of the players used their allotments for this game, resulting in a box filled with a dozen or more people. Thankfully, all of them are family of Jacob's teammates. It makes things . . . interesting.

"So, you're the one who wrote that app?" one of them, a bubbly, curly-haired woman named Rachel, asks. "I just downloaded that last week. Girl, let me tell you, that has been a godsend. I've been able to do so much more, and Jerry's been happier too! He's been able to see that I'm not just wasting time being some WAG. Now, let me ask you . . . think you can write a day trading app?"

I chuckle, sipping the flute of champagne that comes with the box seats. "I could, but I doubt it'd be better than what's out there. Why?"

"A deal Jerry and I have. Each season, we take one game check each and we get to invest it the way we want. He does it in real estate, and he's made some good deals. But I do day trading. I'd like to squeeze out another three percent."

"Why's that?" I ask, trying not to let on that her blithely playing with thousands of dollars makes me a little twitchy. I mean, my job doesn't have me scraping to pay the bills anymore . . . but it's not like I can drop money like this on a whim.

"Whoever gets a bigger return gets to be in charge of our anniversary celebration," Rachel says, giggling. "Last year, I won, and I think Jerry liked it. So this year, I want to go whole hog. Leather, chains . . . he might be a football stud, but if I can get that three percent, he's gonna be my little bitch."

I gawk, then laugh. "You should talk to my boyfriend, Derrick. He'll—"

"Oh, we all know Derrick," Rachel whispers. "Half the players and wives listen in. Congrats. That was one hell of an interview, girl! Now come on, game's about to start."

We sit down, me in between Derrick and Daniel, who insists that I call him Dad. He's still recovering from his heart attack, but he looks a lot stronger in just a few weeks, and we make up for his lack of strength with our own cheering.

"You still don't have any clue what's going on, do you?" Derrick whispers as he leans over during one of the timeouts. "Didn't get to read that book?"

"I tried, but I've been kinda busy," I deadpan. We both chuckle, although it's not too dark a chuckle.

It hasn't been very easy, dealing with the aftermath. So far, Susannah's trying to cover her ass, being as 'cooperative' as possible in the hopes that Derrick and I don't go after her with a civil suit. But that's not the hard part. While the Monday show after our getting back together had plenty of respectful, supportive callers and guests, Derrick's had to deal with a little backlash from some of his female fans.

There were a few emails from pearl-clutchers who didn't appreciate that he called me his 'dirty slut' in our phone sex recordings, but he handled it with his usual aplomb that what consenting adults do and say in the privacy of their own sex lives isn't up for judgement by folks who aren't involved. I cringed a little when he reminded everyone that he hadn't invited them into his dirty talk, but it seemed to shut the critics up.

The other backlash was related to his appeal, at least partially, being because of his apparent 'availability,' and he shattered quite a few fantasies when his girlfriend came on the air and we publicly said we love each other and were moving in together.

We've both been a little bitter about people feeling entitled to an opinion about something that's none of their business, and we've both dealt with trolls and perverts who've sent in daily requests to 'see the Kitty Kat,' along with their 'suggestions' as to what they'd do with me.

Quincy, Derrick's manager, has been pretty supportive. He worked with Derrick to make sure that the new producer, a married woman named Janet, is totally professional, and he's done a good job of screening out the assholes and opportunists who've applied to be the new co-host.

"Hey," Derrick asks, leaning over, "you okay? Looked lost in thought. They still giving you problems at work?"

I shake my head, smiling. "No. A few slimy comments, but nothing I can't handle. If anything, your show's actually become a big hit around the office."

Derrick laughs, our laughter being drowned out as a massive roar goes through the stadium. I look out, and most of the cheering fans are for the away team, so I guess it was bad for us.

"Uh, what happened?"

"Big punt return," Daniel says, his eyes fixed on the field. "I'd say we're going to give up at least a field goal. They've got first and ten on the twelve yard line."

I nod, half of what 'Dad' just said going straight over my head, but I can see the position on the field, and I make sure to watch as the defense lines up. I memorized Jacob's number, and I jump out of my seat cheering as number ninety-two bum rushes through and tackles the quarterback for a big loss.

"Go, Jacob!"

"Big sack!" Dad cheers, grinning. "That's the way to collapse the pocket!"

"Huh?" I ask, glancing at Derrick. "Uhm, I'm just glad I remembered who the quarterback was."

Derrick grins, leaning in. "I think after my lesson, you can at least remember that much."

I blush, my body tingling as I think of our last-minute 'football lesson' that turned into sex after Derrick had me bend over as the 'center' and he got behind me for the snap. He gave my right cheek a swift smack and then smoothed it over with a grabbing caress, and feeling his strong hands on my ass triggered a need for something more than football knowledge. Apparently, it was the same thing for him because we almost ended up late to pick up Daniel after finishing up our 'lesson'.

"I hope the real center and quarterback don't end up like that."

"Who knows?" Derrick chuckles. "Come on, let's keep watching."

The game's first half goes well, and when halftime comes, it's still close. "Time for some snacks," Daniel says, getting up. Because of his heart attack, his diet is much stricter than it used to be, and he's not allowed alcohol or fatty foods, but today, he said he was taking a very rare exception and splurged on a small plateful of buffalo wings already. "I'm gonna grab some bites from the veggie tray. You guys want anything?"

"They got any nachos back there?" Derrick asks. "Feeling like cheese."

Daniel nods and walks off slowly. I watch him go, then turn back to Derrick. "You sure he's okay getting two plates?"

"He's fine. It's just right over there and it'll let him feel more independent. Besides, I had something else I wanted."

"Oh?" I ask, reading the low rumble in his voice. "What's that?"

"Like maybe I should have taken Jacob up on that cheerleader outfit offer," he whispers in my ear. "Minus the panties."

My throat goes dry, and I look into Derrick's eyes. "Behave yourself . . . and we'll see what happens when we get home. For now, though, I need a drink."

I get up and head to the back of the box, where Daniel is piling tortilla chips onto a big plate. "Here, let me help."

He looks over, then nods. "Is Derrick behaving himself?"

"As much as he normally does," I reply with a chuckle. "You know how he is."

"I do," he says, glancing back. "It's funny, but I guess he's always been meant for that show of his. He's always had a way with words, even when he was younger and wouldn't say much unless he really knew you. He's still a little old-fashioned, though, in some ways. Hopefully, that was my and his mom's doing. He just needed a very special woman to complete him. I'm glad he's found her now."

I blink, touched. "Thank you."

"You're welcome. I wish his mother could've been here to see it. Vanessa would have liked you a lot."

I look up, wiping at my eyes. *No raccoon eyes, no raccoon eyes . . .* "I wish I could've met her," I finally say, not trusting my emotions. "Let's get the rest of the grub, go enjoy the second half, and you can tell me what kind of woman she was."

The rest of the game goes well, and it ends on a happy note as Jacob's team gets a close win. "Nice . . . home playoff game next week," Derrick says as we leave the stadium. "He'll enjoy that."

I smile, putting my arm around his waist. I don't know what exactly that means, but I loved being by Derrick's side and knowing that he's there for me just like I was there for him today. We've been tested, and though it wasn't pretty, we withstood the potential hellfire.

"You two go on, I'll be fine," Dad says when we reach the car. "I think after a game like that, I'm going to just go relax, and I'm sure for you two, the evening is just starting. I'll grab a taxi home and catch you later."

He flags down a taxi as if it were nothing, and we watch him get in, leaving Derrick and me holding each other in the chilly wind. "So . . . how was your first football game?"

I chuckle and hug him. "I enjoyed our little practice game more, but it was fun just being there with you guys. So what are we going to do?"

"I say we hit up Jacob's after party," he says. "I could use some adult supervision."

I laugh, and we get in his car, driving to a nearby nightclub. Walking in, I'm surprised to see a familiar face. "Elise?"

She looks like a million bucks in a sparkly, tight-fitting club dress, and when she turns around, a huge grin breaks across her face.

"Hey, babe, why didn't you tell me you were coming?"

"Kind of spur of the moment . . . but what are you doing here?" I ask.

Derrick gives a nod to Elise, but before he can say anything, someone calls his name from across the room and he turns. "Go," I tell him. "I'll catch up in a minute. Tell Jacob good game for me."

"I will," he says, kissing me on the cheek.

Derrick leaves with a wave, and Elise turns back to me. "So, what are you doing in town?" I ask as she leads me over to a table where another woman is sitting. "Hi."

"Hi," the woman, who honestly, I would never expect to be sitting with Elise, says. She immediately ignores me though, gushing to Elise. "Check it, babe! I was talking with some of the girls, and you'd never believe what Christian K is up to."

"What?" Elise asks, and I suddenly get it without her explaining. She's in town working. Guess a gossip columnist has to follow the gossip.

The woman looks over at me and smiles, then back at Elise. "You sure your friend here is up to hear about it?"

Elise sighs and grimaces. "With that, I'm not sure even *I* want to know," Elise says. "Why do the handsome ones have to be so fucked up?"

Her friend laughs, sipping at her drink. "Well, if you don't want to hear that, I've got an even better story to tell you."

The music's starting to heat up, and we have to lean in close to hear. "What?"

"You're never gonna believe it."

Elise grabs her drink, downing half of it in a single gulp. "Okay, I'm ready. Spill it!"

"Okay, well, check out across the room," the girl says, gesturing. "See him?"

I turn with Elise, seeing nothing until I recognize the guy at the bar. I almost missed it because his infamous hat is missing and the lights are landing on his bald head at all angles. "Is that?"

"Yep," the girl says. "Keith Perkins. You know, the country star?"

Elise hums, nodding. "The one who's been gathering the awards? What's he doing in a club like this?"

"Who knows? He seems to be going incognito without the hat, and maybe there's a little more to him than his public image says," gossip girl quips. "Anyway . . . watch him."

We do, and while I only see a man who's out having a good time, he seems to ignore all the women who hit on him, all of them beautiful. "Get my point?" the woman says.

Elise nods. "Yeah . . . players gon' play, but this one ain't playin' . . . interesting. Gotcha. Two more rounds on me."

"I think I'll go see Derrick," I whisper in Elise's ear. "I'll let you work, find your next scoop. Come see us with Jacob up in VIP when you get the chance?"

"You got it," Elise says, giving me a kiss on the cheek. "Have fun, babe. And congrats on the win."

I go find Derrick, who's toasting with Jacob. "To the future . . . well, I'm not gonna jinx you yet."

"Good, because I don't need any jinxing," Jacob says, chuckling. He clinks glasses with Derrick, then sees me. "Hey, Kat. Enjoy the game?"

"Had a ball," I quip. "But I think it's time to party."

And party we do. While we can't go overboard—Jacob's still got at least one more game and we have to drive home—we still enjoy ourselves. Jacob spends most of his time upstairs chatting with nearly every pretty woman who comes his way, but he's still gentlemanly with them.

I can see why Derrick likes him.

"Hey, wanna dance?" Derrick asks me as his ears perk up. "I love this song."

I nod my head, taking his hand and swaying with him down the stairs as the DJ plays a remix of Rhianna's *Only Girl*, and find a space on the dance floor. We're dressed nowhere near as fancy as some of the clubgoers, where undone buttons and high hemlines seem to be the norm . . . but I don't care as I sway with Derrick.

Turning around, I grind against him, humming happily as I feel something start to swell. "Is that for me?"

Derrick growls, lowering his lips to my ear. "I need you. Alone."

"Well," I reply, reaching back and cupping his cheek, "tell Jacob bye and let's get out of here."

The fresh air outside is brisk, but after the heat of the club, it's refreshing. Walking back to the car, we pass a park, stopping to take in the lights and the large, full moon that's peering down at us from over the trees. Suddenly, a fountain starts up, spraying into the air and underlit by deep red and blue lights like something out of a Disney movie. "Wow," I whisper, hugging against Derrick in the cold air, "it's beautiful."

"It is," Derrick agrees, hugging me tightly, his front pressing into my back. "Kat . . . thank you. For everything."

"Thank *you*," I reply softly, looking up to see him with a faraway look on his face. "Derrick? Penny for your thoughts?"

"Hmm?" he asks. I giggle and snuggle against him, feeling his still stiff cock at my back. "Mmm, this is such a romantic setup . . . you and me, alone, with the gorgeous fountain, but all I can think are dirty thoughts. I can't help it. That's what you do to me."

"Oh, really?" I ask, giggling a little. I look back into his eyes, which are glowing red and blue, reflecting the fountain's lights. "Tell me. I wanna hear every filthy thing."

Derrick lowers his voice to that sexy purr he knows drives me wild, a small smile dancing on his lips. "Like I want to get you back home, rip these clothes off you, and worship your body and fill your pussy so full you can't walk right tomorrow."

I grin, turning around and pressing my breasts against his body. "You want to fill my pussy so full of what . . . your long . . . thick . . . throbbing . . . cock?" I ask, drawing out the final word in that way that I know drives him crazy and reminds us both of just how far we've come. I reach down, running my hand over his bulging jeans, humming. "Seems that's exactly what you want to do."

Derrick gasps and nods. "Then let's go home. I think I owe you a nice, long massage tonight."

Epilogue

DERRICK

THE CHURCH LOOKS BEAUTIFUL, and the springtime air is warm, the scent of flowers wafting in from the trees outside. I feel a little cooped up in my suit, but that's okay. Today isn't about me.

It's not really about Kat either, although it's a very big deal for her. With her sister happily married and our own relationship being on track, today's sort of the capstone to her own circle of trust.

It's one more sign that fairy tales can happen. One night, after we made love, we lay in the dark and she explained a theory about happiness being an island in a sea of misery, comparing love to a small Styrofoam cup.

I hadn't really understood the whole significance of her theory, but I promised to make our island the biggest, happiest one I could, and she smiled as she fell asleep in my arms. I decided that meant I was doing good. It's a growing process for us both.

Her whole life, she's been betrayed by every man whom she's ever given her heart to. And while I've not been perfect—I don't think any man is—the worst I've done over the past few months was forget to pick up Chinese takeout for dinner one night when she asked me to. Thankfully, the local spot down on the corner delivers in ten minutes flat.

Still, she's had a lifetime of insecurities and fears to get over, and we've conquered them together. I finally knew she was totally over it when she unpacked her last bag and turned in her key for her old place. No need to worry about a place to go or needing to leave because I've hurt her. Since then . . .

"Hey," Kat teases, looking so beautiful in her dress that I have a hard time taking my eyes off her. "You're daydreaming."

"Can you blame me?" I ask, taking in her peach-colored curves. We're in the back. There's still time before the ceremony starts, and I'm helping her with last-minute adjustments. "This sort of thing . . . let's face it, I get off on this sort of stuff."

Kat smiles and turns to snuggle against me. She's not perfect. She's flawed, and there are always going to be those little dark places in her heart. But they're fading day by day in the light of our love, pure and never-ending.

"You big softie."

"Hey, I did my cardio last night," I tease with a wink. "At least, you didn't complain then."

Kat chuckles and hugs me tighter. "Okay, time to get ready. You're sitting up front, right?"

"Right," I reply, giving her another squeeze. "In fact, if I want that prime seat . . . tell your mom to have fun today. And tell Jess that you're a far hotter bridesmaid than she is."

Kat smiles and pats my chest. "Go on, no need to kiss my . . . well, not right now, at least."

I laugh and head into the sanctuary, settling into a seat in the second row on the bride's side. I've come to know most of Kat's family, and I'm sure I'd be accepted in the front row if I asked, but I guess I'm still sort of old-fashioned that way. Front row is for family only.

The church fills up, and when the music starts, I stand along with everyone else to turn and watch the procession. When Kat comes down the aisle, my mouth goes dry.

She's so stunning, even though I just saw her earlier. The sunlight streams through the high stained glass window behind her, making her hair glow with inner health and beauty, truly my angel.

Watching her, the peach fades, replaced with white and lace, and I imagine her walking toward me. Yeah, according to stereotypes, women are supposed to be the ones who fantasize about weddings . . . but I'm fine being a romantic at heart. Maybe that's why I'm so good at being the Love Whisperer. In fact, that makes me more than fine with being romantic. I'm damn proud of it.

During the whole ceremony, I know that Kat's mom and her man say things, but my eyes never leave Kat, even after Jessie catches me staring and smirks, elbowing her little sister.

At the reception, as soon as I can, I have Kat in my arms on the dance floor, swaying to a slow song from back in the day. I'm not downing it. Hell, I've played a little Vanessa Williams on *The Love Whisperer* from time to time myself

"You know . . . you're the most beautiful woman in the room," I tell her as we move to the music.

"Thank you," Kat replies. "Although you should occasionally blink. It'll help with those love goggles you've got on."

I laugh lightly and pull her in tight, lowering my voice intentionally, adding a little growl of gravel to the velvety smoothness so that it vibrates against her ear.

"And that dress is something else. Makes me wonder what you've got on underneath it."

Kat casually shimmies in my arms, winking. "Is that a question? Remember that red set with the cami and boy shorts?"

My eyes glaze over as I think of that special set. Sure, we've bought other, sexier sets together, but that first set we played together with, the way I'd slipped the strap off her honeyed skin with my teeth . . . it's special. My cock thickens in my pants, and I nod softly.

Kat sees I'm in la-la land and chuckles. "Well, this dress is way too strappy and low-cut for that . . . or any bra at all. But those boy shorts, the ones you love because they show the bottom curve on the outside of my cheeks and are so sheer you can see every bit of my pussy? I've got on those . . . and nothing else."

"Fuck, Kitty Kat," I groan, pulling her closer. "Every damn day, you know just how to drive me wild. Your mom and Bob had better cut the damn cake or I'm sneaking you out of here early for another peek and nibble of that delectable ass."

"Well, I suppose you could have some frosting . . . before your dessert," she purrs. "But I'm thinking the same thing as you."

Kat

"So everyone, that wraps up another evening. I'd like to thank everyone for joining me, Derrick King, for The Love Whisperer. I'll be taking a few days off, but don't worry, I've got plenty of stuff recorded for you. Tomorrow's show is a special episode on weddings: the good, the bad, the Bridezillas. So until I'm back, love yourself and each other. Goodnight."

The song starts, and I reach over, flicking off my radio and putting my stuff away. The office is almost totally deserted, but that's fine. I enjoy having these hours with just Derrick in my ear as I do my work. I guess going two for two on number one-rated apps across multiple platforms and another expected hit with our new game gets me a few extra benefits, and one of them is that I get to pick my own hours now . . . except for meetings.

I'm going to keep riding this for a while longer. I'm motivated, and taking a risk in doing another solo app after we wrap the game, but that's okay. A simple, easy to use standalone program that helps you lock down your devices and prevent spyware is something that's been in the PC market for a while, but it keeps being ignored in the mobile market. No longer, not when I'm done.

It's a high-profile project because while the inspiration came from our incident, the potential implementations could be amazing in securing governmental agency phones from tapping. I told Derrick that we could be the first beta-testers because since the big deal with Susannah, we haven't been as bold in phone conversations or FaceTime. We save our real dirty talk for the bedroom when it's just the two of us, with the phones in the other room.

Still, we both miss the little thrill that comes from showing off for each other.

Getting behind the wheel of my car, I catch the end of the outro music for *The Love Whisperer*, then change the channel. The new show format has been awesome, simpler and more conversational with just Derrick. He's still got a producer. I talked with her once when I called in, but they decided to skip the co-host role and now the on-air is all Derrick.

People seem even more responsive now that they know he's happily in a relationship. It was rocky there at first when he lost the 'available' appeal, but people have come around, and he says it adds believability to his advice, even though he's always been pretty spot-on.

According to Derrick, after the initial short-term dip, his ratings are stronger than ever. So much so that the bigwigs have been talking to him and Quincy about going the syndication route, and he even got invited to LA to be a guest panel member for some TV show. He hasn't decided about either opportunity yet though, saying he's happy with what he's got at work and at home.

I get home and change quickly, missing the sensation of having him here. We've both been working so hard the last few weeks, getting the programming just right on a difficult segment of coding, and Derrick's been tied up with recording his extra shows so he can do some extra project that he's been really secretive on. A few months ago, I would have been worried and distrustful . . . but that was then.

Now, love and trust are together, and I've never doubted his intentions for a moment.

"Besides," I murmur as I quickly change clothes, "the good mornings and even better nights are that much sweeter when we spend every spare moment wrapped up in each other's arms, whispering dirty things in each other's ears."

I'm just slipping on my sexiest heels, not for height reasons but just because I know Derrick likes my legs in these, when he comes in from work.

"Hey, babe. Good show. Loved the caller who wanted advice on self toys."

Derrick comes over and gives me a kiss on the cheek, hugging me from behind. "Thanks," he growls, nibbling at my ear and sending tingles down my spine. "Fuck, you're so damn gorgeous, Kitty Kat. Those heels make me want to bend you over and lick down the line of your legs before flipping you onto your back and making them become 'in the air' shoes.

I raise an eyebrow, moaning lightly as he licks at the curve of my earlobe and traces a single fingertip along my upper thigh. "Why aren't we doing that, then? Let's stay home, order in, and change into something more . . . comfortable while you get a taste of my pussy and I get a sip of *your* cream. Then we can eat to regain our strength and fuck again . . . all night long."

Derrick moans and kisses my neck again before releasing me and stepping back. "I wanted to do this differently, more . . . something, but I can't wait anymore."

Reaching into his jacket, Derrick takes out a plain black jewelry box. It's narrow, but I don't care about the box . . . I care about the look in his eyes and the love in his heart as he opens the box to reveal a beautiful diamond ring. It's not gaudy. It's classic, a simple platinum band with a single square-cut diamond in the middle.

"Derrick . . ."

He takes my hand, kissing my knuckles softly. "Kat, you thought you didn't deserve a fairytale, that it was rare. And while it's true it is rare, you most definitely deserve the happily ever after, and I hope that you'll choose to spend it with me, as my wife."

There's no other answer I can give except a choked nod and a small squeal of excitement. "Yes . . . with all my heart, yes."

Derrick slips the ring on my finger before sweeping me up in his arms, spinning me around. "That's my Kitty Kat. Thank you for giving me my dream."

I hug him tightly, kissing his lips hard. "No, thank you. Thank you for showing me that I didn't need a fairytale fantasy. What I needed was real love from a real man. After that, the dream will happen on its own."

Our kiss deepens, my silky dress letting me slide down Derrick's body as our joy quickly mixes with intense heat. I can feel his cock already hardening for me, and my nipples are stiff and electric against the slick fabric. Getting on my knees, I look up at him. "Now, I think I want to start our celebration. You can call the delivery guy while I have a suck of your big—"

"Don't say it . . . unless you want me to be too distracted to order," Derrick chuckles. "Mmm . . . sexy, smart, loving, mine, and oh, so dirty in a good way. My Kitty Kat."

I reach for his waistband, undoing his belt while I grin. "I want General Tso's chicken. And as for your being distracted . . . well, just think—after our food, you can bend me over the couch and fuck me any way you want. But first, I'm going to enjoy a taste of this amazing cock."

I draw the word out the way I always do for him, knowing that it's driven him crazy since day one, still does today, and hopefully will for many more happy years of dirty talk.

His cock pops free, and I look up at him. He grins down at me, telling me what he knows I want to hear. "Go on, Kitty Kat. Suck my cock down your pretty little throat like my naughty girl."

My mouth waters, and I immediately swallow him whole. Dirty? Maybe, but nothing could be better.

We'll have to call the family to tell them the news . . . later.

The End. Thank you for reading. If you enjoyed the book, please leave a review by just clicking HERE. If you'd like to listen to this as an audiobook, it's available on Amazon or Audible.

Let's stay in contact! You can join my mailing list here. You'll never miss a new release and you'll even get 2 FREE ebooks!

Book 2 in this series, Elise & Keith's story, is now LIVE! Read Dirty Laundry HERE. Or read on for a 2 chapter preview!

Get Dirty (Interconnecting standalones):
Dirty Talk | | Dirty Laundry | | Dirty Deeds | | Dirty Secrets

Dirty Laundry

CHAPTER

One

ELISE

"YES, sir. I'm on it, sir. By Monday, of course." I sigh, rolling my eyes as Donnie, my boss, somehow manages to both ream me out for not delivering yet and make me feel like I can totally accomplish my latest assignment.

I'm not sure how he manipulates people so well, but he does. It's a gift, I guess.

Hanging up, I look at myself in the mirror, making sure my disguise for today is in tip-top shape. I'm not famous, but my face is known enough that I want to be sure I'm not recognized. My blonde hair is tied up under a dark brunette wig that falls down in perfect mermaid waves, my usually slightly made-up face is fully done like I'm some YouTube makeup tutorial, and I'm dressed in casual clothes that scream money in quality, not flash. I've got on the one pair of designer jeans I own, a perfectly slouchy tee, and a fluffy soft hand-knit cardigan.

With the addition of my huge sunglasses and heeled booties, I'm off . . . looking just like one of the other millions of twentysomethings, out for coffee and to run errands. Which is exactly what I need, nondescript from the masses.

It's nowhere near my normal look, but that's what makes it a great disguise. Glancing at my watch, I realize I'll need to take a cab if I'm making my first observation point on time. At least I can turn the receipt in for reimbursement because taking cabs all over the city is definitely above my pay bracket.

I hope Donnie isn't going to be a prick on the expense report this time.

After a quick ride, I order a coffee and a blueberry muffin before sitting down at what's become *my* table over the last week, taking out a notebook full of scribbled notes. To an interested observer, I'm working on a movie, or maybe a TV show, or something similarly vapid. I assume an aura of 'don't-fuck-with-me' and pretend to work, which makes a great cover because I am actually working, just not on what it seems.

Keeping my head still behind the shades, my eyes move left and right, not missing a thing. From the obviously morning-after coffee date, to the mom juggling two kids while bribing them with muffins that look just like mine and will put those two into sugar overload in ten minutes, to the old man reading the paper. I've worked long and hard on these skills. They're more vital to my career than the ability to type quickly.

It's not long before my target appears. Keith Perkins, the country music star who's topping charts and winning awards left and right. He walks in to order his morning cup o'joe. He's not really in disguise, just wearing jeans and a t-shirt, but the missing cowboy hat and tennis shoes instead of boots seem to be all the disguise he needs to go about unrecognized in this town. Then again, this isn't a big country town. I bet he couldn't pull this off in Nashville without getting mobbed.

He tells the barista his name is Kevin instead of Keith, but I don't think she even looks up. In fact, I know she doesn't look at him, because if she did, she'd be drooling like I've been for the last five days since I started my assignment.

There's something about the way he moves, like coiled power waiting to spring into action, that makes me hum with anticipation. Combine that with a build that's tall and wide-shouldered, with powerfully built arms and a tightly muscled waist that's so narrow that he can't wear normal jeans without squeezing his thighs and leaving his waist baggy . . . the man's walking sex on a stick. He's infused with energy in such a way that you can't help but wonder what he could do with it.

Or what he could do to me with it.

I shake my head, a small smile tilting up one corner of my mouth. As if. That's never gonna happen. I'm not the sort who gets wooed and swept off her feet by handsome stars who then proceed to wine and dine me before making my toes curl. No. With my job, I have a better chance of my name ending up pinned on a voodoo doll than my body being pinned to a bed.

My job is to follow Keith and watch that fine ass and dimpled smile as much as possible to find out his secrets. Once those secrets are in hand, I'll write a damn good story for the online gossip rag I work for. It's not my dream gig. Hell, I've hated it at times, but it's interesting and pays the bills. I wanted to be a real investigative reporter. I wanted to follow in the steps of Woodward and Bernstein, exposing the back-alley machinations and dirty laundry of those who really deserve it. Those in power who are trying to fuck the average Joe.

Too bad most of the reporters on that gig are just as dirty as the assholes they're covering. So I get to watch and report on celebs. But it pays the bills, so here I am lusting after the mark I'm following in preparation to expose all of his dirty laundry to readers who circle like vultures. Sometimes, I feel sorry for people like Keith. He's not into drugs or acting like a jackass, and I've even listened to his music. It's music to make you feel good. And make my panties wet, but that's his voice. He could read his grocery list and I'd be all ears.

Knowing his routine, I start to gather my things, ready to follow out a few seconds behind him. As he walks out the door, questions run through my head, mental preparation for what's coming. *Where are we going today, Keith? The recording studio? Maybe the quiet spot at the gastropub you like to write at that has those bacon cheeseburgers that I have no idea how you eat and still have a six-pack? No jelly there. Or maybe just some errands? I could really use some errands so I have more to complete your picture.*

He doesn't answer, of course, but I carry on the conversation with myself as if he does. *Sounds good, I can learn more that way. Maybe after your errands, you can take me home and fuck me stupid? Make that tight ass of yours good for something . . . pounding into my needy pussy. How's that for a plan, Keith?*

God, I need a man.

It's been months since my last boyfriend, the bastard. While I'm known for being a spontaneous, up for anything kinda girl, I don't sleep around and have pretty discerning taste. Which, of course, is how I find myself fantasizing about Keith's ass as he walks down the street, sort of looking down as he walks, maybe to hide his face from the public or maybe because he's got his own internal dialogue going. It's too much to hope he's thinking about the sexy brunette in designer jeans and sunglasses he saw in the corner of the coffee shop and how he'd like to take her home and make all her dreams come true, but fuck it, I'm allowed to fill in the blanks here.

He pauses in front of a store and looks back, so I step over to a potted plant in front of a store as cover, jostling the sidewalk traffic flow as a younger guy on rollerblades yells at me, "Watch it, bitch!"

I scowl, not wanting the attention, and quickly bury my face in my phone but sneak looks out the side of my sunglasses as I catch my breath.

Focus, Elise. Get your brain out of the gutter and do your fucking job!

Suitably chastised by my own more responsible half, I continue on, following Keith into . . . a grocery store?

Wouldn't have expected Mr. Fancy Country Singer to be buying his own food. With online delivery and personal assistants running rampant around this town, I just never imagined him buying his own jars of basil pesto. Still, the fact that he does is cute, sweet, and maybe even a bit humble. I like this down-to-earth potential tilt to my story, so I sneak a few pics of him pushing his cart around the store, an old-fashioned piece of paper in his hand as he goes over his grocery list.

Following at a distance, I grab a few things totally at random as cover while I try to scope out what he's buying to see if there's anything interesting that'll tell me his secrets.

Bread . . . boring, it's not even fancy, just plain old wheat bread. Steaks . . . no surprise, although I wish I could afford a nice rib-eye every now and then. Speaking of USDA prime beef, God, I could take a bite of his biceps. Yummy. Milk . . . so 1990. Wait, not milk. He's buying milks, two different kinds of milk . . . skim *and* whole, a half-gallon each. And the skim milk is that special type for people who are lactose intolerant.

That's unusual, right? I mean, if you drink milk, you're not likely to go for two drastically different fat contents. Unless he cooks? Maybe the skim is to drink and the whole is to cook?

Hmm, could be. But then, why the lactose intolerant one? I've tasted it myself, and no matter what the makers say, it's crap compared to the real thing.

I keep following as he walks . . . into the feminine hygiene aisle. *Jackpot.*

Why would a notoriously single man, one whom women literally throw themselves at and are routinely rebuked, be buying tampons and pads? Because he's not single anymore! The little news ticker in my brain rolls by . . . *Hearts break all across America as Keith Perkins confirms he's off the market, ladies. News at ten o'clock.*

He's stockpiling his house. By the looks of the third box of goodies he tosses in the basket, he's got damn-near a full medicine cabinet in there. I sneak another pic for proof and follow him up toward the front of the store.

Choosing the line behind him, I consider maybe taking a chance to say something. It's risky, but I might be able to tease some nugget of information out of the potential encounter. After setting his items on the conveyor belt, he looks at me.

I smile my biggest, flirtiest smile, expecting him to see stars. This smile has gotten me into more private rooms, parties, and information trades than I could say . . . unless you're paying.

But from Keith, nothing. Not even a returned smile. His eyes slide over me and then back to the conveyor belt as he watches the little display show each item as it's rung up.

How rude!

The whole encounter, Keith ignores me and barely speaks to the cashier. Most of the noise is grunts and mmm-hmms coming from him in response to the cashier's chatter. She doesn't seem to know who he is either. I get that we're not in a country town, but do none of these people listen to country music? Or music period?

You wouldn't think he'd be able to take off his hat and be incognito, but apparently, he can. Clark Kent, eat your fucking heart out. He pays—cash, I notice—and grabs his bags, disappearing out the door in a hurry. Shit, did he make me?

I pay for my mismatched bread, soda, and candy bar and hustle out behind him, wishing I hadn't grabbed that bag of tater tots as part of my cover for going down the frozen food aisle because it wasted precious time telling the cashier I'd changed my mind about them. I'm so busy looking left and right down the sidewalk, trying to find his bald head above the crowd, that I don't notice when he steps out right in front of me.

His chest is like running into a brick wall, bouncing off a slab of iron hard muscle that barely gives. I cry out in surprise, more of a startled squeak really, but before I fall, he captures my arm in a tight grip. For a split second, we're in tight proximity and I can feel the thrum of hot control resonating from him, and it makes me drunk. Suddenly, I'm aware of where my hand is, and it's cupping something big, warm . . . and I bet it would get even bigger if I had a chance. I feel my face heat and am momentarily thankful for the caked-on makeup to hide the flush racing along my cheeks.

The makeup can't hide the shiver that rushes through my body though, straight to my core as I'm reminded once again how fucking sexy Keith is. "Oh my gosh, I'm so sorry," I finally squeak out in a voice that's about an octave higher than I normally have. "I wasn't watching where I was going."

It isn't until I'm finished that realization hits me, and I start praying this was accidental. The last thing I need is his figuring out that I'm part of the press and that I've been following him.

Keith looks down at me, no small task considering I'm five seven in bare feet and usually feel part Amazon by the time I get high heels on. Even in running shoes, I can stand eye to eye with the average man.

As I look up, though, I realize I could wear my highest heels and he'd still be taller than me, still be able to bend me over and fuck me senseless. God, every thought I have of this guy is about sex. Either I'm really that desperate to fuck, he's that sexy, or both. Either way, I need a new vibrator. Hello, Amazon Prime, you are amazing. Two-Day shipping? Yes, please!

Luckily, my traitorous eyes are covered in sunglasses so he can't know what I'm thinking, but regardless of whether he can catch my vibe or not, he doesn't seem impressed.

"Well, maybe you should watch where you're going then," he half growls, steadying me for a moment. "This isn't the sort of place for daydreaming."

Without another look, he strides off down the street. I stare at him, too shocked to even stammer a reply.

What an asshole! I think for a split second before I realize that yeah, I was following him, but he didn't know that for sure!

A tiny thought jumps through my mind, reminding me how hard his body felt, how strong his grip on my arm was as he kept me from falling. And yes, the feeling of what's inside his jeans, even if it was only for a microsecond. For a moment, I'm torn. Should I keep following him? Or now that he's had eye-to-sunglass contact with me, would that be too suspicious? I decide the risk isn't worth it. Besides, I think I have exactly what I need.

There's a woman in Keith's life. It isn't me, but that doesn't mean I'm not going to tell the world about it.

Get ready, Keith. Your dirty laundry is getting hung out to dry.

CHAPTER

Two

KEITH

"WHAT THE FUCK, TODD?" I explode into my phone as I do my damndest not to hurl my computer across the room to shatter into a million pieces against the wall. "Have you seen this shit?"

Through the phone, I hear Todd, my manager, trying to placate me. "I know, Keith. And I'm sorry. I'm looking into it as quickly as I can."

Quickly? I'm paying Todd a lot of money to make sure this isn't something that needs to be handled quickly. In this particular matter, I've made it clear that this should *never* be an issue. "Todd, the headline is 'Keith, who's the girl?'" I fume as I keep reading. "Fans want to know who's captured the heart of the rogue country star. Why would they even think there's a girl? I'm not dating anyone. Everyone knows that."

Todd sighs, and in my mind, I can see him now, sitting at his antique oak desk, the little vein in his left temple pulsing to his heartbeat. "That's just it, man. Everyone knows you don't date, and that's . . . odd for a celebrity of your success. I tried to get you to do some image work . . . show up for a few awards shows with another star, but nooooo, you didn't want to hear it. So people get curious."

I've heard all of this before, but I hate being fake. There are too many wannabes and fake ass people in this business for my liking as it is. I refuse to be one too.

"Well, fuck everyone's curiosity. My private life is my own. I sing songs, I make records, ones that have won some pretty sweet awards. I put on concerts, and we've done some damn good shows, I think. But that's it, I'm not available for public comment on my private life. I don't ask what they do with the life-sized posters I sign for them, and they don't get to ask what I do in my home."

Todd clicks into business mode, no longer trying to appease me, beginning the same conversation we've had over and over again for all the years we've worked together. I didn't hire him because he's a friend but because he knows the damn business. "Keith, there's nothing to be ashamed of here. You went grocery shopping and bought supplies for your daughter. Maybe it's time you tell the truth."

I inhale deeply, counting to ten before I let it out, willing it to calm me. It's maybe only slightly successful. "We've talked about this. No. Carsen is only twelve years old, and I want her to have as normal a childhood as she possibly can. If people know about her, she'll get hounded nonstop. She'll need a security detail to go to school, for Christ's sake, and never be able to grow up on her own. Never mind the fact that people are going to do some simple math and figure out that I fathered a child when I was still in high school. That'll start a whole other heap of questions, ones I don't want to fucking go into. The public isn't entitled to know about her, to have an opinion on what she's wearing or how I'm raising her, or fucking bring up her mother. No."

I can hear the resignation in Todd's voice. We've had this argument too many times. "I know. And I understand. It's gonna happen at some point, though. She can't stay hidden forever."

I chuckle darkly. "The hell she can't. If Hannah fucking Montana could pull it off for years, so can I."

Todd groans. "That was a fictional Disney show. And let's face it, I doubt you want your daughter doing what Miley Cyrus is doing in the real world now."

"I know it's fictional, dumbass. But I'll make sure Carsen has her fairy-tale Disney ending. She deserves that."

"Fine, fine, I can see I'm getting nowhere with you," Todd says, the exasperation with me obvious. His tone changes to one intended to be more placating. "Really, Keith . . . is Carsen okay after all of this?"

"Some bitch reporter made my little girl's first period into an expose about how I've supposedly got some new fucktoy. Ten million people now know what brand of fucking maxi pads I bought for her!" I growl, pissed off. "How do you think Carsen is doing?"

I hear Todd gulp and have a little mercy on him. He's kept my situation secret for nearly five years, a century in celebrity terms. "Sorry, man."

I shake my head, sighing. "No, it's okay. She's doing fine, mostly. She didn't realize that the feminine shit was what brought up the questions. Thinks it's just the usual speculation."

Todd hums, and I can hear the steel in his voice. He's a damn good manager, a good man overall, really. "I'm gonna fix this. I'm not sure how, but I'll see what I can do."

"Do your best. And do it fast, Todd." I grunt as a goodbye before I hang up. As soon as I do, I realize Sarah, my older sister, is standing in the doorway and likely heard everything I just said.

Sarah's leaning against the doorframe with her arms crossed, her long brown hair hanging down nearly to her waist, the same color as mine if I didn't keep my head shaved by choice. "Little rough on Todd there, weren't you?"

I can see the disapproving look in her eye, reminding me so much of Mom. We both got our height and physique from her, although thankfully, I inherited Dad's wide shoulders, or else I'd look like a ripped string bean.

"Not really," I reply evenly. "It's his job to handle things, to make sure nothing like this happens. But it did, so now he can fucking fix it. Fast."

Sarah sighs, giving me an amused eyebrow. "Why didn't you just call me? I could've gone to the store and there wouldn't have been an issue. You know, if I go buy maxi pads, nobody gives a shit."

I sigh, feeling trapped. On one hand, I know she's right. On the other hand, every time I'd have to do it, I'd feel like the world's shittiest father. It's a no-win situation. "I know, Sarah. And you know how much I appreciate everything you do . . . for me and for Carsen. But I'm her dad, you know? She needed something, and it's my job to provide it, so I went to the fucking grocery store. It shouldn't have been a big deal."

I plop to the couch, elbows on my spread knees and my head hung low. It's been hard, raising a little girl without her mother, no help from her grandparents, and only my big sister to turn to. I can't even ask more from Sarah. She's a beautiful young woman with her own life to live. It'd be unfair for me to demand she be even more of a surrogate mother to Carsen. And no matter what . . . "I just didn't want to be a failure of a father."

Sarah sits beside me, putting an arm around my shoulder like she did when we were little and I had to turn to her for comfort in the bad times. "You take good care of her, Keith. No doubt to anyone who knows you two how much you love that little girl. She has everything she needs right here with you, but you don't have to do it alone. I love that girl like she's my own. Damn-near raised her right along with you, remember?"

I place my hand on hers, patting it. "Thanks, Sarah. I know you love her, and I don't know what we'd have done without you all these years, but I hate that something that should be simple, like getting groceries, just isn't anymore." I sigh. "Hell, maybe I need a break. Just step away from the spotlight for a few years until Carsen gets older?"

Sarah shakes her head. "No chance in hell. You have worked your ass off to chase your dream, Keith. 'All those years' you're talking about? I remember them too. I remember you working days at shitty job after shitty job before singing nights. I remember my working a full-time job and bringing Carsen to some seedy places to hear you sing when she was just a toddler. I remember you holding her to your chest with one hand, writing songs with the other while you hummed her to sleep at night."

I smile slightly, remembering those nights too. "She couldn't sleep as a baby unless I was holding her."

"And she still loves you just as much," Sarah reminds me. "So all that hard work? You made it, Keith. You got your dream, and you need to grab onto it with both hands and hang on tight for as long as the ride goes. Because you know what the rap god says."

I nod. Sarah's always been more into hip hop than I am, but I know the lyrics. "When the run's over, just admit it's at an end."

"And in the meantime, get as much as you can out of it," Sarah adds. "So yeah, it's awkward right now, and the fact that something happened that is beyond your control is killing you . . ."

I try to interrupt to disagree, but she talks over me. "Please, Keith. You're the biggest control freak I've ever met. And this hit you out of left field and you don't like it. But suck it up, buttercup. It'll blow over, and trust Todd to make sure it does. In the meantime, you know you've got a moment, maybe two or three. Hang onto them and give you and your daughter the rest of a life together afterward."

I huff, knowing she's right. "Fine. You're right. As hard as I've worked to make a career singing, I'll give it all up in a split second if it's bad for Carsen though. You know that."

Sarah smiles, reaching up and rubbing my head like she used to when we were kids. "Of course you would. But look around you, Keith. She's fine, goes to a great school, has great friends, lives in a gorgeous house like nothing we could've ever imagined when we were kids, and is happy."

I smile, looking around. You could probably fit our childhood home in just this room. Hell, this house has more bathrooms than we had rooms back then. We've definitely moved up in life since those days.

"Thanks, Sarah," I finally say, leaning back and relaxing some. "You know how to make things sound right."

She nods, and I'm struck by how far we've come, brother and sister against the world. Needing a lighter moment before those childhood memories take over my brain, I tease her a little. "You sound just like Mom."

She grins, sticking her tongue out at me. "Well, thank you. I'm choosing to take that as the compliment I'm sure you intended it to be."

I laugh, giving her a side hug. "Yeah, definitely a compliment, Sis."

CHAPTER

Three

ELISE

I CAN'T QUITE BE sure, but it feels like I'm floating into work as I walk down the sidewalk. It's only been two days . . . but what a two days. I knew that story was going to be hot. I was ecstatic when Donnie agreed to give me the top header with the biggest page square footage and a big byline on our site's homepage. I've already snapped screen grabs of it for posterity. It's tabloid trash, but one day, those disguises and stalker skills are going to land me my dream job as a real investigative reporter.

I'm not picky, obviously, considering what I'm doing now. But I would like to do more than tabloid celeb hunting. Still, it was some damn fine surveillance if I say so myself. Well, other than when I ran into Keith. That was some newbie shit there, but he didn't seem to figure out I was a reporter, at least. If anything, he probably thought I was just a fan girl trying to get an autograph or maybe cop a feel . . . which I certainly remember, even if that was a tidbit I couldn't publish in order to cover my ass.

Wonder if he's still trying to figure out who at the grocery store scoped him out for the expose?

I pause for coffee, greeting my coworkers Maggie and Francesca as they linger around the pot waiting for refills. They look like a study in opposites. Maggie is tiny, a deceptively curvy blonde who rocks the nerdy-librarian look while maintaining an appearance much younger than her twenty-five years. She's a little shy but a total sweetheart once you get past her armor.

Meanwhile, Francesca is an exotic and willowy brunette who carries the practiced presence of her younger years in pageants. She never fails to mention she was second runner-up Miss Teen New Jersey. No wonder I detest the bitch sometimes.

So they're polar opposites in personality, with Maggie being more shy and reserved to Francesca's extroverted cockiness, but coffee is the eternal common denominator.

Francesca sips her coffee, toasting me slightly. "Congrats on the country singer story, Elise. Got everything you could want with that one."

The words are right, but there's a cattiness to her tone that's always there with her. She's always a bit chilly with anyone she perceives as a threat and sometimes an outright bitch if she doesn't get her way.

I pour myself a mug and make sure to keep my voice neutral. "Thank you. It was hard work so I'm glad it paid off."

She laughs, putting more meaning to words than I'd intended. "Oh, trust me, I do plenty of hard work for my stories too," she says as she almost disgustingly slurps down a mouthful of coffee, hinting at her meaning. "It pays off in some ways more than others."

With a wink, Francesca refills and sashays to her desk. I shake my head as Maggie half chokes on her coffee as she finally gets the meaning. Leaning in closer, she stage-whispers. "Did she just mean . . .?"

I smirk, giving Maggie a glance. "Of course. She's totally been fucking Donnie to get the prime stories. Has been for months. Why do you think her reports are always from fancy parties, galas, and red carpet events? Hello, preferential treatment. You seriously didn't know?"

Maggie blushes a little and shrugs. "Well, I knew she was doing something to get Donnie's attention, and the rumors are always flying. But she's so casual about it, just throwing it out in conversation."

I grin, smacking Maggie's arm. "You're so cute when you go Dorothy Gale on me. Remember, hun, this ain't Kansas. Besides, I can't say I'm jealous. I'd rather work for my stories than get them by giving Donnie blow jobs under the desk. Can you imagine the dust bunnies under there? And eww on sucking his gross dick. I like my facials at the spa, thank you very much."

I half-feign a full-body shudder of disgust, and Maggie laughs. "Ew. Now I'll have that image in my head all day. Thanks a lot, Elise. You suck!"

I grin, blowing Maggie a kiss. "Well, in the right circumstances, yes, I do suck. Even been told I'm pretty good at it. But I think we've established that it's not happening here."

I scan the room with a pointed finger. "Yup, not happening, not happening, not happening, and never, even if he was the last male on Earth and we needed to repopulate the species. So . . . what are you working on now?"

Maggie laughs again, brightening my day. I love making Maggie laugh and blush. She's so easy since she's a bit innocent, and I've got no shame in my game and generally give zero fucks. "Nothing great. I'm currently looking into a senator who's supposedly cheating on his wife. But I've been undercover as a copy-making volunteer in his office for two weeks and haven't seen anything other than a man who works too many hours. Seems like a bust."

"Sorry about that. At least he's not cheating. Hell, that alone would likely make me vote for him, considering the options lately."

Maggie grins, nodding. "Yup. He's even polite. I've been wearing my cutest tight skirt and blouse whenever I go by, and he keeps looking in my eyes."

"Maybe you don't have the equipment that entices him?" I ask, making Maggie laugh. "What? He wouldn't be the first politician to reach across the aisle for entertainment."

"Nah," Maggie says, smiling. Waving fingers at me, she walks off. "See you later, babe."

Refilling my coffee to the top, I head to my desk too but am sidetracked by Donnie's yelling. "Elise! Get your ass in here!"

Damn, you'd think a great prime story would at least get me twenty-four hours of peace, but apparently not. I consider saying as much as I sit in the chair across from Donnie, but when I see how red his face is, I decide to leave it be. Fuck it, I don't need the headache. "What's up?"

Donnie's in a pissed off mood for some reason. "You've got proof on the Perkins story?"

I nod, confused but answering anyway. "Of course. Pics of him in the store, putting things in the shopping cart, including maxi pads in the hygiene aisle, and then again at the register for a close-up. Why?"

Donnie sighs, running his fingers through his thinning, greasy hair, and again I'm reminded why I could never get to the top the way Francesca does. I might be a girl who enjoys sex, but I've got standards. Donnie ticks none of my boxes. "I just hung up with Perkins' people. They want a retraction and correction."

My jaw drops open. It happens in our business from time to time, but it's never happened to me. I'm too damn good at my job. "No way. I followed him legally, pics are in public places, thus legal, it's obviously him, and I didn't say anything that could be libel. It's all true."

Donnie smiles, relieving me a little bit. "I know. That's what I told the guy who called too, but I just wanted to check."

"I appreciate that you had my back," I tell him honestly. Donnie's a sleazeball, but he's a dedicated sleaze. He won't back down from a story he prints unless he has to, and that usually involves lawyers. "So, what now? We're obviously not pulling the story, right?"

Donnie shakes his head, reaching for the bowl of jellybeans he keeps on the corner of his desk and popping three into his mouth. "No, actually, when I told him that wasn't going to happen, he had another idea that's pretty interesting. He proposed a series of interviews, probably three or four at least—but maybe more—with Perkins himself."

Perkins himself? At the words, my pulse quickens. I can't seem to keep my thoughts about him not tied up in how fucking sexy he is. "Really?"

Donnie nods. "They're doing some damage control and wanting to write their own narrative about his life. Control the narrative, you know?"

"That sounds great!" I exclaim gleefully, and not totally professionally. "When do I meet with him?"

Donnie laughs, almost like he's amused I'd ask. "I'm thinking Frannie can take this one, Elise."

My jaw drops. Oh, hell no! Giving the best initial slots to Francesca because she's giving you her slot? I get that . . . but to take a story from me? "Like hell! This is my story . . . a follow-up from my expose. It should go to me and you know it, Donnie."

He narrows his eyes at me, not liking that I questioned him, but I'm right. This is my story. A small piece of me wants to stamp my foot and yell *Mine*! but since that's not likely to get me what I want, I quickly figure out a different tactic.

"Donnie, look. This story should go to me, and I know you . . . appreciate Francesca's work," I choke out, almost gagging to have to say that, "but she's going to be busy with red carpet events for the next two weeks when those new blockbusters come out. You know those comic book movies make big bucks and get big stars at the premieres."

Donnie makes a humming sound in the back of his throat, seemingly in no hurry to hand down his decision while I'm waiting on pins and needles. Do I need to bring up the fact that the whole office knows Francesca's using her . . . assets to get ahead with head? Finally, Donnie speaks. "Okay. You can do it. Interviews with Perkins, and I want all the dirty details, ins and outs of his life, all of it. Can you do that?"

I nod, relieved. "Of course!"

Getting up to leave before Donnie changes his mind, I stop at the door when he calls my name. "Hey, Elise? Just FYI . . . Perkins is pissed as fuck for the story because everyone knows he's majorly private. And he'll know who you are from the byline. You might have six feet three inches of raging cowboy to deal with. Be ready. And get those secrets."

I nod, my mind focusing on the words *inches* and *raging*. "Yes, sir."

CHAPTER

Four

KEITH

"I CAN'T BELIEVE you think this is the best way to deal with this," I growl at Todd through the small screen on my phone. He cringes slightly at the vehemence in my voice, even though he's a thousand miles away and probably thanking the fates for inventing FaceTime. It's not really his fault. It's the upper management at the record label that decided on this hair-brained scheme. He just has to play the messenger, and he's the only person available for me to take out my frustrations on.

So I do, copiously. I need to hit the gym and relieve some of this stress. "Really? How is an interview going to make my life more private? Sing songs, play music, go the fuck home . . . that's all I ask."

Todd sighs at the repeat of the mantra that's been the driving force for my career for the last few years. Yeah, I tour, but always in the summer when Carsen and Sarah can come along. During the school year, I play one-shot TV appearances or so-called "secret shows" where it's marketed as a last-minute gig and usually stuffed with radio personalities and listeners who win tickets. It works for me because I'm usually only gone for a weekend before getting back home to Carsen and my quiet life.

Todd calls it 'keeping my name out there' . . . like I need more promotion. I've got the career I've always dreamed of if the nosy paparazzi would just leave me the hell alone.

"Do we need to do this when I can be there to wrangle you?" Todd asks, deciding to just say fuck it and ignore my protests. "Or can you do this on your own and not be an ass? This is happening, like it or not. The label's already told the paper, and if you back out—"

"Then the shit really hits the fan," I growl. I'm this close to calling his bluff. What stops me is the fact that if I don't talk to this paper, the label will, and not everyone there understands my need for privacy. "Fine, fuck it. I'll be a fucking gentleman."

"Good," Todd replies. "So make sure that you represent yourself in a way that won't make the label folks shit their pants. Okay?"

I sigh, feeling like a deflated balloon. "I'll be fine. You know I can bullshit and be charming when I need to be. I get it . . . follow the party line. No woman in my life, obviously. Stick to promoting the new album and next tour. Nothing too personal."

Todd winces, and I can feel the other shoe about to drop. "Well, not exactly. We sold them on the idea that this is an all-access interview series, and—"

I cut him off, nearly losing my shit again. "All-access? How the hell am I supposed to keep Carsen a secret if it's fucking all-access?"

Todd rolls his eyes. "As I was saying, we call it all-access because then it seems like you're giving them everything, but then you corral them some. There are going to be personal questions. Answer them as honestly as possible without giving anything away that you want kept secret."

"And if they pry into areas that I don't want to talk about?" I ask.

"It's called playing coy, for fuck's sake. Every actress in Hollywood has been doing it since they invented film! You give a smile, a deceptive answer, and let your charm deflect. But by telling them and viewers that it's you completely uncensored and open, they'll hopefully quit asking questions. Especially when they see you're just a nice guy who wants to keep to himself, living out his dream of country music."

I laugh. He's got a few points. "That actually *is* true, so I think I can sell that. Okay, honest . . . to a point. Charming and genuine. Promote. That it?"

Todd claps his hands together, satisfied. "I think that's probably a tall enough order for today. You good? Really?"

I take a big breath, trying to focus. "Yeah, Todd. I'm good. Thanks for talking me off the ledge. You know I hate attention like this already, and with Carsen, it's hard to keep from freaking the fuck out."

Todd, who's kept my secret well, nods. "I know, Keith. Everything you do is for Carsen and for the music. That always shines through, even when you're being an ass. That's why I'm still working with you."

I laugh. "Naw, that's not it. You just like those platinum albums on your resume and my pretty-boy face."

Todd barks out a laugh, getting up from his chair. "Yeah, that's it, of course. Your mug. Speaking of, you'd better get cleaned up. The reporter will be there at four. Dinner service arrives at six for you two to take a break, and then interview number one ends at eight. I'll help you arrange a few things for steering, but if you think you're good, I've got a decent trio that's looking at becoming a bunch of solo acts."

"Why?" I ask as I run through a mental list of what I need to do . . .

starting with locking Carsen's room. Thank God she's got her own bathroom.

"Same shit as always. One thinks she's better than the others . . ."

"Damn. Good luck," I reply, thinking about one thing. In four hours, a reporter will be asking me questions, digging into my past, my thoughts, and my heart.

It sounds like hell.

As soon as I hang up with Todd, I work like a madman, calling in for an emergency cleaning from my housekeeper as I scrub every trace of Carsen from the common areas. After that, I plaster a smile on my face and get dressed to kill, hoping that at least my country boy charm can carry me through some of this train wreck.

When the doorbell rings promptly at four o'clock, I force myself to inhale deeply a few times, attempting to calm my nerves. The most important thing is that Carsen is over at Sarah's for the night and I've got a plan in mind for an 'all-access' grand tour that goes nowhere near her room.

You never know just how eagle-eyed and sneaky reporters can be. Carsen's door is locked, so if the reporter checks it, she'll probably think I've got some red room of pain hidden upstairs. But honestly, I'd be better with that than if she exposed Carsen.

I open the door and am immediately struck stupid. The woman standing on my front doorstep is gorgeous. She's tall and lean, but with curves in all the right places, barely contained in the slim-fitting dress she's wearing.

Her blonde hair is pulled back in a ponytail, fully exposing her high cheekbones and the graceful length of her neck. Her blue eyes hold a hint of amusement at my obvious freeze, and something tickles the back of my mind. She seems familiar, but I think I'd remember a woman this beautiful, even if I only glanced at her for a moment.

"Mr. Perkins?" she says after a moment. "I'm Elise Warner from The Daily Spot. I'm here for the interview."

I nod, but I'm still checking her out, if I'm honest, blood rushing to my cock instead of my brain, so it takes a second for what she said to sink in.

"Wait. Did you say Elise Warner? As in the reporter who started this whole clusterfuck in the first place?" I fume, and she nods. "Oh, fuck this."

Before I even think about it, I slam the door and walk off into the house. She should know to leave it alone, walk away and maybe send someone else. Someone I don't want to crucify for fucking with my life. But does she?

Of course not.

Instead, she starts ringing my doorbell over and over like a damn five-year-old. *Ring-ring, ring-ring.*

I snarl in frustration, turning around halfway down my hallway, and stalk back, yanking the door open. "What?"

In her defense, she doesn't look cowed by my grumpy assholeness, instead lifting her chin up defiantly. "You're right, Mr. Perkins. I am the one who reported that you seem to have some interesting things happening in your life. That's my job . . . to report on things our readers find interesting. And now it seems our jobs align. Mine to interview you and you to be interviewed . . . by me. Or perhaps there was some misunderstanding with your record label? Maybe you should call them? Or I could, if you'd rather."

I narrow my eyes, taking her measure. She's bluffing, but somehow, she hit on the one thing I don't want to do—call the label and tell them I'm not doing this. That happy bunch of assholes would probably just put out a fucking press release saying I'm off the market and probably start selling tickets to some fake engagement party they set up for PR. Instead, Todd's voice echoes in my ear. Charm her, tell some stories, get on with life. *I can do this. I can wrap her around my little finger, no problem. It's gonna suck big hairy balls, but I can do this.*

"Fine. Come on in."

I leave the door standing open and walk to the living room, not even checking to see if she follows. But she does, of course, closing the door with a soft click, and then her wedge heels swish on the tile floor until quieted by the rug.

She gestures to the chair opposite where I've claimed the expanse of couch, and I simply raise one eyebrow, but she takes it as permission and sits down daintily before taking out her phone, a small notebook, and a pink sparkly pen. Seriously?

"Okay, Mr. Perkins, I'd like to go over my thoughts for the interview series first so we can make sure we're on the same page. Is that okay?"

She smiles like she's trying to soothe an angry bear, and hell, I guess she kinda is. I lean back, letting my arm stretch out over the back of my couch, relaxing a bit.

"Keith."

Elise, who's checking her notes, looks up. "Excuse me?"

I chuckle, rubbing at my head. "For the love of fuck, call me Keith. Not Mr. Perkins. That was my dad."

I see her mouth twitch a bit and she mouths, 'for the love of fuck' before shaking her head, seemingly amused at my random turn of phrase. Still, she blushes just slightly, and I find it . . . well, she looks even hotter now. "Okay, Keith. And please call me Elise. Does that sound like a plan?"

I nod as graciously as I can muster, which is basically not at all. Hot or not, she's in my private territory, and I'm doing my best to just be polite. "Sure."

"So, I'm thinking that you're obviously an enigma and your fans want to know more about you, especially since you tend to shun the spotlight. That's really rare in this day and age, when most stars can't seem to hog the spotlight enough."

"I like having my privacy, that's all. Always have."

Elise nods, leaning forward. "And I think a series of interviews will give us a nice peek into your life. I understand your point of view."

"Is that so?"

Elise gives me a heartstopping smile, nodding. "I know you don't believe me, but yes. So maybe a past, present, future setup or something more along the lines of your professional life and personal life mixed in with tidbits about your history in each? All in all, just a bigger, better picture of who you are. It'll satisfy the fans and keep reporters like me, but with a lot less morals, off your doorstep. I'll know about the structure as we see where the interviews naturally lead. Anything you want to add or that's off limits?"

My first thought is that everything is off limits, but I know I can't say that, so I simply nod in agreement before I think better of it. "Actually, Elise . . ."

The name sounds sweet on my tongue, making me remember just how damn sexy she looked all fired up, standing in my doorway and calling me on my shit. Her cheeks are still a bit flushed from the fiery exchange, and now that she's leaning toward me, I can see her voluptuous breasts pressing fully against her dress.

It helps, and the idea that was hatching in my head a moment ago suddenly seems a lot more possible. I turn on the charm, dropping my voice a bit. "Elise . . . this is obviously not by my choice. I'm very much a private person, and I like to be in control . . . of my image, of my music, of what I do and don't do . . . honestly, I like to be in control of everything. So these interviews chafe against that by their very nature. How about we make a deal, you and me?"

I don't miss the way her breath hitches when I mention being in control. Deliciously interesting. She licks her lips, her little pink tongue darting out, and I have a flash of her tongue licking me all over. My cock twitches, and I realize . . . maybe this won't be as bad as I thought.

"What kind of deal did you have in mind?" she asks, her voice a bit breathy. I smile, knowing I've got her on the hook.

"Let's make a deal that for every question you ask me, I get to ask one back. You want to know me, but that's very one-sided. Of course, I won't be writing a tell-all expose of your private life like you seem to want to do about me. So the least you can do is make this a little easier, a little more conversational and less of an interrogation. What do you say?"

She bites her lip, thinking about it, and I want to soothe the bite with my tongue. Or shit, maybe bite her lip myself while she fucks herself on my fingers. "I don't know—"

"I'll keep it just between us," I reassure her. "Just think of it as a little pain to go with the pleasure. What do you say?"

Part of me hopes she says yes to the deal so that I have an upper hand. Part of me wants her to say no, and then I can show her out the front door and not do the interviews at all. But the biggest part of me, or maybe just the *hardest* part, wants her to say yes because I want to push her, see what she'll share, how honest she'll be when I poke and prod at her deepest secrets.

Honestly, if she left right now, I'd be jacking off to thoughts of her on her knees sucking me off within seconds, not sending up praise at the lack of interviews.

Curious for her answer, I wait silently, eyes locked on hers.

Let's see who wins.

CHAPTER

Five

ELISE

THIS IS NOT GOING how I thought it would at all. I was expecting a bit of country boy charm, some hospitality, and maybe some pat interview answers. I figured I'd have to work to get deeper, tease out Keith's personality for the articles. I was prepared to dig, to have to wiggle my way into his trust so he'd relax and be real with me.

What I didn't expect was his huge body, clad in jeans and a white button-down shirt that seems to be molded to his bulk, looking so damn sexy when he opened the door. I guess I should have. I ogled his ass for an entire week to get that scoop.

For some reason, the bare head and feet made him seem casual, comfortable until he'd realized who I am. He definitely lit up then, anger flashing in his eyes, and I got a hint of the cold fire in his core.

It's that cold fire that seems to draw me in. I don't feel like I'm in control, but instead, we're jockeying, wrestling for who gets to take charge.

He's clearly doing these interviews begrudgingly, which makes his deal all the more unusual. I don't think for one second that he wants to know a damn thing about me, some annoying reporter digging into his private life when he wants desperately to keep it private.

And so we're in this little silent war, my body saying one thing while my professionalism says another. After all, why would he want to ask me questions?

I realize the answer. He told me as plain as day. It's a control move. His way of showing that even in a situation beyond his control, he's in power here. So we keep wrestling, doing our little dance and seeing who gets to be on top.

But really, is that so bad? To let him demonstrate some semblance of being the boss here, if it gets me what I want . . . him to answer my questions. Right, that's why I'm thinking of sweaty bodies pinning each other to the floor, or a bed, or . . .

Fuck it. It's not like I have anything to hide with my boring life, so he can fire away with his questions.

Decision made, I meet his dark eyes to see fire flashing there. So much anger . . . at me or at the situation, maybe both? Or is what I'm seeing as anger just passion?

I straighten my back, keeping the stare contest going. "Tell you what, Keith. I'll agree to your deal . . . *If* you answer honestly and fully any question I ask and help me write an interesting, exciting story about you. You do that, and I'll return the favor. Complete and full honesty to any question."

He studies me, and I can feel him visually taking my measure as an opponent before he gets up, towering over me as he offers a hand. I shake it, noticing that his large hand engulfs mine. "Deal. Fair warning, Elise. You just made a deal with the devil for your soul."

I grin at his dramatics, but there's a little swarm of bees in my belly concerned that maybe there's more truth to what he's saying than I'm expecting. I expected Keith Perkins to be a little bit of a bumpkin, a good ol' country boy who might be a little hostile but still stunned by the chic city girl with smooth verbal skills. Instead, he's controlled, and he's obviously a damn sight smarter than I've given him credit for . . . and that makes him all the more attractive. And a hell of a lot more dangerous.

We settle back more comfortably in our seats, and I pick up my phone, starting the voice recorder before setting it on the table in front of me as he sits back down with the grace of a tiger in his lair. He doesn't react to my recorder, but I explain anyway, covering my ass. "I hope you don't mind. Recording the sessions is just part of the deal, to make sure I'm correct with any quotes." I give him a slight death glare, remembering how his label wanted a retraction and correction as if I'd been incorrect about my reporting.

He doesn't say anything but gives me a look of tortured pain. I figure since he's not arguing, I might as well run with it and charge ahead. "So first, let's get the basics out of the way . . . the Wikipedia version of who Keith Perkins is. Tell me about yourself."

He sighs, rolling his eyes, and I know it's exactly the kind of question he's had to answer a million times before. But I need it direct from the source for the articles, and it helps break the ice a little, gets him talking on comfortable ground.

Finally, he starts. "My name's Keith Tiberius Perkins. I'm a musician, a singer-songwriter. I'm thirty years old, born and raised in Idaho in a tiny town nobody's ever heard of, including some of the people who lived there. As soon as I graduated high school, I left home for Boise to play in local dive bars and clubs. I even had to use a fake ID to get in because I was underage.

As far as my mom was concerned, I might as well have run off to New York City or even hell, judging by her reaction. But I learned, worked hard, and after a few years, moved to Nashville to play in hole-in-the-wall dives there with every other dreamer. Got discovered one night, signed a contract with my label, and now here I am, years later, hit songs and awards later, doing interviews I hate."

I grin. He'd been doing so well until the end there. I do wonder, though —why leave Nashville? They'd worship him around there. What brought him to this area of the country, not exactly New York but still, not quite the center of country music?

"Sounds like you're living the dream, huh?"

Keith smirks, then remembers where he is and grows serious again. "Yeah, I worked hard for a lot of years on my music. Still do. That's all I want to do . . . write songs, sing them for people, and go home. Alone."

"Damn, dude, like a dog with a bone. Let it go. I get it. I'm in your man cave that's the size of a McMansion, but I'm really not trying to be a bitch here."

He shoots forward in his chair, giving me a fierce look, and I realize I said that out loud, not in my head. "Excuse me?"

Shit.

Backpedaling, I try to smooth over the accidental out-loud monologue. "Sorry for saying that out loud, but not for thinking it."

I smirk at him, virtually daring him to puff all up in anger again.

Instead, he sits back in the couch, pointing a finger at me and dropping his voice to a sexy commanding growl. "My turn. Tell me about yourself, Elise Warner."

I smile, liking this game. If a bullet point list of all things me is what you want, I'll give it to you, asshole. You're not in control of things yet.

"I'm Elise Warner, twenty-six, grew up here in East Robinsville, and went to school at State where I got my journalism degree. Did some small-time reporting for the local paper before getting hired by *The Daily Spot*, where I write celebrity tabloid crap but get to keep my investigative skills fresh. And this interview series is a big deal for me, so don't fuck it up. Please."

He huffs out a surprised laugh. I don't think he was expecting me to be so honest or so confrontational with him. By his smile, I think he likes it, too. He quickly asks the same follow-up question I did. "So, living the dream? Is this what little Elise wanted to do when she grew up?"

I shake my head, letting the 'little' comment slide. I'm all grown up, buddy, and you damn well know it. "No, not really. I like investigative reporting, but I wish I could do something more . . ."

Unexpectedly, I stumble for words, searching for something big enough to explain my heart while Keith looks on, interested. "Go on."

"Just, I want something more impactful," I admit. "Fight for the little guy, expose the bad guys, that kind of thing. But that's a hard gig to come by, so I'm working my way up. If I was in your story, I guess I'm still in the dive bars in Boise but working on that big move to better things, chasing the dream."

He hums, seemingly thinking about what I've said. I want to keep the ball rolling, to capitalize on the bit of sympathy I seem to be getting from him, so I decide to address the elephant in the room, the main reason I'm here.

"So, your professional life is golden, all you could've dreamed of. What about your personal life, Keith? What's happening on the dating front? Who are you buying maxis for? Who's the milk for, Keith?" I ask with a conspiratorial tone.

He growls, literally growls at me like an animal. It's like nothing I've ever heard, and on some primitive level, I'm scared and know I should run for cover from the apex predator with his sights on me. But on a deeper, instinctive level, my blood just started singing through my body, pulsing at a focal point behind my clit.

Holy shit. Maybe it's a little caveman-ish, but it's fucking sexy as hell too. Unconsciously, I squeeze my crossed legs tighter, needing some pressure for relief. But he notices. I expect him to start yelling, but instead he just smirks and leans forward again.

His voice is quiet, gravel as he answers, seemingly puzzled by me. "You're forward, aren't you? No finesse or foreplay. Just jumping into the question you know is most likely to set me off. No, I'm not dating anyone, nor am I looking to. Maybe the supplies were just so I can be a gracious host. Need a tampon, Elise?"

I can't help but defend myself a bit. He's somehow getting to me despite my best attempts to get under *his* skin. The score is definitely in his favor right now. Needing to get back in the battle for control, I fume. "No, fuck you very much. It's the reason this all started, that speculation, so why not address it from the start? Besides, foreplay is for people who don't know what they want, who need to warm up to the idea. I get the feeling that neither of us is like that. I know what I want . . . your secrets. And you know what you want . . . to not tell me. I'm not going to trick them out of you. Just bold honesty."

He tilts his head, searching my face for something. "Okay. But there's one thing you're wrong about."

I raise an eyebrow in question. "What's that?"

Keith smiles, but it's a predatory full baring of his teeth, more threatening and conquering than humorous. "Foreplay isn't for people who need a warm-up. Foreplay can be the best part if it's done right."

He pauses, and I know I'm breathing faster than I should be, considering I'm just sitting on a couch talking, but damn, can he talk. Every word is measured for effect, and I feel more bare than if I'd even answered a question.

The answer is written all over my face, my body. "And are you good at foreplay?"

Keith nods, his smile changing slightly, becoming as seductive as it is confrontational. "Bold honesty, huh? Very. Okay, Elise . . . tell me about *your* dating life."

It's not a question, it's an order.

I want to be bratty back, call him on his bossiness, but I realize that would be counter to my mission here, so I give in and willingly share. "No, I'm not dating either. I work too damn much, and my last boyfriend was an ass. I'm not hung up on him or anything. It's been months ago and was casual at best, more like fuck buddies than a real relationship. But I'm just . . . no, not dating."

He grins, a real one this time. "Point proven. Fuck buddies don't need foreplay. Just get in, get off, and get out. You're just not used to getting more. So much more that it becomes a necessity, an integral piece of the bigger action, not something to be rushed through or skipped." Every word he says is seduction, meant to make me squirm for him and I'm fighting the urge, forcing myself to be still.

I bite my lip, considering his words, my body screaming that it wants more, too. "Well, you may be right. But tell me, Keith. For someone who's not dating anyone, you sure do have some insight into the inner workings of the human mind and body. How'd you get so . . . smart?"

I stumble at the last second because I almost said sexy, and I'll be damned if I'm giving him that kind of ammunition, but he seems to know that 'smart' wasn't my first word choice judging by his cocked eyebrow. "I said I'm not dating. Never said I was a saint."

Before I can ask a follow-up question, the doorbell rings and Keith rises from his seat to go answer it. I can't help but watch him as he moves with graceful power toward the hallway, returning a moment later leading a guy wearing black pants and a white chef jacket toward what I can only assume is the kitchen. I follow, drawn by both professional and personal curiosity.

As the cook tells Keith about the menu and warming times, I hang in the doorway, taking in Keith's no-muss appearance. His jeans have ridden down low on his lean hips, showing the waistband of his underwear as he reaches up and his shirt hem raises with his arms.

Wondering if he's a boxer brief kind of guy, I let my eyes dip down to his crotch and see a nice bulge that makes me picture him dropping those pants and taking his cock out for me. As my eyes drift back up, I see that his arms are crossed over his chest, showing off biceps that strain against the white cotton of his shirt and make his shirt ride up to expose a tiny sliver of his stomach. I have to admit to myself that want to run my hands over his abs, feel and caress each ridge.

When the cook takes his leave, Keith turns to meet my eyes. "Hungry?"

There's an undertone to his voice, an awareness of the fact that I was just checking him out. But I see a gleam in his eyes. He's checking me out too, which just increases my desire. Before I can tell myself not to say it, I answer him honestly. "Starving."

There's a rumble in his chest, but he seems to remember his game plan before I remember mine, still lost in some fantasy of him bending me over the kitchen counter and licking his dessert out of my soaking wet pussy. He opens a cabinet door, grabbing plates, then glasses and silverware. "Follow me."

After serving up healthy portions onto the plates and a quick warming in the microwave, we sit at the table in the kitchen nook. There's tension between us now, but it's not awkward. If anything, it feels good, flavored with the little intimate touches like using a microwave. It's like Keith's saying *I know you find me sexy. I don't need to bend over backward to impress you more than I do naturally.*

It's natural and heady, like I'm a stick of dynamite and he's waving a lit match around, and I'm dangerously close to begging him to light me up because everything in me says that he damn sure could.

I try to get my head back in the game, reminding myself that no matter how fucking sexy Keith may be or how horny I am, that's not happening. I'm a reporter, and my name isn't Francesca, goddammit!

I need to be professional, get him to answer some fresh questions, dig a little deeper into who he is. Discovering his secrets, writing a great article series . . . that's the goal here. Not getting my pussy licked before getting a creamy ending to my fantasies.

Keith seems to read all of my dirty, naughty thoughts, but he chooses to let me simmer in my need and goes over to the fridge. "Wine?"

I nod, curious that he didn't offer me a beer. "Just a half glass. Still on the clock, you know."

I wish I hadn't said it the moment it leaves my mouth. It's a reminder that regardless of any flirting we might have been doing, and how fucking hot Keith makes me, being here is my job. My job to tell all the things he'd rather keep private.

It's like a bucket of cold water has been dumped on our whole interaction, and I can see it in the sudden increased tension across Keith's jawline.

Dinner and the rest of our evening proceed with conversational questions and answers, but not nearly as personal and telling as our earlier talk. There's none of the burning taunting now, just a polite aloofness.

It feels colder, robotic even as he answers in what amounts to one word, sometimes one-syllable answers. And though I could write a whole book about how hot Keith is in person, how commanding his presence is, I'm not sure that's exactly where this all-access story needs to go.

That fact feels like . . . my secret.

CHAPTER
Six

KEITH

TEN MINUTES.

I was totally right.

Fuck. I'm amazed I lasted this long.

Our evening of interviewing is barely over. I'd shut the door behind Elise no fewer than ten minutes ago, and here I am, in my shower, jacking off. I run a soapy hand down my stomach, grabbing my already thick cock in a tight grip, moving slowly up and down.

Foreplay, I tell myself, and moan at her denial of needing it. Shit, she doesn't know it but we've already started our foreplay. All evening has been an exercise in seduction and denial on my part, and she's gonna love every hot minute of it. Every moment, from the instant that I knew she was into me and I wanted her too, it's been a slow, tortuously seductive dance, half with our bodies, half with our words.

The way she challenged me . . . delicious. Her inquisitive and prying nature . . . sublime. And her body . . . I couldn't write a song good enough to describe how perfect she looked, the twinkle in her eye, the flush on her cheeks, the way her breath caught at times, and how she'd pressed her thighs together when I growled at her.

I picture Elise slipping her cotton dress over her head and letting it puddle to floor as she stands in my foyer in just her bra and panties and those ridiculous wedge heels that still made her calves look scrumptious.

In my mind, she drops to her knees in front of me, eyes begging for my cock, but she waits for my nod of permission before taking me out. I tease the head of my cock with the ball of my thumb, imagining it's her hot tongue licking me like a lollipop and then begin to pump in and out of my fist in earnest as I visualize taking her mouth, her throat.

I place my other hand on the wall, leaning into the thrusts, wanting more, wanting her. She's the sexiest fucking thing I've seen in months and she knows it. But she wants me to take control too, even though she's worried about being so vulnerable. It's so fucking sexy. I need to show her how foreplay can be dirty and satisfying at the same time.

Raw need pulses through me as I talk to the empty shower, my voice a whispered rasp in the steamy air. "That's it, take it, Elise. Suck my cock down your pretty little throat and make me come. You're gonna swallow every drop like a good girl, aren't you?"

I can see her nodding around my mouthful of cock, hungry for it, and with a few more strokes, I'm a goner, crying out harshly as I come all over my hand and the shower wall violently, jet after jet shooting from my cock as I spasm in ecstasy.

As I come back down from the high, I'm panting, my knees shaky as I lean my head against the shower wall to steady myself. Fuck. I haven't come that hard in a long time. I'm not sure that's a good thing though, considering I just mind-fucked the one person who could and would royally fuck me over, exposing my secret to the media.

But I want her. Fuck, do I want her, and reading her eyes, she wants me too.

I need to get myself in control. *Control?* I ask myself, laughing as I spray down the shower wall and make sure everything is washed down the drain. I'm such a control freak. I just need to remember that with her tomorrow during the interviews.

Except I know, on some level, she wants me to take control, to fight her for it until she has no choice but to give in to me. With her, I'll have to earn the power position, but once I have it, I'll give her just what she needs . . . a hard fucking with her at my mercy. Hell, that's what I need too.

The thought makes me shiver, and I feel another thrum down my spine to my balls. No, she's too dangerous. I have to make sure I don't get sucked back into a teasing flirtatious conversation because no good can come of that. I groan out loud, the thought of getting sucked back in making the pictures I'd just used to jack off flash across my mind, and my cock thickens again.

Already.

It's noon the next day, and I'm jittery with anticipation of Elise's visit. I've done the best I can to prepare, taking Carsen to school before putting myself through a brutal workout that has hopefully left me too exhausted to get a fucking hard-on.

Honestly, I'm not sure if I'm nervous or excited—maybe both? I'm still dreading her asking me questions, knowing that I'll have to carefully avoid too much honesty about my life, but another side of me is ready to demand it of her. I'll ask her everything I want to know, and somewhere in that interrogation, maybe she'll decide I really am an ass and will leave me alone.

A tiny voice in the back of my head whispers *that's not true*, and I know my conscience is at least partially right. I don't want to know everything to scare her off. A small part of me just wants to know everything about her, period. The gentleman side of my mind wants to know what she needs in a man, wondering if I'm man enough to give it to her. The dirty side, though . . . it wonders if she'd be just as sassy with my cock stuffed in her mouth.

When the doorbell rings, I instinctively look upstairs, mentally reminding myself that Sarah picked Carsen up after school to go to the mall and then out for sushi, knowing that she couldn't be here for this.

I open the door, and all I want to do is gawk at the sight in front of me, but I force my face to remain stoic as I take her in from head to toe. Her blonde hair is lightly curled today, soft waves that I want to gather in my fist and use to guide her where I want.

She's wearing a t-shirt with a logo I don't recognize stretched across her tits, a slim cotton skirt, and a pair of low-top Chuck Taylors that are cute as fuck on her. She looks young, bite-able like a fresh cherry, and curvier than a mountain road.

Thank God I wore tight jeans today because I need that pressure to keep my cock from growing too big in their stretched confines. Even my workout isn't helping. I can feel the tingle already.

My body's immediate and fierce reaction to her presence pisses me off. It makes me feel wild and out of control, and I don't like it. I'm the one in control. Always.

So I take out my body's betrayal on her, barely grunting before turning and walking, not to the living room, but deeper into the house this time. We didn't get through the whole house. She might as well see some more this time.

I hear her sigh of frustration behind me. I can virtually hear the eye roll too, but she closes the door and follows me without complaining. It gives me an ounce of satisfaction that even if my body's out of control, she's still doing what I want her to do.

That slight lift is broken when I hear her behind me, her shoes squeaking quietly on the tile flooring of my hallway. "So, we're back to grumpy and asshole-y? I'd hoped we'd made some progress yesterday."

I don't answer, just head into my music room. I have an office as well, but this room is where I've done some of my best recent work. As she walks through the door, I close it behind her, locking us inside these four walls without ever turning the actual lock.

Elise looks around, eyes jumping from the art on the dark-paneled walls, to the awards in a case in the corner, to the bar, to my collection of old vinyl and their record player. "You jam in here? Or is this where you come to brood about how you want your girl back, your dog back, and your truck back?"

I hold back the chuckle, not wanting to give in an inch, not even for an old joke about country music. "This is my cave, basically," I admit, letting my voice be honest, slightly soft, and in reverence for what this place means to me. "It's a warm and cozy place that I can hole up and do my music away from everyone and everything. I write all the time these days, in little note-books I always carry with me, but this is where it all comes together. This is where scribbled notes turn into songs, where melodies that play on repeat in my head become harmonies between instruments and voices. This room is my music. The recording studio's just . . . production. This is where the magic happens."

Elise looks taken aback at the openness in my voice, in what I'm telling her. And it's hard, so fucking hard to let her into this room, this place in my soul, but somehow, talking about my music feels safer, easier than anything else she might ask about me, my history, or this supposed mystery woman I'm hiding. Music. I can always take it back to the music because I can talk about that for hours.

"It feels sacred in here. Thank you for sharing it with me."

There's no insincerity to her voice, no note of teasing, just truth, and it makes me feel better for sharing something so personal. She's right. The music has always been pure, even when sometimes performing hasn't always felt pure. But that's not the music's fault. Here, I can tell the truth. I can take my soul out for inspection, see where it's tattered and frayed, and see if I can somehow stitch it all back together long enough to make it through the next day.

And Elise seems to understand this. It's because of that, more than anything else, that lets me gesture to the couch. She plops down on the end, pulling her recorder out of her bag before slipping her shoes off.

Once she's satisfied with the recorder setup on the table, she curls up in the corner of the couch like a kitten, ready to ask me questions. But I have one for her first as I sit on the opposite end.

"Do you listen to my music?" I ask, maybe a bit more harshly than I intended. "To country at all? Or are you into like electronica dance shit?"

I gesture at her shirt, taking in the logo and the lushness of her tits all at once. She looks down at her shirt, then back to me. "Actually, I do listen to country some. It's not always my first choice, although that's definitely not EDM either. If I'm jamming on my own, I'll usually pick rock . . . Highly Suspect, which is who this t-shirt depicts, or Cage the Elephant, stuff like that. But if a song is good, the beat hits you in your chest and the lyrics make you feel, I'll listen to any genre. Even country."

She says the last part teasingly, and I'm a little relieved to hear she's not some super-fan who's just trying to get closer to me with these interviews.

I've been lucky to not have any obsessively dangerous fans like some artists have. My fans seem to be mostly down-to-earth folks who just like to two-step a bit, maybe get a little rowdy for a party anthem, or have something to keep the dusty roads a little more tolerable as they get to work. But I'll admit that I wanted her to at least be familiar with my music. It's integral to my soul, and I'm curious to know what she thinks about my music, even if that makes me vulnerable.

Elise takes my question and turns it around smoothly, not like an interview but . . . almost like a date or something. "What about your musical tastes? What do you listen to?"

Been there, done this question before, so I answer using my usual country charm story. "My mom used to sing Patsy Cline to us, played us all the classics . . . Johnny Cash, Hank Williams One and Two, Reba McIntyre, George Strait, and more, so I always have a soft spot for those. She also played a lot of that sixties rock, when country and rock were sort of walking hand in hand some. The Doors, CCR, and of course, Lynyrd Skynyrd."

Elise smiles, humming a few bars. "I've jammed a little CCR. *Run Through The Jungle* is a damn good tune."

I nod, impressed. Most people who only pretend to like Creedence use one of their more famous songs, but Elise somehow plucked my favorite right out of her head. "But I like newer country too . . . Jason Aldean, Dierks Bentley, even Blake Shelton, but don't tell him I said that. Can barely get a hat to fit on that melon of his already."

She grins, but I'd bet my favorite guitar she doesn't even know who Blake Shelton is beyond his TV show fame or maybe his famous blonde girlfriend.

"You said you write all the time. What inspires you to write a song?"

I think for a moment, then shrug. "Everything. You ever go about your day, see a mom sitting on a park bench with a baby in a stroller and then a guy in a suit walks up? That's a song . . . about love, responsibility, doing whatever it takes to make your woman light up when she sees you at the end of a long day. Or the guy on the side of the road, lost in his own mind and missing the life he once had. His story is a song. Watching the news and seeing a tragedy, that's a song too. Even a party, letting loose and having a great time with friends. That's a song. Every experience, every emotion . . . they're worth having, worth feeling, worth sharing. It's addicting, that ability to connect through words and notes, transform something surreal and hazy into something palpable and visceral."

Elise is biting her lip, looking at me with delight, and I realize I think I just gave her a good quote for her article even though I was talking off the top of my head. Guess I can talk smoothly without even trying.

My attention is drawn to Elise's mouth, watching the small white flash as her teeth press into her bottom lip before her pink tongue darts out, licking her lips to soothe the bite and leaving them shiny.

I want to taste her mouth, to abandon myself to my inner desires and let loose the reins of my lust. Before I can move from the other end of the couch, though, she asks another question, saving me. Or maybe saving her, I don't know. "So once inspiration strikes, how do you get it to song . . . music first, lyrics first, both simultaneously?"

There's a dirty joke in there if ever I heard one, but I try to refrain, sticking to the safer topic of music, especially since it's why she's here. It'll help me just enough to stay in control of myself.

Although I can't help riling her up. It's just so damn fun. "The short answer is yes, all of those. Depends on the song. I've had melodies that I couldn't find words to, or lyrics all laid out that just needed a tune, or sometimes, I just sit and pick at a guitar and see what happens. I had one set of lyrics that sat in the drawer for three years before I got the music right, and another that hit full on, both coming hard at once."

Elise looks around the room again, her voice a little shaky at my last words. "And this is where the magic happens?"

I wonder what she sees when she sees this space, my private place. Does she feel the music in every molecule the way I do? Does she see the awards, the lineup of guitars, the pictures of me with favorite artists I've met, or does she see the hours I've spent in here with my eyes closed or staring at the guitar in my hands, sweating bullets as I try to combine inspiration with perspiration? I wonder what she would say if I told her about that side of things, but that's not what I ask her.

"So that was a bunch of questions in a row. Seems like it's my turn now, according to our deal."

She laughs, a soft acquiescence in her nod. "Hit me. What do you want to know?"

God, woman . . . so much. Everything. What's her favorite flavor of ice cream? Does she like candlelit dinners or fun nights out? Has she ever had eight and a half inches of thick cock up her ass?

But I try to focus, or at least to keep my horniness in check. What do I really want to know about her?

I eyeball her, curled up in the corner of the couch with her arms wrapped around her knees, perfectly at home in my room, my presence, her cheeks flushed as she waits to see what I'm going to ask.

Finally, I know. "Tell me a secret."

It's not a question but a demand, and I want to see what she shares when given an open-ended opportunity. She's demanding all of my deepest, darkest secrets, so it seems only fair to own hers too. And I want to see . . . she's filling my head with all these dirty thoughts and desires. Just how dirty is that mind of hers?

Her puffy lips frown, but it seems to be in thought as she searches her mind for what she wants to say.

Finally, she narrows her eyes, looking at me defensively. "Okay, this might not seem like a big deal at first, but let me tell the whole thing before you judge."

I nod, and she takes a steadying breath, which makes me curious what exactly she's about to spill. "I like to . . . knit. Scarves, sweaters, socks, hats, anything I can get a pattern for. I knit."

I can feel my face scrunch up in confusion. "Knit? Sweaters? This is your big secret?"

I know I just said I wouldn't judge, but come on. She's gotta be fucking with me, especially after all the emotional shit I just shared about my music. She wants my deepest secret, wants my daughter exposed even if she doesn't realize that's what she's doing, and she tells me that she knits? Seriously?

I can feel the flames of anger licking at me from inside, and I shake my head, poison dropping from every word. "I thought we had a deal, Elise. But if you want to shit on the arrangement, fine. We'll go back to pat PR answers. Get up, get out of my room. Let's go back to the living room, the kitchen . . . somewhere less personal to me."

She stands, breath heaving as her tits rise and fall, pointing a maroon-tipped finger at me as she speaks just short of a yell, her eyes sparkling with anger. "I said to wait to judge, you asshole! But by all means, jump to conclusions that I'm giving you a superficial answer. FYI . . . I've literally never told anyone that."

She grabs her bag and shoes, stomping barefooted toward the door. I can hear the truth in her vehemence, and it surprises me. I jump to my feet, reaching out but not stepping toward her. "Wait."

Again with the orders, but she doesn't seem to mind given that she stops immediately, looking back at me over her shoulder but not saying a word.

I sigh, gesturing toward the end of the couch. "You're right, I shouldn't jump to conclusions. Sit back down. Please."

The nicety feels foreign on my tongue. I'm used to telling people what to do and they do it, no please or thank you required, except maybe to Carsen or Sarah since I try to be less of an ass to them.

Elise returns to the couch but perches on the edge, ready to rage again at any second as I stand in front of her, looming. It feels telling, symbolic. She's wild chaos, on the edge, and I'm ordered control, caging her in.

I keep my voice steady and look her directly in the eye. "So you knit."

She lifts her chin, and the posture suddenly feels very heated with her lips mere inches from my crotch, looking up at me with fire in her eyes. I feel my cock twitch in my jeans, thickening and straining to be closer to her. My fingers dance over my thighs, playing invisible chords to keep from grabbing her by the hair and taking what I already know I want so desperately.

Needing to stop that freight train from crashing into us for both of our sakes, I sit on the coffee table, my knees wide on either side of hers, my eyes waiting impatiently for her to continue. Finally, she sighs and nods, relenting to my unspoken request for her to continue.

"Yes, I knit. So the story is two-sided, I guess. When I was a kid, my parents would ship me off to my Gran's house every summer. It was awesome and occasionally boring as hell, especially for an active kid. I couldn't run through the house. She had all of these really fragile things that I swear only old people or people with too much money have."

I chuckle. I know just what she means. My grandmother had a carnival glass lampshade in her dining room. God help anyone who even stomped through that room and made the shade even twitch.

"So Gran taught me to knit, probably to keep her doll collection in one piece," Elise says before I can interrupt. "Every night after dinner, we'd sit on the porch and listen to the cicadas buzz, and we'd knit. That first summer, I made my first scarf. I was so damn proud of that ugly thing that I wore it to school every day, no matter the weather."

I'm trying to picture a miniature Elise, blonde hair sticking up every which way and wearing a scarf with shorts and a tank top. It's cute and makes me smile a little. "What color?"

She tilts her head at the question. "It was yellow, like the sunflowers in Gran's yard." She smiles too, but I can see she's not really here with me. Instead, her mind's far away, long ago in this moment.

Blinking, she continues. "So I kept at it, making stuff all through school and eventually nobody even wanted the things I made any more, so I started shipping them off to charities. That's one side, that I honor this gift of a skill my Gran gave me by helping as much as I can, anonymously of course. And the other side of the story? Why the big secret?" Elise grins saucily. "Well, I have an image to maintain. Part of my work is going to clubs, the whole party scene . . . seeing who's there and what's happening and reporting on it. I'm spontaneous, a fly by the seat of my pants kinda girl most of the time and that's what everyone expects of me. But knitting is my time to recharge, just me in the silence of my apartment."

I can see that she's telling the truth. Never would've seen that coming, and maybe that's the point. "Okay, so you knit. I promise not to tell." I make a zipper motion across my lips and she grins. My eyes focus in on that smile, her lush lips pulled wide and I want to devour her. She must feel the pull she has on me because her smile falters, her lips parting slightly to invite me in. I meet her gaze, knowing my lust must be written all over my face, but I'm surprised to see the need so plainly on hers too. It's all I can do to stop from moving closer, but I restrain myself by sheer will. My voice is gravel as I try to force lightness into the heavy moment.

"I think I'd like to see that. Think you could model some for me?"

She giggles a feather-soft baby's breath of a laugh, which suddenly becomes vibrant and bubbly as she plants her palms on my chest and pushes me. I'm aware of her touch on an animal level, wanting to push her back, down on the couch, pinned underneath me as I ravish those lips and neck along the way to tying up her wrists with her old yellow scarf.

She keeps laughing, shaking her head. "Asshole, just for that, I might actually do it! I'll expect pictures of you in it to go along with the story in return though."

She thinks I'm kidding, but in this moment, I'd probably do that . . . for her.

CHAPTER

Seven

ELISE

SETTLING into my desk at the office, I'm already sipping on a huge coffee knowing I'm going to need the caffeine hit today. I've barely even turned my laptop on when Maggie stops by, perching daintily on the corner of my desk, her feet swinging.

"So, what's he like?" she asks, almost vibrating. "Tell me everything!"

Her excitement is infectious, especially since she's truly excited for me, not just pumping me for info to steal my story. Well, maybe a little jealous too. She is the office's self-proclaimed biggest country fan.

I grin, teasing her with a long, dramatic pause. "Why, Maggie," I finally say after taking a long sip of my coffee and setting the mug down, "you're an eager little beaver, aren't you?"

Maggie laughs, tugging at a lock of her hair. "Of course! This is like the assignment of the year, and we're all curious about what you're going to write up on the elusive Mr. Perkins."

We? Yeah, right. I know quite a few people who don't really care, but for Maggie, Keith Perkins is right up her alley. I look up, trying to collect my thoughts, both for the first article in the series and to explain our encounters, knowing that I can't possibly explain how he makes me feel . . . how his powerful presence makes me want to climb him like a tree or maybe kneel at his feet.

For my own safety, I'm definitely leaving out the bit where I swore he was going to lean in to kiss me yesterday after I pushed him in the chest, and definitely how fucking bad I wanted him to.

"He's actually a lot different than I thought he'd be," I finally reply. "I was expecting a good ol' boy vibe, even with the awkwardness of the forced interviews, but he's . . ." I pause, searching for the word I want before continuing, "intense. He was definitely pissed when he figured out that I was the one who wrote the original article and that I would be the one interviewing him. He slammed the door in my face."

Maggie, whose idea of rude is to not offer you a cookie when you stop by her desk, gasps. "Oh, my gosh, he did not!"

"Oh yes, he did. But we seem to have worked it out," I reply, leaving out the arrangement I made on answering questions tit-for-tat with him. "The interviews have been going really well since then. I haven't got any real dirt, no hidden secrets, but he's letting me in. I feel like he's at least being honest and not totally PR with me. I think I'll be able to show a real and deeper picture of who Keith Perkins is. Not just the image he portrays on stage."

Maggie looks like she's about to swoon, and I'd bet fifty bucks she's got one of those huge Keith Perkins posters at home. "Speaking of stage, didn't I hear on the radio that he's doing a local private show this weekend?"

I nod. It was something we went over right at the end of last night's talk . . . it's hard to call something as intimate as what we're doing an inter-view. "Yeah, he is. That's actually our next interview date. He said that we could do a field trip and he would get me a front-row seat for the show. I'm hoping to get backstage access before and after too so I can see his whole process for a show. I think that'll be a slam dunk for the article . . . him in his element, doing what he does."

"So you're going to his private show with a front-row seat and backstage access?" she asks, blushing as she clutches at her chest and sighs dreamily. "That sounds like heaven! Surely, you'll get some juicy details there?"

I smile. Maggie's too cute not to. "Honestly, I haven't found any dirt . . . really, none at all. He's a bit of a controlling jerk, but no deep, dark secret that I've been able to find yet."

Maggie pouts. I don't think she likes the idea of Keith being controlling as much as I secretly do. "Well, you know Donnie won't be happy with that. You're going to need to find something."

I wave it off. "I know, but I swear he's basically boring . . . he writes, he does shows. I don't know what else he does with his time."

Maggie taps the tip of her nose, smiling as if she's got the perfect idea. "And there's your story. What's he do in his free time, because you know he doesn't write and sing all the time. That's what he's hiding."

I purse my lips, mulling that over. Maggie looks young and innocent, and many a mark have taken her to be naive, and well, she is cute in a way that makes you want to pat her head like a sweet puppy sometimes. But she's also a shrewd and brilliant investigator who uses her gifts to her benefit without getting jaded or down from the dirt she digs up. "Hmm, maybe you're right. I'll have to stick my nose into that area . . . carefully. But this weekend, I'm staying with the performance aspect because I know that'll be interesting. Trying to dig up what else he does in his free time could be a dud, and it's risky. But thanks, Mags."

She smiles, planting her hands on the corner of my desk and transforms back to looking cute enough I want to stick her in my backpack and take her home. "No problem! I'm just as curious as you are. Lord knows, there's a whole lot of women who'd love to know what makes that man tick, and I bet you'd be up for a promotion if you can figure it out and let us all know."

With a hop, Maggie is off my desk and off to do her own thing, leaving me tapping at my keyboard. I'm not sure what I want to say yet, and her comment about wanting to know what makes Keith tick rings a bit true and close to home.

He's been angry, dismissive, and downright rude to me in some moments, the perfect target for one of those bloodletting exposes that can get a shitload of website traffic. I'd have no problem with ripping him apart if that's all he was.

But it's the other moments where he's attentive, open, and intriguing. Not to mention, he's just so damn sexy when he gets all bossy and gruff. I've always gone for confident men, but Keith is on a whole different level. It's not confidence. It's raw power over his domain. And fuck, do I want to be in his domain.

That means I'm not being objective, and that makes me hesitate before I start to write. The words come slowly, slow clicks of my old-fashioned keyboard that start to string together, slowly becoming like machine gun spurts of words, long pauses shortening until I find my stride.

This first article, it's going to be mostly surface, about a country star who cherishes his privacy but is allowing his fans a peek into his private life. I'm careful to paint an accurate picture, including his gruffness and larger than life presence along with his passion for his music.

By the time I hit my two-thousand-word goal for the first feature, I think I've managed to hit all the points I need to, both the basics and giving hints at a deeper picture. There are no groundbreaking dirty secrets, but even if I had any, I wouldn't want to spill too soon anyway. But I've got a solid, intriguing hook so readers feel a more intimate connection with Keith and to the series for follow-up feature reads.

After some edits, I hit *Send* and submit it to Donnie with a smile.

Now . . . what am I going to wear to Keith's concert?

CHAPTER

Eight

KEITH

PULLING up in the service's rented Lincoln Town Car, I tell my driver to let the engine idle for a moment as I take in Elise's apartment building. It's pretty standard for East Robinsville, far enough from the downtown center to be needing a coat of paint, but probably close to work for her and has rent that fits her paycheck. Seems safe enough, I guess, although the homeless guy lounging up against the corner seems a bit out of place. I'm about to hop out to ring the bell when the bodyguard in the front seat does it for me.

Fuck.

I swear sometimes I forget that I can't just do shit like that, even if it should be no big deal. But since I topped the charts for the first time, the label keeps putting in new rules on their 'investment.' Number one, I can't do shit when I'm dressed in my usual boots and hat, making me more recognizable. Chances are, it'd be fine. But just in case, that's what the bodyguard is here for. I sigh, leaning back in the seat . . . until I see her come out.

Behind the dark tint of the car window, I can look my fill as she comes closer. And what a fill it is. She's strutting, but not in an overt way, just a subtle natural feminine roll of her hips. And oh, sweet mercy, her legs, just thick enough to make them sensual, covered in slightly torn white denim that looks painted on. She's got on slouched black cowgirl boots, and I wonder vaguely if they're new, but when I scan up . . . my breath catches in my chest.

She's the epitome of country sexy, with her hair curled and fluffy, makeup that looks sultry and sexy, not too dark but not too bright either. She's got a face that could sell about ten million pickup trucks back home right now, and that might be a conservative guess.

But what grabs ahold of my attention is the fullness of her breasts, pushed up high in the simple black tank she has on. I can see the outline of a bra, but that makes it even sexier, like she's dressed down but dressed up at the same time. She's somehow managed to be both girl-next-door and femme fatale all at once, and my cock surges in my jeans. I press my palm against the fullness, willing it down by sheer mental force.

I clear my throat, needing to get my head on straight before the door opens. I wish I could step out, greet her like a lady, but I can't. Security rule number two . . . stay in the vehicle unless instructed by the guard.

Sigh. All it took was for one dickhead to threaten one guy, and now the label's gone apeshit whenever I have to be 'the artist' Keith Perkins. Sometimes, I miss the days when I showed up by pulling around back in my pickup and grabbing my guitar case out of the truck bed.

But as she ducks in, climbing in beside me, I forget about my first world problems and try to make up for my apparent lack of manners.

"Holy fuck, Elise. You look gorgeous."

Okay, so maybe my manners aren't quite up to snuff after all. I can't help my mouth, except around Carsen, and even then, I slip up every now and then. I am human.

She doesn't seem to mind, though, judging by the smile that breaks across her face. She's checking me out too, and I swear her gaze lingers on my crotch for just a split second longer. Or maybe that's wishful thinking on my part and she's checking out my belt buckle.

"You too, Keith. You look ready to rock . . . I mean, ready to country?" she teases.

She laughs at her own joke, but I chuckle, dropping a wink for her. "Definitely ready to rock. Just don't ask me to dance."

She laughs, and it's comfortable for a moment, just sitting next to each other on the leather seat, two people just . . . I don't really know. The feeling is broken, though when my phone rings shrilly, shattering the silence.

I stifle a curse and fish it out of my pocket. Glancing at the screen, I answer. "Hey, Todd."

Todd, who's in either LA or New York, I'm not sure and don't really care to find out, sounds energetic. "You good to go tonight, man?"

"Yeah, I'm good. Thanks for checking in. Security and driver were right on time. I'll do a gear check when I get to the venue."

"Good, good . . . what else?"

I roll my eyes at his usual pop quiz, glad he can't see me. For fuck's sake, I'm a pro. "KCTY radio sponsor, promote the summer tour and the new single."

"Perfect. You've got this, man. What about the reporter? She's coming to the show tonight, right? It'd be a good image for her to highlight. Maybe some pics of you onstage or with fans to help kick the grocery store ones down the image search on Google?"

The reminder pisses me off, and I know the grit is in my voice because Elise flinches beside me. "Yeah, she's right here. I'll tell her what you said."

Todd sounds apologetic, and I can understand why. He knows the interviews are a pain in my ass. "I know you can't say much with her right there, but are the interviews going okay? Tell me if you need a rescue or if we're going to need some spin doctoring."

I glance over at Elise, who is pointedly staring out the window, but I know she's hanging on every word. "It's fine. A bit rough at first when I slammed the door in her face . . ."

I see Elise crack a tiny smile, confirming my suspicion as Todd sounds like he's about to have a coronary. "No you fucking didn't!"

I chuckle, reaching over and patting Elise on the knee. "Actually, I did. But we came to an agreement and it's been fine since. She's . . . she's good."

Todd laughs, while I can see Elise blush lightly at my compliment. Or maybe it's my hand on her knee, which I still haven't lifted yet. "I can't imagine what your agreement is, and I probably don't want to know, do I?"

"Nope, you don't." I'm not even sure what our arrangement should be called. I'm just wondering if she could stretch across the backseat so I could touch every inch of her silky skin.

Todd lowers his voice, virtually whispering in the phone as though Elise could hear him, and I smirk over at Elise, who's smiling back, her eyes gleaming as she stretches out a leg for my perusal. "Any suspicions on the you know what front?"

I think for a second how to answer in a way that won't make Elise suspicious, and part of me is reminded again why I have to be careful around her. I've got miles to go and secrets to keep. "So far, so good."

Todd sighs in relief, and in the background, I hear someone holler out his name. "All right then, man . . . listen, I gotta cover some fires on this end. Have a great show. I'll be in touch."

"Sure thing," I answer easily, glad I don't have his career. "'Bye, Todd."

I hang up, turning to Elise, who's still not taken my hand from her leg. "Sorry about that. Manager always checks in before a show to make sure I'm not gonna screw something up."

Elise looks thoughtful for a second, then gives me a raised eyebrow. "So, you're here alone, basically. No big crew, no manager clearing the way, no team of stylists getting you primped and teased up for stage. That seems . . . unusual."

There's not a question in there, but I treat it like one anyway. A part of me wonders if Elise sort of likes it that it's just me and her. It's more intimate this way.

"For tour, there's a bigger crew and a whole team of folks that travel with us. I mean, I don't need a huge backup band, but I do like to have a consistent crew for that. But for shows like this, I try to keep it simple. I've done bar gigs my whole life, so I don't need a bunch of guys telling me how to tune my guitar or what to wear. Damn sure don't need a hair stylist," I say, taking my hat off to run a hand across my bare head. "Although I should get Gillette to sponsor my next tour."

Elise laughs, moving her leg but scooting a little closer. "Holy shit. Did you just make a joke? I didn't think you knew how."

I smile, leaning a little closer to stage whisper in her ear. "It's been known to happen . . . on rare occasions. So consider yourself lucky to witness one."

I turn my head, and Elise locks eyes with me, the magnetic pull between us shimmering in the air. "Oh, I definitely feel lucky."

There's another one of the increasingly frequent moments where I'm this close to grabbing her by the neck and kissing her, but the car stops with a slight jerk, bringing my attention to the front seat, where the bodyguard is already moving to our door.

Without thinking about it, I grab Elise's hand, her soft warmth immediately sinking into my skin and forming some sort of bond between us. She looks down, then up, where I catch her gaze with my own.

"I'll get out first. Follow behind me and we both follow the guard," I explain quickly. "Things shouldn't be bad, not many people out here right now, but don't stop and don't look scared. Smile and look friendly."

Elise nods her head, but her eyes give away the panic she feels.

A tiny part of me thinks evilly, 'Not so great on the other side of the paparazzi lens, is it?' But another, maybe more nobler side of me wants to protect her from the fear and the pain. Mostly, though, I just want to get us in the backdoor of the bar as quickly and safely as possible.

We step out of the car, and the flashes immediately go off. I basically drag a stiff Elise to the door, a smile frozen on her face as I smile and wave, and I only stop once to sign one autograph for a little girl holding a sign that says *Keith, I'm too young to see the show tonight so will you sign my poster?*

I know I really shouldn't, but the kid's cute, and just a little younger than Carsen. The beaming smile she gives me as I ruffle her hair is worth the delay, even if my bodyguard is a little abrupt, shoving us inside and slamming the door behind us. We're thrust from the light to being alone in the dark. We're not really, because I can hear people onstage setting up, and there are no doubt radio people already out in the bar, but backstage in this little alcove hallway, it's just the two of us.

I can feel Elise's body pressed tightly against me, her hand still grasped in mine. She's so close I can feel her heart hammering in her chest, and her breasts heave as she catches her breath.

"Wow, that was insane," she whispers, our eyes adjusting enough that I can just start to see her face. "How can you do that all the time?"

I shake my head, wanting to brush a lock of hair out of her face but not wanting to let go of her hand. "That was nothing. When I'm on tour, it takes four guys to get me in the building because there are hundreds of people yelling your name, grabbing at you, and shoving Sharpies and more in your face."

She hisses, obviously imagining what that'd be like. "Shit, no way could I do that."

In the sub-twilight dimness, I cup her face, tracing her cheekbone with my thumb, marveling at the texture. "You okay, Elise?"

I feel her nod, but I can sense the tension in her body, and even though I damn well know I shouldn't, I dip down, catching her mouth with mine, needing to make sure she's okay. It's soft, tender as our lips press together for the first time for real and move against each other.

I feel her free hand move up, and she lays a flat palm against my chest, but she's not pressing me away. She's using it as leverage to get closer to me, wanting more.

My hand moves from her cheek to grip the back of her neck, encouraging her and taking that touch of control I need. She responds to it with a moan of enjoyment and desire, opening to let me take the kiss deeper.

Our tongues tangle, and it's like getting hit by white-hot lightning. Her body galvanizes and she lunges into me, the softness disappearing into almost a thrashing battle for dominance. It's just for show though. We both know I'm going to win this. She wants me to—she just wants me to work for it.

And I do, overpowering her even as she grabs my belt loops, pulling me in tighter, and when she feels the hard ridge of my cock against her belly, she moans. I grind against her, letting her feel what she does to me.

Vaguely, from seemingly far away, I hear my name being called, and it's like a bucket of cold water. I pull back, wiping at my mouth. "Fuck. I'm sorry, Elise. That can't . . ." I curse, not believing that just happened.

Elise understands my muttering, nodding. "Me neither . . . conflict of interest. For work, I mean."

I know it's the right thing to do, step away from the woman who has the power to ruin me, but goddamn, do I want to press her up against the wall and take her raw, hot, and fast right now. I think if we'd met under different circumstances, I'd fucking do it.

I haven't dated in . . . well, ever since I got custody of Carsen, but I'm not sure I could date Elise anyway, even though she is the most interesting woman I've met in a long time.

What I really want right now is to fuck her mercilessly until her eyes roll up and she's fuck-stunned from being pounded over and over. But with a steadying breath, I grab her hand again, loosely this time, and lead her through the dark corridor backstage to my green room. As we approach, a busy looking guy with a clipboard claps at me as he proclaims to the heavens like his redemption just emerged from the dimness. "Oh good, you're here. I'll be happy to get you anything you need tonight, Mr. Perkins. Anything now?"

I growl, still on edge. What I need . . . is what I can't have. "No. Just give me fifteen, ten, and five-minute warnings. That's it."

He nods, smiling broadly. "You got it." With that, he hustles out to the next thing on his list, leaving us alone again.

Shit.

I can still feel my cock throbbing in my jeans, and I know Elise can see it, the way she's looking down at my jeans.

And we both know that if we rush . . . yeah, we could get it done before I go on stage.

WHAT THE FUCK, *Elise? You can't be doing shit like that, no matter how irresistible Keith is. Work . . . remember work? The interview series that is going to jump start your career, maybe get you a gig with a real magazine, not celebrity trash fodder. Get your shit together. You don't get paid to feel that thick, throbbing cock pumping in and out . . .*

Wait. Okay, start over.

Stop thinking with your hormones and think with your head! Get your shit together and do your fucking job!

Better. Mental pep talk complete, I move around the room, feeling Keith's gaze follow me, burning into my neck, my back, my pussy and my . . . well, everything. My words aren't helping. The power in his eyes is breaking me down.

I need to reset us, calm down the flames still licking at my insides, the need pulsing in my clit. Taking a deep breath, I dive back into reporter mode, locking the door on my inner sex-starved bitch for now.

"Green room, huh?" I ask with forced sarcasm. "Seems pretty . . . standard. No bowls of just blue M&Ms, buckets of Popeye's chicken legs, or fancy champagne. What's in your rider for requirements?"

Keith hasn't moved, standing stock-still as he watches me, making me feel like prey that he could pounce on at any moment, or not, solely at his discretion. Even if I wanted to, I couldn't resist him.

"No rider," Keith says in a low, sexy purr. "The venue always comps my beer and some bar food after the show and supplies water bottles before and during. But I'm not some asshole who needs caviar and Cristal. I'm just here to sing songs, shake hands, and go home."

I nod, taking it in. He's so much a dichotomy. On one hand, he's commanding, on the other easygoing. It's . . . unique. "Seems easy. Maybe even too easy."

Keith chuckles, his eyes flashing again with humor, desire, and power. "Definitely nothing easy about me."

Before I can question that statement, there's a knock at the door, and Keith turns his head, breaking our eye contact for the first time since we entered. "It's open."

The door opens slowly before a herd of guys comes barreling in, loud and big and . . . loud.

Really, it's just three guys, but it's a small room, so their appearance and energy make the room feel claustrophobic. Keith moves to greet the group, a big grin on his face as he bro-hugs and back-pats each one. "Hey, Slim, you're not going to have that nickname much longer."

"Man, fuck you," *Slim*, a slightly chubby guy who's wearing a jean jacket, says with a laugh. "Good to see you. You don't want to know what the other offer I had for the weekend was."

"What?" another of the guys asks. "I turned down playing backbeat for a folk-opera fusion. Let that sink in . . . Folk. Opera."

"Try a studio session for a Prince tribute band," Slim replies with a shudder. "I mean, I can play bass to anything but . . . fuck me, a slow-dance version of *When Doves Cry*? Fuck my life. And Prince would be pissed as hell at the hatchet job they're doing."

After a round of laughter, Keith turns to me. "Elise, these are the guys. We've been playing gigs together for years. Guys, this is Elise. She's a reporter, doing a couple of articles about me."

One of the newcomers, a lean guy with long, shaggy blonde hair makes a whooping noise, grinning widely to show off perfect, square teeth that are almost a little too big, giving him almost a feral look. "Ooh, writing an article about our Country Star? Want me to tell you all of his dirty little secrets? I'm Jim, by the way. In my day job, I'm the lead singer in a blues band."

I grin, my eyes jumping from Jim to Keith as I shake Jim's offered hand, teasing. "Actually, that'd be great. Maybe you can give me all of his juicy secrets?"

Keith jumps in, his voice amused but still brooking no argument. "Shut your mouth, Jim. You too, guys."

He looks at the other two. Slim, whatever his real name is, nods, and Keith continues. "She's interviewing *me*. Got it?"

There's a hint of possessiveness to Keith's tone, and something else I can't quite place . . . a warning, maybe?

But the three guys seem to catch Keith's meaning loud and clear, whatever it is. They nod in unison, and Jim speaks up. "Got it, boss man. But maybe I could share some gig stories? Tell her about the time that chick crowd-surfed up to the stage and damn-near jumped your bones before security could snatch her off the stage?"

I'm grinning, already visualizing how that snippet is going to add some flair to my next article about Keith's performances. "God, yes . . . tell me more about that!"

He glances to Keith, obviously silently asking permission, and Keith gives the approval, shrugging. "Well, you damn-near already told it, so you might as well go ahead."

The next thirty minutes are spent listening to Keith and the guys banter, joke, and reminisce about past tours and shows. I finally figure out that Slim and Eric are one and the same, and it's interesting to hear about their time on the road together as they obviously have a long history and a deep friendship.

"Wait, let me ask you one thing," I interrupt Eric as he goes on about a time he was painted up on stage. "You guys talk about lots of different music. You're not just country?"

"I prefer country," Eric says, "but with us mainly working in the summers, we can pick up other gigs that sound interesting . . . or pay well. Besides, while Keith won't admit it, he can do a pretty stellar *Sweet Child O'Mine* if you get him drunk, or sometimes if you just beg hard enough."

I blush, thinking about begging Keith for anything, and say nothing. As I listen to another tale, Shane asks Keith, "Hey, remember that time Sarah brought us all chili dogs and we ended up puking ten minutes before the show? God, that show sucked."

I wouldn't have even caught the namedrop if the temperature in the room hadn't just plummeted at the same time the tension in Keith's entire body sprang tight. Shane cuts his eyes to me, wide and panicked. He looks like he wants to crawl into a hole and make sure someone's hidden all the pointy things nearby.

I look at Keith, questioning. "Obviously, a story there?"

Keith glowers but finally relents, although her voice is ice. "Sarah is my sister. She comes on the road with us in the summer sometimes, kinda acts like my assistant. She's not to be included in the article. She has her own life and doesn't need mine fucking hers up."

He gives me a hard look, daring me to disagree with his decree. I give him a tiny smile, acquiescing for now but knowing I'll need to do a bit of digging to make sure there's nothing hinky about the sister he was obviously hiding. I mean, if there's nothing there, why not just say up it up front? "Fine."

Before the tension in the room can settle, the kid with the clipboard pops back in without knocking. "Fifteen minutes."

Keith hops up before the kid can leave, calling out to him. "Hey, can you take my guest out to her table? It's reserved up front."

The kid actually looks at his clipboard for a moment, and I have a split second where I kinda want him to say no, just to see what Keith will do.

But eventually, the kid waves at me with his board. "Follow me," he blurts out before muttering something under his breath.

I glance at Keith, who is searching my eyes for something, his eyes narrowed like he's analyzing me. I'm not sure what tell-tale sign of my possible dishonesty he's looking for, so I smile warmly. "Have a great show! Break a leg . . . that's what you say, right?"

Finally, he relaxes slightly and speaks dryly. "I'll see you in a few. I'll be the cowboy on stage in the hat."

I shake my head, rolling my eyes. "I'll be the girl in the front row, yelling 'yee-haw' louder than everyone."

Keith actually smiles as the guys laugh. "Good lord, woman. Do *not* do that. Or you're likely to get kicked out for being drunk."

I grin, considering doing it just to mess with him.

As the kid sets me up at my table, a fresh bottle of beer magically appears from a passing waitress. I yell out 'thanks' but she's already gone.

A few minutes later, I've taken some notes on the show attendees. Most are fans wearing t-shirts from Keith's last tour, with a pair of radio djs wearing polos with their KCTY call letters on the chest and a slew of half-naked women all giggly and girly as they wait impatiently for Keith's appearance on stage. I try not to feel catty about them, but I can't help it . . . some of these bitches need a muzzle and a tranq dart.

Shit, maybe I'm the one feeling possessive.

When Keith finally emerges, it's a riot of noisy yells and clapping. As he greets the crowd, I can see just how comfortable he is on stage, his energy creating a buzzing sort of high among the crowd. He starts singing and it's magical. I didn't tell him this, but once I got this assignment, I did my homework like any good reporter.

I've listened to all his biggest hits, both the ones that sold millions and the ones the critics raved about, which ironically aren't usually the same songs. I've heard him sing about parties, about women, about dads, about long drives home, and more. But none of those hours spent with Keith blasting through my earbuds prepared me for this. His deep tenor is amplified until it vibrates my chest, making me feel his words, both physically and metaphorically in my heart.

I can see how the emotions of every song resonate for him, both upbeat and subdued. It's amazing how in this entire room full of people clamoring for a piece of him, it feels like he's singing just to me, and I'm sure if I asked every person in the crowd, they'd feel the same way.

It's in the tilt of his head, the way his eyes slowly move across the space, connecting with people, how he even winks at a couple of those giggly women with a sign proclaiming *Keith, we love you!*

As he sings his latest hit about the girl he wants but can't have yet, he bends down low, right in front of me, reaching out a hand. Even though I held his hand earlier, when I touch him on stage like this, larger than life, I swear I light up just like a teenybopper at a Justin Beiber concert.

And I don't care. I'm swept away because he really is singing to me right now. *Baby, take my hand; we'll buy a little piece of land; it'll be just me and you; forever, if you say, 'I do'.*

Okay, obviously not singing to me like he means what he's saying, but his eyes are locked on me until the end of the song, and then he kisses the back of my hand like the gentleman he's decidedly not. With a wink, he tears off across the stage as the band changes tune and Keith starts belting out his most famous party anthem.

I'm still swooning a bit, plopping back in my chair when I feel a tap on my shoulder.

I look up to see a young guy in a button-up and jeans standing there, and he smiles and leans in, whisper-yelling in my ear. "I'm Ethan. I'm with the bar crew. Mind if I sit with you for sound checks?"

I nod, mouthing "Sure" as I gesture to the chair. He sits down and I go back to watching Keith rock the crowd for a few songs. My legs are still shaky, knees knocking under the table as I catch my breath from singing along. Keith is strutting his stuff, grinning and playing his heart out over to the right side of the stage, but I notice a tight look on his face when he looks back at me, eyes bouncing from me to Ethan.

I shrug in an attempt to let Keith know it's no big deal, because I really don't mind sharing the primo table, but he seems stiffer than he was just a moment ago. He finishes out the song but keeps playing a guitar riff as he resets the microphone center-stage right in front of me.

When he stops, he takes the microphone, his eyes radiating power that takes over the room. "Thanks so much, everyone. I have to tell y'all a secret if you think you can keep it quiet."

He looks straight at me, daring me to say no as the audience responds en-masse with a resounding 'yeah'.

Keith nods, adjusting his hat a little to pull it down, making him look like an old-time gunfighter or something. "I love playing shows just like this one . . . small venue, tight-knit crowd, with everyone singing along. It's closer, intimate when I can hear you singing and see your smiling faces. So I just wanted to say . . . Hello."

Without even pausing, he rolls right into one of his older and lesser-known songs, but somehow one of my favorites. *Hellooo, girl; C'mon over here and let me get to know you; Hellooo, girl; gimme five and you won't believe what I can show you . . .*

As Keith hits the chorus, Ethan leans over, whisper-yelling in my ear again. "Was the transition from music to speaking to music okay for you? I think it sounded a bit tinny on the right."

I nod at him, smiling and mouthing 'it's good' and returning my attention to an obviously scowling Keith. Shit, what's wrong with him?

After a few more songs, which feel forced and not quite as casually comfortable as the vibe had been earlier, Keith wraps up and takes a bow. I rise with everyone else, clapping like a maniac and sticking my fingers in my mouth to let out a piercing wolf-whistle instead of the yee-haw I threatened.

Keith smiles at the crowd but doesn't even glance at me as he struts off stage. Piped-in music begins playing as people get up and take to the dance floor, building on Keith's energy to get their groove on.

Ethan nods and gives a little wave as he heads off to talk to a guy behind the soundboard at the back of the floor. Honestly, I don't know what to do. Should I go backstage the same way I came out? Wait here for clipboard kid?

I drain the last of my beer, now hot from being ignored while I focused on the show, and I decide to find my way back. After all, I'm supposed to have all-access to Keith, so surely, they'll let me backstage?

When I get to the edge of the floor, I see Keith's bodyguard and make my way over. "Hey, I'm Elise . . . from earlier. Can I go meet up with Keith now?"

He doesn't even answer. Hell, I'm not sure if he looks at me since his eyes are covered in sunglasses, but he bumps his head to the left so I take that as a yes and quickly scoot on through to the curtained backstage area.

I'm a little fuzzy on how to get to the green room, but I'm shuffling along in the dark when two hands reach around from behind me, one grabbing loosely at my neck and tilting my jaw up and the other firmly around my belly, pulling me back against a hard body.

I'm frozen in fear for an instant before I hear Keith's voice growling quietly in my ear, "What the fuck was that, Elise? What kind of games are you playing?"

Before I can speak, he moves his hand over my mouth, muffling my questions . . . my explanation of whatever has set him off. Keith grinds against me, and I can feel his cock, thick and hard, even more so than during our stolen kiss before the show, and I'm instantly on fire for him. All the flirting and eyeballing we've been doing is coming to a fever pitch between my legs, my pussy thrumming like a guitar string.

I arch my back, circling my hips, wanting to feel him, wanting to make him lose control the way I am. I whimper, trying to beg if that's what it takes, but before I can, he continues.

"Leaving me with your taste still on my lips, and you're already sitting with some asshole for my show? Think you can cock tease me and make me jealous? Guess what? It worked."

I try to shake my head, wanting to tell him that it was just a sound guy, but he doesn't give me a chance, and I can barely form a coherent thought anyway because he's licking and nibbling my neck.

"You've been wanting me since the first second we saw each other," he whispers as he works his way up to my ear. "You've been dreaming about it, haven't you? And I'll let you in on one of those juicy secrets you always want—I've been wanting to fuck you since that first night too."

The words explode in my brain, and I moan against his hand as Keith's lips move lower, to the curve between my neck and shoulder. His hand on my waist fumbles with my button, but he gets it undone.

"Shove your jeans down," he growls. "You were naughty, so take your punishment like a good girl, Elise."

I don't know what punishment he has in mind, but *fuck, yes* to whatever it is. He can fuck me right here in the middle of the backstage area if he wants. Hell, he could shove me down on the dirty stage in front of the crowd and I'd happily take him. I'm that gone.

I push my jeans down, leaving my lace thong because he didn't tell me to take my panties off, and on some instinctual level, I want to do what he says. Exactly what he says.

I feel his hand, broad and rough, caressing the cheek of my ass, and it makes me shiver in anticipation.

Before I realize what he has in mind, he lifts his hand, popping it back down on my cheek with a loud smack. I cry out, but the sound is muffled as he presses his hand tighter across my mouth. And then he does it again, and again . . . three times total, and I'm a quivering mess.

I've never felt this on fire before. My pussy's quivering, almost dripping down my inner thigh as I give him total control. Keith is undeniable, a force of sexual nature that I don't want to resist. I just want him to fuck me, hard and pounding and mind-blowingly . . . and make me his dirty secret.

Keith grabs the strip of lace, pulling it tight against my soaking pussy and whispering hotly in my ear. "Are you gonna come for me? Just from me smacking your delectable ass?"

I shake my head. As on the edge as I obviously am, I need more, my hips bucking as I look for relief. Keith laughs darkly. He knows I'm lying. "Need me to rub your hot little clit? Make you come all over my fingers?"

Whimpering, I look over my shoulder, meeting his eyes in the dark, begging silently. He grabs a handful of my tender ass in his calloused fingers, squeezing hard, and I know—hell, I hope—I'll have his fingerprints there later.

When he lets go, his fingers dive around my hip, tapping little smacks right over my lace-covered clit. I'm so on fire it only takes a few, and I detonate, my body shaking and convulsing as I press his hand tighter on my mouth, muffling myself so I'm not too loud.

As I come back down from the high, I pull his hand down, gasping for air as I still writhe against him. I feel him bend down, grabbing my jeans and trying to pull them up, and it's like a wakeup call.

Holy fuck . . . I just *fucked* my assignment. Well, not fucked, but I might as well have. And I've never had anything blow me up like that. I can't imagine what he could do to me pounding that thick fucking cock into me, but I damn sure want to find out.

I can't get my racing thoughts corralled, so I start to button my jeans back up. "That guy . . ." Keith growls, and I turn, placing a hand on his cheek.

"That guy . . . was the sound tech. You had me in the palm of your hand all night."

I can hear Keith's teeth grinding before he gives in, his voice velvet over gravel. "Fuck. Get in the damn car. Let's go."

CHAPTER
Ten

KEITH

STUPID.

So fucking stupid.

I was so on edge, but that . . . I can't believe how I exploded when I saw her. It wasn't like she was eye fucking the guy. Sure, he was some young stud, whispering in her ear, getting her smiles. Fuck that. I felt played and pissed, but apparently it was only my mind playing tricks on me, not Elise.

But I basically attacked her when I saw her uncertainly stumbling backstage, even if she didn't seem to mind. Instead, she went with it, giving me all the sexual energy that I knew she kept inside her. The feeling of her body writhing against me, the sound of her ass smacking under my hand . . . my God, she's perfect.

As long as I live, I'll never forget the moment she pressed my hand tighter on her own mouth as she vibrated through her orgasm, covering my hand in her sweet cream.

I wanted to taste her, to drop to my knees behind her and bury my face in her ass as I feasted on her. I wanted to shove her up against the wall and fuck her so hard they'd have heard her screams over the music on the dance floor. She'd have let me, too. I fucking know it.

At least I didn't lose that much control of myself. But I've damn sure done enough to screw myself up in a big way. Because as hot as that was, and as much as we both wanted it, she's still the reporter digging into my private life.

As we sit in the car, speeding back to her apartment, it's hard to focus on that when my fingers are tingling with the desire to grab her again. It doesn't help my cock any when Elise puts her pink-nailed manicured hand on my thigh, making me turn to look at her. "The show was awesome."

She's trying so hard to settle me, the tension obvious. I stare at her hand for a moment, trying to decide on the best course of action. Cold professional or hot lover? Inside, I feel like I'm both right now. I want to push her away, to keep my secrets safe . . . but the other side of me wants to make Elise mine, to show her what it really feels like to have a man take her completely and fully.

What keeps Carsen safest? Finally, I decide that's the only real result I need, regardless of what my throbbing cock wants. I can't push her away. She's so smart she'd just keep digging. And I can't trust her either.

Decision made, I play somewhere in the middle, taking her hand loosely in my own . . . not quite professional, but decidedly not the guy who just spanked her ass and made her come.

Giving her my best attempt at a 'fan-friendly' smile, I answer her evenly. "Thanks. Those really are my favorite types of performances, even better than the huge arenas stuffed with fans. Those are great too, the roar and energy of the crowd, but the smaller shows where I get to shake hands with folks, see their faces as they sing along . . . it's more intimate and more satisfying."

Shit, ten seconds in and I've already fucked up and betrayed what I'm thinking. That's definitely not what I meant to say because 'intimate' and 'satisfying' do not have me thinking of the show anymore.

Apparently, Elise's thoughts track the same way, and she lowers her voice just in case the driver and bodyguard up front can hear. "He really was the sound tech, Keith. Not that I'm at all upset about the misunderstanding."

I cut my eyes over at her, and she's smiling broadly, her whole face lit up, but there's a flash of uncertainty in her eyes. I know what she's saying, and I guess she's got the same fears running around in her head. I can't be a *total* asshole about this.

I sigh, running a hand across my head, and turn to face her fully. "There's obviously something between us, chemistry for damn sure. But—"

She interrupts, placing a hand on my forearm, giving me that pitying look that I know but so rarely get. "It's inappropriate while I'm interviewing you," she says, sighing softly and making this hurt a little. "I agree. Maybe later, we can see where this goes, or maybe not? But I need to be as impartial as possible while I'm writing this series."

I nod, relieved knowing she's at least partially right. "Elise, I told you the first time we met . . . I'm not dating and not looking. I have my reasons that are not up for discussion or for reporting. But they won't change, not even when the job's done."

She bites her lip, nodding, and all I want to do is lick the sting away where she's worrying it between her teeth. It hurts. It hurts a lot. So many years, sleeping alone in an oversized king bed for no reason other than my bedroom would look ridiculous with a twin-sized mattress in it. So many nights sitting up alone after Carsen's gone to sleep, wishing I had someone I could share those things with that I can't even share with Sarah. Too many years, but I have to protect my daughter, and that means I can't let Elise in further.

"I understand. Won't say I'm not disappointed, but I get it," she says bravely, trying to keep her voice light but not really quite making it. "You've got a lot at stake here. You're a big country music star and I'm a tabloid reporter."

I nod, and she smirks, but it feels sadly ironic. "Funny thing is, I've shared more with you, stories and connection, not just chemistry, than I have with anyone in a long time. Maybe ever. I know your original arrangement was just to even the playing field a bit, but I have to tell you, I like you. I like talking with you, hanging out. You hide it in a lot of ways, but you're a good guy, Keith. Not too many of those out there."

I smile, genuinely shocked by her words. "I don't know that anyone's ever called me good . . . good for nothing, maybe?" I joke. "And I didn't feel good backstage."

Elise smirks. "That wasn't good. That was bad. But in that case, bad was fucking awesome."

Her words draw me in, and I can't stop my fingers from gently grabbing a curl of hair that's hanging by the side of her face, twirling it around my finger. "I like you, too. Definitely made this whole interview thing a hell of a lot better than I thought it'd be."

All too soon, the car stops at the curb in front of her apartment. It's late, after two in the morning, and the street is dark and deserted. When the guard opens the door, I get out too. "Gonna walk her up."

The guard takes another look around, then dips his chin once. I chuckle. I've already ditched the hat and changed shirts. The most noticeable thing about me right now is the Town Car with a muscle-bound man in black in the front seat.

As we get a few feet away, Elise whispers. "That is so weird. That's one scary ass dude."

I laugh. Our thoughts are so similar. "He's just doing his job, and I appreciate that. I try not to be an annoying asshole that makes the security team's life hard, but I couldn't sit in the car and watch you walk to the door alone. Better say good night at the door though. If I try to go up, he'll shit a brick."

Elise stops on the steps by the door, turning to face me, and puts her hands on my chest. "Probably best if you don't come up anyway. I'm not sure I have the willpower to not . . ." She stops, and fuck, do I wish she'd finish that sentence, tell me what she'd do if we weren't fighting this thing between us.

Before I can ask, she leans in, kissing my cheek with her velvety soft lips before moaning lightly.

She lingers, and I can't take it, groaning. "Fuck it, Elise."

I pull her closer, encircling her waist in my arms, and turn to take her mouth once again. She's right there with me, kissing me back as she wraps her arms around my neck.

I squeeze her ass, knowing she's likely sore from the earlier spanking, and she cries out softly, opening her mouth, and I take advantage, invading her with my tongue to taste her.

Easing the sting, I rub her cheeks through the denim, cupping her and pressing her against my raging cock. From behind us, I hear a polite interrupting cough.

Shit, the bodyguard and the driver. I forgot about them, lost in Elise . . . again. Literally minutes after agreeing that we can't do this, and I'm holding her, the two of us making out like horny teenagers at the end of prom night. I take a big breath, pressing my forehead to hers and firmly cupping her face.

"I have to go. Now. Or I'm gonna throw you over my shoulder, run to your apartment, and bury my cock in your pussy so deep, so hard, you'll feel empty without me there."

She shudders, placing her hands over mine and squeezing. "You do have to go. Because if you do that, I'm sure as fuck gonna let you. Hell, I'd beg for it. But . . . we can't."

Grinding my teeth, I agree. "We can't."

"We have a dinner interview tomorrow. That still okay?"

I laugh softly, inhaling the scent of her hair, the innate purity underneath the scent of beer and sweat from the bar. "I'll probably still be jacking off from the raging blue balls you've given me tonight . . . repeatedly."

Elise leans in and whispers in my ear. "If it'll help . . . my vibrator might need new batteries by morning."

I moan, knowing exactly what she'll be doing and wishing I were the one doing it to her. "Fuck. I'll see you tomorrow, and I promise to behave if you do."

She's quiet, not promising me back but still with that little smile on her face. "Elise?" I question. "Do we have a deal?"

She grins, but sassy as fuck and not apologetic at all. "Sorry, yeah. Behave. I was just picturing you stroking that thick cock I felt in your jeans, coming all over your hand but still not stopping because you're still rock-hard . . . for me."

I growl, but instead of grabbing her like I want to, I step back. It's the hardest thing I've ever done. "Watch it, woman. Don't poke the bear. You just might get attacked. See you tomorrow night."

She doesn't answer, just nods and smiles, but as I turn toward the car, I hear her hushed whisper. "I fucking hope so."

———

By lunchtime, I've already made up my mind about Elise and our situation. That is, before changing it at least twenty times.

Maybe we could have a little fun after the interviews are done and with a clear understanding that whatever things we get up to are not to be written about. There's a chance we could be . . . well, I don't know, fuck buddies? Friends with *very* good benefits? More? the little voice in my head whispers to me in my weaker moments.

But that's playing with fire and I know it. Elise is an investigator at heart, curious and wanting to know things. I saw that when she was just chatting with the guys.

And the one most likely to get burned there is Carsen.

I promised myself years ago after what happened that I wouldn't do anything to jeopardize her ability to have a normal childhood, and fucking a tabloid reporter damn sure isn't the brightest idea I've ever had.

I'm still flip-flopping when Sarah comes in the kitchen, cautiously giving my grumpy ass a wide berth. She's come over to pick up Carsen again so I can keep up the façade of a publicity-shy loner bachelor. "So, did the show suck last night or something?"

Caught off-guard, I give her a confused look, realizing I've been dipping a cookie into some milk for so long the poor damn thing has dissolved and I've got nothing but a chocolate chip between my fingers. "Huh? Not that I know of. Why?"

"Well, usually, the day after a show, you're buzzing a bit, ready to tackle the day," she says, coming over and rescuing my plate of cookies, grabbing one and munching on it contentedly. One of the ways I reassure myself when things are tough . . . eat cookies with Sarah and Carsen. "But you're wearing a cloak of 'fuck off' right now. Ergo, did the show suck?"

I laugh at her, loving that she knows my routine to a T. "No, the show was great, as usual. They loved the songs, even did an old one I haven't performed in years. *Hello Girl.*"

Sarah nods, doing some more chocolate chip deduction with another cookie. "That's not in your usual set list. Anything in particular make you feel like singing that?'

I shake my head, not wanting to let her in on the truth. "I dunno, just felt it."

She hums, and when I look at her, her eyebrow is raised as she dunks her cookie, obviously seeing through my bullshit. "So, wasn't the reporter going to the show last night? That wouldn't happen to be her favorite song or something, is it?"

I laugh. Close, but no cigar. "Hell if I know. Elise isn't even a country fan, really. More of a rock person she says, good taste in rock at least. But she went to the show last night. Must've done her homework too because she sang along with almost every song." I say, thinking back to how she looked as she belted out my words, my songs. Everyone was singing along, but somehow her doing it felt like winning a prize.

Sarah snaps her fingers, grinning impishly. "That's it. It's the reporter. Spill it, Keith."

I know my eyes are wide, panic showing, because Sarah continues, her smile dimming but her voice becoming more intense. "It's all over your face when you talk about her. And no woman just memorizes a bunch of songs for an assignment like hers. What's her deal?"

I force my emotions back under control, schooling my face into a calm dismissal despite her comment about Elise dropping a bomb into my emotional calm. "She's fine. We've had a few interviews now. The first article is already published, mostly just basics. Record company was happy."

Sarah shakes her head and downs the rest of my milk, including the soggy cookie bits in the bottom. "Nice try at diversion, big guy. You forget I grew up with you and know all your tells. That's what Todd and the record company want to hear. Tell me about her."

I swallow, trying to speak in a way that won't show my hand too much, even though Sarah has always been able to read me like a book. "She's a tabloid reporter. The one who printed the first article that started this whole mess, actually. But she's good, seems to want a real story, not a made-up melodramatic one, which is better than I can say for most of the vultures."

Sarah interrupts, not interested in Elise's resume. "Yeah, yeah, yeah . . . work, work, work. Tell me what *she's* like."

"Fuck, Sarah . . . what do you want to know? Her damn cup size and favorite food?"

Sarah smirks, hopping up on the kitchen island and swinging her legs back and forth. "Funny that's where your mind goes. Question is, do you *know* her cup size and favorite food?"

I duck my head, busted and pissed as fuck about it. "Maybe."

Sarah claps like this is a good thing. "Finally! Hallelujah and pass the peanut butter, my prayers have been answered!"

I growl, glaring at her pure . . . glee. "What the fuck are you so damn happy about? This is bad, Sarah. Really fucking bad."

Sarah shakes her head, not clapping but still smiling. "No, it's not. You took this vow of being alone like some martyr, sacrificing your own happiness for Carsen in a misguided notion that it's somehow better for her. But she doesn't need that. She's a happy little girl who has everything she could ever want . . . but one thing. She needs you to be happy with her, with your work, and with a partner. Show her what love can look like."

I sigh, wishing it were that easy. I love my sister, but sometimes she can be a bit idyllic. "What? I don't love Elise. How could I? We just met, for all intents and purposes. I just . . . want her."

Sarah puts her hand on my shoulder, patting it gently. "Fine. So you don't introduce her to Carsen. But you take a little joy in life for yourself.

She's the only woman who's even intrigued you in all these years. I never said anything before because I could see that about you. And I can see that you're fighting this now. But maybe . . . don't?"

"What about the articles? It's not exactly professional for either of us to be fucking while she's writing a tell-all expose on me," I exclaim. "And it gets her closer to the truth."

Sarah smirks, shaking her head. "Uhm, I'm sure more than one article has been 'researched' that way, especially in showbiz. At least you two can go into it with eyes wide open. Talk to her, see if you can figure out how to tell her what she needs to know for the articles without putting Carsen at risk. It could work. And judging by the way you're behaving, it's gonna happen sooner or later anyway, so best to get in front of it. Control the outcome, Mr. Control Freak. You can't tell me you haven't been going over every possible scenario already. Just pick the one where you get to have a little fun for a change."

Fun. My own sister, telling me to have fun, which of course means get my fucking freak on. "I can't believe you're telling me to fuck the reporter. This has bad written all over it."

Sarah grins and punches me in the arm. "Well, a little bad can be a good thing sometimes, little brother."

I groan, remembering how Elise said something similar just last night. And now, my sister. "Ugh, don't. For the love of fuck, do not. You're my sister, Sarah. Just hush."

She laughs, miming locking her lips as she gives me a sassy look and walks out of the kitchen, calling for Carsen. "Carsen, c'mon, honey. Grab your gear and let's roll. Don't forget to think of a chick flick for us to watch. Something romantic . . . maybe Enchanted?

Quieter, I hear her mutter under her breath. "Mmm, McDreamy . . ."

I shake my head, definitely not wanting to know who my sister fantasizes about.

Carsen runs through, bag tossed over her shoulder, grinning. "Bye, Dad, we're leaving."

"Hey, wait a second, young lady," I declare, holding up a hand. "I at least need a hug bye."

She grins, wrapping her arms around my shoulders, and I pick her up, giving her a big hug. She's still so young, so fragile, and if I were a stronger man, maybe I'd be able to keep the promise I gave her. But I'm weak, I'll admit it.

Elise lights me up like no woman ever has, and I can't hold out much longer against my desire. I've got to figure out a way to keep Carsen a secret, keep her safe, but give in to this thing with Elise, at least a little to let the pressure off.

Giving Carsen one more squeeze, I give her a kiss on the cheek. "I love you, baby girl. You know I'd do anything for you, right?"

She looks at me weird, like I've lost my damn mind. "Of course, Dad. I love you, too."

I set her down, and she's off with Sarah, already talking about ordering pizza. "And popcorn too! Okay?"

Sarah laughs, nodding at Carsen before looking at me, giving me a little wink. Before I know it, they're driving away in Sarah's SUV and I'm alone.

Elise won't be here for hours, not until dinner time. But I'm already craving her, her breathy moans as I picture fucking her like I have every time I've jacked off since last night.

If I'm honest with myself, it's not just the sex I'm after though. I want her smiles, her laugh, for her to tell me about her day.

I want to know her. That's the scariest part of all.

CHAPTER

Eleven

ELISE

MY FINGERS ARE FLYING across the keyboard for this second article. It really is some of the easiest writing I've ever done. It's like I'm just pouring myself out on the pages, and I know the hardest part will be keeping myself under the word limit.

"So tell me about your first performance."

Keith's recorded voice is deep and casual, sending warm ripples through my body as he chuckles in my earphones. *"Wow, that takes me back. It was . . . fourth grade. My school's talent contest, and I knew that I wanted to sing my ass off. I couldn't play well enough yet, but I got my hands on the instrumentals to some Garth Brooks."*

"Garth Brooks?" I asked, laughing. *"You didn't."*

"Oh, I had the whole getup, from that solid black colored shirt to a black cowboy hat. The only other song I could get the chords to was Shania Twain, and I looked like hell in a dress."

I smile at our mutual laughter. *"So, what happened?"*

"Well, I was nervous as hell when I got up there, even though I'd practiced for a month straight. But I closed my eyes and started singing. The response was good, and so I kept going. Everything was good up until the bridge."

"What happened?"

"Let's just say I'm a better singer than dancer," Keith says with a laugh. *"There's a reason I don't do dance numbers in my shows now. A whole month of practice in front of the mirror at home . . . not enough. Still, I got a standing ovation, which I guess set the bar pretty fucking high for future performances."*

I snicker to myself and work in some backstory of his years perfecting his craft on small stages in dive bars before I segue into my experience with Keith's local show, the way he kept it pretty low-key and wasn't some hard-to-work-with diva star but instead was easygoing and casual with the small backstage crew and band.

I add in how he talked about his fans with sweeping compliments and appreciation, making sure to highlight the little girl he'd stopped and signed an autograph for. The guys' stories from the green room add a bit of a rock 'n roll element and tour absurdity that makes Keith feel like a perfect blend of country good ol' boy and rock star god that I know will tickle the fancy of even the non-country fan readers.

It's hard to stay objective, though, when I talk about the concert itself. More than once, I find myself deleting whole passages as I gush like a fangirl about his command of the room, the way his voice vibrated through my body to enflame my desires, or the sexy swagger and the way his ass looked in his jeans as he strutted back and forth across the stage. Sure, some of it can be in my final cut. I need to entice the readers and maybe make a few panties wet, but I can't come off like some newbie with a total crush on him . . . even if I'm starting to feel that way.

I most definitely leave out the moments in the dark backstage. Those are ours, whatever they were. Even now, with his voice talking through the recorder, my body heats as I remember the feel of his hand smacking down on my bare cheek, the taps on my clit. I can feel the blush in my cheeks as I remember our agreeing that we can't pursue anything and then seconds later, going at each other again.

It's like we've crossed a line, and no matter what, it can't be uncrossed. The pull between us is too damn strong.

I've never felt anything like this before. Even though we haven't seen each other that many times, the time we've spent together has been intense, full of deep conversations and sharing about ourselves over long hours. I've had whole relationships that lasted months that haven't been as deep as the sharing that Keith and I have done. Add in the explosive chemistry, and we're so fucked.

Well, I am.

If something happens and people found out, Keith comes out like a famous music star. The worst someone might accuse him of is slumming it with a reporter to try and get a better angle. A little naughty, but nothing all that bad.

I'm the one who's compromising her professional morals. Even if I'm not doing it for the story, which I'm definitely not, no one would believe that. They'll think I'm just as bad as Francesca, using my body to get ahead professionally. And quite frankly, too many girls get chewed up and spat out by the industry once it gets out that they fuck their way around. There'd be no chance in hell of my ever getting out of the sleazy tabloid circuit. No chance of getting the job that I really do want.

As much as that should give me pause, and normally it would, I know that if Keith had come upstairs last night, there's no way I could've said no.

Underneath my desk, I have to cross and uncross my legs just to relieve some of the pressure as I think about the ridge I felt in Keith's jeans, the jealous possessiveness as he punished me in the dark.

My hands drop from my keyboard to press against the top of my shorts just over my pussy. My mind is back to picturing him stroking himself, imagining his groans as he cries out my name when he comes, thick spurts of cum coating his hand.

Fuck it . . . professional morals be damned.

I want Keith.

I want him in a way I've never wanted a man before. Something about the way he's both soft and rough unexpectedly does it for me, and if I have a chance, I'm going for it. If I get burned . . . well, I can try starting over writing books. They say every reporter has their own version of the Great American Novel kicking around in their heads. Might as well put mine out there.

Decision made, I shake my head with a smile and take a deep breath, attempting to refocus on my article.

As I read back over it, I know it's good. Really good, maybe the best I've ever written. I know for sure it'll make our readers feel like they've actually experienced what backstage with Keith is really like. Donnie will like this one without a doubt. It paints Keith in a positive light but has just enough exciting dirt from the tour stories to be intriguing. It teases, and while it doesn't say anything bad about Keith, it does let the reader fantasize just a little.

It's more than a usual 'man on the stage' piece, delving into Keith's performances from day one to now, along with his thoughts on the whole journey he's been on. I've even got a lead for the next story . . . where does Keith go from here?

With a flourish, I hit *Send* and lean back in my chair. Two down, at least another couple to go, but Donnie is going to expect some dirt now that I've set up Keith as the hero in this tale. He needs a dark moment, but I really don't know if there is one. I'm beginning to think that Keith really is just who he says, a guy who wants to write, sing, and be left alone.

There's a tiny voice in the back of my head reminding me of what Maggie said about finding out what he does in his free time, and I make a note to ask some questions about that tonight. Selfishly, I want to ask about his 'why no dating, now or later' rule, and as I get dressed, I try to decide if I can do that without sounding like a whiny cling-on.

Realizing the time, I decide casual is the order for the day and grab black leggings and a soft pale blue sweater I knit last winter. The neckline is wide and hangs off my shoulder. I'm still not as good as Grandma ever hoped, so I slip on a lacy purple bralette underneath. I change panties too, into a matching purple thong that nestles softly between my cheeks, making me bite my lip thoughtfully.

Yeah, I'm going in with all thoughts of being professional tonight, but if something happens, I don't want to be wearing ugly granny lingerie.

I drive quickly to Keith's place, my mind whirling as I try and think of questions to ask . . . but really, all I want to do is hang out with him, to see where this evening takes us.

I knock on the door, expecting to have to wait, but instead I hear a voice from inside. "It's open."

I swing the door open, and my first thought is that Keith seems to have had the same thought of casual comfort. He looks downright edible, grey sweatpants hung low on his hips and a tank top stretched across his chest. I can see tattoos peeking out along the neckline and twisting down his arms in thick bands of design that I've never seen before. They're intricate, they're detailed, and I want to trace them with my tongue.

My eyes are running across his chest, down his thick arms to his clenched fists. He's here not to talk, not to have a casual dinner. He's here to conquer, to take what he wants. And fuck, do I want to give it to him.

"Elise."

It's not a question, it's an order, and I look up as a shudder races through me. I can see the lust he's holding back, the control he's using just to stand in front of me. I want to test it, push him and see where his limit is, if for no other reason than my own sanity, which is mind-numbingly lost in his presence. "Keith, what are you thinking right now?"

He doesn't step toward me, but his whole body seems to vibrate as he growls quietly, his eyes blazing with need. "Right now, I'm thinking that I want to bite that bare shoulder, leave a mark while I hold you in place and pound into you from behind. I want to make you scream my name and fill you with my cock and come until we're both satisfied."

And I'm done.

I haven't even made it in the door yet, not a single interview question asked, but I can't hold myself back like he is. I don't have the iron will he does.

Instead of answering, I drop my bag inside the door and jump into his arms.

In a testament to his strength, Keith doesn't even flinch when he catches me, his large hands easily cupping my ass and holding me high as I wrap my legs and arms around him, hanging on. He presses into me, taking my mouth in a heated kiss. I hear the door shut behind me and vaguely realize he must've kicked it shut because his hands are squeezing me, kneading my cheeks roughly.

He slams my back against the door, using it as leverage to get one hand free. He dips his free hand under my sweater, tracing my hip, up my side, and finally grabbing a handful of my breast. His thumb swipes across my lace-covered nipple, already hard for him, and I arch for more. "Fuck . . . Keith . . . fuck, I can't—"

He pulls me to him and holds me against the door, leaning his head back to meet my eyes.

"Tell me no, Elise," he grates out, control and choice battling in his eyes and his voice. "Tell me to put you down and stop this. Because if you don't, I'm gonna fuck you. This is my point of no return. I fucking need you."

The last part is nearly a whisper, and I'm not sure he meant to say it, but as much as he needs me, I need him more . . . need him to fuck me, make me come apart under his hands. His tongue. His cock.

I cup his face and try to insert some steel into my voice to show that I'm doing this of my own free will. "Put me down."

I can feel the power it takes him to do it, how much he doesn't want to, but he does, letting my pussy slide down every inch of his rock-hard abs and cock. His fists are on either side of my head, knuckles pressed to the door, his breathing so heavy I can feel it on my cheeks. "I need . . . an answer."

That's the sweet with the rough I want, that edge where he's in control but just barely, hanging on by a thread.

Once my feet touch the floor, I push him back just a half-step, giving me enough space to grab the hem of my sweater, pulling it up and off before dropping it to the floor next to us.

I meet his eyes again, my fingers fidgeting with the hem of his tank top. "Didn't want you to ruin my sweater. Keith, yes. I need you, too."

I see the instant he recognizes what I said, his feral grin hot for a split second before he growls. "Fuck!"

Grabbing me and tossing me over his shoulder, he strides further into the house, an area I haven't seen before, but now, it's upside down and my attention is mostly caught by the way Keith's back and ass are flexing under my weight as he moves.

I get a sense of a dark blue bedroom before he tosses me unceremoniously onto the bed, and I bounce. If I wasn't so turned on, I'd be giggling and yelling, but right now, what I want is to be fucked as hard as Keith can give me.

"Pants. Off," he orders, his voice iron-hard. I hear the undertone. He asked, I gave him control, and now . . . I'm *his* to do with as *he* wishes. My choices are over for now.

I'm already hurrying to do what he says, but as he rips his tank over his head, I freeze, taking in the picture in front of me.

His chest is broad, covered in tattoos that would take my tongue hours to trace, and I make a note to do just that. His stomach ripples with muscles, lines and ridges that all flow together before dipping down to a V on the lower half. The lines disappear into his sweats, which are tented with obvious evidence of his arousal.

Keith cups his cock through his pants, blocking my sight for a moment, and I look up, knowing my desire is all over my face. But it's all over his face too, his blue eyes intense and focused on my still legging-covered pussy.

"Take them off," he warns me, his jaw clenching. "Or I'm gonna rip them off and tie you up with them. I need to see your pussy, taste you, feel you come on my tongue. Last warning."

I wiggle, trying to slip the leggings off gracefully, but I'm distracted by Keith's hand rubbing up and down his cock through his pants.

When I finally get my leggings down to my knees, Keith gives in and grabs them, pulling them the rest of the way off before grabbing my knees. He spreads me wide, leaning in close enough that I feel the brush of his nose through the lace as he inhales my scent.

His face is buried in me, and I feel his hot breath dance over the small holes in the lace and against my burning skin. "They match. Your pretty purple panties match your lacy bra. Did you do that for me, Elise?"

I bite my lip, not sure if I should tell the truth, but when he traces a finger along the fabric at my hip, I gasp, unable to hold back from him any longer. "Yes, for you."

"Mmm, naughty girl," he moans, pulling the hem of my panties to the side, exposing my pussy to his gaze. "Fuck, you're soaked for me. This tight, little pink pussy wants my throbbing cock, doesn't it?"

I don't answer this time because I can't, but I lift my hips toward Keith's mouth, and he takes my invitation, licking a long line up to my clit, circling it with the tip of his tongue before sucking on it hard. I cry out, balling the comforter in my fists as I buck my hips, desperate for him to do it again. "Please."

My wavering plea triggers him even more, and he yanks my panties off, immediately diving back in. Switching targets, he strokes his tongue over my outer lips, tasting my softness before using both hands to spread me wide.

With a jolt, his tongue pierces into me, and he finds a rhythm, fucking me with quick, stabbing licks as he moves a thumb up to tease my clit in small circles that drive me wild.

My body is thrashing back and forth on the soft bed, my head whipping from side to side as I rise higher and higher, but I need more. It's so damn good, but I'm greedy and I want more.

"More . . . Keith . . . please."

Keith hums, the vibration shooting sparks through my pussy, but he complies, pressing one thick finger into my pussy and licking at my clit lazily. He strokes his finger in and out, looking up into my eyes, his voice deep, water over gravel. "This what you need, Elise? Want me to fill your pussy with my fingers and suck your hard little clit?"

I reach for his head, trying to direct him where I need as I give in to begging. "Fuck. Yes, Keith."

Finally, he gives me what I desperately need, slipping in another finger to fill me and pumping them in and out, curling up to my front wall to hit that spot that makes me see stars. He takes my clit in his mouth, sucking hard and flicking the tip of his tongue across it so fast it feels like butterfly wings.

I curl up, my shoulders lifting off the mattress as every muscle in my body goes tight with how good it feels. I linger on the edge, feeling trapped in bliss before Keith hums and I'm rocketed over the edge, screaming out as I come. I shudder and shake helplessly, chanting his name and reaching for him, not sure if it's to make him stay between my legs or to make him move. Everything feels so good, but it's too much, overwhelming me with pleasure.

Everything unhinges, and I collapse back on the comforter, tears leaking from the corners of my eyes at the intensity. Keith kisses up my belly, dropping one wet kiss to each breast before kissing me hard, his fingers still softly thrusting deep inside me. I whimper, cupping his face as he pulls back, confidence and sex appeal radiating from every pore of his body.

"That was fucking delicious," he says softly, his fingers slowing. "Taste."

He takes his fingers out of my pussy, bringing them to my mouth. I don't even think. I just suck his fingers, licking and nibbling on the calloused pads.

Keith watches my mouth, licking his lips in anticipation. "Fuck, Elise. I want you to do that to my cock. Suck me down just like that, but if you do, I'm gonna come down your pretty throat. And I don't want that right now. I want to come deep in your pussy. It's all I've been thinking about."

I nod, writhing under him, but he wants more. "Tell me."

I moan, reluctantly taking his fingers out of my mouth to give him my plea. "Fuck me, Keith. God, please, fuck me. No mercy, no questions. Fuck me hard. Use me. Make me yours."

He stands, yanking me to the edge of the bed by my ankles and throwing my legs up high on his shoulders. Grabbing his waistband, Keith pulls his sweats over and down his cock, which springs out hard and already oozing precum like jewels from his tip. Just like I imagined, he's huge and gorgeous, thick veins running along the shaft that I know are going to light my nerves on icy delicious fire.

He grabs his cock in his hand, reaching beside him to the bedside table for a condom. I'm sad when he's covered, the beauty of him encased where I can't marvel at it. I want to foolishly plead for him to take it off, to take me raw, but then he teases my opening with his head and I completely forget. I don't need to see him. I need to feel him deep inside me.

I drive forward with my hips, my pussy trying to suck him in as I try to wrap my legs around him. Before I do, though, he reads my need and obliges in one deep thrust, going balls-deep and forcing every breath of air out of me in a gasp.

He stretches me just on the good side of pain, my eyes rolling up because it's so overwhelming. He doesn't give me a minute to adjust to his girth, immediately retreating and pumping back with force, his balls slapping against my ass. I can feel my inner walls clenching against him, desperate to feel every nerve turned on in ways they've never been before.

Keith grunts, his eyes never leaving my face as he thrusts harder and harder. "Squeeze me just like that. Fuck, Elise. You're so damn tight."

I try to do as he says, clutching at him, both with my hands on his forearms as he holds my hips and with the muscles deep inside me. He strokes into me, filling me with every thrust.

As he leans forward, pressing his body against me more and taking me fully, I bend my legs, folding myself in half as my knees roll next to my shoulders. I say a little prayer of thanks for my yoga habit as he pounds me even harder at the new angle, the head of his cock rubbing that spot inside again. A deep whine of hunger starts in my chest, and I stare up at him, my mouth dropping open as I feel myself caught helpless again, swept up in another orgasmic wave that'll shatter me when it finally crests . . . but I don't care as long as I feel him come first.

He grabs my hands, forcing them to the bed with our fingers entwined, and I realize I'm his total prisoner. This powerful man is pinning me to his bed, both with his hands and with his body as he speeds up, his strokes getting harder and more intense with each slap of our hips.

All I can do is take him, enjoy the sensation of every inch filling me up and the control he has over me.

"Oh, fuck," I force out between deep breaths that ripple through my entire body. "Keith, I'm gonna come."

His eyes are hard as he meets my heated gaze with a commanding shake of his head. "No, not yet. You come with me, when I say."

His voice is tight, so I know he's close, but I don't know if I can hang on as I thrash below him. "I—"

Keith lets go of one hand and grabs my jaw, just above my throat but still cutting off my words like a switch. "Look at me, Elise. Do not come yet. I want you to come all over my cock, squeezing me in your perfect little pussy. I want to ride out our pleasure together."

His words aren't helping me wait. He's teasing me on the edge even more. His hands tighten in mine, and his hips hammer me even harder, and as I cry out, unable to wait any longer, he roars as I feel him jerk inside me.

"Fuck, yes . . . Elise!"

I clench and squeeze as much as I can, lifting my hips to meet his as he slams against my thighs, working to prolong our orgasms together. Our eyes are locked, never leaving each other as we both pant our way through the pleasure and the return to earth.

A smile is already breaking across my face when I see the stern look on Keith's and I sober.

He grinds against me as he scolds me, his eyes still burning with desire. "Mmm, that was so damn good. But you came before I said to."

For a moment, I think he's kidding, and I tease back. "What are you gonna do? Punish me?"

He smiles back, but it's predatory, and a little chill mixes with the heat of his cock still pulsing inside me. "Yes. Yes, I am."

If this were any other man, I'd be pissed. As if he's in charge of me? I'll come when I damn well feel like it, and just count yourself lucky you got to be here for it.

But the tiny voice deep in the back of my mind reminds me about his punishment before and surprisingly, how much I liked it. He talks as if he wants me to be a good girl, but being bad sounds so much more delicious, so I consider playing a bit coy.

I let that voice win, smirking. "So should I turn over for my spanking then?"

Keith shakes his head, pulling his cock out of me, and I immediately want him back, feeling empty without him inside me. He slips the condom off, tying it off and tossing it to the trash, where it drops in like a jump shot.

"No," he says, turning his attention back to me. "I think I'm ready to come down your pretty little throat now. Don't flip over, Elise. Get on your knees."

So help me, I do. And eagerly, at that. Both because he told me to and because I really do want to taste him the way he tasted me.

He's already thickening again by the time I get on my knees, his gorgeous cock bobbing in front of me. Keith gathers my hair in his fist, and I look up at him through my lashes.

I stick the tip of my tongue out, teasing his head with the faintest touch and moan at his taste. "Mmm, you taste good too."

But Keith is done with teasing, all pretense gone as he pulls my head back, bending my neck so that I'm forced to look him in the eye. "Put your hands behind your back, Elise. Suck my cock down your throat and make me come. Take your punishment like a good girl."

I have a flashback to him saying that last night and how good that made me feel, and I know for Keith, I do want to be his good girl. I do as he instructed, clasping my hands behind my back and opening wide as Keith presses his cock into my mouth. He stretches my mouth too, my lips as wide as they can go, but I don't stop.

I hollow my cheeks, sucking him deeper and letting him direct my pace with his hold on my hair. He pushes into my throat, and I gag slightly, but Keith doesn't pull out. Instead, he retreats into my mouth just enough to let me breathe while he strokes my hair. "Shh, just relax. Breathe and let me fuck that sweet little mouth."

He doesn't ask, but he looks at me questioningly, so I blink, humming my agreement. Keith moans as his cock jumps in my mouth, making me feel . . . good. He starts slow, thrusting further with every stroke until he's deep in my throat. He holds me there for a split second, and I work to relax, wanting this, wanting to make him lose control. He pulls back with a shudder and then does it again, and again. I open up more, amazed at how much of him I can take, letting him invade my throat and take me fully.

The next time he holds me, pressed so close to his body that I'm forced to hold my breath, I swallow and hum again.

He loses it, that sexy control snapping like a rubber band as he grips my hair tighter and pistons wildly in and out of my mouth, growling. "Fuck. Swallow it, Elise. Swallow my cum like a good girl."

I gulp and suck as Keith roars his release, trying to catch every bit as he shoots his salty-sweet cum down my throat, but it's so much I lose some and it runs down my chin, dripping onto my chest. And he's still coming, holding himself deep in my throat again as he jerks. When he's depleted, he leans back, looking down at me with wonder in his eyes.

"God damn. That was . . ." I can tell he's searching for words, and then his mind settles and he smiles. "Mmm, good girl."

I grin, pleased that I've made him brainless. "Thank you. I aim to please."

As he watches, I use my thumb to gather the bit of seed on my chin, slipping it into my mouth with a moan of delight at his taste on my tongue. Then I rub the drops on my chest into my skin.

He groans at the sight and scoops me up from the floor, raising me to my feet and taking my mouth in a deep kiss. "Very good girl."

CHAPTER

Twelve

KEITH

IT FEELS strange yet appropriate to do the interview in bed, although I'm not sure if that was my idea or Elise's. Either way, it's a brilliant one.

As we curl up naked over delivered pizza, Elise turns to me, putting her voice recorder in the space between us. "So, we've done the history of Keith Perkins in article one. Article two is all performance-related, with an emphasis on the show experience I had at your local venue gig."

I raise an eyebrow at her, and she laughs, stretching out with one pink-tipped foot to kick me. "My entire performance?"

"I didn't include any of *that*, of course. Despite our current situation, I do know where the lines need to be drawn. And yes, none of what we've done tonight is ever going to see the light of day. I promise you."

There's a hint of something in her voice that I can't place. I grasp her chin in my hand, gentle but not letting her look away and hide from me. "Are you okay with where we are right now?"

She sighs, her eyes dropping, but she answers, scratching at her lovely hip as she does. "Personally, yes. Professionally, no."

I narrow my eyes, needing to understand. This is maybe even more important than even the interview itself. "Explain."

She drops her pizza to the box, climbing up to her knees and sitting back on her heels. I refuse to be enticed by the sight of her breasts pressed between her arms, but she's still so sexy and beautiful, it's hard not to notice.

"Okay, so look, there's this woman at my office, Francesca. She's ambitious, always wants the best assignments, and if I'm honest, she's a pretty good writer. But she gets the cherry assignments because she's sleeping with the boss. Our gross, older boss."

I'm looking at her, still not sure where she's going.

"And because she slept her way to those assignments, it doesn't matter how well she writes them. She could be Mark fucking Twain, and everyone will discount her because of the way she got there. I don't want to be that girl. I'm a good writer, and this series means something to me. It's my first shot at something real and not just . . . well, rumor mill tabloid fodder. And I think it means something to your fans and is good for your image. But I'm not the woman who trades for inside information on her knees."

My gut tightens as my blood boils. "Have I done anything to make you think this is a quid-pro-quo situation? That I'm going to tell you my deepest, darkest secrets because I fucked you?" I know my voice is too loud by the way she winces at my reply.

Elise's head drops, her chin almost touching her chest as she shakes her head.

My voice is hard, even as I work to quiet my volume. "Is that why you fucked me?"

I'm holding my breath as I wait for her to answer. She doesn't realize that it may be the most important question I've asked her the whole time I've known her.

Elise's eyes snap to mine, her cheeks flushing with anger as she squares her shoulders, glaring at me as she yells. "No! Of course not. That's why I'm so fucking torn up. I wanted this. Hell, I want to do it again right now. But I shouldn't when it could mess up everything I've worked so damn hard for. But you're just so damn . . . irresistible. You drive me fucking crazy."

I pounce on her in reply, slamming her to the bed underneath me and covering her mouth with a kiss, demanding entry and tangling my tongue with hers. Our bodies press together, and even though I've come twice in the past two hours, I can feel a tingle in my cock as it starts to raise its head again.

Once she's breathless and I know she'll be quiet for a second, I pull back, looking into her sapphire eyes. "You drive me fucking crazy too. No, we shouldn't be doing this. For more reasons than you know, but someone I consider pretty smart told me that if I fight this, I'll regret it. So I'll take what I can get with you, Elise. We do the interviews, you do the stories, and whatever this is . . . it's between us, not a thing to do with your work. Can you handle that?"

She bites her lip like she's actually considering what I've proposed, and at first, it pisses me off. I'm laying it all out there and she's fucking hesitating. But then I realize I'm not laying it all out there. And as much as I'm holding back, she's making a pretty ballsy career move by agreeing to be with me outside of the interviews, and suddenly, I appreciate that she's considering so carefully.

While she thinks, I decide to tilt the odds in my favor and I move in, suckling a spot in the curve of her neck I found that she likes, and she leans to the side, giving me more access. It's all I need. I know I've won. I give her tender skin a little more, biting gently, just enough to leave a mark, but I know it'll fade in minutes as I lick over the spot, soothing the sting.

Elise sighs happily, stroking her fingers down my back. "I can handle it."

I grin into her shoulder before pulling her back up to sit opposite me, and I sit back, recognizing that my cock is half-hard . . . guess I do need at least a little bit of time before I'm ready for full action again.

"Fine. You've got thirty minutes before I take over again . . . so hit me. What questions do you have?"

She looks flustered, my move from seduction to business making her spin. "What?"

I raise my eyebrows at her, teasing as I set a timer on my phone. "Thirty minutes. Twenty-nine and fifty seconds now. Better get some questions done or article three is gonna be a hard write." I scold her teasingly.

Elise laughs, going along with me, but not before teasing me back. "And what happens in thirty—twenty-nine—minutes?"

I let the smile drop off my face, the dark need shining through. "In twenty-nine minutes, I'm shoving you face down in this bed, grabbing your arms behind your back, and taking you again, banging your hips so hard your ass will be bright pink when you leave. Next question?"

I see her shudder, the heat rising between us already, but she rallies, pulling herself together. With a quick reset of the recorder between us, she starts.

"Okay, history . . . check. Performance . . . check. What about your personal life? What do you do when you're not on stage and not driving me crazy with want?"

I stutter, trying to figure out how I'm getting out of this when she's hitting too close to topics I'd rather leave alone. "What do you mean? Are you already turning stalkery on me?"

She laughs, shaking her head and pushing at my chest playfully. "No, but like, take me through a typical day, a typical week in the life of Keith Perkins. What do you do all day, all night?"

I hesitate, quickly trying to edit my day to leave out any mention of Carsen. "Well, I get up, get coffee, and run errands like everyone else. I normally work out just before lunch, and I spend a big chunk of the afternoon writing songs, playing music. I don't know, just usual stuff, I guess."

Elise is scouring my face, and I wonder if she can see through me. It has to be the biggest gap-filled schedule in history. I mean, seriously? I gotta figure out a hobby to throw in or something.

"Wow, that's really . . . boring," she says before laughing self-consciously. "What do you do that your fans would be surprised about or would like to read about? Hobbies, activities? Any secret fetishes?"

Whew, I guess I dodged that one a little. "If there was, I'm pretty sure that'd fall under our previous agreement about *not* being in the article," I say with a wink.

Elise grins, biting her lip even as her nipples crinkle at the meaning of my words. "Fair enough . . . thought I'd just slip that in there for my own curiosity. But really . . . hobbies, activities?"

I try to think of something. In the few seconds that I have to consider, I throw out a lot of ideas. Star Wars? Too nerdy. Pro wrestling? Please. Baseball cards? Where's my collection? I'm stumped and stumble for anything. "Well, not really a hobby, I guess, but I like being outside. I try to go camping, hiking, fishing, and hunting occasionally, that sort of thing. I've got a couple of ATVs and a parcel of land out in the mountains. I like to escape out there. No TV, phones, or Wi-Fi. It's just nature, clean air, and waking up with either the sun or my own body's needs. It helps me recharge away from everything. I always do that before and after summer tours, catch the spring blooms and the fall leaves turning colors. Makes everything else seem a little less impressive when you see the things Mother Nature can do."

I see her eyes soften as her mouth silently repeats what I just said, and I know she's mentally making a note for another quote. I like that she hears something important in the things I say. I work for days, sometimes weeks to make a song say just what I want to convey, but I rarely do that on the fly while talking to someone.

But somehow with her, it comes easily. I just open up, and what comes out seems to be right.

"Okay, my turn," I say, picking up a pepperoni and chewing it thoughtfully. "Why aren't you seeing someone?"

Her jaw drops, and she glowers at me, mock-outraged. Okay, maybe not quite mock. "That's not fair! I asked you an easy one and you're coming back with the big guns."

I flex my biceps at her, deadpanning. "Damn right, they're big guns."

She groans at the cheesy joke but turns thoughtful as she ponders her reply. "Okay, if I want honesty, I've got to give honesty. Just know that I'm already ready with my next question, Mr. Perkins."

I smile but gulp, glad that I've got a few moments to figure out how I'm going to get out of answering what she wants to know. I knew it was a risk, but I really do want to know the answer. Elise is so gorgeous, smart, and funny, I don't understand how someone hasn't snatched her up and slapped a ring on her finger.

"Well, I grew up an only child," she starts, looking shy again, "so initially, I was a little socially awkward. I had a good family, I told you about Grandma, but still, I was a little awkward at first. By high school, I'd figured out how to fit in, but I suspect that had a lot more to do with how I developed physically than emotionally."

She gestures to her bust and I make a low wolf-whistle. "Mmmhmm, I can see how you might be distracting for a teenage boy because you're damn well distracting a fully-grown man."

I'm teasing a little, but I feel my cock as it jumps in response to my eyeful of her lush tits.

Elise laughs, her eyes darting down to my rising third leg. "Yeah, well . . . high school was fine, and then I went away to college. I was . . . serious. At least more serious than people expected me to be. I guess because I'm blonde and a bit bubbly, people expect me to be an airhead or an easy lay. So I had to work twice as hard for professors to give me the grades I deserved, and I avoided guys for the most part because every time I'd try to date someone, I'd instantly get treated like brainless arm candy. I dated a bit after college, thinking it'd be easier once the frat boy mentality ended, and I did find a few guys who'd grown out of that. Including Trevor."

I try to hold in a growl when she says his name. I don't even know him, but I already hate him because his name is on her tongue. "Trevor?"

She smiles, seeing right through my question with a hint of amusement. "He's a chef, a really good one, actually. We met at a club. I was there for work . . . seeing who was out, what they were doing, and who with. He'd been there for a nightcap after a late closing. We hit it off, dated for a few months. But mostly, we just met at the club and hung out afterward."

I hear the code for 'fucking all night' and it riles me up even more. I know I'm not exactly planting a flag on new territory, but I know how I feel about the thought of her with other men. "What happened?"

She smiles sadly, fidgeting with the sheet. "He had an investor dinner. Invited me as his girlfriend, asked me to entertain the wife of the investor. Be the little lady for him. And I was happy. I was fucking proud to do that for him. Until the dinner." She shakes her head, remembering. "It was just the four of us. I thought it was going well. Everyone was talking, laughing, and when Trevor and the investor started talking figures, I was trying to help him, talking up the success he'd had, but he basically told me to shut up. Not in those words, but degrading enough. I sat there at that dinner and realized he didn't respect me at all. Just wanted me to sit still and look pretty, just another piece of arm candy. And so I got up, excused myself to the restroom, and walked out. When he called later, yelling about how I'd embarrassed him, I just told him goodbye and hung up. I still think I should've yelled, fought with him about it, but really . . . what would be the point in that? I'd already seen who he was inside, what he thought of me, and I was done. Better to just move on, right? That was about a year ago, and I just haven't found anyone who interests me since then." Her eyes meet mine, and she blushes. "Until now, I thought maybe I'd just missed the boat on good guys."

The silence that drops over us seems to press me toward Elise, enveloping me and urging me to take her in my arms and ignore the so-called 'professional' side of what we're supposed to be doing. My phone dings, the thirty minutes up, and with a breath of relief, I cup her chin in my hand, leaning in for a sweet kiss.

"You deserve so much more than that, Elise," I whisper when the kiss breaks and I pull back, just enough to look into her eyes. "I want to hear all the things you have to say. Truly."

She smiles, cupping the back of my neck and scratching lightly. "And you will . . . after. If I recall, you made me a promise?"

She purses her lips, daring me to renege on the words I spoke earlier. If it were anyone but Elise, I'd think there's no way they could go from such an emotionally revealing conversation to thinking about sex so quickly, but I can see the truth in her eyes. For her, everything was part of the foreplay that I teased her with during that first interview.

The vulnerability she shared, she needs to close it back off. We're seeing each other in a different light, accepting the complexities, but it's time to be vulnerable in a different way.

I kiss her softly one more time, a smacking sound as our lips caress each other, and I make sure she's good before pulling back, my voice hardening just the way we both need. "Elise. Lie on the bed, face down, and stick that perfect ass up in the air for me."

She grins hugely and immediately moves as I instructed, going even further and placing her crossed hands at her lower back for me. She remembers, and that sends another little thrill up my spine. She remembers exactly what I told her I was going to do to her sweet body, and if she's going to be this good then she deserves that I be just as good in return.

I line up behind her on my knees, running a fingertip down her spine and watch as she arches so prettily, her ass spreading a little, showing me a hint of her little pucker. I wonder if she's ever had her ass kissed before. If not, she's about to find out what it feels like.

I scratch my fingernails up her thighs to the globes of her ass, the skin smooth and unblemished, making me want to watch it pink up under my hand. Instead, I spread her ass wide, exposing her tight little asshole again and already wet pussy to my eyes. I dip down, kissing her cheeks, getting closer and closer to her asshole as she circles her hips, chasing my kisses, wanting my licks. "Oh fuck, Keith, what are you doing?"

"I'm going to make you feel amazing before fucking you as hard as your body can take," I promise. "Now . . . tell me if you want this."

Elise's breath catches, and she looks back. "I . . . yes. First time for everything, and you . . . yes."

My chest warms as I give her what she wants, licking a long line from her clit to her ass with the flat of my tongue, and Elise cries out, a shockwave wracking her body.

I rest my cheek on the fullness of one globe, watching as I use a finger to dip into her wet pussy, spreading her honey up to her asshole and circling it slowly.

"Have you ever been taken here, Elise?" I can feel her tensing underneath me, but she's lifting her hips toward my teasing finger and she whimpers softly.

"No, just . . . a finger once."

I groan, making up my mind. "Mmm, good girl. I'm gonna take this ass, Elise. Be the first one to fill you up, come deep inside you as you cry out at how good it feels. But not tonight. You need some prep before I can fuck you like that. Do you want that?"

She nods against the bed, and I can see her juices dripping down her thighs.

"Good. Now don't move."

I leave her there, face down, ass up in anticipation as I hop off the bed to reach the nightstand. I watch her eyes follow me, but to her credit, she doesn't move at all, ready for me to take her as I promised. I quickly roll the condom on, assuming my position behind her once again.

Moving behind Elise, I slip a finger deep inside her pussy, coating it and moving up to tease her ass. She shivers, whimpering again as I line up my cock with her pussy and slowly, oh, so slowly, slip my cock inch by inch into her, and my finger millimeter by millimeter into her ass. Her ass clenches, and she whines deep in her chest.

"Relax. Breathe and push against me. I won't hurt you."

I can feel her tensing, convulsing against the intrusion, and then with a big exhalation, she relaxes some. I go slowly again, slipping my finger in and out of her ass as I pump my cock in time until I'm seated fully in her, cock and finger. I stay still, letting her adjust to the fullness.

She cries out again, but it's in pleasure. "Yes."

"You okay?" I tease, wiggling my hips a little. "Think you can take it all?"

She grunts, turning to look back at me with all the sassiness that I'm already coming to appreciate. "I need you to move. Fuck, Keith . . . move."

I grab her crossed wrists with my other hand, pinning them to her back and giving me leverage as I piston my hips, slow and easy. I can feel her clenching around me, pushing her hips in time to fuck me back, and her pussy gets even wetter.

As I pump into her pussy, I start to move my finger in her ass, just little thrusts in and out, but she notices and arches even more. "You like that? You like my cock in your pussy and my finger in your ass? Filling you up. You want that? You ready for more?"

Her voice is hoarse as she begs, surrendering herself to me. "Fuck, yes. More."

I give it to her, thrusting faster and rougher, slamming into her pussy with everything I have, timing my thrusts in her ass to fill her completely and then leave her empty and wanting. "I'm going to let go of your hands, Elise," I grunt between deep breaths to keep up with my frantic, powerful fucking. "I want you to rub your clit, pinch your nipples for me. I'm going to overload your body, but you can take it. You can take it all, and hold on until I tell you to come. Can you do that for me?"

She nods, and I let go, watching with pleased delight as her hands move exactly where I told her. I can feel her fingers blurring across her clit, the pulses immediate around my cock and my finger. I speed up, slamming into her as I push her into the mattress, pounding her body with all of my strength.

"That's it. Your nipples, your clit, your pussy, your ass . . . all mine."

She cries out, and I know she's almost at the point of no return. I'm throbbing just as much, holding on with only the strongest of wills as I give her a couple more thrusts before I'm unable to hold out any more. I growl, my voice rough as I order her. "Come for me, Elise. Do it now."

I rain a handful of smacks on her ass cheek, feeling the gush as she comes, covering me down to my balls in her juices. Her muffled scream fills my ears, making me come too, shouting out my release as I bury myself as deep as I can go, pulse after pulse shooting from my cock.

The only thing that would make this even more perfect was if I was busting deep inside her, feeling her body taking all of me deep inside her.

In the almost reverent silence that follows, I pull out of her ass slowly, pressing my body forward to lie on top of her, still inside her sweet pussy.

I kiss her shoulder, her neck, her cheek as she recovers from the onslaught before she turns toward me, reaching up for a kiss on her swollen lips. I soothe them with a lick before nibbling her earlobe and tugging on it between my teeth. "Mmm, your thirty minutes starts now."

She laughs, sighing happily. "I'm renegotiating terms. Five-minute grace period between transitions. I . . . I can't even breathe right yet."

I lay another kiss to her shoulder before pushing up to take care of the condom and get a warm, wet washcloth, which I use to gently, carefully clean her. "I think we can do that. Deal."

We spend the whole night like that . . . talking about nothing and every-thing, then devouring each other again and again. Somewhere in the early morning, we fall asleep tangled in each other, her head pressed to my chest. But when we wake up, we do it all over again.

It's not always the same, but that doesn't matter. Whether it's me going down on her, her sucking my soul out through my cock, or any of the positions we end up in, it's all delectably perfect.

Eventually, after a particularly intense mid-morning session, I need a shower, but Elise elects to stay in bed, passed out from all the times I've taken her. I'm smiling as I shower, overjoyed at how good last night went. Elise is amazing . . . responsive, open, brilliant, funny, sweet. And most of all, her sass. She's everything I could ever want.

If only the timing were better and she wasn't a reporter who could crash my whole life to ashes. But as long as we keep this what it is, we should be fine. More than fine, judging by last night. I come out of the bathroom, releasing steam to the bedroom as I towel dry my hair.

I see the empty bed and grab a pair of sweats, thinking to track Elise down for a late breakfast.

As I walk down the hall, I hear it. Voices. Not just Elise. She's talking to someone. As I step into the kitchen, I see Elise, wearing one of my black workout t-shirts, so huge it drops down to her thighs, her obviously freshly-fucked hair pulled up in a messy knot on top of her head.

And she's smiling, talking to . . . Sarah.

Before I can say or do a single thing, the back door opens and Carsen comes barreling in like always, her voice announcing her long before her head pops around the corner. "Daddy! Guess what I did on my girls' night with Aunt Sarah?"

She freezes when she sees Elise, and I see everyone's eyes cut to me, Elise's jaw dropping as Carsen covers her mouth with her hands.

Fuck.

Thirteen

ELISE

THE FROZEN SILENCE stretches out for a seeming eternity, the four of us caught in some sort of crystalline pattern that binds us immobile but just needs a single tap in the right direction to shatter and set us free . . . if only we could.

I can see the fear on the little girl's face as she looks at me like I'm a monster, and Keith is looking at me with barely-contained fury. I'm not sure what's going on here, but I do know that the girl just called Keith 'Daddy.'

That changes everything in more ways than one. Before I can even let my mind roll through the possibilities, both professional and personal, Keith takes control of the situation.

He kneels to gather the girl in his arms, giving her a hug that seems to make her more nervous at first, judging by the way she's stiffens, her voice pleading as she hugs him. "Sorry, Dad. I'm so sorry."

Keith pats her back and then meets her eyes, stroking her hair with a feather-soft caress that tells me that no matter what, he loves this girl . . . his daughter. He. Has. A. Daughter. My mind races, jumping from question to question . . . *holy shit, how? I mean, I know the logistics. But with who? And why didn't he tell me?*

"It's okay, honey. It's fine. I'll take care of everything."

And I realize . . . *this* is the big secret.

With a frown that I can tell is as much fear as it is his being upset, he stands and introduces us. "Elise, this is Carsen and Sarah. Ladies, this is Elise."

I move forward to shake Sarah's hand first, figuring it's the safe move for right now. Things are in a very precarious balance, that crystal lattice I felt earlier starting to strain . . . if I don't want a disaster on my hands, I have to do things very carefully. "Keith's sister, right? Shane mentioned you back-stage, told a funny story about some chili dogs on tour."

She smiles at me, but it's tentative, especially as I move closer to Carsen and offer the girl my hand too. "Hi, Carsen. Nice to meet you."

She looks at Keith, but at his nod of approval, she takes my hand and shakes. "Nice to meet you, too," she says in a quiet voice. "Are you . . . the writer?"

I've never felt like this before, like everyone in the room is terrified . . . of me.

The girl who came barreling in, loud and vibrant, is now almost shivering as she clutches at Keith's waist.

Keith looks at Sarah but talks to Carsen, the siblings communicating through some form of telepathy that only they share. "Honey, Aunt Sarah is going to take you out for a bit of lunch. Let me finish talking with Elise here. And when you get back, I can't wait to hear all about your night out. Okay?"

She nods, silently moving over to Sarah and they walk back out the door, but as she goes, Carsen looks back once more. "Sorry, Dad."

Sarah looks between Keith and me, and I can feel the threat in her eyes, warning me not to fuck with her family. Seems alphaness runs in the DNA around here.

The door closes, and Keith rubs at his head, growling softly, looking like he's about to start head-butting the nearest hard surface to make the pain go away. "Fuck. Fuck. Fuck."

He walks out of the kitchen to the living room, and I follow, perching on the edge of the couch as he paces back and forth in front of me. He pauses as he identifies the path he's tracing in the plush rug and locks a stern gaze on me.

"Let's get this clear up front. What you just saw, what you just heard . . . that is not for public consumption. You can't include anything about it, not even a hint, in your articles."

It's an order, hard and fierce, but underneath the harsh tone, I can hear the pleading. It cuts me to the core, and I shiver. For a man like Keith to be reduced to begging for his daughter . . . she must mean the whole world to him. I know that no matter what, I can never do anything to hurt her. "I completely understand that, but . . . what the hell is going on? How does no one know that you're a dad? You have a daughter, Keith."

He starts pacing again, his right hand waving as if he's trying to pluck the words he needs out of the air. "It's a long story and not many people know it. But all of them are loyal to me. And they know that I would burn the world to ashes before I let anything happen to her. Promise me you won't write about her."

I'm torn because this is the dirt I've been tasked to find. This is my ticket to a ground-breaking interview series that could launch my career. But I know I didn't come by it the way I should have, and whatever Keith's story is, he has every right to keep Carsen a secret if he wants to. It's not moral—hell, it's not even right to expose Carsen. She's just a little girl, and judging by the way he's reacting, he definitely wants to keep her existence unknown.

I also hear the threat about burning the world, and I have no doubt that he'd do it in a heartbeat, me included in the flames.

"I promise," I solemnly say, holding my hand over my heart. "I won't write about her if you don't want me to. But I don't understand why she's such a secret. Tell me, Keith. Please. All the things we've already shared? Articles be damned, tell me."

Keith stops, seeing I'm being very serious, and turns to face me, his hands clasped behind his back. Probably to keep them from shaking as I see his shoulders twitching. "She's the secret I always keep. I don't let the world know about her because I want Carsen to have as normal a childhood as she possibly can. She goes to a regular school . . . without bodyguards. She can go to the park or the mall with her aunt and nobody knows who she is. Carsen comes on tour with me and can walk around in the crowd without a second glance. I want that for her . . . the gift of being just a normal kid. If people find out she's my daughter, all of that would change. Paparazzi would chase her, take pictures of her, and fans could approach her. I won't let that happen. I won't let my daughter be turned into some fucked up tabloid fodder celebutante."

I flinch, knowing that's why the vibe in the kitchen was so chilly. They'd all assumed that as a tabloid reporter, I would throw them under the bus and cash in on the big scoop, drastically changing their whole world with one broad sweep of my pen, exposing Keith's deepest secret.

I'll admit there was a tiny piece of me that considered it, but it's that deep, ugly part inside us all that plays devil's advocate, tempting the part that dreams of bigger and better things.

The larger piece of my conscience knows I would never reveal something like this if Keith doesn't want me to. I've been silent too long, my thoughts ping-ponging as I study all the angles of the problem, and Keith comes to stand in front of me, looming over me but somehow feeling as though he's begging on his knees.

I look up at him, and I can see it in his eyes . . . the pain, the fear, the confusion. I reach out, putting my hand on his stomach. "Keith, I won't write about her. I won't say a word. I promise. Will you tell me everything though? I feel like we've shared so much, our bodies and our souls naked as we've talked about everything. But this is huge. I feel like you've been hiding this big piece of who you are, even as I was telling you everything with nothing held back. This is about trust."

He sighs, sitting down in a chair next to me with his elbows on his knees, head hanging low. "All of this is a hundred percent off-the-record. I'm not kidding, Elise."

I nod, putting my hand over my heart. "As God is my witness, I promise you Carsen's name will never see the light of day."

Keith nods and begins. At first, his voice is slightly tentative, filled with pauses, and I'm reminded of how I sometimes type. "When I was a kid, I had a girlfriend, Janie. She was my high-school sweetheart. We wanted different things. She wanted to settle in our small hometown, and by then, I was already dreaming of Nashville and being a musician. When I left after graduation for Boise, it was amicable enough, I thought. We didn't know it at the time, but she was pregnant."

"How'd she . . .?" I ask, feeling stupid as soon as it leaves my mouth.

Keith shrugs. "I was a teenager, in love, and stupid. Anyway, shortly after I left, she moved away to live with her grandmother, keeping the pregnancy a secret. That sort of town, you understand. Only her parents knew and they were disappointed, wanted her to go away to her grandmother's too. She gave birth to Carsen and then stayed with her grandmother for almost two years after having her. The two of them did a great job raising Carsen. She was a lucky baby, loved and well cared for."

"She didn't tell you?"

Keith shakes his head. "But when Janie's grandmother passed away unexpectedly, Janie couldn't do it alone and didn't want to go back to her parents. She showed up on the doorstep of my crappy, rundown hovel of a studio apartment with an almost two-year-old toddler on her hip. I hadn't seen her in years by then.

"She begged for forgiveness, and it wasn't like I could turn her away. She had my daughter with her. She moved in that day. It was awkward at first. We didn't really have feelings for each other anymore, but we'd made this amazing little person together."

I can't help but give Keith a sad smile. In one short statement, he told me so many things about himself and the sort of person he is. It doesn't even matter about the rest. But still, I need to listen, to know the details. "What happened?"

"I did," Keith says softly. "I would go back and forth from being mad at Janie for taking those two years of Carsen's life away from me to thankful she'd done this selfless thing to let me chase my dreams unencumbered, even if she thought it was because I wouldn't be able to support them, financially or emotionally. I mean, I'd left her . . . them, even if I didn't know it . . . for what? To play in smoky bars for drunks for all hours of the night? But she gave me this incredible gift. Carsen stole my heart the moment I laid eyes on her.

"We'd been living together for about six months when Janie didn't come home after work one day. I was scared something had happened to her, but I had a gig at a new club, the biggest one I'd ever played. I had to leave Carsen with a neighbor, and I called Janie over and over between sets."

"No answer," I say, reading where this is going.

Keith shakes his head again, his voice hitching as I see tears well up in the corners of his eyes. "The next morning, her parents called me. Janie had been walking home, crossing the street, and a drunk driver hit her before running into a pole. Janie didn't make it. She died instantly. The driver died too. The police had called Janie's next of kin, her parents. Not me, because I wasn't her husband. I was just the father of her child whom she lived with."

I can see the hurt in his eyes, and my heart aches to soothe Keith's pain. So much pain, more than any one man should have by himself. "Keith, I'm sorry."

He nods, plunging ahead because he has to unburden himself of this weight. "It messed me up bad for a while. Luckily, Janie's parents were fine with Carsen staying with me. They could've fought me for custody, especially since I was barely scraping by back then. But they agreed that Carsen needed to be with her father. I think they felt guilty over what happened with Janie before she left home, and having that reminder wasn't something they could handle. That's when Sarah came to Boise to help me. She stayed with me in that shack of a room, taking care of Carsen. Hell, taking care of *me*. And that's when I got another call.

"That night, the same night Janie had been hit . . . there'd been an A&R at the new club and he'd liked my sets. He told me to get my ass to Nashville, that I was good, had potential but had some growing to do."

A&R . . . industry term for a talent scout. "What did you do?"

Keith laughs bitterly. "I was in bad shape, but Sarah knocked some sense into me, literally and figuratively. So we moved to Nashville, the three of us. I played there for a while, learning as much as I could, and one night, that same guy came in. That's when I got a contract and the machine of my 'career' started really turning. At first, it wasn't really a conscious decision to keep quiet about her. But when things started happening fast, I realized how quickly my life was changing and was scared what that would do to her. I wanted her to have as normal a life as possible."

"How many people know about Carsen?" I ask curiously. "The record company has to know."

"Their lawyer does. It's part of the whole copyright estate thing," Keith says, "but not too many people, actually. Only those I truly trust."

He doesn't have to say it, but I'm obviously not one of those people, but now I know too. He's quiet, the weight of everything he just said heavy in the room as I digest it all.

"So? What do you think?" he asks. "Devoted father? Misguided fuckup?"

I stand, moving in front of him, and kneel down between his legs to bring myself to the same level and look him directly in the eyes. "I think you sound like a wonderful father who loves his daughter very much."

"Thank you." I can feel his relief at my positive judgment. "I haven't told anyone this in a very long time. Elise, can I trust you with this?"

There's no doubt in my mind or my heart as I nod, taking his hands. "I know that even though I'm saying yes, you'll have doubts. That it'll take time for you to trust me. But Keith . . . yes. I will never tell, and if I can, I'd like to get to know you more, and Carsen too, if you're okay with that?"

He scans my face, looking for any trace of lie, but I'm telling the truth. I may not quite understand Keith's vehemence at keeping Carsen a secret, but if that's what he wants, I can support him and not be the weapon of destruction that obliterates the normal life he's built for his daughter over the last decade.

He leans forward, kissing me softly but holding my chin firmly in his palm. After a moment, he pulls back. "Thank you."

I press my lips to his once more, relief and joy filling my heart. "Thank you for telling me. I know you're scared."

A thought occurs to me, and I smile as I lean back. "Is this why? I mean, why you don't date?"

He dips his head once, smirking a little. "Carsen has already had it so tough. Too many deaths, and then she's forced to keep this big secret so that her life can stay the way it is. That's heavy for a kid. She's happy the way things are, so I want to keep it that way. I promised to keep my focus on her and my music, make things as simple and easy for her as I can."

I sit back on my heels, putting my hands on top of my thighs and tilting my head questioningly. "But what about you? Don't you deserve to be happy too? It's good for kids to see their parents loved and in love. That's how they learn what a relationship can be. Did it ever occur to you that by locking yourselves away, you're taking away both of your opportunities to have that? You're teaching her that to be a good parent, you have to be a martyr."

"No, I never thought about that until recently," he admits, looking a bit shell-shocked by what I've said. "Giving Carsen a normal life has just always been the priority. But it seems you and Sarah share the same point of view. She said something very similar to me. Let's say it pushed me over the edge toward us . . . you know." He lets out a huff. "This is all just a bit overwhelming."

"Points for your sister. I owe her a box of chocolates or something," I reply. "You're not the only one feeling overwhelmed. Because I just found out that the guy I'm head over heels for is not only majorly out of my league, but he's a fucking awesome dad who takes great care of his daughter."

He smirks at me, leaning forward, and his aura of confident command slips back into place like a familiar glove. "Head over heels?"

I bite my lip, again blushing furiously. "Uhm, can we pretend like you didn't hear that? I feel like we've maybe done enough expose for the moment. Oh, speaking of expose . . ."

He looks at me, his eyes narrowing, but I at least seem to have distracted him from my slip of the tongue. "Two things. One, on the article front . . . we really are going to have to come up with something more exciting than fishing as a hobby. I don't know, maybe like you're into bows and arrows or something?"

"I've shot a bow three times in my life," Keith says but shrugs.

I grin, figuring we can come up with something. "And two, can you maybe tell Carsen I'm not the boogieman? She looked terrified of me."

He laughs a bit, and it sounds foreign after the deep conversation we've just had. He pulls me into his lap, my legs hanging off the side of the chair as he wraps his arms around me, his hands resting lightly on top of my ass.

"What's wrong with fishing? I like to fish. And yeah, I can talk to Carsen about you. She knows to avoid questions, so I think she felt bad that she accidentally spilled the beans."

I smile, feeling something pressed against my panties that certainly tells me Keith's accepting this more and more. "Well, she probably wasn't expecting to find me in your kitchen in the middle of the morning."

Keith growls, nuzzling into my neck. "I think I like you in my kitchen. And in the living room. And in my bedroom. Shit, definitely in my bedroom."

He nibbles at me, tickling my neck, and I squeal, squirming as I playfully fight back even though I love it. He pauses, looking at me intensely. "Are we okay, Elise? Really?"

I scratch my fingers through the morning scruff on his face and over the slight prickle of hairs on top of his head as I meet his eyes. "Yes, Keith. We're okay. Except that Sarah and Carsen are going to be back soon and I'm still wearing just your t-shirt and nothing else. Awkward. Especially since you're making my panties wet again."

Keith hums, squeezing my ass tightly. "Can't have that, now can we?"

With a single exhilarating swoop, he stands, holding me with one arm under my knees and one behind my back. "Seems like a quick shower is in order. Maybe I can help with your back?"

I purr, scratching the back of his neck lightly. "You can help everywhere."

EVEN THOUGH ELISE is dressed again, in the same leggings and pale blue sweater she wore here yesterday, it's still awkward when Sarah and Carsen pull up out front as I'm kissing Elise good-bye.

Apparently, the shower wasn't fast enough even though we really did just wash up. Our bodies spent from the night and morning and our minds racing with all the revelations, we just soaped up and rinsed off. Although I did take my time helping Elise dry off. Thoroughly.

With one more soft kiss, she bounds down the front steps toward her car, waving shyly at Sarah and Carsen, but the truth is in her eyes, which are shining bright. Her words come back to me . . . *head over heels.*

There's still a lurch in my gut, a moment of worry rearing its dark head. What if she's bounding off to go tell her boss she just got the best story ever and that's why she's so damn happy? I shake my head, letting the thought go. I need to trust her. She said she would keep this secret, and everything about her said she was telling the truth. The look in her eyes . . . if I'm to ever become the man I want to be, the father I want to be, I need to trust those eyes.

Sarah gives me an appraising look as they come inside, her face neutral even as she looks at me hopefully. "Well, how'd it go?"

For some reason, I decide to be playful. "Well . . . I hear that they've got good land for sale in Costa Rica, and we can live there for the rest of our lives quite well."

Sarah sticks out her tongue and punches me in the shoulder. "Come on, I'm being serious!"

I grin, putting an arm around her shoulders. "Better than expected, for damn sure. She says she'll stay quiet about the whole thing. I want to believe her, but I might've also been a bit threatening."

Sarah grins, elbowing me in the side. "Threatened her? I'm thinking that didn't go over too well."

Actually, she climbed into my lap and told me her panties were wet . . . "Well, okay . . .maybe I didn't exactly threaten *her*. Just told her that I'd burn the world to ash to protect Carsen if need be."

Sarah pats my chest, smiling. "That's not a threat. That's a promise, because I'd be there with the matches to help you light the flamethrower."

We walk in the kitchen, where Carsen is already sitting, a pen and piece of paper in front of her on the table. She's all business. "Again, I'm so sorry. I didn't expect that you'd have, uhm, company when I came in."

She's blushing, but she continues, looking more like the world's smallest lawyer or politician than a little girl. "What's the fallout? Whatever needs to happen, I understand. But please, please do not make me change schools."

She's poised like she's going to take notes on some new security protocol, and it makes me grin, but it also makes my heart ache. Most of the time, I still see her as the little thing that used to curl up in my lap and fall asleep to cartoons.

But she's growing up, too. And she needs to know that life is more than sneaking around to avoid the media. In that, maybe I do need to change, while still figuring out how to protect her. And I thought learning how to play guitar and sing at the same time was hard. "Carson, baby. It's okay," I tell her, cupping her face. "This is your home and you did what you have every right to do. I'm sorry that I've put you and Sarah in a tough spot, but I talked with Elise. She's agreed to not write or say anything about you."

Carsen's frown softens, and she looks like she might actually smile. "Really? That means I can stay at my school, right?"

I nod, taking her hand and giving it a squeeze. "Yes, we'll ride it out for now. I trust Elise and I think we should have faith that it's all gonna be fine." Maybe that's not entirely true yet, but I'm hopeful and I think parents are allowed to paint an optimistic picture for their kids. At least I hope so, because I'm trying hard to be positive here and not freak out now that Elise is gone, maybe putting my family on the news.

Carson nods, grinning. "Okay, if you say so. Is Elise like . . . your girl-friend now or something? Do you love her?"

Wow, what a lot of stuff to dump on my head at once. The little girl who's had my heart her entire life, asking all this stuff about Elise . . . how the fuck do I answer this?

I need to reassure her that nothing has changed, that she's still my prior-ity, but the things Elise said about being a good example, not a martyr, come back to me. Besides, I do need to be honest . . . I know I feel something for Elise, I just don't know what yet.

"Baby, it's still soon to say I love her, but I like her a lot. And that's new for me, maybe enough for now. I don't think I could fall in love with a woman unless you got along with her too. You're the most important thing to me, Carsen."

She smiles, giving me that look that I'm sure all parents get when their children think we're talking like a silly, senile idiot. "I know that. But if you like her a lot, and you want me to get along with her too, don't you think I should meet her? I mean, more than just a freak-out in the kitchen where I froze like a dork? I want to meet her."

I look up to Sarah for her opinion but she shrugs her shoulders. I think back to what Sarah told me before about living a little, having a bit of fun, and what Elise told me about showing Carsen what a relationship should look like, and my decision is easy.

"Okay, baby. Elise said she wanted to meet you too, and to let you know something."

"What's that?"

I lean in, whispering in her ear. "She says she's not the boogieman. So . . . is dinner good?"

Carsen looks like she's thinking for a minute, and I kick myself a little. For fuck's sake, the kid just caught Elise half-naked in our kitchen two hours ago. Even if she's asking to meet her, I need to slow my roll here and not move too fast. But my daughter surprises me every time. "Yeah, but we're gonna need the supplies to make s'mores out back if she's coming for dinner. Oh, and Aunt Sarah? You need to make those chipotle chicken wraps you kick butt with."

I laugh. She's not reconsidering. She's making the damn menu. I smile at her, ruffling her hair. "All right, kiddo. We'll get the supplies. But also, let me call Elise, see if she's available for dinner tonight, okay?"

Carsen rolls her eyes. "She's your *girlfriend*, Dad. Of course she's available."

Sarah snickers, and I can read her face clearly. *If only things were that easy.*

———

When the doorbell rings as dinner approaches, I'm nervous. I've never done this, introduced someone I'm interested in to my daughter. Hell, I never thought I would do this, at least not while she's still a kid.

But fate intervened, I guess, and here I am. I'm excited for Carsen to get to know Elise though. I think they'll like each other.

At least I hope they do or I'm fucked. Elise looks stunning. Her hair is pulled up, but curls cascade down her back and her cheeks are flushed. She's wearing a pink tank top that shows a hint of her cleavage, but she's thrown on a sheer jacket with a floral design all over it that dips long in the back over her jean-covered ass and a pair of white Chuck Taylors.

It's more 'city chic' than what I've seen her in before . . . but it's cute and I like it. She looks sweet and sexy, all rolled up into one tempting package. "Come in," I greet her, taking her in my arms. "You look beautiful."

I kiss her lips lightly, aware that we probably have an audience spying from the kitchen. So I keep the kiss quick, and Elise hums. She probably understands. "Thank you. And thanks for actually greeting me instead of stomping off like Conan the Barbarian."

I chuckle. I have been a bit of a grumpy ass. I look down at her, lowering my voice just in case. "You ready for this?"

She smiles, her lips wavering a bit, but she nods. "Yes. I'm ready."

I take her hand, holding it between us for a split second before turning and leading her into the kitchen, where Carsen and Sarah both scuttle back from the edge of the doorway. Busted, you little spies.

Sarah recovers first, offering a hand again but with a decidedly warmer tone than earlier. "Nice to meet you, Elise. I'm Sarah, this big oaf's sister."

I can feel the tension in Elise's hand lighten at the casual comment, and I make a mental note to thank Sarah later for making this easier. She's always known how to help make things easier for me.

Elise shakes, then offers her hand to Carsen. "Hi, Carsen. Your dad said it was your idea to invite me over for dinner, so thank you for the invitation. And I heard something about s'mores?" she asks, looking around the kitchen. "Mmm, I love s'mores."

It's perfect. She's not treating Carsen like a little kid but is being genuine and treating her like the young lady she is, as much as I forget that sometimes. We head outside to the backyard. It's one of my favorite family places around the house, a large flagstone patio with a fire pit and loungers that opens up to a green yard, blue pool, and a hot tub. "Whatcha think?"

"Can I live in your hot tub?" Elise jokes. "That thing's bigger than my bathroom."

"No peeing in the pool!" Carsen declares somberly before grinning. "But sure!"

I assume my place at the grill to get the chicken going, Sarah having already made her chipotle rub. "Hope you like things hot and spicy."

Elise smirks and glances over at Sarah. "Does he know what he's doing?"

Sarah laughs, nodding. "With the grill? Yes, he's a total pro. With teasing you? Well, I'm just going to pretend he's innocent."

They laugh, and I'm glad to see they are starting to bridge the gap between them. Carsen brings me the chicken, and I pat her on the back before letting her get to know Elise.

"Elise?"

"Yeah, Carsen?"

"So you love my dad?"

I'm surprised and glad I haven't had a drink yet or else I'd choke. I know I should jump in to save Elise, but I'm kinda curious what she'll say. Instead, I just lay out another chicken breast and adjust the fire to the right level.

Obviously, she doesn't love me, despite her earlier slip of tongue. It's too soon for that, but we've definitely got something here, I think. Whatever the original reason we met, whatever the excuses we've used to start talking, we've left the idea of it being just an 'interview expose' long behind. So I'm interested to see what she'll say.

I can feel Elise's eyes on my back, but I'm not letting on for a second that I'm eavesdropping and instead pretend to mess around with one of the chicken breasts. Still, I'm holding my breath for her answer.

"We haven't known each other that long, but I definitely like him," Elise says with frank and open honesty that warms my stomach. "I want to get to know him better. You too, if that's okay?"

I hear Carsen hum, and the smile in her voice is evident when she replies. "I'd like that too. I asked him the same question."

"Oh, and what did he say?"

Carsen laughs. "I can't tell," she replies sassily. "I can keep a secret."

Elise laughs back, obviously 'served.' "You got me. I can keep a secret too, though. I promise, Carsen."

The last bit is solemn, truth in her every word. I hear it, and Carsen must too. She lowers her voice some, but she's like me, she's got a terrible whisper that tends to carry. "He said he likes you too . . . a lot."

I can't help it. I have to know Elise's reaction, so I look over my shoulder, ignoring the grill temporarily. My tongs clatter, and Elise hears me, so I see her looking at me like I just caught the moon, a wide smile on her face and her eyes glittering.

"Is that so?" she says. "Well . . . let's see how he cooks before I say anything else. I'm a liberated woman. I want a man who can at least cook for me once in awhile."

Conversation continues, with me mostly butting out to let the ladies get to know each other. Maybe, just maybe, I put a little extra attention into the chicken so that by the time we sit down at the big table, dinner looks scrumptious.

"Well, what's the verdict?" I ask after two minutes of silence.

Elise looks up, wiping the corner of her mouth. "I'd say . . . I like it a lot."

Carsen giggles and forks some sliced and grilled corn. "Just wait until Dad makes s'mores. He does them just right, browned and not flamethrowers."

"What if I like flamethrowers?"

"Everyone likes a good flamethrower," Sarah jokes, inserting herself. "Useful for . . . difficult ex-boyfriends."

"Oh, I'd love to hear that story sometime," Elise says with a wink. "Just in case."

I swallow, getting up. "I think I'll go get the marshmallows and stuff."

The only regret I have as the four of us toast and prepare our s'mores is that I'm not using a real wood fire. Maybe another time, I could take Elise out camping, do it right.

Nobody complains about the lack of smoky hints though, and I notice after she's finished that Elise has just a little smear of chocolate and marshmallow on the corner of her mouth.

"Hold still," I growl, leaning in close. Elise smiles as I kiss her, licking the sticky mess before tasting her even more delicious mouth.

Carsen groans, pretending not to gag. "Ugh, LD moment."

Elise laughs, pulling back a little. "Uh, what's a LD moment?"

"Lovey-dovey," Carsen explains in that *adults are so ignorant* voice. "It means get a room. Some of us are innocent. Like Aunt Sarah."

We all burst out, but I have to know something. "Carsen, do you know what 'get a room' means?"

She smirks, nodding. "Yep, it means you're grossing everyone out with your kissy faces, so go kiss somewhere else. I have watched Netflix, you know."

"Yep, that's exactly what it means, little daughter of mine. And yes, your aunt is totally innocent."

Sarah, Elise, and I stifle giggles at her innocence, and I'm reminded again just how sweet this age is, on the cusp of teenage drama but still young and naïve. With her Netflix comment, though, I make a mental note to double-check the parental control settings. A dad can't be too safe with his little girl.

I know it's impossible, but I want to preserve this time for Carsen as long as I can. It's sweeter and better that way.

After the mess of s'mores, we clean up and Carsen heads upstairs for a shower.

"What do you think?" I ask Sarah as we clean up the dishes, Elise outside wiping down the table.

"I think . . . good job, baby brother," Sarah says. "I like her so far."

I tell Sarah goodnight and watch with joy as she gives Elise a hug. "He's a good one," she says when they part. "Stubborn as a damn mule, but good. Don't break his heart."

Elise shakes her head, not letting go of Sarah yet. "I won't. I know he's a good man."

Sarah heads home, and as soon as the front door closes, I grab Elise to my chest, hugging her tight.

"Think it went okay? Did they like me?" she asks as I run my hands down her back.

I kiss the top of her head, nodding. "It went better than okay. They loved you. I think Carsen is gonna hold you to that promise to teach her to knit though."

I can feel her smile as she lays her head on my chest, humming happily. "I hope so. I meant it. I haven't done a single stitch with anyone since my grandmother died. It'd be nice to share it with someone else, even if only for a minute. I think Grandma would like that."

We're quiet for a minute, just swaying in the foyer as we hold each other tight. I feel a little torn. I want to invite her to stay . . . but at the same time, it's so fast. Maybe taking a few hours' break might do some good, let this all settle in. For Elise, for me, and mostly for Carsen. I definitely don't think she's ready for her dad to have sleepovers.

"Thank you, Elise," I say, my voice gravel as I resist letting her go. "This was better than I ever would've dared dream. And right now, even though I know you should go home and have a good night's sleep in your own bed, the only thing I can think of is taking you upstairs and burying myself inside you, telling you thank you over and over again."

Elise pulls back, looking up at me and placing her hands behind my neck. "Thank you. You let me into your story, your family, your world tonight. And I know that's not something you do lightly. And as much as I'd love for you take me upstairs right now, we shouldn't. It was a big night for Carsen too. Be with her tonight. Make sure she's okay with all of this."

One statement, and it sums up how she's breaking down my every wall, every defense. Whatever fucked up gossipy rag story brought us together, Elise is good at her core. She cares about people, about my daughter and how she's doing after a good but pretty risky night.

"Good idea . . . but still," I growl, backing her up against the door, taking her mouth in a passionate kiss. I gather her hands in mine, pressing them to the door above her head, forcing her to arch. I hold her there with one hand, the other moving down to cup her throat, lifting her chin up to meet me, kiss for kiss, breath for breath.

I'm not even sure whose air I'm breathing anymore. It's ours, mixed between the two of us in panting gasps as we fight for more from each other.

I press against her, grinding my cock against her softness, and she gasps. I take advantage and dip my tongue in to taste her. It's hot, heavy, and heady and I want more.

But we can't, not tonight.

Not with Carsen here, especially when I need to check in with her and make sure she's okay with all of this. With a groan of unsatisfied frustration, I pull back and press my forehead to Elise's.

"When can I see you again?" I groan, my control wavering. "Because it's stupid, but I need you soon. I can't imagine going to sleep without us coming together."

Elise's eyes are still locked on my mouth as she licks her lips, and I know exactly what she's thinking. With a blink and shake of her head, her eyes clear. "Huh? Oh, I should go into the office tomorrow. Write the next article, and I need time to work in your 'dirt' without exposing your real side. How about the day after?"

I think for a second, knowing it's probably for the best. "That works.

What about if we go out to my little piece of land, ride ATVs or hike? We could get you a bit of 'behind-the-scenes with Keith Perkins, Country Star' out there for the next article. And then, there's a little cabin. It's rough, but we could stay overnight."

Elise smiles like she just won the lottery. "That sounds like the best plan I've heard in ages. Except . . . by rough, you do have plumbing, right? And heat?"

I laugh, letting go of her hands. "So high-maintenance. Yes, there's plumbing and electric. Heat is handled by a wood stove, but it's a small cabin so it's enough. Besides, if you get cold, I can probably come up with some ways to warm you up."

CHAPTER

Fifteen

ELISE

AND SO, *in an ironic twist, the story that brought us into contact with Keith Perkins was easily explained.*

I pause, pondering before highlighting the whole paragraph and deleting it. "Nope, just won't do."

"What won't do?" Maggie asks, making me jerk my head up. "Let me guess, Keith's got a girlfriend?"

Ouch, close to the bone. "No, it's not that," I reply, lying my ass off while trying to distract my friend. "I just . . . I have a lot of information, and it's been harder trying to figure out what's supposed to go in this one and what goes in the next one."

Maggie nods, taking a seat on the edge of my desk, a familiar spot for her. "So what's his big secret then?"

I smirk, knowing I'm lying, but it's the lie that Keith said was okay when I texted him. "He was out running errands, and if you can believe it, his maid was having a bit of a situation and he was just doing her a favor."

"Uh, by buying half the aisle?" Maggie asks, lifting an eyebrow. "Nice boss. I think if I had that problem, Donnie's response would be to ball up a copy of *The Times* and chuck it at me." She doesn't sound remotely convinced.

I shrug, wanting to change the subject as quickly as possible because the more I think about it, the more ridiculous it sounds. "Keith's just boring, really. His only unusual hobby is archery. Next time, I'm going to get some shots of him practicing. But other than that, he's just a normal guy. So . . . what's with your face?"

"My face?" Maggie asks, rubbing at her cheeks. "What's with my face?"

I look closer, squinting as I confirm my suspicions. "You're . . . glittering. What the hell have you been up to?"

"Oh, well . . ." Maggie says, blushing. "That undercover at the senator's office didn't pan out, so Donnie has me following another angle. There's this club out by the airport, Petals of Heaven—"

"Oh my god, Donnie has you, of all people, at a strip club?" I ask, gleefully shocked. "I mean, not that you don't look the part but . . . well . . ."

"Don't worry, I'm not stripping," Maggie reassures me. "I'm a cocktail waitress, so the glitter's more for showing up under the blacklights."

"What does Donnie have you out there doing then?" I ask, worried. I've heard of Petals. It's one of those places where you don't ask questions most of the time. You don't want to piss off the owners.

"They get a lot of celebrity patrons, apparently," Maggie says, waving her hand. "One of Hollywood's big *family* men, in particular, has been in three nights in a row now, having himself a particularly good time in the private rooms in the back. I don't have pics yet, but I think I'll be able to. Someone's going to have some explaining to do!"

"Wait, what is this?" I ask, surprised. "You're liking this assignment, aren't you? Our innocent little librarian has a naughty streak to her? What happened to the Maggie who was scandalized when someone told her that her ass looked good in a dress?"

Maggie blushes and shrugs. "She's still there. I guess I get caught up in the fun of the bust, that's all. Speaking of busts, tell me how the interviews with Keith are going. I need boring and nice right now, honestly."

I lean back in my office chair, humming. "He is nice, actually. Still sometimes a bit of a commanding asshole, but . . . well, it's the good kind of commanding asshole. I'm feeling good about the interviews."

"Feeling good, huh?" Maggie asks, lifting an eyebrow. "Sounds like you're feeling good about *him*. You starting to like him?"

"No!" I protest, maybe a bit too strongly. There's no way I'm going to let anyone, even sweet little Maggie, think that I'm getting this story Francesca-style. I can't even let them think that I'm interested in Keith. "I just . . . it's nice to be pleasantly surprised, that's all. He's hot but boring."

"I see. Well, I think—" Maggie starts, but before she can finish, I hear a yell from down the hall.

"ELISE!"

"Oh, great, what's he want?" I mutter, looking at Maggie. "Any ideas?"

"Maybe Donnie wants to say great job and give you a raise?" Maggie asks, then grins. "It'd be a first, but hey, miracles *do* happen."

"We'll see," I answer as I get up. "See you later."

I head down the hall to Donnie's office, where I find him behind his desk, popping jellybeans into his mouth. "What can I do for you, Donnie?"

"Have a seat," he says, pointing as if I don't know where the chair is. "I wanted to talk about your third article."

"What?" I ask, surprised. "Donnie, I barely got the outline done and sent in to you."

It's company policy that all articles other than editorials need to be outlined and sent in to Donnie after the website got burned to the tune of a half-million dollars for not verifying a claim. It could have been worse.

"I know, I checked it over," Donnie says, popping another jellybean, this one black licorice by the looks of it. "And while I normally let you just run with your gut, you always back up your shit. I'm worried this time."

A compliment and a concern in one sentence. That's a first. "What're you worried about? There's nothing that'll get us a lawsuit in there."

"That's exactly it!" Donnie exclaims. "Elise, we won't get sued, but we won't get read either! This article . . . it's boring as fuck. My God, a story about the Pope's diet would have more sizzle than this! This is just . . . listen, if I wanted to read this type of fawning bullshit, I'd buy *People!*"

"What can I say, Donnie?" I ask, ignoring his dig. "This series is different. It's good, I think. More in-depth and driving readers with a real insight into Keith. His music, his life, let them really get to know the man. I've included some interview snippets from some calls I made to his manager and some of the club owners from Boise and Nashville that he used to play in, to give the readers a sense of how much he's grown."

"Growth . . . now you sound like *Reader's Digest,*" Donnie gripes. "Come on, Elise! We run on dirt, smut, and knowing who's fucking who! Not how Keith Perkins learned to play guitar at the age of six and what might be next for him with this summer's tour!"

I'm trying to keep my cool. I'm walking into deep waters now with Donnie, and while I'm not technically lying yet . . . I'm not being honest and frank either. "I've gone through everything in his background, online searches, criminal record, everything available. And when I talk to Keith, he seems to be real. He was pissed about the record company springing the all-access interviews on him initially, but he's been forthcoming. I'm telling you, Donnie, there's just nothing salacious. The man's just an All-American sort of dude."

I hope it's enough, that he believes me and doesn't pry any further. Donnie may have questionable morals when it comes to Francesca, but he's a crack reporter and can smell a story long before anyone else does.

"Dammit, Elise. There's something!" he yells, slamming his hand down on his desk and sending jellybeans rolling everywhere. "Nobody is this fucking whitebread. Nobody can become as famous as he is without having at least a fucking parking ticket in his background. There has to be *something*. I don't want this to be a big waste of fucking time. Find me something, or I'll get someone who can."

"What?" I gasp, my face paling. "Donnie, this is my story—"

"I know it is! So do your damn job!" he yells, his face getting redder as his voice carries. I know the people out in the office can hear him reaming me out. "Even Pollyanna Maggie out there has more dirt in her life than you've written about Keith. Now, I'll let you write part three the way you want, but end it with a teaser about some *legit* dirt for part four." His voice drops dangerously. "And you'd *better* get it, one way or another. Am I clear?"

"Clear. I'll find something." I say as I nod, but my gut churns.

"Then get the fuck out of here and finish up part three. What are you going to do for the next interview?"

"I convinced him to get out of his house. I'm hoping that the change of scenery will get him to open up more. If I thought there was anything worth reporting on in the house, I'd have stayed, but he's shown me every room . . . the only person who'd find it interesting might be the Style section."

Slightly placated, Donnie starts scooping up his jellybeans and putting them back in his bowl. "Where are you doing the interview?"

"His land outside town," I reply honestly. "Get to know his country boy roots. I'm hoping it'll let me in past his image, getting back to who he used to be. You know what I mean?"

Donnie nods, his eyes pinching slyly. "Okay. Get a thread with the unvarnished Keith, and then tease that out. Even if it's just innuendo, I want something, Elise. Now get the hell out of here. You owe me part three by the end of the day."

"On it," I reply, getting up. Going back to my desk, my head aches and my heart twists.

Dirt . . . well, I know dirt. I know some life-changing, bomb in the middle of the room sort of dirt. But I promised two people that I wouldn't disclose it. And I won't.

But what sort of dirt on Keith can I come up with that'll be okay and still keep Donnie off my ass?

I've got a lot of work to do.

CHAPTER
Sixteen

KEITH

THE WEATHER IS PERFECT, late enough in the spring that my t-shirt and jeans are all I need for the days while the nights are going to be cool enough that Elise and I are going to have no problems snuggling up next to the fireplace in my cabin.

"It's been too long since I've been up here," I admit as we pull off the deserted dirt road onto the grassy shoulder at the trailhead, shifting my truck into park. "Guess I got too caught up with stuff this past winter. By the way, are you sure about those clothes?"

"What about them?" Elise asks, turning and sticking out her chest. "Don't think I'm covered enough?"

I take a look at her tight blue tank top, the valley between her breasts deep and proudly displayed before clinging to her stomach and hips. Her legs are just as displayed, as Elise showed up wearing a pair of tights that show every curve of her body.

"You look amazing," I tell her honestly, "but I'm just worried. It's a five-mile hike to my cabin. Are you sure those tights are what you want to wear in the woods?"

Elise grins, shifting her knees and giving my eyes a little treat that sends a warning twinge down to my cock. "I'll have you know, Mr. Country Music Star, that these are top of the line trail runner's tights, and the person who sold them to me at the store told me they're better for me than those old ass Levis you're wearing. They support and compress my leg muscles, giving me just what I need."

"And I thought I had what you needed," I joke, making her blush. "Just one thing."

"What's that?"

"Stay behind me on the trail because if I have to spend five miles looking at your ass in those tights for the whole walk . . . well, we won't last five miles before we scare the local wildlife."

Elise grins, biting her lip. "Maybe I'll want to take a break from walking . . . we'll see. Come on, let's get the packs."

I could have come up here yesterday and brought the ATVs down, or there is an old fire trail that I could take if Elise and I wanted to bounce and jolt our way for ten miles going around the backside of the mountain, but hiking up for a weekend just felt more real.

I help her with her pack before grabbing mine. "Come on, and if your pack gets too heavy, tell me."

"I'll have you know, I was a Girl Scout. I did go camping . . . once or twice," Elise says, grinning. We start off, and as we take the trail, a comfortable silence drops around us. It's not totally quiet, of course. There's plenty of natural forest sounds, but there are no cars, no traffic. Just us.

"Wow, it feels like another world," Elise says quietly as we hike. "It's . . . it's kinda like you."

"How's that?" I ask, thinking how she nailed it in one single sentence. She's got a gift for it, that's for sure.

"Well, on the surface, it's a little intimidating, beautiful but imposing at the same time," Elise replies, her eyes still in the trees as we walk. "Then you get this sense of nothing going on, like it's just boring and calm . . . but if you really look, there's a lot going on. You just have to be quiet and let it unveil itself to you. You're a lot like this place, I guess."

I smile, reaching over and taking her hand. "And they say *I'm* the songwriter. Come on, if you think this is nice, wait'll you get a view of the cabin."

It takes us about ninety minutes to make the hike, taking our time because there's really no need to rush. Elise does tease me a little as we go up one hill, pushing past me to give me a very inspiring view of her ass flexing as she makes her way up the trail. I probably could've made the climb quicker on my own, but I'll admit to being more than happy with my slow, distracted pace since it gives me more time to admire Elise's assets as we reach the crest and start down the other side.

"Just up this side trail," I tell Elise as I unlock my gate and hold it open for her. "Don't worry about the signs. They're mostly to scare off hunters."

"Do you get hunters out here?" Elise asks as she eyes the *Private Property, Trespassers Will Be Prosecuted* signs. "Or at least, have you had to prosecute anyone?"

"Once I found the water tank a little low. Someone had obviously refilled their water bags, but I've never had a break in," I tell her, taking her hand. "Don't worry, we're perfectly safe." I lock the gate behind us as we resume the final stretch of our hike.

"Is that what you call it when we're alone together? Doesn't feel safe to me," Elise jokes. "To be honest, it feels . . . thrillingly dangerous, like the world's sexiest rollercoaster."

Conversation trickles off as we climb the last hill, the hardest one, actually, and we have to lean into the slope. It's not that bad, but I am carrying three days' worth of food and supplies for a weekend on my back.

I'm curious what she'll think of the cabin. It's definitely different from my house in the city, but as we crest the hill, I feel relieved. Her eyes widen and her hands pop up to cover her exclaimed, "Oh, my gosh!"

"You like it?"

She looks at me, a smile stretching over her beautiful flushed and glistening face. "It's perfect! It looks like something out of a painting."

I like that she can appreciate a rustic log cabin, even one as small as this. It's one of the things that sold me on the property too. I don't need glitz and glam. I bought this place as a getaway because of the privacy and rustic charm.

"Well, come on then," I reply with a grin. "Let's get down there, get the fire going so we can have some hot water for later, and get things going!"

We go inside and drop our gear, and Elise seems enamored with the small space. The main room is a square with a bed to the left, a couch area to the right around the woodstove, and a working kitchen along the back wall. The bathroom is through a door off the kitchen. Bare-boned and simple, like I am at my core. The only concession to simplicity is the large hammock on the all-weather back porch, where Carsen and I have watched sunsets on numerous occasions.

"This is perfect," Elise purrs, setting her bag down on the kitchen table-slash-food prep space. "And it's ours all weekend?"

"Until we either have to go back or run out of food," I joke, watching her. I like seeing her here. It feels right somehow. Watching her stretch out and wiggle on the couch, my cock thickens in my jeans and I know what I need.

"Come here," I half-growl, feeling in touch with my inner wild nature. Elise's lips are twisted in a little smirk that says she already knows what I want, and her hips are doing a tantalizingly sexy sashay as she comes closer.

"What for?" she asks, laughing happily when she's in arm's reach and I grab her, kissing her deeply. Our bodies twist and tangle as I lift her up, walking her back to the couch and forcing her to clutch me tightly as I bend her backward.

There's no worry, though. I've got her securely in my arms, and as she moans when she feels my cock press up against her thigh, I set her back upright, my heart hammering in my chest. "We need to get out of here," I growl, "because I really want to show you some things . . . and if I don't get you outside in the next ten seconds, I'm going to rip those tights off and devour your body until you can't walk anymore."

"Sounds good. I do want to see what you have to show me," she purrs, running a hand over my chest. "I have some things I want to show you too."

I groan, pressing into her touch for a moment before getting under control. "No, really. I have every plan to fuck you until we collapse of exhaustion tonight, but I want to show you the land out here first. And if we don't leave right now, there won't be hot water, and I'd like to help you wash up after I get done burying myself inside that tight little pussy of yours."

She shudders in my arms, nodding. "God, I love how you talk to me. And I like that plan, but maybe I don't need hot water when I've got you."

She's pouting, but it's playful and I can see she's teasing me. She's been just as excited as I am about exploring the area. I pull her close one last time, grinding against her belly, and give her ass a good smack.

"Out, woman. Let's go."

She pulls away to walk toward the door, and I smack the other cheek for good measure. She looks back over her shoulder, sass and brattiness in her eyes, and I shrug. "I'm all about equal treatment, so the right had to get what the left got."

"I'll remember that later," she says. "Your ass is mine, country boy."

Outside, it's still picture-perfect beautiful, and after showing Elise how to fire up the small generator I have and starting the water pumps, I lead her to the parking shed for my ATV. "Hop on."

"And if I want to do the driving?"

I grin, mounting the ATV and firing it up. "After you know the local trails, I'll be happy to let you. Safety first, though."

Elise gets on behind me, pressing her breasts to my back and wrapping her arms around my waist, her hands dangerously close to my crotch. We ride, and I goof a bit, having fun and stopping to show her bits about the trail and property. Reaching the top of a ridge, I come to a stop at the beginning of a small trail. "Here's a nice spot. Can't take the ATV up though."

Elise gives me an amused look but says nothing, which I appreciate. I'd hate to ruin the surprise. "So how'd you get into the outdoors?" Elise asks as we go. "You seem totally at home here."

"Guess being country's always been in my blood," I explain, smiling. "My dad would take me out, sometimes into the mountains. We'd go fishing, camping . . . Dad wasn't a hunter, but we had fun. There was this lake up at Lucky Peak that I loved to go swimming in. We had some good times there." I fall quiet, not really wanting to talk about my parents and their reaction to my 'damn-fool' career, so I decide to turn the questions back on her. "What about you?"

"Other than those six months with the Girl Scouts, I've never really spent a lot of time outdoors," she admits, grinning. "I did a few nature walks when I was in college, but those were more parks than real nature. I mean, you could hear the cars if you listened hard enough. Not at all like this."

"Well, check this out then," I tell her as the path ends in the clearing. I found this place on my first trip up here, and as Elise takes it in, I can tell she's just as enchanted as I was. "It's the biggest reason I bought the cabin."

"It's . . . you've got a fairy forest," Elise says, looking around. The trees here are all pines, shooting high into the sky and shadowing a lot of the clearing, and for just a moment, I can imagine sparkly little creatures fluttering between the branches, intent on making magic.

"I never thought of fairies before, but it is magical," I agree. Taking her hand, I lead her on. "And up here is the best part."

I don't know how a creek this high up in the hills is able to form a pool, but it does, with a soft grass bank and half of the pool in the shade, the other half in the sun. "Have a seat. I'd say swim, but it's a bit cold except in July and August."

Elise sits down, letting me gather her in my arms as we lean back, my leg cocked to the side to let her press her body against me. "And you don't live here all the time why?"

I laugh softly, brushing a lock of her hair away from her cheek and inhaling the soft aroma that is naturally Elise. "If I thought I could, I might. But Carsen needs good schools, and besides, if I were up here all the time, I'd have to have visitors, all that shit. Ruin the scene. So I save it . . . for special people and for special occasions."

Elise turns, looking up at me and taking my hand. "Thank you. I know this is a crazy way to meet someone, but . . . I really am glad I followed you that day."

"So that *was* you," I confirm, chuckling. "Took me a while. Those sunglasses and wig are a hell of a disguise. So, how's the story coming?"

Elise sighs, leaning back and I can hear the worry in her voice. "Good and bad. Part three is done, but Donnie insists on dirt for part four. I don't think posing some archery shots is going to be enough." She spits out in disgust. "Hell, I wouldn't put it past Donnie to make up some random shit and publish it, and that's exactly what you don't want to happen, so we've got to come up with something. Got any ideas on a scandal I can give you that is juicy but won't be too embarrassing?"

I look up to the blue sky, trying to think and hoping to find an answer in the clouds. Partying on tour? Too hard to keep up appearances this summer. Drinking and drugs? I don't need that sort of attention. "Hey, what if I had a girlfriend? I just keep her locked up in my love dungeon and never let her out." I wrap Elise up tight in my arms, growling into the soft skin of her neck.

Elise giggles, wiggling away from the tickles of my nibbles. "I don't think that's the kind of thing you want getting out. Women would be lined up around the block for the *Yes, Mr. Perkins* experience."

"Well shit, I don't know, but we have all weekend to figure something out. For now, I have an idea." I hold her tight again, nuzzling in her hair and taking in her sweet girl-sweat and sunshine scent.

But she twists in my arms, surprising me with a smack of a kiss before scurrying towards the pool. I know the first few feet are shallow and mostly sandy bank, and likely freezing, so when she drops down and dips her hands in with a glint in her eyes, I can fully read her intentions.

"You'd better not, Elise. That water's fucking ice cold. You wouldn't dare." I warn her.

"Hell yes, I dare." and with a whoop of delight, she throws handfuls of water to splash at me.

I hop up, charging at her like she waved a red flag in front of a bull, and she retreats into the knee-deep water, where I follow her, splashing her with my stomping steps. "You've done it now…" And I grab her, splashing her with the frigid water as we both laugh and shiver.

"Holy shitballs!" Elise yells. "It's fucking cold!" But even as she complains about the water, she's reaching down, tossing more my way.

I laugh, and for the next few minutes, it's a water war of freezing proportions, both of us getting soaked but not caring in the least. Our calves and toes quickly numb, but the warm sun on our bodies helps. When we're both breathless, dripping, and smiling, I help her back on the bank, laughing as I stroke her wet hair. "Truce, I won't splash you anymore."

"How about you let me drive back as a peace offering?" she asks. "Do that, and maybe I'll let you join me for the warm-up shower."

"Deal," I reply, kissing her softly. This kiss feels different, like we're not getting ready to fuck but just . . . foreplay. Her lips are tender and soft, and when her tongue touches my lip, I caress her tenderly, holding her close before pulling back. "Thank you for letting me share this with you."

Elise takes it nice and slow, controlling the ATV on the ride back down, listening as I give her clues and point out where to turn. By the time we get back, the sun is getting low, which is great because we'll have plenty of hot water for our showers.

Elise brakes and turns off the ATV, pulling off her helmet as she looks out at the golden valley below the cabin. "I keep getting my breath taken away. It's beautiful," she whispers.

"Not as beautiful as you," I murmur, hugging her from behind. We watch the sun disappear behind the mountain, then push the ATV into the shed. I turn back to Elise in the fading light. "It'll get chilly up here quickly now. I'll grab some firewood, get that started for some heat while you wash up."

"And what if I don't *want* to wash up?" she asks, sassy again. In response, I come over and pull her close, growling lightly.

"I might just have to spank you," I threaten. "Hard."

Elise hums, pressing her breasts against my chest and squeezing me close. "I don't know if you understand what punishment means . . . because that sounds exactly like what I wanted anyway."

I hum, reaching down and cupping her ass, squeezing it as I whisper in her ear. "So you like it when I spank you? Hold you down and make your ass pink up so pretty for me?"

She bites back a moan, but I hear it even as she nods, grinding her hips forward to brush against my cock. Turning her around, I wrap a fistful of her hair around my hand, splaying my other on her belly as I lean down, nipping and sucking on her neck. Elise cups my head, holding me still. "Harder. Please . . . God, you make dirty feel so fucking good."

I nip her again, licking her skin and making her jump, pressing her ass against my now raging cock. "You want me to mark this pretty neck, leave bruises to show how well you've been fucked?"

She nods, and I have to give my lady what she wants, sucking harder and licking lines to find the next treasure spot to mark with my kiss. As I do, I grind my cock against her ass harder, finding a rhythm as I ride her through our clothes. Needing more . . . more skin, more contact, more of Elise surrounding me, I use my hold on her to walk toward the cabin, leading her inside.

"Sit," I order as soon as we're inside. "I wasn't joking about how cold it'll get. Once I'm in your pussy, I'm not going anywhere."

She sits, breathless and blushing, and I love that she looks like she's ready for me to take her, claim her any way I want. I quickly start a fire before turning to face her.

"Forget the shower. Show me your tits, Elise."

I expect her to pull her tank off, but instead, she stretches the neckline low, letting her tits pop up, the tank pushing them up like they're being cradled on a serving platter for me to feast on. I pull my shirt off in response, showing her that while I might be in charge, we're still equals. "Now touch your nipples, pinch them for me."

She looks at me from under her lashes, mouth already parted as she pants, wanting more. She reaches up and pinches her right nipple, rolling it between her finger and thumb and whimpering in desire.

I reach down, unbuttoning my jeans and sliding them down my hips a bit, my already hard cock tenting my boxer briefs. I slip my hand down, cupping myself through the thin fabric to show her the outline of my thickness. "Is this what you want?"

Elise whimpers again, the firelight starting to dance in her eyes as she nods. "Yes."

"Then say it. I want to hear it from those sweet lips of yours."

Elise's knees spread on their own, and I can see the contours of her pussy lips against the wet fabric, her eyes dark with desire. "Please . . . I need to see your cock."

"And what do you want to do with it?" I tease, toeing my boots off. "Do you want to suck it into that sassy mouth of yours?"

She nods, licking her lips. "I want to suck it, to choke on it . . . I want to feel it in my pussy . . . I want to feel you in my ass. I want you . . . everywhere."

"Do you, now?" I ask, letting my jeans drop the rest of the way to the ground before stepping out of them. "Has anyone ever fucked your ass, Elise?" She shakes her head, but her eyes never leave my cock, her desire for me to claim her in every way written across her face. "And do you think your tight little virgin ass is ready for my thick, pulsing cock?"

Elise pinches her other nipple, gasping and replying breathlessly, "No . . . but I want it anyway."

"I promise you . . . when you're ready, I'm going to fill your ass and make you scream my name," I rasp, hooking my thumbs in the waistband of my shorts. "But first, you need to get down to your panties. Fair's fair."

Elise scrambles to comply, nearly ripping her boots off to yank her tights down her long, sexy legs. My cock throbs watching her breasts bounce as she tumbles off the couch, kneeling in front of me before sitting back on her heels, looking up. "I can be very good," she winks.

"I know," I reply, teasing my underwear down some before stopping. "You do it. Suck my cock, baby."

Elise's eager hands pull my underpants down, my cock springing out to almost slap her in the tip of the nose. She's so hungry for me. Grabbing a handful of her hair, I take control. "Open."

As soon as her lips part, I feed my cock to her, deeper and deeper into her warm mouth. Elise moans, looking up at me as I start pumping my cock in and out of her lips, grinning. "I can see it in your eyes, Elise. Don't try and fool me . . . you want to show me you're the real boss here, don't you? That you can make me lose control and come down your throat."

"Mmm-hmm." Elise vibrates around my shaft, reaching up and fondling my balls.

I growl, shoving my cock down her throat. Elise swallows, taking it all but gagging as I hold my cock buried in her throat. "Is this what you want? Want me to fuck your pretty lips, let your throat work me every time you swallow?"

She nods slightly, her movement inhibited by my hold on her hair. I pull back, pausing to let her breathe for a moment, but she's already going back for more, so I fuck her mouth harder, pumping in and out as she tries her best to take me balls-deep with every stroke.

Still, I hold back, not hurting her but watching as she moans around me, her hands slipping down between her legs to start rubbing her panty-covered pussy.

"That's it, baby . . . rub that sweet pussy for me and get it nice and wet, because I'm gonna fuck you all weekend long." She cries out around my cock, and I see her hand move even faster, matching my punishing pace as I fuck her mouth. I'm already so damn close. "Elise . . ."

She looks up at me, and I hold her in place, tracing her pink lips with my head. "Do you want my cum inside you?"

Her tongue darts out to lick up the drop of precum already beading, her eyes answering my question. "Fuck, I want that too." Pulling my cock away, I tug her to her feet, half dragging her to the couch before I bend her over the arm, letting go of her hair.

"Grab that cushion, and if you let go, I'm *not* going to spank your ass, and I know how much you want me to spank you, baby," I tell her, getting behind her perfect, peach-shaped upturned ass. "God, you look fucking gorgeous, you know that?"

Before Elise can reply, I smack her right ass cheek, watching it pink up as I kneel behind her. She gasps, her legs spreading, and I get a great view of her panty-covered pussy. Reaching up with both hands, I pull them down and toss them across the room, already forgotten as I bury my stiff tongue in her pussy.

"Fuck!" Elise screams as I lick her wet folds, sucking and slurping hungrily. She's sweet and delicious, just what I need to quench the thirst inside me. "Keith, oh, fuck . . ."

I find the glistening jewel of her clit and lap at it with rapid little licks that leave her wiggling her hips as she chases me, desperate for release. Growling, I reach up and smack her ass, harder this time. "Don't move or I stop."

Elise freezes. I don't think she even breathes as I tease her opening with first one finger, then two. I slowly slide the length of my fingers in and out, feeling her pussy squeeze around them as I go as deep as I can. "Hands. Elise, hold yourself open for me. Fuck, I need to see you taking my fingers in your tight little pussy."

She does as I ask, pressing her cheek to the cushion and grabbing her ass to spread herself wide for my feasting. "Fuck, so pretty and wet for me . . . taking my fingers like you're gonna take my cock."

Slowly but powerfully, I finger fuck her pussy, letting the tip of my tongue skate across her clit, her lips, and up to her asshole. She whimpers, and I bite the fullness of her cheek before soothing it with my tongue. "It's mine, Elise. And I'm going to lick and suck and fuck you anyway I want."

I can't see her face pressed down to the cushion, but I see her body relax as she presses herself to my tongue, ready for whatever I give her.

I curl my fingers inside her, pressing along the front wall and sucking hard on her clit. I feel vibrations start to course through her body, and its only seconds before she comes. "Keith!" she squeals, trying to stay still for me but overwhelmed. "Oh, fuck!"

She's still convulsing around my fingers when I stand up, my cock pulsing with my racing heartbeat. Precum is oozing out, and I can't wait to slam inside her, but I stroke myself a few times, coating my cock with the juices from my fingers as I memorize the sight before me. She's so fucking gorgeous, waiting for me to fill her up. I can feel her soft lips pulsing, trying to suck me inside. "This is what you need, isn't it? Take it, take my hard fucking cock balls-deep."

I bury myself all the way in, our hips slapping together, and I grind inside her, feeling her pussy clench and relax as she adjusts to the fullness. "Fuck, Keith . . . I feel so full."

I reach back and smack her ass again, seeing the pink handprint I leave behind. "Mmm . . . your ass looks so good when it's red like this."

Elise moans, her pussy squeezing even tighter around my cock in response to the smack. I pull back, slamming into her again and making her back arch up. Reaching around, I cup her breasts with one hand while grabbing her neck with the other. She freezes, looking back over her shoulder but not resisting as my fingers close around her throat.

"Trust me," I whisper as I start pumping in and out of her. Elise shudders, her eyes never leaving mine as I stroke my cock faster and faster, our hips smacking together. Elise's eyes sparkle, and I can feel her pulse all around me . . . in her pussy, under my thumb along her neck, and under my palm at her breast. With every beat, it urges me to go harder and give her more.

"Your pussy is fucking choking my cock," I grit through clenched teeth. "This tight little pussy that's mine now, isn't it?"

"Yes," Elise cries out. "It's yours. I'm yours. Give it to me, fuck me and give me everything you've got," she says as her pussy gets impossibly tighter with every filthy word.

She reaches up to grab my wrist. For a moment, I think she's going to try and pull away, but she instead pulls me tighter, urging me on.

I speed up, feeling her body start to quiver again, and I look in her eyes. "I can feel you're close, Elise. Tell me."

She shudders, her voice and body both begging "Please, Keith . . . I need to come. Can I?"

I growl. "Come for me, baby. All over my fat cock. Cover me with your sweet cream."

My words are all Elise needs, and her fingernails tighten on my wrist, breaking the skin as she marks me too. Her eyes flutter as she pushes back, her pussy spasming around me as she starts to come again. I can't hold out, and I barely pull out in time to spurt all over her beautiful ass, covering her in thick streams that gleam in the firelight. I collapse, rolling us to the floor with Elise in my arms.

We lie on the floor, the soft light from the stove illuminating the cabin, until a strange sound breaks the silence. "What was that?"

Elise giggles, blushing a bit. "Uhm . . . my tummy. I'm hungry."

I laugh and sit up, helping her to sit with me. "Well then, I have plenty to feed you with. To start, how about some Dinty Moore beef stew?"

"Dinty Moore?" Elise asks, smirking. "And here I was thinking I was going to get three-star quality meals."

"Hey, it reminds me of the better times with my dad," I explain, helping her up. "And besides, it's quick and filling because you're gonna need your energy later. I'm just getting started."

CHAPTER
Seventeen

ELISE

WE SPEND NEARLY all of the next thirty-six hours entangled in each other over and over, and it feels like my every sex fantasy come to life, but somehow, there's more than just sex between us now. In the mid-morning hours, after another round of him taking me, claiming me, pounding me into the mattress until I screamed out my release and he growled in my ear, we're still and relaxed. Finally exhausted, but I can't control the warmth that spreads through my body.

Lying on his chest, scratching and petting at the tattoos that traverse his skin, it feels comfortable. Especially as he twines a section of my hair around his finger and then releases the curl. We're naked, but maybe more so emotionally than physically.

There's been a change forged between us. There's still a bossy gruffness to Keith that is all him, but the defensive asshole seems to be mostly gone now that there's no big secret to tell.

Sometimes when he looks at me, I can still tell that there's a hint of doubt in his eyes, a constant demand for me to keep my mouth shut. But that's understandable when he's had this looming secret for so long and hasn't shared it with anyone new in years. I'm a risk, and we both know it.

Good thing I don't intend on tattling his story to the public, not at all. In fact, I feel special that he chose to share it with me. Granted, it was initially by force with Carsen barging in like that, but Keith could've shut down completely. He could've stopped the interviews, sent me away, and called in lawyers to force me to keep my mouth shut. But he didn't. And I think it's because he wants this . . . whatever this is between us, just as much as I do.

So I've spent the weekend reassuring him with my words, with my body, with everything I have that he can totally trust me and that I'm feeling this thing inside that would never let me hurt him. I wasn't looking for it, and I certainly didn't think I was gonna feel this way about the jerk who slammed a door in my face. But now that I know why, I understand. And that protective streak is damn sexy.

A man who will go to the lengths he has so his daughter can grow up safe and happy? Every girl should be so lucky. And lying here in Keith's arms, I feel like I'm a lucky girl too. Safe, peaceful, cherished . . . and I want to return those feelings to Keith, be his strength when he needs it, and most importantly, protect him and Carsen at all costs.

"What are you thinking?"

I blink, looking into Keith's eyes as I snuggle up to him more, pressing against him gently. "I'm thinking that I wish we could just stay here like this, in this perfect little bubble, away from reality and responsibilities. Just sleep and hike and fuck, and then do it all again."

He chuckles, tracing his thick thumb across my lips, and I pucker, kissing the pad and darting my tongue out for a quick taste of his skin. He presses into my mouth, and I suck his thumb like I've sucked his cock so many times already as he swirls across my tongue. "And when we run out of food?"

"There's some old wisdom . . . country boys can survive?" I joke, licking his skin again. He tastes like sweat and sex, and I bite my teeth down gently, holding him there so I can circle my tongue around him. "Mmm."

He groans, and I feel his cock jump, responding jealously and wanting my attention lower. Keith moves unexpectedly, pulling me beneath him and pressing my hands to the bed above me. "I think I like your plan," he purrs, touching his forehead to mine. "I could stay inside your tight little body, your hot silky walls caressing me all day."

I smile, writhing against him, pressing my wrists against his restraint even though I don't want him to let me go. I just want to test him, make him press against me harder, force him to dominate me a bit rougher because we both know I can take it.

It's a new awakening for me. I've never really experienced anything like it before. But in giving in to Keith, I've found my body responding more to every touch, every stroke of his fingers on my skin. He drives me wild, and I feel like a different woman from when we first met . . . stronger and more satisfied than I've ever been.

He leans down, kissing me fiercely before biting at my lower lip, hard enough to make me whimper. "There's just one thing. I promised you pancakes on the way home, and if we stay for another round, I'm gonna wear you out so much that we'll have to go straight home so I can be there when Carsen gets home from school."

I pout, puffing out my bitten lip. "I don't want pancakes. I want you. One more time before the real world intrudes?"

But even as I curl my hips, searching for his touch, my traitorous body responds to his promise of pancakes and my stomach growls loudly. I guess cans of chili and stew aren't enough.

Keith smirks down at me, pushing up a little. "See? I need to feed you. I promise we'll get another chance, but you've got to be sore."

He moves one hand down my body, soft caresses meant to soothe as he traces my breasts, my belly, and across my hipbone. Sweet, but oh, so tantalizing, and as he brushes across my mound, I quiver, whimpering again.

He's right, I am sore from our repeated rough couplings, but I'm still hungry for more. I'm addicted to Keith, fully head over heels even if I've never said that to him again, and I want every caress and every orgasm he can give me. I arch my back, but my stomach growls again, betraying me. "Dammit."

Keith laughs, cupping my pussy and making me hiss, both in heat and a little ache before he bends down and kisses me just above my belly button. "Don't worry, Elise. I know what you need. Food and maybe a little recovery time, then I'll make you cream all over my cock again."

I sigh, knowing he's right. He stands, pulling me up with him, his thick cock sandwiched between us.

Keith hisses at the contact, pulling back reluctantly. "Get dressed before I change my mind," he growls mock threateningly. I'm not scared. Hell, I want to push him a little further just to find that line of control he skates on the edge of every minute of every day, and then shove him past the boundary.

So I do as he says and get dressed, but I do it with every bit of sexiness I can muster. I find my panties on the floor and bend over, exposing myself to him as I pick them up. I can feel his eyes blazing on my skin and I look over my shoulder, delighted to see his gazed fixed on me. I can see his cock hard, throbbing, wanting him to change his mind.

Loving that my tease is working, I flick my panties, getting them turned right side out before inhaling, and holding them out to him. "These are dirty from yesterday. They smell like sex. I need fresh ones from my bag."

I walk past Keith, who is as still as a statue, and lay the panties against his chest where he grabs them in one fist. "What?"

"Souvenir," I reply as I dig in my bag, again exposing myself to him as I grab a tiny scrap of satin and pull it out, holding it up where I know he can see it from his position behind me. I dip even lower, slipping first one then the other pointed toe into the undies and pulling them slowly up my calves and to my knees.

When I get mid-thigh, Keith growls. "Stop."

I look back, a smirk already on my face. But when I see him, it vanishes, my mouth dropping open as I see Keith with my sexed underwear wrapped around his cock as he jerks himself.

"You think you're in charge here? Your little pussy is what needs a break. My hard cock needs a release, you little tease."

I bite my lip, eyes focused on his hand slipping up and down his length, rubbing the silkiness of my panties against the velvet of his skin.

I try to explain my bratty behavior, knowing it's already useless. "I wasn't teasing you. I want you. I want you to fuck me . . ."

Keith's face is hard, feral, and sexy as fuck as he speeds up, shaking his head. "Oh, no, I already told you. Pancakes. But now . . . look what you've done."

I glance down again and whimper, wanting him, and I move closer but he stops me. "No. Leave those panties wrapped around your thighs so you can't move. Bend over again and show me that wet pussy."

I do as he says, spreading my legs as wide as I can with the confines of the satin at my thighs. "Put your hands behind your back. No touching."

Again, I obey, leaning to one side so I can see him behind me. "That's right. Watch me. I'm gonna jack my cock off with your sexy little panties, come all over them. And you're not gonna move. Stay right there and show me how soaked your pussy gets from watching me come."

I cry out, desperate for his touch, my touch, needing to come. "Tell me. Tell me what you feel, Elise."

"I need . . . God, I can feel my heartbeat in my clit, begging for release."

His eyes leave mine, locking on my pussy, and he groans, squeezing his cock tighter. "I can see your cream coating your thighs. Your pussy is so hungry for my cock that I can see your lips pulsing, searching to pull me inside."

I buck my hips a bit instinctively, opening wider to his fierce gaze. God, I never thought someone could come from not even touching, from just words, but watching Keith, I'm about to come and I haven't even pinched a nipple.

"Mmm, so pretty. I'm fucking close. You want me to come?"

I nod. He's driving me so insane with lust, I know I could come just from seeing him erupt. "Fuck yes, Keith. Fuck my sexy panties. Come all over them. Show me how you jerk yourself, thinking of my pussy surrounding you. I want to see you explode while you look at my needy pussy."

I'm getting dizzy from standing slightly upside down and from panting with lust, but I'm not moving. Not until I see what I want. Thankfully, only a few hard strokes later, Keith comes with a roar, jets of white pulsing out of his cock and ruining my panties. Well, not ruining them . . . making them better.

I'm gasping as I watch him, forcing myself to stay still even though the need to touch myself is overwhelming.

Keith's breathing is labored as he finishes, a few last jerks as he gets every drop out. He smiles, taking in my body with his adoring eyes. "Such a good girl, Elise. Not moving even though I know your pussy must be begging for release."

He stands there just like that, watching me, eyes moving from mine to my soaked slit. "How close are you? Are you about to come from watching me? From standing here with your dripping pussy on display for me to jack off to?"

I whine, mad at myself because I couldn't hold myself back even if I tried. "Fuck, Keith. I'm so close. So fucking close."

He moves closer and stuffs the cum-covered panties in my mouth, and the flavor of his essence coats my tongue, making me moan at the deliciousness.

He gives me a hard look. "One lick, Elise. That's all you get, you naughty cock tease. Come on my tongue or you'll have to wait until we get home for some relief. It's a long, hard drive home, baby. You don't want to wait, do you?"

I shake my head, my thighs quivering, so close to the edge I think his breath might be enough to send me over.

He leans closer, inhaling my scent like it's the finest of wines and making me wait even longer. Oh, my God, do it already! "You smell so sweet. I know you're gonna taste like honey on my tongue, coating me as I lick you down while you taste my cum on your gag. Don't drop it, Elise. Bite down and taste me while I give you your one . . . good . . . lick."

He leans forward, his hands spreading me wide, and the flat of his tongue presses against my clit, tracing through my soaked lips, up to my asshole before fluttering there, never breaking contact but still . . .

I detonate. From just one lick, shudders wrack my body as I see stars. I cry into the makeshift gag, his flavor bursting on my tongue sending me spiraling again. My knees buckle, and I start to pitch forward but he grabs me with one arm, supporting me as I lose all control, futilely trying to breathe oxygen into my blackened vision when Keith grabs a gentle handful of my hair, pulling me up to stand in front of him.

Supporting me from behind, he reaches around, taking the panties from my mouth and letting a rush of sweet, cool oxygen flood my body. Placing his lips by my ear, his breath is warm as he holds me tenderly. "Such a naughty girl, but you took your punishment fucking beautifully."

I grin, finding the strength to stand up on my own. Keith reaches down, grabbing my still pristine panties that are twisted and stretched around my thighs and pulls them up, smoothing the stretch of material between the cheeks of my ass. "Keith . . . I have so much to say."

"Over pancakes," he promises me, stepping back. He takes my panties and inhales deeply, savoring their scent. "You're right, these are mine now."

He puts them in his backpack, cinching the top closed. "Get dressed. I'm feeding you some fucking pancakes on the way home."

Fuck yes, pancakes sound like heaven now, my body on empty after the intensity of what we just did. With one lick.

That's all it took.

We take the ATV down, Keith using some ramps in the back of his truck to put the vehicle inside before he ratchet-straps it in place. "Just one thing," I tell him as we sit in the cab, finally finding words. "You have to promise me something."

"What's that?" he asks, smiling as he sees me regain my equilibrium and a little bit of my sassiness.

"Promise that if you start wearing my panties, I have your permission to include that dirty secret in the articles. And maybe take a picture . . . but I'll keep that to myself," I say with a saucy wink, the imaginary image of a big, rough country boy like Keith even getting one tree-trunk of a thigh in my tiny panties quite laughable.

He laughs, twisting the key in the ignition before pointing a finger at me. "Not happening . . . the wearing, the story, and most definitely, not the picture."

We start back toward the city, stopping at a restaurant known for its weekend brunches, and my thoughts return to the promise of pancakes and coffee. God, coffee . . . I need a thermos full considering how blissfully worn out Keith has made me.

"Just a moment," Keith says, getting a hat from the back and pulling it over his head. "There."

"You just going in here, thinking you won't be recognized?" I ask, laughing.

He chuckles, shaking his head. "Actually, if I don't have a cowboy hat and tight jeans on, most folks don't even give me a second look. Especially when I pull out the *fancy* disguise."

He pops open the console, pulling out a pair of thick black-framed glasses, slipping them on. He looks like a sexy nerd, and I'm reminded of my earlier thoughts that Clark Kent could learn a lot from this guy. Then again, maybe Keith is from Krypton . . . he certainly is the cock of steel, at least.

"So, what do you think?"

"I think if you throw on a fake Boston accent, you could pull that off in the middle of Kentucky and nobody'd bat an eye," I say, impressed that the glasses actually do a decent job of disguising him. I should know since I've had some pretty stellar disguises in my investigations. "So does that mean I get to hold my boyfriend's hand and not have to worry?"

"Damn right," Keith says, and he's true to his word as we go inside. Also true to his word, the hostess doesn't even give Keith a second look before leading us to a table by the window. The waitress gives us an appraising double-take as she takes our orders of orange juice, coffee, and pancakes, and worry starts to twist in my stomach. Despite what's growing between us. We absolutely *can't* be public.

As she walks off, I lean over, trying to keep my voice low. "She knows."

He grins as he wiggles the glasses at me, totally assured. "You don't know that. Maybe she just thinks I'm hot."

My fears are confirmed, though, when she returns a moment later with the steaming cups of caffeine nectar. She leans forward, her voice careful. "Uhm, excuse me, but are you Keith Perkins?"

I freeze, curious how he's going to handle this, and admittedly, my journalist gene kicks in a bit. He gives her a confused look and tweaks his voice a little to make it sound totally un-Keith-like as he replies. "Who? My name's Adam. You must have me confused with someone else. Sorry."

He flashes her an innocent smile and shrugs his shoulder. She looks at him for a second longer before sighing wistfully. "Sorry, sir. You just kinda look like him. You've never been mistaken for him before? He's a country singer."

Keith smiles wider. "Not that I recall. And I'm more of a rock guy myself. Ever heard of Highly Suspect?"

She smiles back, and if this girl starts flirting any more openly, I'm going to know right where to stuff my first handful of pancakes. "Nope, can't say that I have."

Keith nods, adjusting his glasses. "Good band. You should look them up."

Seemingly appeased, she heads off to check on our pancakes. I'm grinning behind my coffee cup, damn proud of myself for not laughing and blowing Keith's cover.

"Have you even heard a single song by Highly Suspect or did you say the first rock band I mentioned in a desperate attempt to distract her?" I ask. "And by the way, she was flirting with you."

"Maybe both," Keith admits with a chuckle. "The distraction worked, but I gave them a listen after you mentioned them. They do have a good sound. And even if she was flirting . . . I'm taken."

I smile, my heart melting at the simple statement. "You surprise me, Adam. Just when I think you're a gruff asshole, you're sweet too. Keep it up."

We're halfway through our stacks of pancakes when I see someone I never expected to see working her way through the tables. Her eyes cut my way and lock, the surprise obvious on her face even if her eyebrows don't move because of all the Botox. She turns, bee-lining straight for us. "Shit. Incoming."

Before Keith can even question me, Francesca stops by our table, all airs and elegance. "Elise, darling! What a surprise to see you! Out for a bite of brunch? They do have the best mimosas here." She says it like she's sharing national secrets, whispering slightly and gesturing to my non-champagne orange juice like we're besties.

I force a smile, knowing it's fake, but Francesca can't tell the difference anyway. I don't know if it's because I've given her so many dishonest smiles or if she just doesn't care. Not bothering to correct her assumption about my juice, I tell her neutrally, "Good to see you too."

Francesca dips her chin demurely, her eyes zeroing on Keith. "Ooh, aren't you going to introduce me to your friend?"

She knows who Keith is, I'm certain of it. Hell, Donnie and she have probably had some gross form of pillow talk about my article series, but she's playing coy. Fuck that.

"Of course. Francesca, this is Keith. Keith, this is a coworker of mine, Francesca. She works with red carpets, galas, award ceremonies, that type of thing mostly."

Keith is polite as he shakes her hand, and I can see on her face that she's thinking he'll be impressed by what I said and by her good looks.

But what Frannie doesn't know is that Keith knows about her too, and her hopes are quickly dashed. "Oh, yeah, those are all events I mostly avoid like the plague if I can help it. The vampires and vultures are out in force there."

I smile, keeping my giggles inside, as Francesca seems a bit miffed at his dislike of her favorite arenas to see and be seen. "Well, yes . . . I'm sure they're not for everyone. So, Elise," she says, directing her focus on me. "How're the interviews going?"

"Oh, great," I reply, jittery until I feel Keith's foot touch mine under the table. *Keep it together, girl.* "Keith was showing me some of his hobbies, like hiking and archery. A bit of outdoorsy stuff for the next article."

Francesca sniffs, literally sniffs like she's smelled something distasteful. "Outdoorsy? Sounds . . . interesting." Her tone says she obviously finds it anything but interesting.

Keith interjects, saving me. "Elise was a natural out there. I'm sure some reporters wouldn't be willing to get dirty . . . hiking, riding an ATV, shooting a few arrows. But she jumped right in. Anything for a story, right?" He says it with a true smile, but I can see by the flint in his eyes that he remembers what I'd told him about Francesca.

"Oh," Francesca replies, giving me a worried look like everyone doesn't already know how she gets her assignments. "Uhm, well . . . sounds like you've got some good scoop, so I'll let you two finish brunch. I'm off for a hair appointment. See you Monday."

After Francesca leaves, I freak a bit, gasping. "God, do you think she suspected anything?" I whisper, trying and failing at not looking guilty. "I'm pretty sure we were just eating when she came up, nothing suspicious. Right?"

Keith smiles, patting my hand. "I think we're fine, nothing sketchy. Am I *your* dirty little secret now?"

He's teasing, but there's a hint of truth to it, and a bit of hurt too. I try to corral my thoughts. "Honestly, there's a piece of me that wouldn't mind shouting from the rooftops. But that wouldn't be great for either of us right now. Professionally, it'd be career suicide for me, and you would have those vultures flocking around so fast your head would spin. And that's dangerous . . . for Carsen. Neither of us can afford for suspicions about a flirty breakfast to get out."

"Touché, you're right. There's a part of me that'd be right there next to you on the rooftop, but . . . Carsen is first, always." Keith responds, picking up a piece of bacon and munching on it as the gravity of the situation sinks in. "I will say, Francesca has barracuda written all over her. She's the one giving favors to your boss, right?"

I shudder, nodding. "Yes. Ugh, so gross. I just imagine . . . jellybeans."

"Huh?" Keith asks. "Jellybeans?"

I explain about Donnie and his crystal bowl of jellybeans, and he nods, trying to chuckle, but I can see it. The spell's broken and there's a dullness to everything now that reality has crept back in, the risk of what we're doing more real.

We finish brunch, but as we walk back out, we don't hold hands.

It feels too dangerous.

CHAPTER

Eighteen

KEITH

"SO, HERE WE ARE," I muse as I drop Elise off at her place. "Thank you for a wonderful weekend."

Elise gives me a ghost of her normally megawatt smile, still worried about running into her co-worker at the pancake joint. "I should thank you. Keith, about the restaurant . . ."

"There's nothing we can change about it now. She'll either suspect something's up between us or not," I reply evenly. "The best thing you can do is make sure your story is a knockout and you drop enough hints of dirt that your editor's going to be happy. Just make sure of one thing."

"What's that?" Elise asks, brightening a little.

"When you tell the world how much you're addicted to my big, fat cock . . . don't skimp on the size," I joke. I'm trying to lighten the mood, ease her mind, but I know her career is serious to her. And as much as we're both enjoying this growing thing between us, I don't think either of us is ready for the fallout of everyone knowing. But I don't want to end our amazing weekend on a suspicious, fearful note, so some prodding to get Elise to smile seems warranted, even if it's a bit less bright than her usual megawatt grin.

Elise finally laughs, shaking her head. "What, are you kidding? That's my *big* lead-in! I mean, it'll *hook* them in for sure!" She holds up her finger, bent at the knuckle into a hook shape.

I laugh but grab her hand. "Don't even joke about that, woman. Or I'll have to remind you just how big and *straight* it is when I'm bottoming out in that tight little pussy."

Elise laughs, blushing a little. "I've already told you, you're the worst at punishing my brattiness. That sounds like a reward."

I look around to make sure we're alone on the street, and I lean forward, sipping at her lips, driving her crazy wanting more. I pull back and she chases my kiss. "That's enough for now. You've got work to do."

She sits back in her seat, full bottom lip protruding in a pout. "You want to come inside?"

I smirk, knowing that if we do, work just won't get done. "Maybe next time. Right now, you're gonna go in, work your magic on another story, and I'll call you later. And Elise, don't you dare come without me. Save it for me."

She nibbles at her lip, then nods. "I take it back. You're better at punishment than I give you credit for."

I smile, hitting the unlock button for her door. "I know."

I grab her chin and give her one more kiss, fiery hot and powerful to stoke her fire one last time before she goes inside. As she closes the door behind her, walking to her apartment building, I take a deep breath and adjust myself in my pants. I might be able to keep my control when she's with me . . . but she pushes me to the limits. I wouldn't have it any other way.

Driving home, I sing to myself a few bars of something that's been floating through my head. I don't quite know what the song is yet, just one of those little ditties that float through my head from time to time . . . but this one feels like it could be one of those that turns into something.

Getting out of my truck at home, I'm barely in the door before Carsen's hounding me, a hundred questions pouring out of her ever-curious mouth.

"So what did you do? Did you take her to the creek? What about the ATVs? Did you see any deer?"

I laugh at the way Carsen is bouncing and dragging me inside by my hand. Carsen's always enjoyed going to the cabin, but I think she was even more excited for someone new to experience the beauty and fun we always share there.

"Slow down, honey. Let me at least get my pack in the door and get these boots off, and I'll answer your questions. Think I can do that?"

Carsen nods, stepping back before coming closer again to hug me tightly. "I missed you."

I hug her back, kissing the top of her head before looking up to see Sarah watching us with a smile on her face. "How was it?"

"Good," I reply, letting go of Carsen and putting my backpack down. "I'll get that later. Let's see, my weekend . . ."

I give Carsen and Sarah a rundown of what's happened the past forty-eight hours, a heavily edited version, of course. "And after the pancakes, I dropped Elise off at her place so she could start work on her story," I finish, leaning back and sipping the Coke Sarah got me while I was telling Carsen about cooking chili. "Like I said, it was fun."

"So, do you like her? Is she your girlfriend now?" Carsen asks.

I take another sip of Coke and lean forward, watching Carsen carefully. "Do *you* like her? Because yes, I like her a lot."

Carsen smiles, nodding. "She's cool, Dad."

"Remember, baby, that no matter how much I like Elise, you're always my number one girl, right?"

Carsen rolls her eyes, and I feel like sometimes she thinks I'm about fifty years older than I actually am. "I know that! But I want you to have more than just me and Aunt Sarah."

I reach out, and Carsen comes over, plopping into my lap. She used to fit on one thigh, snuggling up to my side to watch cartoons. Now, she's tall and all gangly limbs, but I'll happily hold my little girl anytime she'll let me, knowing it's getting more and more rare as she gets older. She's wise beyond her years sometimes, and it strikes me just how fast she's growing up. "I love you, Carsen."

She looks at me, no doubt in her mind. "I know, Dad. I love you too."

Behind her, I see Sarah give us a nod and get up. "Think I'll start dinner for tonight. How's my famous biscuits and gravy sound?"

"Awesome!" Carsen says. "Uhh . . . so does that mean I have to go do my homework now?"

"You'd better," I mock growl, making Carsen bounce up and run off with a laugh. I laugh too and watch her disappear before looking at Sarah.

"So you were fine taking care of her this weekend?" I ask her as soon as Carsen's out of earshot.

"You know I adore that girl. Don't you even think about that. Carsen's right. Elise is good for you." Her tone takes a more serious note. "If she's it, you need to circle the wagons, make sure she fits with you and Carsen. Dinner went well, but you need more time together. Both you and her, and the three of you."

"The four of us, you mean. You're a huge part of this too, Sarah. Carsen has only had you as a mother figure. I don't want to ever replace that, but I want to see if this can go somewhere. Who knows, maybe add to our ragtag motley crew."

Sarah reaches up to hug me, lightly kissing my cheek. "I like that plan. Let's see if we can do dinner this week . . . the four of us."

CHAPTER
Nineteen

ELISE

CHECKING MY DRESS, I realize that I'm even more nervous than when I came to interview Keith the first time.

I know why. I feel like this is a test. Dinner before was to make sure I'd keep my mouth shut. Then, this thing between Keith and I was . . . physical, primal, but not emotional.

This is more personal. This is to see if my edges fit in with Keith's family and their edges. Figuring out if it's an easy, smooth fit or a forced one that leads to friction and fraying. I'm praying it's the former, because I really like Keith. It is emotional now.

Hell, I'm pretty sure I more than "like" him, even if I'm not ready to put a label that big on it yet. But I will admit, to myself, at least, that I want to see where this goes . . . beyond the interviews, beyond casual hookups. I want to see him as a father and get to know Carsen and Sarah more, because they're important to Keith and that means they're important to me.

And hence the nerves. We're not doing anything fancy, just a casual dinner at a restaurant near downtown. But I want this to go well. Really well.

Walking in, I'm suddenly unsure whether Keith would've given his real name. "Uh, hi, I'm supposed to meet someone here at seven?" I tell the bored looking hostess. "I don't know what name it's under though."

"You can check," the hostess replies, waving a hand vaguely behind her. I look around, and after two passes, I see Keith sitting in a back corner, facing the wall. I'd know that bald head and set of wide shoulders anywhere. Plus, the fact that Carsen is waving wildly at me is a sure tip-off. But I don't see Sarah. I hope she's here.

Heading over, I'm not sure what to do. Should I kiss him in front of

Carsen or just sit down like it's no big deal that I'm invading a family dinner as a trial run? "Uh, hi."

Keith stands up to greet me with a hug and a quick kiss, and I see he has on his Clark Kent glasses disguise again and an oversized polo shirt that amps up the nerd effect.

It's cute, but still sexy as he gives me a smirk. "So glad you could make it."

I smile, taking the seat Keith motions to, next to him and across from Carsen. "Of course. I wouldn't miss this. I've been excited and nervous about it all day!"

He smiles, leaning in to whisper in my ear. "Don't be nervous. They both already like you."

Just like that, the swarm of nervous butterflies is gone and instead I'm filled with warmth, reassured that this is going to be okay. "Where's Sarah?"

"Right here," Sarah says behind me. "Sorry, had to use the ladies' room."

We sit down, chatting about our day, and I quickly realize that Carsen and Sarah are raptly watching every exchange between Keith and me and have matching wide grins plastered across their faces.

"What?" I ask, feeling heat rush to my face after we place our orders. "You guys don't like fish?"

Carsen giggles a little girl laugh but leans towards Sarah, talking low even though we can all hear her. "Check out her eyes. They're sparking like fireworks. Think that's Dad or makeup?"

Sarah hums, obviously used to Carsen's sense of humor. "Ask her." she tells Carsen as she gives me a wink.

Carsen leans back to me. "Do you wear makeup?"

I grin, catching on. "I do, just a little to bring out my features. But you know the trick to looking your absolute best?" Carsen tilts her head, eager for the answer. "Being happy. Always makes you glow from within." I wait a half a beat and then we all giggle like only females can do and I feel a knot unfurl in my belly even more.

"I was too nervous to say anything last time, but I really love your hair. It's much cuter than your dad's."

Carsen grins, her eyes shooting to Keith as he rubs at his head, which is covered with a few days worth of stubble on top. "Think I'll grow it out until the next show. Helps with the anonymity."

"Brother, was that a five-syllable word? Elise, I think you've worked miracles! He's doing more than grunting like a grumpy ass," Sarah teases.

"Hey, I do more than that." Keith protests, "I talk. Sometimes."

"Ugh, man speak, woman understand," Sarah jokes, grunting as Keith glowers at her, but I can see the twitch of laughter at the corners of his mouth as he fights to keep a straight, stern face.

We eat for a few minutes, comfortable and chatty with each other when Carsen pipes up. "Hey, got any plans tomorrow?"

I wipe my mouth with my napkin. "Nothing really. What's up?"

Carsen looks at Sarah, who nods. "Aunt Sarah is taking me shopping so I can find a dress for the school dance. It's going to be epic . . . the dance and then it's my best friend Kaitlyn's birthday, so I get to sleep over at her house after. You wanna go shopping with us?"

She's speaking so quickly and animatedly. It takes my brain a moment to catch up to my ears. "Shopping sounds like something I might know a thing or two about," I say carefully, looking at Sarah, not wanting her to think I'm stepping on her toes with Carsen. But she's smiling and seems excited about the idea too. "Sounds fun! What time?"

Keith gawks, looking around the table. "Are you sure?"

Carsen bounces excitedly while Sarah smiles. "We'll pick you up at four? Then we can grab some dinner to bring home while we're out."

I smile back at them both. "It's a date!"

Keith mock growls. "I don't know whether to be happy you are all getting along, or scared you're going out without me."

Sarah laughs. "Oh, you'll be there with us . . . in cash form, Daddy Big Bucks." We all laugh as dessert is served and Sarah promises to tell me all Keith's embarrassing childhood stories.

Dessert is wonderful, caramel cheesecake for me, and after we pay—I notice Sarah uses her credit card, probably another layer of protection—we walk outside. "Thank you," I tell Carsen. "You were right, the cheesecake was to die for."

"Anytime," Carsen says, giving me a quick little hug. "I can't wait until tomorrow. Can I get some heels too?"

"Let's talk about that in the truck," Sarah says with a knowing grin, taking Carsen by the shoulders and steering her away. "We'll be waiting."

The two of them walk away, and I'm left with Keith, who's been quiet through most of dessert. "You okay? You've been a little quiet."

"This was the best family dinner out we've had in years," Keith says quietly, taking my hand as I lead him toward my car. "Carsen really likes you. I was just taking it all in."

"She's a great little girl," I answer honestly. "Sarah's done a good job being a mother figure for her. But . . . do you think she'll be worried if Carsen and I become friends?"

"Not at all, we talked about that already," Keith says. We reach my car, and he pulls me in close. "You're a wonderful person, and I'm glad you're getting to know my daughter."

I put my arms around Keith's neck, looking up into his eyes. "I'm happy to know my nerdy boyfriend has such a sweet family."

Keith chuckles and pulls me in close for a kiss. It's tender, and while there's a little bit of fire underneath his touch, it's restrained for now. Still, I moan, slipping my tongue over his once before pulling back. "Just in case they're spying on us again."

"I have no doubt they are," Keith says, smirking. "Carsen because she's curious, Sarah because she wants to make sure I behave."

"I happen to like when you don't behave," I purr, pressing my body against his. "I missed you."

"I know. I missed you too," Keith rumbles. "And if you can be a good girl for just a couple more days, you and I can have plenty of time together to make sure you get a heaping dose of—"

"You'd better stop," I warn him, my heartbeat speeding up. "Or else we're going to have a not-family-friendly moment in this parking lot."

Keith smirks, stepping back to create a small space between us but leaving his hands on my hips, and I leave mine wrapped around his neck. "I never thought I'd be doing this, but it feels right with you."

I nod, feeling my heart swell in my chest. "It does feel right. This feels big, Keith." The last part is almost a whisper, feeling like a confession as I wait with bated breath to see what he says.

"I know. I didn't think things could happen like this, so fast and with a less than friendly start. But there's something about you, about us . . ." He says as his eyes are searching mine.

"I feel like that too. Keith, I never thought it was real . . . but I really think I'm—"

"Not here," Keith says, putting a finger to my lips. "I feel it too, but when we say it, I want to be able to take you, claim you and have you claim me back. And I can't do that in this parking lot with my kid a few cars away."

I nod, the warm assurance of Keith's feelings sinking in. Suddenly, I pull him to me, kissing him hard, claiming his mouth in a turnaround that leaves him stunned for a moment before he kisses me back, cupping my ass with his hidden hand to give it a squeeze. I can feel him swell, and when I pull back, Keith's breath is fast and deep, his eyes glowing with desire.

Keith nods, breathing deeply as he regains his control. "I need to go. Are you sure about taking Carsen shopping?"

I nod, smiling. "Absolutely. Girls' shopping trip sounds like fun, and I want to get to know her."

"You're amazing," Keith says before lifting my hand to his lips and kissing my fingertips sweetly. "Goodnight, Elise."

"Goodnight," I answer, watching him go as my fingertips tingle from his kiss. Despite the oversized polo, he is still an amazing figure as he walks away, his ass perfectly filling his jeans and flexing enough to give me good dreams tonight.

Very good dreams.

CHAPTER

Twenty

ELISE

It's only the third time Carsen's asked me, and I'm happier than ever that she's asking. It was a little awkward at first, despite the good dinner we all had yesterday. I can understand this isn't about Keith and me. This is about how I fit with Carsen and Sarah . . . and that's going to take a little longer to adjust to.

But Carsen has loved having our undivided attention, giving a fashion show-worthy walk and twirl with each dress she's tried on. It's helped us relax, the giggles taking us over more than once, and making the conversations with Sarah more comfortable as Carsen changes into another possible dress selection.

"I think it looks great, Carsen . . . but I'm not sure it's my favorite," I admit. "What about the black one?"

"No way, that looked so old lady," Carsen replies, making me wince inside. I thought it looked beautiful and classic, but then again, to Carsen, twenty-one is middle aged. "What about the red one?"

"NO!" Sarah and I say simultaneously, making me grin. Sarah smirks too and explains. "Honey, I know you want to look grown up, but that's just not something a twelve-year-old should be wearing. What about the blue one?"

"I think that's my favorite style, but I like it in green better," Carson says. She looks at us both and we give her double thumbs up, all in agreement on her choice.

With the dress decided on, we move on to accessory shopping. "So, are you looking forward to the dance?" I ask.

"Well . . ." Carsen says before blushing. "I think Max will be there. I hope he asks me to dance."

"Max?" I ask, catching Sarah's shrug out of the corner of my eye. "A boy from school? Does your Dad know about this Max?"

"Of course not!" Carsen says. "Daddy would freak out if he knew Max gave me a card for my birthday. He said I'm cute. And he's like, the cutest guy in my class. And it's not like Dad can come to the dance and do the whole intimidating dad thing anyway." She raises a finger to her lips, "Ssssh, it's a secret."

I smile. "Who's a secret? Your dad or Max?" Carsen smirks, and I can read her answer all over her face. "Ah, so *both* of them are top secret."

Sarah smiles, but shows that she's heard every word. "I'd just like to point out, you shouldn't use your dad's desire for secrecy against him, you know?"

Carsen nods, trying not to look guilty. "I know. I know that if everyone knew, we couldn't do stuff like this . . . walk the mall and shop. Unless the big scary guys came with us."

I'm struck by how mature Carsen really is because most kids would be shouting about their famous dad all over Instagram and demanding special treatment. Hell, I know some adult children who act that way. I've written stories about some of them. Instead, Carsen is chill, understands the risks of fame, and seems content to be exactly who she is, secrets and all.

Accessory shopping is quick and easy. Carsen might be on the budding cusp of womanhood but her tastes are simple and elegant. A thin necklace and set of earrings later, and we decide on an afternoon snack at the food court.

I'm about halfway through my ice cream cone when I get a prickle on the back of my neck. Wiping my mouth with a napkin, I glance around discretely.

"You okay?" Sarah asks, sipping a Coke. "You look like you've seen the boogeyman."

"No . . . but I do feel like I'm being watched," I reply. Across the food court, I see why. Francesca is sitting near one of the pillars, a wide, floppy hat on her head but still, I know her too well to be put off by a simple hat. "Shhh-oot." I manage to correct myself. "We should go."

"What's wrong?" Carsen asks, instantly on alert.

"My co-worker," I reply, giving Sarah a pointed look.

Sarah catches my meaning. "Alright, honey. Grab your stuff and we'll go shoe shopping somewhere else."

Carsen doesn't dilly-dally, but Francesca seems to be faster. Just as I'm grabbing my purse, she comes over, a big, fake smile on her face. "Elise, it's so good to see you again!"

I glower, annoyed at her intrusion . . . again. "Francesca, figured you'd still be at the office today. Cut out early?"

Francesca laughs, an obviously fake tinkle like a bell. "Oh, I'm just out shopping for a gown for the premiere next weekend. Thought I might treat myself, you know. I was just grabbing a half-caff frappe when I saw you out with . . . sorry, I don't remember your names."

"Sarah and Car," I answer, praying I can keep this short and not have to give Francesca any more information than I have to. She might cut corners to get ahead, but she's got good instincts.

Shit, I should have used fake names. At least Francesca will likely assume Carsen is Sarah's daughter.

"So, what's got you out?" Francesca asks, her eyes clicking from bag to bag on the table like she's taking mental notes. Fuck my life, she probably is.

"Just out for some girl time with my friends," I reply. "Listen, I'd love to stay and chat, but we really need to roll."

As we walk away, Carsen doesn't seem to realize the significance, but Sarah gives me a worried glance. "Is everything okay?" she asks quietly while we close the trunk of her car and Carsen's getting into her seat. "Should I tell Keith?"

"No . . . no, I don't think he needs to worry," I answer softly. I give her a nod, attempting to convey that I think we're clear and that I understand how important this is . . . to Carsen, to Keith, to Sarah, and now, to me. There's a wiggle in the back of my mind that finds it odd that I've seen Francesca twice recently, considering we never run into each other, but I let it go considering the place is popular and is near some of the busiest streets in town. Francesca could have been legit dosing on caffeine and shopping, just like us. "I'll handle it."

"Okay," Sarah says, her voice still a little tense. She's probably kicking herself as much as I am for coming to a popular shopping center.

I should've had a better plan for that. Hell, I can do disguises that'll fool people all the time . . . yet I forgot to even come up with some fake names for Sarah and Carsen, a cover story, anything. I do it all the time when I'm working a story, but it hadn't occurred to me to do it for a simple shopping trip.

That's a mistake I won't make again.

"Listen, Sarah?" I ask as we're still outside the car. "I promise, I'll handle this. I'll do my best to keep Carsen and Keith safe."

Sarah studies me for a moment, then nods. "I hope so. I believe you."

CHAPTER

Twenty~One

KEITH

FOR THE PAST a week and a half, it feels like a new routine has established itself in my life. I wake up, make sure Carsen's good for school before Sarah drops her off, then grab a workout before spending a few hours putting together tunes. That little ditty in my head keeps developing, and as I work on it, I'm more and more convinced it can be a good song . . . maybe even my best.

Sometime during the day, Elise either calls or comes over to talk about this and that for articles, showing me rough drafts on what she's got. More often than not, she stays for dinner, and on those nights, the whole evening is a heady mix of professional and personal as we talk about music and tours and then roll into deep late-night conversations about everything and nothing. One night, she'll hang with Carsen and we'll be all about what's on TV. The next, Elise and I damn-near have ripped the headboard off my bed as we fucked ourselves into a near coma just from an intense quickie before Carsen got home from school.

It's been amazing to watch how Carsen, Sarah, and Elise have bonded so quickly and easily, although I'm even further outnumbered now, but I wouldn't change it for anything. I'd worried so much for so long, assuming that I'd be alone until Carsen was grown, turning off that part of my heart, my soul.

But Elise makes it possible to have a connection with my daughter and still have a safe haven where Carsen knows she's my priority. That takes a special woman, and I'm glad that it's Elise.

We haven't retraced those steps we were taking in the parking lot, saying how we feel. We haven't had a night alone to address those feelings the way I want to. But looking over at her, I smile.

She's at home in my house, washing up the dinner dishes from our date night-slash-interview and loading the dishwasher the way I like. It's a small thing, really, just a nuance of daily life, but the simple fact that she's comfortable doing it here, in my home, makes all the difference.

It resonates deep inside me, a fiery ball of joy singing out at her presence in my life, completing a puzzle at my core that I didn't even know was missing a piece. I feel solid with her here, and I need her to know that.

Standing in the doorway with my arms crossed over my chest, I watch for one more second before I interrupt her, "Elise." There's already gravel and heat in my voice, but I can't and don't want to control it.

She looks over at me, a question in her eyes. "Keith?"

"Leave the dishes for later. I need you now. Come with me." I can see the moment of hesitation on her face, the way she weighs whether she should sass me back, but she must sense the weight in my words. I'm glad. I don't want to punish her tonight. I want to love her, fuck her, be inside her body so deep she feels my imprint there forever more.

Tonight, I don't just want her body. I want her soul and her heart. It's only fair because she has mine.

I press off the doorframe, turning to walk down the hall, feeling her presence behind me as she follows me to the bedroom. As soon as she passes the threshold, I turn, closing the door behind her.

Her eyes track me, her breath already shallow and fast as I slip my shirt over my head and toss it to the floor. I stand in front of her, and I can feel her gaze as she traces the tattoos along my chest and arms. "Strip for me, Elise. I want you naked."

She doesn't rush to do as I command. Instead, she takes advantage, knowing her own power even as she submits to what I want. Slowly, she slips the straps of her dress off her shoulders, looking up at me through the fringe of her lashes, a flirtatious faux-innocence on her face as she holds it to her chest.

With a dramatic flair, she lets go and it drops to the floor, puddled at her feet in a whoosh. She steps out, kicking it out of the way and standing before me in her bra and panties.

I take a mental snapshot. "So fucking beautiful, Elise. Take it all off. Show me everything."

She reaches to unclasp her bra and slips her panties down her legs. She stands still, hands at her sides, confident in herself as she should be. She's a work of art and I'm a lucky fucker to get to see her this way. No falsity, no pretense, just bare and exposed and vulnerable.

It's a gift she's bestowing on me and I know it. I walk around her, memorizing her full beauty, trailing a finger along her arm, across the back of her shoulders, around to her collarbone, down between her cleavage, and along her hips.

"Michelangelo himself could not have created a creature more beautiful than you," I murmur as I trace my finger across her stomach, dipping into her shallow belly button and continuing across to the other side.

She is virtually vibrating with need by the time I stand in front of her again. I undo my belt, dropping my jeans and then my boxer briefs to stand nude in front of her too, letting her see me just as bare, just as vulnerable. "Keith . . ."

My cock is rock-hard, straining to get closer to Elise as I hold back, needing to do this right, wanting more than just the gift of her body. I take a half step back and speak from the depths of my soul.

"Elise, there's nothing to hide behind right now," I reply softly, my voice intense with emotion that fuels every syllable. "Just you and me, naked physically and emotionally. I told you before that I felt it too, but that I wanted to be able to claim you, mark you as mine when I said it."

Her eyes, which had been roving over my form, are now locked on mine, her lips parted in anticipation. "I didn't think this was ever going to happen to me, but you came in and crashed my world in more ways than one. You challenge me, you make me wish for things I never thought I would. Elise . . . I love you."

I can see the glitter of tears in the corners of her eyes, but she doesn't let them fall. Instead, she takes a deep breath and puts her hands behind her back, not only offering herself to me but making her look even more beautiful. "I didn't see this coming either . . . any of it. I want more with you, with Carsen, than I have any right to want. I love you too, Keith."

It feels like vows, like we're making promises beyond this moment, the gravity of the situation pulling us together. I close the distance between us, wrapping my arms around Elise and taking her wrists in my hand as our lips meet in a passionate kiss, sealing our words with our actions.

Our tongues tangle, the fire burning hotter, brighter as we press against each other, moans and skin melding into one being.

"Take me, Keith," Elise begs breathlessly when our lips part. "Claim me, mark me as yours."

My whole body starts to tremble at her request, knowing this is more than we've done before, physically, emotionally and spiritually, because she is giving herself up to me all the way to her soul, the way I am hers.

Turning, I lead her over to the bed, still keeping my hands on her wrists, as if by encircling them I'm closing the circle that's between us, forging our bond stronger even though I don't have to 'command' her at all. "I need to worship you. Every inch of your fucking delicious body is mine. Lie down."

I release her and she lies down, her arms and legs splayed out like she's making a snow angel in the white sheets, and it gives me a dirty idea.

Stepping into the closet, I grab a few of my rarely used ties and make my way over to her. Slowly, methodically, I tie her to the bedposts, forcing her to spread even wider, her body open and available.

"You okay?" I ask, running a finger down one silk tie to her wrist, tracing her skin all the way to the inside of her elbow. "Not too tight?"

Elise smiles, but she's writhing, trying but unable to get more contact between us. "No, I need you. Fuck, Keith . . ."

"No, my love," I rumble, leaning down and kissing her lips softly. "Not fucking. Loving."

Elise mewls as our lips brush against each other so softly that only the electricity between us guarantees that we're actually making contact. "Mmm . . ." I murmur against her skin as I kiss down her neck to nibble at the hollow of her throat. "You look fucking stunning like this, all tied up for me, your eyes just as open as your long legs are. Is this what you want, Elise?"

"Oh, God, yes. Yes," Elise groans as I lick her collarbones. I perch on the edge of the bed, wanting to touch her but knowing if I do, I'll abandon all self-control, and I don't want that.

"Your body . . . so sexy and smooth," I purr before running my tongue over her skin between her breasts, nibbling on the soft skin. I kiss over, watching Elise's eyes as I grow closer and closer to her nipple. I can feel the stiff pink nub drag over my throat and chin before I take it between my lips, sucking hard before biting down just enough to make Elise arch her back, moaning in pleasure.

"Keith . . . yes."

"Sex with you is like nothing I've ever had," I add, kissing down her body. I finally climb onto the bed between her stretched out legs, running my palms up her inner thighs as I look at the soft, delectable lips of her pussy. "You're smooth all over . . . and delicious."

"If you—" Elise tries to say, but her words are cut off as I lean down, covering her pussy with my mouth and kissing it lovingly, tracing my tongue from base to clit while my lips caress hers. Elise's breath catches, her words dissolving into a long, guttural moan that's deeper than I've ever heard her make before.

Guided by her sounds, I make love to her body with my mouth and tongue, sucking on her pussy lips before stroking her clit with my tongue in quick, soft little flicks that have Elise arching her back and trying to press her pussy against my mouth.

"Oh, God . . . I'm so going to make you come when you untie me," Elise groans, showing me her strength and sassiness. It's what I love and what makes her so special. She can take all I have and not wilt but come back wanting more. I nip at her thigh for her comment though, knowing that even though it's meant to be punishing, it only fuels her higher.

But all of my focus is on her as I lower my mouth again and devour her. I'm unrelenting, cupping her ass and lifting her to my eager tongue as I stroke and suck on her clit, my ears listening for the moment when she's about to come. "That's it, Elise. Let me hear what you like. Tell me."

Elise's breathing deepens, her chest heaving as she grunts out. "Keith . . . lick me, suck me . . . please . . ." before she's lost for words, one keening cry escaping with her air. She's almost vibrating on the bed as I lap at her clit, and I know the moment's here. Raising my head, I look into her beautiful eyes. "I love you."

Elise's breathing deepens, her chest heaving as she starts to quiver, almost vibrating on the bed as I lap at her clit, and I know the moment's here. Raising my head, I look into her beautiful eyes. "I love you."

Elise's answer is torn from her lips as I bite down lightly on her clit, ripping the orgasm from her body in a tidal wave that makes her throw her head back, screaming in pleasure as she covers my face in her delectable juices. I suck, taking everything she has, letting her ride it out slowly until she's limp, unable to even look down at me as I raise up from between her legs.

I come around, kneeling over her and tapping her cheek with my cock. "Open for me, Elise. Suck my cock down that amazing throat of yours. I'm gonna fuck your face, baby. Can you take it like this?"

She opens wide, her tongue poking out to lick at my tip as she nods. Slipping into the wet warmth of her mouth, we both moan at the sensation. "You like that? You like my thick cock in your sweet mouth while you're tied down at my mercy?"

Elise nods again, hollowing her cheeks and sucking hard. Her eyes tell me everything I need to know as she uses what little range of motion she has to bob up and down on my cock, getting it wet and throbbing for her.

"That's my good girl. Suck that cock, baby. Suck me hard."

I lean forward, grasping at the headboard with one hand and tangling the other in Elise's blonde locks. I'm getting deeper with every thrust until she's taking me fully into her throat as I fuck her face.

My eyes are locked on her, watching as my cock disappears into her puffy pink lips, her eyes gleaming with need. I'm so close, but not this time. Not now.

Elise moans in disappointment when I pull out, gasping as she looks at me with lust. "I wanted to taste your cum."

"I know, but I want to seal this moment inside you," I promise her. Moving down, I kneel between her spread legs, grabbing her inner thighs as I stare at her. "I need your pussy. Are you ready?"

"Oh, my God, Keith. Inside me, please. Fill me." Her hips are bucking, trying to get closer to my cock, but she's limited by the ties, unable to get what she desperately needs.

I move my hands higher, spreading her lips and lining up my cock with her entrance, teasing her. "Whose pussy is this?"

She cries out, "It's yours. My pussy, my heart, my fucking soul, Keith."

An even better answer than I'd dreamed of. I reward her with a sharp thrust, going balls-deep in one motion, forcing a satisfied cry from her throat. I hold her hips up, her back arching as I pound her mercilessly, the pleasure overwhelming my shredded control.

"Fuck, Elise. You too . . . my heart, my soul." I grunt, accentuating every word with another powerful stroke of my cock. "I love you."

Elise's eyes fill with tears, but she's smiling so I know they're happy tears, and I feel her pussy quiver. "That's it, come all over my cock," I encourage her. "Squeeze me so tight with that little pussy. I can take it, and I'll fill you so full you can't even hold it all."

With a final thrust, she shatters in my arms, writhing and pulling hard on her arm restraints, but I don't lose rhythm, keeping the driving force hard and deep as she cries out my name over and over like a prayer.

Her voice rises as her pussy clamps around me, and the pressure is too much. I come hard, my balls pulling up tight and my spine tingling before I crash over and shudder my pleasure, emptying into her.

Pulling out, I jerk my cock a few last times, covering her pussy lips with the last few spurts of my essence, needing to mark her inside and out.

I shake my cock a few times, wanting every drop on her, and then use the head to smear it around on her. It's primal, probably something that would turn some women off, but that doesn't matter in this moment.

What matters is that I need to mark her and that Elise wants to be marked by me. Her pride at being covered in my cum is just as palpable as my delight in seeing her dirty like this. *Mine.*

I untie the restraints, gently rubbing her wrists and ankles to get the circulation back as I kiss each one delicately.

"You okay?"

She smiles, stretching and squirming around like a pleased kitten as she curls up into a ball. "So much better than okay. Only one thing could make it perfect."

"What's that?" I ask before realizing what Elise needs. Sliding behind her, I gather her in my arms, my finally sated cock nestling against her ass as I wrap myself around her as much as possible. "That's perfect."

Twenty~Two

KEITH

I LOOK AT CARSEN, unable to tell her exactly how I feel. Part of it, I guess, is that seeing her twirling in her dress, looking more mature than I've ever imagined possible scares the shit out of me. What happened to the little girl in pigtails who'd wake up in the middle of the night and beg to climb into bed with me so that I could keep the monsters away?

There's no evidence of that little girl now as she struts and twirls, looking comfortable in the short one-inch wedge heels that Sarah and Elise talked me into letting her wear. The other part of me is so damn proud of my little girl and the young woman she's growing up to become. It's an oddly oppositional pull to want to see who she can be while at the same time wanting to force her to stay my baby forever.

Carsen comes over to me, wrapping her arms around me in a hug. I look down, seeing just the hint of mascara and blush that Elise did for her, and when she smiles, she looks so much like the woman she's going to become it makes my heart ache. "I love you, Daddy. I'm sorry you can't take me to the dance."

"It's okay honey," I promise, rubbing my freshly shaved head. The label wants me to get some new photos done for the next album and summer tour, and that means 'Keith Perkins' needs to be in full effect. "You look beautiful, baby. More like your mother every day. Did I ever tell you about the time I took her to our first high school dance?"

Carsen shakes her head, making me sigh. I know I don't talk about Janie much, but Carsen should hear these stories. Her mother loved her so much, and it certainly wasn't Carsen's fault that we fell out of love or what happened in the end.

"Come over here and sit down," I reply, noticing Sarah and Elise quietly moving toward the exit. I can see they understand. This is our time. "Over the years, Janie and I went to a few dances together. But the very first one was a winter formal. I wore what had to be the ugliest suit in existence. But she looked gorgeous in a white dress with little blue flowers on it. It actually looked a lot like what you're wearing now."

Carsen looks down, delight obvious on her face as she runs her hands along the skirt of her dress. "Really?"

I nod, smiling a little at the memory. "I was so nervous I didn't know how to dance at all. But your mom helped me, just swayed back and forth with me. It was a great night, the first of many. And that's what tonight will be for you too. The first of many greats as you grow up. I know she'd be real proud of the young lady you're becoming."

Carsen's eyes are shining, and when I open my arms, she runs into them, giving me a big hug and laying her head on my shoulder, climbing into my lap a little. She barely fits, but that's okay. I hold her tight, knowing that my little girl is growing up so damn fast. Too fast, and I want to freeze time right here, where she's on the cusp of leaving her innocent childhood behind and becoming a teenager.

A teenage daughter? What the hell am I going to do?

I don't know how to raise a teenage daughter. Hell, I barely survived my teen years with my sanity intact. I know I'll have my hands full when she starts being interested in boys, that's for sure.

But as I look around, I know I'm not alone. Sarah and Elise are still in the doorway, holding hands and watching the scene between Carsen and me with watery smiles. They're so different, yet so vital and similar.

Sarah has been there for me almost since the very beginning, sacrificing so much to make our lives work as I chase my music dreams. She's been essential to my becoming a true man, and she's never complained.

And Elise has fit in nearly seamlessly to our little family, bringing with her sass and joyfulness, and a love of life that's reignited the passion in my own heart. It's not what some would call a picture-perfect life, but it's perfect for me, and I'm so damn thankful for it.

Sarah glances at her watch. "All right, young lady. Go grab your purse and let's go."

Carsen runs off to her room and Sarah pats my shoulder. "Good job, Keith. I was scared you'd end up locking her in her room and not let her go."

I smile, knowing that I'd considered it, but I also know I can't stop my little girl from growing up. "It definitely crossed my mind, but I figured you two would stop me."

Elise chuckles and comes over, sitting on my knee and putting her arms around my shoulders. "Well, I'm the bad influence here, so the plan was for Sarah to distract you while I showed Carsen how to sneak out a window. I figure it's a life skill that'll serve her well."

I growl at her. "You'll teach her no such thing."

There's a moment where the unsaid threat hangs in the air, tension coiled around us, then it breaks as we all bust up laughing. Elise leans into me and gives me a smack on the cheek. "Okay, we talked about it but I wouldn't have actually shown her how to sneak out. Probably. Maybe."

I love her brattiness, knowing that she's joking and wouldn't actually lead Carsen astray, but to tease me about it is enough to warrant a bit of a spanking later, the kind that leaves us both more than satisfied, and that makes my smile more than a bit predatory and we both know it.

Sarah clears her throat, turning toward the hallway. "Well, on that note, I'll be leaving now. I'll pick up Carsen and bring her home tomorrow mid-morning. Maybe be dressed this time?"

I grin, but Elise blushes. It's a pretty sight and makes me want her round ass the same flushed pink color.

As Carsen jets back into the room, I call out some last-minute reminders. "You've got your phone to call if you need anything. Have fun, baby. Sarah will pick you up at Kaitlyn's tomorrow after your sleepover, and then you can tell us all about the dance. Behave, young lady!"

Carsen runs back, a knowing look on her face as she kisses my cheek. "I love you too, Dad."

And then she's gone in a flash, so much sooner than I expected. I sit in my chair, stunned at how fast it happened. Sarah gives me one more smile as she follows Carsen out to the car, and they're gone. To my baby's first dance.

The silence is deafening but slowly becomes filled with promise and potential as I realize we're alone all night. I meet Elise's mouth in a soft kiss, pulling her body flush to mine. "Thank you for being here tonight. I know Carsen liked that we were all here to celebrate her first dance, and she was thrilled with the dress you found."

Elise smiles, snuggling tighter against me and melting into my arms. "I'm glad I was here too. She looked beautiful and I think she liked the story about her mom."

I apprise her carefully, running my hand up and down Elise's arm, knowing I'd have to talk with her about this but hopeful there isn't a problem. "That didn't bother you, did it?"

"Of course not!" Elise says, sitting up and smiling. "A girl needs her mother, even if it's only through stories. She's lucky to have had a mother who loved her and a dad who can tell her those stories. Plus, Sarah is a great role model for her. She's a loved girl."

"She is. And so are you."

Elise smiles at me, obviously pleased. "I know it's fast, but I'm hoping that I can be . . . well, not a mom—I think Sarah's got that role covered—but at least a good friend and role model for her too."

"I think it's not too early to think about that," I reassure her, giving her another kiss, already getting lost in her sweetness. Suddenly, there's a shrill beeping from the nearby kitchen. Sitting back, I laugh a little sorrowfully. "Goddamn phone. I'd better check it anyway in case it's Carsen."

Elise lets me up, and I go into the kitchen, where it's sitting on the counter, still ringing away. I check the screen, but it says unknown number. Normally, I'd let it go to voicemail considering not many people have this number, but it could be Carsen calling from a friend's mom's phone or something, so I pick up. "Hello."

There's a moment of silence, then a man's voice comes on, sounding muffled but still distinctly male. "Keith Perkins?"

"Who's asking?" I reply, the hairs on the back of my neck standing up.

"Mr. Perkins, we need to meet," a voice says, more clear now and almost . . . snooty sounding. "I've come into some information I think you'd be rather interested in. Write this address down. 3489 Johnson Boulevard, right off Main. Be here in one hour."

"What?" I ask, wondering if this asshole is drunk or something. "What are you talking about? Meet for what?"

Elise steps in my field of view, a concerned look on her face. "Everything okay?" she mouths silently. I shrug, and she lifts an eyebrow.

I hold up one finger, asking her to wait a second to fire off the questions I can see in her eyes, and focus on listening to the man on the phone. "One hour. 3489 Johnson Boulevard," he repeats. "Do not be late, Mr. Perkins. I'm certain you won't like the consequences if someone else were to get this information before you do."

There's a click and the line goes dead as the man hangs up. I stare at my phone for a moment, feeling like I've just been punched in the gut.

"Who was that?" Elise asks as I set my phone down. "What's wrong, Keith? You look pale as a ghost."

"I don't know," I reply, trying to keep my voice level. "A guy said that he has information I'd be interested in. Gave me an address and said to be there in an hour."

"What?" Elise asks, shocked. "What are you going to do?"

I shake my head, running my hands over my smooth dome. "I don't know."

I search my memories, replaying the conversation again, looking for clues what this could be about, a sinking feeling in my stomach. He said I wouldn't like it if someone else got the information. That sounds like a threat, whatever it is. Of course, my brain leapfrogs to Carsen first, since she's always my greatest secret, but there's no reason for anyone to know about her.

Elise, ever the investigator, stays calm, trying to be helpful. "What's the address? Maybe we can look it up and get a clue?"

"3489 Johnson," I recite for her, and her jaw drops.

"Oh, my God!" she gasps, her voice trailing off into a whisper. "No way."

"What? Do you know the address?"

She nods, her face frozen in horror. "That's my office, Keith. That's the address of *The Daily Spot.*"

Elise's office. Okay, keep it cool . . . "We should go. Maybe it's just about the articles?" I say hopefully, knowing I'm full of shit even as I say it. The man didn't introduce himself like it was a professional call, and he specifically said he had information I wouldn't like.

The truck ride into town is silent, both of us considering a million possibilities for what we're walking into.

Pulling in, it looks like a normal office building on a weekend, empty and just waiting, recovering after a busy week before it gets swarmed again on Monday with worker ants trying to hustle a buck.

The main parking lot is empty except for one Mercedes parked up front. "Guess that's the mystery man."

Elise's voice shakes, and her hand comes to cover her mouth. "That's Donnie's car."

My phone buzzes again, and I look to see I've got a text message. *Upstairs, sixth floor. Front's unlocked.*

Elise reaches out, and I take her hand as we go inside, the empty, nearly dark lobby making things even more foreboding. We take the elevator up to the sixth floor, stepping off and following the only light visible, a dim glow that brightens as we approach. "Is this . . .?"

"My office," Elise whispers in reply, pointing at the etched glass. "At least, the lobby."

We open the door and follow the glow to another office, where inside, we find a round weasel-looking man sitting behind a large desk. Even before he speaks, the crystal bowl of jellybeans on the corner of his desk tells me exactly who he is. "Donnie."

Donnie doesn't look surprised, but instead his ruddy face glows, obviously pleased. "Keith! You don't mind if I call you Keith, do you? That whole Mr. Perkins shit is for people who aren't friends, and I think you and I are going to be very good friends. Elise . . . so good to see you too. I wasn't sure I'd be seeing you tonight." He pauses, a comical sneer on his face. "Oh, who am I kidding? Of course, I knew you were at Keith's tonight!" He claps his hands twice, like he's overjoyed at our being here, as if this is some twisted fucking social call.

I don't respond, keeping my gaze on the man. I don't trust him. He's too at ease here, delighted at calling the shots as we come running to his territory when he beckoned. I sit in one of the chairs in front of his desk, wanting to show that I don't perceive him as a threat. Elise follows my lead, sitting in the other chair, but she looks scared and disgusted at the same time.

As we sit, there's a sound behind us and Francesca walks in, shutting the door behind her and going over to Donnie's side to perch on the narrow built-in bookshelf behind him. Putting a well-manicured hand on Donnie's shoulder, she sneers at Elise, smug satisfaction rolling off her in waves.

Donnie looks over his shoulder for a moment, patting Francesca's bare knee like you'd pat a strange dog on the head. "Thank you, Fran. We're just getting started."

She smiles wanly at him, but I catch the flash of disgust in her eyes at his touch. His eyes stay locked on her leg so Donnie doesn't notice her reaction.

Donnie turns back to Elise and me. "So, Elise. I have to say, I've been mostly pleased with your work. It's well-written and if I was running *Country Music Weekly*, you'd probably be getting a raise. However, this is the goddamn *Daily Spot*, and your articles are decidedly lacking on . . . juiciness."

He says the word juiciness with emphasis, spittle pooling at the corners of his mouth. Reaching over, he picks up a small handful of jellybeans and pops a few in his mouth.

Elise starts to speak, but Donnie waves her off. "Don't bother telling me there's nothing again. You've already said it enough, and I'm well aware that you're lying. After all . . . you've given me all the dirt I need."

Elise's eyes snap to me, but I keep my eyes locked on Donnie, trying to get a read on him. Looking at Elise, he smirks, chewing his jellybeans like a cow with its cud as he grins smugly. "I suspected there was more, that you were holding out on me. So I assigned my favorite reporter to investigate."

I let my eyes tick up to Francesca, remembering how we'd run into her at brunch. I'd dismissed it to reassure Elise, but it hadn't been a coincidence at all.

For her part, Francesca adjusts herself self-righteously, like the cat who just got the cream. She even seems to preen a bit as she re-crosses her legs, an obviously practiced move designed to look sexy.

I look back to find Donnie still eyeing Elise with a leering appraisal. "You're quite good at following a mark, Elise," he continues, his jaws never stopping as he smacks his way through another candy. "Seems you're quite a bit less adept at being followed. Usually, you never even noticed."

Donnie smiles at Elise like she's prey he's preparing to devour, but even though he's insulting her, I'm the real target here. I know that with every bit of dread running through my blood right now. My fingers tighten on the arms of the chair, and it's only thirty years of self-control that prevent me from grabbing him and jacking him up right now.

Francesca interrupts, puffing up even more as she giggles, but the sound is more mean-girl than sweet. "You really should be more aware. I followed you for days . . . to Keith's, to the cabin, to dinner, to the mall. The cabin was a little hard, but nothing a good telephoto lens couldn't fix. And you never suspected a thing!"

"You backstabbing, dirty little bitch—" Elise says, starting to get up, but Donnie claps, getting our attention again.

"So, as Francesca was following you, looking for the dirt *you* were supposed to be finding, we discovered something rather interesting. It didn't take long to figure out that you two are sleeping together. A bit salacious to fuck the talent, Elise, and definitely a bit of slumming on your part, Keith."

"Fuck you, you fucking dirt-peddling slimeball," I growl. "So what if two consenting adults are having sex? Is this what passes as shocking news these days?"

Donnie laughs, looking at me like I'm dense. "Well, it could be a good story. Trust me, as they say, sex sells. But more important is what it led us to discover. It seems that in addition to fucking a tabloid reporter, you seem to be doing it to buy her silence . . . about your twelve-year-old daughter."

I can't stop the growl that tears from the depths of my chest, and I hear Elise gasp next to me. I'd known walking into this tonight that this was probably what was coming, but hearing it straight from this asshole's mouth is more than I can take. I'm going to tear his heart out and shove a crystal bowl of jellybeans in its place.

"Whatever you think you know, you'd best keep your fucking mouth shut about it," I threaten, my lip curling.

Donnie steeples his fingers, regarding me coolly as he opens a file folder on his desk, spreading out picture after picture, along with detailed reports of our outings. "If I had a dollar for every person who's threatened to kick my ass over what I find out, I'd be rich enough to get out of this gig and retire," he says, pushing the photos toward me.

They're sharp, hi-def, and show a variety of things. Sure, there are a few of me and Elise getting romantic . . . but what's even more hurtful is me hugging Carsen. Of us at the restaurant. Of me with my little girl. There are others too . . . of Carsen by herself, or with Sarah when she's getting picked up. "There are a couple of possibilities here, but what happens is totally up to you."

"What do you want?" I snarl, only the thought of ending up in jail and Child Services taking Carsen away from me keeping me in my chair.

"Well, this can go one of two ways, and I'm being gracious enough to let you choose," Donnie says greasily. "Option one, you will pay me a half-mil each year that you want this secret to stay quiet. My understanding is that Carsen's twelve. So probably, you'll want to wait until she's at least eighteen. So let's say $3.5million to make it easy?"

"You son of a bitch," Elise rasps, but Donnie plunges on.

"Option two, I'll publish an exclusive story breaking the news of your secret child and the relationship you had to keep it quiet. Either way, I win. I get money from you directly or I get notoriety for breaking a huge story and make money on clicks and sales. Win-win either way for me."

I'm furious, and it's taking every bit of my control to keep from jumping over this desk and pounding this weasel's face. Elise is mad too, but not nearly as controlled as I am.

She's like a screeching wildcat, vaulting out of her chair to slam her hands down on the desk, sending Donnie's jellybean bowl tumbling to the carpet where it bounces. "What the fuck, Donnie? You can't go around black-mailing people! You cannot publish this story. She's just a little girl!"

Donnie laughs mockingly, his voice pitching high into a screeching falsetto that's clearly a mockery of Elise's voice. "You can't blackmail people! She's just a little girl!" He laughs again, leaning back in his chair. "Of course I can. You think this is the first story to get squashed this way? If only you knew the celebs and their secrets in my little black book of dirt. So many juicy stories, all ready to be hung out like dirty laundry for everyone to consume. Or, for the right price, washed and sanitized and never to see the light of day. Why the fuck do you think I stick around this shitrag of a 'news source' with the shit pay and bennies? I get ten times that off the books. You can help the Save the Donnie Foundation . . . or the world can find out about you. Your choice."

I clench my hands in my lap, trying to get ahold of myself. "I'll sue you and this piece of shit tabloid you're running. I'll burn this place to the ground and piss on the ashes."

Donnie shrugs, unconcerned. "Go ahead. But since what I'm reporting is the truth, you'll lose. It won't matter by then anyway, because I'll have already published the story and gotten the sales and the money off your secrets. You'll just add fuel to the fire by suing."

"And in the meantime, I'll make sure every sleazy paparazzi I know is at your house. They'll follow Sarah, try to get interviews and pictures with Carsen. What she's wearing, which boy in school she thinks is cute. Do I need to continue?"

He's right, and I hate that he's thought of this from every fucking angle, obviously experienced at doing this while I'm stumbling. Like he said, this isn't his first round of blackmail, and I bet he's got a basketball team of lawyers ready to cover his ass.

I feel outplayed. He's planned ahead, and I'm still reeling, hoping this is a nightmare I'll wake up from any minute. All I can think of is kicking Donnie's ass, and while that might be worth it for a few short seconds, it'll just land me in a lawsuit. Seeing the resolve on my face, Donnie offers a consolation. "You don't have to decide right now. I suspect getting those kinds of funds prepped is time-consuming, even for someone like you. I'll give you some time to decide. The article is already written, ready to be public with one click if you don't have the money ready to transfer to my account . . . oh, let's see. Today's Saturday . . . so how about by five o'clock Monday? Understood?"

I dip my chin once, knowing I'll need to evaluate the risks of this propo-sition carefully. I've got roughly forty-eight hours to figure out what the fuck to do, and I figure I'll need every minute. "Fine. Elise, let's go."

"See you at work Monday morning!" Francesca calls out nastily as we leave the office. We say nothing as we get in the elevator and leave the office.

The truck ride is awkward until Elise breaks the silence, rating. "I can't believe this! I knew Donnie was a sleazeball, but this is beyond what I'd ever imagined."

She's pissed, which helps, but I'm furious, and my mouth is running away from my brain. "Just like a paparazzi, always looking for juicy gossip even it ruins people's lives."

I see Elise flinch, knowing my comment about Donnie likely hit a little close to home for her too. I clench my teeth, biting back the rest of what I wanted to say as she looks down into her lap, cringing. "I never ruin people's lives," she says, so quietly I can barely hear her over the noise of my engine. "Just report stupid shit about them. Nothing like this."

"But even that stupid shit hurts people, Elise," I growl, watching the road ahead. "Even what you think is stupid can be important to others. All of this started because you reported something seemingly inconsequential, but look what's happened. My buying some fucking maxi pads for my little girl's first period has turned into a $3.5 million blackmail proposition."

She makes a small sound, hurt by my words, but I'm angry, lashing out. "I should've fucking known better," I mutter, shaking my head as I get off the freeway and head toward my house. "Should've done the fucking articles and sent you on your merry way and you wouldn't have found out shit. I told myself I wasn't going to get involved while Carsen was young. She's my number-one priority and I let myself get caught up." I bang a fist to the steering wheel, frustration and anger bubbling past the boiling point in my veins. "I knew better, I fucking knew better."

"Keith, I'm sorry!" Elise cries out, her voice choked with anguish. "Really, I am. But this isn't my fault. Maybe we should've been more careful, but it was bound to come out eventually. You can't keep her a secret forever!"

"Like hell I can't! I've kept her hidden for ten fucking years!" I half yell, pulling over and glaring at Elise. "We were doing just fine until I thought I could have more, and look what's happened! I hurt the one person I'm supposed to protect!"

Elise blinks, her eyes looking like I just slapped her. Her eyes brim with tears, but she's too strong to cry, and instead, her face hardens. "I think you should take me home."

"Fine."

Neither of us says anything as I turn at the next light, pulling up to the curb by Elise's apartment five minutes later. She's out before I even put it in park, stomping toward the door, her hurt morphing into fury.

I'm so angry I don't even watch her go inside, just peeling out from the curb to get away from this nightmare that's become real. The ride home is maddening, my mind replaying everything Donnie said about my options and then hearing everything Elise and I said when we fought.

Yeah, I know I was in the wrong to say she started it. But I'm not exactly in my right mind. I'm not pissed at her. I'm a grown ass man and it was my decision to let Elise in. I'm just pissed about the situation and that I can't rewind time and figure out a way out of this.

Getting home, I walk inside and am instantly surrounded by silence. Sarah's at home, Carsen's at her sleepover, and Elise . . . isn't here. I have a momentary thought to have Sarah pick up Carsen early, just to be safe, but I hold off knowing that if her world is about to implode, she deserves one more night of innocent fun.

Sitting on the couch, I put my head in my hands. The quiet void surrounding me echoes the emptiness in my heart, which is quickly filling with anger. Not at Elise, not at myself even, but where it should be directed . . . at Donnie and his scheming. How did this get so fucked up?

CHAPTER
Twenty-Three

ELISE

WHAT THE FUCK JUST HAPPENED?

In the thirty minutes I've been home, I feel like that question keeps coming back into my head, like I'm stupid drunk or something and the world just isn't making any damn sense.

Donnie wants to blackmail Keith. And according to what I heard from the slimy, jellybean scarfing son of a bitch, he's done this before. Maybe lots of times. I always knew Donnie was an asshole, but every good editor has a strong streak of that in them. Can't get to that job without it.

But there's being an asshole . . . and there's this. And while I'm so disgusted with Donnie that I'm not even thinking of going to work on Monday, I'm hurt most by Keith.

He blames me for this shitstorm, or at least for starting the snowball down the hill. And from a certain point of view, he's right. But I've done nothing but help him hide Carsen since I found out about her, actively lying to Donnie and putting my job in jeopardy by not reporting it in the articles. Hell, I went to him with ideas for out and out lies to use that he could live with so that he could keep Carsen a secret!

It doesn't matter. Even if he's mad at me, I'm going to help him. I *have* to. I love him and Carsen, and I'll do whatever it takes to help them. That's what love's supposed to be, doing the right thing and taking care of those you love, even if it hurts you.

So that means I'm going to step up and do anything. Except pay the money, obviously. I don't have that kind of cash. I never really even considered whether Keith did either.

His fame, his wealth hasn't been a factor in our relationship at all. I love him for the bossy, intense, protective way he loves me and Carsen, not because of some sordid angle he's manipulating like Donnie insinuated.

I spend hours lying on the couch, not sleeping but just tossing and turning as I think, testing and discarding every idea my brain comes up with, my frustration growing as I think through the whole situation from every angle.

I flip-flop between anger, raging at the empty room around me, to crying in frustration, hot tears slipping down my face. It's just not right, it's not fair. Somewhere around midnight, I have an epiphany.

I need help, someone to bounce ideas off. And Keith doesn't want to talk to me right now. But right and fair . . . innocent ideas in a sadly dark world. I know someone brilliant who might be able to work some magic for me. Someone right, a little innocent, and whose sense of justice and fairness will make sure I might actually have a chance to conjure up righteous justice out of thin fucking air.

With crossed fingers, I call Maggie. She picks up after three rings, the background of her call telling me what's up even before her falsely abrasive voice comes on.

"This better be good because it's the middle of the night and I'm at work."

"Maggie, I need your help. Can you come over?"

Maggie's voice immediately changes, going back to the kind, open voice that I know and adore. "Elise, are you okay?"

"Yeah," I reply, glad I didn't take a left turn into Crazy World where Maggie's a jaded bitch like she sounded at first. "I just need your brain. Can you come?"

Maggie sighs, and I know the answer. "Not for a while. Closing's at two and then I have to clean up. Want to come to the club? It might actually help my cover, if you don't mind. Otherwise, I won't be able to get there until three thirty at the earliest."

I look down at myself, already schlubbing in sweats and knowing my face is red and splotchy from the tears. What the hell, it's not like anyone'd expect me to be going to see Maggie . . . not where she's undercover. "Yeah, it'll take me a bit to get presentable. But I'll meet you there. I've never been to a strip club, Maggie. What should I wear?"

Maggie sounds happy, and she probably is. "Nothing flashy. You're better off if you don't take attention from the working girls. They're . . . touchy. Just jeans, something casual and comfortable. Tell them you're looking for Megan."

I nod, then remember she can't see me. "Okay, I'll be there in a few."

After I hang up, I take her advice and keep it simple, just jeans and a t-shirt, not dumpy but not flashy. My hair and face are a lost cause, though. Five minutes of scrubbing only makes my cheeks and eyes look like I'm tweaking out or something. I pull my hair into a poufy messy bun that takes advantage of a freshly fucked look and slick on little bit of lip gloss. Looking in the mirror, I know it's barely passable, but fuck it. It's all I've got in me right now, and I head down to catch a ride over to the club.

The Uber driver gives me an odd look when he pulls up, verifying the address. I smile. Guess he doesn't drop off many single women to a female strip club at one in the morning.

The bouncer at the door looks like a monster, muscled and tattooed and looking more like an MMA fighter than a late-night doorman. His biceps are bulging against the crisp white button-down shirt he has on, his black jeans are slung low on narrow hips, and his boots look heavy enough to crack a skull with a solid kick. He's intimidating. Every pore of his body exudes a dangerous coolness that lets you know up front that he could fuck you up and walk away without a scratch. Oddly, it reassures me. There's no way shit goes down in this club without Mr. Chill here taking care of it. Maggie couldn't be safer, and in re-evaluating him, I guess you could call him handsome in his own way. Kinda the way a lion is pretty . . . from afar, and when it's not looking at you like dinner. I'm not sure how this guy is looking at me though. His eyes are hidden behind mirrored shades, probably for the intimidation factor.

He obviously notices me though, raising an eyebrow just enough that I can see it over the rim of his glasses as I approach. "You here hunting your man?" he rumbles in a voice that promises violence if someone pushes him too far. "We don't want any old ladies causing problems."

I shake my head, giving him the most reassuring smile I can muster right now. "No, just meeting a friend. She works here . . . Megan? Short, pretty, and sweet as pie?"

The smile he gives is so fleeting that if I wasn't watching his face intently, I'd never know his mouth had even twitched a quarter-inch at the edges or that his chin dipped maybe a half-inch. "Meg's here, all right. I'll waive the cover for you since you're her friend."

I nod my thanks and step inside, uncertain about this but desperate for help. Inside, it's dark and smells like a mixture of stale beer and floral perfume with an undercurrent of cigarette smoke that immediately scratches at the back of my throat. When Maggie told me she was working at a strip club, the first thought that came to my mind was sleazy, but the tasteful decorations and the women I can see are way too high-quality for that label. Maybe . . . erotic? I'd need my thesaurus at home to really get it right.

The music is thumping, the heavy bass pulsing through my chest as a stunning woman wearing black heels, lingerie that basically consists of a few skinny strings, and a seductive smile is twirling and working up and down a pole on stage. It's an amazing display of strength and grace, and the acrobatics momentarily stun me, but when someone bumps me from behind, I remember to move and work my way toward an empty table off to the side.

There's no way I'd want to be close to the action here, looking at the leering faces of the jackals surrounding the stage. It's a shame too, because for all of the sexual arousal hanging in the air, the dancer's routine is as beautiful and elegant as it is sexy.

Randomly, a thought pops in my head to check out a pole fitness class, but before it can solidify, Maggie struts up. She's glittery still, but at least she's wearing a top and clothes, although I don't think I've ever imagined Mags in a black bustier top and miniskirt before. "Hey, honey! You made it, you must *really* need some help. Want me to grab you a beer, or do you need something a little stronger?"

I consider asking for a shot, but I know I need to keep my head straight to figure a way out of this. "Just a beer. Gotta keep my head straight. Anything good on tap?"

Maggie nods, adjusting her glasses. "Sure thing, let me grab one of the local brews and I'll see if I can take my break in a few."

"That's fine. I know I'm intruding on your work, so whenever you have a minute is fine. At least there's a show," I reply, indicating the girl on stage, who's currently hanging upside down with her legs so splayed she sort of looks like the letter T. I'm jealous. I don't think I could get my legs that wide apart even if Keith were . . . nope, don't need to go there right now.

Maggie grins and bounces off, and I'm struck by how even in this club with her tits popped up and her ass hanging out, Maggie comes across as cute and sweet. Sexiest Girl Scout candy striper in the whole world, and she's working undercover in a strip club.

Maggie has an innocence about her even when I see her banging on her tray as she claps for a particularly difficult trick the woman on stage is performing. I follow her sightline and see the buxom brunette flashing her panty-covered pussy to the audience as she stands on one foot and raises the other leg high, splitting vertically in the air like a gymnast as she leans way far back. It's almost a ballet-like position, minus the leotard and tutu. And then when she grabs the pole, flipping herself up onto it again, the audience goes wild, clapping and whistling.

Holy crap! I *definitely* need a pole fitness class if it can teach me how to do that.

Maggie brings me a beer, and I lean back, sipping it as another girl makes her way on stage.

"Hey, baby, you enjoying the show?" a guy asks, coming up. He's a little tipsy but not drunk, and while he's not hideous, he wouldn't be my type even if I wasn't seeing Keith.

"Sorry, just waiting for my girlfriend to take a break," I reply, letting him draw his own conclusions. Thankfully, *girlfriend* has so many different meanings. The guy looks intrigued for a moment, and I wonder if he's going to press his luck, and I cut my eyes toward the door for the bouncer just in case. The guy immediately chills out and shrugs in defeat when he sees the bouncer look this direction, and he takes a step back, tossing back the rest of his drink.

"Have a nice night," he says simply before disappearing back toward the stage.

For the next hour, the scenery turns into a blur of sweat, stale smoke, glitter, and thumping music between two slowly-sipped beers. Maggie never does get a chance to take a break, but when the sound guy gets on and says that Tina Tempest is the last act and they need to clear out, the patrons comply quickly.

"I need to change and I'll sit down with you," Maggie says, looking tired but still concerned about me. "More privacy out here than in a back room."

When Maggie comes out a few minutes later, clad in a tank top, baggy sweats, and Ugg boots, I can't help but crack a big smile. She's wiped all the makeup off her face and pulled her hair up into a cute off-center ponytail, looking more like an eighteen-year-old girl on any college campus in the US than a strip club waitress. Or more importantly, a reporter. All traces of her night in the strip club are wiped clean.

Well, except for the glitter sparkling in her cleavage. "You look great. How do you do that . . . sexy sweetheart to girl next door in two minutes flat?"

She looks pleased at my compliment and sits down, pulling her knees up to her chest and curling up like a tiny spitfire ball of cuteness. "Just how I was made, I guess. I'm totally not a femme fatale type for sure."

"Speaking of femme fatales, you won't believe what Francesca has been doing," I growl, glad I've got the two beers in me or else I'd be throwing shit, I'm still so fucking angry.

"What?" Maggie asks, sensing my displeasure. "She didn't . . . stab you in the back, did she?"

I laugh bitterly, nodding. "Like it's nobody's fucking business. She's been following me, on Donnie's orders! Me! Like I'm a target."

"And?" Maggie asks, not getting upset yet, "What did she find?"

I stop, immediately defensive. "How do you know she found something?"

"Because you've been sitting in a strip club for over an hour waiting to talk to me, ergo, she found something," Maggie explains matter-of-factly. "If she hadn't, you'd have just told me the story and called her a stupid bitch on Monday. Am I right? So what did she find?"

"Well, I can't exactly say everything she found," I reply before taking a deep breath. Fuck it, right now I need to trust someone with some secrets, or else I'm going to be spinning my wheels and going nowhere. "But she figured out pretty quickly that Keith and I are dating."

Maggie reaches out, putting a hand on my arm. "You two are . . . dating?"

I nod, pushing on. "There's more, but that's not my secret to tell and I promised I wouldn't. Suffice it to say, Donnie made it sound like Keith is just fucking me to keep me quiet. But that's not it. I love him, and he loves me."

Maggie smiles, leaning back in her chair and giving a little fist pump to the stale sky. "That's awesome, Elise! I mean, I hate you too—you got the hunkiest guy in country music and you held out on me . . . but I understand why you didn't spill that around the coffee pot at the office. So, what's the problem?"

"Donnie gave Keith an ultimatum," I reply, loving Maggie totally in that instant as she cheers for me. "He said Keith either has to pay him three and a half million dollars to keep quiet or Donnie will publish a story with the secret Keith doesn't want to get out and get his money that way. Donnie set it up pretty well. Apparently, he's blackmailed other celebrities too so he's got experience. Keith has until Monday night to decide."

Maggie looks pissed, slamming her tiny little fist on the table and making my two beer glasses rattle. "Donnie is such a creep. I'm honestly not surprised he's pulling something like this, nor that he's good at it, considering how long he's been in this business. He's manipulative and a great strategist. But there's always a weak point to every plan. We just have to find it and exploit it," she declares, holding up first one finger and then another like she's making a to-do list.

I sigh, hope lighting bright for a second before I crash back down. I look at the last dregs of beer in the nearest glass and realize it looks a lot like my life right now, a room temperature puddle of piss. "There's no weak point. I've been thinking for hours now. The only way to keep Donnie quiet is to pay him off, and I don't trust that he wouldn't get the money and then publish the story anyway. We both know he's fine with double-dipping considering that he slept around on his ex-wife with Francesca."

Instead of joining me in my misery, I can see Maggie's brain turning. I quiet down, watching the wheels spin as she talks silently to herself, until suddenly, her face breaks wide in a huge ear-to-ear smile. "I know what the weak point is, but you're not gonna like it."

"What? Anything, God. Help me!"

"The weak point is Donnie. He literally gives zero fucks about keeping his life private, flaunting things most people would hide—like sleeping with Francesca—so that he's untouchable. And in doing so, he assumes most folks do actually give a shit and want to keep their secrets just that . . . secret. He targets people he thinks will do anything, pay anything, and he's set his sights on Keith."

I see where she's going, and I nod, feeling a light at the end of the tunnel as she continues.

"Donnie's entire plan hinges on that initial supposition that Keith will want to keep this quiet, and that he'll do anything, and that will be enough to get the millions. I think he'll likely take the money and publish too. That's just the sort of snake he is. Probably not even give Francesca a decent cut of it either. He'll just keep stringing her along until she's too deep in to ever go anywhere else, then cut her free when he finds his next fresh-faced girl willing to sleep her way to the top."

Maggie nods sadly, sparing a bit of sympathy for Francesca. I guess I can understand why. That, and Maggie's the reincarnated spirit of Marsha Brady. "That's right up his alley. So, based on that, the secret is coming out . . . whatever it is. Keith just needs to get in front of it. It's the only way. Go on the morning talk show racket and apologize for the drug use and check into rehab . . ."

I give her a severe look, my inner feelings flaring up. "He's not on drugs."

Maggie smirks, knowing she's been caught. "Had to try. Maybe apologize for the . . . red room of pain and explain that you're into it too?"

I laugh, wondering if Maggie's brain is really as innocent as she seems. "Nope, not it either. Really, I can't say. But I know Keith isn't going to want to publicize it. He's worked his whole life to keep this secret."

"Well, I have to say, I don't think he's going to have a choice about whether it gets out," Maggie says, shrugging reluctantly. "But he can decide *how* it gets out."

My jaw drops as something comes back to me. Donnie said the record company's initial push to have Keith do the interviews with me was so that they could . . . control the narrative.

Quietly, I murmur the phrase to myself, like a magic incantation that can change the very fabric of the universe. "Control the narrative."

"What?"

Maybe . . . maybe it can. Getting excited, I reach across the table and grab Maggie's hand. "We have to control the narrative. Donnie's power is in that he's the only one with the information, but what if he wasn't? Keith could do the morning show racket and tell it himself. Then Donnie won't get the blackmail money and he won't be able to publish it and get the exclusive breaking news. It takes away his power and lets Keith control the narrative! Control the narrative! You're a fucking genius!"

Maggie laughs, cute and self-conscious now. "Well, sometimes yes and sometimes no. Just glad this seems to be a yes-time for your sake. So, you're really not going to tell me the secret?"

"Nope, but I'm gonna need your help getting Keith on TV the day after tomorrow *without* telling the shows why and keeping the whole appearance *Top Secret* so Donnie doesn't find out and try and jump out in front of the whole thing. Can you do that?"

"Yeah, I can make a call or two and make that happen for a top name like Keith," Maggie says. "I know a few people down at the local station, and if it's Keith, they can probably get him on the national circuit if we promise them a big enough prize. But shouldn't his manager do that though?"

"Well, that's my next problem. I have to get Keith on board with this plan because he's not going to like it," I reply, sighing a little. "He's not going to like it at all. We kinda had a fight about the whole thing. He didn't really blame me, exactly, but he was mad at himself for dating me because it's led to this whole drama. He's got some definite anger toward the media and paparazzi, and I've got this huge glaring neon sign on my forehead, blinking 'REPORTER' in big capital letters right now, and it's got his shields up."

"Well, this isn't really your fault, exactly, but maybe it is time for you to do something a little different if you're pursuing something a bit longer term with Keith," Maggie counsels me. "Not saying you're not good, Elise. I mean, you've taught me a few things in the time we've worked together, but a gossip reporter and a country music star don't exactly sound like a match made in heaven. And we both know you're too good for this job anyway. Maybe you really could parlay this series into something with one of the legit music industry magazines? Or do some investigative journalism that's not so, I don't know . . . gossipy? Not like you can go to an award ceremony after-party on Keith's arm and be trusted if you're publishing all the drunk hookups on Monday morning," she says jokingly, but she's on target.

I sigh, knowing Maggie's right, but there are so many variables up in the air. "I know, and I'll have to figure that out. But right now, I just want to figure out this thing with Keith. Thanks so much . . . Megan."

I give her a little smile as I use her cover name, glad that our conversation has been private even in this club and trusting that she will help me. Giving the bouncer a nod of thanks as he *ushers* out a few overindulged guests, I leave, stepping into one of the waiting Ubers.

I've got a lot of shit to do, and not a lot of time to do it in. So the only question I have is . . . do I wait until sunrise to talk to Keith about this . . . or wake him up at three in the morning to deal with it?

Twenty~Four

KEITH

I STARE at the walls of my kitchen bleakly, my mind constantly replaying that smug asshole telling me that I'm going to pay him or he'll expose Carsen to public scrutiny. Like any teenage girl needs that! I'm furious at Donnie, but maybe even more at myself.

I couldn't sleep at all last night, racked by anger and punishing myself for being a total dumbass. I was so worked up by what Donnie said, and my anger at the situation, that I took it out on Elise. I know that was a really shitty thing to do. She didn't deserve to have me give her shit, especially since she never intended for this to happen.

But I have to push that to the back burner and figure out what the fuck I'm going to do about Donnie's threat. The problem is, I've drawn a blank as to any course of action.

I can't sue him. He's right that it wouldn't do any good because it would be too slow-moving to stop him, and he is telling the truth.

I can't go beat his ass into a pulp. That'd get the cops involved and only get Donnie what he wants, a fat payout in the form of a civil suit.

I even had a dark few minutes late last night, well, early this morning, where I thought about hiring a hitman and taking Donnie out. Problem solved. But that's not who I am, nor is it the legacy I want to leave to my daughter. And as much as it sounds like a solution, I know it's just one for a TV show ending where the good guy gets away scot-free every time. Reality is a lot different, and as the hours go on, I'm still trying to figure out my way past the harshness of that reality.

I'm still stumped, slamming my fourth coffee at eleven in the morning when Sarah and Carsen come blowing in, all girly giggles and excitement. "Daddy, oh, God, I had the best time! You wanna hear about it?"

My head is pounding and I'm worried as shit, but I can see the swoony hearts in her eyes like some old-school cartoon.

Still, it's hard to find the will to be happy for her. All I can think about is that my baby's first dance was probably going to be her last because by the next one, she'll need security guards and won't know whether to trust people's friendship because of who she is or because of who I am.

It makes my blood boil, and I realize it's carrying over as Carsen and Sarah have stopped giggling, looking at me worriedly.

"Daddy?" Carsen asks, her smile disappearing and breaking my heart. "What's wrong?"

I thought about telling Sarah during one of my more desperate moments of trying to sort this all out, but I held off, hoping I'd be able to find a solution before scaring her with all of this. But she can see things aren't right. "What happened?"

I try to school my face into a calm mask and shake my head. "Nothing, everything's fine. Hey, Carsen, can you go hang out upstairs for a few minutes? I need to talk to Aunt Sarah about something, and then you can tell me all about the dance, okay?"

She nods, but I can see that she's not fooled by my forced calmness. "Sure, Dad. Holler when you're done and I'll tell you about it."

"I can't wait, baby," I reply, giving her a hug as she passes me to head upstairs. It hurts, because I know even as she hugs me that her world's about to shatter, and that like Humpty Dumpty, it can't be put back together again.

"So tell me what's going on," Sarah says, going over to the cabinet next to the plates where she gets out the Tylenol she keeps there. "And take these. I can see you wincing every time the sunlight sparkles in the window, and you kept wincing every time Carsen laughed. Guess you didn't sleep?"

I shake my head slowly, taking three Tylenol along with a glass of water, which somehow tastes a lot better than it should. "That fucking bastard is trying to blackmail me."

"What?" Sarah asks, shocked but trying to keep her voice down. "Back up, start slow, and omit nothing."

I actually don't tell her everything, just giving her the basics because I just don't have it in me right now. "And in the end, that jellybean loving motherfucker said if I don't pay up by five tomorrow, he's going to publish."

Sarah nods, biting her lip as she thinks. "And Elise? What does she say about this?"

Fuck. I thought my headache was doing better after telling the story, but Sarah's reminder brings back the pain around my temples. "Well, I was so fucking furious that I might've said some things . . ."

"Keith, you stupid son of a bitch," Sarah says softly, reprovingly. She sighs, waving her hand. "What did you do?"

"I might've blamed her for starting this whole mess with her first article and told her that if I'd just done the damn articles and kept her at arm's length, I wouldn't be in this mess now . . . and that I knew better than to date her," I reply. "It hurt her, and I dropped her off at her place. I haven't heard from her since then."

"This isn't her fault and you know it!" Sarah says, still trying to keep her voice down but managing to yell at me all the same. "From what you just said, she's been putting her own career at risk to keep this secret. She's done everything she can. It's not her fault a coworker got suspicious when she saw us at the mall."

I rage. "I didn't even know about that! Until I saw the pictures of the three of you out shopping. Why didn't you tell me?"

Sarah grimaces. "We thought it was just bad luck. It's a mall, Keith. We thought the woman was shopping."

"That wasn't a coincidence. She followed Elise there and Elise didn't know it. Hell, she followed us all, and none of us caught her. She had pictures of us all." I huff, fuming as I remember the stack of photos.

Sarah snorts, shaking her head. "So you're mad at Elise because she should've recognized something you didn't even notice. How many times has she been followed before? What about *you*?"

I rub across my head, the calluses on my hands scratching on the smooth skin up there. "I know! I fucked up. I know that, and I spent most of the night divided between wanting to tear this Donnie asshole's head off and wanting to tear my own off for hurting Elise. What am I going to do?"

Sarah studies me for a moment, then comes over, putting a hand on my shoulder. "You're going to man up, like you always do. Call her, have her come over, and the three of us are going to figure out what to do . . . together. That's what family does, Keith. We'll stick together, through the good times and the fucking bad times."

I nod, knowing she's right, and I grab my phone, dialing Elise's number. It rings and rings, my hand drumming on the countertop in frustration as my mind runs in a hundred different exhaustion-and-caffeine-fueled directions before switching over to her voicemail. *"Hey, this is Elise. Leave me a message or send me a text. Check ya later!"*

"Uh, hey, Elise," I say, clearing my throat before I can continue. "I just wanted to say that I'm sorry. Can you call me back, please? We need to figure this out . . . and I need you."

I hang up, looking at Sarah, knowing my face shows my disappointment, my anger, and my sadness. She pats my shoulder again before giving me a little side hug. "She'll call back. She loves you, brother."

The reassurance feels empty even as it gives me a little whisper of useless hope. "But what if—"

Before I can finish my sentence, the doorbell rings. Sarah and I look at each other, and she gives me a nod. "I'll get it in case it's reporters."

There's a brief silence as she walks to the door, but when it opens, she laughs before calling out. "Hey, Keith? It is a reporter, but I think you'll want to see this one."

My heart speeds up and my jaw drops as Elise walks into the kitchen. She looks stressed, dark smudges under her eyes and her skin pale. Honestly, it looks like she had just as rough of a night as I did, and I know I look like hell too.

Still, I've never seen anything more beautiful in my life as I get up, crossing the kitchen to stand in front of her, wanting to embrace her but knowing there's something I need to do first. But I have to touch her, reassure myself that she's really here and not some insomnia-induced hallucination. Holding her upper arms gently, I wait for her to look up at me, needing her to see the truth in my words as I speak. "Elise, I'm so fucking sorry. I was scared and mad and I took it out on you. I shouldn't have. I love you."

I lift my head to look her in the eyes, and she's smiling a little, but it's tremulous and her eyes are a little sad. "I know, Keith. I'm sorry too. For starting this whole mess. If I hadn't put you on Donnie's radar, you wouldn't be in this situation now."

"We," I correct her, reaching out and taking her hands.

"Huh?" she asks, looking confused.

For the first time in what feels like a year but has only been less than twenty-four hours, a smile that isn't one of bitterness comes to my face. "*We* are in this situation. You, me, Sarah, and Carsen. You've made a place in this family, and I want to work with you to figure out what to do. This affects us all."

Elise stutters, a single tear rolling down her cheek as I gather her in, and she hugs me hard before stepping back. Wiping at her face, she takes a big breath and I can see her putting her emotions away, at least for now, and getting down to business. "Okay, good. Good, because I've got a plan and it'll work. But you're going to hate it. Can we sit down?"

I nod, gesturing to the living room, and we all sit down. I make sure to guide Elise to my side on the couch, needing to be in contact with her. Sarah sits across from us in one of her favorite easy chairs, leaning forward, her eyes darting between the two of us. "Judging by appearances, you two look like you got about thirty minutes of sleep last night . . . combined."

"Actually, I got about an hour," Elise admits. "But it sorta sucked. I was too busy trying to think and working some angles. I wanted to come over here to talk about it with you . . . but I wanted a full plan in place before I did. I was just worried you'd say no outright if I didn't have a full plan."

"Why do I feel like I'm repeating myself?" Sarah asks the sky, then sighs. "Start at the beginning, omit nothing."

Elise starts, telling us about visiting her friend at a strip club. "You told your friend about us? At a strip club?" I ask incredulously. "But . . . why?"

"Maggie's one of the smartest people I know," Elise replies. "I edited things and didn't say a thing about Carsen, and Maggie's someone who will respect that. And she gave me the idea that we've got to get out in front of this."

"What do you mean?" Sarah asks. "Get in front of it how?"

"Right now, Donnie's power lies in one thing only," Elise explains. "He thinks you're only going to consider one of two options. Let it blow up in your face and maybe try and deny . . . or pay up. But there's a third option."

"What?" I ask, even though I see Sarah's face dawning in realization. "Okay, guys, little words, haven't slept."

"We go public first," Sarah says, nodding. "Then we're in control."

Elise nods. "Keith, Carsen's going to become public knowledge one way or another. I don't trust Donnie not to take the money and then publish anyway. He's got zero fucks to give and nothing to lose. Hell, he'll come out way ahead that way and I'm sure that's his idea already. But if you go first, get out there and tell the story, then Donnie's going to have nothing. And you get to control the narrative."

"But . . ." I answer, taking a deep breath, trying to get my brain to line the fuck up and think straight. "It means going public."

"And we do it the right way . . . talking about Donnie's blackmail attempt," Elise explains. "Don't you see? This isn't just about you and Carsen. He's done this before and he'll do it again. You have a chance to control your narrative, but you also have a chance to control Donnie's narrative too. Let everyone know what a sleazeball he is, blackmailing and threatening people to create tabloid gossip headlines for cash. Get in front of both stories. It's the only way."

I shake my head, feeling desperate as my whole world seems to be turning to quicksand that's slipping through my fingers before sucking me down to my doom. "No. That defeats the whole purpose. The only thing I care about is keeping Carsen's life how she's used to. I'll just pay the money and pray that he keeps his word about not publishing the story. He's gotta have at least a little honor among thieves. If he's done this before and breaks his word now, nobody'll trust him in the future when he pulls the same shit, don't you see? It's the only scenario where she has any chance at being left alone."

Suddenly, Carsen steps in from the hallway, where she's obviously been eavesdropping. Part of me wonders for how long, and I'm too exhausted to be upset. "No, Dad. This guy's a bully, and the only way to stop him from hurting other people is if we stop him. Just tell people about me. That's what he's holding over your head? Who cares if people know you're my dad? I'm proud of being your daughter and I don't care if everyone knows."

If only it were that easy. "Carsen, you don't understand, baby. If everyone knows you're my daughter, it'll change your whole life. You might have to get security, change schools, always be on the watch, and never know who your real friends are. It'll change everything."

"I know, Dad. I understand, really, I do," Carsen says, coming over and sitting on the other side of me and Elise. "But, it's the right thing to do. Don't let a bully win. You're stronger than he is, and I'll be okay with whatever we have to do."

I'm torn. Carsen looks so certain, sitting next to me so tall and proud. I know she's strong, but she's still just a little girl and I wanted her to make this decision when she was a little older. I look at Sarah and Elise, and they're both nodding, agreeing with Carsen.

"Keith, she's right. It's the right thing to do. And you said we're a family, so we can do this together, support each other through whatever this storm brings," Elise says.

I look at Carsen, searching her eyes. Keeping her a secret has been my main focus for so long, and that's coming to an end, apparently. I'm terrified. Most of my instincts are telling me to just grab her up and go hide, leave music and everything behind. But she's right, I'm stronger than that.

And I don't want to leave.

I want to have a life with my daughter, my woman, and my sister, this crazy family unit we've created where we all fit together somehow, bringing happiness and growth and love into each of our lives in a way I never expected.

"Okay, I'll do it," I reply, leaning forward and putting my face in my hands, exhausted and knowing I can't wait. "Elise, set it up."

I thought she'd be happy, but she knows what this is costing me. Not in terms of money like Donnie wants, but it's costing me all the same in my peace of mind, which is going to be sorely lacking for a long time, I suspect.

Elise's eyes are somber, serious as she reaches into her purse and pulls out her phone, dialing quickly. "Maggie, it's a go," she says simply when the line's picked up. "Work your magic."

I hug Carsen to me tightly, hating that her world is about to change but knowing it's the only way.

Donnie needs to be stopped, and I can do that.

Twenty~Five

ELISE

SITTING IN THE 'GREEN ROOM,' waiting as the makeup people do last-minute adjustments to Carsen's wardrobe and makeup next door, I'm struck by last-second indecision. "Keith, are you sure about this? I mean, I know it's my idea, but it's your decision. Nothing has been done that we can't undo. We can stop this train if you're uncertain."

Keith glances out the door at Carsen, who looks like she's having the time of her life as a makeup artist and hair stylist give her the full celeb treatment, then he shakes his head. Crossing the room, he grabs my waist, pulling me to him. "No, I'm not sure, but this is what we're doing. My manager agreed with the plan too. And though you're right, as much as I wish I could turn back time and not have to disrupt Carsen's life, that would mean not having you. And this, us . . . I've got to believe it'll be worth it in the end."

I bite my lip, trying to stop the words I've already said so many times from spilling out again, but I can't help it. I might be forced to say it another ten thousand times, but I mean each one. "I really am sorry, Keith. I never meant for any of this to happen. I can't believe Donnie is such an asshole, and if I could take it all back, I would. Except for you, of course."

Keith's hands move down to cup my ass in a firm grip that gets my attention, and I'm glad the green room is only us for the moment. "Stop apologizing. I think we've both apologized enough. We haven't done anything wrong. It's Donnie and he's forced my hand. He expected me to roll over and give in, but he's threatening my family, and I'm more of a bite than bark kind of guy."

I feel a warmth spread throughout my body and my nipples tighten in my sensible, professional bra that I'm wearing. "I've noticed that . . . the biting, that is. I happen to like it sometimes. Although your bark is pretty loud too."

I'm intentionally trying to lighten the mood, even if I am starting to get massively turned on. But Keith needs this. He's been a growling beast of a reluctant man all morning. But I love him for it because I know it comes from a good place. He loves Carsen, and he wants the best for her. This is just one of those situations where the best path forward isn't the one he planned. But he's still doing it, and that's why I love him.

"I just hope the hosts go easy on us," he says, raising his hands enough that he's not quite making me want to dry hump his leg in the middle of a TV studio but still making his point. "You know, with Carsen and everything."

"Really, Keith. I know this is the exact opposite of what you've wanted for Carsen, but I think it'll be for the best," I reassure him, running my hands over his broad chest. He looks handsome in his button-down shirt. "You won't have this constant threat hanging over your head. I just hope the fallout isn't too bad."

"It'll be whatever it is, and we'll handle it," Keith says, gaining confidence. "I promise."

Sarah and Carsen come in from make-up, and Carsen looks like she's actually having fun. She's not too made up, which I know Keith was worried about.

"Wow. So this is a green room?" Carsen asks, coming over and grabbing a bottle of water. "I thought it'd be green, but the walls are just blah wallpaper. And they said there'd be cookies!"

Her nerves are obvious, even if she is pretty awed by the whole production of a morning television show. Keith walks over and kneels down in front of her.

"Carsen, honey . . . are you sure about this? Of all of us, this mostly impacts you. I'll happily pay the money and we won't have to do this. Everything can stay just as is. Say the word, and I'll make that happen."

Carsen looks thoughtful for a moment, and I'm glad she's taking this seriously because this really is going to impact her life in a major way.

"I know, Dad. It'll be okay. You can't let this guy bully us around though. It's not right. But maybe being the daughter of the world's best country music star won't be so bad. Maybe you can even take me to school every once in a while?"

There's a knock on the door and a production assistant pokes her head in, looking slightly bored by all of this, as if changing people's lives is just part of her normal Monday. Then again, I guess it is. "Time, everyone. Follow me, please. We'll get you over to set."

Walking across the TV studio, it's interesting to watch the quiet chaos going on behind the cameras while the two hosts gab on about the latest political scandal getting headlines. We reach the 'on deck' spot, and Keith reaches out, holding my hand on one side and Carsen's on the other. Sarah places a stabilizing hand on his shoulder.

I can feel him take a deep, fortifying breath, knowing he's about to go to war . . . against Donnie, against the paparazzi, against his own secrets. "Hey."

"Huh?" he asks, looking over. I give his hand a squeeze and a small smile.

"You're not doing this alone. We've got your back."

Keith nods and gives my hand a squeeze back. "Thanks. I love you."

The show kicks to commercial, and a flurry of activity erupts. Keith is herded over to a couch in the middle of a set made up to look like one of those 'in-your-house' style living rooms. A quick sound check makes a tech adjust Keith's microphone, and the host comes over, shaking hands with Keith before sitting down and assuming her perfectly trained chair pose that looks ridiculously uncomfortable.

"Ten seconds!" a producer calls, and Keith gives us a thumbs-up, but I can see him forcing his emotions in check and prepping mentally for what he's about to say.

"Three . . . two . . . one!"

The overly perky morning host immediately starts up, grinning nearly orgasmically. "Welcome back to *Good Morning*! We have a special surprise guest for you, an exclusive you'll only see here on KTSR-TV this morning. I have to tell you, this was a surprise for me too. When I got the call from my friend, I said she had to be pulling my leg . . . but I've known her for years, so I was able to convince my producers to give this a shot. You see, we don't even know why this guest is visiting today, it's all top-secret, hush-hush. But I can tell you he's one of my favorites, so forgive any fan-girling I might do in the next five minutes."

I think the host's actually telling the truth and is a fan. The professional side of me knows that definitely works in our favor, although the personal side of me will want to rip her extensions out if she starts eye-fucking my man.

Crossing my arms over my chest, I watch as she gestures to the side. "Please welcome one of the hottest country music artists today . . . Keith Perkins!"

There's a bit of silence, and I guess that in the production booth, they're mixing in a few clips of Keith performing as the host starts up again. "Breaking onto the charts five years ago with his first big hit, *Gonna Do It The Country Way*, Keith Perkins has, over the past three records, consistently been one of the top ten artists in country today. With enough party to draw in new listeners and enough roots to have even old-schoolers impressed, Keith's star just keeps rising. Keith, welcome."

The host reaches over and shakes Keith's hand for the cameras, eyes starry as she looks at Keith, and I have to giggle a little bit. I'm pretty sure that's what I look like too, but I'm the lucky girl going home with him tonight. Not her, so she can suck it.

"So, Keith, we're thrilled to have you with us this morning. According to what I was told yesterday, you have some type of announcement you'd like to make? Are we talking your usual summer tour already? If so, put me down for two VIP tickets!"

"I'll remember that when tickets go on sale," Keith says on stage, "but unfortunately, tour info isn't why I'm here this morning."

"Okay, what brought you here this morning then?"

"Well, if you're a fan, you know I'm pretty quiet about my personal life. I always have been, just keeping that line between my professional life and my day-to-day stuff, you know? And recently, there were reports speculating that I may have a woman in my life."

Even from here, I can see the host's eyes light up, and you can virtually see her salivating for the story even though she must be reading between the lines since Carsen's already made up and in the wings just off camera behind Keith.

"Are you saying there is someone in your life? You're gonna break some hearts if that's the case!"

Keith nods, his smile widening before dimming by half. "Well, yes . . . but there's more to it. You see, when that story broke, I did have a young woman in my life, but not the way everyone thought. I'm not much for dating. It's kind of hard to do when you're . . . a single father."

The host plays it well. She can't have been that stupid to not see the similarity between Keith and Carsen, but to anyone at home, you'd think she'd just been kicked in the gut she's so shocked. Her mouth gapes open and closed a few times like a fish before she speaks. "A father? Oh, my."

Keith nods, his voice gaining strength as he gets into his tale. "You see, for a long time, my daughter, Carsen, and I have been a team, along with my sister, who's the biggest help ever. Carsen has been my number-one priority, and part of that responsibility was keeping her safe. I felt that the best way to do that was to keep her out of the public eye. She's a twelve-year-old girl. She deserves to have a normal childhood, and that's what I've worked damn hard to give her."

The host nods supportively, her eyes cutting to Carsen as I see a production assistant tap Carsen on the elbow. "So your daughter, Carsen. Is that the young lady I see off-set here? Carsen, would you like to join us?"

Keith nods, turning to look at us, and Carsen bravely walks to Keith, sitting down next to him on the couch as the host looks on with a smile.

"Wow, so very nice to meet you, Carsen! It must be awesome to have the one and only Keith Perkins as your dad."

Carsen smiles, looking at Keith and taking his hand. "I guess. To me, he's just Dad though. He makes me do my homework, clean up my room, all that stuff."

The host laughs, turning her attention to Keith. "So, you've kept Carsen a secret for all these years. What's changed now?"

Keith smiles, but it's bittersweet. "Well, after that article came out, my record label got the brilliant idea that I should do a series of interviews so a reporter could write an all-access story about me. Maybe you've seen them?"

The host nods, totally engrossed in every word of Keith's story. "Of course I have. Actually, I have printed copies of them backstage in my dressing room. Maybe you can sign them later?"

Keith chuckles. "Sure. I'd be happy to do that for you. So, the interviews were going well, but the real news wasn't what was in the articles. It was the reporter, Elise Warner. During the process of the interviews, I fell in love with her, and she fell in love with me. We've been dating for a little while now. Carsen and she get along well, and we're just trying to find our way."

For the first time, the host looks genuinely shocked, and she looks over at me, her eyes a mix of *go, girl!* and *I hate you, bitch!* She looks back at Keith, her grin still mostly professional but at the same time, she's eating this news scoop right up. "Wow! A daughter and a new love interest! Can Elise come out too?"

I squeeze Sarah's hand, wishing I could take her with me, but we'd decided that it'd be best for her to stay off-camera. It's not her style, and besides, it's good for at least one of us to stay unrecognizable.

With a shiver of nerves, I head over to sit beside Carsen. Keith stands up and gives me a hug, which eases my nerves a little bit. And when we all sit down, he stretches a long arm out along the couch back, marking us both as his.

"Welcome, Elise! I must admit, I'm a bit jealous and I imagine there must be thousands . . . I take that back, millions of women with shattered dreams right now. Tell us, how'd you claim this one?" She smiles as she points at Keith with a thumb.

She laughs a bit, but as far as I'm concerned, she's right. Keith doesn't give me a chance, though, leaning forward and shaking his head. "I'm the one who needed to claim her. Elise is a great woman, and I'm lucky she puts up with my grumpy ass."

Carsen giggles and looks over. "Dad, you can't say ass on TV!"

We all laugh a little, and the host jumps in. "Don't worry, we're on a ten-second delay. So . . . wow! What an announcement! We appreciate your sharing with our viewers this morning. What prompted you to come forward and not stay mum like usual?"

Keith's smile falls, and his face clouds as he lets a hint of his anger pierce the happy buzz of this morning's announcements. "Well, that's the bad side of this business. Most people have been nothing but positive and are happy to read stories about my background and music. I've tried when I do go out to perform to give back to them, because I know if it wasn't for them, I'd be still working honky tonks out in Boise. But there are others out for blood and dirt and any juicy tidbit they can find. Vultures, that's what I call them. And they take that information and exploit it, looking for a way to make a buck off someone else's life. I was recently given an ultimatum to either pay three point five million dollars hush money to one of these people, or he would publish a story exposing Carsen's existence. Total blackmail."

The host gasps, and I can see the crew members' shock and disgust. These people might like a little titillation themselves, but they're legit journalists, not tabloid bottom-feeders. "Oh, my gosh, that's awful! I'm so sorry."

One of the camera guys adjusts his angle to get what I assume is a full-frame close-up of Keith as he continues. "This man had his mistress, who is also a reporter, follow us . . . me, Elise, Carsen, and my sister. She took pictures of all of us, both in public and in private, using a telephoto lens, which is illegal and feels like such a personal violation. He was counting on his belief that he had all the power because he knew about my desire to keep Carsen out of the public eye." Keith pauses, his eyes meeting Carsen's with an apology obvious in the stress on his face. "So my choices were to pay him off or let him publish the story, which would let him get richer from clicks and sales. I couldn't let that happen. Schemers like that shouldn't be rewarded for their misdeeds."

The host nods. "So, by coming forward on your own, you preemptively cut him off at the knees?"

Keith nods. "I just want the opportunity to tell the truth of my story. I have a daughter, who is an amazing young woman, and I'm in love with Elise Warner, who through some stroke of luck is actually in love with me too. And as much of a bombshell as I know this is, I hope everyone will be respectful in their handling of this news and not overwhelm my family."

Keith looks at Carsen, then me, and I can feel his gaze like a physical touch, knowing that he'll protect us no matter what. The host is obviously trying to think of a next question, and when she touches her ear, I know that someone in the booth is feeding her words because she's so stunned.

Finally, she gets it together. "Wow, Keith. That's horrifying, and I'm so sorry that's happened, but I'm glad you came to *Good Morning!* to dispel any rumors before they got started." Her voice takes on a more serious tone as she asks, "Can you tell us who attempted to blackmail you?"

There's a sense of breath-holding suspense as I see more than one person lean forward, eager to see if Keith is going to name names. While all of them show some signs of disgust at the idea of blackmail, they've all got the secret shame that they're just as gossipy as the next person, wanting to feed on someone's secrets. To some degree, it's human nature to be nosy, but this is well beyond curiosity.

"Yes, the man who tried to blackmail me is Donnie Jardine, the editor-in-chief at *The Daily Spot*. The reporter who took the illegal photos and was complicit in his plan is Francesca Knauss, also of the *The Daily Spot*."

The host's eyes snap to me, her eyes widening. "Elise, isn't that the online magazine you work for? The one who's published your articles about Keith?"

I nod, knowing this was something we'd have to answer. "Yes, it is. Donnie Jardine is my boss." I look directly into the camera. "However, effectively immediately, I quit."

Twenty-Six

KEITH

MY STRENGTH HOLDS out until we get backstage, where in the dressing room, I've had enough. I sag into the couch, too exhausted to even unbutton my shirt.

"Enough . . . no more," I say, leaning back. "Tell the whole world to piss off."

"Once we get home," Elise says, kneeling next to me. "You can let us take care of you . . . family."

I nod, leaning back and attempting to relax for a second. I shouldn't be so tired, but that was the hardest thing I've ever done. I've spent so long keeping quiet about Carsen, and serving her up on a fucking platter for the morning news went against every code of honor I have. But I have to trust that it's the right call.

Carsen's privacy is a fucking impossibility now, though, because as we're leaving the studio garage, the driver and bodyguard are talking up front in code. But I know what they're saying.

There are paparazzi right outside the garage waiting for us. How the hell did they get over here so damn fast? After the interview, we whisked through the back halls and were out in minutes.

But they're already here like vultures, waiting to snap and pick at the remains of our privacy even after I've literally given them everything I have and more than I ever wanted to.

"Just get us home safely," I call up front, leaning back into the leather seats. "I can't do any more publicity today."

"Of course, sir. Make sure everyone's buckled up back there . . . sometimes, I have to punch it."

Carsen seems to be handling it well so far, still smiling, and it brightens my mood just a little.

As we drive out of the garage, the paparazzi swarm the SUV with their cameras and phones and faces pressed up against the glass. They're knocking and slapping at the windows, their yells a jumble of noise I can't understand except for my name over and over. Carsen cringes, the fun of being a 'celebrity' temporarily snuffed out, and she gets her first scary lesson in the price of her new identity.

Donnie, if I do see you again, I'd love to shove my fist so far up your ass people would think you're a puppet. *Damn you for doing this to my little girl,* I think in anger toward Donnie, even as a wave of guilt washes over me at the part I might've played in this mess too.

I realize the driver is barely rolling and look out the front window, seeing a group of daredevil cameramen standing in front of the vehicle, their lenses zooming through the untinted front windshield to try and get a shot of us in the back.

"Mother truckers," I growl, censoring myself at the last second. I'd say run them over but that's probably not a good idea. "Should we just keep rolling or do we need to stop?"

The driver and guard don't even respond to me. They're too busy doing their thing. It makes me glad that they're here and that they're well-trained for these situations.

Deciding I'd be better served by not distracting them, I turn my attention to my family sitting around me. Carsen and Elise both look horrified while Sarah just looks disgusted, but all of their heads are whipping back and forth, taking in the swarm still calling out and banging on the vehicle. Hearing a particularly hard slap behind me, I whirl around to see several reporters behind us too. We're completely surrounded on all four sides, barely inching forward as the horde moves step by step with us.

"Oh my God, Keith! I had no idea. I'm so sorry . . . is it always like this?" Elise asks, her voice small, but there's an undercurrent of anger. *That's my girl.*

I can feel Carsen's eyes on me, wide with fear, and I try to reassure them. "No, it's not usually like this at all. Maybe at some kind of awards show, where there's lots of media coverage and cameras flashing, but even then, it's nothing like this. Especially not in my daily life. No one usually follows me around, desperate to get pics. Still, might be a good idea to lie low for a bit until this whole thing dies down. Guess it's a good thing the house is stocked with everything we need for a few days."

Elise finally tears her eyes away from the chaos surrounding us and looks at me. "Right. I guess that Plan W-T-F is going into play?" she dead-pans, but there's still a touch of fear even as she tries to joke.

A small smile plays at the corners of my mouth, even though we're still in a rather precarious situation. I reach over and hold Carsen's hand, giving it a little squeeze.

"It'll be fine, honey. I promise."

After a few more minutes of tension-filled progress, we make our way into the street and the driver is able to find a hole in the human shield surrounding us, speeding up and getting us out of the area by punching it through a yellow light. Once we hit the highway, we all breathe a sigh of relief, the pressure ratcheting down as we put miles between us and the studio.

There are several idiots gathered around the house as we approach, but they're outside the gate and they move out of the way as we go on through. As bad as it was, I know it could've been much worse, but thankfully, we're home safe and sound now.

Heading inside, I see Elise and Sarah already getting out the coffee for us and hot chocolate for Carsen. Carsen is pulling off her 'fancy' clothes as soon as she steps inside, eager to get comfortable.

"I don't know if I want to be a celebrity," she says, looking out the window. "Guess there won't be too many girls-only shopping sprees in the future."

"Oh, I don't know about that. If we need to, maybe we can get a cool female bodyguard, like our own personal Wonder Woman," Elise says thoughtfully, giving Carsen a comforting smile. She turns the stove on, pouring milk in a pot to warm it. "Come on. Hot cocoa with marshmallows always make everything seem better." I appreciate the calm and sweet way Elise is handling this with Carsen, helping her find a moment of lightness even as we're all freaked out.

Carsen smiles back, but it's weak and I know she's pretty shaken up by what happened. There's a big piece of me that wants to just gather her in my arms and run away where no one would be the wiser, keep her safe and secret forever. But that ship has sailed and now, we adapt, grow stronger. It's going to be tough, but looking around the kitchen, I know that Carsen has the best support system a little girl could ask for. Still, I go over and hug her tight.

"You did great today, honey. Did you know the first time I had to go on live TV for an interview, I got so nervous I puked all over the green room?"

"No way!" Carsen exclaims. "But you did it?"

"I did. And you were a pro today in comparison. You've already got me beat."

She laughs a bit more fully at that, which soothes the anger still coursing through my veins like a salve. We look up as Sarah sets a cup of coffee in front of me and hot chocolate in front of Carsen.

The four of us sip at our cups, sitting quietly on each side of the table as our minds replay the morning's events in a comfortable few minutes of silence. We're all just taking the day in.

Always the planner, Sarah finally jumps in, setting her mug down and breaking the silence.

"So, now what? We can't just hide out here forever. We got as far as the morning show interview, but we haven't really made a plan for what happens now. Keith, what are you thinking?"

I hum, still wishing I could wake up and this all be a nightmare. For it to not be real. I drain the rest of my coffee, promising myself that after yesterday's overload, I'm not going to have another cup, and think for a moment before answering.

"Well, I need to check in with Todd. I told him I'd do that the second we got back here. Just taking a moment. I'm sure he was watching, but he needs to know about every detail and the ride home after." I intentionally don't say the word paparazzi, not wanting to bring it up any more than I have to in front of Carsen.

"After that, I do think we'll need to be a bit scarce for a bit. No coffee runs or errands for me. And Carsen, you're going to have to take a few days off school. I'll call the school. I'm sure they understand and can have your homework sent here."

"Aww, Da-ad," Carsen says, then stops when she sees my face. "How long, though? I wanna talk to my friends."

"You can, honey. We'll just be a little more reserved until all of this dies down. It won't be long. There will be something else they'll be buzzing over soon enough. Maybe after a few days, we can see if any of your friends want to come over."

Carsen's eyes twinkle. She's never had her friends here. She always has to go to them. "Really?"

"Really . . . but let's not rush things. First, we need to see what we can do. Elise . . ."

I look at her as I say her name, and I see that she'd been staring at Carsen with a sad look on her face as I told her no school.

"I'm sorry, Carsen," she whispers. "Really, I am."

Carsen, who's probably already in her head planning a sleepover with her best friend, smiles at Elise. "No apology needed. This isn't because of you. It's that jerk boss's fault."

Carsen gets up from her spot at the table, hugging Elise around the neck. I can see the shock on Elise's face as she pats Carsen's back. Elise's eyes are bright with unshed tears as she whispers into Carsen's hair. "Thank you, honey."

It's a heart-warming sight, and even though the situation sucks ass, I'm glad that Elise and Carsen are bonding so much. It eases the knot in my gut about bringing a woman into my life while my little girl is still so young.

As Carsen sits back down, she ducks into her hot cocoa, obviously not wanting any more attention right now. I smile, knowing she's going to be okay. She's a tough cookie, that girl of mine.

"Elise," I say, waiting for her eyes to meet mine. "We need to stay together, not be spread out across the city. You should stay here for a bit while this dies down, not just overnight."

"Oh, Keith, that's not necessary. I don't want to intrude," she says, looking pointedly at Carsen. I know she's trying to say she shouldn't stay over if Carsen is here, but fuck that. I want her here with me, where I can keep her safe . . . and fuck her whenever I want.

"No arguments. You're staying here," I reply in a more commanding tone.

Carsen chuckles. She's probably never heard me use it with anyone but her before. "Don't bother arguing. Once he uses that drill sergeant voice, just forget it."

"Oh, his 'drill sergeant voice'? Is that what you call it?" Elise asks, giving in, but in her way. She's going to stay . . . but she'll give me plenty of sass while she does it, too. Lowering her voice, she mock-whispers to Carsen loud enough for everyone to still hear her. "I usually call it his caveman voice . . . but I'm no dummy and I only say that in my head so as not to poke the bear."

Carsen laughs, her eyes twinkling as she glances at me and mock-whispers back. "Poke the bear? Is that when he gets all growly and grumpy?"

I keep my voice deep, but the amusement is obvious as I interrupt them before they can go further. "That's enough, you two. I'm right here and can hear you making fun of me. Next commentary outta either one of you gets punished."

Carsen smirks, giving me a raised eyebrow. "I'm basically grounded already. What else you gonna do, Dad? Spank me? I'm too big for that now."

I laugh at her joke, thankful she seems to be moving on from the trauma of the morning. I harrumph at them both, crossing my arms over my chest and looking down at them mock-threateningly.

Elise laughs too. "I know . . . he's the worst at punishments, isn't he?"

Elise's eyes are flashing fire as she teases, and I silently promise her with my eyes that she'll definitely be getting a punishment later. Maybe exactly the spanking she obviously wants.

Sarah interrupts us before things go on, probably for the better. "So Elise, for tonight, we're good, but do you need me to pick up anything from your apartment? I can have someone go with me, just in case they're scoping your place, but I can get whatever you need."

"Oh, would you?" Elise asks, relieved. "Thank you! Yes, I need some clothes and bathroom stuff. But mostly, I need my laptop and my knitting bag. Maybe while we're cooped up here, I can show Carsen a few stitches?"

Carsen's face lights up as she realizes that our new family dynamic could have some benefits for her as well as me. "That'd be awesome! Thank you."

A plan in place, Carsen asks to be excused, wanting to see if her phone has blown up with texts from friends at school. As she gets up, I give her a final bit of warning. "Remember, honey. Don't say too much. Just that I'm your dad."

She rolls her eyes at me. "I know! Don't worry."

I sigh, knowing she'll do her best. "Just . . . be careful. Everyone's going to be asking you questions. And I want you to . . ." I reply before stopping, seeing Sarah's tiny shake of her head. Let her fly on her own, Keith. Even if it scares you. "Just be careful, baby."

Carsen leans over and kisses my cheek, "I will. I love you, Dad."

"I love you too, Carsen."

Sarah gets up, grabbing her keys from the board next to the door. "Well, no time like the present. I'll grab the hunkier of the guards and stop by your place. Think you can text me a list of what you want before I get to your place, or should I just ransack it and grab what I think you need?"

Elise laughs, taking out her phone. "I'll have it for you. Don't stress if you can't, though. Seriously . . . it's not like I need to meet any deadlines. I'm kind of unemployed at the moment. Be careful, okay?"

Sarah *pshaws*, waving it off. "I've spent years knowing how to look normal after leaving this place, and I'll have a cute guy with me who knows how to kick ass. He can even help me pack."

Having a caveman moment, I let out a growl. "But don't let him touch her stuff, especially not her clothes."

Sarah smirks, twirling her keys in her hand. "Oh, really? I figured he could pack up her bras and panties while I got her makeup. No?"

I growl, but I know she's messing with me. She knows better than that. I just couldn't control myself. "Get out of here . . . and thanks again, Sarah."

She sticks out her tongue and heads for the door, and I hear her calling to the driver before she gets too far away.

Once it's the two of us, Elise comes over to me and I push back from the table, spreading my legs wide to let her step between them. She sits down on my left thigh, wrapping her arms around my neck. "Are we okay? I mean, *really* okay?"

I encircle her waist with my arms, nuzzling her neck, pressing my lips to her racing heartbeat to feel the soothing arousal she brings me before answering. "Yeah, we're okay. At least, we're gonna be."

I pull back, grabbing her chin with my fingers in a firm grip so she's forced to look into my eyes. "Elise, I love you. All of this drama, that's outside of us. What I want is right here . . . you, me, Carsen, and Sarah. That's all I need."

I see her eyes soften as she sighs, letting the rest of the guilt she's been feeling slip away from her conscience. "I love you too, Keith. I still feel so bad it's all turned into this . . . this shitstorm," she says, gesturing toward the world outside before laying a hand on my chest. "But I wouldn't change this right here."

I growl, covering her hand with mine and clasping it to my chest. "Stop worrying yourself or I'm gonna have to smack your ass for it every time."

She grins, raising an eyebrow. "You are so bad at punishment." She leans in, kissing me sweetly. As our lips part, I slip my tongue into her mouth, exploring and tasting. I feel her relax into me, and I rear back and smack her cheek where she's lifted it from my lap.

"Hey!" she gasps as I grab a handful of her ass, kneading it firmly, spreading the heat from my hand and turning the outraged gasp into a deep, throaty moan. "God, yes."

I nip at her chin, licking the spot before pulling back reluctantly. "There's more where that came from, but while Carsen's distracted with her friends, I really do need to call Todd. Make sure everything is okay on the professional front."

Elise sighs in disappointment and acceptance, placing her head on my shoulder. "Do you need me to leave while you call?"

"What? No way. We're done with secrets around here. Everything in the open, at least between us. Okay?"

She hums happily but still gets up to let me get my phone. "Okay."

Grabbing my phone, I dial and Todd picks up on the second ring. "Hey, Keith! How are you doing?" His voice is serious, not his usually chipper clip.

"Well, all things considered, I guess I'm okay. Still, I think I'd rather be in the Yukon right now. How's it looking on your end?"

"Good and bad, if I'm honest."

I freeze, not liking the sound of that. "What do you mean? Tell me."

Todd adjusts, and I can hear a *tap-tap-tap* sound that tells me he's fiddling with a pen on his desk. "The media is having a goddamn orgy with the news about your 'secret daughter,' still-frame shots of the show are already hitting online news sites, and there's lots of speculation about why you've hidden her, where her mom is, that sort of thing. We kinda expected that though, right?"

"Yeah. You got a press release ready about that, though, I assume. What else? There's obviously more, judging by your voice."

"Yeah, that's the bad news. Donnie and the tabloid already lawyered up. They contacted me within minutes of your accusations on TV. They're talking about suing you for slander."

"It's only slander if it's not true. And it's definitely true."

"Yes, I know. But we're going to have to fight it, since it's your word against his. I've already contacted the local authorities. They're sending out a detective this afternoon to talk to you and Elise. You're going to have to file a report so the paper trail starts on our end. With no real evidence, there's not much a DA can do, but at the same time, a civil suit could be a possibility."

"A civil suit? You've gotta be joking."

"Don't sweat it, man. The lawyer from the label I talked to said that there's no jury in the country that'd find against you for trying to protect your little girl. And if Donnie says one bad thing about Janie, about your past, any of it . . . I'll have his ass nailed to a board so fast he'll wonder what the fuck hit him. Just hang in there, bud. And no talking to reporters. Other than Elise, that is."

CHAPTER
Twenty~Seven
ELISE

WHEN THE DOORBELL rings at about three in the afternoon, I jump, dropping the Ritz and cheese that I'm trying to eat to calm my nerves.

Sarah, who's been a great calming presence since coming home, gathers up a few dishes that still have food on them. "Hey, Carsen, let's go watch a movie upstairs while your dad talks to the police officer. 'Kay?"

Carsen goes without complaint, and Keith answers the door after checking that one of the guards is with him. "Hello, Officer. Please come in."

I don't know what it is, but as soon as the guy walks through the door, everything about him screams 'cop.' He's in his mid-forties, and he's got on a pretty decent suit, but I think it's his eyes that make the difference. They say he's seen some shit, and that despite Keith's celebrity status, there's a lot of other things he'd rather be doing on a Monday afternoon.

It makes me like him, relaxing some. If he'd come in starry-eyed and asking for Keith's autograph, I know I wouldn't trust his ability to handle a case like this. But his air of professional indifference and just-the-facts seriousness seems like a bigger help. He offers a hand to Keith, then me, shaking them in turn. "Detective Morrison. Nice to meet you, Mr. Perkins . . . Miss Warner."

Keith directs Detective Morrison to the living room, and we sit on the couch next to each other, holding hands.

Detective Morrison pulls out a small notepad and pen, along with a voice recorder, and begins. "I've already seen the interview you did this morning. Just for my records, I'll need you to confirm everything. You said the threat was over your daughter. Is that correct?"

Keith nods, leaning forward, his elbows on his knees. "Yes, and that I'm dating Elise. The threat was to publish both of those things."

"Can you tell me how the threat was made?"

With a large sigh, Keith starts telling Detective Morrison about the suspicious phone call and our late-night meeting with Donnie and Francesca.

Detective Morrison writes in his notebook as Keith talks, but he looks up sharply when the $3.5 million blackmail is mentioned. He seems to search Keith's face for a moment, then motions for him to proceed.

As Keith wraps up his retelling with the Monday five o'clock deadline, Morrison hums. "And what happened then? Did you approach him in any way? Touch him at all?"

"No. I was furious and I damn sure wanted to. But in that moment, I was just thinking about keeping everything quiet for Carsen's sake. As mad as I was, I needed to figure out my play, not rush in hot-headed and make things worse. So we left."

Detective Morrison turns to me. "Miss Warner, you were there to witness these events? Anything you'd like to add?"

I shake my head, wondering what Morrison's hinting at. "No, that's exactly what happened. Maybe add in there that Francesca and Donnie are sleeping together? Not sure it's relevant, but I'm not covering up anything for them."

"Okay. Mr. Perkins, so after leaving, where did you go?"

"Why? Do I need an alibi?" Keith says, getting a little pissed. "I'm the one getting blackmailed here, for fuck's sake. No, I was here at home, and nobody was here with me. But there are cameras. The feed is recorded so there's video of me coming in. No person to really confirm, but video of the whole house for the whole night."

Detective Morrison scribbles something down and then turns to me. "So, Miss Warner, you weren't here that night? Where were you?"

Keith sighs, his anger evaporating as he looks ashamed for the first time. I squeeze his hand. "Well, we had a bit of an argument about the whole thing, so Keith dropped me off at home. Later, I went to see a friend to help me figure out what we could do. I went to the club where she waits tables, and we talked while everyone cleaned and closed up. Lots of people saw me there."

He nods his head once, his eyes skimming his notes. "Okay, I will need the video from the cameras and the names of the people who saw you that night."

Keith and I nod, still not sure what that has to do with Donnie's blackmail. "I'm feeling like I'm being charged with something here when Donnie is the one who committed a crime. What's going on?"

Detective Morrison looks at us, and it feels like he's scanning us for mistruths or misdeeds, like he's a living lie detector.

Finally, he caps his pen and puts it back in his suit pocket. "Mr. Perkins, I believe you and your accounting of what happened. That's important for you to understand because I don't think you're going to like what I say next.

We received a phone call this morning, shortly after you went on-air, in fact, from Donald Jardine. He reported that you came to his office two nights ago, angry about an article he was publishing. He stated that you were violent, aggressive, pushing him against the wall and breaking things throughout his office. He said you then punched him several times, in the abdomen and across his cheek. I went to see him at the hospital this morning."

"That son of a bitch!" Keith seethes, getting to his feet. "I never laid a hand on him! I wanted to, but I didn't."

Detective Morrison doesn't even flinch. He's stone cold as he gestures back to the couch. "Please sit down, Mr. Perkins. Remember how I said I believe you?"

Keith takes a big breath, obviously steadying himself, and sits down. "Sorry. I didn't lay a hand on him," he says more calmly.

"I've been doing this a long time, learned a few things along the way. One of which is how to read people. Mr. Jardine doesn't particularly strike me as an honest character, just based on his storytelling. It was full of sensationalism that made sense with his particular profession. I took pictures of his injuries. I visited his office too, took some evidence shots there as well. My gut tells me he saw you on TV this morning, concocted this story, and went so far as to have someone punch him to give the story credibility."

I blurt out in shock and frustration. "So what do we do?"

"Stay right here at home, get me the tapes and the names of your alibi witnesses, and wait for me to write up this report."

"That's it? I'm just supposed to sit here and wait?" Keith growls. "My family's being threatened, and I'm supposed to sit on my ass?"

"Yes, exactly that. And leave your cameras on and recording just in case. I think this will be pretty quick once the alibis check out, but if Mr. Jardine is willing to blackmail you, and I suspect intentionally injure himself to make you seem violent, he might be willing to play hardball in other ways too. Just stay put and I'll be in touch."

Keith shows Detective Morrison out and comes back to sit next to me before pulling me into his lap to straddle him. He holds me tight, pressing his cheek to my breasts, breathing heavily as he calms down. "This is so fucked up. I can't believe he's saying I beat him."

I scratch my fingers along his jaw, letting the scruff tickle my fingers, letting my man know that I'm here for him. "It'll be okay. Detective Morrison seems to be on our side and will check everything out. Donnie's a media pro with strategies and manipulations at his fingertips, and this is his move in response to our going public. He wants to create drama and questions about your character to save his own skin. But we know the truth, and that's enough."

"You know as well as I do that sometimes the truth isn't what people want to hear," Keith says, pulling back and looking up into my eyes. "They want scandalous secrets and dirty laundry, told with dramatic flair. It makes them feel better about their small lives. Most folks don't get that a small life, just you and the people you love living simply, is the best thing to have. They want for more when they have the best thing a person can wish for."

I lean back, marveling at the wisdom he spouts off so easily. "You're a good man, Keith Perkins. I love you."

"I love you too, Elise," Keith rumbles, looking at me with desire as the mood changes. There's still anger, but it's against something we can't change right now . . . but we can celebrate us and what we have.

He grabs my hair and the back of my neck, and I eagerly go to him, opening up as he plunges his tongue in to twist with mine. He cups my breast through my t-shirt, letting his thumb trace back and forth across the already pebbled nub.

Gasping, I push back, even as my body betrays me and my hips grind in Keith's lap, knowing what it wants. "Keith, we can't . . . Sarah and Carsen . . ."

He grins evilly, not even glancing in the direction of where they went. "Are watching a movie upstairs. I'm in charge here, Elise. And we need this . . . something normal, something that feels right."

He waits for me to protest, but he's right. I need this as much as he does, to let the drama outside our doors disappear and get lost in each other's bodies for a moment. I nod, and his grin widens as he lifts me off his lap. "Get on your knees. Suck my cock between those pretty lips, looking in my eyes like you know I love."

As I move to the floor between his legs, unbuckling his jeans, he runs the pad of his thumb over my lips and I suck it into my mouth, teasing his pad with my tongue. "Mmm . . . like that?"

Keith's eyes are locked on my lips, watching his thumb disappear and reappear from my mouth. "Yes, just like that. Suck it like a good girl."

When I finally manage to get his jeans open and boxer briefs pulled down, his cock springs free, thick and hard. There's already a drop of precum at the tip, and I lean forward, keeping eye contact as I lick the delicious drop, moaning at his sweet masculine taste. "God, I love your fucking cock."

Keith gathers my hair in his fist, keeping it out of my face as he looks down at me like a king. "I need to see. I want to see every inch of my cock disappearing into your hot little mouth. You can take it, Elise. Show me . . ."

With every beat of love in my racing heart, I take him to the root in one motion, holding him deep in my throat as I press my nose into the soft hairs at the base of his cock. I hold my breath as long as I can, hollowing my cheeks against his shaft and massaging the head of his cock with my throat, swallowing again and again before lifting back up, gasping for air.

I do it again and again, both of us getting more aroused with every thrust. With just the head of his thick cock in my mouth, I look up at Keith through my lashes like he wants, knowing the sight of my lust, my love on my face as I suck him does wondrous things to him. "Like that?"

Keith growls, nodding slightly. I return to my task with a gusto, bobbing up and down on his cock as I keep my eyes on him, my panties getting wetter with every stroke of his cock over my tongue. I don't go deep throat every time, but I give him all I can, licking and worshipping his cock with all that I am.

Keith groans above me, running a soft hand on my cheek as our locked gazes tell me to stop. I pause, circling his head with my tongue and waiting for his command. "Your hips are bucking the whole time you're sucking me. Is your pussy nice and wet for me, baby? Are you getting off on having my cock fill your mouth?"

I nod, pulling off his cock but still pumping him with my right hand as I answer. "Fuck, yes. I'm soaked from your taste, from having you in my throat. I fucking love it."

Keith smiles down at me, his cock jumping in my fist as he hears me return his dirty words and thoughts. "That's a good girl. Slip your jeans down a bit. I want you to touch your clit while I fuck your face. You don't come until I'm splashing down your throat and over that beautiful face of yours though. You hear me?"

I nod, hurriedly shoving my jeans and panties down my thighs. Sitting back on my heels, I spread my legs as wide as I can and slip my fingers into my folds. I moan at the slickness I find there, and Keith leans forward, looking down at me. "Is this what you want?"

"Fuck, yes," Keith says, his voice rough and deep. "*Just* like that. God, your pussy is perfect."

He watches for a moment, taking his cock in his own hand and stroking himself in time to my movements against my clit. We build together slowly, his fist pumping his cock while I slip another finger into my pussy, pushing them in and out in sync with his hand until we're both moaning, my chest flushing as I feel the orgasm build within me. Suddenly, Keith reaches for me, grabbing my hair again and pulling me forward. "Give me your fingers. I want your taste on my tongue when I come."

I move my honey-coated fingers to his mouth, and he sucks them in, licking them clean before pushing them back between my legs. I'm watching his hand move up and down right in front of me, and I see him squeeze himself hard just behind the head, milking a drop of precum out.

"May I?" I beg, opening my mouth for him, sticking my tongue out, wanting that drop so badly.

Keith taps his head to my tongue, and his taste bursts across my tongue again and I can't help but lick and lap at him for more. He moans, guiding his cock back into my mouth. "Mmm, fuck. Take me in your mouth again and rub that clit. I want to feel your moans all the way to my balls."

I take him in deep again, holding him there and humming, and Keith growls as he starts to fuck my mouth, his hips jerking as he fully takes over. "Dammit, Elise. I can't hold back. You feel too fucking good. Get there, because I'm about to come down your throat. I want you choking out your orgasm around my cock as I fill you."

I moan in happiness at his compliment as I speed up my fingers, blurring across my clit, moans and gasps coming from us both as we get closer to the edge. Keith lets out a grunt, trying to be quiet but failing spectacularly. I can feel his balls tighten and his cock swell even as he chokes out his order. "Come. Now."

As soon as I feel the first hot jet of his cum splash the back of my throat, I shatter into a million pieces. I'm slurping to catch every drop as Keith keeps pumping his hips, driving his cock into my mouth, crying out in a strangled gasp as his climax overcomes him and he throws his head back, filling my throat with his cream.

My clit is pulsing as my pussy clenches around nothing, hungry for Keith's cock. I'm floating, darkness surrounding me as flashes of white spark across my vision behind my closed eyes as I feast on his sweetness, both of us so caught up that he doesn't pull out but instead stays inside me for every pulsing release.

Finally, I collapse, laying my head on Keith's hip and humming out in satisfaction. Nuzzling his cock, I lick at the softening skin, mewling in pleasure and contentment. Thinking he's laid back on the couch too, I'm surprised when he speaks up, his voice still full of heat and desire. "Elise, I need to taste that orgasm. Give it to me."

I smile, reaching down between my legs again and rubbing gently across my sensitive pussy, coating my fingers. "For you."

I look up, keeping my head on his thigh as I offer my fingers to him once again. He holds my hand, drawing the essence of my scent deep inside him, searing it into his mind and soul before sticking his tongue out for a long, lapping lick along their length. "Mmm, so fucking good. Come here. Taste . . ."

He pulls me up from under my arms, depositing me sideways in his lap, and takes my mouth in a kiss. As our tongues slowly tangle, I can taste myself on his tongue, and I know he must taste himself on mine too. Somehow, it feels filthy and dirty, but at the same time it doesn't. It's the joining of two souls, mingling as one and making something new, something better. It couldn't be more perfect.

He was right. That was just what we needed.

CHAPTER
Twenty-Eight

KEITH

FOR WEEKS, the firestorm has raged, surrounding and consuming reputations like they're nothing. Between me, Elise, and Donnie, I'm not sure any of us will survive the ugly gossip and snide commentary from the tabloids, who seem to be playing the odds and supporting both sides of the story, even though ours is the truth.

Donnie and *The Daily Spot* basically wrote Francesca off, leaving her to fend for herself as they focused on their own spin-doctoring. She went the Hollywood path, and after a few too many tabloid mentions of her sleeping her way to the top and harsh speculation about basically everything she'd ever written, she checked herself into a 'health retreat' due to exhaustion rather than suffer a public mental breakdown. While she's still a bitch who had no problems trying to stab my family in the back, I can't help but feel a twinge of sympathy for her. A tiny one. But we've all got shit to bear right now.

It's been hard for both me and Elise to deal with all the craziness. The speculation was so random and out-there, I couldn't believe anyone would think it was true. One night, some stand-up comedian on late-night TV thought it'd be funny to question the magical powers of Elise's *vajayjay* to get more than just secrets spilled.

I'd been a second away from calling Todd to see if anything could be done about it, but Elise distracted me, teasing me that maybe her pussy was indeed magical and that I should probably check it for rabbits. I had to spank her ass pink for that bit of brattiness.

By the time we were exhausted and satisfied, it'd been too late to call Todd and I let the cruel joke go, realizing that Elise's distraction was probably the best idea.

But we keep watching the headlines and celebrity gossip shows when Carsen isn't around, needing to know what's being said about our interview stunt and the whole situation with Donnie. Even I can tell that the paparazzi and tabloid shows are repeating the same story now and that there have been no new developments they're aware of.

It's all a waiting game now, the police charging nobody so far and the lawyers on both sides waiting to see who blinks first. Todd tells me that the lawyers don't want to jump the gun early since a police report going against us could torpedo our case even before it begins.

So we sit and wait. Hiding out doesn't feel right. I still feel like yelling from the rooftops that Donnie is a scumbag, maybe actually punching him for good measure since he's using that claim to garner sympathy like the master manipulator that he is. But Todd assured me that that's not a good idea, and Elise and Sarah agree with him. I know I'm not thinking straight on this issue, so I'm trusting their judgment.

Other than the sneaky viewing of the shows and the drama outside our door, sitting at home has been oddly easy. We've spent long hours eating, playing board games, watching movies, and hanging out just the four of us.

I work off my stress in my home gym and in my music room, furiously creating dark licks on my guitar that I'm not sure are country or sometimes angry metal. It's helpful, and each night as I set my guitar aside and look at my red, aching fingertips, I feel better.

It might be hostile outside these walls, but in here, we're safe, cocooned together and bonding more and more each passing minute.

Emerging from my shower following a good afternoon workout, I grab a beer and look out the window to the back porch and the setting sun. I can hear Elise and Carsen talking outside, but it seems like they're speaking in code, their backs to me so I can't see what they're doing.

"So go under, over, pull a loop, and then cast off the left."

"Okay, but what about this piece?"

Curious what they're up to, I quietly sneak out the back door, moving to the side so that I can see them better. To my heart-warming surprise, my girls are sitting face to face on the patio lounger, their legs crisscrossed, mirroring each other as Elise teaches Carsen to knit. It's a beautiful picture, tender and sweet as they giggle at the uncooperative yarn. The soft laughs feel like a balm to my soul with all the anxiety lately, and I can see Elise being maybe not a mother to Carsen, but motherly.

I never realized just how much Carsen needs that. She has Sarah, and always will, but this feels different and special. My little girl can only be happier surrounded by more love, and I realize that Sarah was right all along about my dating.

I catch movement out of the corner of my eye and look up, where I see Sarah standing in the window of her bedroom, giving me a nod. I give her a nod back, and she smiles before stepping back, giving us a moment of privacy.

I'm glad, because nothing could compare to this moment right here. The woman I love sharing one of her passions with my little girl, teaching her so much more than just skills with yarn.

Elise must feel my eyes on her because she looks over, grinning as she holds up her little patch of yellow. "Hey creeper, you just gonna stand there and watch? Come on over and see what we're working on."

Carsen looks up, delight written across her face, "Look, Dad! Elise helped me get two whole rows done."

I look at the small tangle of knots and loops she's holding up, clueless whether it's right or wrong, good or bad, but she's proud of it and that's all I need to know I'm proud too. "Great job, honey! So what are you guys trying to make?"

"Well, since we don't know how long we're in for," Elise says, "I figured this was a perfect time to learn. And we'll start with the same project I started with, a coaster. Simple, small, and it'll keep us busy. Be productive, all that good stuff."

I plop onto the lounger nearest them, sipping at my beer and watching the pink sunset light wash over their faces, thanking the fates for bringing me this moment. A little beauty with the ugly, a bit of joy with the pain. I hop up, suddenly inspired.

"Keith, you okay?" Elise hollers as I head inside.

"Fine," I yell back, not stopping. "Don't move."

I grab one of the notebooks scattered throughout the house and rush back to my perch on the chair, a song taking shape in my mind already. This is different from the angry, rage-fueled metal-country that could still make some damn good songs. This time, as I sit and watch my girls knitting and chatting, I feel peace and gratitude and love.

I watch the sun set on another blessed day.

I think about the storm raging beyond our doors and my need to keep my family safe and surrounded by love.

Before the last sun ray dips below the horizon, I'm done. It's not a ballad, it's not a party jam . . . it's something else. It's a good one too. I can feel it in my bones.

Born of pain and hardship, lit by love and appreciation, and filled with my heart and truth, it might just be the best song I've ever written. I set the notebook down, eyes taking in the progress Elise and Carsen have made on their projects and on their developing relationship.

I'm a lucky fucker. I drink the rest of my forgotten beer, not even minding the warm suds but just wanting to drain the bottle before dumping the glass in the recycle bin. Behind me, the door opens and Sarah sticks her head out. "Hey, guys. Dinner's almost ready. How about if we eat out here tonight?"

"Yay!" Carsen says, obviously giving her two cents while Elise flashes a thumbs-up. Sarah looks at me and I give her a nod.

"Sounds good."

"Okay. By the way, Keith, your phone just buzzed. Think you got a text."

I sigh, wishing I didn't have to step back into the reality of the world outside, wishing I could just stay in our safe, cozy hideaway. But reality comes calling no matter what, so I know I'd better deal with whatever has happened now.

Grabbing my phone, I see it's a text from Todd. *Call Me ASAP.*

It must be important because he picks up on the first ring.

"Holy shit, Keith. Are you watching this?"

"Watching what? What happened?"

"Turn the TV on. Do it now."

I head into the living room, snatching the remote off my couch and jabbing the power button. "So what am I looking for?"

"News. Shit, any news."

I click a couple of times as Elise, Sarah, and Carsen come in, likely hearing my raised voice even from outside. I find the news and see a blonde pseudo-pageant-looking reporter talking in dramatic tones, as if the world were hanging in the balance.

"That's right, Joanna. What we saw here today was something I don't think anyone was expecting, especially Donnie Jardine. Police arrested him at the offices of The Daily Spot *this afternoon, reportedly rushing in with multiple arrest warrants. Simultaneously, they raided his home, executing more search warrants. Police and crime scene investigators were seen leaving with several dozen boxes of evidence. No official word yet what the boxes contained. Speculation is that they contained evidence proving the multiple allegations of blackmail that were brought to light earlier today."*

My fingers half numb, I put the phone on speaker so we can all hear. "Todd, what the fuck is happening? What are they talking about?"

Todd's glee is evident even through the phone line. "It seems Francesca had a surge of conscience and started naming names. You'll get the list later, but there are some heavy hitters in music and media . . . and they fought back. A little late, considering most of them already paid him, but they've got lawyers that make ours seem like goddamn *Night Court.* And with Francesca now turning on Donnie . . . he's going down for sure."

"So they arrested him?" I ask, stunned. "I mean, I'm glad he's going to be prosecuted, but what does this mean for us?"

"Well, Schrodinger's cat is already out of the bag. Everyone knows about Carsen now. But you don't need to stay at home anymore. The complaint against you has been dropped. It's up to you, but we have a good case to go after the tabloid since Donnie committed these felonies under their employment umbrella using staff to do his dirty work. I'm gonna be honest, it's the only way to get money. By the time the other lawyers are done picking Donnie's financial bones, he won't have two nickels to rub together."

I look to Elise, wanting her opinion. She shakes her head, speaking up. "The tabloid itself didn't do anything other than what it's designed to do, which is report gossip. I hate it, but it's the truth. This was all Donnie, his evil scheme and power play. Besides, I've still got a friend working there, so going after *The Daily Spot* would just hurt people like her, and she is a good person, just doing her job."

"I agree. Leave the tabloid alone as long as they agree to never publish a single story about my family. Ever. I just want this to be done and over. If Donnie gets his, I'm happy. Oh, except there's one more thing . . . Francesca. Tell the cops if she is the one who leaked all of this and is willing to testify against Donnie, I won't file a complaint against her. That's how much I want this over."

I look to Elise for approval, and she nods.

"Okay, all clear then," Todd says. "Feel free to go out when you want. But Keith, you'll definitely need to take a driver and guard for a bit until all of this dies down. It won't be instantaneous, but if we're lucky, a Kardashian will get pregnant again and that'll be all the talk and they'll leave you alone." He laughs, and we hang up, looking at each other in shock.

Carsen is the first to break the silence. "Does this mean Elise has to go home now?"

My eyes snap to Elise as I answer Carsen, trying to decipher what she's thinking as I jump in the deep end with no life vest. "No, it means she *can* go home now. But only if she wants. I'd rather she stay here with us. This can be her home now too. If that's okay?"

My words hang in the air, the question a huge turning point in our family. Elise looks at Carsen, the hope obvious in her eyes. Carsen, in all her innocence, seems unaware of the weight of the situation and responds casually. "Cool! I want to finish a few more rows on my coaster tonight before dinner. Pretty sure I'll need your help. And next, I want to try a blanket."

And without a care in the world, she walks back outside and plops down on the lounger, returning to her knitting.

Elise and I let out long-held breaths, and she laughs softly. "Well, I guess that's that. I'd love to stay."

Sarah pats Elise on the shoulder, a twinkle in her eye as she whispers quietly. "Welcome to the family." Sarah heads back into the kitchen to grab a platter of fried chicken and walks outside with it.

As soon as we're alone, I scoop Elise into my arms, holding her tight as I push a strand of hair behind her ear. "I meant what I said. I want you to stay. Tonight, tomorrow, forever," I tell her, looking into those eyes that I know I can't live without. "I love you."

She blushes, the pink lighting up her cheeks and making her look like a sweet angel. "I love you too. And I want to stay. I can't imagine not being here now, with you and Carsen and Sarah. You're . . . home."

Her words hit my heart like sweet arrows, and I take her mouth in a soft kiss as I grab a handful of her firm ass in my hands. It's just the right thing to do. Soft and hard, gentle and rough, all the things she makes me think and feel . . . each one of them is better than the last. And only Elise can draw them all out of me.

There's a tap on the back door and we break apart to see Sarah smirking as she hooks a thumb behind her. "Dinner's ready, lovebirds."

CHAPTER
Twenty~Nine

ELISE

HOURS LATER, dinner has been eaten, stories have been told, and laughs have surrounded us for hours. Finally, the tension and dread that have underlined the last couple of weeks has fallen away.

After we clean up, Sarah wipes her hand on the dish towel. "Well, fam, I'm off to soak in my bathtub before sleeping for at least twelve hours in my own bed. Now that we're not on lockdown, I'm going to head home. Call me if you need anything."

We say our goodbyes and Sarah leaves. Soon, Carsen crashes out too, falling asleep almost before her head hit the pillow. It's a little slice of heaven when she asked if Keith and I both could tuck her in.

After closing her door, Keith pulls me close, kissing my forehead as the gravity of what our family could be sinks in. Detouring through the kitchen to snag two nightcap beers, we snuggle on the back porch, talking and looking at the stars.

"I'm going to grab another," Keith says, sighing happily. "I think I've earned it today. Want one?"

"No, thanks. I think I'm going to change into my jammies. I'll meet you back in five?"

Keith heads to the kitchen and I go to our bedroom. Wait . . . *our* bedroom. God, that feels good, and I'm going to love getting used to saying that. Quickly, I dig through the big drawer where I'd dumped the clothes Sarah had brought over for me, looking for PJs. I guess if this is our bedroom now, maybe I'll have to claim more than one drawer in the dresser.

Shuffling things around, I see a flash of red lace. I fish around a bit, pulling out a lacy teddy I'd bought but never worn. Sarah brought just the thing.

Slipping my clothes off, I change into the teddy and check myself in the full-length mirror. *Looking good, Elise. And now it's time to be a little bad.*

Sticking my head out the window, I see Keith below, his back to me as he watches the moon. "Keith, can you help me with something?"

I wait, standing tall and proud in the middle of the room as I hear him come inside, his bare feet still clumping on the carpet. Thank God he's a country singer. He'd never make it as a ninja.

"What do you ne—" Keith asks as he steps inside, but his voice tapers off into a groan as he sees me. "Holy shit."

I smile and arch my back a bit, knowing the pink of my nipples is visible through the fine lace. "I think this might be a bit too revealing. What do you think?"

"God damn, Elise," Keith says, his eyes wide and his jaw still a little slack. "You look sexy as fuck. Turn around, let me see all of you."

I do as he says, turning a slow circle to let him see all of me, but I look over my shoulder, wanting to see his reaction to the tiny string between my ass cheeks.

I don't have to wait as Keith nearly pounces across the room to grab me forcefully from behind. Excitement sends shivers down my body as I expect him to shred the lace, hurl me across the bed, and ravish my body however the fuck he wants . . . but this is Keith, and as always, he's in control.

"You tease me . . . but it's a good tease," he whispers in my ear, running a gentle finger along the edge at my cleavage, smiling as goosebumps break out along my skin. "But you're not going to make me lose control first."

His hips grind forcefully against my body as he turns me around, his full cock already pressing to my clit, but his touch is reverent as he traces along the slim strap at my shoulder.

"Do you like it?"

"Like?" Keith asks, lifting one strap and easing it off my shoulder but leaving my breast still covered. Tracing his finger down my arm, he shakes his head once. "No. I fucking love it."

He reaches behind me, grabbing the tiny thong and pulling it up, making it rub along my pussy as I gasp at the sensation. I feel the bottom slip between my lips, and the string rubs against my asshole, making me shudder as Keith leans down, whispering in my ear.

"I'm going to fuck you in this, this sexy red lingerie that makes me so fucking hard for you. I'm gonna leave it on you and just slip this little string that's splitting your ass over to the side so I can get my cock in your hot pussy. Do you want that, Elise?"

My head nods like a bobblehead, desperate for what he's saying to happen right now. "Fuck yes, Keith. Do it now. Fuck me."

But he steps back, his hand rubbing along the bulge in his jeans, and my pussy gets even wetter, knowing he's gonna fill me with his thick cock. "Oh, Elise. You know better than that. Who's in charge here?"

I bite my lip, knowing this is part of the tease, although it doesn't always feel like a tease . . . it just feels natural. For a second, I'm reminded of him telling me in our first interview that foreplay can be the best part if it's done right, and fuck, does he do it right. "You are."

"That's right, good girl. Get on the bed, on your knees and face down."

I hurry to do as he says, grabbing a pillow to lay my face on as I lift my ass in the air. I can feel Keith move behind me, his presence filling the room and my senses. He pauses behind me, running a gentle, intimate hand over my right cheek so softly that it almost feels like a whisper of wind. "That's a damn pretty sight, your fine ass turned up for me."

He grabs a handful of each of my cheeks with his large hands, kneading and massaging, spreading me open wide to his gaze. "Look how wet your pussy is. I've barely touched you and your cream is soaking down your thighs. Time to taste."

Without letting go of his powerful hold on my cheeks, he bends down to bury his face between my legs, tracing his tongue in a long line up my inner thigh to my center before repeating it on the other side. I shiver at the sensation, so good but not nearly enough. I lift my ass more, tempting him, taunting him, hoping he'll give me what I desperately need.

I should've known better. *Smack!* His hand pops down on my cheek, fire exploding from my ass through my body before re-centering on my desperate pussy. "Bad girl. I know what you want, and I'll give it to you. But only when I'm ready. Until then, let me take my time."

I whine, the heat from the spanking warming my body and leaving me wanting more. *Smack!* He spanks my other cheek and I glare back at him. "You . . . you fucker. You know *exactly* what you're doing."

"Damn right," he says, his eyes never leaving my ass. Keith gently rubs to soothe the sting, his smile showing how pleased with himself he is for spanking me. "Needed your pretty cheeks to match this lace."

The flash of pain gone, his touch gets rougher again, and he spreads me wide, the thong string pulled off to one side to let him have full access to anything he wants. Holding my breath as he leans forward, ready for his tongue on my pussy, I clench the blanket underneath me to prepare for the expected bliss. But that's not what he does. Instead, he starts on the outside, at the base of my ass before his hot, wet tongue moves toward my higher center, and I feel him flick against my asshole, making me squirm in delight.

He holds me tighter, locking me in place where he wants me. "You're mine, Elise. Every part of you . . . mine."

I nod, overwhelmed by the wonderful sensations of his tongue on my ass, but it's not enough. "Tell me."

"Yours," I moan, my hips bucking uncontrollably even though he has a tight hold on me. "Everything. It's all yours."

"Mmm, good girl," he murmurs, licking me again, his tongue slipping over my ass before moving down to tease at my lips. I spread my knees wider, letting him in deeper, and he takes the invitation, fucking my pussy with his tongue before circling my clit.

"Ohh, fuck . . . Keith . . . feels so good."

He's teasing me, tracing patterns with no sense so I can't expect his touch, making me feel so good without letting it build too high, driving me crazy as he feasts on my body.

He moves a finger to my ass, letting the thick digit press inside slowly and deliciously, never pausing his torture of my clit. Deeper inside he goes, and I feel a sense of being so full, so wonderfully impaled, and this is just the beginning. I push back, wild for more as I moan and cry out, begging him.

He slips his free thumb into my pussy, filling me as he finger-fucks me faster and faster, filling my ass and pussy simultaneously.

Suddenly, he sucks my whole pussy into his mouth, thrashing his tongue across my clit. I explode, my orgasm pounding through me, tremors wracking my body as I bury my cries in the pillow.

I'm still coming when I feel him pull back, his jeans dropping and his hard cock thrusting deep inside me in one long stroke. It sets me off again, and I keep spasming, my walls fluttering around his thickness as he pounds my body relentlessly.

"Fuck, fuck, fuck," I squeal nearly incoherently as my spine fills with fire. I arch and reach back for him, trying to get all of him that I can. Keith is tugging the string of my thong tight over my left cheek, and he grabs my hands behind my back, locking them in place and forcing me to be still for him. "That's it," he says as he roughly, wonderfully hammers my pussy. "Keep squeezing me like that. Let me feel you milking my cock, your pussy sucking the cum out of me."

I squeeze my pussy as hard as I can, wanting to drive him as crazy as he's driving me, wanting him to reach that tipping point where he loses control.

"Harder," I growl as I regain my voice. "Fuck me . . . I want it, Keith. Come in me and fill me up."

He grunts, his hand twisting around the thong, and I feel the lace loosen around my lower half, falling to the bed beneath me as he tears it from my body. Now that his hand is free, he buries it into my hair as he leans over me, still pinning my hands behind me as he covers me with his body to rumble in my ear. "You think you can take me harder, Elise? Be careful what you wish for."

I nod, and he takes my breath away, slamming into me harder than ever before. Holy fuck . . . this man is more than I ever could have imagined, even after all the fucking we've done before. This is right on the line, the undercurrent of pain making the pleasure even better.

I know I'm going to be sore after, and I like the thought that he'll be imprinted on my body inside and out, heart and soul. I'm his forever, and he knows it as he makes me totally his.

"Yes . . ." I choke out in a strangled cry as my body tightens and explodes in another orgasm, his name a prayer locked behind lips frozen in exhilaration, caught in the waves of pleasure spreading from my pussy out to my fingers and curled toes.

Somewhere in the haze, I hear him behind me, his voice trembling as he's on the edge too. "Just like that, Elise. Fucking milk me like a good girl."

I have just enough energy left to squeeze him in a vise grip, giving him all I have.

"Shit, so tight . . . it's so good," Keith grunts. His cock swells, and I feel him slap into me a final time, his cock exploding deep inside me, the warmth of his seed coating my insides and making me softly weep in satisfaction.

As we pant, trying to catch our breath, I collapse to the bed, Keith still on top of me and inside me. Gathering me in his arms, he kisses my cheek, tasting my tears. "You okay?" he whispers, concerned. "I didn't hurt you, did I?"

I smile, moaning happily. "So much better than okay. So much better."

I feel the rumble of his laughter at my back, and he kisses my shoulder before slowly pulling out. I feel the loss instantly and wish he were inside me still. I'm too exhausted to look up, but I hear Keith pad to the bathroom and walk back to the edge of the bed.

"This might sting for a second."

I hiss as he presses a wet washcloth to my sore pussy, but almost as soon as the shock of discomfort starts, it passes and a soothing warmth takes its place.

"Mmm, that feels good. But you might have to kiss it all better."

"Normally, I'd give you a smack for that sass, but maybe I'll take mercy on you for now."

I chuckle, looking at him from half-hooded eyes. "Maybe just save it for later?"

"I can definitely do that."

After a minute or two, the washcloth loses its warmth and Keith sets it aside, gathering me to curl up to him as he wraps his arm around my shoulders.

He covers us over with the blankets, tracing his thumb along my shoulder. "I love you."

I look up at him, seeing the honesty, the depth, the truth in his eyes and knowing it's all we ever need to say.

"I love you too, Keith."

ELISE

I CAN'T BELIEVE how nervous I am, sitting in the dressing room backstage. It's the first night of Keith's new summer concert tour, and it wasn't until I looked back that I realized he's always started his summer tours in his home state, Idaho.

Some investigative reporter I am. Luckily, since I quit my job with *The Daily Spot*, I've been doing freelance reporting so I was able to come along. Freelancing has been better than I could've ever hoped, letting me work on whatever stories interest me. With Keith and Carson's permission, I even did a whole new in-depth profile on our new family, and *Rolling Stone* snatched it up at a good premium. Not quite *The New York Times*, but you really can't get much more respect in the music industry media.

Ironically, the tabloids have left too. With no more secrets—well, none that are that big, my wonderfully aching ass tells me—the buzz of intrigue has died off. There's just nothing there for the paparazzi to pick clean.

I'm even doing a weekly blog post for a country music site called *Life on the Road with Keith Perkins*. So even while we're on tour, I get to work and spend time with Keith. It's the best of both worlds. Paparazzi still show up in droves for awards and concerts, but it's settled down enough so that we can live pretty quietly at home.

Carsen is safely back at school, at least for another week until her summer vacation starts, and then she and Sarah will join us on the tour starting in San Diego. Best of all, Keith and I can usually sneak out for coffee without hassle as long as he skips the cowboy hat and wears the Clark Kent getup.

I've come to like the faux nerd version of Keith, and we've definitely put those glasses, along with some of my wigs and disguises, to good use over the last few months. He plays my nerdy computer repair guy in glasses and a polo, or I'll pretend to be his personal lap dance stripper thanks to the moves I saw at Maggie's gig. Keith says it's sexy to have a blonde one minute and a brunette the next, and I'm thinking of ordering a short red wig for some extra spice. I think a red-haired version of myself might be a bit more bossy, and it'll be fun to see if Keith can handle that. Ha!

But today, Keith is in full cowboy mode in his tight jeans, plaid button-down shirt, hat, and boots. He looks hot as hell and I'm reminded again how lucky I am that everything has worked out this way.

It could've been very different. If I hadn't written the initial article. If we hadn't given in to our attraction. If we hadn't gone public with our story. Hell, if Donnie hadn't tried his blackmail schemes.

There are a thousand what-if's, but they've all led to this moment right here. We're happy, in love, with our careers doing well . . . and I've got my very own dominant sexual beast of a country music star to satisfy every desire I could ever imagine.

There's a knock at the door, and from the other side, I hear the head roadie, a balding, leather vest-wearing guy holler in his smoke-lunged voice, "Fifteen minutes to stage time!"

Jim, Shane, and Eric stand, moving toward the door. "All right, man. See you in ten next to the stage for our pre-show cheer to kick off this year's tour," Jim teases.

As they leave, I turn to Keith, who's shaking his head good-naturedly. "Oh, I need to see this cheer! That's definitely going in the first story about the tour."

Keith grins, shrugging. "Of course, but you know, I think I'm going to need to read these posts before you make them live. This isn't all-access, so I might need to make sure you're not telling all of my dirty secrets."

I can hear the teasing heat in his voice, and I come close, whispering breathily in his ear. "Oh? And do you have some dirty secrets, Mr. Perkins? Please tell me . . . I'll do *anything* if you'll tell me."

"I might have one or two secrets left in me," he rumbles, his voice just on the line between teasing and sexy. "Want to hear one?"

I bite my lip, looking at him with faux-innocence as I nod. He spins me, shoving me flush against the door and whispering hotly in my ear. "My secret is that I'm gonna fuck your pussy with my fingers, make you come all over my hand. And then I'm going to play my concert with your taste, your scent marking me. When I wave to the crowd, it'll be you I'm thinking about. Your fucking cream so sweet on my fingers as I blow kisses to all the fans. Take off your panties, Elise."

I rush to do as he says, yanking my maxi skirt up and pulling at my thong. Keith grabs my wrists, stopping me in my tracks. "Wait. I didn't know you had that on. You know how much I like those."

I do know. That's exactly why I've taken to wearing them more frequently. Keith caresses my bare cheeks, humming happily. "Leave it on."

I nod, and keeping my skirt gathered in my hands, I press my cheek to the cool wood of the door, arching my back and pressing my pussy closer to Keith. He stands behind me, wrapping his arms around me and dropping his hands to my hips, urging me open some more.

I spread my legs a little wider, giving him access, and feel him chuckle behind me. "Oh, no, you're gonna spread those pretty pussy lips for me. Hold your skirt with one hand and then open yourself for me. I need one hand for your sweet little clit and one to fuck your pussy."

I do as he says, and as soon as he touches me, I cry out softly, knowing this room might not be soundproofed. "Oh, fuck, Keith. That feels so good."

He goes fast, his fingers moving across my clit in hard sweeps, and I feel his cock grinding against my ass, turning me on until I'm soaked and I want more. "There's not enough time. I want—"

Keith interrupts me, tugging on my ear with his teeth. "You've got three minutes, Elise. Then I'm walking out that door for the show. I want your cum on my fingers. You need to get there. Squeeze my fingers and imagine it's my cock filling you up and come for me like a good girl."

He shoves his fingers deep inside me, pressing them forward to my front wall, his other hand grinding against my clit. It's so good, and all I need is to fall off the edge, gasping and coating his hand. It's hot, intense, dirty, quick . . . but sometimes, that's just as good as the times we've spent hours slowly teasing each other to multiple orgasms.

Before my vision even clears, I'm spinning and dropping to my knees as I wrench Keith's jeans open. I look up and give him a flirtatious smirk. He's not the only one who can tease his partner. "Two minutes and you're walking out that door, Mr. Perkins. You need to come down my throat before then. Or else."

"Or else what?" he growls, gasping lightly as I lick his shaft from base to tip.

"Like you said, you're walking out that door. So get there, cowboy," I say as I wink at him.

Before Keith can respond, I take his whole cock deep in my mouth and suck with everything I have, immediately bobbing up and down on his cock and loving the intoxicating musk of his natural scent. Keith groans loudly, planting his palms on the door behind me and spreading his legs wide as he tries to fuck my face. But I'm faster, holding his hips, slurping and hollowing my cheeks as I suck, hungry for him.

I squeeze his balls, tugging gently as I hum, gazing up at him with the innocent look that I know he loves. He groans, his orgasm rocketing through him, and he shoots jet after jet of sweet warmth down my throat and I swallow, satisfaction buzzing in my head as I take every drop like the good girl I am.

He pulls back, yanking me up from the floor to kiss me fiercely. "Damn, Elise. Now I'm gonna be thinking about burying my cock in your pussy the whole damn show."

I wink, dabbing at the corners of my mouth like a lady. As if I missed a single drop. "It'll probably be your fastest show ever. Don't forget to blow kisses to the crowd."

Keith lifts his hand to his mouth, inhaling deeply and then licking a taste of my honey from his fingertip. "Mmm, I have a feeling this is gonna be a great show."

He tucks his shirt back in, helping me adjust my skirt so we both look more or less put together. Hopefully, no one will be able to tell we just fucked backstage. Then again, this is music . . . this might not be out of the ordinary.

We speed-walk through the dark curtained hallways and I remember the first concert I went to where Keith fingered me in a jealous fit backstage. It all seems like a dream, so perfectly impossible but somehow true and real.

"Okay, you ready?" Jim asks when Keith joins them. "Pain don't hurt!"

"Glory never dies!" Shane adds.

"And chicks dig scars!" the others yell, making me laugh.

"Kick some ass!" they all finish, heading out on stage to the cheering crowd. I'm just as loud, but this time, though, I'm just off stage. Which in some ways is better. I can see my man more easily.

Keith grabs the microphone, looking out on the crowd. "Helloooo, Boise! Are you ready to sing along with an old hometown boy?"

He leans an ear out, listening to them scream wildly. "That's what I thought!"

I watch as he brings his fingers to his mouth, blowing a big kiss to the crowd before looking over at me and winking. I almost melt, and I'm glad nobody can see me swoon.

God, this man is so damn sexy and amazing. And most importantly, he's *mine.*

I watch transfixed as he sings song after song, working the stage like a master. It's a bigger setup than the small shows I've seen at home, and it's exciting to watch him use the space, flirting with the audience as they watch him with rapt attention, singing every word back to him.

Knowing the big closing is coming soon, I'm surprised when I hear the music play on with a soft beat as Keith takes off his guitar, handing it to a stagehand.

He approaches the mic and pulls off his hat, wiping his forehead. "Hey, Boise. You mind I do something a little different tonight?"

Yelling back their agreement, he continues. "You see this yellow scarf tied up on my microphone?"

His fingers run along the length of yellow fluff tied to the top of the stand

and hanging down to almost brush the stage. I blush, knowing why it's there but not noticing it before.

"Well, it was made for me by someone really special to me. She joked one night that I could tie it to my mic like Steven Tyler, a little rock star style for this country boy. In fact, she dared me that I wouldn't do it. And you know what I had to do, right?"

I can hear a mutiny of voices yelling back, mostly seeming to agree that Keith had to do it. I laugh, thinking of Keith saying, "hold my beer," but I still get warm and fuzzy inside because Keith did put the scarf I'd knitted for him on his mic and promised he'd do it every show for the whole tour.

"That's right. I put the damn scarf on the mic, because contrary to some folks' opinions, I'm not a stupid man. And when your woman tells you to do something, you'd best do it. When she dares you to, well then, you damn sure better do it!"

There are some hoots and hollers, and I grin. That's right . . . his woman. And he makes it sound like I'm in charge. If they only knew.

"So the woman who made this scarf for me is here tonight. You think I could bring her out and introduce you to her?"

My jaw drops as Keith looks over at me, waving me onstage. I shake my head no, honestly terrified. I'm not shy, but shit, this is on another level. There are thousands of people out there. No fucking way. I'm the one behind the camera and keyboard, writing the stories.

Keith grins, talking to the crowd again. "Oh, looks like she's shy, but I promise she isn't. She just needs a little incentive. Hey, Elise?"

I glare at him, and he smirks, "I *dare* you to get that fine ass out here with me."

Fuck, he knows I'm coming out there after his whole speech about my daring him and his following through. I take a deep breath and step out onstage.

The wall of supportive sound that hits me as I step awkwardly out helps unlock my knees, and as I give a little wave, I even hear a few wolf-whistles, which helps even more. Still, it seems like Keith is miles away as I walk the few yards to him in the center of the stage.

As soon as I'm close enough, he takes my hand, pulling me to his side and kissing me fully . . . in front of everyone. But it settles the swarm of butterflies in my belly a bit, even as it starts another type of fluttering in my body.

There's some noise again, but it seems to be a mix of cheering, more wolf-whistles, and a lot of 'awws.'

Keith releases me, spinning me out to let the whole crowd get another look at me. "So everyone, this is my woman, Elise. Elise, this is . . . everyone."

The crowd goes wild again, and I see lots of people waving, but even more phones being held up, recording this craziness. "So, I've got one more song to play for you, but I thought maybe you could help me with something first."

Keith moves the microphone out of the way and looks at me, our eyes locked as he slowly drops to one knee. The crowd roars again, a physical force that nearly knocks me over as my head spins. From the corner of my vision, I see a two-man crew run onstage with a camera and a boom mic above us and realize they're beaming us to the big jumbotron screens for the audience.

Oh. My. God. What is happening? Is he doing what I think he's doing? Oh, my God.

Keith takes my hands in his, looking up at me. "Elise, I wasn't looking for you. I didn't think this was in my cards, at least not for a long time, maybe never. But you came into my life, full of sass and refusing to take no as an answer. And we somehow fit together perfectly. You have given me so much . . . your heart, your trust, your love. And you have mine too . . . all of me. I love you and I want to spend the rest of my life making you as happy as you make me. Elise Warner, will you marry me?"

From somewhere, he's pulled out a ring and is holding it at my fingertip, his eyes shining hopefully. The tears are already rolling down my face as he waits, the shock and beauty of the moment overwhelming me.

I can't get a word out. My head's spinning so much, so I nod. "Yes, Keith. God, yes!" I finally whisper. "I love you."

He slides the ring on my finger, and I can't even see it as he swoops up, hugging and spinning me, and I can finally breathe, joyful laughter filling the air as I cling to him. "I love you so much, Keith."

He sets me down, and I realize the crowd is still going crazy, a deafening roar of celebration coming from every direction.

Holy shit, I just got engaged on stage at a concert. My fiancé's concert. Whose life is this?

Keith grabs the microphone again, still holding my hand. "Thanks, everyone. I think that went okay. What do you think?" he teases.

They cheer again, and Keith looks back, giving some sort of signal. The stage lights dim, and I see two stagehands come out, one with Keith's guitar and another with a stool. I think at first that Keith is going to sit down and sing, but he gestures to me instead.

I settle on the hard stool, thankfully remembering to sit up straight as Keith strums a few chords. "All right, Boise. I started this new song when it seemed like everything that could go wrong had gone wrong. It was angry, it was bitter . . . a real country song."

That earns a few laughs, and Keith continues. "But when I looked at the things that really mattered, that was all I needed to realize just how lucky I am. The song changed . . . because Elise changed me."

The first notes are soft, and anyone who doesn't know Keith might think they're plaintive . . . but this is the Keith I've been able to get to know more over the past few months, the one who is controlled, and reflective . . . and who just asked me to marry him.

> In the darkest of nights
> When I'd near given up hope
> You held me close
> And you saved me
>
> As the storm raged on
> I had no fight left
> You stood, sheltered me
> And you saved me
>
> You showed me love
> You showed me light
> You taught me pain was worth it
> If you were the prize
>
> It's a whole new world
> It's a beautiful day
> As long as you're by my side
> It'll be a helluva a ride . . .

The End. Thank you for reading. If you'd like to listen to this as an audiobook, it's available on Amazon or Audible.

Let's stay in contact! You can join my mailing list here. You'll never miss a new release and you'll even get 2 FREE ebooks!

Continue on for an excerpt of Dirty Deeds! Dirty Deeds is Maggie's book!

Get Dirty (Interconnecting standalones):
Dirty Talk | | Dirty Laundry | | Dirty Deeds | | Dirty Secrets

Dirty Deeds

Prologue

SHANE

I LEAN BACK, keeping an eye on the club from my position near the wall. On the far side of the club, Marco the bartender is mixing up a pitcher of margaritas for one of the tables while looking cool as a cucumber in his dress shirt and vest, the sleeves on his cranberry-colored shirt rolled up to just below his elbows. Seeing me, he gives a little salute with two fingers. I return it, knowing that within a few minutes, I'll have some refreshment myself.

"Hey, Shane, you want to switch?" Nick, the guy I have working the door right now, asks. "I gotta piss."

"Yeah, I'll cover the door for a bit. Just hurry. I want to do a walk-around."

"No sweat," Nick says, heading toward the back. I take over the door, leaning back in the stance that allows me to keep an eye on the floor while still keeping the door under control.

Nick takes his time. He always does, which is one of the reasons I'm the bouncer in charge here, but I'm not upset as I see a tight, petite blond make her way toward me. "Hey, Shane," she says, handing me a big beer mug filled with Coca Cola. "Marco said you were looking thirsty."

"Thanks, Meghan. You doing okay?" I ask, taking a moment to appreciate the wide-eyed cuteness that is Meghan. She's only been here about a week, but there's something about her that draws my eyes to her again and again, and not because I'm doing my security job. "No troubles with the tables?"

"Of course not," Meghan says, giving me that shy, sweet-girl smile that I've started looking forward to. "Actually, I've got a friend coming in later.

Uhm, if a tall knockout chick comes in asking for me, you mind pointing her my way?"

"Sure enough," I promise her, an unfamiliar smile crossing my face. I almost never smile at work, but Meghan seems to pull them out of me without even trying. "You two gonna discuss cookie baking or something?"

For a split second, I see the most beautiful shade of pink as her cheeks blush, but then she ducks her head shyly. "No, she's just having a tough time with a guy she's seeing and wants my advice. I think she mostly needs girl talk, you know?"

"Sure," I lie through my teeth. "I'll keep an eye out. Be safe out there."

Meghan nods, sashaying away. She tosses her hair back over her shoulder, her hips hypnotizing me with each swing left and right. On her, the sexy moves seem unintentional, not a practiced performance like the other girls here. Nick comes back and I drain my Coke before patrolling the floor. It's not really needed, but letting the customers have a silent warning helps stop about ninety percent of the shit that can happen around here before it even starts.

As I move around the floor, my eyes tick back to Meghan as she works her tables. It's almost like I'm circling her, edging ever so closer, tempting fire and keeping the best view of her that I can. Her uniform miniskirt hugs her tight ass like it was painted on her, and as she bends down to put a pitcher of beer on a table for six, I swear she's showing off especially for me, popping her ass out in a fantasy-come-to-life move.

Maybe it's just me, or maybe it's Meghan's natural charm, but I can't help watching every move she makes. The way she licks a thumb when she splashes something on it, the way she shows her cleavage as she moves in her uniform bustier corset . . . it's all so damn seductive, and the contrast between the shy girl she is around me and the sex kitten she acts like while working makes me wonder which is more real.

Meghan straightens up, turning and looking over her shoulder at me, adjusting those thick-framed 'nerdy' glasses that push her from cute to hot as fuck. She seems surprised to find me watching, her eyebrows lifting behind the frames, but I catch her biting her lip to hide the little smirk tugging at her mouth. She's fucking with me, she's got to be. I have to hold back a growl as she goes over to her next customer, striking a pose beside the table as she takes their order.

I'd never let any of the fucknuts who frequent this place lay a hand on one of the girls, but I keep a special eye on Meghan. It makes some of the long shifts a bit easier, and stocks my spank bank with plenty of imaginary material . . . Meghan bent over the bar as I take her from behind. Or maybe twirling around a pole in one of the private rooms just for me. The dangerous fantasies are the ones where I picture her in my bed . . . hair a mess with flushed cheeks, wearing nothing but the smile I just put on her full lips.

I alternate door duty with Nick, letting him do the next floor sweep per protocol. A static position sometimes makes me antsy. But for right now, I lean against the doorframe, appreciating the best view of Meghan in the house.

I continue my scan of the room, checking customers, the bar, and the stage, but my eyes always return to the tiny, sweet blonde that is slowly driving me insane. "God damn, what I would do to you if I had a chance," I whisper to myself, knowing the heavy rock music will obliterate the words before anyone can hear them. Still, as if by some form of ESP, Meghan taunts me, crouching down with her ass near her heels to hear a guy's order. He's looking straight down her bustier at her tits and I have to hold myself back from beating the shit out of him just for looking at her. My restraint is rewarded as she rises back up, shifting her skirt back into place and giving me a bigger peek at the curve of her ass. She heads towards the bar to turn in the order, but I see the way she peeks over to check if I'm watching.

Two can play that game, little girl. I casually reach down and adjust my cock, my face hard and stoic as I give her a disapproving look. She squeaks I think. I can't hear it, but the way she jumps a bit and her mouth flies open, I imagine the shocked sound coming from her throat. I laugh to myself, but I'm not sure if she won that round or I did.

Still, I keep my cool, keeping myself under control as the night wears on. Meghan's friend shows up right before closing time, and the two have a long sit-down talk while Marco and I finish up the cleaning.

"Thanks, Shane," Meghan says as they get ready to head out the door. Her friend's gone off to use the ladies' room, and it's just us for a moment. "I always feel . . . good when you're around."

"I just want to make sure you stay safe," I reply, looking down into her adorable face. "After all, this is a gentlemen's club."

Meghan chuckles and looks around. "Not too many gentlemen in this club. But I'm glad there's at least one. Thanks again, Shane."

My name on her lips is a tease that makes me want to taste her mouth as she says it again. But her friend comes out, and the two of them leave. Meghan gives me a little finger wave as the door closes. Oh, my sweet little innocent one . . . if only I were a gentleman.

If only.

I'm anything but, which is why it's safer if you stay away from me.

CHAPTER

One

MAGGIE

"HEY, Marco! Can I get a pitcher of Miller Lite for table fifteen, please?" I yell over the throbbing bass of the music in the club . . . and get ignored again. "MARCO!"

He looks over and gives me a half-understanding nod before grabbing one of the plastic pitchers and filling it with . . . well, fudge it, it's beer at least. I roll my eyes, frustrated that I have to drag the bartender's eyes away from the stage. He's been here for years, and you'd think he'd be immune to this after seeing dancers for hours five nights a week.

But he isn't. Obviously, as evidenced by the way he's staring at the stage. He moves a hand, and I think he's going to adjust his crotch, but instead, his hand lifts to his head and he slicks his already meticulously coifed hair into place. In my head, I nag him. Adjust whatever you need to, your crotch or your hair or your suave designer clothes. Just do your dang job so I can do mine. Not too much to ask, is it?

"Here you go, Meghan," he says, sliding the pitcher the last few inches to me. I notice that he doesn't apologize that he's ignored the order I placed on the bar five minutes ago, nor that the delay will likely affect my tip, not his. His eyes still haven't left the show onstage either. Such a butt-nugget.

With a sigh, I turn to see what's got Marco so blasted distracted at the moment. I know from the music that it's Allie's turn on stage. Besides being one of the people I can call a friend around here, she's an amazing dancer, definitely too good to be stripping in a place like this. I watch as she spins around the pole, her legs splayed wide in the splits for several rotations as she flips her head around, making eyes at a guy in the front row.

In a flash, she pulls her legs in smoothly, locking them around the pole and lying back in a death-defying backbend move that puts her eye-level with her prey, although she's upside-down and his eyes are locked on her boobs, not her face. I see her smirk and then kick her legs over, rising to stand tall in her high-heeled red stilettos. It's impressive, even from just an athletic point of view, although I'm sure most of Allie's fans aren't really interested in how much she's had to train and work for her unworldly strength, balance, and flexibility.

The guy picks up a green bill from the stack in front of him, and Allie slithers down to take it, blowing the guy a kiss with her plump, heavily lipsticked lips, knowing she'll have the whole pile before her time onstage is up.

I clap loudly, cheering her on, knowing that the cash will help her out with her debt situation. She's a nice girl, my best friend in this club, and still way too good for this joint.

Still clapping, I don't hear Marco approach. "She's something else, isn't she? Even you can't keep your eyes off her. Can you blame me? Unless . . . that's your thing?"

I laugh, glancing over at him to see a questioning look in his dark eyes. He seems more excited about the idea than I would've expected because he knows me better than that. I shake my head. "You know I don't swing that way, but I can appreciate talent and hard work. Especially in my friends."

"Calm down, Little Miss Goody-Two-Shoes. You know I'm not going near that chick with a ten-foot pole. I like my dick where it is, thank you very much."

I narrow my eyes at him, attempting to appear threatening, but we both know it's not the threat of my tiny little librarian-looking self that has him shaking in his Italian loafers. It's that our boss has taken a rather obvious interest in Allie lately. And no one dares go against Dominick if he's even considering marking some of that territory for himself.

"If you're still interested, your Miller Lite is getting piss-warm and table fifteen is looking mighty thirsty," he says, smirking. "I guess they're not into Allie. They seem to be paying more attention to their beers and their MIA waitress."

Shishkabob! My tip is definitely going to take a hit on this table if I can't turn it around with a little extra sugar. Hoping that maybe they like nerdy girl-next-door types instead of out of this world exotic beauties like Allie, I fluff my girls up in the black bustier that serves as the top half of my uniform and grab the pitcher to walk it over.

"Here you go, fellas. Didn't want to interrupt your view of Allie's special talents," I say, going heavy with the flirty innuendo as I lean over, confident that while my full cleavage is on display, they're locked solidly in the cups and won't spill out for an unintended nip slip.

Not that anyone would mind. Except me, of course. Petals from Heaven may be the sort of club where the female persuasion exposes their body parts to the spotlights, and my uniform is decidedly sexier than I would choose myself, but I've never felt like I was expected to do more than deliver drinks. Unless I wanted to, which I definitely don't.

The guys' eyes all lock to my chest, same as always, and their eyebrows lift. Gotcha, boys. So Allie isn't their cup of tea, but I am. Well, it takes all types, and it's sort of encouraging to know that a girl like me can be compared to a goddess like Allie and sometimes get the nod. Maybe my tip won't be so bad, after all.

I take a moment to pour each of the four guys a mug, feigning a lack of skill that makes the suds at the top spill over the lip and down my hand, the white foam looking decidedly like something more seductive than beer. I might be kinda innocent, but I'm not as schoolgirl innocent as I look, and I know how to tease.

I give the last guy his drink and then casually lick the bubbles from my fingers, letting my pink tongue curl out before sucking a tip into my mouth. All four guys' jaws drop at my innocent display before the one closest to me grabs my hand.

His blue eyes flick up to me as he holds my hand in a near-crushing grip, grinning drunkenly. "Let me help you with that."

Before I can say yes or no, he moves forward, his blond hair falling into his face as he quickly swipes his tongue against my finger and sucks it into his mouth. *Fudge! Danger, Will Robinson. Need to back this play up without causing a scene.* One of the hallmark rules of working in a club—don't cause a scene unless you really, really need help.

Instead of freaking out, I give my best girly giggle, jerking my hand back and squealing. "Ooh, that tickles!" I laugh as I shake my hand loose. "You shouldn't be so naughty!"

"Honey," Blondie says, half getting up, "if you want to see naughty—"

Out of nowhere, Shane appears behind me. He's part of Petals' security team and the star of too many of my midnight fantasies to admit. I can't see him, but I can feel his presence like a physical force pressing against my body. It's comforting, a little scary, and also frustrating. I can't help it, Shane's just . . . well, he's as sexy as chocolate cake, and probably just as dangerous for my health.

Shane growls, his voice low and dangerous. There's no weakness, no compromising with that voice. Fact is, Shane's not afraid of anyone or anything. He might be the only person in the club not afraid of Dominick. "No touching. Or I'll be the one touching you."

The threat is apparent, and the guy's face shows his fear that Shane will kick his ass. Shane's words have the opposite effect on me, though, and my mind is filled with an image of him touching me, his strong, thick fingers tracing lines along my private silky areas, teasing and tantalizing me before taking me roughly.

Back in reality, finger-sucking guy has his hands up wide, backing down immediately. "No problem, man. Sorry, won't happen again."

Shane lets out one more growl before stalking off. I never even made eye contact with him, but under the slip of dark denim they call my miniskirt, my panties are soaked from being that close to him, having his voice wash over me, and that flash of fantasy.

Needing to save the tip, though, I smile at the forward guy, and he does at least offer an apology to me, a rarity in this place. "No problem, honey. Security is just really protective of us. I'm sure you understand."

"I can certainly understand why," he says as his eyes float down my body, taking an extra moment on my chest, my crotch, and the length of my legs sticking out of the skirt before tracing back up again. Despite my petite height, this slip of a skirt combined with my heels make my legs look a mile long, and it feels like it takes him forever to uncomfortably peruse every inch. "We're good for now, but keep the pitchers coming all night."

He says the last part in a filthy little cadence, emphasizing every word, and I can hear the obvious double-entendre. I nod and giggle, reverting to my innocent girl shtick as I promise to keep them coming.

I walk away, smiling as I hear the guys start loudly talking to each other. Two can play that game, and we're both hoping to get lucky, just not in the same way. Tip me, tip the stage girls, and get out so I can get some fresh meat at my table with another full wallet.

It sounds crass, even to myself, but it's the reality. No one is coming to Petals from Heaven strip club to find love, and really, no one is coming to find sex. Well, I guess some of the guys do come in with the fantasy of having an amazing night with a woman who ticks all their mental boxes, but the odds of that are worse than winning the Powerball.

I don't really get it. Guys crowd in with their other guy friends, pay fart-tons of money for cover, drinks, and tips, then go home to flog their bishop? Why the game? Just watch some porn or something and take care of business.

Unless the guy is paying for a private show, where they're not supposed to whip it out, but according to my dancer friends, they pretty much know they've got a fifty-fifty chance that they're going to be dancing while the patron gets down to business.

Ew. Just gross.

I make another round of my tables, getting refills, flirting, dropping off checks, flirting, collecting cash . . . and more flirting.

As I work, I keep an eye out for any patrons who might be . . . somebody. That's my real job, scouting for celebrities, major or minor, politicians, CEO bigwigs, Instagram-famous people, or anyone else who might be interesting and tends to frequent this particular club.

On one hand, they're usually the best tippers. On the other, they're why I'm really here, working as Meghan, a cocktail waitress at a strip club, undercover for the tabloid gossip rag I work for. Neither job is my dream come true, but since no one is knocking on my door to write for *The New York Times*, online trash talking pays my bills.

I got the assignment to get a second job at Petals two months ago, and to my surprise, they hired me right away. Petals is known for being exclusive and VIP-preferred, so I'd been nervous about their hiring plain Jane me. But I'd been hired as a waitress on the spot based on my resume and my other . . . ahem . . . assets. So far, the undercover gig has paid off in a couple of smaller celebrity-sighting stories, but I feel like there's something bigger here. I just don't know what it is yet.

But Petals from Heaven is sort of the place to go if you're a celebrity who wants a taste of the salacious life but you don't want to get caught out on the town because of your wife, your girlfriend, or just your reputation. There's a sense of discretion at Petals, and Dominick fosters that, making sure the A-listers get what they want, whether it's private rooms or flashy top-notch service. Plus, Petals employs some of the most beautiful dancers I've ever seen in my life. It's almost artistic, just nearly naked too. With this combination, something gossip-worthy has to happen eventually, and I want to be here to report on it.

Ironically, this undercover gig is pretty sweet and is paying more than half my bills now anyway. It was an odd realization that the writing and research I love to do and went to school for are actually less financially rewarding than playing airhead and slinging drinks.

Not sure what that says about our society, but it's not anything complimentary.

I hear the DJ talking loudly over the mic, adding some hype to our last performer of the night and telling everyone in the club to get their last drink and get the fudge out. He doesn't use those words, of course, but I censor them in my head like I sometimes do.

I drop one last pitcher and the check at Finger-Sucking-Guy's table and he clears his throat. "Uhm, hey, so I don't wanna piss off the bouncer or nothing, but what are you doing tonight? Wanna party?"

I forcefully contain my eye roll, choosing to twirl my hair around my finger and kicking my voice up an octave. I deal with this at least once a week. Can't get the dancer, go for the waitress. "Oh, no. Sorry, honey, I can't. I've got school in the morning, so I'd better be a good girl and get home."

The reality is, I've been out of school for over three years, but they always believe this excuse because I look a lot younger than my twenty-five years. I still get carded when I buy wine.

Luckily, he takes the refusal gracefully, or maybe he's worried about Shane showing up again. "Mmm. Yes, you should be a good girl. Get right to bed."

It's still flirty and slightly sleazy, but at least he's not arguing with me. I give a wink and turn, flouncing off to close out my other tables.

Once everyone's gone and the club is cleaned up, I head backstage to change. Pulling on sweats and a long-sleeve T-shirt, I'm thinking of only a few things. Mainly getting home, taking a good long shower to get the left-over smell of the club off me, and then collapsing into bed. After all, I've got to be ready for work at ten . . . and my boss hates it if I'm late.

CHAPTER

Two

SHANE

REACHING DOWN, I wrap my hand around the handles of each keg, lifting one with each arm. Marco needs the help restocking or else he's going to be here until sunrise, so I normally help him out by carrying the kegs up from downstairs while he brings up the bottles he needs and sends in our orders for the suppliers.

My arms are a little tired by the time I get the two kegs up the stairs, and it's with a grunt of relief that I set them down. Marco's working the register, checking his money against the Point of Sale system. "You have a good night tonight?"

Marco nods, smirking a little. "Yeah, pretty solid. Decent tips, and with the eye candy from Allie's new routine, I can't really complain."

He waggles his eyes at me, like he expects to chatter on about Allie's tits or something. It feels like a test. I'm just not sure if it's a bro one or seeing if I'm aware that Dominick has marked her as off-limits.

Doesn't really matter either way. I'm a fucking professional and I know that I *do not* get involved with any of the girls here, whether they've been tabbed by Dominick or not. So Marco's going to be disappointed in my answer. "Yeah, she's good. She's been working hard and it's paying off."

A couple of the girls come into the club from backstage, and I'm thankful for the break from Marco's slick vibe. Time to do my actual job and not just help out. "Ladies, let me walk you out."

They murmur their thanks but basically ignore me, especially Tina, who's already gabbing away on her phone, telling her babysitter that she's on the way home. I get it. They've got men talking to them all fucking night, and ninety-nine percent of it more or less leads to 'I wanna fuck.' They just tune it all out. It's a survival instinct.

I don't mind. Walking the girls out is one of my usual duties and the one I take the most seriously. There's always a chance that some 'fan' might not be able to check their fantasy at the heavy door, and I'm here to ensure that doesn't become a problem. I make sure they get in their cars safely and then watch from the doorway to make sure they pull out alone.

It's a little sad, really. I can't imagine any of them as little girls thinking, 'Hey, when I grow up, I wanna be a stripper.' But life sometimes doesn't go according to plan, and we do what we need to so we can get by. So when these girls are under my supervision, they deserve respect and safety, and I'm gonna give that to them, even if no one else in their lives does.

After the girls are gone, I head back inside, seeing Meghan swinging through the saloon-style doors from backstage. She looks young, even more so than usual in her sweats and oversized T-shirt. She could pass as a college freshman on any campus in the US.

She's 'just' a waitress, but in my opinion—not that anyone asks me. I'm not paid to have an opinion—she's the best-looking girl working here. She's absolutely gorgeous when she's done up for a shift, all poufy blonde hair, big doe eyes with fake lashes, puffy, kissable pink lips, and a sexy rack atop a tiny body. She usually favors a sort of 'naughty innocent' look, and there's a reason she's getting more tips than any other waitress.

But my favorite is her 'after shift' style, when she's fresh-faced with her hair pulled up, wearing her big owlish glasses and jeans or sweats. She looks cute and sweet, and small enough I could pick her up and put her in my pocket . . . or over my shoulder. She's almost shy, walking into the main room like she's making sure she's allowed to come in before committing to the movement. She sees me and smiles, walking with more confidence.

That smile feels like a secret view not many people get, like it's a lazy morning at home with a lover look, even though it's damn near three in the morning and we're at a strip club. It makes me . . . Shaking my head to let that train of thought go, I call out to her. "Meg, you ready to go?"

She nods, giving me a little wave and a thumbs-up. "Yep. G'night, Marco. See you tomorrow night."

I have the urge to stick my elbow out for her, gentleman style, but the no-touching rule extends to staff. Unless asked, don't. And I'm the enforcer of the rules, so there's no way in hell I'm going to let myself break them. So I clamp down on that urge and have to be satisfied with opening the door for her. Still, I do let myself take a moment to admire her pert ass as she walks through. I can't help it.

Outside, I ask her the same generic question I asked Marco, but I hope for a better answer from Meghan. "You have a good night tonight?"

Meghan gives me a nod, adjusting her glasses and giving me a tired smile. "It was okay. Good tips, even from that one table," she says, and we both know exactly what she's talking about. "Thank you for that, by the way. I didn't even have a chance to react before you swooped right in."

I shrug, not letting Meg know that when she's on shift, I always keep an extra eye out for her. She's just so . . . innocent. "That's my job. Already had my eye on that table anyway. They were giving bad vibes."

She nods in understanding. She's been here long enough to get those gut feelings too. "Well, I appreciate your being the bad guy so I could be the good girl."

I tease her, knowing it's a bad idea but unable to stop myself. "And *are* you a good girl?"

My voice has dropped a little, low and gravelly. Meg always makes me feel this way, like a caveman on the verge of dragging her off to have my way with her. She makes me yearn to control the situation, control her, but I have to settle for controlling myself.

She giggles, but it's not the false one she gives guys in the club. She sounds nervous and . . . flirty, maybe? "I try to be, but sometimes, it's hard to be good."

There's a hint of sex to her voice, but it feels like there's more truth to what she said than a casual coy response. It's maddening, the way we seem to dance around each other, half innuendos and comments that just toe the line between 'playful banter' and 'outright suggestion,' but I can't go further. It's too dangerous, and not because of her.

Before I can think on it too much, we reach her car and the silence of the early morning dark is broken. "Hey, honey! You ready to go?"

I'm instantly on alert, shoving Meghan behind me as I turn to see the finger sucking asshole who was putting the moves on her earlier. Considering that it's now a good hour after the last patron was out the damn door, we're way, way past the bounds of appropriate behavior.

He's leaning up against the car next to hers like he's waiting for her. While it's against the official rules, some of the girls will do date-nights with patrons on the side, almost sugar daddy style. But Meghan isn't the kind to do that sort of thing, and I don't consider for a second that she told him anything but a polite version of "fuck off".

Even if she did, I'm not letting her leave with him. Not her. Not with a guy like him.

Instead, I shift my left foot forward while covering Meghan with my body. "You need to leave, asshole. The no-touching policy extends to when we're closed too. So get in your car and take a fucking hike."

Blondie pushes off the car, facing me fully, and I do a quick assessment. He's big, at least six feet, but I've got a few inches on him, and though he looks muscled, it's in a gym rat way. Not the look of someone who's surprisingly strong because of real manual labor.

Most importantly, he doesn't have that air of 'I'll fuck you up.' He seems on the verge of drunk and a bit prissy, like he's used to getting his way.

Well, not tonight. Instead, Blondie talks about Meghan like she's not even here, and as she almost shivers behind me, I know that if a line needs to be crossed, I'm going to cross it. "We're partying tonight. She told me to wait for her."

"No," I declare, bringing my right hand slightly up while tilting my hips to protect against a bitch move kick to the balls. "Leave now."

I see the fire flash in Blondie's eyes as he steps closer, and Meghan steps forward a bit too, leaning around me and setting me on edge because she's too close to this jerk.

"I can't," she says sweetly, trying to de-escalate things before I put this asshole on the ground right here in the parking lot. "I've got early school tomorrow, remember? Sorry, baby."

I tense just a little as I hear the code word all the girls have for trouble. They'll call patrons just about anything—honey, daddy, sugar, sweetie—but the rule at Petals is that 'baby' is the safe word that'll get security on a patron like white on rice.

I already knew he was full of shit, but Meghan just let me know for certain. I shift a little more, knowing that the beating is about to commence. I just have to make sure Meg's safely out of the way before I start.

Blondie's either too drunk, or probably too stupid, to notice. "C'mon, baby. Just a quickie. We don't even have to leave. I've got some goodies in my car so we can party right here. Big Guy won't mind, right? I can slip him a few bills."

He reaches for Meghan's wrist and it's automatic from there. In a move that's so fast that most people don't even realize what's happening, I deflect his hand, directing it down and back while grabbing his wrist in a sweeping motion as I twist it up behind his back. In less than half a second, he's fully hammer locked, and in the next half second, he's pivoted away from Meg and toward his own car.

I slam him face down on the hood, lifting his wrist while twisting his hand to maximize the controlling pressure on his shoulder, finding that edge where the pain is balancing on the razor's edge right before his arm dislocates. "She said no, asshole."

Blondie yells out in alarm, struggling from pure instinct. "Hey! Hey! Ow! Fuck, man."

I press him into his hood some more, using my booted foot to kick his legs out from under him, holding him in place easily even as he struggles.

"Meghan?" I chance a quick glance behind me to see she's frozen, her face a mask of shock. I raise my voice a bit, knowing she needs a bit of command. "Meghan."

She shakes her head, her vision clearing as her eyes meet mine, wider than usual behind her frames. "Yeah . . . yeah?"

My voice is clipped, all business. Right now, I don't have time for emotions. "Get his wallet out of his pocket. Read his license for me."

She's shaking but does as I order, coming close and with delicate fingers, reaching into Blondie's back pocket and withdrawing a brown leather wallet.

"What the fuck, dude? You're robbing me now? I just wanted to talk to her."

He has another burst of energy and thrashes underneath me, making Meghan jump back. I grab his neck with my free hand, thumping him head first into his hood, not hard enough that he can't drive out of here . . . yet. "Shut up, asshole. Meg?"

She opens the wallet, finding his license inside, and starts to read out loud. "Miles Jacobson, 3654 Sidewinder Trail. He lives here in East Robinsville."

I nod, giving her a professional smile. "Good girl. Now put it back, carefully. And Miles, if you so much as fucking move, I'm going to break your arm."

I emphasize my point with a little yank on his shoulder, encouraging him to be still while Meg puts his wallet back.

Waiting until Meghan's stepped back and is safe, I yank him off the car to growl in his ear. "Miles Jacobson of 3654 Sidewinder Trail, you are banned from Petals from Heaven. If I ever see you even close to this block again, I'll take special care of you. It won't be over quickly, and you will not enjoy it, I promise you."

"But—"

"*If* you ever see my girl here anywhere at all," I interrupt him, "you'd best run the other fucking way because if you so much as lay an eye on her, I'll fuck you up so badly, your own mother won't be able to identify the body. *If* they find it. Clear?"

He nods jerkily, weeping softly and sober as a judge at the turn of events. I don't feel sorry for him at all. He probably thought a little more forceful asking in the deserted parking lot would lead to Meghan partying with him, willingly or not.

Fucking pricks like him, thinking they're entitled to whatever they want just because they want it.

Still, I don't have time for a philosophy lesson. "Meghan, open the car door."

She moves from behind me, and I keep an eye on her movements, making sure no other threats pop out of hiding in the dark lot. I pull up a bit on Miles's arm, the pressure forcing him to stand in front of me. I prisoner-walk him to the side of the car and push him in, where he clumsily falls into the driver's seat, yelping as his shoulder gives him a warning twinge at the release of the hammerlock. "Fuck, man, I'm gonna—"

I lean down, keeping eye contact as I cage him in with one hand on the roof and one hand on the door. "Think about your next words and where you're making your threat. Goodbye, Miles Jacobson. I don't want to ever see you again."

I give him a hard stare, memorizing every detail of his face and his car, down to the company parking garage badge hanging from the rearview mirror.

Stepping back carefully, I slam his door and then give it a swift and solid back-kick with my hard-soled boots, denting the panel. It's not enough. I'd rather break his jaw or the glass out of every window of his fancy car, but it'll have to do.

I stand, stoic and solid, still threatening as Meghan hides behind me again. He peels out of the lot, but I catch the 'Fuck you!' he yells out the open window.

Not worrying about his need for the last word, I turn to Meghan, gently putting my hands on her shoulders. She's trembling for real this time, and so tiny I have to be careful not to accidentally hurt or scare her with my roughness. It's more difficult than I thought. I'm still on edge, and this is the first time I've touched Meg other than to shake her hand the first night we met.

"Are you okay?" I ask. "It's all over now."

Her eyes are glassy, but she nods, biting her lip. My thumbs are tracing circles on her arms, soothing her and soothing me too. This could've been bad, really bad, and I'm glad I was here to keep her safe.

"You're okay. He's gone, and you're safe," I murmur softly. "I'll always do my best to keep you safe."

She suddenly collapses forward, all the energy keeping her upright whooshing out as she falls against me, shaking and rambling. "Holy fracking . . . he could've . . . fluffernutter . . ."

She says some of the words like she's cussing, even though she's decidedly not, and even in the midst of the insanity, it makes the corners of my lips tilt up. I've noticed it before, and in some ways, Meg sounds a lot like someone's churchgoing cousin.

She's sweet, an innocent little darling who doesn't belong in a rough life like this. She's way too much of a good girl for someone like me. I gather her closer, wrapping one arm around her shoulders, and lead her back inside the club.

"Marco. Hey, man!" I call out as the door closes. "Get your ass out here!"

Marco pops up from below the bar after a few seconds, already teasing. "Took you long enough. I need your help grabbing another case of—"

His words cut off when he sees Meghan, and he rushes out to get on the other side of her. Despite his player tendencies, he's got a decent heart and knows a girl in need when he sees one.

I squeeze off the growl of 'Don't Touch' that threatens to pass my lips when he grabs her hand, but together, we get her sitting at the bar.

"You got a pen and paper?" I ask as Meghan shivers, putting her head in her hands.

Marco rushes behind the bar again, grabbing a tumbler and filling it with ice and water before setting it in front of Meghan. "Yeah, yeah. Here you go." He grabs a notepad and pen from beside the register, and I write down Miles's information and description, along with his vehicle description and license plate.

I push it back toward Marco, who looks the information over. "This guy. He's banned from the club, from the whole damn block, and definitely from Meghan. Pass the word."

Marco reads the note and nods, knowing that my request isn't directly to him, but to Dominick. His club, his rules, but for something like this, Dominick will definitely agree with my assessment of the appropriate response.

Pocketing my note, Marco turns to Meghan. "You okay, sweetheart? You look pale. Need something a little more than just ice water?"

She shakes her head, then seems to reconsider. "Can I have a scotch? Just a little sip to settle my nerves?"

It's part of Meghan's magic. Here she is, scared out of her mind, and I swear she sounds like little girl who's asking to have a sip and not get in trouble for it. Marco smirks, turning to grab a shot glass that he fills to the brim with the amber liquid before setting it in front of her.

"Don't sip it. Just shoot it down so it can work its magic, warm you back up."

She picks the shot up with delicate fingers, and for a moment, I wonder if this girl has ever even done a shot. If not, she's about to be in for a rude awakening.

But she tilts it back, opening her throat and swallowing it down with ease before slamming it back to the bar top. Wiping her lips, she offers Marco a hint of a smile. "Thanks. I needed that."

All on its own, my cock jumps right to attention in my pants, wondering if she'd swallow something of mine down her pretty little throat, and if I could put a bigger smile on her face than what the scotch has.

Fuck, I've gotta get my head on straight. Now is definitely not the time for me to be thinking dirty thoughts. Hell, there's never going to be a time for me to think that about Meghan. Even if she wasn't too damn good for someone like me, I'd break a sweet little thing like her.

Still, I can't help but put my arm around her, mindlessly patting and rubbing her back, even though I'm treading dangerous territory for us both. "You gonna be okay? We can hang out here as long as you need," I reassure her. "Whenever you're ready, I'll walk you out to your car again. Make sure you're safe. 'Kay?"

She sighs, looking up at me, her pupils black and large behind her glasses. "Actually, do you think you could drive me home? I'm not much of a drinker, and I have a feeling that scotch is going to knock me out in three, two, one . . ."

She smiles a tiny smile, but it sounds like she's telling the truth. This is a girl who can sling drinks like a certified pro, but one shot knocks her out for the rest of the night. And no, my dirty fucking thoughts don't avoid the innuendo there either.

"Yeah, I can do that," I reply, even as part of me says this is a bad move. I've wanted her for weeks, and my instincts are going apeshit. *Bad move, Shane. Bad move.*

Doesn't matter. The smile she gives me is more than enough to overcome whatever my mind is saying. I turn to Marco, who's cleaning the shot glass carefully. "Will you let Dominick know I'm leaving my truck here overnight? I'll drive Meghan's car to her house and cab it home."

Marco gives me an evaluating look, and I again appreciate that for all his slick player persona, he's actually a pretty solid guy and is making sure that I'm not running some game on Meghan when she's shaken up.

I must have passed his test because he nods and sets the glass aside. "Yeah, I'll let the boss know. Take care of her."

With a nod, I help Meghan up. I walk her back outside, head on a swivel as I look for any threats, any sign that Miles Jacobson got a shock of courage and came back, but all seems to be quiet and dark. We make it to her car, a nondescript little thing that looks like it sort of hangs together by sheer force of will.

Meghan digs in her bag for her keys and hands them to me. I do a slight double-take as I see her keyring has a fucking pompom on it. A puffy fluff of soft fur that's white like a rabbit's tail. It suits her.

I hold the passenger door for her and make sure she's buckled in before I go around. "You ready?"

"Yeah. And thanks, Shane," she says, giving me a smile that could melt Ebenezer Scrooge's heart. I pull out, still keeping watch for anyone who might be following us, and head away from the club, toward the main road.

"Where to?" I ask, and Meghan gives me directions to her apartment from there. As we drive, I have to admit I'm interested to see where she lives.

A tiny piece of me is disappointed when I pull up outside a regular apartment complex, just one like a hundred others around town and not some special, secret hideaway with unicorns in the driveway befitting the fairy-princess sparkle of this girl. I walk her to her door, planning to get her safely inside and then call a cab . . . from the parking lot, not wanting her to feel weird about being alone in her apartment with the huge, scary guy from work.

Hey, I know what I look like, and yeah, I use it around work to my advantage. I'm surprised when I turn to go and she calls out, "Shane!"

I turn, hearing the fear returning to her voice. "Yeah?"

She's clutching the door, the toe of her Ugg boot digging in the carpet, looking for all intents and purposes like the scared little girl she is. My heart melts even as another side of me growls possessively, wanting to claim her as mine.

She takes a deep breath, biting her lip, but her voice is surprisingly strong when she speaks again. "Do you want to come in? Have a cup of coffee or something?"

I pause, most of me wanting to say no. This has bad idea written all over it. We're pushing four in the morning, I'm with a girl who's had a scare and might be slightly drunk, and for the past two months, she's jumped to the top of my fantasy list as she ticks boxes on my mental fuck list I didn't even know I had.

But I can man up, be the security she needs, and not let on that she's slowly driving me insane every time she looks up at me in those glasses. That half of me wants to comfort and soothe her, to tell her she'll never be hurt . . . while the other half of me wants to rip her clothes off and make her hurt so damn good she screams in blissful agony before I empty my balls deep inside her body.

"Are you sure?" I ask, keeping my voice calm. "You're home, and you're safe. I can just call a cab."

She doesn't answer, just gestures with her hand into the apartment, inviting me in. I walk past her, careful not to touch her or crowd her so she doesn't spook again. Keeping my steps casual, I feel dirty as my heavy boots cross the threshold into her apartment, and I feel an intense, sudden need to just take them off and not pollute her space.

Her apartment is cute, just like her. Her living room is full of soft furniture, with fuzzy blankets thrown over the arm of an old, overstuffed sofa and a floral coffee mug sitting on the table. The room is white and beige and all the other shades of . . . white. With a few highlights of pink.

I'm nervous to sit on her furniture. I think of the places my pants have been, and I'm afraid I'll sully it up just with my presence. But she motions for me to sit, so I do. "Uhm . . . thanks. It's a nice place you've got here."

"Thanks. Just hold on a moment, would ya?" she asks, bustling off to the kitchen. Moments later, she's making coffee, by the sound of the clinks I hear.

I look around and see a huge bookcase filled with books. I don't recognize any of the titles, but whatever type of books she reads, she's got a shitton of them. "You're a reader, huh? Lots of books in here."

Her laugh from the kitchen is slightly self-conscious, and I hear the click-thunk of a knob being turned through the open doorway. "Yeah, I read . . . a lot. Little bit of everything. Non-fiction, like historical stuff and biographies, and fiction too, romance, drama, mystery. You read much?"

I grin, even though she can't see me. Romance, drama, and mystery? *God, you're fucking perfect, Meghan.* "No, can't say I'm much of a reader," I reply. "I'm more of a dumb jock type."

A minute later, she appears with a tray, holding two cups of steamy coffee and the fixings. "I wasn't sure how you take it."

She sets the tray down, and I lean forward to grab a cup. "Black is fine. Sugar at this time of night gets me jittery."

She scrunches her nose and adjusts her glasses again. "Ew, too bitter for me. I like lots and lots of cream."

Oh, for fuck's sake, she's really testing me here. If it were any other girl, I'd think it was intentional. But Meghan seems completely oblivious to the effect she's having on me.

She sits down next to me, and I watch as she adds enough creamer and sugar to her cup to make it basically coffee-flavored ice cream before taking a sip and sighing happily. I sip my own coffee, and I have to add another mark on this girl's list of accomplishments. I haven't had coffee this good since a vacation to Chile two years ago.

There's a comfortable silence as we both sip before she breaks it, looking at me earnestly. "Shane, thanks again. That was some scary intense stuff tonight. I'm glad you were there."

I nod, setting my cup down on the tray. "It was no problem, Meghan. I'm glad I was there too."

She flinches a little, and I'm afraid she's having a bit of a flashback, so I slip my arm across the back of the couch, not touching her, but she scoots closer, curling into my side, so I place a light hand on her shoulder. "I usually think of myself as capable of handling whatever comes my way, and I've dealt with some handsy customers, but if I'd been alone in that parking lot tonight . . ."

Her voice trails off, and I know she's imagining all the ugly things that could've happened. "It's okay," I reassure her. "You're safe now."

CHAPTER

Three

MAGGIE

I WAKE SLOWLY, feeling warm and fuzzy-headed and safe. It's funny, because normally, I have to be yanked out of sleep by the harsh braying of my alarm clock just to make sure that I can get to work on time. But a quick glance to my left confirms that it's only eight o'clock, and I've got time. So I curl tighter into a ball before stopping because my pillow feels harder than usual.

The thought makes me stop and actually wakes me up, because I'm not in my bed. I'm on my couch underneath one of my throw blankets, the clock I saw was my microwave, and I'm curling up to a hard body . . . the very hard body of Shane.

His breathing is even and slow, still asleep, so I take stock. He's lying half reclined on one end, his boots hanging off my couch and his muscular left arm lying across the back of the couch in a protective position, like he wanted to hold me but didn't. Meanwhile, I've got my cheek pressed against one nearly iron-hard but delightfully warm pectoral and my left leg's half draped over his like the world's biggest body pillow. It feels . . . good. Safe.

I hum softly, and Shane stretches slightly in his sleep, his muscled arm descending slowly to lie on top of the blanket, almost instinctively cupping my butt.

I have a momentary freakout as my body thrills and *fully* wakes up in a lot more ways than just shaking off the last cobwebs of sleep. Did we? No, no. We're both fully dressed, and I'd definitely remember that. I have no doubt that having sex with Shane would be something a girl would never forget. Considering I've had a few fantasies about him over the past two months . . . yeah, I wouldn't forget it.

At that thought, my core fills with warmth, making me squirm slightly.

The leg I have thrown over his lifts, and I feel the hard fullness of his dick. Sweet mama's fairy tales, he's . . . I don't think I could even fantasize about someone this amazingly put together.

Shane moans lightly in his sleep from my pressure, pulling me to him and grinding against me ever so slightly, and I gasp as electricity shoots through me. Unfortunately, the sound seems to wake him and he stirs beneath me. He rubs my butt, pressing into me again as he stretches and groans. The sound alone turns me on, and I bite my lip, lifting my head to look at his face.

Shane blinks and smiles sleepily back at me before I get a close-up view of the second his face goes from smiling 'good morning, sweetheart' to frowning 'oh, shit.'

Sigh. I never should've even pretended he'd be happy to wake up here with me, even if we didn't do anything. I mean, I'm just a nerdy girl next door, and he's so far out of my league it's not even funny. He's the sort of guy who has girls like Allie and the other dancers drooling over him.

It's only because Shane's so nice, and that I basically begged him to stay like a little girl last night, that he's here. But I was truly scared after the parking lot incident.

I can feel the blush rushing across my cheeks, and I do my best to try and smooth all this over before I die of embarrassment. "G'morning. Guess we fell asleep?"

Smooth one there, Maggie. State the dang obvious, why don't ya?

Shane smiles back softly, though, lifting an eyebrow. "Guess so." Suddenly, he notices his hand on my ass and maybe the feeling of his morning wood against my thigh, and his smile disappears in an instant. "Oh, uh . . . sorry."

He lifts his hand off my butt, and I lift up, trying to disentangle myself from our compromising position before my heart fails. "Thanks for staying last night. I was pretty freaked out after everything. Think that guy will stay away?"

Shane's face hardens, and it's reassuring to see absolutely no doubt in his eyes. "He'll stay away, or he'll wish he had. But you're safe, okay?"

I dip my chin, feeling silly that he's still reassuring me, and deciding I need to act a bit more blasé about the whole thing, put it in my past and move forward. I'm supposed to be a tough girl, not a scaredy cat.

Decision made, I stand and straighten my back, rolling my shoulders back to look as tall as I can, which isn't much considering my petite five-foot-nothing self. "Let me put on a fresh pot of coffee—"

Shane interrupts, straightening up himself. "Thanks, but I'd better get going. Need to get my truck before tonight's shift starts."

A tough ball of disappointment forms in my gut, but I plaster a fake smile on my face anyway. I mean, I was pathetic enough to almost beg him to stay last night. I shouldn't keep the streak going. "Sure, of course. Want me to give you a ride back to the club?"

"No, thanks, I'll grab a cab. I'm sure you've got plans today," Shane says, getting up. I do have plans. I mean, I have to go to my other job, but he doesn't know that. And there's something about the way he says it that sounds like a dismissal, not like he's fishing for me to hang out with him.

"Yeah, busy." He folds the blanket and lays it on the arm of the couch, and something about that strikes me as so domestic, so tame considering he's a wild beast of man who didn't hesitate to put the beat-down on that guy last night.

The contrast makes me feel dizzy, or maybe that's just him and how he makes me feel inside. I walk him to door, one hand on the doorknob as I turn and look at him again. "Thanks for last night."

Shit, that sounds like I mean something else, something decidedly more vulgar, and I can feel the blush warming my cheeks. Even Shane smiles a little, and I quickly try to get myself out of this quicksand I've stuck myself in. "I mean with the guy at the club. And bringing me home."

I know I look like a total fool, and Shane seems amused by my awkwardness. He gives me a little grin that leaves my heart hammering even more in my chest and chuckles. "You're welcome. Just doing my job. Well, mostly," he says with a pointed look at the couch. "But I'm glad I was here."

I think he's trying to make me blush more, and to be honest, he's succeeding. "Uh . . . me too."

Shane clears his throat, and I have a half-second to wonder if he's serious that he liked being here. "I'll see you tonight?"

I nod, thinking that I wouldn't miss a shift at Petals for the world right now. "Yeah, I'm working dinner to close tonight, so I'll see you later."

There's a moment where it seems neither of us knows what to do, so I finally lean in for a hug.

I mean, heck. I slept draped over the guy like he was a body pillow last night. A hug doesn't seem all that intimate, right? And we're colleagues, work buddies even. And work buddies will sometimes give each other a hug.

Except when I reach up and wrap my arms around him and press my chest toward his, all I can think about is how good he feels. My breasts tingle as they smoosh against his hard chest muscles, and my body feels every bit of his hand splayed on my back. I can almost read the way his fingers adjust their pressures, his thumb pressing against one of my 'dimples' for a moment before his fingers take over, alternating like he's playing a piano before he pulls me tighter and his musky-manly scent fills my senses. I have to bite back the moan in my throat.

"You be good," Shane says with a tantalizing ghost of huskiness in his voice that makes me think maybe he liked the hug as much as me. With one last full, white smile and a little two-finger wave, he steps out. "And take it easy."

As soon as he's gone, I melt back to the couch, a wistful sigh mixing with the floomp of my cushions as I flop.

"Damn, that man is hot with a capital *Oh, yeah!*" I sigh, knowing that he's also incredibly off-limits, for so many reasons. First, there's my waitress job where the no fraternizing rule is strictly enforced.

Second, there's the fact that I'm undercover for the tabloid and he doesn't even know my real name. He thinks I'm Meghan, not Maggie. Major buzzkill to be mid-flagrante delicto and for him to cry out your name, except it's not yours but rather the alias you gave him.

I won't even touch on the third reason, considering that contemplating how out of my league he is won't do my self-esteem any favors. I know I'm a catch, and I'm picky because I can be, but Shane is in a whole other dimension of gorgeousness.

Shaking my head, I rally and grab a cup of last night's coffee, nuking it in the microwave and dropping in three sugars and a lot of milk, just the way I like. The caffeine and sugar are just what I need to get dressed and into the office for my check-in and assignment update.

Yeah, big plans, that's me. Get off work and go to work. If I'm lucky, I might be able to squeeze in a workout at the gym to try and keep up my girlish figure.

Living the dream, baby.

———

The big open 'bullpen' of *The Daily Spot* is humming when I get in. Of course it is. A lot of my coworkers have been here for a couple of hours already, trying to make the noon update deadline. We may be a gossip rag, but that doesn't mean we don't have a schedule. Seven in the morning for the pre-work and water cooler crowd, noon to catch the lunch-timers, and then at six to give everyone a late-night update.

As soon as I log into the computer, my instant messenger box opens in the corner of the screen. It's my new boss, Jeanine. *Hi, Maggie! Come to my office ASAP.*

Shoot, wonder what she wants. She's definitely better than my old boss, who was a skeevy jerk. Actually, he was worse than that, but he went out in a blaze of glory . . . publicly. *The Daily Spot*'s reputation took a hit, but at the same time, website traffic is up. I guess it's true—controversy creates cash.

Jeanine's been here a little over a month now, but I don't have a good read on her yet. She always seems serious and cold, and she communicates in snippets of sentences rather than in full, embellished diatribes. I'd bet money she's never so much as cracked the spine of a book of poetry. No time for that prosaic nonsense.

So a tabloid full of gossipy blurbs is probably right up her alley. Actually, I read her biography when she took the editor's job, and she's worked in some legit journalism too, but still, the woman communicates by the five Ws —who, what, when, where, and why—almost exclusively. She doesn't even bother with how. That's my job, I guess.

I don't waste her time by responding to the message. I just lock my computer and head her way as quickly as possible. Knocking on her doorframe, Jeanine doesn't even look away from her computer, although she does wave me in with a quick little flutter of her fingers.

Ah, well. I sit in one of the chairs, waiting for her to finish whatever she's working on and speak first.

Jeanine hits her *Enter* key with a flourish that's sure to break her keyboard before too much longer and looks up, giving me a professional smile. "Maggie, how are things? What have you got for me?"

I swallow, knowing she won't like my answer. "Honestly, not a lot right now. There hasn't been even a pseudo-celeb in the club in over a week. I wrote that one up for last Saturday's edition, remember? The headline was *Bad Boy of Soaps Gets Glitter Bombed*."

Jeanine is silent, but she nods so I think she at least remembers the story. I'll admit, it wasn't that big of a story. I mean, sure, the guy's made a few housewives fan themselves, but ever since he came over from New Zealand, he's been getting himself in so much trouble the biggest story is whether the INS is going to let him renew his work visa.

Jeanine's grey eyes narrow at me as she purses her blood-red lips, her expression making her look even harsher than usual. "Glitter. Oh, yes."

She says it with a sneer, like the sparkly confetti is unwelcome contagious merriment. But that's what it was, if you count getting smacked in the face with a dancer's glitter-covered hiney a 'bomb.' But he's single, not dating anyone, and most fans don't really mind if a guy like that gets up to no good.

With a shake of the head, she continues. "I've received word that a certain All-Star basketball player will be clubbing sans the missus at a rather high-end venue tonight. I need you to go in, look the part, and see if he's up to anything devious. If so, get pics and write up his delinquency. If he's being a good boy, take pics of the sketchiest thing you see and write it up as supposition for why he's out alone. Trouble in paradise type story. Got it?"

I fidget and tug at the sleeve of my blouse. "I'd love to, but I'm already working tonight. I can probably get someone to cover the later part of my shift and catch up with him after the liquor kicks in though. He'd be more likely to behave badly then, anyway."

I've agreed, but only partially, and Jeanine definitely catches the difference. Her face goes hard, a mask of iron determination. "Maggie, my dear. Are you a waitress or are you a reporter? Because it sounds as though you're turning down a sure-bet reporting assignment to sling beer to drool-mouthed drunks. If you'd rather wait tables, by all means, feel free to do so. However, if you'd like to be a reporter, I'll need you at Club Noir all night in case Jimmy Keys shows up."

The threat is obvious, and while I only took the waitressing job as a means to get sordid stories, it is a big part of my life now. I have friends who work there, and the money is great. Dominick is tough, but he's a good boss, and I won't lose the waitressing job for calling out on one shift.

But missing this assignment from Jeanine will definitely cost me the reporting gig, so with a sigh of resolve, I plaster a saccharine-sweet smile on my face. "Of course, I want to be a reporter, Jeanine," I reply, while inwardly wondering if working for this gossip rag can really be called reporting. "I'll get my shift covered so I can be at the club well before the target arrives and will have a story submitted by tomorrow."

Jeanine doesn't compliment me, just smiles shrewdly, knowing her intimidation worked and I'm solidly ensconced in my place once again. '*My place,*' of course is at least one notch lower than her, as everyone in the office has quickly learned that Jeanine carries her job with a superiority like a cape that swishes along behind her like a pissed off queen. And everyone knows that in her right hand is her scepter, which she'll beat over your head if you push her far enough.

She doesn't even bother answering as she turns back to her computer, just waving me off as her attention goes back to whatever it is that she's focusing on now that her favorite little petite social wallflower knows what to do.

Summarily dismissed, I head out to my desk, digging my phone out of my purse. I think and text one of the other girls at the club. She's a dancer, but considering she's new and nowhere near as good as Allie, her paychecks could use the help.

Hey, Sarah, can you cover my shift tonight, please? Last-minute thing came up.
She replies quickly, happy to cover.
Sure! I'd love a bonus Friday shift.
Thanks! I owe you one. Anytime you need me.
With a sigh, I set my phone back down and get to work, scanning Instagram accounts for celeb news, checking Twitter feeds for vague posts, and although Jeanine would never admit it, searching other tabloid sites for their stories to see if we can do a story better justice. Twice, that's hit for me, being able to read between the lines and get a juicy tidbit that someone else left behind.

It's a hard knock life for me.

CHAPTER

Four

SHANE

I KNOW it's not quite professional as I scan the room, but when eight o'clock comes and goes and I don't see the petite figure of Meghan working the tables, I get worried. I've been looking forward to seeing her all day, ever since waking up with her snuggled against me, and to not see her . . . well, it just feels weird.

Especially after we both said we'd see each other tonight. Marco won't know anything. He sleeps most of the day, and if it wasn't for his slight tan, I'd swear he's a vampire, and most of the dancers are the same. Instead, I find Sarah, a newbie dancer who's wearing a lot more clothing than normal as she carries a pitcher of margaritas through the club. "Hey, where's Meghan?"

Sarah delivers her pitcher, earning her 'tip' with a little flirt and a shake of her curvy hip before giving me a smile. "Oh, I'm covering her shift. She texted saying something came up."

"I see. What happened?"

Sarah shrugs, already walking away as another table waves for her attention. "I don't know what though. Sorry."

I grit my teeth, knowing Meghan was fine when I left this morning. I thought she was even looking forward to seeing me when she came to work, and I'll admit that I've spent a decent amount of time today with some extra pep in my step at the thought. Sure, something innocent could've come up, but after the incident last night, I hope she's okay.

But the question, the doubt creates a tension in my gut that twists and gnaws at me. What's worse is that I can't even do anything about it. I've got a job to do here, and it's not like Sarah could cover *my* job.

"Hey, Shane."

I look over from my perch by the door to see Marco waving at me. We're in between dances, so he doesn't have to yell or use the walkie-talkie system we have. Getting up, I walk over, still keeping my eyes on the patrons. "Yo, Marco."

"That was Dominick on the phone," he says. "Asked to see you in the office."

I nod, walking over to Logan, the other guy working security tonight, and ask him to cover the door for a minute while I talk to the boss. Logan's a MMA fighter who works here part-time to help cover costs. With his bald head and trimmed goatee, he's intimidating enough that I don't have to worry.

Comfortable the floor is secure, I head upstairs to Dominick's office and give two quick raps on the door. A moment later, a deep voice inside calls out. "Enter."

Even though I was invited in, I open the door slowly, both to give anyone inside time to get decent and so that I can make sure some goon isn't going to grab me as I enter.

Dominick isn't a guy you mess with, and while I never have, I don't want to be caught unaware. But all seems chill as I enter, Dominick sitting behind his large mirrored desk.

The whole room is done in contemporary modern lines, mirrors here, low-slung leather chairs there, all surrounded by sleek black shiny walls. Of course, those are one-way mirrors that look onto the dance floor and audience area downstairs, but they're good quality so the noise in here is barely noticeable unless Dom turns on the speakers. Dominick is watching, always watching what happens in Petals since it's his club, his territory.

I sit in one of the white leather chairs, although I don't dare get comfortable and familiar in his office, not with the Desert Eagle I know he keeps under his desktop. Instead, I lean forward, appearing poised and ready for anything. "What can I do for you, sir?"

Dom's the only man I call sir, and while I don't like it, it makes my life a lot easier. He drums his fingers on the top of his desk, looking at me with those perceptive eyes of his. If I ever needed a reminder that my life is perilous, those eyes are a perfect one. "Shane, Marco tells me there was trouble last night. Explain."

It's an order, and one I know to obey. I give Dominick the full-detailed version of last night's incident, knowing withholding anything would be seen as a betrayal, finishing with Miles's name and information being posted behind the bar for Marco and shared with the rest of the security team.

As I speak, Dominick spins the gold pinky ring he wears. It's filigreed but has been passed down in his family for a long time, so the decorations are nearly worn as smooth as a new wedding ring. It should look stupid, my upbringing telling me that real men don't wear rings, especially pinky rings.

But Dominick pulls it off with style, the ring fitting in perfectly with his custom-made deep navy suit and silver tie.

He radiates wealth and power, and though he's a few years older than me and about twenty pounds lighter, I'm pretty sure that if he and I ever threw down, it'd be one hell of a scrap. And that doesn't count if Dom fought dirty, in which case all bets are off.

Dom knows my evaluation of him, and in some ways, that helps me. He knows that I view him not with fear but with the respect of one warrior to another, and because of that, he gives me respect back. He nods and folds his fingers together. "And after the incident?"

I nod, knowing what he's talking about and that honesty is the best policy here. Marco would have told him that I left my truck here and drove Meghan home, and that I didn't come back to pick up my truck at all.

Better he hears the story from me than find out later from someone else, and he will find out because he has an uncanny way of always knowing things.

"Meghan was in shock, asked me to drive her home, which I did. I offered to call a cab from the porch, but she asked me to come in for coffee. We talked, and she calmed down. At some point, we fell asleep on her couch. I left her apartment this morning and she seemed fine."

Dominick's fingers tighten a little before he unlaces them, setting them almost casually on the arms of his office chair. I'd be fooled too if it wasn't that I know his right hand's about six inches from that Desert Eagle of his. "You slept with her?"

I nod, speaking quickly but calmly. "I feel like that's a trick question, asking one thing but meaning another. We slept on the couch, fully clothed. If you're asking if I had sex with her, the answer is no."

Dominick nods, his hands relaxing and going back to turning his ring. "Well answered. I do feel the need to remind you of our no-dating policy, both the dancers and waitresses being strictly off limits."

"I'm aware."

Dom nods, smiling tightly. "Beyond my policy and its enforcement, although I don't know Meghan well, I sense that a man like you would break a girl like her. And then I would be called upon to break you for the misstep. Am I clear?"

Like that exact thought hasn't been running through my head since I felt the flawless curve of her ass in my hand and the soft pressure of her thigh against my cock this morning. I tilt my chin in deference, blinking once. "Crystal clear," I answer. "No worries."

I pause, taking a moment to let Dom know that I'm not just spouting some fear-inspired bullshit, then continue. "Well, actually, I am concerned. But not about that. It's Meghan."

"What about Meghan?" Dom asks. "Do you feel she is under threat still?"

I shrug, tenting my fingers in my lap. "Not sure. When I left, she seemed fine, even said she'd see me tonight because she was scheduled to work dinner to close. But she got Sarah to cover her shift. I'm sure it's nothing, but I wanted you to be aware."

Dominick's eyes flick to the black walls, seeing through them to the dance floor below where the familiar but faint bass beat is telling me Allie is on stage. "I'll have Allie call Meghan," Dom finally says. "They're close, so she can see what's up and why she ditched her shift. Tell Allie to come up after her performance, please."

Hearing the dismissal, I rise and walk out of Dominick's office, feeling like I just received a pardon from the firing squad. Even knowing I'd done nothing wrong, Dominick is one of the few men I legitimately fear. Even now, leaving his office, there's one percent of my brain that expects to hear the *snick* of him drawing the hammer back on his pistol.

The fact is, Dominick is ice-cold and all business, willing to do whatever is necessary, regardless of where the law or public opinion lies on his actions. This time, though, I'm safe, and I get downstairs to wait behind the curtain backstage for Allie to finish her set.

As she comes though, her costume is wadded up in her hands, and she jumps slightly, not expecting me to be standing there, and she squeaks a little. "Jesus fuck, Shane! You scared the hell out of me!"

"Sorry, didn't mean to startle you. Dominick wants to see you for a second."

She bites her lip, and I can see she's nervous, but there's something else in her eyes too, but it's gone too fast for me to identify it.

She lays her costume down, grabbing a towel and patting herself off so she removes the beads of sweat without disturbing the waterproof makeup and glitter too much. She's got a couple more dances coming up tonight, and Allie's a girl who absolutely hates to do touch-up work once she's got her 'costume' on. It's interesting the things you learn working in a strip club. Girls' makeup habits being one of them.

Thinking of girls' makeup makes my brain flash to Meghan and the way she can go from sultry to fresh-faced in a flash, and in my jeans, my cock twitches. Thankfully, I prepared for tonight, and I'm wearing my tighter compression briefs, and my semi-chub goes unnoticed.

"Thanks, I'll head up now."

I hold the back-stairwell door open for her, giving her a nod as she walks by before I head back out to the floor to resume my door duty. Yeah, Dominick might have Allie call her, but I'm going to have to check on Meghan tonight to satisfy my own questions.

I just need to make sure she's okay after last night's incident, and maybe moreso after this morning's awkward wakeup.

CHAPTER

Five

MAGGIE

"WHAT A FREAKIN' waste of time," I mutter to myself as I look around the club, wishing I wasn't here. As ordered, I've gotten dolled up, paid the rip-off twenty-dollar cover charge to get into the fancy-schmancy Club Noir, supposedly the hottest night club this side of New York. I've sat here at a table, nursing two weak girly drinks for the past four hours, tipping the waitress generously as she gives me looks.

I've spent since eight o'clock tonight looking like the world's biggest club loser, hanging onto my seat and turning down the guys who have approached simply because this chair has the best view of the door, the dance floor, and the stairs up to the VIP section.

And did Mr. Basketball Star, Jimmy Keys, make an appearance in said VIP section? Did his twenty points and eleven rebounds a game ass even show up?

Of course not. The closest thing I've seen is a guy who's about six four and looks like he might make a good basketball player.

So now, as people start to pair off and head out to continue the night in private, I'm almost fifty bucks in the hole for the night. I have no story, and based on my last text to Jeanine, my boss is somehow pissed off at me for the whole thing.

Not to mention that by giving up my shift, I've lost out on a couple of hundred dollars in tips. Grabbing my purse, I head home and flop into bed, growling the whole time.

———

The morning isn't much better, and I spend most of the day Saturday just stewing and trying to get Jeanine to unclench her sphincter.

Pulling up in front of Petals, I'm just hoping that we've got a big crowd. The parking lot looks good, so Hello, Dolly! I've got a shot of not ending the week on a bad note . . . if I'm lucky.

I slip through the door without anyone noticing me, a plain-ish girl in oversized sweats and a hoodie that hides my face, helping me be invisible. Except to Logan, who's on door security and does his job, giving me a quick once-over to make sure I'm allowed entry. I give him a small smile, but he returns his attention to the door, dismissing me without a word.

Backstage, I change, putting the last touches on my makeup and giving my hair and my girls one last poof as I cross my fingers for a good night. "Here's to hoping we've got high-rollers who like fifties over fives."

Looking over, I see Allie slipping into lingerie for her performance tonight and giving me a cockeyed grin. If you'd told me a few months ago that hanging around a bunch of half-naked, or sometimes fully naked, women wouldn't make me bat an eye, I'd have laughed my butt off. I'm no prude, but it's not like my real life has offered many opportunities for in-depth analysis of panty styles, grooming habits, and ways to highlight your best assets.

But these girls, the ones I call friends, are real and open. They've given me a lot of insight into men, some good and some bad, and most will be the first to give you a Cosmo-worthy tip when you have an unfortunate pimple or need a hair plucked from a spot you can't quite reach.

"Hey, Allie, sorry I missed your call last night," I reply, glad I get to wear real underwear as Allie fiddles with her four ounces of 'stage costume.' "Everything okay?"

"Yeah, I heard about what happened Thursday night from Dominick," Allie says, straightening up. "I just wanted to make sure you were okay. You are, aren't you?"

She looks at me, her brown eyes warm with concern, and I blush, nodding. "Yeah, totally fine. Just had to take care of something unexpectedly for a friend, so Sarah covered for me. I think it's almost time for her next school loan payment, so she seemed glad to get the weekend shift."

I feel guilty for not being completely honest, but I can't exactly explain that I was working my other job as a reporter, no matter how good of friends we are. Allie's too close to Dominick, and I've got to keep that screen between us. It sucks too, because honestly, I'd count Allie as one of my closest girlfriends. And she doesn't even know my real name.

"Marco said Shane took you home."

It's a statement, not a question, but I treat it as one anyway. "Yeah, I was pretty shook up, so he drove me home. It was nice of him."

I purposefully leave out that he spent the night and the awkward morning departure. Allie grins, shaking her bouncy curls and boobs at the same time. "Nice? I'm sure Shane would love to hear you describe him as nice. Because trust me, there isn't a single nice thing about that man. He is bad . . . in the best way."

Her voice goes all breathy at the end, and I'm struck with a twinge of jealousy. I cover that with a smirk and zing her back. "Hmm, sounds like someone has a crush. Better not let Dominick hear you talking like that."

Allie flushes instantly, stammering and shaking her head. "No, no, no. Listen, Shane's got the whole bad boy persona going on. Hard body, tattoos, you know."

"He's got tats?" I ask, surprised. I mean, I'm not that surprised, but I've never seen Shane in anything but his normal long-sleeved shirt. It makes me wonder when Allie saw him.

"Yeah, and before you ask, there was a night right before you started where Shane had to deal with three drunken frat boys. One of them got a handful of Shane's shirt, and we all got an eyeful of some pretty impressive eye candy. Actually, that was the only damage Shane took."

My pulse is hammering in my chest and I can't help it. "Wish I could have seen that."

Allie grins. "But you also know Shane. He's a badass, to be sure, but he's got that golden core to him. There's a deep-seated decent streak about him. Dominick's a different creature altogether. It's not a façade with him. He actually is a bad guy."

She says 'bad guy' like most folks say yummy cake, and I wonder exactly what is going on between the two of them. Part of me hopes it's not what I think. Allie's the kind to let her heart get broken in a futile quest to redeem the bad guy.

Before I can question her further, she gives her boobs a little shake and blows me an air kiss. "Anyway, off for my first set. Make sure you clap for my back walk-over move."

I smile. "You know I will. It's really a brilliant hook for your routine. I've seen guys' eyes just about bug out of their heads when you do it. Well done!"

She gives me a high-five and sashays out to wait backstage for her music cue. I quickly join her out on the floor while she's just getting her hips rolling for the crowd, immediately realizing that my section is already nearing capacity. Tossing a quick wave to Marco, I hustle over, jumping into the routine of getting orders and drinks.

As I work, I scan the room, sensing a vibe of tension for some reason. Usually by now, there's an ambiance of wicked abandon, wild chaos barely restrained. Too many guys are looking around the room too, ignoring Allie even as she hits her sexiest moves.

But instead, everyone is on edge, sitting up and looking over to the right, even as Allie comes off stage and the new girl takes over. Her approach is a different style from Allie's elegant grace, but the confidence and sex appeal are all there and should be garnering the crowd's attention.

Hmm, something's got to be up. I wonder what's over there? I try to look surreptitiously, especially since it's not my section and I don't want to be seen as a table poacher, but I just have to know.

Holy Mama Llama! That's Jimmy Keys, all six-foot-eight inches of millionaire himself, here at Petals, not at Club Noir like he was rumored to be last night. He's sitting back, two girls already hanging out with him, a bottle of very expensive bubbly sitting on the table.

The devil on my shoulder wants to tell Jeanine to suck it because this waitressing cover just might pan out after all. Mr. Basketball getting his drink and dance on at a regular club without his wife is one thing. Getting his jollies off at a strip club with a table full of what totally looks like his boys is another.

I can definitely use this for a story in *The Daily Spot*, but I need pictures as proof. I move to the far end of the bar, calling out an order to Marco and staying back to wait while he makes my drinks.

I pull out my phone, which is against the rules, but I need to take the risk. Acting like I'm checking my messages on my phone—*yep, nothing to see here, folks*—I quickly pull up my camera and fire off a burst of pics rapid-fire style. Score! Knowing when to cut and run, I don't even check the pics before shoving my phone back in my apron pocket. If they're fuzzy, well, it's not the first time we've run with unfocused photos, and these aren't even of UFOs or Bigfoot.

I'm just in time as Marco sets my drinks down. "One JB on the rocks and one draft beer for table nine," he says, grinning. "Good times tonight, huh?"

"I'm guessing you mean the bar tab?" I ask, and Marco nods. "Yeah. Good times."

I deliver my drinks and check in with my tables, my eyes flashing back to Jimmy every few minutes. I hear some guys cheering and laughing and look over to see his boys all riled up as Jimmy stands from his seat. He's grinning but not seeing a damn thing as his eyes read one thing and one thing only. Lust.

I can easily see why as Sasha, a stunning blonde from Russia, takes his hand and leads him straight into the back hallway where the private rooms are.

Not just a score, this could be a jackpot! Family man basketball star getting a private lap dance. I can see the headline now.

Once upon a time, I'd have been ashamed of peddling gossip like this. I would have been even more ashamed that a public person like this is acting so . . . dishonorably, but after a few years of tabloid work, you get numb. It feels like there's a sense of justice to it sometimes, at least. Jimmy trades and exploits his image as a family man, banking millions on his mantra of 'being a real man who treats his woman like a queen,' with endorsements, speaking fees . . . heck, the man spoke in front of a ten-thousand-seat church once. But something tells me his wife won't be too happy with her husband getting a private, one-on-one show from another woman.

Before I can even question more deeply, I follow them down the hallway, staying back and acting casual so no one suspects anything. They go to the big room that is used for private lap dances, and Jimmy sprawls out while Sasha saunters over to pick out whatever music she's going to use, temporarily leaving the door open.

I pause, leaning against the hallway wall, and take out my phone, clicking on the screen as though I'm texting but silently taking shot after shot. You can only see a bit of Jimmy from the side, but with the shots I got earlier being of his face, the clothing and his height instantly identify the faceless image as Jimmy.

I slip my phone back into my apron again before Sasha turns to close the door, knowing this will be a job well done and a hit story. I'm about to turn back onto the floor when I hear an angry voice behind me. "What the fuck are you doing, Meghan?"

I jump, startled and fearful as I look around. Shane steps forward from the end of the hallway, where he was standing in a dark corner. Considering he's wearing black pants and a smoke gray silk shirt, he's damn near a ninja.

His face is hard, his jaw clenched as he grabs my hand and drags me over to his hideaway corner, standing in front of me to block me in. "Shane, I—"

He shakes his head, looking down at me with iron-hard eyes. "Spill it."

Thinking fast, I pull out my airhead act, letting my voice rise girlishly. "Oh my gosh, Shane. You scared the poop outta me. Are you just skulking over here in the dark?"

Put the attention back on him. Good job, Maggie. I can play young, dumb, and broke all night long. But he's not having it at all. "One more time, Meg. What the fuck are you doing back here?"

I look into his dark eyes, which are boring into mine, and I can't help it, my gaze drops to the floor submissively. I try to work my way back up, letting my eyes trace the multitude of tattoos visible on his forearms where his sleeves are rolled up. I've never seen them before, and they're fascinating.

As I get higher, I follow where the tanned skin peeks out, and I can't help but wonder how much of his shirt I'd need to unbutton in order to see the tats on his chest.

But my gaze stops at his mouth, not able to meet his eyes again.

Deciding that a speck of truth will work better than my airhead act, especially since he's seen it with patrons before, I swallow my fear and let out a whisper. "Look, I'm a huge fan, okay? I just wanted to get a better look at him."

Shane grins, cocky and obviously holding back his laughter. "You're a basketball fan?"

I manage to look him in the eye, seeing his disbelief. "Well, maybe more of a Jimmy Keys fan than the whole sport. I always liked his wholesome family guy image. Seems that's not real, though, considering he's got Sasha grinding in his lap right this second. I just . . . I wanted to know for sure."

Shane tilts his head. "I've been around here longer than you. Even good guys are bad sometimes, and bad guys are good sometimes. No one is a simple character all the time. People are more complex than that."

I swallow, more of a gulp, honestly, and my eyes dip down again, intent on studying the buttons of his shirt and wondering about what's underneath the thin, dark fabric in front of my eyes. "So, which one are you, a good guy or a bad guy?"

From my peripheral vision, I see Shane's hand move, but I still freeze when he cups my chin, tilting my head back and forcing me to look up at him. There's heat in his eyes, a tension in his body as he leans forward, basically looming over me due to our height differences.

"Weren't you listening, Angel? I'm both good and bad. I suspect you are too."

The throaty, deep challenging purr of his voice drives the breath from my lungs as my pussy clenches, moisture almost immediately wetting the cotton of the good girl undies I'm wearing. Yeah, I am a good girl . . . but I so want to be naughty with him.

I suddenly realize my jaw is hanging open in his hand, and I force my mouth shut, my teeth clacking together. "I don't know what you're talking about."

Shane's thumb traces along my jawline, sending another thrill down my spine to stoke the heat inside me. "Pity," Shane softly growls, looking both amused and disappointed. "You looked so pretty with your mouth wide-open and waiting. Waiting for something . . . to suck on."

A shudder racks through my body, unbidden and uncontrollable at the image that brings to mind, and it takes every ounce of willpower I have to stay standing and not drop to my knees to immerse myself in obedience just to feel the intensity of what he's promising.

There's a moment of tense quiet where I think he's waiting to see what I'll do, and I wonder if he actually thinks I'll give him a blowjob right here in the hallway.

While the thought might be hot, it's definitely not something I'd actually do, even though my body's saying something very, very different.

Finally, he stands to his full imposing height, no longer angling over me, and he crosses his arms, his feet splayed wide. The mood has changed, seemingly at his whim, going from heated sexiness to all-business in a flash.

His chin dips as he lowers his gaze to look me in the eyes again, and his voice loses the growl, becoming softer but at the same time less intimate. "I was worried about you last night when you gave your shift away. Everything okay?"

I get the sense he was disappointed, and maybe a bit worried I wasn't here, either because now he thinks I'm some wilted flower who can't handle a jerk customer or maybe because he just wanted to see me.

Maybe both, to some degree? my mind asks, the hope mixed with the arousal that is pulsing its way through my body. I try not to let that hope plant too deeply and tell my hormones to calm the fudge down.

"Everything's fine," I finally reply. "Something just came up with a friend and she needed my help."

That's true, or as close as I can get to it. Jeanine isn't exactly a friend, but she did require my help.

Shane doesn't look convinced, his eyebrows lifting as he studies me closely. "A friend needed help? That's . . . vague."

Dang it, every time I try to play him, even a little bit, he calls me on it. He's giving me a little wiggle room here, maybe because he wants to find out more or maybe because he's just being nice, but he knows something's up.

Stuck, I shrug, hoping to play the one trump card most women have. "She thought her guy was stepping out on her, so she wanted me to do a little recon, see if he was being honest about where he was. He actually no-showed, so I gave up my shift to slowly drink in another bar for no good reason. I'm a bit bitter about the loss of tips, honestly. I'm out fifty bucks for the night."

It's just enough of the truth that it rings honest, and Shane's eyes soften as he accepts the expanded version of my story. Giving me a slight nod, he smiles, his white teeth flashing in the dim light. "Okay, just wanted to make sure you didn't have a freakout after I left. And next time, before you go drinking alone at some random club, call me and I'll be your cover story so you don't get caught spying on some friend's dude."

I nod, too stunned at his casual offer to say anything. Is he serious? If he were drinking at a club with me, watching my surroundings would be the last thing on my mind as I got lost in his brown eyes and powerful presence. Although last night would have been a lot more fun if I could have taken Shane out on the dance floor and shown him that I might not be on Allie's level, but I can work it myself a little . . . with the right guy.

"I'd better get back to my tables, see if they need anything," I say, clearing my throat and my mind. "Gotta make up for yesterday to pay the bills."

Shane chuckles. "Sure. And stay out of the private room area, Meghan. It's no place for a good girl like you."

I almost tease him about being a bit bad too, throwing his own words back at him, but something about his calling me a good girl feels nice, and instead, I just bask in the compliment as I hit the floor again.

CHAPTER

Six

SHANE

FOR THE NEXT WEEK, I keep an extra eye out on Meghan. It's not that hard, honestly. I keep an eye on the entire club anyway, and I've been paying attention to Meghan for at least the past month regardless. She's just so tempting that I can't help myself.

But now I find myself making sure that her area is even better behaved, that nobody gives her any grief even as I keep my distance physically. My attention never wavers from her tiny body as she swishes around the tables, leaning over provocatively to flash the fullness of her lush tits as she flirts harmlessly, giggling her little girl laugh and playing her airhead act every night. The guys love it, and the few girls who come in love it too. They just see her as the totally relatable girl next door.

Every flirt, every move, every time she makes eyes with a customer, it feels like she's taunting me. But deep down, I know it's her usual schtick as a waitress.

Every girl has one, dancer or waitress alike. They have to in order to survive in a place like this. They find a mask, a mantle of fakeness they put on like a Halloween costume when they hit the floor. For some, they become sweet or sarcastic, and for some it's femme fatale flirty or bitchy snippy. They find the personality type that attracts the customers, and the best girls know how to read their customers and behave accordingly to get the big tips.

For Meghan, that's her natural innocent bubbliness. It's disarming, enchanting, and very effective camouflage. I've watched her for long enough to see how smart she really is, and that while she's innocent and maybe even naturally flirty, she's no airhead despite her act. It's in the flow of her words, the way she shoots guys down even as she compliments them, and how she can subtly manipulate every table into falling in love with her. She's quickly gotten a small group of regulars who come not to see the dancers, but to get their beer and liquor with a side of her sweetness.

They see her as the girl they always wanted in high school, the good girl whose sparkling eyes and smile say she'll be honest and pure . . . but that underneath is a kitten waiting to be unlocked if she can find someone able to teach her.

Although, I'm not entirely sure that part is an act. I remember the way she blushed at my tawdry comments, her eyes dropping even as her breathing quickened, and her awkwardness the morning after we'd slept on her couch.

I don't think the innocence is all that fake, and though it shouldn't, that just ramps up my interest in my little angel Meghan all the more. Because I know, deep down in my guts where the good and bad sides of me swirl in constant tension, that I could unlock that sex kitten.

All I'd need is one opportunity. Much like the thought I had in her apartment about sullying her white couch with my griminess, I can picture dirtying Meghan up—lipstick smeared across her face by my lips, long blonde hair a mess from my hands tugging and pulling her at my will, my cum all over her tits in her black bustier uniform as she sags, spent from spasming helplessly around my cock before I marked her as mine.

Suppressing a groan, I shake my head, trying to clear it. Meghan's taken up so much real estate in my damn mind, I'm having to wear my compression shorts every time she's on shift, or else I walk around with a tent in my trousers.

Needing something more, I head over to the bar for a cold drink. No booze. That's unprofessional . . . but the bar has more than liquor. "Hey, Marco. Can I get a Coke when you get a chance?"

Marco doesn't look my way, too far in the weeds with orders to talk, but he flashes me a thumbs-up so I know he heard me. While I wait, I lean against the bar, surveying the room. Meghan and two other waitresses are hustling about, Sasha is on stage crawling on all fours toward a front-row guy in a nice suit who looks like he's going to have a stroke with as red as his face is getting, and every table is full. Best of all, the patrons are behaving themselves. It's a good, easy night at Petals.

My eyes are drawn back to Meghan, and before I know it, Marco clears his throat from right beside me. Shit. I never even heard him approach. And in my job, letting myself get that distracted is dangerous.

"How's she doing?" Marco asks as he hands me a Coke, no ice, just like I always have it when I'm on duty. "Any problems after the parking lot guy?"

I shake my head, taking a swig of the cold Coke. "No, she's been fine. Seems to have moved on."

Marco wipes the bar beside me with his towel, even though it's already spotless. He's a neat freak and compulsive in keeping up appearances both on the bar and in his personal habits, so I know it's not just for show. I wait, knowing he'll speak when he's ready.

"So if she's all good after the incident," he says, flipping his towel over in a quick quarter-fold before tucking it in the strings of his work apron, "why are you staring at her like you expect her to need you to run in like a knight in shiny fucking armor to slay the dragon?"

"Maybe because some people attract the dragons?" I ask. "She's different, you know? The other girls in here, they're more experienced and harder than she is. They can handle their shit and not blink twice about it. But Meghan has a softness to her. Dragons are attracted to that and would burn her to ash without a second thought just to ruin her tenderness."

Marco laughs a big belly laugh, his smile flashy. "That was some fucking panty-dropping poetry, man. Hold on, I gotta write that down."

He actually grabs a pen and paper from behind the bar, scribbling chicken scratch notes that only he can read. That's Marco, a dapper, fastidious dresser, a decent bartender with a neat freak fetish, but his handwriting is so messy I doubt even an expert can decipher what he puts down.

Marco tucks the paper away and looks up at me. "Shane, you said she attracts these types that can burn her up, right?"

"Yeah."

Marco nods. "One question then. What color dragon are you?" His laugh is gone, his tone serious and his eyes intense, reminding me that behind the affable exterior, there's the soul of an alpha male. "Oh, make that two. Who's protecting her from you?"

It's a question I've asked myself for the past week, but instead of answering, I take a drink from my Coke and lift it in salute to Marco. "Thanks for the drink. Better get back to the door."

I give Thomas, one of my fellow security guys, a nod, which he acknowledges, and we rotate positions. I resume my relaxed but ready, arms crossed front door stance, scanning the room.

As I do, something catches my eye. There's a patron at a side table, far from the stage, in a hoodie with a ball cap on. Not too unusual, since not everyone wants to be recognized at Petals, but something about him sets me on edge, like he's trying to not be noticed or seen. Every time the waitress in his zone comes by, he slinks down, turning his face even farther away from her.

I press the button in my ear, triggering the walkie talkie. "Hey, did you catch a sight of the hoodie guy at table twenty-eight coming in? I don't like the way he looks."

Thomas's voice comes back in my ear, and I see he's on the other side of the club, easing his way over. "He came in while you were taking a break.

Had sunglasses on but took them off once he sat down. No clear visual, but no red flags."

Thomas is okay. He knows how to handle himself, but he's not the best at faces or at spotting fake IDs. Twice, I've cleaned up behind him when he's let in underage kids. "Thomas, man . . . sorry, but can you come back and cover the door for a second? I wanna get a closer look."

Thomas is quick on the reply, which I appreciate. "Sure, no problem. On my way."

I see Thomas coming and then look back at the hoodie guy to see Meghan has approached the table. Twenty-eight is just on the edge of her zone, and obviously, the girl working that area has given up on Mr. Hoodie.

Meg seems fine, her usual smile on her face as she greets him to take his order, but then I see her face fall as she steps back. Before I can even take two steps, the guy's hand shoots out to grab her wrist, and I'm reacting, sprinting for her.

I sweep between them, my hip forcing the guy's hand free as I use my left arm to sweep Meghan behind me, and I'm struck with déjà vu as I realize hoodie guy is actually the parking lot fucker.

"Miles Jacobson," I growl, my right fist clenching, "I told you that you were banned. In fact, I told you that your own mother wouldn't even be able to recognize your body if you showed up here, but yet, here you are."

He looks at me, clear-eyed and sober and spoiling for a fight after the beatdown I gave him. "I just wanted to apologize, but this stuck-up bitch wouldn't even let me."

He leans to the side, trying to make eye contact with Meghan, spitting out words quickly. "Sorry I scared you the other day. I was drunk. Just didn't want to be banned. I bring clients here, you know."

He sounds like that should mean something. It's almost comical. I resist the temptation to bend down to his level—it would compromise both Meghan's security and mine—and instead grab him by the front of his hoodie, pulling him to his feet. "Correction. You *used* to bring clients here."

Before he can react, I twist his arm up behind his back at the same time I shove him belly-first into his table, bending him over and knocking the wind out of him. "Agh!"

"Exactly," I growl as I yank him up, applying a half-nelson to his other arm to walk him toward the back. I'm trying to not make a scene on the floor, but a few people are applauding already, and I just have to trust that Thomas will have already activated our standard protocol for unruly guests. I know I'm right when Logan meets me by the door to the back.

"Boss will be down any second. What's the plan?"

I don't bother answering him, knowing I'll have to explain again when Dominick arrives. Speak of the devil. Just as I push Miles through the doors, Dom emerges from the private staircase he has to his office.

"Shane, what seems to be the problem with our guest?"

Meghan, who's been nearly glued to my back, answers before I can even open my mouth. "It's him. The parking lot guy."

Dominick looks to me for confirmation, and I nod, jerking Miles's head up to face Dominick. "You fucking assholes! I'm going to call my lawyer!"

Wrong fucking answer. Instead of laughing, Dominick's voice drops to a silky, amused tone, his cadence slow and clear. If you don't know any better, he sounds civilized, maybe even casual. But if you pay attention, you can hear the coldness, the lack of fucks he gives about whatever shit Miles is spouting "Ah, Mr. Jacobson. Yes, I do know your name, as well as your address and vehicle information. Since I don't take my girls being accosted in the parking lot of my place of business lightly, I took it upon myself to get to know your business too. By the way, how is your hedge fund going? You seem to have hit a rough patch, isn't that right? It'd be a shame if your whole deck of cards came falling . . . falling . . . down."

Dominick's creepy menace permeates the room, and I can feel Miles's skin getting clammy under my hold as he begins to realize just who and what he's messing with. He stammers, and I swear he sounds like he's on the edge of crying. "Look, I'm sorry. I just wanted to apologize and hoped to not be banned because of a misunderstanding. I can see that was a mistake. I'll just go."

Dominick strokes his chin, but there's no doubt or softness in his eyes. "Yes, I do think we should go . . . out the back, perhaps?"

Dominick's eyes meet mine with his judgment and sentencing of Miles complete. I nod, understanding, but gesture behind me with a lift of my chin. We've got company, and he doesn't want to say more.

Dominick follows my gesture, his face softening instantly as he spies Meg's blonde locks. "Oh, Meghan, I'm afraid Shane casts such a huge shadow I lost sight of you for a moment. Are you okay, honey?"

She seems more angry than fearful, her voice tight. "Fine. Thank you."

Dom smiles, charming as ever as he comes around, taking her hand and patting her on the shoulder. "Very well, then head back to the floor and resume covering your tables. We'll escort Mr. Jacobson out."

Her eyes dip to the floor, but she lifts them instantly. "Uhm, Dominick? Can I ask you a favor?"

He's a dangerous man to ask that question, but I'm curious what she's going to ask. He inclines his head, the curiosity on his face too. "You may ask."

"Can I have a word with Mr. Jacobson before you throw him out?"

I can see the smile on Dominick's face as he motions with a wide sweep of his hand for her to proceed. She steps in front of Miles, all five foot nothing of her puffed up and standing tall. Curious to see what she'll say, I lean my head to the side, making sure that my grip is still strong. She meets Miles's eyes with no problem, and I'm damn proud of her.

"I wish I'd had the chance to do this before," she says before her right fist flashes out pretty damn quickly in a straight punch that smashes perfectly into Miles's nose. I might be able to dodge it, but most people would have no chance, especially since no one would see it coming from an angel like Meghan. The crack is unmistakable as Miles squirms in my arms, cursing a blue streak as blood streams from his ruined nostrils. "Fucking bitch. You'll pay for that. Let me go!"

Dominick puts a gentle arm around Meghan's shoulders, guiding her again toward the door to the club. "Well done, I must say. And quite surprising, which is a rare occurrence for me. We'll take it from here."

She nods, shaking her hand a little as she heads back to the floor. As soon as the door swings closed, Dominick turns back to me, all the polite softness gone from his face. "Now, shall we go outside? I hate to get blood on the tile back here. The cleaning staff tends to gets rather upset."

Logan opens the door, and we scan for any cars in the dark rear parking area, knowing that there won't be any but always checking to be safe.

I heave Miles through the doorway and out into the dirty backlot. It's closed in on three sides between the building and two sides of chain link fence. It's perfect for what I need to do, especially when Logan stands sentry at the backlot entrance, ensuring our privacy.

"Now. I was polite inside," Dominick says as he unbuttons his jacket, "but let's be clear now. You're not going to forget this fucking lesson. You will not come here. You will not come to this neighborhood. Shane, make sure those lessons stick."

I step forward, my boot flicking out to catch Miles just above the kneecap. His leg hyperextends, and he gasps in pain, dropping his hands so that I can punch him in the temple.

"How dare you fucking touch her? You're not good enough to even lick the floor she walks on, asshole," I growl as I follow up with a big uppercut that catches Miles right in the teeth. I feel my knuckle split, but I don't give a shit as he rockets nearly straight, his hands blindly flying out.

"Excuse me, Shane," Dominick says as he steps forward. He's rolled up his sleeves, his sinewy forearms rippling as he grabs Miles by the ears and drives him backward. Dominick's not as formally schooled as I am. He learned his techniques from the streets, and he fights dirty.

"Shane's nice," Dominick says as he knees Miles in the balls. "Sometimes, too nice. So let me continue. If I hear that you've been within a half-mile of this club, or within a half-mile of Meghan, this is going to seem like a walk in the fucking park. *If* I decide to let you live, you won't leave the hospital for a long fucking time. Do you understand me?"

By this point, Miles is sobbing. "Y–y–yes," he blubbers, tears mixing with his blood. "Please."

I'm disgusted by this piece of shit. Begging for what? Mercy? Like he would've given any to Meghan if he'd gotten her alone in his car? He's weak, preying on a woman when she's defenseless. Although, after that jab to Miles's nose, maybe she wouldn't have been quite the meek mouse he expected. The thought gives me a hint of satisfaction.

Miles continues to cry, his pleas to stop peppered with threats of lawsuits, still not understanding that we don't handle things like that at Petals. Dominick looks offended at Miles's breakdown and winds up, kicking him in the stomach hard enough that I'm pretty sure Dom missed his calling as a field goal kicker. "Shane, before Miles leaves us, make sure he'll be jacking off left-handed for the next two to three months."

"Certainly, sir," I reply, stepping forward again. Miles tries to fend me off weakly, but I grab his right hand without a problem, goose necking it before punching him in the ribs just for fun. "This way, asshole."

It's harder to lead Miles out to his car, mainly because he's taken so much of a beating his legs can't really support him. It takes both me and Logan to get him across the lot.

Finally, we reach his car, and I twist Miles's wrist a little more, making him whimper. "Keys."

Using his right hand, Miles finds his keys, holding them out to me. "Unlock your door."

He pushes a button, and I open the door, looking into his teary, fear-streaked eyes. "I'm not a bad guy," he whines. "I just wanted to say sorry."

"I'm sure. But you know what?" I ask, lowering my voice. "Now you understand fear. Now you understand what she felt when you grabbed her wrist tonight. How she felt when you came at her in this parking lot. Now you understand that for all your macho bullshit, you're just five seconds away from being someone's little bitch. Put your hand in the door."

The realization of what's about to happen clears away some of the haze in his eyes, and he starts shaking his head, a whine coming from deep in his chest. "No! Please, no—"

I force his arm out, slamming the door on his fist. There's a crack, and he cries out, dropping to his knees. "My hand!"

"You have until I count to twenty to be out of the parking lot . . . or else, your neck is next," I say, picking him up and heaving him into the driver's seat of his car. "One. Two. Three."

I'm bluffing about the neck part, but it does the job. He leaves as quickly as he can, running over the curb as he pulls out just as I reach twenty.

Turning, I head around to the back door of the club to report to Dominick. As I walk, I know that on some level, I should be bothered by what I did tonight.

A two-on-one beating that left a man broken, bleeding, and with only fate to decide if he lives through the night should give me pause.

But the fucker deserved it for what he did to Meghan the first time. And the fact that he showed back up to intimidate her again?

A part of me hopes he does die, all snug in his fucking bed tonight, choking on his own blood. And if he doesn't die, he spends the next week pissing dark brown and looking like he picked a fight with a steamroller, because if he shows his face near the club again, I will kill the son of a bitch. Consequences be damned.

Whatever it takes, because Meghan deserves to be treated with respect.

CHAPTER

Seven

MAGGIE

STRETCHING ON MY SOFA, I lean back, sighing. Thank goodness I'm off today from *both* of my jobs. After last night's craziness, I need a day to recover, unwind, and settle my mind. My hand is sore from where I punched Miles, and typing this afternoon might be a bit of a challenge, but I'm not the least bit sorry.

The light throb is a reminder that I'm a strong beast of girl who can put those killer cardio-kickboxing class and elementary school Tae Kwon Do moves to good use when needed. Getting up, I doctor a cup of coffee and plop back down on the couch, turning on old gameshow reruns as background noise as I curl up with my laptop. For some reason, listening to Richard Dawson asking what the survey said gets my creative juices flowing.

I click around, checking my emails, Instagram, and Twitter to see if there's anything I can cull into a story for the tabloid. There isn't much. An Instagram girl famous for her booty seems to be stiffing her video editor, both literally and financially. I also cobble together a quick hundred-word blurb about a celebutante dining at the fanciest restaurant in town with her brother, noting that they're rarely seen together in public. It isn't much, but it'll keep Jeanine happy enough to not bug me on my day off.

Nothing's really smashing ground-breaking journalism, but it's what I've got. Fortunately, I'm still riding high on the Jimmy Keys expose story I was able to write based on his appearance in the club. Jeanine ate that up like candy, just like I knew she would.

I'd even written a couple of follow-up pieces about the fallout when his wife found out, and then when he admitted to having a sex addiction and was seeking treatment.

I think his reaction's a bit overblown and probably more to save his reputation, considering he was just getting a lap dance. There's no need for the melodrama, but the cynical side of me wasn't surprised to see the pedestal-living pseudo-hero fall to Earth with a crash.

After a few more minutes of clicking around, I find myself staring at the TV screen mindlessly rather than digging for more juicy stories. Sure, it's a waste of time, but it feels good to laugh as a bunch of pseudo-celebrities swap one-liners and give double-entendres for answers to ridiculous questions. It's light and bright. Nothing they're saying really matters, but that's what makes it fun.

Setting my laptop aside, I give in to the draw of the show, but after a few minutes, my phone rings. I mute Charles Nelson Reilly, circa 1978, to grab it, seeing it's Allie.

"Hey, Allie. What's kickin'?"

"Are you serious right now?" Allie asks, sounding outraged and amused at the same time. "You punch an asshole customer out last night, and today, you're all casual, 'Hey, Allie, what's kickin'?' Bitch, you'd better start spilling the story."

I grin, loving how she's blunt and straight to the point. She also shows that she cares that way. The more direct she gets, the more she likes you. "It wasn't that big of a deal."

Allie guffaws. "Actually, pause right there because I need to see your face when you tell this story. I gotta see how much of your bullshit you actually believe. What are you doing right now?"

I look around my apartment, at the muted show I'm watching, the nest of blankets wrapped around me on my couch, and me still in my pajamas. "Literally, nothing. Why?"

"Perfect. I'm picking you up in fifteen minutes and we're going for mani-pedis so I can hear it all. Okay?"

"That sounds great, actually," I admit, grinning. When Allie makes me offers like this, she always insists on picking up the tab. "I'll be ready."

We hang up, and I hurry to get ready, pulling on shorts, a T-shirt, and flip flops before retying my ponytail and swiping some mascara and lipgloss on. It's not fancy, but it's what I've got on short notice. I'm just making sure my mouthwash is doing its job when I hear a knock, and I know I'm out of time.

Of course, when I open the door, Allie looks like a million bucks. Her chocolate hair is hanging straight down her back, her makeup is impeccable but perfect for daytime, and while she's also wearing shorts and a T-shirt, she manages to look like a Pinterest pin while I look like a fashion don't list victim.

"Are you planning on handing out heart attacks today?" I ask, and Allie grins.

"Nope, that's your job. You look gorgeous," she says.

I smooth the wrinkles out of my T-shirt and laugh. "You must be high! Come on, let's go. Who's driving?"

"Like you have to ask," Allie says, dangling her keys. "Come on, I'll drive."

Forty minutes later, we're sitting in matching pedicure chairs, my feet already feeling softer as they soak in eucalyptus-scented water. "Mmm . . . nice."

"So, what color do you think?" Allie says, flipping through the color guide. "I'm thinking dark navy blue, something that'll stand out."

"Yeah . . . I don't think so," I reply, flipping through my own copy. "Hey, what do you think?"

I hold up my card, a pinkish light lavender that just caught my attention. Allie grins, giving me a thumbs-up. "Totally you. It's so sweet I need to check myself for diabetes."

I stick out my tongue, and Allie laughs. A few minutes later, our technicians take our choices and get to work, buffing and smoothing our feet until they tingle.

As the ladies really get into their work, Allie looks over at me, leaning back in her chair. "Okay, now spill it."

"Well, I was working the floor," I begin before giving her an edited play-by-play of last night's events. Of course, I have to leave out names. We're in public, and I know that name dropping could bring unwanted attention. "So, anyway, I socked him in the nose."

"You caught that motherfucker in the nose?" Allie asks, barely containing a fist pump. "How'd the boys react?"

I think back to the shocked looks on Dominick and Shane's faces, and I grin. "I surprised them pretty good, I think. I'm sure they thought I didn't have it in me. Honestly, I didn't think I had it in me either, but watching the way he was trying to weasel, I just knew I had to fight back. Or else."

"Or else what?"

"Or else I was going to be afraid of jerks like that my whole life," I reply. "And you know what? It felt really good to stand up to him that way. I think the guys probably scared the bejesus out of him more though. Hopefully, he won't try coming around again."

Allie gives me an odd look, like I must be having the sillies or something. "Uhm, he definitely won't come around again if he knows what's good for him. I'm sure they beat the shit out of him. Did you see the guys again last night?"

I think back, then shake my head. "No, Bossman came in and told me I could take off early, considering everything. He even comped me the missed tips—reached into his pocket and slipped two Bennies in my hand like it was nothing. I was so surprised, I went straight home and slept like the dead till late this morning. Why?"

Allie seems uncertain if she should say more but finally hums to herself and makes a decision. "Well, I saw the boss's hands later. He had a few scrapes, and his right shoe was scuffed. And I'm thinking your knight had more of an axe to grind."

"How so?"

Allie bites her lip before replying. "Later, when he was walking us out, I noticed that one of his hands was bandaged. I asked, and he said he was fine, but . . . if I could give you a guess, I'd say your knight laid a major asswhipping on your motherfucker."

I let that sink in.

Dom and Shane beat Miles up . . . for me. I should be horrified at the caveman-like behavior, disgusted that they sank that low instead of . . . what? Using their words? Not saying pretty please and calling the cops?

I scoff at my own line of thinking. It's not like this is kindergarten, and I know Dominick protects the club and his girls fiercely. They used brute force because they're able to and that's what the situation called for, especially after Shane gave Miles a threatening talk the first time around.

I mean, even I got a shot in, so their beating him up isn't all that different from what I did, right? Maybe more aggressive, taken further, but I know that deep inside, I'm not upset at what they did.

I'm thankful they defended me that way, made me and all the other women Miles has likely tried to intimidate safer with their actions.

"Well, I'm glad then. If I never see that poohead again, it'll be too soon."

Allie chuckles, shaking her head. "Poohead. I swear the universe missed out on one of the greatest jokes in history when you weren't named Pollyanna. Then again, you don't seem upset by the news."

"I'm not, honestly. It was . . . I guess you could say it was noble. From a certain point of view."

Story complete, our conversation turns to other matters. Allie chats about what she's been up to, mostly sticking to some new clothes she picked up online the other day before grinning. "And guess what?" she says, not even giving me a chance to guess before she rattles on excitedly, "I got another job!"

She's giddy, almost dancing in her seat, making the lady working on her nails look at her sharply. "Miss, I cannot do the contours correctly if you keep moving."

"Sorry," Allie apologizes, turning back to me. "So, yeah, new job!"

"Oh, my gosh, are you quitting?" I ask, worried. Allie's my best friend. I couldn't imagine what work at Petals would be like without her.

She laughs, shaking her head. "Of course not. Nothing pays like the club. But this is a shot at some classical ballet. Two classes a week to adults who want to stretch and tone and feel graceful. It's not much, but it's a start, and I can use my training for more than splits and spins on a pole."

"That's so awesome, Allie," I reply honestly, grinning. "If I could hug you or high-five you right now, I so would!"

Even though we don't move, the nail tech by Allie gives us a shrewd look. It's just that I know Allie's been busting her butt to make some sort of inroad on her dream of working in the ballet world. She trained for years, even to the point of injuring herself to try and get more turn-out on her feet before an eating disorder put her in the hospital.

Even just her dancing in a strip club is a step for her. I think it shows that she's at least a little confident in her body again. Sure, she's got bills a mile high, but in almost every other way, I think she's almost a role model for me.

Finally, when our nails are done, I'm able to give Allie a congratulatory hug, both of us keeping our nails away from each other in a weird forearm patting embrace.

I'm truly happy for her to get this job because I know she misses ballet. She has an empty room in her apartment lined with mirrors so she can dance and improve. I'd teased her about her voyeuristic sexcapades the first time I'd seen the mirrors, but when she turned on some music and began swaying and leaping through the small space, I knew exactly what that room was for her.

It's her sanctuary. I guess we all need one.

"Come on, let me buy you a cupcake to congratulate you on your new gig!"

Allie grins but refuses. "Thank you, and maybe later, but I should get going. I work tonight and need to get ready. You working?"

I glance at my watch, surprised at how late it is already. "Yeah, I'm only doing a partial shift tonight though. I'll be in at ten 'till close. But come on, one cupcake? I'll make it double-fudge red velvet."

Allie glowers at me, then grins. "You're buying."

CHAPTER

Eight

SHANE

"ROOM CHECK," I say quietly into my ear mic, notifying Nick, the guy working the door. It's just another Sunday night at Petals. You'd think Sunday would be the lightest night of the week. I mean, East Robinsville has a lot more churches than strip clubs, but it's not. It's not quite as busy as Saturday night, but Sundays aren't slack either.

There are quite a few patrons. Maybe it's a carryover from their Sunday morning activities, or maybe it's the fact that they're not looking forward to Monday, but the customers seem pretty chill.

But tonight just doesn't seem the same. Instead of the shitload of things I should be watching for, including but not limited to making sure the customers behave, that the dancers are comfortable, and that Marco's not getting stiffed at the bar, I find myself waiting for Meghan. I even know her schedule, and she's not supposed to be in for a little bit, but that's not stopping me from anticipating her arrival.

Trying to rein my attentions in, I scan the floor. The new girl on stage seems to be doing all right, although I can't remember her name. Candy? Caramel? Something with a C that's definitely fake.

Most of the patrons are watching her with rapt attention, except for the bachelor party that seems more intent on roasting the groom-to-be, leading to some raucous laughter from their table. They haven't gotten to their lap dances yet, but from what I see, I'd say the bride-to-be has nothing to worry about. Her beau's got a look on his face that says he's enjoying himself, but he's just putting up with his buddies' antics and he's going to behave.

Still, I scan each face for a moment, making sure it's just good ol' boy fun and not going to be an issue before continuing my threat assessment of the room. It's a normal Sunday crowd, with guys in just about every age bracket, wealth bracket, and confidence bracket . . . and three girls, two of whom are having 'nights out' with their guy friends.

Petals is a decent place, more high-class than most country clubs, so we don't get too many low-life types. Still, there's always a mix of folks to keep an eye on, especially in Dominick's place where he rules with an iron fist. The inherent combination of guys full of liquid courage and sexy women flirting with them is a dangerous equation, like sparks near dynamite . . . unless the rules are strictly followed.

So I keep my eyes open. From my perch, I can angle to the side and see behind the curtains on the far side of the stage. I see when the backdoor opens and Meghan walks in, a backpack thrown over her shoulder, her sweats and tank outfit in place but with full fuck-me hair and makeup going, probably done at her apartment. It's an oddly endearing combination, the sweet and the sexy all mixed up.

Giving Nick a nod to keep an eye, I step away from my station, needing to make sure Meghan is okay after the shitstorm last night. I'd driven by her apartment after I got off shift, hours after Dominick let her go home early, and I barely managed to keep from banging on her door.

But the single glowing light in the living room told me she was home, and I let that be enough to soothe the beast inside me. Besides, my hand was still pretty busted up, and it would have freaked her out to see my knuckles that way.

Backstage, I lean against the doorframe and watch for a second like the pervert that I am, enjoying the way she gently moves to the music pumping through her earphones as she touches up her makeup in front of the big light-up mirror. Her eyes meet mine in the glass, and she smiles, turning around to face me.

"Let me see it."

For a heart-stuttering moment, my filthy mind thinks she wants to see my cock, and it instantly hardens, liking that idea a lot. But as she walks toward me, it's not my crotch she grabs, it's my hand, lifting it to see the bruises and scrapes along my knuckles.

"I'm fine, nothing that won't heal in a day or two," I reply softly. Thankfully, I patched up my hand last night—hydrogen peroxide to clean it out, and then NuSkin does a lot to cover the damage.

She runs a feather-light fingertip over the roughly crinkled skin, her voice soft. "You did this for me?"

In my pants, my cock surges again, and my compression shorts are not up to the job this time. Instead, I'm resisting the urge to take her hand and press it into the wall above her head before taking her mouth in a strong kiss. "Of course. Asshole had it coming. That's no way to treat a lady, especially not you."

She blushes a bit, her cheeks pink with pleasure. "Thank you. That's sweet."

Before I can reply, she bends down, laying little butterfly presses of her lips along my knuckles, like she can kiss my injuries away. "Meg—"

"I'm nothing special, just . . . me," she says, looking up at me with emotion in her eyes that makes me want her all the more. "And no one has ever done anything like that for me before. Thank you."

I growl, wrapping a hand around the back of her neck as I step closer to her, our bodies a mere whisper away from touching. "Don't say that. You are beautiful. You can haunt a man's dreams, his fantasies, filled with your laughter, your sighs . . . and your screaming his name in pleasure. You're special, Meghan."

A small whimper escapes her lips as she looks up at me, her lips parting, almost begging for me to take them in a kiss. I shouldn't. I can't . . . for so many reasons.

But she's irresistible. I need to know what she tastes like. I have to experience the taste of her skin, whether it's the sparkle vanilla cupcakes she makes me think of, all sugar and sweetness. Or if there's the musky undertone that has haunted my dreams, the sexual essence of a woman that I sense burning just beneath the surface.

Instead of tasting her lips the way I want to, I trace my free hand down her arm, slowly and steadily to take hold of her hand. Bringing it up, I inspect her knuckles too, noting that they're looking a little bruised even in the dim light of the hallway. "Are you okay? That was quite a punch you landed."

She nods, her eyes so wide as I kiss her knuckles, one by one, letting my tongue slip out to lick at her as I caress her skin. She's even more thrilling than I thought, electric vanilla fireworks that make my head spin.

As I heal her not-at-all-injured hand with my ministrations, I look up to meet her eyes. "Not sure any of us saw that coming from such a sweet, innocent thing."

She smirks, a fire sparking deep in her eyes as she gathers herself for a sassy reply. "Who says I'm sweet and innocent?"

I chuckle, flipping her hand to kiss her fingertips and palm. They're silky soft, and in my mind, I can imagine this hand holding my cock in front of her open mouth for me to fill. "Angel, everything about you says sweet and innocent. That's what's so fucking dangerous. You don't know what you're playing with. You make me want to dirty you up, shock you with the filthy things I want to do your body, and tease at that sweetness until I can drink up every drop of you like candy."

My words galvanize Meghan's body, leaving her panting, her breath smelling like sugar with a faint hint of coffee, making me want to sip the flavor from her lips. I don't think she means to say it out loud, but a soft hiss escapes her pink lips unbidden anyway. "Yesss."

I cup her jaw in both hands, forcing her eyes to meet mine and lock. The next words are the hardest words I've ever spoken, tearing from the depths of my stomach like coughing up nails. "But we can't. You know the rules. Dominick would kill me. Literally, most likely. And you deserve better than me. You see me as a dangerous thrill, but I'd ruin you. A night with me would leave your pretty pink pussy in tatters from fucking you so rough because I'm not a gentle lover. I'd take you hard, wringing your orgasms out of you until you passed out in exhaustion. I'd give you so much cum, your pussy couldn't even hold it all and it would run down your legs."

Her eyes are dilated, wide and soft as if I'm whispering sweet nothings in her ear. I thought she'd be shocked, maybe even offended by my crude words. Some of me hoped she would be, that she'd be repelled and maybe we could end this dance between us. But it seems this angel has a bit more devil in her body than I thought.

Every bit of me wants to make good on my words, toss her on the chair in the corner and earn the first cries of her orgasm with my tongue between her legs. With the way her skin tasted, death by Dominick's hand might be worth it.

As much as I don't want to, I have to tell her the rest, leaning in to smell her hair before whispering in her ear. "As much as that excites you—and yes, my cock is throbbing at the idea too—I'll break your heart, Angel. I'll take what I need, make you a dirty mess, and leave. It's what I do. I'm a bastard, a motherfucker who only hurts those who let me in. You deserve better than me."

I pull back from her ear, letting her see the truth of my words in my eyes, on my face, knowing that even if I wanted to, I can't keep her. That's not who I am. It's . . . impossible.

The spell is broken, my words sinking into her head, her heart. I can see the moment her desire and arousal turn to hurt, then anger. She pulls back, putting space between us, and I hate it instantly, missing the feel of her so close.

"I see," she says, turning on a heel and heading toward the lockers. I want to chase her, push her to the ground, and take her like the predator I am. I want to bury myself inside her, feel her spasm as I stake my claim on her body, mind, and soul. *Mine.*

But this is the right thing to do. Let her push me away for her own sanity and safety. I can take it, even if it hurts. And right now, it does hurt, both in my gut and in my balls.

Just before reaching the curtain to the changing area, Meghan turns back, her eyes flashing dangerously. "You say I deserve more. That's for me to decide. Don't act like you get to make decisions for me. Is this just a game to you? Get me all riled up and then squash me with some lame justification that sounds more like a carrot on a stick enticement than a real warning? Well, fu–forget you."

She pushes the curtain aside, and I feel like I just got punched in the gut. She almost cursed at me. If I needed any more proof, that tells me how hurt she really is. Fucking hell. That was the last thing I wanted to do. I just couldn't help myself. She calls to me without even meaning to, and I'm barely holding back, for her sake.

She leaves the curtain open, stomping her little body over to her locker and ripping her scrap of a miniskirt out. She glares at me over her shoulder and then pulls it on over her sweats, only dropping them once she has the scrap in place.

I don't bother telling her that when she bends over to grab the sweats from the floor, I can see the bottom of her ass cheeks, so grabbable and bite-able. And the peek of her good girl panties, white with lace trim against her tan flesh, does more for my fantasies than any fancy lingerie ever has.

She snatches her black lace bustier off the hook, holding it to her front like a shield even though she still has her tank top on.

She makes a shooing motion with her hand, swatting the air at me like I'm an annoyance. "Weren't you just saying you would leave me? Well, go ahead. I've got to get ready for my shift."

I should, I absolutely should. But I can't walk away when she's so mad at me. Instead, I assume my security guard stance, my feet planted firmly on the floor with my arms crossed over my chest, eyes daring her to test me. With a huff, she turns back to face her locker and rips her tank over her head.

The expanse of her back beckons me, and I want to trace the line of her spine with my tongue, make her arch beneath me as I fuck her from behind. She quickly fastens the bustier, not needing any help, and then leans forward, shimmying slightly and doing something to her tits, but my eyes are fastened on the flash of her ass again.

It's delectable, just enough that I could massage, knead . . . and spank it until it's bright red. It's taut, perfect, the type of ass that could grip my cock until we're both crying out. That peek is going to taunt me all night and for a long time to come. After slipping her heels and apron on, Meghan struts toward me looking like a fucking Valkyrie in petite-fairy form.

I hold my position, expecting her to either stop in front of me for another scathing dismissal or maybe push me out of her way. But she does neither.

Instead, she turns her body to step around me, not even brushing me with a faint touch of her skin. That stabs my heart more than anger or violence somehow. It's a dismissal. It's her saying that she understands and isn't going to waste her time on me any longer.

The scent of her lingers in her wake, and with a deep breath, I draw it in, knowing it might be my last chance to savor it. I let it sear its way into my brain for the upcoming lonely nights and empty beds, when the weaker side of me gnaws at my mind and tells me I could have had the most beautiful, flawless woman I've ever seen next to me. Even if only for a moment.

It takes me a while to settle my nerves, and I wipe at my cheeks and forehead, dismissing the moisture on my fingers as just sweat from the heat back here.

It's gonna be a long fucking night.

CHAPTER

Nine

MAGGIE

HOW DARE HE? I fume to myself as I move around the tables, catching as many orders as I can. *That arrogant son of a biscuit!*

Shane had me all fired up and ready to break the rules. He talked about Dominick, but I know that rule too.

The first day I worked here, before I'd even met Shane, Dominick had gone over his employee rules. Number one of which, and the one that seems the most pertinent right now, considering my wet panties, was no fraternizing between staff.

Considering what I now know about the way his eyes follow Allie's every move, it seems a bit hypocritical. But he's the boss, and if he wants to break his own rules, I guess he's allowed. Although, maybe he really does just watch her from afar. Allie has never said otherwise.

At the time of my sit-down with Dominick, I'd just been concerned about getting the undercover job without his being suspicious, and the rule seemed reasonable. I totally understood, but now I'm frustrated. Shane has me so . . . darn it, all I can do is try and avoid him. But he's a dang moving target all night, working the door, working the floor, and with those dark clothes of his, he's like a ninja when he wants to be.

At one point, he settled into a position on the far wall, so I asked Sarah to switch sections with me, and she did, albeit with a questioning look.

I had a few moments of glee at getting away until Shane switched stations too, glaring at me as he took up his new perch. Ugh, fine. Play your games, but I'm not playing.

Even as I tell myself that, I know it's not true. I'm pissed, I'm disappointed, but if he told me right now 'one-time ride . . . get on', I'd hop on his dick so fast he would see stars.

I sigh, shaking my head. Why do bad boys have to be so hot?

How is that even fair to us mere mortal girls? I mean, I know that I shouldn't be looking at guys like Shane.

I should try to find a nice guy. One who'll take care of himself and his family, who might not be perfect but will love me and any children we have. I need a guy who wants that too, a simple, happy life. That's what good girls are supposed to do.

But with Shane, I feel such a connection. And I'm no fool. Chemistry like that is rare, and if once was all I got, I'd go for it and pay the emotional price later.

So I spend the night alternating between ignoring him and glaring daggers at him.

Marco doesn't slow down, though. He's got drinks to get ready and customers to serve. Still, he's not heartless. "Hey, Meghan, here's your pitcher for table forty-five, but what's up with you tonight? You okay?"

I huff, trying to make my voice light and bubbly but failing miserably. Still, I gotta try. "Yeah, I'm fine. You?"

Marco laughs, shaking his head. Good bartenders are half-baked shrinks, and Marco's no different. "Nice try, sweetheart. Last night hit you harder than you thought?"

"No, it's not that," I reply, hoping he doesn't push the issue. What Shane and I did in the back was probably close enough to being over the line, and as pissed as I am at Shane and his sexy bad self, I don't want him to get in trouble. "Just one of those nights, I guess."

"I can dig that," Marco says with a chuckle. "We all get them. By the way, I heard you put the smackdown on Mr. Creepazoid last night. That right?"

I grin a little, showing Marco my knuckles. "Yeah, I got one good punch in before Dominick sent me home."

Marco takes my hand and looks it over, giving a small whistle. "Sweet. Glad that Shane and Dom took care of the rest though. You mad at that?"

He looks at me questioningly, and I know that he's giving me an evaluating question, one that might have multiple layers to it. But regardless of the legality of the beating, my reply is quick and honest. "Oh, heck no, definitely not mad at that. I appreciate their having my back. Tonight's just a weird night."

Before I can stop it, I glance over my shoulder at Shane, who is watching my exchange with Marco with eagle eyes, even from across the room.

Marco follows my eyes and sees Shane looking our way. "Hmm, not really my business to get involved in. But Meghan?" He waits for me to look back at him before continuing, "Don't go barking up that tree. He might've saved you a couple of times, but he's no Prince Charming. And you know the rules."

Marco's eyes pointedly flick up to the camera at the corner of the bar. I understand. Dominick's always watching. You just never know when. "Best to stay in your own lane, especially around here. I wouldn't rat you to Dom, but I'm also not going to lie to the man if he asks."

I sigh, nodding. "I would never ask you to. Not trying to court trouble. Just . . . a weird night."

I know I'm repeating myself, but I don't want to take the risk of exposing what happened backstage. At least I can be assured that Dom didn't see that. He's never put a camera back there to give the girls some privacy. Or that's what we've been told. "Okay," Marco says, giving me a shrug. "Just be careful."

"I will, thanks. Thanks for listening," I reply. "Anyway, back to work."

I grab the pitcher Marco poured for me and deliver it to table of what looks like personal trainers, who seem to be out for more work talk than to watch the performances on stage. At least, while they remark on Tina's dance on stage, they're peppering their comments with remarks about her 'intercostals' and 'core stability' as much as her boobies.

After another hour, I've managed to push Shane from my mind, too busy slinging drinks to see if his eyes are still following my every move.

At least he's not positioned in my section anymore, the security team's rotation putting him on the other side of the room now. Thank goodness for small favors. Besides, I'm nearing the end of my shift, and I can't wait to go home, slam a Nytol to put me out quick, and dream of a tomorrow without a certain bad boy both frustrating and arousing me.

I come back around, checking on one of my loner tables, a single guy. He's my age, maybe, but his eyes look wiser than my twenty-five years and his suit easily costs more than my car. He has a worldliness to him, watching the performances almost as though they are artistic displays, not tawdry fantasies of the flesh.

As I come nearer, he raises a manicured hand. "Can I get another Macallan, miss? Actually, I'm headed back for a private dance with Allie. Can you bring the bottle back, Rare Cask Single Malt?"

I nod, surprised. Allie's very particular about her private dances, and her rates are pretty exorbitant. "Of course, sir. I'll keep your table reserved for after?"

He dips his head, rising to stride confidently to the back, and I head back to Marco to order the bottle service. With the bottle and a fresh glass on my tray, I head back to Allie's usual private dance room, the one closest to Dominick. It's the best room in the back too, mirrored and with a pole, but with a luxury feel to the supple leather seating and soft lighting.

I give one sharp rap as warning and then slowly and invisibly enter, pouring the scotch for the customer as Allie selects her music from the playlist in the corner. I give her a wink as I turn to leave, and she winks back. Considering that he just ordered a three-hundred-dollar bottle of scotch, it's gonna rain in here.

As I head down the hallway, I see a large guy striding toward me. He's wide, and the black of his jeans and T-shirt blend with the dimness of the hallway, although the moving laser lights bounce off him. He looks cold and calculating to a degree that seems to almost chill the very air around him. Our security guys are pretty badass themselves, but there's something raw about this guy, a missing element to his soul.

He's ugly as sin too, with a bald head that gleams lightly in the dim light and squinty eyes. His left ear's all types of screwed up, what I think some people call cauliflowered, like an alley cat that's had one too many scraps over the garbage cans.

I walk past him, hugging the wall and drawing myself in tight to seem as small and unimportant as possible, knowing that I'll have to tell security to keep an eye on him. Even still, my back ripples in goosebumps as I slide by.

This guy zings my red flags as a definite potential problem. I'm almost to the corner when I hear a fast ra-tat-tat sound, but it's barely audible over the loud bass-thumping music on the main floor. My brain takes a split second to register the sound as gunfire, but it's not until I hear Allie scream that I turn and run toward her. It's stupid. I shouldn't be running *toward* gunfire, but all my brain is telling me is that my best friend may have just been shot, and I have to help her.

I see the guy in black running out the other end of the hallway as I stop in the doorway of Allie's room. She's crouched in the corner and covered in blood splatter but seems to be uninjured. She's just frozen in shock, her eyes wide as she stares at what used to be a human being slumped on the couch.

My brain seems to shift, taking all of this in, not in panic, but in still-frame shots like my eyes have turned into a camera. I see the scotch-drinking suit guy, obviously dead since he's got three bullet holes in his chest, slumped over on the couch, blood pooling brightly across his white shirt.

I see the other holes in the wall and can only assume that Allie's alive because she was near the wall when the attack happened. Maybe she hadn't fully gotten into her routine, or maybe she was getting ready to drop her bra. Whatever the case, there's a bullet hole in the wall just about a foot from where she's cowering, and it's by luck or fate that she's not wounded too.

"Allie—" I start before Dominick blasts through the door that leads to his office, charging down the hall like a raging bull.

"What happened?" he yells, his face taut. "Allie?"

Dominick pushes me out of the way, rushing in the room and gathering Allie in his arms, blood and all, as he checks her over. I somehow find my voice, pointing down the hall. "He went that way. Big guy, in all black, black and cold eyes. Had a screwed-up ear."

As I speak, the security guys surround me, so fast and quiet I didn't even realize. Nick turns, his voice hot with anger. "On it, Boss."

He races down the hallway, following the direction I pointed. Shane grabs me, turning my face to his chest, where I burrow in without hesitation, needing something solid to hang on to because this is all too surreal. "I've got Meghan."

Dominick never takes his eyes off Allie, but he talks over his shoulder to Logan, the last of the security guys. "Take care of that."

Logan nods, moving closer to the suit, and Allie flinches. Dominick picks Allie up, heading toward his office, and Shane moves me quickly and steadily to the dressing room, dragging me to my locker and pulling out my backpack.

His voice is urgent but quiet in my ear. "What do you need outta your locker? Anything?"

He's shoving my wallet, my phone, my makeup, and clothes into my backpack. "What? What do you mean?"

He glances back once but then returns his attention to my locker, giving it one last scan before closing the door. It's nearly empty, except for maybe that chocolate chip muffin I brought in last week and had sort of forgotten until now.

He slides the backpack onto one shoulder before turning and looking into my eyes. "Meg, we have to go. You can't have seen what you just saw. They won't allow it. We gotta go. Now."

CHAPTER

Ten

SHANE

MY HEART'S hammering in my chest as I peek out the back door of the club, scanning the lot carefully. It's nearly deserted. The soundproofing is good and nobody heard the shots. If it wasn't for Dominick getting on the radio, nobody on security would have known.

So there isn't a panicked rush of customers running for their cars. Part of me wishes there was. It'd help cover what I'm about to do. Instead, I'm forced to lead Meghan across the parking lot by her arm in a quick walk, looking more like I'm escorting a drunk customer than helping her flee for her life.

I aim for my truck. It's closer than Meghan's car, and a lot more secure. Hitting the unlock button on my remote, I shove her in the rear seat of the crew cab from the driver's door, hopping in behind her and yanking my door closed. I'd like to be gentle, but right now isn't the time for gentleness. It's the time for action.

"Buckle up," I instruct her, and thank fuck, she listens and sits up, reaching for the belt as I start the truck. It takes all of my willpower to pull out of the lot calmly and not put the pedal to the floorboard and peel out. I know that Nick's still out here somewhere, and Logan might be around too. I can't take the risk that two guys, one of whom I trained, might react.

Right now, eyes on us is the last thing we want. The parking lot cameras are bad enough. I know Dominick's going to check the tapes when he notices that Meghan and I are gone, but hopefully, he'll be so distracted with Allie that we're far away before he does.

It's not that I don't care about Allie. She's a nice girl who I hope is fine, but I know Dom cares about her. He'd never touch a hair on her head. Meghan, though . . . I have to protect her.

Meghan is quiet, curled in on herself, with her feet in the seat and knees hugged tightly, obviously in shock as we hit the highway.

As my truck growls its way up to eighty, chewing up pavement and spitting out miles and minutes between us and what she saw, she finally settles. I watch her out of the corner of my eye, never taking my awareness off the road in front of us or the cars behind us to make sure we're not being followed. Can't be too safe.

I can see Meghan willing her mind to focus, taking deep breaths that she holds for a two-count before letting them out slowly. Still, after five miles, her body is still shaking, her hands trembling as she reaches up to adjust where the shoulder belt is rubbing against her bare neck. And when I meet her eyes in the rearview mirror, they're wide, but with a turn of my head, I can see that they're at least clear as she starts processing things. "What are we doing? Where are we going?"

I nod, shifting my eyes back to the road. "Those are great questions. And I promise to answer them, but what you really need to know right now is that I'll keep you safe. I'm taking you somewhere secure until all this blows over."

She opens her mouth to ask more questions, always inquisitive, but right now, we don't have time for her to be curious. I hold up my right hand, silencing her. "Angel, I promise. Just give me a minute to get us where we need to be."

The nickname subdues her, even as her eyebrows perk up. She's so smart. Her mind ticks along in a way that's impressed me since I first met her. But she closes her mouth, looking around as I exit the highway and head to a deserted lot on the outskirts of town, just before we get to the truck stops that mark the way west.

I pull in next to a covered car, knowing that underneath is a four-door sedan that looks like a million others on the road. That's the point. I want us to look like any other car that might be out right now, and as 'un-Shane-like' as I can get.

Grabbing her backpack from the floor, I rifle through and grab her cellphone, leaning forward to drop it to the floorboard. I do the same with mine and then grab a duffle bag from behind the seat. "Okay, when I say go, open your door calmly, get out, and get in the car next to you. I'm doing the same."

"What about our phones?" she asks, reaching forward. "Why did you put them in the floorboard? I need that."

I place a hand on her forearm, the touch electric as I feel the tremble of her muscles underneath my fingertips. "Nope. They're traceable, like my truck, and we've got to be ghosts until we figure out what's going on."

She sputters, looking at me with renewed fear in her eyes. "Traceable? Ghosts? What the heck are you talking about?"

"Go," I order. "There's time for answers later. I promise you that, but for now . . . go."

I open my door, snatching the corner of the dust cover on the sedan and pulling it back, revealing a ten-year-old Ford before grabbing the spare key from the magnetic box hidden in the rear wheel well and climbing into the driver's seat. I hit the unlock button, relieved when Meghan opens her door and buckles up, her eyes full of questions, but she keeps her silence as I start up the Ford.

Thank fuck.

With a turn of the key, we're back on the road, heading way out of East Robinsville. As we drive, the reality of the situation hits me.

Fuck. This has gone so damn sideways.

How much do I tell Meghan? There are secrets piled on top of secrets around her, and the layers go so deep that sometimes even I don't quite remember which way is up.

How much does she already know? It's common knowledge not to cross Dominick, but just how much does she understand?

She's quiet in the seat next to me, scanning around us occasionally but mostly watching the scenery blur by, but I know her silence won't last long. She's just too curious.

"Your truck?" she says after a bit, and I shrug. "What's that mean?"

"I mean that if it gets stolen, it gets stolen," I reply. "That lot's pretty out of the way. Decent chance it might be unnoticed."

"And this thing?"

"Just an old car. I promise to explain. Just wait a bit longer."

My answer silences her for a bit, and it's almost dawn when we pull over at a no-tell motel in the middle of nowhere. I know where half a dozen of these places are around the area, places that are desperate enough to take cash without too many questions but not so rundown as to become crack houses that'll attract the attention of the police.

I run inside and rent a room under a fake name, paying cash before parking and shepherding Meghan inside. Closing the door behind us, I lock it and peek out the window. We're clear.

But as I look back to see Meghan perched on the edge of the bed, so tiny but her eyes sparking with anger, I know the grace period of time I asked for is over. Hell, considering the worn-out carpet, dingy walls, and patched bed cover, I'd be pissed too, even if I was clueless about the rest.

"Okay," I start before she can say anything. "Where do we start?"

CHAPTER

Eleven

MAGGIE

I STARE AT SHANE, who's looking for the first time since I've met him less than a hundred percent sure of himself. If anything, he looks frightened, which scares the schnitzel out of me. "Okay, so we're wherever this is," I start.

I look around us, my nose upturned at the dingy motel room, noting the large crawly thing underneath the table in the corner and reminding myself not to go to sleep without covering every pore of my skin. "And seemingly safe-ish, wildlife notwithstanding. Now what the frick is going on? Why aren't we at the police station reporting a murder? Shane!"

He sighs, running a hand through his hair, and steps away from the door to sit down on the edge of the bed, still watching me with those eyes of his. "No matter how I spin this, you're likely to freak the fuck out, but you're in the middle of it now, so I'll dive in as delicately as I can."

I nod, just wanting him to tell me already. "Delicate, not delicate. Just get to the truth, Shane. I'm not following you one more step without it."

He nods and strokes his chin. "Deal. So, do you know who that was back at the club?"

I shake my head, turning to face him and criss-cross applesauceing my legs between us, needing the space to keep a clear head for this conversation. "The suit or the shooter?"

He eyes sharpen, and he sits forward, his voice immediately hardening. "Either."

I shrug, refusing to break his gaze as I stare back at his face, making sure he understands me clearly. "No idea. The suit was drinking Maclellan in my section for a bit, the expensive stuff, and he took Allie back for a lap dance. I took the scotch in and Allie was picking music in the corner. She gave me a thumbs-up, and I silently wished her luck."

"And the other guy?"

I take a deep breath, hating the fact that I have to try and relive those few moments but somehow knowing that it's important. "I saw him coming down the hallway. That guy chilled me just with this . . . I don't know . . . aura. Next thing I know, big man was shooting up the place and Allie is screaming bloody murder. You were there for the rest."

He nods, letting that sink in. "Okay, the shooter is a hired gun. Hitman. Assassin. Maybe if you tell me more, I might be able to tell you who he was. The list of men with the skills and either the guts or insanity to make a hit inside Petals is pretty small. The suit was Carlos Rivaldi, bastard son of Sal Rivaldi. Names mean anything to you?"

I shake my head, and he scoffs lightly, smiling a little. "So fucking inno-cent. Let's rewind. Meghan, you know Petals is a money laundering front for the mob and Dominick is The Boss, right?"

I squint, making sure I heard right. "Wait, Boss? Money laundering?"

Shane nods. "Boss. As in, Boss of the Angeline family."

I shake my head vehemently, but after a moment, my brain whirls. I think back to some of the customers, the business meetings in Dominick's office, and the large security team that has always made me feel safe. Petals is a small club. There should be no reason they always have three and some-times four guys working security. I thought it was because of the clientele, a sense of fancy-schmancy to make the celebs feel like VIPs.

I gasp, looking at Shane. I knew Dominick was a shrewd businessman, but the level of what I've walked into . . . did my former boss, Donnie, know when he came up with this idea for me to work undercover? Does Jeanine know? Do they even care that I'm covering stupid celeb gossip in a freaking mob club? Oh, my God, everything I've been doing suddenly seems so much more dangerous. My reporter senses felt like there was more to Petals, but something like this never even occurred to me. How could it have? It's crazy. "Dominick is The Boss? Holy frack. But . . ." My words stutter, another thought jumping forward. "Oh, no! Allie!"

Shane shakes his head. "Allie is fine. She's Dominick's. Well, she isn't, but she might as well be by the way he looks at her and I suspect feels about her. He wouldn't touch a hair on her head unless she directly betrayed him. That's why I'm confused."

"Confused about what?" I ask, the reporter in my head pushing back the fear. It's not hard. Right now, I'm pretty sure that information means life, and Shane's about my only source of more information.

"Dominick is the head of the Angeline family, who are basically mortal enemies of the Rivaldi family, even though there's been peace for years. It's been a Cold War in the area, two sides that posture and talk a lot of shit, but nobody's been willing to actually draw blood. Still, it's not like Carlos Rivaldi was welcome inside Petals. So why was Carlos in Dominick's club? The Rivaldis have their own bars, their own club. So why would he be at Petals?"

He looks to be thinking for a moment, but my mind has already begun rolling, considering angles and strategies and manipulations. It's what's given me my best stories, being able to see all the possible motivations and consequences of people's actions. "Maybe he was a spy? Or you said he's the bastard son. Maybe he's pissed at that label and wanting to stir stuff up? Or maybe someone just invited him to come check out the show and have a drink? It could be anything."

Shane rubs his jaw, his words coming slowly as he considers my comment. "You're right. Carlos could've been spying for his daddy, in which case Dominick would be pissed as fuck and could've hired the hit. There's another option though."

"What's that?" I ask, nodding when I understand a moment later. "Dominick invited Carlos."

Shane nods. "If he thought he could bring Carlos on board, it'd have changed the entire game in this part of the country. The Angelines are the big dogs by far, but it wasn't always that way, and the Rivaldis do have some pockets of power. Sal Rivaldi's getting up there in years. The issues between the two families started with Dom's daddy. If Dom and Carlos thought they might be able to forge an undercover alliance and get Sal to retire quicker, either voluntarily or the hard way . . . Daddy Sal might have heard about it, and he's not the kind to forgive treason, even from his own blood."

I swallow, feeling like I want to throw up. Down the rabbit hole, and I'm still not sure how deep I've gotten. "He'd kill his own son?"

Shane nods once, chuckling darkly. "Carlos is his bastard son. He just found out about him a few years ago and there's no love lost. Apparently, Sal had a one-night stand when he was trying to make inroads with the Colombians, and he left Carlos's mom with a souvenir."

"And he never knew?" I ask, and Shane nods.

"I don't know the full story, but apparently, Carlos just showed up, wanting his birthright and being pretty fucking aggressive about it, from what I hear. Sal ran the DNA, but not much else he could do about it."

"So either Dominick killed his arch nemesis's son, in which case, I'm guessing Sal will be pretty POed, even if he didn't like the kid. Or someone, maybe even Sal himself, sent Carlos to his death on Dominick's turf. It sounds like the beginning of a mob war," I comment and shake my head. "And I got a look at the ugly mug who did it. Great."

Shane's face pales as he looks at me. "You might be the only one who did, too. Allie was near the edge of the sofa, right? And she had blood on her chest and face, so she couldn't have seen from that angle. She'd have been facing Carlos, her back to the door. But you saw the hitman face-to-face. Could you identify him?"

I nod, biting my lip. "I feel like that's a question you should automatically say no to when you're talking mob hitmen, but yeah, I'd recognize him anywhere. That face, the squinty eyes and cauliflowered left ear . . . I could probably sketch him for you, if that's helpful. I'm not an artist, but it'd be close enough."

"Yeah, we'll see if we can get a pencil and some paper because we need to know who the hitman is so we can figure out who hired him," Shane says, sighing. "I can't believe we're talking about your sketching a hitman."

"But why can't we go to the police? They could help us," I ask, almost pleading with him, and Shane laughs harshly. "What? That's their job!"

Shane looks at me with pity in his eyes and smiles bitterly. "Both families have the police in their pockets. The only way to be a cop above Desk Sergeant in East Robinsville is to be friendly with one family or the other. If we go to the cops, we'll likely never be seen again because they'll turn us over to whoever wants us the most."

"As in?" I ask, fearing the answer even before Shane says it.

"Meaning whoever's willing to pay more for our silence. Knowing some of the cops in this town, they'd do the job for the families and might even try to collect from both of them if there's money in it."

Hating that answer and needing more, I run through the whole evening again in my head, something wiggling at me, but it's not until I see the blood spatter on Allie's favorite costume that I realize what it is.

"Hey! What about the cameras? The security? How'd the hitman even get inside without being seen? He should be on cameras all over the place. There should be all sorts of images of him, not just my memory."

Shane nods but gets up to pace the carpet. "Yeah, but that's only helpful if it's Sal's guys fucking with Dominick. If Dominick did this, he'd erase the recordings. All it takes is a single button push on his system. That'd leave him just one last loose end to clean up."

Shane gives me a pointed look, and I realize he's telling me that if Dominick is behind this, he'll want me killed. If Sal did it, Dominick won't hurt me, but Sal probably will. I'm messed up either way. "So, where does that leave us? You're Dominick's guy."

I leave the question as to whether he'll hurt me unasked, but he knows that's what I need to know. Shane walks to the curtained window and glances out before turning to me, looking at me from across the room with intense eyes that burn with . . . something.

"It's more complicated than that, but I swear to you, Meghan, I would never, ever hurt you. I work at Petals for Dominick, but I'm not in the mob, not one of his guys. I promise with my very last breath to keep you safe."

"And how do you plan to do that?" I ask, my heart pounding as the intensity of Shane's words hit me. In another light, another situation, they'd be the most romantic thing a man has ever said to me. I feel the sting of tears in the corners of my eyes, but refuse to let them loose, even though this is all so overwhelming.

Shane doesn't have the magic answer I was hoping for, instead being a bit vague. "We'll figure it all out."

For a moment, I think about telling him that it's even more complicated than he realizes because I'm not just a cocktail waitress at Petals, but an undercover reporter using the job to get stories for a celebrity tabloid. Part of me wants to tell him everything, because deep down inside, I feel this almost instinctual need to be totally honest with him.

We've danced around each other for two months to the point that earlier tonight ,we nearly kissed, despite knowing the rules. We both know that we want the other, and that the only reason he'd gotten me so angry at him earlier tonight is that he's under my skin.

But that seems minor in comparison to mob hits, and honestly, I don't think telling Shane that I've been lying to him is going to ingratiate me to him.

And I need him right now, to stay safe, to stay alive.

So I let the truth die on my lips, keeping that secret.

For now. I only pray that before this is all over, there's a chance that I can tell him the truth. Because just once, I'd like to hear him call me Maggie instead of Meghan.

CHAPTER

Twelve

SHANE

FOR A MOMENT, Meghan looks like she's got something to say, maybe something important that dances on the tip of her tongue, but with a sigh, she deflates, biting the words back, and I'm curious what she was going to tell me.

Maybe something about the shooter? Big guy, cauliflower ear. I can think of a few suspects, but I'd need more to be sure since the ear doesn't ring a bell at the moment.

Still, the look on Meghan's face. I have to know what she's thinking. Unable to stop myself, I cross the room, crouching in front of her and tilting her chin up, forcing her to look me in the eye.

"You're safe. We're okay right now."

She bites her lip, and I can see the sheen of fear in her eyes. Tears form on her lower eyelids, and I pull her to me, hugging her close. She lays her head on my shoulder as I rub up and down her back.

I hear her sobbing gently, her sniffles breaking my cold heart wide open. "I . . . I never . . ."

Nothing should make something as sweet as her cry. Ever. I lean down, bringing my lips close to one perfect shell-pink curve of an ear, and breathe deeply of her scent, which is undercut with the acrid stench of fear that still can't overwhelm how beautiful she is. "Shh, let it out. I've got you."

She quakes a few more times, burying her face in my chest as she clutches at me for a moment before taking a steadying breath, but even that sounds a bit shaky. She might have pulled herself together by sheer will, sealing over the cracks in her worldview with Scotch tape, but she's still fragile, and that tugs at every heart string I have.

As she pushes back from me, a watery smile on her face, she's trying so hard to be brave. "I'm not sure why I'm even crying. It's just a lot to take in, you know? Guess I'm a bit overwhelmed. And mad! I'm mad I didn't see what was going on when it was right there in front of my face. I feel stupid, and I'm definitely not. I was just focused on the wrong things and didn't see the forest for the trees."

Her voice is stronger by the end of her rant, her fire making me reevaluate just how fragile she is. I think she's made of stronger stuff than I gave her credit for, and the momentary breakdown was the anomaly, not her usual default when things get tough. It's an odd reassurance that her sweetness is tempered with some iron, like pretty cotton candy on a steel core.

I lay a light kiss to her forehead, comforting her, but the touch of her skin to my lips is like fire in my veins and blood rushes to my cock. "Meghan."

The heat in my voice is evident, and she looks up at me, her eyes flickering too. "Yes."

I don't need another word as I drop to my knees on the carpet, and Meghan spreads her legs as wide as her skirt will go, letting me between her thighs. I press the growing bulge in my jeans against the side of the bed, looking for any relief as I get closer to her while trying my damndest to be respectful. She just saw a shooting, had a breakdown . . . the last thing she needs is my intensity. I force myself to sit back, making my jeans tighter to the point that my cock and balls are painful, but I take a deep breath, regaining a modicum of my unraveling control. "I think Dominick does a good job of hiding the truth from those he doesn't want to see it. He's cultivated an image of being a high-class businessman, and only those who need to know the truth do. Hell, some of the guys in his organization probably don't even realize he's The Boss at the very top. That's the way he likes it. Low-key and calculated. But Meghan, I'm not lying when I call you an angel. You have no place in this mess, and I'm sorry you got caught up in it."

I didn't realize it, but I've been rubbing small circles on her thighs with my thumbs, soft and gentle but getting higher and higher.

Her breath hitches, and I can smell her arousal, like vanilla and sugar, as her muscles contract beneath my fingertips. She leans back, her shoulders thumping lightly against the wall as she bites her lip, looking down at me. "Shane?"

I force my hands to stop moving, instead grabbing hold of her thighs and squeezing her flesh with a tight grip. "Yes, Angel?"

"What are you doing to me?"

I clear my throat, but my voice still feels gravelly, rich with lust and need as I look up at her. "What I want to do is run my hands up higher, take your panties down, and bury my tongue so deep in your pussy that you scream my name the way I've been dreaming for weeks."

She lets out a mewl, her hips fighting against my hold to lift toward me. "Oh, God. I've wanted that too."

I squeeze one last time, forcing myself to let go as I roll back, my cock screaming in pain as my jeans nearly become a goddamn tourniquet. "But you already said you're overwhelmed. I will never take advantage of you. That's not how I do things. You're not ready for this, for me. Not now."

With all my willpower, I get to my knees and push to stand up, pressing a palm against my throbbing cock, hoping the attention will relieve the pressure, but it just makes me want to arch against my hand.

Meghan's mouth opens when she sees the bulge in my jeans and a little squeak sounds out from her throat. "You're . . . big."

I force myself to stay still, not giving in to the urge to release the pressure of my zipper and show her exactly how big I am, but my cock jumps anyway, desperately wanting to be closer to her mouth as she sits forward, just inches away from my crotch. She watches me, the tip of her tongue coming out to trace one plump lip, and I have to turn away. "Fuck, Angel. Don't look at me like that, all wide-eyed and open-mouthed. All I can think of right now is how much I want to slide my cock past those full, pink lips and into your hot mouth. I wonder if you could swallow me to the hilt?"

I tilt my head, watching her throat work as she swallows. "I wonder that too."

Her voice is breathy, a sex siren so damn close to making me crash on her shores.

I rub my cock through the denim once more before balling my hands at my sides, wrangling control back of my lust-addled body before I need to punch myself in the thighs. "I need—"

Meghan interrupts, her voice soft as she looks up at me. "Yes."

I smirk, wishing I could finish that sentence the way I want but knowing that I'm right, and fucking Meghan right now will only make her regret it more later.

A deep part of me says to do it anyway, fuck her and take what I want while she's willing to give it. But I'm not an animal, and if I'm going to be between her thighs, I don't want her to hate me for it tomorrow.

She'll hate me enough from all this mess. I don't need to add to my karmic bad shit list, so I hedge, turning away and squeezing my eyes shut. "I need you to take a shower, get cleaned up while I make some calls to see what the word on the street is. Then we'll sleep for a few hours. I want to be back on the road by sunset. This place . . . it won't be safe for more than twenty-four hours."

My words don't register for a split second, but when they do, her mouth closes hard enough that I hear her lips smack together, and I glance back to see her blushing, looking down and embarrassed by my denial. "Shane, this is maddening. One minute, you make me feel like the sexiest woman in the world and then you turn—"

I lift her chin again, meeting her blue eyes. "Angel, don't do that. Never, ever doubt yourself. Fuck knows, I want you, but I'm trying real fucking hard to be a good guy here and keep my promise. You . . . you deserve a good man. Not me."

She stands to study my face, her body so close to mine that my cock is straining for her. Her eyes soften, then sparkle, and I can see the sass in them before she even speaks. "Fine. I'm getting in the shower. But Shane?" She pauses dramatically, lifting to her tip toes and leaning toward me. "Nobody asked you to be a good man. And I happen to have some fantasies involving you . . . and a shower."

With that parting shot, she bites at my jawline, the stinging flash of her tiny teeth on me making my blood boil. She turns to swish to the bathroom, but I reach out, smacking her ass through the denim miniskirt.

The pop is loud in the silent room, but her cry is one of pleasure, not of pain. She glares at me over her shoulder, but I can see the spark of interest in her eyes and make a mental note of that. *Oh, Angel. You do have a little devil inside you, and those wings might not be the purest white either. Fuck me, but it makes you even sexier.*

But as the bathroom door shuts behind her, I know I can't go there with her, no matter how much we keep crashing into each other. The whisper of the shower through the door is pure torture, but with this sword of Damocles hanging over our heads on a single silken thread, I can't let myself get any more distracted by the pleasures that she offers me or the ones I could readily give to her. I can't, because I have to keep her safe. I have to get us both out of this mess. That's all this can be, or we'll both end up dead.

The fact is, even at my best, I might still end up getting us both killed, but I have to try. And I need a clear head for this. The dire thought is enough to calm my raging desires and let my brain focus on the tasks ahead. Taking a moment to at least undo my zipper and let my cock have a little bit of relief , I dig in my duffle to pull out a burner phone.

I dial Chucky, a guy who's more a tool than a friend, but someone good to have on your side. He's gotten in trouble a few times with the law and walks in that gray area where what he does can be legal or illegal simply based on whose computers he's doing it to and who he's working for. The line connects, but it's silent, as always, because he waits for you to speak. "Chucky, it's Shane. Ran into some issues at work."

His voice, high-pitched and wheezy, comes through the line like it always does. "Shane. Good to hear from you, man. Heard there was some carnage."

Chucky speaks like everything is a video game come to life, and I doubt he's ever seen actual carnage or he wouldn't throw that word around so carelessly.

"What have you heard?" I ask, not only for curiosity's sake but to know how fast and far the word's getting out. I can judge the heat on me and the severity from that.

"Heard a legacy man went down on enemy soil," Chucky replies. "That true?"

I consider how much to tell him, but I need his help, and getting information comes at a price, usually telling or confirming information. And this isn't too bad. Chucky can't use it to hamstring me. "True. Professional hit on Dominick's turf. Carlos Rivaldi."

Chucky whistles low and long, knowing that there's always a ticking time bomb between the Rivaldi and Angeline families, just waiting on the spark of ignition, which this could be. "That is a problem, isn't it, Shane? You do it?"

"No," I growl, wanting him to understand this one hundred percent. "Did you forget who the fuck I am? I had nothing to do with it. Hitman came in and out clean, and we were all chasing our tails to catch him, deal with Carlos, and get the girls out."

"Girls? What girls?" Chucky asks, and I can hear the excitement in his voice.

Shit. He didn't know about the girls yet. "Girl was in the room when the show went down, uninjured. Another was in the hallway, also uninjured. Come on, man, it's Dom's club. What did you expect?"

"Hmm, either girl see the hitman?"

Trying to appeal to his nature, I use his vocabulary. "Maybe. That's why I'm calling, Chucky. I got an innocent that needs protection, needs to disappear for a while, maybe long-term respawn."

Chucky laughs in my ear, not harshly but he's not buying it yet. "Good one, but don't bother, Shane. Just tell me."

I try again, knowing I don't have a lot of time. "Look, Dominick's keeping the dancer safe. She's his. But this other girl, she's mine. Not like *that*, but I promised her I'd keep her safe. Also, right now, other than the camera, she's the primary witness who can identify the hitman and help figure out who's behind the whole thing. I need you to see what you can find out. Let me know how much shit we're in here and if we should be hiding from Dominick or Sal or both of them. I don't fucking know."

Chucky huffs, sarcasm dripping from each wheezy exhalation. "Oh, sure, just all that. No problem. Would you like for me to get into the IRS D-base while I'm at it?"

"Please, Chucky," I beg, wondering how much more horse trading this guy's going to need. For Meghan, I'd be willing to bargain away every chip I've got, and maybe promise a few more down the line. "This is important."

Thankfully, Chucky lets me off the hook, humming for a second as I hear his keyboard clacking away in the background.

"All right, Shane," Chucky says finally. "I'll see what I can find out. But this is a big ask and a big owe. I won't forget."

I nod, even though he can't see me, relieved that he's not going into details. "I know, Chucky. Thanks."

CHAPTER

Thirteen

MAGGIE

WHEN I COME out of the shower, Shane is lying back on the bed with his eyes closed. For a moment, I let my eyes trace over him, noting the flops of dark hair he's obviously been running his fingers through, his long lashes, the soft part of his full lips, and his strong jawline. Before I can continue my perusal any lower, his eyes pop open and he catches me leering at him like a creeper. Without a word, he stands and disappears into the bathroom to clean up, giving me time to change clothes. My body's exhausted after all the stress of the night, the fear, and then having a couple of heaping doses of arousal thrown in there with it.

Still, slipping into my after work tank top and some fresh panties helps me regain some sense of normality, and despite my earlier worries, the sheets on the bed are fresh and smell like fabric softener. I promise myself that I'm going to stay awake for Shane, but I'm just so worn out, my eyelids are drooping almost immediately, and the darkness seems so inviting and unavoidable after everything that's happened.

Sometime after I fell asleep, Shane must have decided to join me in bed because when a bad dream wakes me with a barely suppressed gasp, I find myself waking up in his arms.

The dream was horrible. I was back at Petals, but this time, I was in the room ready to dance, and instead of it being Carlos in his thousand-dollar suit, it was Shane watching me with lustful eyes when the door burst open and suddenly, Shane's body exploded in bullet holes.

Still, the feeling of him holding me melts the dream away in an instant, and I relax. His bare chest is warm on my back, the big spoon to my little spoon, one arm wrapped high around my shoulders and one low around my hips. The fingertips of his left hand are just above my panty line, in that small space where my tank top always seems to ride up, but it feels good and reassures me that my dream was just that—a dream.

I wiggle slightly, pleased and comfortable in his arms. When I press my hips back, I can feel him, thick and hard against my peachy bottom, barely contained in his boxer briefs.

I bite my lip to suppress my moan, knowing I'm already wet between my legs. This fire he keeps stoking in my core had cooled to embers while we slept, but it lights to an inferno instantly as I feel him grow even larger against me.

I grind my hips back again, stroking his length between my cheeks, mimicking the lap dances I've seen the girls at the club give. It's amazing, electric to my very core, and my panties feel soaked as I part my thighs a little, still making little movements against him with my butt. But Shane stays still, sleeping through my attempt at seduction. Frack, I'm so turned on, already on the edge.

Maybe I could . . . no, not with Shane right behind me. He begins snoring softly, his breath warm against my hair. He's passed out, deep in sleep and would never know. I'll just have to be super quiet so he doesn't wake up. I know it's a risk, but maybe a quick release will help me deal with him today?

Decision made, I slowly let my fingers trace up my thigh to my center. My panties are soaked through, my clit already pulsing in need.

I rub slowly, circling clockwise and then counterclockwise, teasing myself through the cotton as I chase my own touch.

Slipping my hand inside my panties, I cup myself, sliding a thin finger inside to spread my juices up to my clit. I find a rhythm, trying to stay still, but my hips are circling against Shane, the feel of him against my ass giving me that extra spark, taking me higher.

I bite my lip, stifling my moans, already so close to coming.

Suddenly, Shane's hands tighten around me, his hips pressing forward to squeeze his cock between us. I have a split second of hope that he's still asleep, reflexively pressing against me like he did when we slept on the couch.

That hope is dashed, mortified horror taking its place as he moans, obviously awake, and his hand comes up to cup my breast, pinching my nipple. I don't know what to do, but then he growls in my ear. "Don't you fucking stop, Angel. You started this and we're fucking gonna finish it. Touch that pussy for me. Get yourself off and let me hear you come."

He grabs my wrist, pressing my palm flat against my core with his. I'm still frozen, but as he moves my hand, his fingers rub with mine against my clit in strong, hard circles. He arches against my back, stroking himself along my ass, and I give in, too far gone to stop.

"Shane, oh, my God . . . so good."

"That's it, Angel. Show me how dirty you are, rubbing your hot little pussy while you think I'm sleeping behind you. So fucking innocent. So fucking sexy." Shane grunts, his hips grinding against me in time with his finger, guiding me to his rhythm.

I gasp, thrumming at my clit faster, bucking my hips to get closer to my own touch and then to massage along his length. "Oh, Shane, I'm gonna come."

"Do it," he gasps, his cock throbbing against my ass. "Come for me. Come for me, and I'll give you the same. Get those fingers coated in your honey so I can lick them clean. Fuck, I need to see if you taste as sweet as you smell."

Every muscle in my body tenses, riding the knife-edge of pleasure, and with one more brush across my clit, I cry out, feeling myself release intensely. Shane pinches my nipple hard again, pulling on it as I cry out once more. My body shudders, riding the waves of bliss as they roll through my body.

Behind me, I hear Shane grunt, his body jerking as he pulls me tight against his hips, his cum warm through the cotton separating us. I circle my hips one last time, trying to wring out the last drops of pleasure from us both, but Shane has other ideas. He rolls me to my back, half pinning me as he props himself up on an elbow, looking in my eyes. "Give me your hand."

His fingers encircle my wrist, holding my wet fingers up for his savoring. With a smirking grin, he licks a long line up my index finger before taking it into his mouth and sucking the whole thing deeply. It makes me think of what I could do to him, and my soaked pussy quivers again. I whimper, "Shane."

He hums in appreciation and repeats the sexy move on my other fingers, his eyes gleaming with appreciation. "You do taste like sugar and vanilla, so sweet, but there's more, sexy undertones of a dirty girl. Isn't that right? Maybe you're not so innocent after all, considering you just used me to get yourself off."

My jaw drops, indignant anger racing through me. I press my leg to the side. "You did too!"

Shane smirks down at me, and I realize he's teasing as he gives my fingers a final lick before bending down to murmur in my ear. "Yeah, but you took advantage of a sleeping man, rubbing that tight ass of yours along my cock and touching your little pussy so soft and quiet, like you didn't want to wake me up. But you can wake me up like that any fucking time, Meghan."

I cringe inside, keeping my face steady. Meghan. Not Maggie. I can't believe I just basically had sex with Shane and he doesn't even know my real name. Is that weird? I've never had sex on an undercover job, and I don't know the moral code for that. Actually, we've never even had a date, and that's a new one for me too.

But Shane must see the flash of thoughts on my face because he lets go of my hand where he's been licking and suckling along my fingertips to cup my cheek. "What's going on in that head of yours, Angel? Talk to me."

I bite my lip, mentally racing through potential reactions and outcomes to telling him the truth, and still not sure if this is the best course of action. But I can't do this any longer. He's risking his life to protect me. The least I can do is tell him my real name, especially considering the rest of the lies I've told.

Apparently, there's a big web of lies and deception around us, considering the things I didn't know about Petals. But this is within my control. If it ruins me, if it ruins what I've felt building with Shane for the past few months . . . I'll have to live with the consequences. If it risks my life, that he won't want to protect me . . . I'll walk out the door and do my best to figure out what to do. At least then he'll know my real name, and if he reacts poorly, then I'll know better than to ever tell the rest of the truth.

I look down, unable to meet his eyes. "Shane, my name . . . it's Maggie, not Meghan. I didn't want to use my real name at a strip club. I'm sorry for not telling you before."

I can feel the heat radiating from his body, hear his teeth grinding, but I don't lift my eyes, flinching as he growls. "What the fuck? Maggie? You'd let me fuck you and call out a name that's not even yours?"

I gasp, looking up at him in pain. "We didn't . . . I mean, kinda, but not really."

He jumps up from the bed, his eyes flashing as he paces back and forth before turning to me, legitimately angry and hurt. "Not really? Not sure of your definition, Angel, but what we did is riding a pretty fine line of fucking. Maybe you make a habit of telling guys fake names or not caring what theirs might be, but I fucking don't."

He runs his hands through his hair, growling in frustration. I'm mad too, and flustered by his reaction as I sit up in the bed holding the sheet to my body. I'm not yelling, but I'm dang close as I form my reply. "I'm sorry, Shane. It's just been my work name for so long that I answer to it too. But I wanted you to know in case . . . well, because I don't go around having sex with guys who don't know my name."

Shane grabs his jeans from the chair, sitting down and yanking them up his legs. "Get dressed. We need to hit the road."

Feeling the shift in the room, I'm embarrassed again by his easy dismissal of me. How does he always seem to do that?

"Yes, sir!" I say with all the sarcasm I have, which is admittedly not much. It's childish, but I can't help needling him for his bossiness, the sudden urge to get out of here coming out of nowhere to escape the discomfort of the argument.

He freezes, his voice cold and commanding as he looks at me with eyes that are flashing with warning. "Don't call me that, Angel. Don't mess with things you don't understand."

I know what he's talking about. I'm innocent, not stupid, and a curiosity whips across my mind and through my body. The spanking. The promises. Now this? On the heels of my revelation is another ripple of desire.

There's still plenty of sass in my voice, though, and fiery anger sparking between us as I press him. "Sir? You don't want me to call you 'Sir'? Are you sure about that? Because you seem to like it . . . a lot."

I look down pointedly at the reawakening bulge in his boxer briefs, the dark stain of his cum making him look even bigger and sexier. He moves to stand in front of me, grabbing my hair in his hands and tilting my head up to lock eyes. "You think you want to play? Push me and see where my limits are? Trust me, girl. You'll break long before I will."

I can see the lust in his eyes mixed with wariness as he tests me, but I want to test him back, challenge his assessment that I'm some fragile, dainty little thing. I can take him. Heck, I want to feel him wild and rogue, see what he's got and maybe see if I really can handle it. "Challenge accepted . . . Sir."

I feel his fists tighten in my hair, the sharp bite keeping me present, ready for whatever he says next. "Maggie." It's just my name, but it hangs in the air between us for a moment, meaning so much to both of us before he continues. "Maggie. I think you need to apologize for lying to me."

My mouth opens to argue but snaps shut at his look. This is Shane, yes, but this is a side of him he's never shown me before, a side that I've only seen hints of.

"Good girl," he says, smiling sternly. "Don't make this worse than it needs to be. Seems like I cleaned up your fingers for you rather well, I'd say."

I nod, head still cradled by his hands. "Yes, Sir."

His eyes flash again at the word, and he hums. "I think you need to clean me up too."

My eyes drop to his dick, straining against the cotton right in front of me. "Yes, Sir."

Heck yes, I'm in for this. I've been dying to get a look at Shane's dick after feeling it in his jeans and against my back.

I grip the waistband of his boxer briefs, slipping them over the head and down his legs, and his dick springs free, gorgeous and hard, with evidence of his earlier orgasm still covering him.

I lean forward, laying kisses and licks over the red head and along the velvety shaft, tasting the saltiness of his cum and moaning in delight.

I trace my fingertips along his length, wanting to drive him wild with the light touches all over, nothing aggressive enough to get him off, just enough to tease and torture him. I hear his growls above me, and I look up with what I hope is my most innocent look.

"Fuck, Maggie. Suck me already. You're killing me."

I pause, leaving my tongue out to lick at him like a lollipop as I look up through my lashes at him, smirking. "My apology, my way."

He groans, his hips pressing forward involuntarily, seeking more contact. I give in, sucking more of him into my mouth, but instead of his dick, I choose his balls, letting his length brush along my cheek as I swirl my tongue over one, then the other.

Finally, I lick one long line from the seam of his balls up the entirety of his shaft, and at the top, I swallow him to my throat in one smooth motion. "Oh, fuck. Right there."

Shane holds my head, using my hair as leverage to keep me deep-throating him. He gives tiny little pulses of thrusts, and I hum against him, already feeling him getting close to the edge. I start to gag, and he releases the pressure on my head, letting me catch my breath before he pulls out totally. He lets go of my hair to wrap a powerful hand to his shaft, squeezing himself to stay on the edge.

"Can you do it again?" he asks, looking at me with total adoration. "Fuck, I want to watch you swallow me down, cum and all."

I nod, diving back for more, and Shane's hands tangle in my hair again. He hits the back of my throat, pushing harder, and I hum, wanting desperately to taste him again. Shane pulls back, dragging the head of his cock over my tongue one last time before slamming deep into my mouth.

From above, I hear Shane cry out, roaring for a split second before I feel rope after rope of his warm cum shooting down my throat. I swallow, gulping deeply and not wanting to lose a drop as Shane jerks and shudders, holding me tight the whole time. As he tapers off, I lick along his length, getting every last drop before I sag, all the energy wiped from my body.

Shane pulls back, cupping my face and running his thumb along my cheekbone. The sweet oxygen is like a gift, and I look up at him, knowing my victory is written clearly on my face. But his eyes are serious, something more than I'd expected hidden in their depths. "Maggie. Apology fucking accepted."

I smile shyly, pleased with his response. "Thank you, Sir." And then because I'm a dork and can't help myself, I wink at him sassily. And I'm not one of those cute gum-commercial winkers, so it probably looks like I've got something in my eye.

He laughs, kneeling down to cup my face and lay a soft kiss on my cheek. "Fuck, I really want to throw you on this bed and spend all night buried in you, but we really do need to go. It's getting late and we've got miles to roll."

I have a thought, wiggling to the surface from deep inside, that my name isn't the only thing I'm hiding from him. He might've accepted my name with relative ease, considering it's not too uncommon at strip clubs to use a fake one. But if he finds out the real depth of my lies, I'm scared that no number of apologies, verbal or on my knees, will make that okay to a man like Shane.

Fourteen

SHANE

IT TAKES us a little longer to get going than I thought. Besides Meg—Maggie and me crossing a line that I never thought we'd cross, it took me a while to locate a safe location for us to crash.

It's nearly sunset by the time I say fuck it and we hit the road, knowing that I need to get us out of the area so no one loyal to Dominick or Sal reports seeing us. I still haven't located a safe place for the medium term, but there are plenty of no-tell motels along the highways heading west.

The hardest part is that I don't know how Dominick will react to our running. Or if we show back up. He might understand us laying low until the smoke clears. Or we could be kidnapped and taken to him or Sal. Or worst case scenario, shot on sight. I'm sure that if Dom's innocent of the hit, he'd let Maggie go. Well, mostly sure.

I'm just not one-hundred percent, and that's the problem. As desperate as the situation is, or might be, I don't want to freak Maggie out too much.

Maggie. It makes me shake my head a little as we roll along the highway, the dim light hiding my movements.

I can't believe she lied about her name. Well, I can. I just can't believe I couldn't tell.

One thing I know without a doubt is that I can read people, but she somehow slipped right under my radar. In more ways than one. Without raising a single flag, she's slipped past all of my defenses.

That both irritates and intrigues me, making me want to know more, even if only so that she couldn't possibly hide anything else because I already know it all.

Know her inside and out. My cock jerks at that thought, but I talk it down, wanting to use the road time for a better purpose. I look over at

Maggie, her feet in the seat, her knees pulled up to her chest. Yesterday, I thought that position was a sign of her shock, her curling into herself, but I'm starting to realize it's just her.

It's as if she's trying to be small, non-intrusive, or even overlooked. It's as good a place as any to start with the things I want to know.

"Why do you sit like that?"

Maggie startles a little before looking at me, confusion on her face. "Like what?"

I gesture at her feet, appreciating the way it folds her up and the curve it gives her pert little ass before refocusing on the road. "All curled up. I don't think I've ever seen you sit down with your feet on the floor."

Maggie grins, shrugging dismissively. "I don't know, just always have." She pauses, her eyes flicking up and to the left as though she's remembering something. "Even when I was a kid, my mom would tell me to 'sit like a lady' and try to get me to sit up straight and cross my legs. It never worked, mostly because at my house, all the chairs were so short compared to the tables. I had to sit on my knees or something just to be able to eat dinner for a long time. Later, in school, kids were sometimes cruel."

My hands tighten on the steering wheel, even though I know what she's talking about was years ago. "Kids can be motherfuckers."

"Making myself invisible helped to keep their sights off me. Eventually, I guess it just became habit, along with being invisible. It lets me watch from the sidelines, learn things about people because they don't perceive me as a threat even if they notice me."

It's a deeper answer than I expected, and that she shared makes me happier than it should. "Angel, nothing about you is invisible, and if you ever thought you were, you were fucking mistaken. I saw you the moment you walked into Petals and have been mesmerized by you every fucking day since."

She blushes, seeming pleased, but laughs lightly. "I don't think for a second that you were watching me sling beer when there are nearly-naked women swinging on poles right in front of your face."

I laugh and glance over. "Day one—a pink backpack with a daisy hanging on it. You wore your hair down, curled, and had too much makeup. We shook hands, and I remember that you had hands that were baby smooth."

"You notice and remember a lot," Maggie says quietly. "What else?"

I smile, remembering. "You wobbled on your high heels, and the first night you were nervous, never looking at the stage once but doing a surprisingly decent job waiting tables. By the end of the first weekend, you learned to pull your hair up. It shows off your neck and makes me want to bite it, but I'm guessing it's more to do with how hard you work. You lightened up on the makeup, playing up your big eyes and assuming a young bubblegum airhead persona that is complete bullshit. The customers didn't know, but we all knew you were a smart girl. Innocent, sure, but smart as a fucking whip. And you learned how to strut in your heels perfectly, your ass swishing this way and that. Yeah, I've been watching you every damn day, Angel."

"Oh." Her voice is softly high-pitched, surprise written clearly on her face as her eyebrows raise high on her forehead. "I had no idea. I mean, I noticed you too, hard not to with your whole . . . *you* going on," she says as she moves her hands about, encompassing my whole body, "But I knew the rules and figured if you were going to break them, it wouldn't be for someone like me."

I reach across the console, grabbing a handful of her thigh and squeeze gently. "If I'm gonna break the rules, it's only gonna be for someone like you."

She bites her lip, like she's not sure what to do with that answer, the glimpse of white making me want her teeth on me, marking my chest and neck. "So, what's your story?" she finally asks, trying to get her balance back. "You usually go around playing hero? I know you don't have any tights on underneath those jeans, and there's no S on your chest."

There's interest in her lightly playful tone, but also a bit of worry, and I know she's thinking about our situation. Happy to distract her, I try to give her an edited version of my life, one that won't cause us more problems.

"Well, I guess I do have some hero tendencies, but not usually to this extreme, admittedly. My dad was a real hero. He went to Vietnam right before the US pulled out, and when he got back, he became a cop in the small town I was born in."

"Vietnam?" Maggie asks. "What, are you the youngest of the kids or something?"

"No, it took him awhile after he got back to feel he was ready to have kids. He was older than Mom too. He was almost forty and she was only twenty-six when they got married. Still, he was a good role model, taught me right from wrong, and I grew up always wanting to make him proud."

She lays her hand on mine where it rests on her thigh, holding it tenderly. "I'm sure he would be. You're definitely my hero. Maybe after all this is over, you can tell him how you saved me from a mob hit and the resulting war?" She says it jokingly, like she's trying to make the monster less scary by laughing at how ridiculous it sounds, but the underlying fear is obvious. "I'm sure he would love this story, on the run but not sure yet exactly who we're running from."

I sigh wistfully, shaking my head. "He died about five years ago. He would have liked the story, and I know he would have liked you. I tell myself he's my guardian angel now."

Without thinking, I salute the way I always do, lifting my hand from her leg to bring two fingers to my lips and then raising them toward the sky. "Thanks, Pop."

My hand goes right back to Maggie's thigh and hers goes right back on top of mine. It's comfortable, and I ponder just how strange it feels that a gesture that's only been in my life for about three or four minutes feels like I couldn't go the rest of my life without it.

"I'm sorry for your loss," she says softly, with genuine regret that she won't get to meet him. "He sounds like a great dad. What about your mom?"

I smile, keeping my eyes on the road. "She's great too. After Pop died, she didn't let it get her down. They talked about that, and they agreed that she should do what makes her happy. So she sold the house and bought a little condo in a nice building. She works as a secretary at an elementary school. She says the kids keep her young, even though she's not all that old, really. I'm one of the lucky ones." Feeling like the storyline of my history might be getting into dangerous territory, like how the son of a war vet police officer ended up working door security in a mob-owned strip club, I turn the questions back to Maggie. "What about you? What's your family like?"

Maggie's lips screw up a bit, and she hums quietly before answering. "Well, not as picturesque as yours, but they're good. My parents divorced when I was little, so I bounced back and forth between their houses, but it was an amicable divorce at least, not some made-for-TV drama deal. I see them both regularly, talk to my mom almost every Sunday on the phone."

"How'd you end up waitressing at Petals?"

I can feel her retreat, like a physical removal of her warmth even though she hasn't moved. "Oh, I've done a lot of moving around, this job and that. Waitressing is something I did when I was younger, so it seemed like a good way to make some money."

She's lying. I can tell this time, but I can't put my finger on how I know. Her tone doesn't change, her face is neutral, her body relaxed. And that worries me. This girl, innocent as she may seem, is lying, and she's good at it. Really fucking good at it.

Wanting to tease out what she's lying about, I pick at her answer, keeping it casual and teasing her a little. "This and that? Tell me, what has an Angel like you done before becoming a strip club waitress?"

She smiles, but it's her fake one, too much teeth and not enough eyes. It's a dazzling smile still, but I guess when you've made a woman come and then made her deep-throat you, you get to see a lot of what her eyes can reveal. "Well, I've been a barista, a secretary, a copy girl, a waitress, a nanny, and a personal assistant. It's not quite the Village People, but finding a construction job is really difficult at my size."

Her list sounds real and honest, and I wonder where the lie was in her previous response, thinking maybe it was something else she was lying about. Maybe it was the moving? Or the money? A lie of omission, maybe?

Before I can ask more follow-ups, she redirects us to the current problem at hand. "What do you think is going on back at the club?"

I know pressing her more isn't going to get any results, so I decide to go with the flow. "I don't know. I've got a guy looking into it for us. I'll check in with him in the morning, see what he's heard."

"You've 'got a guy'?" Maggie asks, lifting an eyebrow. "Seriously? That even sounds like we've jumped into the middle of a mob movie. How in the heck did we end up here? I mean, how'd you get in touch with this guy?"

"Burner phone in my bag," I admit. "The phone's off for now, just in case. But I'll check in, and we'll see what he's hearing back home."

She looks at me with calculating eyes, and I'm reminded once again just how smart she is and how careful I need to be with her. "So, on a moment's notice, you snatched me up, switched vehicles to a nondescript sedan that you knew would be waiting in that lot, have a duffle bag packed with at least one day's worth of clothes, cash, and a burner phone, took us to a no-tell motel, and now we're headed to another safe location, and you 'have a guy'? That about sum it up?"

Fuck. She's putting a bunch of shit together pretty damn fast, and it does sound like a fucking action movie script. Scrambling, I try to stay calm and put her on the defensive, a tactic that usually works on most folks. I laugh heartily, not taking my eyes off the road as if I'm not concerned. "Well, when you put it all together like that . . . you're welcome, Angel. You planning to say thank you on your knees too? Because that was a damn fine apology this morning."

She doesn't take the bait, sidestepping the crude, and honestly rude, comment. "Who are you, Shane? You said you're not one of Dominick's guys, not in the mob. But it sounds like . . . are you tied up in all of this?"

I grit my teeth, growling as I clench the steering wheel a little tighter and hoping it'll scare her into backing the fuck off. "All you need to know is that you're safe."

As we've talked, her curled knees had fallen loosely to her left, toward me, but at my harsh words, she pulls away. Her knees are once again clenched tight to her chest in a protective posture. She half turns away, her back mostly to me as she faces the window, her eyes unfocused as the scenery flies by.

It hurts, honestly. I was enjoying talking to her, but I need to keep her from probing in areas that she shouldn't. I realize I likely hurt her feelings, and that despite her brains and sass, she's got a vulnerable side too. Unable to reach her thigh, I rest my hand on the back of her neck, squeezing lightly, comforting and not threatening, I hope. "Maggie, you're safe, and I promise to keep you that way. That's all you need to know right now."

She doesn't answer, doesn't even acknowledge that I've spoken. I turn my attention back to the road, knowing I should give her space. Hell, I should give myself some space to figure out how to handle this, handle her.

Fuck, that doesn't even sound right. Maggie's a grown ass woman with her own mind. She shouldn't be 'handled'. She should be respected, but the situation makes my caveman instincts come out and all I want to do is protect her.

As my thoughts swirl, I leave my hand where it is, drawing small lines up and down her neck with my thumb, soothing her anger, her fear, even if some of it is my fault.

If I'm honest with myself, having her satin skin under my palm calms me too, and that's a fucking problem.

CHAPTER

Fifteen

MAGGIE

WE DRIVE FOR HOURS, only stopping for a bathroom break at a truck stop with a burger joint attached to it. We take the burgers and fries to go, along with some snacks and an odd assortment of cheap undies, a pack of socks, and some souvenir T-shirts so that I can have clothes, and keep driving. It's quiet for a long time, neither of us willing to give in to the stalemate.

He hurt me, and he knows it. I can feel his remorse, but I'm not ready to forgive and he hasn't apologized. Eventually, Shane turns on the radio and music fills the car. It's nothing much, just the regular late-night stuff you get on Top 40 stations, some slow songs mixed in with oldies and a few tunes for the young lovers who might want some mood music. After a bit, I hear him humming along with an old Green Day song, even singing softly under his breath. It's nice. I can tell he has a good voice, deep and mellow with a raw emotion to it that tells me he actually knows this song.

As the chorus begins, he gets louder, and I look over at him, enjoying the mindless way he's getting into it. It feels like a peek into the real him somehow. Without saying anything, I join in, singing along with the radio and Shane, a trio of voices filling the car.

"I've never heard anyone out-sing the original," I say as the guitar music fades and I wonder if September ever really is going to end for us. "You're pretty good." It's an olive branch, making the first move to break the silence between us and I'm curious if he'll take it or shut me out again."

Shane looks over at me, a small smile tilting the corners of his lips. "Dad loved this song. He always thought that even though it wasn't written about the 9/11 bombings or the Iraq war, that it spoke to him. He never was into what we did there."

"But he was a cop."

Shane nods, shrugging. "Dad was more *Andy Griffith* than *Criminal Minds*. He was the cop people came to for advice, the cop who'd walk into a domestic disturbance without his gun and get everyone calmed down. He always told me that he saw too much of the evil men could do to each other in Vietnam and he didn't want to add to it. So the first time he heard that song, it stuck with him."

It's not a truce. There are too many questions unanswered for that. But it's a pause on the inquisition, a recognition that whatever is going on and whoever he is, we can sing along as we run. And that there's something between us, something building. It doesn't have to be adversarial. Goodness knows, we've all got secrets, and maybe I shouldn't judge him too harshly considering the one I'm still holding close to my heart.

By dawn, we pull over to check into another sketchy motel. Shane apologizes for the seedy accommodations as we pull in, explaining why. "Folks around here aren't as likely to remember us and definitely aren't as likely to talk. They don't want anyone or anything putting attention on their own lives."

"Whatever. I just need a clean bed, not a five-star fancy place," I reply, trying to put a positive spin on things. "So, I guess no free continental breakfast?"

Shane laughs. "We'll be in bed during breakfast hours anyway."

My thoughts flash back to this morning in bed and how Shane and I had sex . . . kind of. Wow, was that just this morning? It seems so long ago, time both speeding by like a rocket and dragging like my ass after an all-nighter.

Once we're in the room, Shane pulls the curtains closed and then plops on the bed, lying back and closing his eyes as he stretches out. "You can take a shower first. I gotta work this tightness out of my back before I do anything."

He looks yummy as a bowl of peanut butter fudge, and I long to lick the sliver of his abdomen that shows where his shirt rides up. But I haven't forgotten his earlier words, even if we have ridden in relative civility for the last few hours. "Call your guy."

He opens one eye, giving me a semi-amused, semi-angry look. "No."

I cross my arms over my chest, giving him all the glare that I can muster. Which, considering the difference in our sizes, probably isn't much, but by gosh, I'm gonna try. "Call. Your. Guy. Find out what's happening back home."

I can see that he's trying to think of an argument to get out of this, some way to reason with me, but he settles on being an ass.

"No. Take a shower. I'll call, and we'll see what he says."

Knowing that sometimes, retreat is the finest form of strategy, I acquiesce. "Fine."

Grabbing the micro-sliver of cheap soap off the vanity and missing even the luxury of tiny bottles of cheap shampoo and conditioner, I stomp into the bathroom, closing and locking the door before turning on the water. Instead of stripping off my clothes, though, I put my skills and my strategy to use, listening intently at the door.

I hear Shane dig around in his bag, and then an unmistakable start-up song as he turns the burner phone on. I can only hear his side of the conversation, but it's enough for now. "Hey, Chucky. What do you got for me?"

There's silence for a moment, and I assume Chucky must be giving Shane some type of update. "So, he's a ghost? Probably wishful thinking to hope he left town straight from the job. What about us? Heard anything about my girl, Ma–Meghan?"

A zing goes to my heart when he calls me that. His girl. I like that, even if I know there's more to him than meets the eye. He's hiding something, but at his core, he's a good guy. I'm sure of it.

His girl. It makes me smile.

My sweet musings are abruptly stopped when I hear Shane start cursing. "Fuck. What the hell should we do then? She's got people who are gonna fucking notice if she goes missing."

Missing? I think back to our conversation in the car and wonder again if Shane is a mob guy. I try to think it through. Is he lying about being Dominick's guy?

If so, why would he run with me? Or maybe he's not running *with* me? Maybe he's kidnapped me for Dominick and is making it seem like I need to run so that I'm a cooperative and stupid victim?

But to what end? If Dominick wanted me dead, Shane could've done that multiple times already. We've been driving on some lonely stretches of highway, and he could've dumped my body along any of them and I likely wouldn't have even been found.

Or he could be Sal's guy? Protecting his boss, or heck, maybe taking me *to* his boss?

But Shane has been protective. I at least know that and truly believe that's real. He wants to keep me safe, not turn me over to a mob boss to be handled like a witness in some B-grade movie. He's even bordered on the near-obsessive sometimes, not allowing me to go into the convenience stores at gas stops without him escorting me, even if it's just to pee.

No, I don't think Shane's a gangster, even if he's worked for gangsters. There's more going on, and I'm going to have to stay on my toes since Shane is hiding what that is, but I trust him. Lord help me, I'm listening to my gut and heart more than my brain, but that's what I'm going with.

I hear him wrap up the call with Chucky and quickly hop in the shower, wetting my hair and scrubbing my body as fast as possible. Luckily, the soap is barely better than rubbing sand all over my skin and I've got plenty of reasons to hurry it up. As I emerge from the steamy bathroom, Shane walks past me, his face hard, jaw clenched.

I open my mouth to say something, not even sure what, but he simply shuts the door in my face and I hear the water start back up again for his shower. I pull on the same tank from last night and clean panties and sit down on the bed, fighting the urge to lie back on the scratchy sheets. "Not this time," I promise myself softly. "I have to stay awake. We have to talk. There are too many questions that need to be answered."

It takes Shane awhile, though, and I'm lying down by the time the bathroom door opens. Shane is quiet, tip-toeing to put his clothes over the chair before carefully sliding into bed behind me. Still, he can sense the tension in my body as he lies down, and he props himself up to whisper, "You awake?"

I turn to face him, curling up on my side as he lies on his back. "Yes. What did Chucky say?"

He looks down at me, his smirk visible even in the low light, that amused glint back in his eyes. "Who?"

"Stop jerking me around," I reply. "You know who."

"Were you eavesdropping, Maggie?"

I growl at him, sounding more like a kitten than the tiger I'd prefer. "Well, what did you expect? You're not telling me anything. Two days ago, I was a waitress minding her own business. Today, I'm on the run from the fudging mob—oh, excuse me, *mobs*. Or what is the proper term?" I say, emphasizing the 's' to illustrate just how crazy my life has become in the last forty-eight hours. "And you're hiding stuff from me. Yeah, I eavesdropped. I'm furious. I'm . . . scared."

My voice cracks, the fire snuffed out by the cold fear in my heart. Shane grimaces, like my anger and fear physically hurt him. "Come here, Angel."

He pulls me to him, pressing my head to his chest as he wraps his arms around me, holding me tight, grounding me to him. "Don't be scared. I've got you, and I'll keep you safe."

"You keep saying that, but I don't even know what or who you're keeping me safe from," I reply, even as my body says it doesn't care about all that, the comfort of having Shane hold me telling my traitorous body everything it needs to hear to relax. But I still talk, demanding even. "Tell me what Chucky said."

Shane lays a light kiss to the top of my head. "Not too much, actually. Hitman is in the wind. They figured out who it was without your input. Dominick knows we're gone, and he's pissed and is trying to track us down. But Chucky doesn't know if it's because he wants to protect us or kill us. Dom's playing this very, very close to the vest, which is his style."

I fall silent, trying to take it all in. I know there are more questions to be asked, and I want to be strong and fierce, but this is so far above anything I've ever experienced it's crazy. My brain's being overwhelmed. I just want to go back to the way things were. My boring life was safe. Secure.

I break down, tears trekking silently down my cheeks, pooling on

Shane's chest. He rolls us, my back hitting the bed as he holds himself on his elbow beside me, his thigh on top of mine, splitting my legs.

He swipes at my tears with a gentle thumb, his voice soft but still strong. "Don't cry, Angel. I know this is a lot, but it's gonna be okay."

I know my eyes are glossy with tears, my face flushing as I try to stop the torrent. "Ugh, I'm sorry for crying. I swear I'm not such a baby. Usually I never cry, but this is all so . . ."

"It's fine, Angel. It's your emotions needing an escape. The fear, the nerves, the . . ." He stops and I wonder what other emotion he was going to list because I've got a few in mind. Desire. Need. Hope.

Instead of continuing his list, Shane leans down, catching a tear with his tongue as it streaks down my face before kissing the trail away.

He lays more kisses along my cheeks, moving down to gently kiss my jawline and then my neck. I can feel the shift in him, going from comforting caresses to heated desire, and it awakens the same lust in me.

He talks into the curve of my neck, sending warm shivers through my chest and down my spine. "Your tears are salty, but here . . ." His tongue sneaks out for a lapping touch of my skin. "Here, you're sweet. So very sweet, Angel. It makes me wonder what you taste like all over."

I whimper, his words amping up my desire, bringing my focus to him and him alone, the rest of the world and my fears fading away. I need this, this release from the fear, release from the worries. For that, I need him. The wolves are out there, hunting us, and we don't even know why.

Shane isn't telling me everything I should know about him, and I haven't been honest with him either.

But right now, I don't care. Secrets, lies, risks, fear . . . they all slip away in his arms.

CHAPTER
Sixteen

SHANE

FEELING MAGGIE whimper under my tongue, the sound echoing in my ear, is pure liquid desire and heat being poured into my body. If I were a car, it's a shot of nitro and my engine's ready to tear up the pavement, but I hold back. I want more of those throaty sounds from her, want to make her moan and scream my name.

I know that we shouldn't, not in the middle of this shitstorm. She's going to regret this later, regret me and probably hate me. But I'm a fucking selfish man, and if she wants this now, wants me to make her forget everything else for a little while, I'm going to fucking make her forget it all.

It's cheap medicine for reality, but it'll work. The side effect is that I'm going to make it so that even after this is all done, she is mine, marked body and soul. Then again, I'm pretty sure that the reverse is true, that I'm going to be marked by her as well. A small price to pay for having an honest to God Angel.

I roll onto her, forcing her legs wide around my hips as I press my cock to her pussy and cage her in with my arms. I can feel the heat from her pussy, the thin cotton the only thing between us as I kiss her neck and tug at her ear with my teeth.

She reaches up, her little nails leaving pink lines where she scrapes my arms, tugging me toward her. I lower my body, covering her lips in a searing kiss that leaves us both panting. She looks at me, her eyes full of want and fear and pain and more.

Grabbing her hands, I push them to the bed above her head, her back arching beautifully to press her full tits toward me. "Angel, tell me to stop and God help me, I will. But if you'll let me, I'll make it all better, even if only for a minute. Let me make you forget."

Her eyes are sparkly, the tears replaced with heat, lust, and need. Her voice is breathy, but I hear her clearly regardless. "Yes, Shane. Yes."

That's all I need to unleash the last of my personal restraints, knowing that I'm going to give her everything she wants. I kiss her again, fast and hard, my mouth claiming her perfect lips hungrily before I move along her neck, dipping down to her chest.

Her nipples are hard beneath her tank top, and I take advantage, taking one then the other into my mouth through the thin cotton to suck and bite at her. This poor shirt's going to have to go in the trash. I've stretched it out so much, but that's okay. I'll tear the damn thing to rags if it makes her happy.

She gasps, arching into me once again. I release her hands, yanking the straps of her tank down her arms, freeing her tits to my hungry eyes before pinning both of her tiny hands with one of my larger ones.

"Fuck, Maggie," I rasp, taking in the sight. I hadn't seen them yesterday, only felt their soft weight in my hand as we dry-humped, but they're perfect, soft and full and delicious looking. "Look at these pretty nipples, all pink like candy, making me want to eat you up."

"Please, do . . . all you want," Maggie says, and I remind myself again that maybe she knows, but she may not, just how intense her words are to me.

I lower my head to take her nipple into my mouth, swirling my tongue around again and again to drive her wild before finally sucking her deep, swallowing and feasting on her succulent body.

She cries out, begging for more. I keep suckling her, back and forth between her right and left, as her hips buck beneath me, asking desperately for attention and rubbing along my hard cock.

But her moans are getting sharper, and I lift my head up to look into her unfocused eyes, challenging her. "Are you gonna come just from me sucking on your tits?"

She shakes her head, lifting her hips to grind against me. "More," she begs, but now that I know how close she is, I want to see this up close. "Please."

I lower myself down, but this time, I keep my eyes on her face as I swirl my tongue around her nipple and she picks up her head to watch me.

"You like watching me lick you?" I ask, teasing her nipple lightly. "A voyeur?"

Her eyebrows pull together, her eyes locked on my mouth. "Or maybe . . ." I murmur before I grab her nipple between my teeth, biting just hard enough to keep it in my mouth as I pull, blending a sharpness with the pleasure to see how rough she likes it.

"Ahhh!" she cries out as her head falls back. I know she's on the edge, needing just a bit more to get there.

"Or maybe if I suck hard enough, the pleasure will shoot right down to your empty pussy, clenching on nothing and wanting my cock so damn bad that you can't help but come. Let's see."

At the same time, I pinch her left nipple between my fingertips and suck her whole right areola and as much pale skin as I can into my mouth, drawing hard and deep. I grind against her soaked pussy, thrusting my hard cock to slide over her clit through her panties, pushing her over.

Maggie bucks wildly, crying out as her orgasm washes through her, and I have an up-close view of her face as the bliss overtakes her.

It's the most beautiful thing I've ever seen. Her fingers clench on my arms before going totally straight, her body shaking uncontrollably like a guitar string. She's still shuddering, her eyes closed as I release her hands, moving down her body. I pull the tank over her hips and off, tossing it to the floor before focusing on the soaked mess of her panties.

I trace a light touch through the moisture, pleased that it's because of me, that I did that to her. "God, I'm hungry for your taste again. So sweet, and so dirty for me. Lift your ass for me, Angel."

The meaning of my words hits her hard, and she stops, fresh heat in her eyes as she lifts her ass just like I commanded. I pull her panties down and off too, my cock surging so hard I nearly come just from the evidence of her first orgasm and the anticipation of what I'm going to get when I lick every drop of it until she coats my mouth with her second.

I press her thighs open wide, hovering so she feels my breath, and look up at her, my voice a throaty growl of need. "Tell me, Angel. Tell me what you want."

She squirms beneath me, wordlessly lifting her hips toward me. I shake my head, pinning her hips with my hands, and blow a hot, open-mouth breath across her lips, knowing she's watching me tease her. "Say it."

"Lick me, Shane," Maggie says, spreading her knees out wider and mewling her need. "Please."

I raise an eyebrow at her, moving toward her inner thigh, right on the crease of her center, and licking a slow line with the flat of my tongue, watching as she jumps. "Here?" I ask before doing the same thing to the other side. "Or maybe here?"

She groans in frustration, and I have mercy, giving her the words. I trace her lips with the tip of my tongue before looking up again. "Tell me, '*Lick my pussy, Shane*' or maybe, '*Suck my clit.*' Tell me what you want, Angel. Unleash the dirty side of you, and I'll give you everything."

Her voice is stronger than I would've thought, need giving her power as she mimics my words, looking at me with a sexual energy that has me breathless. "Lick my pussy. Suck my clit, Shane. Make me come all over your mouth. Make me your Angel."

Fuck me, hearing those dirty words come out of my sweet girl's mouth is almost enough to make shoot my load into the bed I'm grinding against, but I manage to fight it off, needing to give all I have to her.

I growl, diving in and running a flat tongue from her entrance up to her clit, repeating it again and again as I watch her. I pay attention, stroking her pussy just the way she likes, switching when she needs it, and giving her everything she wants. She's frozen, her body rigid, hands full of the bedsheet, and her mouth dropped open in an 'O' of pleasure as her tongue curls up in her mouth.

When I focus on her clit, I thrash my tongue across it, fast as a fluttering hummingbird's wing, and she squeals, her voice high and tight, she's so close again. "Oh, God. Shane, don't stop! I'm coming."

I pause just long enough to look up at her, demanding. "Give it to me, Angel. Come all over my mouth so I can drink down your sweetness."

I press her hips down, not letting her move an inch and ravishing her clit with my tongue. It's only seconds before she shatters, crying out above me as her body shudders, her pussy getting wetter with each spasm. I clamp my lips over hers, drinking her honey and swallowing every delicious drop. She's heady, a liquor that I've never imagined before. It makes the world disappear, leaving me with just her while at the same time energizing me. My cock strains even more with every moan of satisfaction Maggie gives me as I sweep over her sensitive skin.

She collapses against the bed, spent as I pull away and sit up. I consider for a second that she might be done, not able to take more after coming twice so hard.

Instead, she inhales deeply, smiling and opening her eyes. She looks hazy, satisfied, but at the same time playful. Somehow, I've tapped into an inner well of sexual energy that maybe nobody's ever seen, and here's the innocent vixen that I've known she's had inside her all this time.

Maggie sees the need on my face and sits up, kissing my lips tenderly. "Now it's your turn . . ." she murmurs as she reaches for my boxer briefs, pulling them down to let my cock free.

"Oh, fuck, Angel," I gasp as she wraps a soft hand around me. "See what you do to me?"

Maggie looks down, gasping softly and looking surprised at my size, like she hasn't already sucked me off. "Oh, Shane," she says breathily.

I help her lie back before drawing my head through her folds as I squeeze tight at the base my shaft, staving off the orgasm that's already drawing too close. I rub the tip of my cock over her clit before pausing at the entrance to her pussy. "I'll try to be gentle, Maggie. I don't want to hurt you, but I'm on the fucking edge."

"Don't you dare," Maggie says, grabbing my forearms. "I'm not that fragile, remember? You won't break me."

"I might," I rasp. There's more honesty in those words than I'd like to admit, but if she wants to take me, I can't hold back. I drive into her with one thrust, balls-deep, and she cries out as I grab her thighs, pulling her hard to me. It takes all of my willpower to freeze, letting her adjust and trying not to come from the tight grasp she has on me. "Fuck, Maggie. You're so damn tight."

She smiles, her voice cracking as the pain and pleasure mix for her. "Or you're just big. Really . . . big."

"You okay?" I ask, giving her a few tiny thrusts, testing to see if she can relax a bit but bottoming out deep inside her.

She moans, biting her lip as her head drops back, and I can feel her pussy walls already quivering around me.

"Damn, Angel," I half tease, my cock throbbing as she clenches me hard, her body massaging my cock even though I'm not moving. "Are you coming on my cock already?"

She nods, crying out as she begins to squirm on the bed, moving back and forth and fucking herself on my cock. I hold myself still, looming between her thighs, watching as she takes my cock, disappearing inside her and coming back out coated in her cream. It's the sexiest thing I've ever seen.

Her energy gives out, the orgasm depleting her, and I take over. Rolling her legs up until I can wrap my hands under her arms, I grab her shoulders for leverage.

I pound into her, pulling and pushing her tiny body under mine and using her pussy to jack myself off as I bury my face in the curve of her neck.

Sucking the tender skin into my mouth, I mark her, needing proof that she's mine, even if only for this moment. Maggie's crying out, holding onto my neck as I drive her harder and harder, my hips slamming against her and shaking the whole bed.

"Shane! Please, come. I need you to come," she begs. Her voice drops off. Her brain's so overloaded that all she can do is moan wordlessly even as her pussy squeezes me even tighter.

Anything my Angel wants, I'll give her. With a roar, I explode, my cock pumping jet after jet of hot cum deep inside her, triggering her once again, and her walls flutter, milking me. She cries, no words possible for either of us as we're both destroyed and remade in the energy of this bonding.

We ride out the waves together, finally crashing to the bed spent. I lift up, not wanting to crush her small frame with my heavy ass, but she pulls me back down, snuggling beneath me.

I chuckle lightly, not wanting to move, not wanting to disturb my still semi-hard cock inside her. "You sure I'm not smothering you? Can you even breathe?"

In response, she takes an audible breath and blows a weak raspberry against my neck. "Yes, I can breathe. It smells like you, manly and salty and sexy."

I bury my face in her hair, feeling a wide smile overtake my face. "Well, you smell like cupcakes and sugar. Is that just you? Or do you buy special soap that makes me want to eat you all the time?"

I move to nibble at her earlobe and she giggles. "A lady has to keep some secrets to maintain an air of mystery."

She says it lightly, teasing, but a beat later, even as we're still connected as one, the reality of the secrets we are both keeping presses down heavily. We both pause, and I pull back to look at her face.

She lied to me about her name. She's probably lying to me about why she's working at Petals, and fuck knows, I'm lying about shit.

But for a moment, we escaped. Just the two of us . . . until reality crashed back in like it always does. We release each other, both of us needing a moment now, and I quietly roll off her to grab a washcloth from the bathroom. Running it under the warm water, I clean myself before coming back with another fresh cloth for Maggie.

I wipe her down, letting her know that while I've still got issues, there's something that I don't want to let go of between us. She watches me silently, her face promising me things I'm not ready to trust just yet, but I want to. When she's all clean, I toss the rag toward the bathroom door before lying down. I feel like that rag, wrung out and used, and I imagine Maggie feels the same way.

"Come here, Angel."

She scoots closer to my open arm, curling against my side like a kitten and placing her head on my chest as I hug her to me. We might be hiding things, but right now, we both need comfort. And I can give that to her. I'll give her anything.

Her voice is a whisper, but there's steel in it, her bravery shining through, even in the face of a problem she never imagined she'd face. "Shane? What are we going to do?"

I squeeze her tighter and kiss her temple softly. "Right now, we're going to sleep. We'll figure out the next step this afternoon."

She sighs softly, and in moments, I feel her relax, drifting to sleep. I lie awake, though, mentally running through every scenario, every possible outcome, the risks of each making me tense.

We're going to have to trust someone, but if we choose wrong, it'll likely be the death of both of us.

CHAPTER

Seventeen

MAGGIE

IN WHAT'S STARTING to feel habitual, I wake up curled against Shane's side, my leg slung over his and my head nestled on his chest and shoulder. It feels right, comfortable. Safe. I snuggle in deeper, and he stirs, pulling me tight and lifting my hand to his mouth to lightly kiss my fingertips. "Morning, Angel. Well, evening, I guess."

I lower my hand to rub his chest. "What are we thinking today? Drive all night, eat crap food, and then sexercise ourselves to sleep?"

Shane cups my chin in his hand, lifting it toward him. "Sounds like fun, but we'll have to see. First, a kiss. Second, we need to hit the road. We slept in, so just a kiss."

He winks at me. I know a kiss between us could easily turn passionate and keep us in this bed all night, but we likely do need to get a move on. I don't know if Shane's burner phone could be tracked, but sitting around probably isn't the best idea.

I scoot up the bed slightly to reach him with puckered lips, but he pulls me astride him in one quick swoop instead. I gasp, laughing a little. "Whoa . . . hey! You said a quick kiss."

My center brushes against his washboard abs, and I can't help but circle my hips a little, the warm prodding of his morning wood standing proud behind me giving me naughty thoughts, even if it is late afternoon. "This does not feel like a quick kiss."

Shane mock-growls, pressing his hips up into me and adding to the sensation as his stiffy nestles between my cheeks and we both hum happily. "I didn't say quick. I said a kiss."

He's teasing, but the gravel in his voice sends jolts to my core. I swirl my hips again, letting him feel the heat and wetness he's building in me, and the tingle runs up my body to make me whimper. Shane grabs behind my neck, pulling me down to meet his mouth in a punishing kiss, his tongue licking along the seam of my lips, demanding entry.

With a moan, I grant him access, twisting my tongue with his, needing more. Forget the time. Forget the miles we need to roll. Fifty miles or whatever aren't going to make a huge difference. What is going to make a difference is the huge hardness pressing against my butt that I need inside me again. I lift my hips, trying to impale myself on his dick, but he stills my movements with strong hands on my thighs.

Breaking our kiss, he looks up, his chest heaving in the space between us. "Fuck, Angel. You're killing me. We really do need to leave. Tonight, I promise."

I whimper, hips pumping in the air as I try to push back. I can nearly feel the heat of his head against my lips. "We can be fast."

His dick jumps at my words, the tip touching my soaked lips, and we both groan. "Shane."

I'm pleading, something I would swear I'd never do, but right now, I need him filling me more than I've ever wanted anything.

With a growled curse, he pulls me down hard, sliding into my wet core easily and pumping fast and deep. "You want my cock, Maggie?" he asks in between each hard thrust. "We're in fucking danger. You get that, right? But all you want is my cock, isn't it?"

I throw my head back, my nails digging into his chest leaving little half-moons where I grab for purchase. I drop my hips in time with him, our bodies meeting in slaps that shake me to the very center of my body. "God, yes. Shane, fill me up. I want it."

I want it . . . and I want so much more. I know we're not being logical, and I'm normally a very safe girl.

But any concerns I might have are obliterated as Shane smacks my ass hard, the sound ringing out in the quiet room. "Such a bad girl. I said a kiss and look what you've done to me, Angel. I can't help but give you everything you want."

I cry out, the thickness inside me and the heat on my ass getting me so close to the edge. "I love being bad. With you. *For* you. You just feel so good inside me . . ."

The honesty in my words make Shane surge even harder, thicker. He thrusts powerfully, slamming deep in my core and I cry out. "Ahhh . . . Yesss . . ."

Shane groans. "That's it. Show me how your good girl pussy can take me like a bad girl. *My* bad girl."

It doesn't take long, my cries mixing with Shane's continued dirty words until I scream, clamping down around his hips. "I'm coming . . . God . . . Shane!"

Shane jackhammers into me, holding my hips still and forcing me to take his punishing thrusts as I spasm in his hands, the waves washing over me. "That's right, come on my cock. Squeeze that tight pussy and milk me. I'll give you everything you want."

I tense my muscles in time to his strokes, and he groans, losing the rhythm as I feel his hot cum filling me. I take over, slowly rolling my hips up and down to take him, coating him with a mixture of our orgasms and pulling every last drop from him as he shudders. It's warm, intense, and I feel emotions bubbling up inside me even as I feel the first drop of his cum squeeze out of my pussy to roll back down his shaft.

I lean forward, pressing our chests together, and Shane surprises me with another smack, to my other cheek this time. I wail in surprise, my muscles clenching against him once more.

Shane chuckles darkly, his eyes sparkling. "Mmm, I'll have to remember how tightly you squeeze me when I spank you, but we really do need to go."

I grin down at him, happy I got my way and knowing he got his way too. I give him a soft kiss, stroking his face and nodding. "Okay, let me rinse off and we'll go."

He grabs a handful of my mess of hair. "Oh, no, Angel. Bad girls don't have time to take a shower. You're gonna ride in that car all night, feeling me between your legs, knowing that cum you so desperately wanted is deep inside you. That you're marked by me."

He runs his thumb along my neck, and though I haven't looked in a mirror since our session last night, I can feel that there's a heck of a hickie glowing on the pale skin there. It makes me tingly inside, proud that he wanted such a visible sign of what we did.

I smirk, running my fingertips along the claw marks on his chest, knowing I'm not the only one marked. "All right, Bad Boy. But then that goes for you too. You're gonna have my scent all over you tonight too."

He grins, wiggling his hips and sending another little tingle through me. "Maggie, I would happily smell like your sugar anytime you'll let me."

The sweetness of the moment is short-lived because as we head out to the car in the golden setting light, I see a familiar face heading our way. Pulling hard on Shane's hand, I point. "Shane, that's the hitman."

Shane follows my finger, seeing the large guy who has already spotted us. We duck and try to make our way through the cars in the lot, shuffle-running toward ours as fast as we can.

No luck, though, as the window in the car next to us shatters violently. "Get down!" Shane yells, shoving me to the ground. The rough pebbles bite against my palms and against my cheek, but that's nothing compared to the fright racing through my body as I scramble behind a tire, hoping I've got enough to protect me.

Seeing that I'm listening, Shane pulls a gun out of his waistband at his back. *What the 'fridgerator?* I didn't even know he had a gun! Has he been carrying that thing this entire time and I just didn't notice?

Popping his head up from between the cars, Shane aims toward the hitman and fires, his shot much louder than the first. Shane fires off three more shots and I hear glass breaking again. "C'mon!" Shane growls, grabbing my hand and pulling me up, placing it on his waistband at his back, right where the gun had been.

He starts to walk carefully but quickly, leading me toward our silver sedan as his head stays on a swivel, scanning in the direction of where he shot. *Pffzt . . . pffzt . . .* two shots whizz by us from behind, more air whooshing than a bang, and somewhere in my head, I realize the hitman has a silencer on his gun while Shane's is ringing loudly as he fires back again.

We sprint, reaching the car in a second that feels like an eternity. Shane yanks the passenger door open and shoves me in, still looking for the hitman. "Stay down."

It's silent for a few seconds that feels like forever, until the driver's door opens and I see Shane again. I start to sit up when I hear the *pffzt* sound once again and Shane grunts. "Fuckfuckfuck."

"What happened?" I ask, but Shane just slams his door, jamming the keys in the ignition before peeling out.

From the floorboard, I stare at Shane, who seems angry, but in control, nowhere near the basketcase-in-shock that I currently am. "Shane?"

His eyes cut from the rearview mirror to the road in front of him twice more before he looks down at me. "You okay? Are you hit?"

I shake my head, wanting to get up but afraid to move from my protected little hole. "No. I'm okay, but what—"

He takes a turn fast, throwing me toward the door, and then another, throwing me forward into the seat, where I plant my hands. His eyes flick their circle again, rearview mirror, front windshield, then me. "You can get in your seat now. Buckle up."

I quickly do as he says, immediately looking out the side mirror behind us. "Is he following us?"

"No, I don't think so. Not right now, at least. But we need to ditch this car."

I've been undercover for stories before and have experienced a lot of stuff, but nothing like this. I feel like I'm in a freakin' action movie, like somewhere along the way, I got mixed up in something way above my pay grade. But I refuse to be the too stupid to live girl who always ends up dead or causing the hero to die because she's running around like a chicken with her head cut off, panicking at every turn.

I take a deep breath, letting my brain click into the reality my life has become. On the run from the mob, with a hitman chasing us down. Heck, I think I've even seen this movie before. The joke falls flat, even in my own brain. With another breath, I realize . . . okay, I can do this.

"Ditch the car? That means we need another one. Do you happen to have another one hidden around here?"

I say it without humor, totally serious and honestly curious considering I don't know how well-prepared Shane was for all this, but Shane laughs bitterly. "No. Don't have another handily stashed unfortunately."

"Okay, we need a shopping center," I reply, thinking quickly back to a stakeout I did once for a story. "An old one where the security won't have been updated. We can steal a car from the lot and not be caught on camera."

Shane looks at me, lifting an eyebrow. "Done this before, have you? Got a juvenile record you don't like to tell people about?"

"No, but it stands to reason," I reply, trying to sound nonchalant about it. I look up and down the streets around us. We're not on the highway but close enough that there are plenty of little strip malls nearby. "There. Turn around."

Shane hangs a U-ey in the street, turning where I indicate, and we pull into the parking lot of a strip mall that looks like it might be on its last legs. There's a bail bonds shop, a Greyhound bus station, a tattoo parlor, a pizza delivery place, and four empty storefronts that look like gaps in teeth. Down the street, I see a newer, fancier looking mall that's probably the reason for this mall's downfall.

He drives across the back row, parking the sedan and turning to me. "Okay, the blue truck beside you," he says, nodding toward a twenty-year-old Dodge that's got a 'For Sale' sign in one window but not too much dirt otherwise. "I'll come around, bump it, and then you're going from this car, through the driver seat of the truck to the passenger side. Put your backpack on and I'll take the duffel bag. Got it?"

I nod.

Shane gets out, and I see a smear of dark wetness on the seat where he was sitting. If it was a white seat, I'm sure it'd be red. Oh, my gosh, he's hit, and he didn't say anything. Anger and fear war in my gut, but I know that leaving his blood here is a bad idea, especially so visible to anyone passing by the car. I reach over, wiping it off with the sleeve of my shirt. It's not much, but at least it turns into a sort of icky streak that'll dry to a dark black soon enough.

Shane knocks once on the window, and I open the door, hopping into the truck. Thankfully, the truck has a bench seat and I slide over easily, buckling up as he does the same. He leans over, hissing only slightly under his breath as he fiddles around with the wires for a moment while I try to keep myself unseen.

"Come on, you son of a bitch," Shane grunts, and a moment later, the engine turns over. It's sluggish at first before catching, and Shane sits up, letting out a hum of satisfaction, but there's a hint of pain mixed in from the movement. "Okay. Let's go."

It's a little surprising when we pull out of the lot casually, not speeding to draw attention, and merge back with traffic. After a little bit, I reach up and grab the 'For Sale' tag and toss it in the back.

"Thanks," Shane grunts, his tone reminding me of his security guard grumpiness. I can feel my body calming, the adrenaline starting to wear off, and suddenly I'm feeling like a nap.

But I know Shane's hurt, and I force myself to pay attention. As soon as we're on the highway, I turn to him, crossing my arms over my chest. "You're hit. How bad is it?"

He looks at me, then turns his attention back to the road, his lips tight as he speaks. "Just a flesh wound. Bullet nicked me. I'm fine."

I give him an appraising look, then shake my head. "Don't lie to me, Shane. I can see it on your face. We're in deep trouble here. If you're hurt, we need to address that first."

Shane reaches over, weaving his fingers into my hair, holding my head in his palm and looking over with affection. "I'm okay. But I need to report in. See if Chucky has found out anything new, because the hitman tracking us shouldn't have been fucking news. Also, I need to know if the hitman is cleaning up loose ends on his own, or if someone sent him after us."

"What's the chances of each?" I ask, and Shane shrugs.

"About fifty-fifty. But whether the hitman is using his own network to find us or one of the bosses, the result is the same. We're the loose end he's hunting. But if one of the families is helping him, we'd know who the risk is and who the safety might be. Then we could decide if we should try to outrun this, lay low, or maybe even go back. Hopefully, Chucky will have some intel."

CHAPTER
Eighteen
SHANE

I PULL over at a large truck stop, parking in the middle of the lot mixed in with the other cars, knowing they'll disguise the truck a bit since there's a chance it's been reported stolen by now. Best guess, the truck was put out there by one of the workers at the strip mall, and if so, they'll notice as soon as they get off shift.

Maggie digs in my duffel, handing me the burner phone. I remind myself to buy a new SIM card for it, but one or two more calls shouldn't be a problem. I turn it on, and before I can even speed-dial Chucky, it rings, and I recognize his number on the display.

Shit, that's not good. I answer, putting it on speaker and staying silent as we always do as he jumps in. "Shane? You okay?"

"Yeah, Chucky. Fine and fucking dandy, except for the hitman who took us by surprise at the fucking motel," I reply, holding a finger up for Maggie to stay silent. "What the fuck's going on?"

Chucky hisses through the phone, sounding upset. "Yeah, I've been watching for you to turn the damn phone back on so I could warn you. Got word earlier today that he's looking for your girl because she saw his face. Loose ends, you know. He wants to disappear."

I reach across and take Maggie's hand, her face remarkably stoic for having confirmation that she's on a hitman's shit list. "Well, he found us already. Got a few shots off, hit me too. Took a nick to the left bicep, but nothing serious. Meghan's fine."

Chucky's voice drops to a whisper, and I can hear him lean into his mic, the wheeze unmistakable. "We need to talk about her, Shane. Your girl is in some deep shit, not just with the hit."

Maggie pales slightly, squeezing my hand, and Chucky continues. "You had me check out all the employees at Petals, and I did. I checked out Meghan Postland and she was clean. But when the shit hit the fan, I ran a wider search, and found a Maggie Postland . . ."

Maggie suddenly yanks her hand back, her knees pulling to her chest in a position I know all too well and was happy to see go.

She's mouthing, "I'm sorry, I'm so sorry," silently, and I can see the fear in her eyes. This isn't good.

My voice is hard as I answer Chucky. "What about Maggie Postland?"

I hear a few clicks, like he's typing on his end, and then he reads. "Maggie Postland, 289 Westminster Drive, Apartment 175."

I nod my head, knowing that's where I'd taken Maggie the night I drove her home. This is nothing new. "Yeah, and . . .?"

"She works for *The Daily Spot*, Shane. That online tabloid rag that reports on celebrities and shit."

Still hoping I'm wrong about where this is going, even as Maggie's head falls and she hugs her knees, I sigh. "You sure? I'm not saying it might not be Meghan, but maybe she answers their phones or something? She told me she'd done some office work before."

Chucky makes a tsking noise, and I can imagine him leaning back and giving me a sarcastic look. "I'm looking at her articles, Shane. She's a reporter. She was the one who sprang that expose on the basketball player. And if I know, they might know—all of them. Dominick, Sal, the hitman."

I nod, and I know I need to have a private conversation. "I gotta go, Chucky. Give me a minute and I'll call back in. Stand by."

I click the *End* button before staring across at Maggie. A reporter. A fucking reporter? My voice is icy, the anger turning my heart cold. "Were you ever going to tell me?"

She doesn't respond, doesn't even move, just sits there, small and curled around herself. She's so scared, so afraid . . . and right now, she should be. Not from me, but from what her presence and digital footprint brings down on us.

"Maggie!"

My voice rings out sharply in the truck, and she flinches but raises her head. Her eyes are red-rimmed, tears tracking down her face. "Yes! I wanted to tell you, but then everything went all to crap and I didn't know how to!"

"Well, do it now. Tell me what the fuck is going on with you," I demand, my voice hard. "If there's even a snowball's chance in hell of keeping you safe, you need to tell me everything. Omit fucking nothing."

She swipes her tears, her eyes flashing fire as she sits up a little, cobbling together the remnants of her courage from deep inside her soul. "Yes, I work for *The Daily Spot* as a reporter. I got a job at Petals a few months ago because we had reports there were a lot of celebrities going there for side action. I was undercover, reporting on that, like when Jimmy Keys came in."

I mentally recall our hallway conversation where she'd been taking pictures of the basketball star and claiming to be a fan. I'd been duped . . . that almost never happens to me. And this girl has done it several times without me even suspecting. If we were in any other situation, I'd be impressed. "I see."

"But I like the job, the people . . . like you, Allie, and Marco. Even Dominick didn't seem like that bad of a guy. I had no idea about how deep things went. I mean, who would expect this? This is for the movies. I just thought it was a popular strip club, exclusive VIP kinda stuff for the celebrities and businessmen. And then people started shooting, and Allie had blood all over her . . . and we started running."

Her eyes look to the left like she's remembering the scene at the club, and she shivers. I have to force the next words out through clenched lips, but I have to know, even if it hurts to ask.

"Is that it? You lied about your name and you lied about why you were there. Is there anything else you need to tell me? Now's your chance."

My voice is a bit softer than before, but still harsh and commanding. Maggie notices and looks at me squarely, still so brave I want to pull her across and cuddle her to my chest.

"I did lie about those things. But nothing else. The things I've said to you, done with you . . . those were all real, all true."

Her eyes are soft, wide and open, letting me see into her soul. She's being honest. I can tell this time because the emotions I see are mirrored in my own heart too. I give a curt nod and turn away. "Okay, let me call Chucky back."

I reach for the phone, but Maggie lays a staying hand on mine. "Now, it's your turn." Her voice is laced with steel. "You've been hiding things from me too."

I look at her, a look of question in my eyes, but her expression is calculating now, the softness gone as she looks at me with a coldness I've never seen before. "*Shane*, is that really your name?"

"Have I given you any reason to doubt that it isn't?" I ask, trying to deflect.

Maggie's eyebrows lift, and she's not going to give up that easily. "I'm not stupid. You seem pretty intertwined in a mob-owned strip club. You had a bugout bag, a stashed getaway car, and you apparently carry a gun that you're skilled with. Those are all things a mobster would have, and I bet somewhere in that duffel of yours are some pretty good fake IDs. But there's also Chucky."

"What about Chucky?" I ask, scared but at the same time impressed. She's seeing a lot. No wonder she's a good reporter. I thought she was smart before. Now I *know* she's smart. And has probably been putting things together all along, just biding her time until the moment was right.

"Earlier, you didn't say you *needed* to call him. You said you needed to 'report in' and see if he had any 'intel'. It made me think back. You weren't close with Dominick, not any moreso than the rest of the employees. He trusted you, I could tell that much, but you were just professional with him. Same with Marco and all of the girls . . . and me, at first. I've been undercover for stories a lot. I can blend into the background easily, being small and underestimated. But that's not how you play it when you go undercover, is it? And I'm betting you've been undercover a time or two before too. So, what are you, Shane? ATF? DEA?"

Fuck. I need to get her on another track real damn fast. Even if it hurts. I make my voice harsh, glaring at her. "Maggie, you're seeing zebras instead of horses when you hear hoof beats. Just because you lied about everything from the moment you walked into Petals doesn't mean I did. I'm a security guard. That's why I know how to shoot a gun. Dom wasn't going to hire some idiot to head his club security team who didn't know how to do anything but use his fists. And Chucky's a buddy who helps me out. That's it."

Maggie jerks when I mention her lies, but she doesn't back down. "FBI?"

I'm a pro, so I know there's no reaction on my face, but that lack of response must be what solidifies it for her. She narrows her eyes, nodding almost to herself. "So that's a yes to the FBI then."

It's quiet in the truck, the gravity of the situation sinking in like a fog of heaviness. It's hard, and I feel my facade of sternness crumbling under her soft but unrelenting eyes. "Maggie."

She lifts a finger at me, silencing me like I did to her earlier. "So, to recap, I'm an undercover reporter for what is mostly a two-bit gossip rag. You're an undercover FBI agent working in a mob-controlled strip club. I'm guessing you're there to investigate Dominick. And now a hitman is chasing us because I'm the only witness to a hit. And we're in a stolen truck with a guy named Chucky as our only backup. That about right? Anything I missed?"

I nod. "Yeah, close enough. My name really is Shane, but my last name isn't Nelson. It's Guthrie. Special Agent Shane Guthrie, Federal Bureau of Investigation."

I hold my hand out, offering her a shake even though we're way beyond that now. Still, it's the only thing that seems appropriate, and she returns the shake, smirking a little. "Maggie Postland. Journalist with *The Daily Spot.*"

We eye each other, so much unsaid between us but neither of us knowing where to start with this tangled web that's quickly unraveling. Finally, she clears her throat and looks at me expectantly.

Maggie hums. "So now what?"

"Now," I reply, "we call Chucky back to see what else he knows. By the way, that's not his real name, but he always says his work is child's play, and he can be an evil son of a bitch when he wants to be . . . so the nickname was pretty natural."

She nods, and I reach for my phone once again. The line connects quickly, silence on Chucky's end.

"Hey, Chucky. So, we're transparent on all fronts on this end."

Chucky's voice is hesitant through the speaker. He's not used to this type of communication. "Just how clear are we talking?"

"Crystal, man. Say hi, Maggie."

Maggie grins and puts on her 'club voice.' "Hi, Maggie."

Chucky doesn't find it funny though. "Fuck, Shane. You can't do shit like that. She's a fucking civilian."

Chucky keeps babbling, but I don't have time for his shit. "It's already done, Chucky. Just be glad she doesn't know your real name. Now what's going on back there?"

Chucky sighs, still wanting to speak his piece about Maggie knowing I'm FBI, but we need to move on, figure out the next step. "Okay, so it's looking like Sal sent Carlos into Petals. Told him it was a power play or some shit, just to go in and see how things were looking, not make waves if he got recognized but to lie low, observe, and report back. Later on, he would use the fact that his son was able to penetrate Dom's HQ as leverage."

What a crock of shit. I know too much about Sal Rivaldi to buy that. "It was a setup then. But Carlos was his own son. That's pretty fucked up, even for Sal Rivaldi."

Chucky's hum tells me he's thinking the same thing. "Yeah, apparently, Carlos was sowing some dissension among the lower lieutenants and Sal decided he needed to clean house. On the down low. He contracted the hitman himself, but he's selling that Dominick killed Carlos for being in his club. Sal's wanted to declare war on the Angeline's for a while, and this way, he's getting a two-for-one . . . rid of his asshole son and riding into battle like some sort of avenging father."

"We can't let that war happen," I growl. "Those two kick off, and the streets are going to turn to rivers of blood."

"No shit," Chucky replies. "You're the one working with the guy. What's he like?"

I shrug, looking over at Maggie. "He's careful, methodical, and strategic. More businessman than loose cannon, even if he is a crime lord. He's scary, but it's like a controlled burn with him. If we let the Rivaldi's get even a small foothold on more power, Sal will destroy the city and everyone in it with his crazy power plays. He's more like a wildfire . . . it'll be chaos."

"That's what I'm seeing too. You want to call it in?"

"Not yet, that's a lot of bureaucratic red tape I'm not ready to jump into," I reply.

Chucky understands and laughs softly. "I gotcha. I've looked at this from every angle to see what the best move is and to be honest, I'm not sure, man. It's your call."

I tap my fingers on the steering wheel, doing the same analysis Chucky says he's done and coming up with the same results.

Maggie clears her throat. "I have an idea."

THE TENSION HUMS in the air as Shane turns to look at me and Chucky goes silent across the phone line. Shane's looking at me with both respect and anticipation, while Chucky . . . well, he's at least not talking. "Whatcha thinking, Angel?"

"You said Dominick is the better choice for the city, and Sal Rivaldi used his own son as a pawn to incite war," I reply, trying to put words to the thoughts that have been tumbling in my head for only a few moments. I'm trying to put it together with what I know about Dominick, the city . . . everything I've learned in my career in journalism. "We have to appeal to Dominick to prevent the war. The FBI can't exactly go in officially and tell Dominick he's their pick as crime lord . . ."

"That's an understatement," Chucky says, interrupting. "But . . . they might be willing to work under the table if necessary."

"Exactly. He's the best option we've got," I add as Shane gives me a pondering look. "And he can help with the hitman, might be the only one who can."

Shane taps his hands on the dash, his head nodding quickly as he thinks. "You want us to go back to Petals? To Dominick?" he asks before his nods change to shakes. "That's a suicide mission, Maggie. No."

I want to challenge Shane, but Chucky interrupts before the stare-off can reach ridiculous levels. "Actually, I'm thinking she's on to something. You could go back, maintain your cover, share the intel, and nudge Dominick the right way."

"Almost right, Chucky," I interject. "If we go back, we go back honestly. We have to come completely clean with Dominick. If we hold back anything, he'll know and doubt the rest of the information. Besides, having a waitress and a security guy going back doesn't carry weight. A reporter and an FBI agent . . . if we go in and show all our cards, he's more likely to believe us and not go after the Rivaldis. It's risky, but it's the best play."

Shane looks at me incredulously. "You want me to tell Dominick Angeline, head of the Angeline crime family, that I've been undercover with him as an FBI agent for a year and that he's had a fucking reporter working as a waitress in his club, and expect to walk out of that room alive?"

I bite my lip, thinking it through. "Yes. Besides, we can offer Dom things that he would want to take advantage of."

"Like what?" Shane asks, and for the first time, I feel like grinning. "What's going on in your head?"

"Dominick's going to be surprised, and angry, that the FBI has infiltrated his organization," I say, knowing the description is kind at best, stupid at worst. "But if the FBI gives him a tacit agreement for some breathing room, a willingness to back him, even if it's under the table . . . he might be willing to help."

I know I'm pushing it, but Shane needs to understand that I'm all in on this, and I need him to be too.

He nods, obviously thinking through what I've said. "We'd need a safety mechanism, something that will make Dominick talk first and hopefully, *not* shoot later." He pauses, thinking for a moment before grinning. "Not a safety mechanism, but a safety *person*. Allie. We use her as a liaison, make sure she's there for the meeting. I don't think Dominick will kill us in front of her."

He's right. I hate to get Allie involved in this mess. She's my friend, and I don't want her to be in any more danger. But I think Shane might have found the only way to insure we get in and out alive and with any chance at securing Dominick's help with the hitman.

"Okay. We'll talk to Allie."

Shane reaches over, taking my hand and giving it a supportive squeeze. "All right, Chucky, you got all that? I'm going back offline. I'll text you the meet info when it's set."

We hang up, and then it's just Shane and me in the truck. The lies, the hiding, and the stress of the crazy situation melt away as we look at each other, our hands touching, leaving just the chemistry, the connection we've had even when we knew we shouldn't, couldn't pursue it.

I feel naked, vulnerable under his gaze like never before. Unconsciously, my knees pull up to my chest, but I don't drop my gaze. His dark eyes stare back at me, and he gives my hand another little squeeze. "Don't do that, Angel. Don't try to hide now, not when I can finally see you. And you can see me."

I let my knees fall to the side, facing him. My voice is quiet but steady as I meet his eyes, needing to see every nuance of his reaction. "Is this real for you? Because it's real for me. And as scared as I am about all this crazy mob stuff . . ." I wave my hand around, gesturing outside the truck, then place my hand on my heart. "I think I'm more scared that this is some pretend piece of the character you're playing and that you're going to walk away from me when it's all done, leave me alone, broken, and not knowing real from pretend."

Shane grabs my arms, pulling me across the seat and into his lap. Wrapping his arms around my waist, he looks into my eyes, his voice raspy and intense. "It's real for me too, Maggie. So fucking real, and I'm terrified that I'm taking you into the lion's den and won't be able to keep my promise to keep you safe. And I can't stand the thought of that. I need you. I love you."

The doubts in my heart burn to ash as he kisses me, the truth of his words resonating through me. Yes, we've only been intimate for a few days, but I don't care. For months, I've been watching him, dreaming of him, needing him. "Shane, I love you too."

He kisses me again, leaning me back in his arms to lay along the bench seat before covering me with his body.

Shane kisses down my neck, and I lift my head to give him greater access. He groans into the soft skin at the curve, sucking to refresh the mark he's already given me as he grinds the ridge of his dick against my core. "I want to take my time with you, Maggie. Worship every inch of your skin, but I don't want to risk anyone seeing us here. Let me get you somewhere safe for the night so I can make love to you."

I look up at him and pout, wanting more, wanting him now. But he's right. We're too exposed here and I feel like I just found the real Shane. I can't lose him.

With one last fiery kiss, I nod and we wiggle back into our seats, buckling up. "First thing, though. We're getting that arm bandaged."

Shane looks at his arm, chuckling before nodding. "Okay. We'll find a pharmacy or something. Just . . . I love you, Maggie. I promise to keep you safe, no matter what happens."

I take his hand, interlocking our fingers, my tiny hand engulfed by his giant one. "I love you too. I know you'll keep me safe. We'll do this together."

He dips his head, handing me the phone. "Call Allie. Don't answer any questions or give her any indication about where we are. Tell her to set up a meeting tomorrow at noon at the club. She needs to meet us at the front door with one guard of Dominick's choosing. Once we're inside, it's Dominick's show. Whatever he feels is warranted, as long as he listens to us."

I bite my lip, suddenly nervous as we're at the point where the poop hits the fan. "Is that smart? Shouldn't we try to limit the guards, give us a fighting chance if things go awry?"

Shane shakes his head, sighing. "If he wants to kill us, it won't matter if there are two guards or ten. Better to let him feel in control about as much as possible, because we're going in with a big favor to ask and demanding that he put the one weakness he has, Allie, at risk at the same time."

I take a steadying breath, turning the phone on and dialing Allie's number, glad I have it memorized. Allie's voice is hesitant when she answers the unknown number. "Hello?"

Good, she's not dancing yet, or maybe she's not dancing at all after the shooting. "Allie, it's me, Meghan."

It feels strange to use my fake name again, but it's all Allie's ever known, and it's like a firecracker to her. "Oh, my God, Meghan! Are you okay? What the fuck happened to you? Where are you? Are you with Shane?"

She's shooting questions rapid-fire style, and I can't even answer one before the next starts. I try to reassure her. "I'm fine. I'm with Shane. Are you okay?"

Her voice is calmer now, but still tight and probably a little worried. "I'm fine too. I was freaked out for a bit, but I'm okay now. The club just went on like business as usual. I don't think the customers on the floor even realized what happened."

I don't think I realized how scared I was that Allie wasn't okay until I heard her voice, getting stronger and steadier as she speaks. Tears of relief fill my eyes, and I lean my head forward, holding in the sniffle as best I can. "Good, I'm so glad you're okay."

Shane waves his hand in a circle at me, indicating I should wrap this up. I guess it's got something to do with tracing the call, or maybe just because we need to get going. His arm has to be burning like fire. "Listen, I need your help with something."

"Of course, anything," Allie says immediately. "I've been worried about you."

"Look, there's a lot going on here that you don't know," I say, wishing I could tell her. "It's sort of safer if you don't for now. I need you to trust me and do exactly as I say, okay?"

Allie's voice tightens, and I can hear her tapping her phone with a thumbnail. "You're scaring me. What's going on?"

"I need you to set up a meeting with Dominick for us. Tomorrow at noon, at the club. There's stuff that Shane and I need to talk to him about."

"Why not just call—" Allie says, but I cut her off, needing to rush this.

"You need to be there to meet us at the front door. A guard's fine if Dominick feels it's warranted, and he can have as many guys there as he wants. We're coming in to talk, and he needs to hear what we have to say, for everyone's sake. If he asks, tell him it has to do with Sal. Got all that?"

Allie sounds confused, but still sort of put together. "Yeah, tomorrow at noon with security. But what's going on?"

"We'll explain everything tomorrow. I need you to be there, so you'll hear everything," I tell her, instantly hoping she'll want to still be my friend after my lies are laid out for her. "This is important, Allie. Please, tell Dominick he needs to listen."

"I'll set it up. Whatever you need," Allie says. "But you promise me, you're not doing anything stupid?"

I have to laugh. We're light years past stupid. "You know me, Allie. I just take after you, my friend."

"That's what worries me," Allie says, laughing a little herself. "Okay, well . . . see you tomorrow?"

"I'll see you tomorrow," I promise, my voice cracking a little. "Check ya later, babe."

I have to hang up before she can reply, the knot in my belly cinching tight. I'm scared now, and it's not the primal, instinctual fear that I've felt for the past few days. This is deeper, both body and mind, and part of it is that, of all the silly shiz, I'm going to disappoint my friend.

Shane wraps a hand around the back of my neck, pulling me toward him and laying a soft kiss on my forehead. He understands, and he'll be here for me. "Good girl, Angel. Let's roll some miles."

CHAPTER

Twenty

SHANE

THE HOUSE ISN'T EXACTLY a mansion in Bel-Air, but compared to the past two nights, it's a glorious luxury. A two-bedroom house in a nice suburban subdivision. It's an FBI safe house, and it feels good in a lot of ways to use it. It means that all our cards are on the table and that I don't need to hide from her any longer.

She might've semi-accepted the car switch without an interrogation, but having a random house stocked with all the goodies we could need would've raised too many questions I couldn't answer.

I'm glad we're being totally honest with each other now, because beyond all this craziness, I really have fallen in love with this brilliant, tiny, innocent woman.

It didn't take sex, or looking back, even a single kiss to start falling in love with her. It was in the snippets of conversation, in the looks that we've shared. It happened when I was willing to go as far as needed to protect her. It was when I was willing to beat a man within an inch of his life for threatening her, and when I was willing to defy a mob boss to keep her safe.

Sex? Oh, I'm not turning that down with my naughty little Angel—never will. It's been more intense, more satisfying, more meaningful than any I've had before. But I loved her even before that, and I think she loved me before that too.

I pull the truck into the garage, dropping the mechanical door and locking it tight behind us before we enter the house. Inside, it's small and tidy, neatly decorated in stuff that's used but clean and kept prepped and ready. I know without even looking that in the kitchen will be a freezer of basic frozen stuff and some microwave meals, and the pantry will have boxed goods. Nothing fancy, but we'll be able to eat.

"Won't the neighbors wonder about us?" Maggie asks, looking around. "I mean, that there are lights on and stuff?"

I do a routine full sweep of the interior, tossing our bags into the bedroom. "Safe houses are set up with a cover story for any nosy neighbors. In the old days, we'd say it was owned by a pilot who'd let flight crew crash during layovers. Nowadays, we tell people it's an AirBnB to make it easier. People usually accept what they're told at face value, and not many would suspect something as wild as an FBI safe house in their family neighborhood."

Maggie nods, looking around. "I never thought you were FBI, that's for sure. You seem like too much of a bad boy to be one of the good guys."

She says it with a teasing note, so I know that she's pleased with both sides of my personality. I grin. "Uh, you hungry? They keep the house stocked, so there's usually some Hungry Mans around here."

Maggie nods, stepping closer. "I am hungry . . . for *my* man. Forget the fried chicken."

Her words hang in the air, heavy with need as she looks up at me with pleading eyes. I cover the remaining space between us in two steps, sweeping her into my arms and lifting her by the backs of her thighs. "I think I can satisfy your hunger."

She wraps her arms around my neck and legs around my waist, her tiny body climbing my larger one like a tree. I devour her, my tongue meeting her hungry one and the two of us invading each other. Faintly, I can taste the sugary coffee she had earlier at a truck stop, the bitterness making the sweetness even more of a treat.

"Lock your ankles around me," I command her, kissing to her ear. "I want to see you fly."

I feel her feet shift behind me and hold her shoulders, dipping her back parallel to the floor. "Let go. I've got you."

Her hands let go of my neck, and she spreads her arms as she closes her eyes. She weaves her fingers into my hair as I kiss down her neck. "Mmm, Shane. I feel like I'm floating. Your kisses are the only thing anchoring me here."

She sounds dreamy, and I smile against her neck, proud that I'm the one making her hazy. No one has given me this much pleasure, and nobody has ever given her what I've given her.

"I want to anchor you to this moment, to me . . . mark every inch of you with my tongue and my teeth so no one doubts that you are mine. Not even you."

Her head lifts, eyes clear as she meets my dark gaze, and her fingers dig into the back of my neck. "Do it. Make me yours."

I return to her neck, leaving sucking kisses along her pulse, feeling it jump under my tongue as the bruise raises brightly against her pale skin. I know these are going to fade in a few hours, but I'm just getting started.

Fuck. I need all of her. I turn, tossing her to the bed and watching as she bounces on the surface, grinning the whole time. "Take your shirt off. Bra too. Now, Angel."

I rip my t-shirt over my head, a ripping sound coming from the exhausted cotton as my muscles tear the fabric off me. I'm covering her before she even tosses her bra to the floor. I'm so ravenous for her and for what she promises me.

Her palms cup my cheeks, lips puckered for a kiss, and I grant it to her quickly before returning my attentions lower. Moving down her body, I lick, kiss, suck, and nibble her upper body, tracing every inch with my tongue and lips and leaving more marks along her breasts as I find the spots that tickle her . . . that tease her . . . that drive her wild.

"Shane . . . ohh," Maggie cries out as I suck on her pink nipples, her nails clawing at my arms as she pulls me tighter. I love that my sweet girl turns into a wildcat in bed, her need making her desperate . . . for me.

I push off, standing by the bed and grabbing at her shorts, pulling them down and off, along with her gas-station wannabe Crocs.

I place her feet on my shoulders, needing to bend down a bit so her short legs can reach, even with her hips raised high, and begin to worship her shapely legs with little kisses on her toes before moving up inch by inch. "These legs have been in my dreams for months, Maggie. Wanting to slide my hands up your thighs every time you bent over a table, wondering how silky your skin would be under my palms, knowing they led to fucking heaven."

"I've been dreaming of the same thing. Just like this," Maggie whispers as I suck on her soft skin. "You make me feel alive."

My mouth makes its way from her ankles . . . to her knees . . . to her inner thighs, where I force myself to pause, knowing I want to indulge but also knowing I want to take my time. I nibble and suck still, leaving no doubt that this pussy is mine, her cheap panties framed by the signature of my marks.

"Did you know?" I ask as I look into her eyes. "Did you know how much I wanted you? That I wanted to risk it all, my career, my cover . . . my life?"

Maggie's breath catches, and she nods "Yes, and no. We were flirting, and I wanted you so much, but I thought I'd never have you. So I flirted back harder, bending over those tables with my ass toward you on purpose, hoping to tempt you into wanting me. You were like a predator, powerful and dominant, and I felt in my dreams that you could be the man I would spend the rest of my life with."

Her words ignite me, my hands finding the edge of her panties. I tug them to the side to gaze upon her pussy before using my thumbs to massage her outer lips, the softness under my rough hands the perfect symbolism for the two of us. Soft and rough, innocent and jaded, but somehow fitting together perfectly. I can see her juices coating her as she gets wetter and wetter. "Fuck, Maggie. I need to taste you."

"Yes, my love," she gasps, but it turns into a giggling rush as I scoop her up the rest of the way and stand, her thighs over my shoulders and her pussy right in front of my mouth. "Whoa. Holy Shitzu!" Maggie exclaims as her hands grab at my head for balance, but I'm holding her solidly in my palms, my fingertips dimpling her luscious ass as I hold her tight.

"I've got you and I'm just getting started," I promise, dipping my tongue into her folds. I groan at her taste, my cock still trapped in my jeans but straining for freedom. "Fuck, you're so damn delicious. All I want is to eat you up."

I lick her entrance, sucking at her clit, delighting at her whimpers above me. I want to drown in her, suffocate in her sweetness. She's gasping, her voice getting thick as she moans.

Gently, I lower her back to the bed, quickly kicking off my shoes and jeans to lay down naked beside her. I watch her pink face as she blinks, grinning at me. "Two more strokes and I would've come. Not sure you could hold me up if I was squirming through that."

"I wouldn't have dropped you, I would've pulled you in even tighter to get every drop." I reply, patting my chest. "Now get up here, you naughty Angel. Straddle me. Sit on my face and let me feast on that pussy."

She blushes a deep rose shade of pink but does it, stripping off her panties before turning so that she's facing my body. She looks down, and I can just see the naughty twinkle in her eyes before she lowers down. "I want to suck you too."

My cock jumps at her words, trying to get closer to her mouth for the pleasure of her murmured words. She chuckles and lowers her pussy slowly, teasing me. It's not nearly enough for what I want to do to her. I grab her hips in a hard grip, forcing her down to my mouth and immediately thrashing my tongue all along her pussy. Immediately, I'm covered in her sweet juices, my tongue in heaven as my nose presses lower and my eyes are covered in the soft weight of her ass. Heaven.

Above me, I feel Maggie lean forward and then her soft touch along my shaft as her fingers explore me delicately. I groan, my knees falling to the sides to give her total access. My tongue speeds up, finding the button of her clit and stroking it quickly, circling around it before sucking softly. I want to mark her, but not here. I'll never hurt her.

She cries out at my attentions to her clit, and I feel the wet heat of her breath just before she takes my head into her mouth, swirling her tongue along the slit to taste my precum. It shifts her hips down—she's so small compared to me—and I lift my hips while burying my tongue deeper in her pussy, my nose pressed between her ass cheeks, but I never stop.

She moans at my flavor, like it's a treat she savors, and the buzz of her moan zings through me. I pull back, smacking her ass playfully. "That's it, Angel. Suck my cock down your pretty little throat. I'm gonna lick this sweet pussy and make you moan around my cock. Moan on me, Maggie."

I dive back into her pussy, thrusting my tongue in and out of her. She's close, grinding her pussy on my hungry mouth and moaning around my cock as she keeps sucking me down. The feeling drives me wild, making me growl against her pussy. "Fuck, that's so good."

"You too," Maggie gasps breathlessly, her hips bucking, wanting more. "Let me feel how much you like me sucking you."

We become louder, our grunts and groans echoing against each other in a cycle that renews with each sound until Maggie freezes, my cock deep in her throat as she cries out her release.

I pull her tighter, burying my face in her so deeply I can't even breathe, but I don't care because all I need is her and the sweet nectar she's pumping against my tongue.

As soon as her spasms stop, I push her off me, pinning her underneath me and slamming my cock into her.

I don't give her time to stretch, wanting to feel those last orgasmic quivers of her pussy, but I slide in and out slowly, needing to feel every bit of her silky walls against my cock. She moans, wiggling her hips as she squeezes me with her pussy, wanting more.

I gather her hands above her head, holding them with one hand and cupping her jaw with the other so that our eyes meet.

"You and me, Angel. I don't know what's going to happen tomorrow, but it's you and me. Together. And if this is all we have, then I'm spending the rest of my life with the woman I want by my side until the end. I love you, Maggie."

Her eyes shine with tears, but her voice is strong. "I love you too, Shane. Tomorrow is tomorrow. You said you were anchoring me to this moment, but I need you here with me. Right now, just be here with me. My man. Forever."

I look over her body, my marks visible along her neck, her chest and tits, her hips, and though I can't see them, I know she's claimed on her thighs and above her mound too. "You are mine, always."

Maggie smiles, nodding and biting her lip. "Yours. And you're mine too."

I thrust into her, harder and more powerfully, my strokes getting rougher as I demand more and more from her small body, but she takes me, fiercer than I'd ever imagined my Angel to be.

Our eyes stay locked the whole time, never leaving each other for a moment, even as we both come hard. We don't even cry out. The whole time, we're nearly silent as our eyes say everything that needs to be said, the only sound the rush of our breath and the slap of our hips.

My cum creams out of her as I pull out and we collapse in each other's arms. Maggie curls against me, falling asleep fitfully in my arms, but I stay on alert.

I'm dreading tomorrow's meeting, knowing it's potentially a suicide mission. But I'm hoping that we can make Dominick see reason.

EVEN AFTER AN ENTIRE morning of Shane's constant coaching about what to do in every possible scenario he foresees for the meeting, I'm still nervous. Noon comes faster than I expected, and my stomach is grumbling as I sit in the passenger seat and watch the streets. "I should have eaten."

"I offered," Shane reminds me. "Nothing better to start your day than frozen breakfast sandwiches."

I laugh, looking over. He's wearing just a tank top, the bright white of the bandage over the taut skin of his arm taunting me. It really was just a nick, didn't even need stitches or glue, but still . . . it's a bullet wound. I nod, "I know, I know."

Shane chuckles and flexes his arm. "You know what I want to do when we get some normalcy again?" he remarks. "I want to go to the gym again. Gotta stay in shape. You wear me out."

I smile, knowing he's just trying to relax me. "I could be enticed into watching you get your buff on."

Our conversation tapers off as we drive up and down the street three times before Shane pulls the old blue truck up outside Petal's front door.

He does a full scan, and then with one last quick kiss, we get out and approach cautiously. Shane knocks twice on the door, and it opens a crack, Nick peeking out. He looks wary and confused at the same time, like he shouldn't be this concerned about people he knows.

"Shane? Meghan? You alone?"

Shane nods "Yeah, Nick. Alone and unarmed. You know Dom's got three cameras on us right now. It'd be stupid not to be. Allie here?"

The door swings open wider, and I can see Allie, her face a mask of confused fear, but when she sees me, she squeals and runs for me. Her long arms surround me in a tight hug even as she starts demanding answers. "What the fuck is going on?"

Her hug has pulled me away from Shane a step or two, and with a quick jerk, he pulls me back to his side and out of Allie's reach. Allie's jaw drops in surprise at his move, and then she narrows her eyes, taking in the visible marks along my neck and the upper swells of my breasts. "Ooh, it's like that?"

She's teasing, giving me a thumbs-up, and I almost even feel like smiling. Until I realize Nick is leering at me like he never has before.

Before he can say anything, though, Shane steps between us, blocking his view. "Nick, we need to see Dominick. Now."

Nick nods once, moving to pat down Shane, looking a little embarrassed by it. "Protocol, man."

Shane allows it but barely manages to hold himself in check as Nick does a more thorough check on me, like I'd be hiding a gun in these shorts. I knock Nick's hands away when he gets a little high on the inner thigh, though. "I'm clear and you know it, pervert. This ain't the airport, and I'm pretty sure that 'don't touch' rule still applies."

He smirks but turns and leads us into the main room. It's well-lit, more like it is when we clean after closing each night than the usual dim ambiance I'd expected.

But it lets me see the room and its inhabitants more clearly. Dominick is sitting alone at a table near the edge of the stage, right in front of the big pole that dominates the middle of the room, a glass filled with amber liquid on the polished wood beside him.

As Nick takes his place, I can see that there's a guard in every corner. Dominick doesn't bother standing, just gestures to the chairs opposite him, and we sit.

It'd almost feel like a double-date, Dominick and Allie on one side, and Shane and I on the other, if it weren't for the pesky fact that things are about to go more than a bit sideways. Well, that and the guards in every corner.

Dominick picks up his glass and takes a sip before setting it down and studying us curiously. "So you asked for this meeting. What is so important?"

Shane looks at Allie, then back to Dominick. "I appreciate your agreeing to meet with us. And I apologize for asking that Allie be present. I know that would not be your preference, but I feel it affords us a certain amount of safety, considering the information I'm about to share."

Dominick's face tightens slightly, just at the corners of his eyes, belying his anger, but he keeps his cool. I can see it now, the aura of power, the comfort in his place in the hierarchy. I'd been fooled that it was just about him being the boss of such a hot club, but there's so much more. Not to mention, I think he has ice in his veins considering the cool tone as he speaks. "There is always risk to sharing information. I hope that you have not set either of us up for any . . . safety issues."

The pause in his speaking makes his threat crystal clear. I don't need to look to know that each of the guards are on high alert, ready to handle us if there's a problem. Or just at Dominick's say-so.

Shane and Dominick stare each other down for a moment, the testosterone and dominance contest drawing out between the two of them for too long, so I break in, hoping to deter the two alpha males from locking horns until one of them's dead. "Dominick, I would like to apologize for lying to you."

My words aren't totally unplanned. It was one of the many different scenarios that Shane and I went over, a way to keep Dominick off balance and willing to listen.

The shock of my admitting to lying does exactly what we hoped, and Dominick's attention diverts solely to me, his eyes now boring into mine with his eyebrows raised in question. "Meghan, you lied to me? Explain."

I start rambling, trying to get out the whole prepared speech at once. "My name is not Meghan. It's Maggie Postland. In certain circles, Petals has a reputation. Apparently, it has several. But I was only aware of one . . . I didn't know what Petals was, what *you* are. I just knew that celebrities of a certain caliber frequent the club for a bit of fun. I work as a tabloid reporter, writing stories strictly about celebrities. I began my job at Petals as a way of investigating these stories and wrote articles a few times."

My eyes tick to Allie, who looks like I just slapped her across the face. I focus on her, the next words not important to Dom, but I insisted on them with Shane. "But while I worked here, I found friends and a place of belonging, a family that worked together, day-by-day and shift-by-shift, to look out for one another. I found a self-confidence and power I never knew I possessed. It hurt every day to lie to them, because I care about them very much."

I look back to Dominick, who's leaning forward a little, interested now. "I didn't know exactly how deep the rabbit hole runs around here, and honestly, right now, I don't care. My concern now is the trouble chasing me, trouble brought because I'm a part of the Petals family."

Dominick's eyes have gotten colder as I've spoken, and I can see the muscle in his jaw working as he clenches his teeth. His voice is a deadly whisper, but at least he's not yelling as he looks around at the guards. "A fucking reporter? How the fuck did you get past the background check?"

I shrug, downplaying my awesomeness because it doesn't seem the time to brag about how many times I've successfully gone undercover. "I'm good at my job. Please feel free to take a moment to Google me. I promise, you'll see I've only written a couple of stories that relate to celebrities attending strip clubs, and I never mention Petals by name."

He holds up a finger, reaching into his vest pocket with his other hand

and fishing out his phone. He clicks around for a moment, and I speak up helpfully. "The only one that probably would've caught your attention is the Jimmy Keys story."

Dominick laughs, setting his phone down. "You broke that story? That guy's a total douchebag, tried to stiff me on the bill too. I was glad he got busted . . . but not in my damn club."

His voice is hard again by the end, and my momentary hope that maybe he wouldn't be too mad, at least about that part of our revelations, are crushed.

I lower my eyes, unable to help it because I know there's worse news coming. "Dominick, please. There's more."

He huffs, sitting up as Allie lays a hand on his shoulder, helping to calm him. He glances at her and nods, waving a hand at me. "It's your show, apparently. Tell me."

I glance at Shane, but he gives me a reassuring nod. I'm doing fine. Keep going. "So, the night of the shooting . . ."

I see Allie flinch and give her a soft smile of apology for bringing up something that must be scary for her to think about. "That night, I was in the hallway after delivering the scotch, so I saw the hitman. I don't think he even registered me at the time. I'm just kinda invisible to most folks."

I shrug because it's the truth, but Shane squeezes my hand, and I know he sees me. He always sees me, and it gives me the strength to continue.

"But yesterday, when Shane and I were lying low, the hitman found us. He's tracking me, tying up loose ends because somewhere along the way, he realized I'd seen him and could recognize him."

Dominick steeples his hands, fingertips pressing together under his chin. "And this hitman chasing you, you want me to do something about it, I take it?"

I nod, the plea in my eyes. "Please, Dominick. Help us."

"Tell me, Maggie Postland," Dominick says, leaning forward again and studying the both of us. "The suit with the scotch. Do you know who he was?"

"I didn't then, but I do now," I admit. "Carlos Rivaldi. This is where Shane comes in, I think."

Dominick looks to Shane, annoyance and anger clearly written on his face. "It appears you've been tagged. You're *it*."

Shane holds Dominick's glare with steady eyes before beginning. "Dominick, I want you to take a minute and think back on the time I've been working for you . . . the things I've done, the things I've seen, the things I've told you."

Dominick smiles, but it feels threatening, not friendly. "Yes, we have done some rather interesting things in your time here. And until this little incident, I thought you were a fine *employee*, one of the best I had. But what's that got to do with this?"

"Have the guys step out for this. Just you and me, and the girls. Trust me. Please."

They seem to be communicating with their eyes, taking each other's measure, but I think it's the 'please' that does it.

Dominick turns, his voice clear and sharp as he looks at the guards. "Leave us. Secure the building perimeter."

The security guys disappear at once, and I hear both the front and back doors open, then close. Dominick waits, then looks back at Shane. "Okay, we're alone. Out of respect for what you've done and the honor you've shown toward all the ladies who work here, I did that. Don't make me regret it. Now tell me what's so important."

Shane nods and leans forward, his elbows wide on the table as he looks at Dominick. "Approximately twelve months ago, word on the street was that Sal Rivaldi was making progress, increasing the size of his operation, but doing it quietly and in small pocket areas that are only loosely in your control. The way things were looking, he was positioning himself to divide East Robinsville, or maybe take over the whole city."

Dominick leans forward, his eyes intense. "And you know this how?"

Shane looks Dominick in the eye. There is no fear, no hesitancy, no apology on Shane's face. "Because I'm FBI."

Dominick explodes, standing so fast his chair clatters to the floor behind him as he slams his hands to the table. Allie and I jump at the sharp sound.

Shane stands too, holding his ground as Dominick stalks around the table to grab him by the shirt. Dominick rears back for a punch and Shane doesn't try to block him, just keeps his voice level. "There's more . . ."

Dominick pauses, and I think for a second that he's not going to punch Shane in the face. But he redirects the punch to Shane's gut, the powerful hit echoing in the empty room.

Allie cries out as Dom rears back again, and I can't sit here and let this happen, so I yell, "Dominick, Sal's declaring war! You have to listen!"

Dominick's head whips to me, one fist cocked back and frozen. "I thought you didn't know anything about that side of the business? Hmm, Miss Postland?" he sneers. "Or is that another lie?"

I'm trying to be strong, but I know my voice sounds weaker than I'd like as I stand up to him. "I didn't before. I do now. I've spent the past twenty-four hours learning so I can try to stay alive. Please listen."

He shoves Shane back, letting go of his shirt, and both men slowly sit, wary of each other.

"That's your freebie because I respect the fuck out of you, Dominick," Shane says as he smooths his hair. "Next time, I'll fight back."

Dominick's eyes narrow, the coldness intimidating as frick even when it's not directed at me, but Shane doesn't flinch. "If you get a chance. But say your piece."

"I was sent in undercover in your operation, another agent in Rivaldi's,"

Shane says, leaning back in his chair. "It took some time to get that agent's information, but I'm giving you all I have. Carlos was giving Sal shit, and you know there's no love lost between the two of them. Sal decided he needed to stop the coup Carlos was stirring up, but for Sal, that's not enough. If he's going to kill his own son, why not use it as a power play? He knew that if he could pin Carlos's death on you, he'd have the Colombians with him when he wanted to go hot around here. So he sent Carlos to Petals on a fool's errand and secretly hired out the hit so it'd take place on your territory. Sal's telling his whole crew you killed Carlos, and now he has the best justification ever to start a war . . . to avenge his son."

"The Colombians do go for family," Dominick concedes. "Never hired a Colombian dancer for just that reason. Too likely to have some bloodthirsty cousin on my doorstep."

"But Sal set it all up—set *you* up. He's making a play for more control, and he's ready to war with you to get it."

I can see Dominick taking in everything, the calculations and strategies running through his mind as he plays out scenario after scenario. He reaches down, picking up his seemingly forgotten drink and draining the rest of it in one swallow.

"That is a lot to think about, many things to consider. But tell me this, FBI agent. Why are you telling me all this? You wouldn't be trying to entrap me into something, would you?"

Shane chuckles darkly, crossing his legs almost casually. "No, Dominick. I'm not trying to entrap you. What you do with this information is your choice—war with the Rivaldis or don't war with them. My thinking is this. There are devils in every world, some more evil, some perhaps less. But they're necessary, to balance out the angels."

Shane takes my hand and looks lovingly at me before turning back to Dominick. "Sometimes, you help the devil you know is the lesser evil in the hopes that they will help you too."

Dominick looks from Shane to me and back. "Ah, so this is where the help comes in. You've given me information in the hopes that I will do something for you too. What is it you want?"

Shane lets go of my hand and leans forward again. "The hitman. I've got a name. I've seen his face now too. He's seen us and is hunting us still. I'm slightly worried about how he's getting his information, but that's a fight for another day, and likely solved if he's dealt with the way I'd prefer. Right now, I need him to stop. Means and methods are yours to decide, of course. If you do us this favor."

Dominick nods thoughtfully and rubs his chin in consideration. "I do not like people who choose to do their dirty work inside my own place of business. It's disrespectful and bad for my reputation, you see? It's in *my* best interest to punish the hitman for his transgression, but I will say that it's for your benefit and hold that over you. Agreed?"

Shane nods. "One more thing . . ."

Dominick smirks, the smug arrogance obvious on his face. "I thought there might be."

"We walk. Maggie and I walk away from all of this safely. Forever. No outstanding threats, no looking over our shoulders. You will never see either of us again."

That hurts, and I glance at Allie, knowing that if Dominick agrees, it means our friendship's over too. But it has to be.

"Agreed. You may both walk away safely, but I will not promise you will never see me again. Having friends in certain positions can be an excellent resource, so while I will not use you frequently, I will keep you available if the need comes up. And . . . Mr. FBI Agent, your East Robinsville privileges are revoked. Permanently. You don't set foot in this town again. Unless it is by my invitation."

There's a carefulness to his phrasing, the details somehow in the words he's not saying. I can see the methodical strategic mind Shane said Dominick possesses, making contingencies until the end.

I feel like we're all pawns in Dominick's chess game, but we're still on move three and he's already planned out his game to the checkmate move.

Shane nods and offers his hand. "Agreed, with one caveat. You will not use either of us in a way that would endanger us, especially Maggie."

Dominick bows his head and offers his own hand. "I wouldn't threaten a man's family. That's how cockroaches operate, and while I may be a devil in your eyes, I'm no cockroach."

They shake, and the agreement's made.

Twenty~Two

SHANE

"OH, my goodness, I can't believe Dominick's going to help us!" Maggie exclaims happily, falling ungracefully to the couch. We're upstairs at the club, in the private apartment Dominick keeps. I've been up here before, mostly on days when Dom's stayed over himself. It's a cush place, small but fancier than anything I've ever had for damn sure. And it's not even his real home, just a crash pad.

After reaching our agreement, Dominick 'offered' us the protection of the club and the use of the place. It wasn't so much an offer as a demand. We're definitely more prisoner than guest, but his protection comes with his rules, so here we are.

I sit down beside her on the couch, pulling her legs into my lap and slipping off her shoes to rub her feet. "He's helping, but we can't get too comfortable in this gilded cage. I'm not certain he won't flip on us. And we still don't know what he plans to do about Sal."

Maggie looks thoughtful, smiling as she wiggles her toes for me. "Honestly, I'm not sure I care. All this mob stuff was happening before, right under my nose, and I was oblivious. If I wasn't in the middle of it this time, I probably still wouldn't know about this potential threat to the city. Maybe I'd be better off, happier in my blissful ignorance."

I run my hand along her calf up to her thigh, marveling at the power in her muscles and tracing the fading marks from last night. "Maybe so. But the power structure that directs the city, from politics, to businesses, to the streets, it's all intertwined, and if things are running smoothly, you don't notice them."

"Kinda like the sewer company?" Maggie asks. "As long as the toilets are working right, you never notice them."

I nod, thinking Maggie's found a pretty good analogy. "You haven't noticed things here because Dominick does a damn fine job of keeping himself seamless. If Sal were running things, you'd know the difference. You'd see it on the news, you'd feel it when you walked around your neighborhood. To be a part of the solution, you have to be aware of the problems . . . all of them, even the scary ones."

Maggie's eyes bore into me even as she leans back against the couch cushion. "Is that why you do it, why you're an FBI agent? To be part of the solution?"

My hands still. I've known this was coming. We dropped these big bombs of who we are on each other but then had to let the issues lie while we got to safety.

Now that we've got the semblance of protection, the tenuous pause on our questions drops away. "Remember how I told you about my dad?"

Maggie's chin dips as she whispers quietly. "Yeah. Barney Fife, more or less."

"Well, Barney Fife, who was about the same size as me, but yeah. He's why I do this. I grew up seeing him help people, sometimes by being a big, powerful guy with a badge, but more often, it was by being an ear to listen to people's problems and help them find a way out of whatever trouble they were having. When I was a kid, it was normal to come downstairs and find that Dad had taken in a stray overnight . . . sometimes a kid, sometimes a whole family, and a few times, a recently released felon who needed guidance to see the better path available to him. We had a couple of tents that Dad would let them use, or if the weather was bad, he'd let them crash on the porch or even inside in winter. I always knew I wanted to be a police officer like him, to help people."

"So, how'd you end up in the FBI?"

"I knew I wanted to be more than a street cop," I reply honestly. "Dad always said that the real criminals were the ones he could never touch, and I thought I could make a difference. So I went to college for criminal justice, and my grades and performance were good enough to catch the attention of the right people. I was given a few scholarships and cranked my way through a four-year degree in three years before reporting straight to Quantico for the FBI Academy. They broke me down and molded me the way they wanted, taught me how to go undercover, that creative problem-solving is an asset, not a rule-bending problem, and so much more. I don't think my dad fully realized the extent of what I'd gotten into, but he knew I was an agent before he died, and he was proud of me. My mom kinda lives in denial about my job, but she's proud too. She just can't handle the constant anxiety when I disappear for long assignments."

Maggie bites her lip, worry written on her face. "So, when this is all over, what will you do then? Will you leave for another assignment? Leave me behind?"

I pull her into my lap, cupping her face and laying a sweet kiss to the tip of her nose. Leaving no doubt as to the truthfulness of my words as I lay my heart open for her, I look in her eyes, my voice quaking with intensity. "Angel, I honestly don't know what happens after this. All I know is that I love you. I want to be with you, know every thought that runs through that brilliant mind of yours, watch you drink coffee ice cream for breakfast every day, and hold you while you sleep every night. I want to grow old with you, have a family with you, and claim not just your body," I rumble as my eyes rove across her skin, peppered with my love, "but also claim your heart. Forever."

Maggie is smiling, the hope shining in her eyes as she takes my hands and holds them in hers, almost like we're praying together. "I want that too, Shane. God, I want that too, to be your haven when you're protecting everyone else, to fill your heart when you've given more than you should, to create a life with you that you want to come back to reality for after a long time pretending to be someone else. I love you so much. I never thought something like this would happen to someone like me."

Our words feel like vows, promises for a future we may not get. There's no preacher, no ring, nobody to even witness them, but none of that matters. I kiss her fiercely, putting every bit of my heart and soul into the breath I give to her and demanding every bit of hers in return. Nothing less than pure honesty between us will ever be enough again.

My body responds, my cock surging inside my jeans as we part lips, panting, and I want to slip inside her sweet pussy once again, be one with her.

But I need to be inside her mind even more, know everything there is to know about my sweet Maggie, so I still her squirming hips, holding her tightly against my thickening cock. "Tell me, Angel. What did you think would happen to someone like you? What did little Maggie Postland think her life would be like?"

She smiles softly, suddenly shy. "Don't laugh, okay?"

My face is calm, more curious than anything, and after she's sure I'm listening, she continues. "I wanted to be Barbara Walters. She's like this spitfire you don't expect. Early in her career, she was seen as this blonde woman who couldn't possibly do a man's job and interview these powerful leaders. But she did, and she used her charm to get insights no one else could, without selling herself short. Nobody imagined she'd accomplish so much, but she never doubted her ability to get the scoop, verbally wiggling and manipulating her way into the interview of the decade, all the while making it seem like it was just a friendly chat. And it gave little me, blonde, sweet, kinda nerdy little Maggie hope that I could do that someday and make a difference."

I take a moment, studying her face before nodding. "I can see it, *Interviews by Maggie Postland.* You sitting in a chair, sipping coffee, and smiling that sweet smile. Maybe not Barbara style, but more like Oprah, maybe, or like one of the late-night hosts?"

"But more serious," Maggie says, and I nod.

"Right. The people you interview would never see it coming until you hit them like a fucking heat-seeking missile and started asking the tough questions. Hell, they probably wouldn't even know they'd spilled government secrets until it was too late, mesmerized by your sweet girl goodness."

Maggie lays two fingers over my lips and then lifts them high, blowing a puff of air across her fingertips. "From your lips to the universe's ears."

I smile, knowing that she's being silly but at the same time, very serious. "What about now? What about your job?"

Maggie scrunches her nose up like a bunny before making a disgusted sound. "Ugh. I'm pretty sure that I'm fired by now. My boss is strict and demanding, and considering I haven't submitted a story in over a week and haven't even called into the office in days, she'll have already started paperwork to fire me. And I'm guessing Dominick won't let me wait tables here anymore, so currently, I'm unemployed."

"And how does that feel?" I ask because she doesn't seem all that upset, which surprises me because I've seen how hard this girl works. If someone could figure out a way to generate electricity from her, she could power half the city.

Maggie grins, sighing happily. "Honestly, I feel free. You have to understand. *The Daily Spot* isn't like working for *CNN* or even *TMZ*. Sure, it was a job, but everyone there—well, nearly everyone—was either trying to scramble their way up the ladder or was bitterly hanging on so they didn't fall down to *Weekly World News* level. It was dog-eat-dog, and not even about important things. Just an overarching sense of desperation and disrespect. And here with you, even though we're basically being held hostage and everything's going to hell right now . . . I feel free."

She smiles, and I'm struck stupid once again at her beauty. I don't know how, or why, but I do think I've freed her of something she's been carrying around for a very long time. Although I bet if I were to dig deep enough, I'd find out that all I did was help her free herself.

From there, we spend the rest of the afternoon and well into the night talking about our lives, our hopes and dreams, books, TV, and everything in between. It's like we're taking our courtship, the little things that most people learn over the course of weeks or even months of dating, and compressing them into a hyper-speed conversation.

But I don't feel rushed at all. Instead, with every revelation from the mundane to the philosophical, I fall deeper in love with this girl, storing away every tidbit she gives me in my heart.

The heat builds between us, embers always burning just below the surface but spark-flashing into flames, and we pause our conversation to make love or fuck, sometimes both. The pulsing music from the club below occasionally gives us a new tempo to match, leaving us both laughing at times afterward.

With Maggie, even when I'm slamming into her from behind, her hair wrapped in my fist as she cries out, her ass pink from my hand and my marks all over her smooth skin . . . even then, it's a hundred percent love.

Finally, we fall into bed together, happily exhausted.

"Well, at least we've done one thing right," Maggie says as she giggles and lays a naked thigh across my leg.

"What's that?" I ask. "I think we've done a lot of things right today."

"Oh, no doubt. But what I meant was that everyone goes to a strip club to indulge in a sexual fantasy, but it's only that, a fantasy. We get to do the real thing."

"Good point. Now we just need to get a pole up here and—"

Maggie tickles me in the ribs, making me laugh. "And I'll make you dance for me!"

I don't answer, but the reality is if she asked, I damn well might do it.

CHAPTER
Twenty-Three
MAGGIE

BY LATE THAT NIGHT, or technically early the next morning, Shane and I finally lift our heads from being lost in each other and the hopes that there's any way this is going to be okay.

Okay, okay . . . we lift our heads from a nap, but as I told Shane, I'm unemployed.

Soon after the club closes, we carefully head downstairs, as Shane says he wants to check in with Dominick. I sneak backstage and find Allie alone in the locker room.

She's dressed in her silky robe, sitting at a mirrored table to remove the layers of makeup she wears for the stage. "Hey, Allie. How was the show tonight?"

She looks up, meeting my eyes in the mirror, and I can tell she's still mad. Guess I can understand. I mean, I did drop a grenade into the middle of her world.

"No, don't do that," Allie replies, barbs in every word that sting as they hit my eardrums. "Don't ask me shit like how my dancing went or how my night was. Like you care when your whole gig here was fake."

Ouch. I step into the dressing room, really trying. Allie's important to me. "I do care. And it wasn't all fake. Yeah, the job, calling myself Meghan . . . but I meant what I said about feeling like I belonged here and that I found a family."

Allie snorts, her eyes glued to the mirror as she peels her fake lashes off. "I don't know if I should believe that. I mean, you're obviously a good liar, so how can I ever believe what you say?"

I sigh, hugging myself and knowing she's got a point. "You're right, but I swear, Allie. You're one of my best friends, not just in *this* life," I say, indicating the club around us, "but in my whole life. You think I didn't want to let you in all the way? I'm sorry I didn't tell you the truth and that it hurt you."

Allie finally turns around to face me. "This is some really fucked up shit you've gotten me into. I didn't know all that stuff from yesterday."

My eyebrows jump as my jaw drops, and I try to keep my voice to a whisper. "You didn't know about Dominick, about the mob?"

Allie shakes her head, whispering back just in case we're overheard. "No! I mean, I knew Dom was a bigwig, but I thought it was just . . . here, as the owner of a fancy strip club. I didn't know he was *big*, like in charge of the city. Who wants to work in a mob-owned strip club?"

I nod, knowing that especially with Allie's background, that's the last place she ever imagined she'd end up. "So, what happened?"

Allie turns back to her table and starts working on her makeup again. "That guy's blood was all over me. Dominick carried me into his office and helped me get cleaned up. He was furious, the anger buzzing around him like a force field, but he was gentle with me. Tucked me in on the couch in his office and went out to talk to the guys."

"That was about the time Shane was hustling me out of the club," I reply. "He was so worried about me. Looking back, it was touching."

Allie finally gives me a ghost of a smile, looking into the mirror. "I bet. I don't know what Dom told the guys. I guess I just avoided thinking about it because I was in shock. He gave me a couple of days off, even offered to let me stay upstairs in the apartment you're in, but I just wanted to go home and hide in my own bed, you know? So he drove me there himself and came by morning and night to make sure I ate and was okay. He took care of me, and when he wasn't there, Nick or Logan was downstairs, making sure I was safe. And then you called with the whole meeting thing, and he said he needed me to be there, for him and for you. And the three of you just sat there and spouted off all this big scary shit like it was normal conversation."

I realize that while everyone always teases me about my innocence, this time, it's Allie whose bubble of innocence was burst. "I'm sorry you found out like that. I didn't know what you knew, but we needed you there because we thought Dominick wouldn't hurt us in front of you."

Allie smiles sadly, turning around to face me. "You used me. I figured out that part, at least, and I guess I can see why. I just wish I could go back to being blind to all of this around me. I mean, Dominick's a great guy who's been taking care of me, a good boss who makes it feel safe here, considering it's a strip club. But now, I'm just . . . lost."

Her words break my heart, and I step closer, putting my hands on her shoulders. "You're not lost, Allie. Nothing here has changed. You're still you, Dominick is still Dominick, and I'm still me. Now, the veil is just lifted and you're seeing behind the curtain a bit. It's shocking, but it's better to know the truth, even if it's ugly, than a pretty lie."

Allie puts a hand over mine and looks over her shoulder. "That's me, the pretty tragedy. Don't worry, I'm just still adjusting. I don't know what to think about all of this. Tonight was the first night I've performed since the shooting. I was just in total mind dump mode, not thinking at all. Although I practiced so much at home that I finally got that spinning death-drop move perfected. It was flawless."

I grin, even as her eyebrows pull together. "I might need to rename the move though. Seems a bit dark, considering what's been happening."

I rub her shoulders gently. "Call it whatever you want. Allie, what's awesome about you is how even in the deepest of valleys, you've never given up. You keep working until you find a hilltop, and that's where you make your stand for the next journey. You sort of helped me, too. So many times over the past couple of months, I kept telling myself, 'be like Allie. She'd keep going.' And it was true."

Allie takes a deep breath, nodding. "I like that. So . . . Shane? Is that where you're standing for your next journey?"

I smile, feeling the mood shift to some semblance of before, when we'd dish about how hot the security guys are and lament Dominick's no-fraternizing policy. Even as she cheered me on, she also thought it'd never happen. Guess we were both wrong.

Grabbing a chair, I sit down next to her, grinning foolishly as she raises an eyebrow. "What can I say except . . . he's amazing, even better than what you used to tease me about. The last few days have been scary, especially when we had to explain the huge web of lies and get everything untangled. But he's been there for me, kept me safe."

I sigh, not fully able to put into words everything I feel about Shane.

But Allie seems to understand, grinning mischievously. "I can see he's been there . . . and there, and oh, over there too, twice, by the looks of it," she says cheekily as she indicates the various marks visible on my body. "Is there any part of you he *hasn't* been?"

I blush furiously, proud of Shane's claiming of me but feeling shy that she's pointing them out so . . . individually. "Yeah, he's a little . . . mouthy . . . and possessive. I, uh . . . I like it."

I can feel my face burning even brighter, and Allie smiles.

"Well, that's what matters. And good God, a mouthy man. Bet he gives the best oral! Lucky girl."

She winks at me, and things feel like they're okay, or at least like they might be okay someday. "Hey, you wanna see my spinning death-drop?"

Eager to get the focus off me and Shane and our bedroom activities, I nod. "Yes! Let me see, girl! But only if you're not too tired after your performances tonight."

"Never too tired for you," Allie replies with a snort. "I could use a few more practice spins too. Come on!"

We go onto the floor, where everyone but Marco has already left, and

Allie takes her place on stage while I sit at the front row center table. In the background, I can hear Marco working downstairs, probably still cleaning up.

She does a few warmups, and within minutes, she's twirling around the pole, high above the stage floor. There's no music, so it has a different feel. Gone is the sexy sway. It's just the quiet intensity and small grunts as Allie *works* the pole. No wonder they do pole dance fitness classes.

Allie does some kick trick that I couldn't describe even if I tried because it happens so fast, my brain can't even register it. All I see is her stilettoed foot kick out, and then Allie is speeding upside down toward the floor in a spiral with her arms spread wide in a T, and I gasp. "Allie!"

Right before her head smacks into the stage, she grabs the pole and rolls it along her shoulder, her legs straddling open for a moment before she settles to the floor in the splits.

As if she didn't just cheat death and defy gravity, she pulls her feet back under and rises gracefully. "So, what do you think?"

My mouth is still hanging wide open, but I manage to yell out, "Mother trucking smurfin' yeah, biz-nitch!" as I clap loudly. "You're my hero!"

Allie smiles, and I can see the pride on her face, even as she downplays it. "Yeah, it's not ballet, for damn sure, but it sure is fun!"

From the side of the stage, I hear a door open and close, and both our eyes snap that direction. But it's only Marco coming up from the stockroom, boxes of beer in his hands.

He sees me and immediately sets them down. "Holy fuck, Meghan! Where have you been? You okay?"

I run over and give him a hug, and Allie joins in. The three of us hug like it's been years instead of days, and even though Marco called me by the wrong name, I feel at home.

It doesn't matter that it's a strip club or that there's more to the story than we planned.

I'm home with these people.

Guess Shane's right. There is a bit of bad girl inside me.

Twenty~Four

I STAND on Dominick's left, Nick to the right as we knock once on the door of the large brownstone near downtown. That we're even here is just shy of batshit crazy, but it's Dom's show. I'm just the muscle who may or may not have to pull out his FBI badge along with a gun at some point.

"You sure?" Nick, who doesn't know the full story, asks. "I mean, this place—"

"If you don't have the balls, Nick, I suggest you leave," Dom says, not turning his eyes from the door. "I'd rather go in with just Shane having my back than someone who doesn't have balls."

Nick swallows but stands his ground. The door opens, and though the muscled man who answers doesn't say it, his surprise is written clear as day on his face.

Dominick doesn't pause or look at all worried as he adjusts the cuffs on his perfectly tailored suit. In a tasteful black, of course, befitting the occasion. "Good afternoon. We're here to pay our respects for the loss."

You can tell the goon wants to object, or at a minimum wants to pat us all down, but what's the use when we're all obviously carrying weapons at our sides? Instead, he steps to the side, giving a respectful nod. "Please come in, Mr. Angeline."

We enter as a group, both for security and to make sure that we can't get separated. Inside, the wake is loud and boisterous, more of a party than the somber affair of a man who just lost his son unexpectedly and tragically. Actually, considering that I hear what seems to be Latin music playing, it sounds like a damn graduation party.

Still, when Dominick enters the room, a hush falls over the gathering and eyes dart left and right, obviously confused about his appearance. The music stops, and the only sound is one kid who's in the corner and obviously doesn't quite understand what's happening as he keeps doing some lame ass jig until someone pops him in the shoulder.

Fortunately, no one pulls a weapon. From an armchair in the center of the room, a man with slicked back ebony hair and large thick-framed glasses stands up. I've never met him, but for the past year plus some, I've made sure I'm intimately aware of his face. He's old enough to be Dominick's father, and considerably larger, but there's no mistaking who the real alpha male in the room is.

Sal Rivaldi might try and push his way into East Robinsville, but Dominick isn't going to let that happen with a breath in his body. Even in his thirties, Dominick is the king of this city and wears his invisible crown like a man with experience and the balls to back whatever play he has deemed correct.

It matters not if the battle is physical or mental. I'd bet on Dominick to win every time.

Looking as if he were standing in his own church instead of the wake of his biggest rival's son, Dominick extends his hand toward the older man. "Don Rivaldi, I wish to extend my most sincere apologies on the loss of your son. Word of his character had spread throughout the city, and you must be devastated."

Damn, he is a slick son of a bitch. Not many men could make an expression of sympathy include a backhanded comment about what a shitstain your son was, while also letting it be known that nothing happens in your city without your knowledge. And the use of the term 'Don'. Very smooth, in that it both gives Sal respect, while at the same time saying he's behind the times. Dominick's never insisted on being called Don. In fact, I've never heard anyone under the age of sixty use the term with him.

Rivaldi dips his chin in acknowledgement but keeps his eyes on Dominick the whole time. "Please, we are past all these niceties. You can call me Sal."

I hide a smirk. Dad used to listen to an old song that sounded a lot like that. Dominick looks genuinely pleased, although probably because in the subtle game of mob bosses, he was just elevated in the Rivaldi family's eyes. "Of course, Sal. And you may call me Dominick."

Everyone notices the infinitesimal put-down. Sal said that Dominick could use his casual name, while Dominick insisted on his full first name. Nearly, but not quite the same level, and Sal knows it. They eye each other for a moment, the tension in the room building, but Dominick stays cool as a cucumber, no tension in his body even though I know he could snap into asskicking mode in an instant. "Sal, the timing may be indelicate, but I wondered if we could speak?"

Sal looks like he might start something but then relents. "Yes, of course." He gestures to the chair next to the one he just vacated. Sal moves to a bar in the corner, lifting a decanter of what's either scotch or something similar. "Drink?"

My training says to never, ever accept a drink from an enemy. Especially alcohol. It's too easy to hide shit in there. But Dom operates by his own rules and instead nods easily, confident that Sal wouldn't be stupid enough to try something. "That would be lovely. Thank you."

Dominick takes the amber liquid from Sal and swirls it in the glass before resting it on the arm of the chair. Sal sits, the excitement obvious in his eyes. He thinks he's gotten one over, that he's actually going to take over the city from a man clearly his better in every way.

I'm reminded of the saying, *'Pride goeth before the fall.'* because Sal has no idea the precipice he's standing on. I take station behind Dominick, while Nick stands a few feet away, his eyes scanning the rest of the group as quiet, tense conversation begins anew.

"I wanted to discuss some things with you," Dominick leads off, still swirling his drink as he looks Sal in the eye. "Some rather troubling things I've heard about your organization."

Sal doesn't move, but the light in his eyes turns more suspicious and the tension in the room pulls even tighter. The room is silent, with only an occasional whispered comment as everyone keeps their eyes on the two bosses. I scan, noting the guy to my left who just unbuttoned his jacket, a sure sign he's getting twitchy.

"What things have you heard?" Sal asks, sipping his drink. Dominick, though, keeps his glass swirling, almost maddeningly. The liquid never stops moving and Dom's gaze never wavers. Motion and stillness, attack and patience . . . both Dominick's strong suits, and something everyone in the room is well aware of.

"Word on the street is that you'd like to expand your stronghold, which I can, of course, understand," Dominick says casually, as if he's discussing the weather. "I can even appreciate your ambition. But you forget your position of power is in *my* city simply because I allow it to be. And your growth, or lack thereof, is also at my discretion."

Sal sneers, his fingers tightening on his glass. "I'm sure you'd like to think that, wouldn't you? But I own parts of this city because I work them when you don't. The people there fear me, not you. They need my drugs, my protection, not yours."

Dominick nods, still unruffled. "Perhaps. But that is because I've let you have the scraps from my table, the areas that are too troublesome for the meager dollars I could wring out of them. Do not think that I've not kept my fingers on the pulse of those areas, nor that I could not cut off that pulse with a single twitch of my fingers if I wished. I haven't concerned myself with your actions. Until now."

Sal feigns a look of surprise, trying to regain his balance. "My actions?

I've done nothing but continue my business as usual. Yet, here we are, mourning my son. Dead in your club, let us not forget."

Sal is playing up the sympathy card with the audience.

Dominick chuckles, playing to the audience as well as he turns away from Sal to look around the room, speaking to those watching. "Ah, yes, Carlos Rivaldi. The bastard son who shows up out of the blue, full of ego and demanding his birthright. Must have put you in an uncomfortable position, not able to deny your blood-son, but he was just so . . ." Dominick pauses dramatically before locking eyes with Sal, "*weak*. And ungrateful for the scraps you gave him. I dare say, he was much like his father. And how did you handle this?"

Sal stammers, his voice quaking with rage and an undercurrent of worry that tells me he's scared of what Dominick might say. "I gave him every chance, and then he gets killed on a simple mission."

Dominick smirks, knowing he's totally in control of the conversation and where it's heading. "No, I don't think you gave him every chance. You knew he was weak, ungrateful, and power-hungry, so *you* had him killed. On my territory. Such disrespect and ugliness. Especially the part where you've been blaming me for his death to anyone who'd listen."

The reaction to Dominick's revelation is instant, the crowd of men all murmuring and looking at one another. Sal rears up, finding indignation in Dominick's accusation. "I would never! He was my *son*!"

"Perhaps so," Dominick says before dropping the bomb I know he's had planned this whole time. "In which case you should know that I am also hunting the *hitman* who conducted his business on my grounds. I will have revenge for that insult, and it will be slow and painful. I'll make sure that he tells me *everything* I wish to know. But beyond that, I would say that having a son who is such a disappointment, who even in a sacrificial death was not able to serve your ends, is punishment enough. Although his mother's Colombian family may not feel the same way." Dominick locks eyes with the dark-haired man we all know is the Colombian's representative at the wake.

Dominick lets that sink in for a moment, silently watching Sal's face for any response as he realizes that his plan is backfiring in his face. With shaking fingers, he downs the rest of his drink, the ice in the tumbler chattering when he sets it down. "So you're not here to discuss war."

Dominick looks amused again and chuckles lightly. "I'm merely here to extend my apologies for your son, and perhaps to share some advice with a fellow businessman."

"Oh, and what's that?"

Dominick stops his swirling scotch and tosses it back in one practiced movement, not reacting at all as it burns its way down his throat to explode in his stomach. He sets the empty glass on the table in front of him pointedly, commanding every eye in the room with his presence. "When you are being allowed to scurry and play like mice, it is best to not draw the attention of the cat. Because once the cat has set his sights on you, it's difficult to circumvent his instincts. His instincts to hunt, to destroy, to own. In the scheme of life, the cat worries not about the mice. They are inconsequential until they become a nuisance. Then, the cat takes delight in playing with them, until eventually, he kills them."

Sal looks a bit flushed, the tip of his olive nose and cheeks ruddy with fury, and maybe alcohol, but he manages to keep it together, trying to save face with the room full of his men who are now looking at him with new eyes. "Excellent advice, I'm sure. Thank you."

Dominick rises, indicating the conversation is over. As he nears the door, Nick and I still shadowing him, he turns around. "Oh, Sal. I was discussing the shooting with my team when a curious thing occurred to me."

Sal, who's whispering furiously to an underling, looks up. "Oh?"

"In watching the security feeds, it seems the hitman never entered the club through the front door," Dominick reveals. "In fact, it seems he entered through a back door and completed the hit during an irregular blip in our surveillance. Most unusual, wouldn't you agree?"

Sal nods, a smarmy smile crossing his face. "Yes, must've been his lucky day."

Bad move, and Dom just won the war without even firing a single shot. With his words, Sal just unintentionally confirmed Dominick's version of events in front of his entire crew. The men look angry . . . at Sal.

Dominick nods, letting things play out with just one more nudge in the right direction to let Sal destroy himself. "I don't particularly believe in luck myself. I believe in planning and strategy. And I asked myself, what would be my plan for a job like this? It took me a moment to come to terms with my answer, admittedly because I wanted to refuse the truth, but truth is apathetic, neither caring whether we want it or not. It simply is . . . true."

In a lightning-fast move that I can barely follow, Dominick turns and punches Nick square in the jaw, sending him crashing to the floor. I drop my foot back to steady my stance, keeping my eyes on everyone but Dominick, knowing he can handle himself with Nick on the floor. Everyone in the room is frozen, on high alert, but not getting involved . . . yet.

"*An inside man*. That's what he needed to get in and out undetected," Dominick growls, bending down to grab a handful of Nick's hair and slamming his face to the floor. "Someone in the club had to let him in the back door and mess with the security feed."

Dominick slams a heel on Nick's knee, the crack audible even as Nick cries out in agony. I see Rivaldi men tensing, but this isn't a matter they can involve themselves in. Dom is beating the shit out of his own man. Besides, they know I've got the drop on the whole room, my pistol in my hand but not drawn yet.

Dominick trusts that I'm watching the room, a huge move on his part, He ignores the gathered men, instead addressing Nick, his voice rising in anger.

"Even once I admitted that someone in my organization had to have been in on it, I didn't want it to be you. You were the good soldier, I thought. But it lined up. It was you. Did you even try to catch him when you pursued him? I doubt it."

Nick is trying to crawl away, but Dominick stomps on his right hand, twisting his heel to get every finger. The bones sound like twigs being broken, and Nick collapses, rolling onto his back and cradling his ruined hand to his chest. "Dom—"

Dominick grabs Nick's shirt, pulling him face to face. "I trusted you, Nick. And you repaid me with betrayal, working for the little mice and their hired gun. For what? Money? Power? You think they'll trust you when you've already turned once?" Dominick sneers in disgust. His voice quiets, the amount of control scarier than if he was raging. "Not killing you today is a kindness for the years of service you did give me. But if I ever see you again, I *will* kill you."

And with the final threat, Dominick lands one last powerful punch to Nick's nose and blood splatters. Dominick drops him, reaching into his pocket with his clean hand to retrieve his handkerchief and meticulously wiping the blood away.

I reach down, taking Nick's gun while Dominick finishes up, turning back to Sal and sounding like nothing's happened. "I'll leave this trash for you. Not sure he'll be of any use to you with a bum knee, fucked trigger finger, and buyable loyalty. But he is *your* man after all. I trust there won't be a repeat of this issue."

Sal looks from Dominick's stone-cold eyes to Nick, groaning in agony on the floor, and seems to realize that he'd severely underestimated just how smart and how batshit-crazy Dominick really is. "No, Mr. Angeline."

Satisfied, Dominick walks out the door, stepping over Nick dismissively. I wish I could do the same, but the anger in me is too much to bear. Nick is part of the machine that put my Angel in danger.

I can't do anything about Sal right now. I can't get my hands on the hitman the way I'd like, but I trusted Nick and Maggie trusted Nick. He was the guy I thought was my most trusted coworker.

So I give in, kicking him as hard as I can in the gut with my steel-toed boot. Nick screams, curling protectively into a fetal position. He probably deserves more of a beatdown, but I'm done.

I follow Dominick out, getting behind the wheel to drive him back to Petals. Outside, we stay silent until we pull away. "Shane."

"Yes?" I ask, looking up into the rearview mirror. If he did want to kill me, this would be the best time. He could shoot me through the seat. He's buckled in, and we're not going that fast.

Dom's eyes meet mine in the mirror, icy grey and hard. "I wanted to handle that myself. It was necessary for an appearance of strength and knowledge," he explains, finally answering the question I'd asked in his office when I checked in with him last night. The conversation had led to some rather unsightly conclusions after I reviewed the remaining security video and we'd talked through different possibilities of what happened. "The hitman on the other hand . . . if you would like, you may have your turn. Or I can take care of that as well. Your choice. For now though, let's go back to the club."

Back to Maggie.

CHAPTER

Twenty-Five

MAGGIE

I PACE back and forth in the apartment, trying my best not to get freaked out. When Shane told me last night that he was going with Dominick on a mission to hopefully prevent the war that could ruin the city, I begged him not to go. I was nearly paralyzed with terror that it was a setup by Dominick.

But Shane said that he and Dominick talked things through, and he felt like he needed to back Dom's play. He also promised he'd be safe before we made love and he left a few new souvenirs along my skin.

But since they left, I've been jittery with nerves that I'll never see him again. Knowing I need to keep busy, I give up pacing and decide to check in with my regular life . . . the one I had before everything went so haywire.

I can't believe that Dominick's let me have access to a computer, but he did. After our first night here, I gave Allie my keys, and she went to my apartment, coming back with some clothes and my laptop. Dominick didn't even ask to go through my files. "Maggie," he said, "anything you have that you've already published can't be pulled back, and anything you have in there that you could publish, I trust you won't." He said it kindly, but the threat was apparent in his simple words.

A quick run through my email deletes most of the spam, but there are several from Jeanine at work. She's left several voicemails on my phone that were forwarded to my email program too, but after two, I turn them off. It's best to go straight to the source.

I grab the burner phone Shane left me, dialing into the office and waiting for the receptionist to transfer me to Jeanine's office line. I get lucky. I'm not left hanging on hold for long.

"Jeanine Matthews."

"Hi, Jeanine. It's Maggie. I wanted to call to—"

Before I can even get my greeting out, Jeanine interrupts me, her voice crisp and hard. "You have some nerve calling in like this. You drop off the face of the Earth, don't return my calls or meet deadlines for nearly a week, and now you just call in? You should've just stayed gone."

She's mad. Still, some professional instinct guides me to try to patch things up so I'm not leaving under the pall of job abandonment. "Ma'am, I had an emergency and I couldn't call in or check emails for a while. I'm back now and trying to catch up."

Jeanine stops her rant, greed tingeing her voice. Toss her a sniff about a headline, and she'd let me get away with murder. "Anything story-worthy?"

If only she knew, but she thinks I'm just a strip-club waitress looking for celebrity gossip. She has no idea about the depth of how things go at Petals, who Dominick is, or any of the things I've learned over the last few days. And this is a story I wouldn't touch with a ten-foot pole. Dominick's shown me some trust. I'm not stupid enough to betray that.

"No, just a family emergency."

It's not really a lie because the people at Petals are my family now, and while it might take me awhile, I plan on regaining their trust, if that's possible.

Jeanine sighs, annoyance making her drag it out longer than usual. "Unacceptable, Miss Postland. We have standards, the least of which is that you turn in quality work on time. Abandoning your job and your duties cannot stand. You're fired," she jeers, obviously enjoying the opportunity to shut me down. "I wish you all the best in your future waitressing endeavors."

I'm not surprised. I figured this would be coming, even told Shane as much when we discussed it. But now that it's real and actually happening, I thought I might be upset. But all I feel is relief . . . free. And it's a bit funny that she thinks getting fired is such a big deal, considering I'm on the run from a hitman trying to kill me. Losing a crappy job is the least of my concerns.

Instead of laughing like I want, I clear my throat, but still, my voice is light, maybe even hinging on giggly when I respond. "I understand, Jeanine. If you could please have the HR department mail me my last check. My apologies. It's been *interesting* working for you."

It's as close as I can get to telling her that she's a shrew whom people mimic at the office. Hanging up, I let the laughter overtake me. "I'm fired!" I cheer as I throw my hands up and laugh uproariously. "Bwahahahaha, I'm actually fired!"

I'm still basically a prisoner for my own safety, but I truly feel free. No more lies—with Jeanine, with Dominick, with Allie, and most importantly, with Shane. Knowing I need to make one more call, I dial my mother, but only to tell her I'm fine, not filling her in on recent events.

Luckily, she wasn't worried about me, saying she figured I was just busy with work and stuff. It's hard to imagine, but it's really only been days since this whole debacle started. It feels like so much longer. So much has happened. So much might happen still. And Mom never has really asked about my job. I think she's still disappointed I didn't become an accountant or a lawyer or get some nice office job where I could meet a 'good man'.

Well, guess what, Mom? I've met, bedded, and laid claim to not just a good man, but an amazing man. And if I live another month, who knows where Shane and I will be? We're moving so fast already.

I feel the smile spread wide across my face, the happiness bubbling out unbidden. I turn the phone off and lay down on the couch, eyes on the door as I wait for Shane to get back.

I have to trust that he and Dominick are going to come back. That I'll be safe again. That I'll have a chance to figure out what to do from here. That Shane and I will figure out a way to be together.

I don't nap, but the time just sort of slips by. Still, when I hear the familiar heavy tread of his footsteps coming up the stairs, I'm waiting for him. "Angel, I'm—"

Shane doesn't have a chance to finish his greeting as I throw myself across the little apartment, laughing and leaping into his arms to smother his face in kisses. With each smooch, relief and happiness course through me. He wraps his arms around me, picking me up higher and using my momentum to spin us in a circle as we kiss.

It feels like I haven't seen him in forever, even though it's only been a few hours. I was just so scared.

Pulling back, Shane looks deep into my eyes. "Damn, Angel. That's a welcome home I could get used to."

I smile, kissing him again, softly this time. "I missed you today. I was worried."

Shane sets me down, cupping my face in his hands. "I told you, we're gonna be okay. Today was a step in the right direction, and Dominick handled Sal like a boss."

"A boss?" I ask, and Shane laughs.

"Well, more like The Boss. It went well, and I think we prevented the war. Sal's guys know what he did, how he tried to manipulate and lie and killed his own son. I don't imagine them charging into Dominick's territory after his display today. Hell, half of them probably want to work for Dominick now, and the other half pray they never have to see him again."

I smile, trying to imagine Dominick as a monster who would make grown men shake in their boots, but I just can't. Dominick is scary, no doubting that, but he's civilized and has a code of honor. I can't picture him getting rough and dirty.

"So, one crisis averted? One to go?"

Shane looks at me, then nods. "Yeah, Angel. For now, all we can do is stay here, wait for intel, and be safe. Dom even found a mole who let the hitman in. It was Nick."

"Nick? Really?" I ask, disappointed. "He seemed like a nice guy."

"Maybe he was, but it doesn't matter," Shane says, kissing my forehead once. "You're what matters. We can relax for a bit. Chucky and Dom are both looking into the hitman issue, so we should know something soon, but for now, all we can do is wait."

He lays his cheek against the top of my head, hugging me close. It's sweet and comforting, but that's not what I want. I don't want to be babied and kept like a fragile doll he's scared to break.

I want to celebrate that things are getting better—freedom from my job, hope that there won't be a war—to celebrate this moment as the gift it is.

My cheek pressed to his chest, I reach down, letting my hand roam closer and closer to his waistband. "Well, that's not *all* we can do . . ."

Shane looks down at me, and I bite my lip, waiting to see what he says, what he'll do. He's searching for something in my eyes, some sign that I'm really okay with everything that's happening.

I can't wait any longer for him to decide and force the issue by lifting up to my tiptoes and using his shoulders as leverage to press my mouth to his. I lick the seam of his lips, begging him to open for me as my free hand reaches down to cup him through his pants.

It's all it takes to wipe away the last of his worries, and it's the last moment I'm in charge. His tongue presses into my mouth, consuming me as he pulls my hair, tilting my face higher toward him.

A moan escapes me, and Shane answers with a growl. Holding me in his strong arms, he carries me across the room into the living room, but our mouths never break contact. Instead, he's guided by some form of internal radar or something until he reaches the middle of the room. He sets me down, immediately ripping my long T-shirt over my head and slipping my panties to the floor.

I stand there, naked and wanting as he pulls his clothes off with almost unnatural speed. His cock is hard, reaching toward his belly button, and I can see a drop of clear precum on the head. I want it and unconsciously, I lick my lips as my knees start to bend.

Shane notices and smirks. "You want to taste me again, Angel? It's yours. I'm yours."

I drop all the way to my knees and look up at Shane from the floor. "Then give it to me."

I stick my tongue out as Shane grasps his cock, guiding the tip to my outstretched tongue, and the flavor of the salty drop explodes across my tongue, making me whimper for more. I want to worship him, to show him that he's my everything.

Shane slides a hand into my hair, holding me still, and slips his tip along my tongue, teasing me, teasing himself as he reads my eyes, nodding. I cover his shaft in little butterfly kisses and lollipop licks until he shudders, his control stretched as far as he can take it. "Fuck, Maggie," he growls, pulling my hair tighter. "Suck me."

It's all the permission I need to take back a bit of control, and I close my lips around him, letting my tongue dance around his slit before bobbing up and down along his shaft, setting a fierce pace.

I hollow my cheeks, sucking him hard and delighting at the sounds I'm drawing from him. I reach up, my fingers digging into the dimples on his powerful ass muscles as I pull him in all the way. He's mine, and I'm his . . . his loving, worshipful woman who can take all he has.

All too soon, though, he pulls back, squeezing tight at the base of his shaft as he shakes his head. "Not yet. I want to come inside that sweet little pussy."

I nod, smiling as Shane offers me a hand, helping me rise from his feet and then immediately turning me so that my back is to his front. The entire skin of my back is pressed against him as I look over my shoulder while he cups my breasts. He guides me toward the couch near the wall. It's big, and when he pushes me over the high arm of the couch, my toes barely reach the floor while he gets me positioned the way he wants.

"Damn, Angel," Shane says, his voice raspy and heavy with need. "You look so pretty like this, ass up in the air so I can see your wet little pussy, so ready for my cock. Only one thing could make it better."

I'm squirming, needy, so when he bends down, I expect a nice lick to my soaked core. But that's not what Shane does, my mouthy, possessive man.

He swipes a thumb through my folds and bites low on my ass, right at the meaty part above my thighs, and the sharp prick of pain blends with the pleasure as he strokes me. I cry out, arching my back for more, but Shane stands, and I look over my shoulder.

He's licking his thumb, sucking my juices from his skin and moaning at the flavor. "Always so sweet . . . but I think I'm turning you into a dirty girl, Angel."

"A naughty angel for my devil with a heart of gold. I am a dirty girl, Shane . . . *your* dirty girl."

The words set him off, and with a growl, he slams into me balls-deep and immediately begins pumping in and out, hard and fast. I reach back, wanting to feel him piston into me, my nails scratching along the skin of his hips. I can't see them, but I know I'm marking him too, little pink lines proclaiming him as mine. I dream that maybe those marks will be permanent, maybe something that we can share.

Shane grabs one of my hands, pulling it to my lower back and locking it in place with a tight grip. His other hand twists tightly into my hair, and I'm at his mercy, pinned down and getting *fucked*. Even to myself, the word sounds filthy, and that turns me on even more. I mewl, whining as I beg him.

"Yes Shane . . . fuck me . . . please . . ."

He pulls me tighter, his voice a low, growling demand. "What did you say?"

I don't know if he likes it or hates it, and right now, I don't care because it's all I can manage to say. "Fuck me, Shane. Fuck. Me. Hard."

He leans over me, covering my back with his body and pressing me into the couch arm, one hand still trapped between us. "Mmm, my fucking *dirty* Angel." He strokes into me again and again, filling and stretching me as I whimper, begging for more. "Come for me."

He suckles the flesh along my shoulder into his mouth, marking me once again, and I feel pushed harder than ever. His cock is so deep, and I cry out in pleasure and pain.

The moment stretches, both of us on the precipice forever, riding that edge before I fall off, crashing into my orgasm, and Shane comes too, ropes of his hot cum filling me. It drives me more, my pleasure drawing out like a rope too, going on and on as I scream hoarsely. I'm calling out his name and swearing that I'm his as his deep bellow accompanies my cries in a symphony as we finish together.

CHAPTER

Twenty-Six

SHANE

WE SPEND the rest of the evening in the apartment, relaxing. For several hours, we can hear the music booming below us as the club carries on business as usual. We'd done the same, continuing our rounds of talking and lovemaking, pausing to eat and chat before our passions overtake us again.

Around two in the morning, Maggie mentions going downstairs to see Allie, but after the run-in with the Rivaldis, I'm uneasy. "Angel, I know Dominick seems to think this is all handled, and I'm hopeful he's right, but sometimes, a cornered animal is the meanest, and I'm nervous Sal is going to be desperate enough to do something crazy."

"But what about Allie and Dom and . . . well, everyone downstairs?"

I nod, hugging her tightly. "I know. But I can't protect them all. I can protect you, though, and it'd make me feel a lot better if you had Allie come up here rather than us go downstairs."

She agrees, and Allie's actually willing to hang out a bit before she heads home so we can all grab some shut eye. Waking up at noon, Maggie and I eat a simple breakfast of Golden Grahams and tea before sneaking downstairs carefully to check in with Dominick.

I knock on his door, my usual two raps, and from inside, I hear him. "Come in, Shane."

We enter, and he turns around from his desk, smirking that he knew simply by my knock. "Please, sit."

He motions to the chairs sitting in front of his desk, and we sink into them. I notice Maggie has her knees pulled to her chest again, her arms wrapped around her legs. It makes me worry, but I know it'll take her awhile to feel comfortable in Dominick's presence now. "Thanks. Just wanted to check in."

Dom nods, stroking his chin. "So you've heard."

I furrow my brow, confused. I came down for a general check-in and to see if there was a way for Maggie and me to safely stretch our legs. "Heard? Heard what?"

Dominick leans back in his chair, relaxing. "Have you been in contact with . . ." He seems to be searching for a word, an uncommon occurrence for a man who uses words like sharp knives. "Your handlers?"

I look to Maggie and then shake my head. "I don't really have one. An unofficial contact, but making official contact is . . . dramatic."

Dominick smiles, seemingly laughing inside. "Perhaps you should check in with them. At least your unofficial contact."

He doesn't seem inclined to give me privacy for the call, so I reach into my pocket and speed-dial Chucky, putting the phone to my ear.

The line connects with silence, and I talk first, keeping Chucky's name out of it lest Dominick get curious for more information. It may be a nickname, but I wouldn't put it past Dom to find out Chucky's real name and entire history in less than forty-eight hours if he was motivated to do so. "Hey, man. It's Shane."

Chucky sounds excited, panting as he greets me. "Damn, dude, you must have balls of fucking steel! Everyone here is talking about how Dominick walked into Sal's house, in the middle of a fucking wake, told all his shit to the whole damn crew, including the Colombians, and then beat the shit out of a traitor. And you just stood there, sweet as you please, with no reaction."

Interesting. Guess they didn't hear about my kicking the shit out of Nick on my way out. Probably a good thing, considering everything else. I never actually met the man the FBI put in the Rivaldi family, but he must not have been present. The FBI wouldn't ignore my beating the fuck out of Nick like that. The boot to the gut on a downed man was definitely past 'appropriate use of force.'

"Yeah," I reply airily, though, trying to play it off. "That's pretty much what happened."

"Weren't you shitting your pants that Dominick was going to kill you?" Chucky asks, still panting a little. "I mean, I know you're in Dom's custody, but it would've been real fucking easy for him to say he was taking you to Sal's and then dump your body in the river. Probably even keep the girl for himself."

I look at Dominick, considering what happened in the car yesterday, and make up my mind. "No, if he wanted me dead, I would be. He's a man of his word and said he'd help, so I trusted him to follow through."

Chucky whoops like a teenager at a pop concert, and I have to pull my phone away for a moment to wince. "That's some top-notch loyalty there, man. Not sure I'd trust anyone that that much, even if they were player one in the game."

"It's not a game, man. Any other updates? Word on the hitman?" I ask, getting irritated at Chucky's casualness considering this is my life. Maggie's life.

Chucky whistles, obviously surprised. "You haven't heard about the hitman?"

There's something to Chucky's tone, a weirdness I can't place. I look to Dominick, who's eyes are crinkling a bit . . . in amusement? "No, I haven't heard. What is it?"

"Sal Rivaldi woke up this morning to find the hitman dead . . . in his living room . . . sitting up in his fucking throne of a chair . . . and none of the guards saw a thing." Chucky delivers the details with dramatic pauses for effect, and it works.

"So, he's dead?" I ask, a little disappointed. The bastard almost killed my woman and put a groove in my left bicep that's going to leave a wicked scar. I wanted to at least get a little bit of a receipt on that.

Chucky laughs darkly, obviously pleased, although I know if he found a dead body in his living room, someone would need to call an ambulance for his heart attack. "Yeah, you could fucking say that. That's not even the best part, though." I wait, knowing Chucky will tell me when he's ready. Finally, he laughs. "The best part is that on the coffee table were a handful of bullet cases, presumed to be the brass from Carlos's shooting, and an invoice . . . for the repairs to Petals's private room!" Chucky is wheezing, laughter taking his breath away, and I can't help but smile. Dominick is a twisted, manipulative son of a bitch and a damn scary motherfucker.

I like him. Too bad we officially have to be enemies when this is all said and done.

Chucky is winding down, getting himself under control while I study Dom, who's openly grinning now. "You know, I gotta ask. Everyone knows Dominick either did it or had it done, but you're the inside guy. You know anything?"

I grin back at Dominick, who's watching me with interest, and lean back before forming a casual reply. "Nope, Dominick came back here after we went to the Rivaldis' and was here all night. It was business as usual at Petals."

"Yeah, figured he wouldn't have you in on any of the dirty work," Chucky says. There's a rustle on Chucky's end, and he seems to messing around with something on his computer from the clicking sounds. "The office thinks you're clear. Word I've got here is that you can make official contact, mission accomplished, and you can exfil now. Report in when you're out."

"Understood," I reply before hanging up the phone. I look over at Dominick, who's still watching me. "Seems the hitman has been taken care of, rather spectacularly. Better than anything I could've done for sure." Dominick tilts his head, a pleased smirk on his face as he accepts the compliment and understands that I'm thanking him while not saying that he actually did anything because that would be dangerous. "We're clear."

Maggie stutters, her voice a near-whisper. "Really? We're safe?"

And then she turns to Dominick, the question in her eyes, knowing he's really the one who decides if we're safe or not. He nods once, his face schooled back into tightly a controlled blankness. "Yes. "Yes, you're safe. But do not forget our agreement. If I have need of you, I will use you as a resource. Otherwise, you will not return."

Maggie nods, then opens and closes her mouth like she has something to say. Dominick waits patiently, not encouraging her but not dismissing her either.

"What about Allie?" she asks desperately. "Can I still talk to her?"

Dominick smiles, and I think I see a bit of melt in that frost behind his eyes. "If Allie wishes to speak with you, I would not prevent something that makes her happy. I personally think you two have had a good effect on each other and make good friends. However, if she doesn't want to talk, I will support her choice to cut you out of her life."

Maggie nods, still encouraged. "Thank you, sir."

Dominick smirks at the turn of phrase and gives me a knowing look. "Maggie," I say calmly, "can you wait outside for a second? I need to talk to Dominick."

She bites her lip, uncertain, but nods. "Yeah, I'll go backstage and see if Allie is here yet. Maybe she can show me her new move again."

She leaves, and both our eyes follow her out. When the door closes, Dominick turns back to me with a look I've not seen before. It's like he's showing me a glimpse behind his mask, to the real man he is underneath the mob boss persona. "She is an unusual find, Shane. I told you once that a man like you would break her, and then I'd be forced to break you as well. I find that perhaps I was wrong. She is stronger than I gave her credit for, although if you hurt her, I think I'd still find myself inclined to take the offense out on you."

"No need. If I hurt her, I'd punish myself more than you ever could," I reply honestly. "Even with your . . . creativity. I do appreciate the way you make a statement, that flair for the dramatic when warranted," I tell him, smiling as I envision the brass balls it must've taken to pull off a stunt like that.

Dominick inclines his head, smirking. "And I appreciated your company last night while I was at the club." The lie is crystal clear, but only because Dominick allows me to see it. He could lie to me easily, but he's telling me in just a few words that he's approving the lie I told, giving him an alibi.

"So, we can leave?" I ask, moving things along. "No offense. Your apartment is nice, but we've stopped the war, sent Sal scampering back to the dark, stopped the threat of the hitman, and you know the truth about everything. It seems our agreement has been met. And I'd like to be able to get some fresh air and sunlight with the woman I love."

Dominick nods, his mask coming back into place. "Yes, same as I told Miss . . . as I told Maggie. I'll reach out if I need you. However, for you in particular, Shane, there is something else. You mentioned that you were placed in my organization, and another FBI agent into Rivaldi's. Is that agent still in play?"

I nod, already seeing where this is going. "Yes, that agent is in place. I don't know his name, though. It's standard FBI procedure. That way, if one of us got outed, we couldn't be tortured to reveal the other."

Dominick nods in understanding. "I thought so. A policy I've used myself when I've had to send men . . . undercover. But, if any information comes up that would be either potentially beneficial or harmful to me, I trust that you will reach out to share?"

He's smiling, but there's an implied threat to his words, and I know that he would see a lack of information sharing as an insult. "Of course. I assume your phone number won't be changing?"

Dominick laughs softly. "Well, it might, but even if so, the number for Petals won't. I'm sure you'll keep that number around."

I nod, then rise and offer him a hand. "You are an interesting man, Dominick Angeline. Regardless of the initial reason for my placement, I have enjoyed working with you. I like you."

Dominick shakes my hand, pulling me closer to his desk. "I like you too, Shane Guthrie. Hope to *not* see you around my town."

I chuckle at his slickness, a compliment tied up in an 'I know who you are' threat with a bonus order to get out of dodge. He's one of a kind.

Twenty~Seven

MAGGIE

IT FEELS weird to walk through the quiet main room of Petals, knowing I'll likely never return. I look around the room, seeing the dinginess to everything in the light of day.

But somehow, it makes it feel comfortable. I like knowing that table nine is a little wobbly so you have to be careful setting the beers down or else you'll have slop to mop up, or that the fastest route from the bar to the private rooms is to take the outside loop even though it's twenty-five extra steps, but there are no grabby hands to get in your way. The biggest thing, though, is knowing that the people here are my friends.

I mean, what else can you say when Allie and a bunch of the dancers and waitresses are here to say goodbye? I have no idea what Allie told them to cover up the reason. But even Marco's here, looking slick as always, even as his practiced smirk looks a little faded at the edges..

I give Allie a big hug, still loving that she's promised we'll get together soon. "I think we'll have to get you a bright slutty red when we get together for mani-pedis next time," she teases, looking over my shoulder at Shane before giving me a wink. "And some sweet gel nails that are guaranteed not to break when you scratch someone's back."

The other dancers laugh along with me while I give hugs all around. When everyone's wished me well, I turn to Marco, who's talking quietly with Shane. The two shake hands, and Marco turns to me. "You know, it's not gonna be the same without you around."

"Oh, you'll just have to be more careful with those harassing comments," I joke, making Marco laugh. I give him a big hug, patting his back. "You make sure you stay out of trouble, you got me?"

"Never." Marco laughs, hugging me back and picking me up. Shane looks a little jealous, which makes Marco and I both laugh. "Relax, Dragon. I'm not gonna try and take a girl who settled for your ugly ass."

Shane laughs, flipping him off. "Fuck you, man."

I don't get the inside joke between them, but it seems good-natured as they bro-hug. Shane shakes hands with a few of the girls and gives a quick hug to Allie, and then we're done. As we approach the door, I look up, seeing Dominick watching us. He doesn't say a word, just stands in the doorway of his office, watching us, but I wave goodbye and smile anyway. Dominick had sent someone for Shane's truck days ago, so it's waiting in the parking lot for us.

I curl into the passenger seat, tears already starting to slip down my cheeks. Shane looks over and wipes them away with a gentle thumb. "Hey, what's wrong?"

I shake my head, kissing the ball of his thumb softly. "It just feels . . . final. Like I'm not going to see them again, you know?"

"Angel, you literally just made plans with Allie for this weekend," he reminds me. "You two are going to be thick as thieves, and I doubt I'm gonna get two minutes of you to myself. That's the definition of *not final*."

I smile through the tears, chuckling. "You're right. It just feels like I'm saying goodbye."

Shane is thoughtful, considering that for a moment, then puts his truck into drive and pulls away. "Well, you are saying goodbye to a lot of things. Your job at Petals, your job at the tabloid, your innocence at how the city runs. But you're starting a lot of new things, like this with me. It's not the end of things. It's the beginning of new things."

I lean across the seat to wrap my arms around his arm, laying my head on his shoulder. "You're right. Let's go home."

It doesn't occur to me that I didn't say 'my place' or 'your place' until Shane pulls into the parking lot of my apartment. "Oh, if you need to go to your house, we can. Sorry. I didn't mean—"

Shane puts a finger to my lips, shushing me. "Maggie, *you* are my home. My apartment in the city is a front, part of the assignment. For the past year, I've basically lived out of a duffel bag. My place is more of a pit stop than anything else. I like your apartment, it's like you, sweet, innocent, warm. If you don't mind, I could use a little more sweet innocence in my life."

I smile shyly, nodding. "Okay, then let's go home."

We walk up the stairs, and I feel like we're walking hand-in-hand to something bigger, better. At the landing, Shane swoops me up into his arms and carries me across the threshold like a bride. It makes me warm and bubbly inside.

He kicks the door closed and bends down for me to lock it, and then continues his trek to my bedroom. He sets me down gently on the edge of the bed before looking around. "Bathroom? I sorta forgot."

I point behind him, and he disappears for a minute. I can hear him digging around, looking for something, and I call out. "You okay? Need something?"

"Nope, got it," he says, then I hear the bathtub turn on, the water echoing out in the quiet apartment. "There, that's perfect."

Shane reappears, pulling me up from the bed. He begins stripping me, and my body responds instantly, knowing what it wants, and I try to kiss him.

Shane steps back, his eyes twinkling in amusement. "Nu-uh, Angel. I will always give you what you want, but trust me to know what you need too."

Confused, I let him undress me the rest of the way and then watch as he strips too. Once we're both naked, he leads me to the bathroom. I've always liked this bathroom. It's why I put up with the rest of the place. The big garden tub is full of steaming water and fluffy bubbles, and there are tea candles lit on the countertop.

The bubbles in my belly rise again, the happiness bursting out as I giggle and turn to Shane. "Are you giving me a bath?"

Shane holds me, our naked bodies pressed together as he kisses my temple. "Angel, we've had a rough few days. And tomorrow, I'm going to have to start the process of becoming Agent Guthrie again. But for now, I want to wash all the roughness away, start fresh and clean and honest with each other. Never lie to me, never hide from me. Give me all of you. And I'll do the same for you."

I nod, tracing a fingertip along the designs covering his chest. "I love you, Shane."

He presses his lips to mine, smiling. "I love you too, Maggie. Now let's get in."

He steps in first, holding my hand to help me in too. I grab a hair band from the tub edge and quickly twist my hair up into a messy bun on top of my head.

We sit, my back to his front with his legs spread wide around me. Settling in the hot water, the suds tickle and tease against my skin. Shane grabs my pouf and pours body wash on it, working it to a foam and inhaling the scent deeply, grinning. "Mmm. I figured it was a special soap that makes you smell so good. Makes me want to eat you up."

I smile, too dreamy to reply as he moves the pouf along my skin, covering my arms and my chest in the warm vanilla sugar scent of my body wash. "I'll make sure to buy another couple of bottles this weekend."

Shane nods, reaching down and motioning for my foot. "Give me a leg."

I raise a foot toward the ceiling, not as flexible as the dancers at Petals, but not too shabby, if I say so myself. I can feel Shane hardening against my back as he washes down the length of my calf to my thigh, where it disappears into the water. He repeats the move on the other leg, his forehead dotted with sweat, either from his arousal or the warm water, or both.

Once I'm curled back under the surface of the warm water, he shifts, pressing me forward so he can wash my back. The pouf drops into the water, and I feel Shane's rough palms tracing along my back, washing the bubbles away and massaging my soft skin. His lips follow the path of his hands, kissing and nibbling along my shoulder and up to my neck. "Angel . . . so sweet."

A moan rolls past my lips, and I feel like I could lie in his arms forever, but I want to do for him what he's done for me. I want to wash all the past, the lies, the fear away. I want him to know that I want to be by his side. Even if the FBI says that we have to move, or that he has to go man the office in Alaska or something, I'll be there with him. I sit up, breaking his embrace for a moment before turning to face him and sitting between his splayed legs.

I feel around for the pouf. Finding it, I use more body wash to work the lather back up as Shane watches me with hooded eyes. "Hope you don't mind smelling like me," I say flirtatiously as I start to swirl the pouf along Shane's chest. "I happen to love covering you in my . . . scent."

Shane growls, his hands resting on my hips and pulling me closer, bit by bit. "Pretty sure I told you I'd smell like you anytime you'd let me. I meant I liked your juices marking me, reminding me and everyone else that I've been between those sweet thighs. But I'll take any damn thing you want to give me, Angel. Although I am hoping that normally I can use some regular soap."

Having washed his thick chest, the bumps of his washboard abs, and along the length of his powerful arms, I move my hands lower. His cock jumps as I lick my lips, leaning in. "Good . . . because time for getting washed is over."

Under the water, I let the pouf go, wrapping my hands around his thickness and giving him a few strokes.

Shane groans, his fingers tightening on my hips. "Fuck, Maggie."

I keep the pace slow, wanting to control how fast he builds, but he bucks against me, fighting for more. I move to straddle one of his thighs, forcing him still, and lean forward, licking his earlobe. "Shane, let me love you. Let me jack you off, let me mark you the way you mark me. Let me . . . let me be your woman."

His body is strung tight, using all of his control to hold back and let me have this. I move down his neck, kissing and licking and nibbling the way he does to me.

I find a spot in the curve that makes him moan as his dick jumps in my hand, and I smile to myself. I latch onto the spot, sucking and nibbling just to the edge of pain before soothing it with a licking kiss.

All the while, I stroke him, every stroke up his shaft timed with a sucking draw on his neck. I'm mindlessly riding his thigh, letting the soft hairs tickle my lips and grinding my clit along his tight muscles. "That's it, my man. So hot and sexy," I purr in his ear. "So strong, you could break me, but you didn't. You woke me. I'm yours now, your sweet angel and your dirty girl.

You like that, don't you?" I kiss back down, finding that sweet spot on his neck and suck again.

I can feel his balls pulling up tight, on the edge of letting go. "Fuck, yes," he groans. "I want you by my side, Angel."

I let go of his neck and lick his ear as I pump him quickly under the water. "You're *mine*, and I'm *yours*," I whisper.

It's enough to trigger him, and he bucks beneath me, raising his hips out of the water. His cock pulses in my hand as he comes, white cum coating my hand. The sight does me in, and I grind along his thigh, finding my own release as he holds me, keeping me steady as I shudder on him.

"Mmm, that was wonderful," I whisper, cuddling against him. "Thank you."

"Thank you," Shane whispers back, holding me close. "For everything."

Eventually, we get clean, and still naked, we walk into the bedroom. Shane throws the covers back, tossing pillows to the floor as he sees my carefully constructed arrangement.

He laughs as I scramble to pick up a few of them. "Why do you have so many fucking pillows? There's like a dozen of them here!"

I laugh, picking up one to swat him on the butt. "Because they're pretty and soft and I like to curl up in them."

Shane tosses me in the bed, climbing over me and caging me in. "You're pretty and soft. And you can curl up with me now."

He lies on his back, one arm stretched wide in invitation. "C'mere, Angel," he says, and I quickly snuggle into his side, throwing one leg over his before he pulls the blankets back over us.

It feels comfortable, right, just like always. "You'll be here when I wake up, right? This isn't all some dream?"

Shane kisses my forehead, tenderly stroking my arm with his hand. "I'll always be here when you wake up. Sleep now, though. You've been through a lot."

I can feel sleep already overtaking me, but I manage to kiss his chin before yawning. "I love you."

Just as I drift off, I hear him reply softly, "I love you too."

Twenty-Eight

SHANE

FOR THREE DAYS, after waking up and deciding that no, I don't need to formally exfiltrate myself from my assignment yet, we've camped out in Maggie's apartment. This time, not because we need to. There's no one chasing us, no monsters looming.

Instead, it's simply because we can. We've enjoyed every moment of being together, and we've had a wonderful vacation 'playing house,' but we have to be responsible too. I've put off the FBI as long as I can, but when Chucky sends me a text to *'get to the office today or else'*, I know I have to go.

But I'm taking Maggie with me. It's not protocol, but fuck if I care. I'm not letting her out of my sight. Not until we're one hundred percent sure that she's safe and we're settled in.

"Are you sure?" Maggie asks as we approach the Federal building. It's small. East Robinsville isn't exactly Los Angeles or New York for a field office, but that's okay. "I mean—"

"I don't give a damn what Uncle Sam has to say," I reply, holding her hand as we approach security. I watch her go through first before laughing as her jaw drops when I put my gun and badge in the bin to walk through the metal detectors. "Guess you haven't seen these yet."

"No," she admits, her eyes going even larger when I flash the badge in its black leather billfold at her. As I replace them, badge in my back pocket, gun in my holster, I realize she's watching me, biting her lip. I cup her chin, bringing her eyes up to look me in the face. "It's okay, Angel. Don't be scared. I'll never hurt you."

She shakes her head, looking left and right to make sure no one can hear her before whispering in my ear. "It doesn't make me nervous. You look hot and tasty as fresh French fries, all confident badass. Especially in that T-shirt."

I smirk, kissing her hard but keeping it fast. I don't want any of the fuckers around here seeing my woman turned on. That's fucking private, just for me and her. I groan, wishing I could shove her into a broom closet or empty office, but there's never anything private in this place.

I take her hand again and start to lead her to the elevators. "Come on, we'd better get this over with so we can get back home."

The ride up to the fourth floor is quiet but slightly tense. Maggie's probably never even been in a normal police station, except maybe to pay a parking ticket, and now she's going to an FBI office. I give her hand a squeeze as the door opens, and we head into the bullpen area. I'm surprised to see Chucky jump up immediately when he sees me.

"What the hell? When'd they let you out of the basement?" I ask, giving him a big hug, bro-patting him on the back. "Damn, Chucky, you lost weight! What the hell happened?"

He steps back, flexing and patting on his considerably flatter stomach. "Yep, Pokémon Go sucked nuts, but getting outside to catch the little fuckers did me some good. Got me away from my desk and even to the gym. Having to watch my diet now that I'm mostly playing Fortnight and my usual Call of Duty team."

I grin, shaking my head. He's a geek, but he's a good face to see. "Battle Royale?"

Chucky grins. "Fuck, yeah, anytime."

I glance at Maggie, who's wearing a half amused, half scared shitless look on her face. "Might be a bit, but soon, man."

Chucky sees Maggie, and he walks toward her, hand outstretched. "You must be Maggie. Nice to meet you. I'm Chucky. I sorta run the computers, you know."

Maggie smiles, shaking his hand. "I remember, and thank you. Nice to put a face to the voice on the phone."

Our reunion is cut short by the appearance of my boss, SSA Solomon. A tall woman in her early sixties with a no-nonsense brown helmet of hair that nobody in the office has the balls to fuck with, she's run the East Robinsville office for five years now. "Shane. How good of you to join us. You two come on in my office."

I look to Chucky for some read on the situation, but he shrugs. Keeping Maggie's hand, we go into the office.

I try to start on the right foot, with introductions. "Maggie, this is my boss, Maria Solomon. Maria, this is my . . . Maggie."

I didn't know what to call Maggie. Girlfriend doesn't seem remotely strong enough, and I can't just go around proclaiming her 'mine' like a caveman to other people. When it's the two of us, fuck, yeah. But in public, probably not exactly politically correct. Although, Maggie's still got a bit of pink tint to the delicate skin of her neck where my lips sucked a day or two ago, and she looks proud of it.

I knew this meeting was coming and at least tried to keep my marks to the skin that'd be covered by her clothes. I smirk a bit, knowing that she's got my claims on her tits, her belly, her thighs, her ass, and she was begging for me to '*fuck her*' just this morning.

It's those filthy words that do me in every time my sweet girl uses them, my dirty Angel who makes me hard as a rock in an instant.

But right now, she's sitting prim and proper. A lady by every appearance, except to me since I know what lays under those clothes and in her dirty mind. While I've been daydreaming, they've shaken hands, and we sit down, Maria behind her desk and Maggie and me in chairs in front of her.

"I haven't seen your report yet, Shane. But I've got Organized Crime calling for a quick and dirty update, so I need a rundown of everything verbally. And then you can start catching up on your far overdue paper-work. Time to be an agent again, Guthrie."

She's mad I haven't finished the job, but fuck it. I was busy. The hard work was done. The paperwork is always the part I hate anyway. It's part of why I'm better undercover than as a regular agent. I mean, undercover just has to get shit done. The paperwork's later.

Still, I do my best to give Maria a rundown even though she knows parts of it from my check-ins with Chucky. Starting with the shooting at Petals, I move on to the hitman, Maggie and me on the run, and I end with my conversation with Dominick as we left.

"I think we parted on respectful terms, all things considered. War averted, Dominick on alert to watch out for Sal a bit more carefully, and the hitman handled so Maggie is safe. My recommendation is to leave the agent in Sal's organization for a bit to make sure that licking his wounds doesn't turn ugly."

Maria looks at Maggie, and I know I'll have to answer a few hard questions later about the details of why Dominick just let me walk out with a handshake. "Anything you'd like to add, Miss Postland?"

Maggie looks at Maria for a moment, sizing her up, and nods. "I guess just that when I worked at Petals, I didn't know about the mob stuff. All I knew was that Dominick ran a tight ship, cared about his employees, and when the crap hit the fan, he helped us."

"That's his style," Maria replies. "But—"

"He didn't have to do all he did for us, but he did," Maggie continues, and for once, I see Maria actually shut up. "I don't know what the FBI's going to do about him. I just want you to know that he is a good man. It's not black and white, criminal or not, and I hope you'll take that into consid-eration for future operations regarding Dominick and his businesses."

Damn this woman. I'd half expected her to sit here, quiet and shy like she sometimes gets, and just nod along with the big scary FBI folks. But the other piece of her, the brilliant mind she keeps hidden behind blonde curls and innocent eyes, is a work of fucking art. Maria smiles, a predator who's seen her prey, and I'm not about to sit here while Maria skins Maggie with poisonous words.

"Maria, I think we should go. I'll type up the report at home and send it in ASAP."

Maria looks to me dismissively and then returns her eyes to Maggie. "You are quite something, aren't you?"

Maggie shrugs but doesn't break eye contact with Maria. "I do what I can."

Maria nods, an amused glint in her eyes. "When we figured out who you are, I had Chucky do some digging. You have quite the impressive resume, Miss Postland."

I'm confused. I know Maggie is a tabloid reporter, but that's not exactly something that would impress Maria. I look out of the office window to the bullpen, seeing Chucky watching our exchange. When he catches me looking, he startles and looks down, shuffling papers.

Before I can ask what's going on, Maria continues, ignoring me for the moment. "Your resume includes undercover work on a number of stories, everything from politics to celebrities. You've been . . . let's see, an intern for a state Senator, a candy striper—"

"Candy striper?" I ask, imagining my innocent Maggie in one of those uniforms. Maggie gives me a little smile, blushing as I'm sure she's thinking the same thing I am.

"As I was saying," Maria says testily. "A secretary, and a waitress in a mob-owned club. In none of those jobs have you ever been detected until after the story came out and sometimes not even then. You've written many articles about mostly frivolous fodder. The FBI doesn't really care who's sleeping with whom—"

"Most of the time," I say, earning a glare. "Sorry."

"But some of your work—the investigative part, the undercover work—is well beyond your current situation at a tabloid," Maria finishes.

Maggie smiles but shakes her head. "Actually, I no longer work for the tabloid. Nor Petals. I've been fired by both."

There's delight in Maria's eyes, and she opens a manila folder on her desk, taking out a small packet and toying with it. "Ah, so sorry to hear that," she replies in a way that makes me suspect she's known that since Maggie walked in. "However, I do have something I'd like you to consider."

She looks at me, then back to Maggie. "Working undercover, finding ways to tell the truth while lying, and finding out people's secrets in subtle ways are skills that are very difficult to teach. Most field agents in the FBI will go through quite a few training courses and never be able to do them effectively. Wouldn't you agree, Shane?"

I nod, knowing that most FBI agents are products of their bureaucracy.

They can grind, they can use the FBI like a bludgeon, but very few can do what I do. "Not many. Are you saying what I think you're saying?"

"Seeing possible solutions beyond the scope of the usual point-to-point way of thinking is also exceedingly rare," Maria says, turning her attention back to Maggie. "It seems you do well with both of these. In short, you impressed me, Miss Postland. And I don't impress easily."

Maggie gulps beside me, and I squeeze her hand. "See? I'm not the only one."

Maggie blushes more deeply, but smiles. "Thank you."

"The FBI has a very straightforward system for becoming an agent," Maria says, toying with the paper in her hands. "But, there is considerably more flexibility when it comes to being a consultant. Especially when you're a relatively minor field office like this one. So I'd like to offer you a job with my team. Very entry-level to see how you do, an internship, if you will. But an opportunity beyond anything you've ever considered before."

Maggie looks at me, shock clearly written across her face as Maria slides the paper across her desk. "Me? Working for the FBI?"

I smile, encouraging her. "It's your call, Maggie. You're free to do anything you want now. If this sounds interesting, go for it."

"Can I become an agent too?" she asks, looking at Maria. She picks up the paperwork, flipping through it for a moment. "I mean, what does a consultant do?"

"Basically, you'd be able to do all the grunt work, but you can't carry a gun or arrest people," Maria says. "But if you want, well, I could set you up on the path for that. I'd discourage it, though. Consultants don't have to worry about rank or getting reassigned away from their . . . significant others."

Maggie nods, then grins at me. It's so beautiful I want to kiss her, right here and now, but I manage to refrain.

For now.

"That does sound interesting," Maggie says, setting the papers back down on Maria's desk. "I accept, but can I have one request? That I work with Shane and Chucky as I get my feet wet. I trust them and want to learn from them."

Maria stands, offering her hand. "Already planned, although you'll get some oversight and training from me too. See you two on Monday then. Get out of here for now."

Just as we reach the door, Maria speaks up again. "Oh, and Shane, I need that report. Today."

I grin, knowing that I can get it done and still be able to take Maggie out for a little celebration later. "Sure thing."

We walk out hand-in-hand, ready for the next beginning. Together.

MAGGIE

WALKING INTO THE APARTMENT, I can immediately tell something is off and I go on high alert. Quietly opening my purse, I reach for my pistol. I scan the living room for anything amiss, keeping my back towards the door I just cleared.

Seeing nothing but trusting my instincts, I walk heel-toe further into the apartment, looking into the kitchen to make sure no one is ducked down to take advantage of the blind spot. Clear. Other than a couple of dirty dishes in the sink, everything looks just like it normally does.

Silently steadying my breath, I breach the bedroom doorway. Before I can fully scan, an arm pops down across mine, knocking my weapon to the floor and continuing the maneuver to twist my arms up behind me.

I'm yanked against a hard body, male, judging by the impressive bulge pressing against me, and a lot taller than me, considering the bulge is pressed to my back, not my ass.

"You forgot to check your blind spot first," a deep voice growls in my ear. "You know what happens now.

My training kicks in, and in one smooth motion, I pop my hips back to knock my attacker off-balance, pull forward in a twisting motion, and dive into a front roll to get space between us.

I grab my gun from the floor, standing in perfect stance with my attacker three feet away with his hands up in surrender. "On your knees."

My voice is hard, projecting power, something Maria's had me work on in training. He lowers to his knees, a smirk on his face as I step closer. "Usually, I'd prefer for you to be on your knees, sucking me off. But this works too. Come here and let me lick you, Angel."

The gig is up when he calls me that, and I laugh, letting the gun lower to my side. "Dang it, Shane! I was doing so well! And you ruined it with your sweet dirty talk."

Shane takes the empty training gun from my hands, setting it on the dresser behind him and grabs around my waist to pull me to him. "Allie even laughed at my training pistol today. She sent a pic to Dominick, who said he thought mine would be pink, not bright orange."

Shane smiles. "How was your shopping?" But before I can answer, he shakes his head, "Never mind, tell me later. But really, you did just fine clearing the rooms and even handling me. But fuck if you don't turn me on when you get all fierce and badass like that. Makes me want to earn your sweetness back, taste the innocence you only share with me."

As he talks, he's kneading my ass, his nose nudging along my belly and down to my core. More brave than shy these days, I begin unbuttoning my blouse, tossing it to the floor.

Shane sits back on his heels, watching me. "More," he demands.

Having learned a few tricks from Allie, I don't obey instantly. Instead, I tease him, tracing a finger along the swells of my breasts, which are almost eye-level with Shane. He growls, licking along the edge of my bra, and I decide maybe teasing can wait. I reach behind to unclasp my bra and shrug it off.

Shane cups my breasts, pressing them together and burying his face in their fullness, groaning as he begins licking my skin, sucking here and there to leave the marks he always wants to see on my body.

Finally, he takes my nipple into his mouth, and my hands tug on his hair, holding him there, wanting more. His fingers work at the waist of my pants, undoing them before he helps them slide down my legs.

I step out of my shoes and then the pants, standing before Shane in just my cotton panties. I asked him once if he wanted me to wear sexier lingerie, but he assured me with his words, his hands, and his cock that he liked my simple bikini briefs. He said they look sweet, like me.

Seems his opinion hasn't changed because he's using his thumbs to trace my lips through the soaked cotton, desire darkening his eyes.

"Lie down on the bed," he rasps. "On your stomach."

Like I need a reason to do as he says, feeling Shane's weight on the bed as he straddles me, his strong thighs supporting him so he doesn't squish me.

"Hold the headboard, Angel."

I look back at him over my shoulder, but his face is unreadable. I move my hands up, holding one of the slats in the headboard.

Shane leans forward, and before I realize what he's doing, he's handcuffed my hands around the slat.

He sits back, pleased with himself. "Good girl."

I laugh, half turning even as my body thrills. We've talked about this, but this is the first time we've taken the game this far. I love it. "Shane? What are you doing?"

I can feel his rough hands tracing my skin, and once in a while, he bends over to lay a sucking kiss or nibble to a spot that entices him. "Celebrating. The first night I came here, I drove you home after that asshole scared you at the club. Your keyring had a fluffy white pompom on it."

I smile, loving that he remembers details like that about me. "I still have it. And?"

"And as of today, you're officially field cleared," Shane says. "Maria texted me the news."

I've been working hard these last few months, both with Shane and at Maria's insistence. I've learned so much, including FBI procedures, hand-to-hand fighting, firearms, and more. And while I've been able to sit next to Chucky as he pores over his computers, learning the in-house intel side, I hate that Shane is out there, undercover without me.

After his last mission, we decided he was going to wait for me so we could do the next assignment together. He took some well-deserved vacation and requested that Maria let him oversee my training, to which she agreed.

Maria's actually excited to have a team available for undercover work as a couple. Apparently, that's rare and makes us uniquely fit for a few different intel-seeking positions. I squeal in excitement at the news, kicking my feet behind Shane, but not dislodging him. "What's that got to do with handcuffing me to the bed?" I ask.

"Look at the handcuffs," Shane whispers, licking my earlobe and making me shiver. I look up to see white, fluffy handcuffs encircling my wrists and laugh. "They're a bit of the old you, soft and innocent, and a bit of the new you, badass. And best of all, they make you all mine."

Shane scoots back, sitting between my legs, and I arch my back, giving him access to my center. "Tell me, Angel."

I groan, more comfortable with the words now, but still only with him. Maria laughs at my cursing workarounds. "Lick my pussy, Shane. Suck my clit. Mark me up so everyone knows I'm yours."

He growls, lowering his face toward my pussy. Right before his tongue touches me, he whispers, "Give me your sugary sweetness, Angel. I want it all."

I'm already gasping from the heat of his breath, so when his tongue touches me, it's like fireworks exploding inside me, and I buck, fucking his face and chasing his tongue. Shane tortures me, his tongue and lips keeping me balanced on the edge, drawing it out until my stomach is quaking and my toes curling in frustrated desire, and I whimper.

"That's what I wanted, Angel," Shane says before sucking hard on my clit. Like a pistol shot, I'm released, my body spasming as I cry my relief.

"Yes! Shane, I'm coming!"

I didn't even hear him unbuckle his jeans, but as soon as I cry out, he's there, shoving his thick cock into me. It paralyzes me, my orgasm stopped almost mid-crash as he fills me like I dream, pushing me higher again already.

"Fuck, Maggie. Finish coming on my cock. Squeeze me with your sweet pussy, and I'll fill you up," Shane says as he starts pumping deeply in and out. "I'll give you what you want."

I tense my muscles, drawing out every drop of pleasure from my own orgasm as Shane thrusts into me. I push back, meeting him stroke for stroke, wanting his cum inside me, wanting him to lose control and experience this bliss. Knowing what will send him over, I look back, biting my lip. "Fuck me, Shane. I love you so much."

With a powerful thrust, Shane bottoms out deep inside me, grunting like an animal as the heat of his cum sears me. It pushes me to another toe-curling orgasm, and my eyes roll back, my mouth trapped open as I pull on the handcuffs. We're going to have to do it again this way. I like it.

Spent, he lies on top of me, keeping his weight off so he doesn't smush me. "That's my dirty fucking girl," he growls lightly in my ear, "and I love you too. In fact, I had a question."

I raise my head, and he meets my lips with his own, sealing our vows of love with a kiss. "What's that?" I ask as our lips part. "And can you unlock me now?"

"Of course . . . if you're willing to lock me up," Shane says, reaching into the bedside drawer and taking out a keyring with a small handcuff key. On the keyring is a golden circle, with a small, beautiful diamond on it. "Think you want to?"

"Is that what you call a proposal?" I tease, my heart racing. "Because if it is, I'm gonna have to call Dominick to teach you some manners."

Shane laughs and unlocks my wrists, rubbing them gently even though the fuzzy trim cushioned my skin from the metal. I sit up, turning to face him and he moves to kneel in the floor beside the bed. "You know you've had the key to my heart for months now. This is just making it more . . . formal. You're my woman, I'm your man. Now . . . Maggie Postland, will you also be my wife?"

I smile, nodding like a bobblehead. "Yes!" I hold out my hand and Shane puts the ring on my finger. I look at it happily, then give him a huge kiss, a sloppy one because I can't stop smiling long enough to pucker properly.

Pulling back, I give him a serious look. "Oh, there's one condition . . ." I say, and his face sobers.

"You know I'll give you anything. What is it, Angel?"

I grin, not able to play serious any longer. "We do that again right now!" I say, nodding towards the handcuffs dangling from the headboard.

"Deal. You're a tough negotiator, future Mrs. Guthrie." He smirks, then tackles me and I squeal, rolling over and lifting my hands for him to cuff me again.

Our future is still full of unknown possibilities and opportunities, but one thing is for sure—us.

This is real. This is love. This is home.

The End. Thank you for reading. If you'd like to listen to this as an audiobook, it's available on Amazon or Audible.

Let's stay in contact! You can join my mailing list here. You'll never miss a new release and you'll even get 2 FREE ebooks!

Continue on for an excerpt of Dirty Secrets, Allie and Dominick's book!

Get Dirty (Interconnecting standalones):
Dirty Talk | | Dirty Laundry | | Dirty Deeds | | Dirty Secrets

Dirty Secrets

Prologue

DOMINICK

THE SHOT RINGS OUT, and before the echo even dies, I'm running to her. I don't care about the rest. I just care about her. I will not allow harm to come to her.

I hear a high-pitched scream pierce the air. Someone's hurt, and I start uselessly praying to anything listening to a devil like me . . . *please, let her be okay*. I'll trade everything I have. The empire I've built can turn to dust if it'll ensure her safety.

By the time I reach the hallway, there's already a small group of my people standing in the doorway, mouths hanging open. Whatever they're looking at, it's the sort of shock that makes people forget themselves, the sort of thing only violence can bring. It's a look I'm more than familiar with.

I don't even have to order them to move. They just part like the red sea as I approach, barreling in to take stock of what's happened. There's blood spray on the walls and a dead guy in an expensive suit sitting in a chair, but he doesn't matter. I'll get the details on him later.

All that matters is Allie.

My heart starts beating again as I see her. She's cowering in the corner, her brown eyes wide with terror. The spatters of blood on her face, on her breasts, on her stomach make me hot with fury, but at least she doesn't seem to be wounded.

Still, the fact that someone has sullied her body, so sweet and tempting and *mine*, makes the insult of a hit in my territory that much worse. My men quickly follow my orders to handle the situation, but my attention never wavers from Allie. She's what counts, and I can't wait to get everyone else out of here.

Thankfully, my men are well-trained and professional. Once they scatter to carry out my commands, I gather her into my arms, ushering her into my office. She's so shocked I finally scoop her up to carry her up the stairs, nudging open the door with a toe before I set her down in a chair, cringing at the smear of blood bright against the white leather. It doesn't matter. I'm just thankful it's not hers.

I fill a crystal glass with whiskey and force it into her shaky hand.

"Drink this."

She glances at it unseeingly and I can tell she's lost in her head, replaying what she just witnessed in her mind's eye on an endlessly-looping, surreal repeat. I remember when I felt like that. In my mind, events slowed and sped up at chaotic intervals, fresh details coming forward to be blurred into confusion by the next replay as something else takes precedence. It pains me to watch my Allie suffer through the same torment.

I lift the glass with a gentle touch, and as it reaches her lip, she drinks reflexively. Encouraged, I tilt the glass up further, and she downs the whole shot.

Setting the empty glass on the nearby table, I take a handkerchief out of my breast pocket. It's silk, but still not fine enough for a creature as beautiful and precious as Allie, but it's all I have.

I squat in front of her, my hand moving slowly so as not to startle her, but she still tries to intercept it.

"Let me," I order, not allowing disobedience. Her hands fall to her lap and her eyes flutter closed, flicking behind her smoky lids. She's made up for the stage, not like I prefer her, fresh-faced with only a hint of makeup to highlight her natural flawlessness.

As I clean her face, I'm struck by how easy it would be to finally give in. She's so close, mere inches from me, eyes closed, lips parted, her spicy floral perfume surrounding me though it's tinged with the metallic tang of blood. She's soft right now, all her defenses lowered in shock, and I could ease her anguish, give her something else to focus on . . . me.

I wipe a smudge from right beside her lip, close enough that our breaths mingle. My thumb trembles, and I take a deep breath.

"Allie," I rasp, my voice a rough rumble. Her eyes pop open, meeting mine, and I can sense that she feels the charge in the air too.

She bites her lip, white teeth bright against the deep red, and her breath catches.

"Dominick?" she whispers, the confusion apparent in her questioning tone.

The sound of my name on her lips, breathy and soft, is a memory I'll keep forever. A better one than the rest of the shit show tonight has been.

But it's enough to wake me from the hazy fog Allie puts me into. I know better than this. I am better than this. I set the rules for a reason, and no leader can be effective if he holds himself to a different standard than he holds his subordinates.

With all of my mental strength, I slam the door shut in my mind, breaking the moment and cloaking myself in my usual stonewall defenses. I stand slowly and her brown eyes follow me. Any other time, this position, with her sitting and me looming over her, my cock at mouth level, begging for her kiss, would be my undoing.

But not now, not here, not like this. I'm a cold bastard, but I wouldn't dare take advantage of her.

"Let me take you home."

She nods, and with an almost childlike innocence, she lets me escort her downstairs to the changing area and then out to my car.

Arriving at her place, I tuck her into bed, wishing I could crawl into the mess of brightly colored blankets with her. I know I can't, but it would be heaven.

Her deep chocolate hair fans out on the pillow and her face relaxes as she looks up at me and smiles tentatively, an angel swaddled in cotton. She looks soft, her usual fierce shell chipped away by the night's events.

I'm sure the shower and hair brushing I forced upon her helped. She'd argued lightly that she just wanted to fall into bed, but I'd known she'd needed care after such a violent experience. And she'd sighed as she admitted I'd been right.

I didn't need to be too forceful. I just reminded her that sleeping with her stage makeup on would be a mess in the morning, and it did the trick. She even gave me a heartfelt smile when she came out in a towel and saw that I'd laid out a pair of pajamas for her.

I pause at the door as she falls asleep, watching the even way her chest rises and falls with each breath. She'd understandably asked me to leave the hall light on, and now the dim light illuminating her lets me see every expression on her face as she fades deeper into slumber.

I should go, leave her to rest. But there's no damn way I'm leaving her.

Instead, I sink into the chair in the corner of the room, watching her, protecting her, possessing her, even if she doesn't know it.

Even if my own morals won't allow it, that's what I'm going to do. I've fought myself to stay away from her, but tonight, things changed.

I could've lost her, and that is one thing I won't allow.

I'll always keep her safe, even if it's from me.

CHAPTER

One

ALLIE

"AND *GRAND JETÉ* . . . soft landing, Brynn . . . and *plié* with your bow. Beautiful!" I tell my student, offering a light applause as the soft classical music ends. "You're getting much better. Your leap must be at least two inches higher than last month."

Brynn, a young girl just out of junior high who decided to ask her parents for ballet lessons for her birthday, beams at me. It's a late start for a ballerina, but she's making leaps and bounds of progress to catch up with her peers because of the amount of work and time she puts forth.

"Really? That's awesome! Thanks, Miss Allie!"

She does a little *pas-de-chat* step of happiness over to her bag, tossing it over her shoulder. "When I get the part as the Sugar Plum Fairy, you'll have to come watch me!"

I smile back, remembering when I used to think being the Sugar Plum Fairy was the best thing in the world too. "I wouldn't miss it for the world."

Brynn leaves the studio in a whirlwind of energy that is wasted on the young. I don't envy her youth, the fourteen-year-old ballerina just starting her career and still living on hopes and dreams, because I was once that girl and tasted firsthand how sour those dreams could turn.

Once, I was the little girl who dreamed of wearing the white tutu and prancing onstage. A couple of injuries and a body that turned into something that isn't quite suited for ballet dancing . . . and now I'm something different. Older, jaded, maybe even a bit cynical. At least where dance is concerned.

At twenty-six, I'm virtually ancient in the ballet world. Not that it matters, considering I left any chance at a professional career behind at barely twenty-one when I injured my ankle, tearing two ligaments.

Nine months of rehab, and it's fine for daily life and even for dance, but not for the daily grind of being a principal dancer *en pointe* in any company worth the work.

It put me in a pretty dark place for awhile, and I did some things I'm not proud of. I don't regret them. I have some good relationships out of them, friendships, and I've made damn good money . . . but none of it's going on my resumé anytime soon.

And that's why I live for teaching the next generation of dancers, wanting to ensure that they have long and healthy careers by taking care of themselves better than I ever did.

The thought of how poorly I treated my body for years makes my stomach turn. I force it all to settle with a deep breath that I hold for a five-count before letting it out slowly, counting the good things I have in my life as I do so. I repeat the process twice more, just as I learned, counting out the beat to maximize my lung capacity before I feel re-centered.

I head to the lobby to see Eileen on the phone. She's one of the dance moms, but thankfully, not like the drama-mamas on television. She just works at the studio, answering phones and doing paperwork to help offset the cost of her daughter Sydney's lessons.

I admire that about her. Actually, there's a lot to admire about Eileen in general. She's a single mom doing whatever it takes to support her child, and though she's not a dancer herself, she doesn't harbor any desire to live vicariously through Sydney's journey. She kind of reminds me of my own mother, though my parents are still happily married and act more like newlyweds than a couple going on thirty years of wedded work. That's what my mom calls it, 'wedded work,' and she maintains that people who call it 'wedded bliss' are just lying to make it seem easy.

Eileen told me once that she'd put in all kinds of work to make her marriage last, but it'd been one-sided then, and now she basically parents alone. I hate that for her, but Sydney is a happy kid, so Eileen must be doing something right.

"Hey, Ei—" I start, but she holds up one finger, telling me to wait a second.

I stand for approximately two seconds before lifting my right leg up to the counter and stretching. It's a dancer thing. Any free moment is spent stretching, bending, lifting, tilting, always working somehow.

Even if I'm in a position where I can't physically move, my brain is constantly dancing, practicing choreography or considering new combinations. It makes the line at Starbucks seem to move much faster.

I've barely begun when Eileen hangs up and squeals, "Are you ready for tonight?"

"You mean they didn't cancel? I swore they would." I feign shock, knowing that my private class tonight definitely wouldn't cancel, considering they paid extra to rent the studio for this lesson. And considering just how much extra, it'd take an emergency for them to break the deal.

"Shut up, you know the ladies are excited. This is a good thing, girl."

She's right and I know it. I'm just nervous, which seems silly considering how many times I've performed on stage and how many classes I've taught.

But this class is different. This class isn't people of all walks of life, toddlers to adults, wanting to add a bit of ballet to their life.

No, this class is a bachelorette party where I'm teaching the bride and her bridesmaids a little routine to use . . . in private.

I'd automatically refused when Donna, the studio owner, had asked me to teach this class. I've always kept the other side of my dance life separate from the studio. It's like I'm two women, two dancers.

But when Donna promised it'd be just the one time and told me she'd share the rental fee with me fifty-fifty, I'd reconsidered. The money is . . . good.

And now, Stripper 101, as I've been jokingly calling it, is almost in session. Eileen, of course, doesn't understand.

"I hear you, Eileen," I reply, sighing. "I just thought that I'd left the sequins and body glitter at the other place. But it's following me."

I glance over my shoulder like there's somebody there, and she laughs as I intended.

"You act like it's a bad thing. You can be Ballerina Barbie and Stripper Suzy at the same damn time. There's no shame in dancing, however and wherever you do it, if you enjoy it and it supports you."

I smile, glad for her lack of judgment. I can't say that I would've ever dreamed I'd be making a living as a stripper, but alas, here I am.

At least I'm fortunate enough that Petals from Heaven, the club where I work, is top quality, VIP only. I'm one of their star performers, able to set my own hours and prices.

It's a far cry from the ballerina I thought I'd be, but at least now, I get to live both sides of the coin, stripper and ballerina. And still pay my bills.

"I still can't believe you don't care about that," I tell Eileen. "I honestly figured that if the dance moms here found out, they'd yank their kids out of my classes faster than you can say 'hell to the no.' "

Eileen's smile is sad but at the same time mischievous. "Honestly, there are some moms who would, so we just don't tell them. All I care about is your ability to teach the kids proper technique, something you are excellent with. You connect with the kids and never, ever make them feel like they're wasting their time or not doing fantastically."

"I love their faces and their hard work," I admit. "Who cares if they make it pro or not?"

Eileen grins. "Exactly. And there are a handful of us who know your gig. We're just waiting for the stars and babysitters to align so that we can come crash one of your performances en masse. Girl, I plan on making your night by making it rain." She giggles, covering her mouth with her hand. "I've always wanted to say that."

I laugh. Eileen's ridiculous sometimes. "That sounds awkward as hell, but awesome. I'd put an extra spin in my pole routine just for you." I bat my lashes at her and we both laugh again. "Anyway, guess I'd better get ready for tonight."

I head to the back studio to set up. Encore Studio is decent-sized, with three rehearsal rooms lined up along the left side of the building with the lobby and other facilities arranged on the right.

Normally, I like snagging Studio One because it's in the front with full glass windows, so I feel like we're performing every time we hold class there.

But for Stripper 101, I'm choosing Three, all the way in the back. It's almost the same size, but with no windows, it feels cozier. My choreography for this group is a bit risqué, including some good floor work, and I'm betting the ladies will prefer the privacy over flashing their business to everyone on the sidewalk.

I set up the music, dipping back into the nineties and naughty eighties for that slow, sexy RnB that straddles the line between sexy and slutty. Even I get the warm tingles when Janet Jackson sings *Anytime, Anyplace*, and I've danced to it before.

That done, I set up the snack table with the sandwiches and cupcakes the maid of honor dropped off earlier. I grin at the little plastic dicks stuck in the pink frosting on top of the cupcakes, thinking that at least there's diversity in the coloring. Although if any of the ladies does find that her man has a naturally blue dick, she should take him to a hospital.

Eileen set up a borrowed frozen margarita machine earlier, so it looks like everything's ready. I change out of my pink leotard and into black booty shorts and a loose tank top with a light sports bra. I could be going to yoga or the gym, but nope . . . Stripper 101 class is in session.

"Okay, ladies. All right, remember, this isn't about the guy. Trust me, most men are easy. If you just show up and show some interest, he's gonna be in there like a rocket. Stripping is about the slow seduction, letting the anticipation build and creating tension. You're dancing for your partner—"

The blonde to my left interrupts me, squealing out, "Jason!"

The bride blushes but finds her balls and says decisively, "Hell, yeah, I'm dancing for Jason."

I smile at her confidence, something the shy brunette had been lacking an hour ago. She's beautiful, and Jason's a lucky guy . . . who's going to get his world rocked after this session.

"Yes, definitely dance for Jason," I say, giving her a wink, "but also for yourself. Find your own strength and sexiness in the moves and seduce yourself just as much as your partner. They'll respond to seeing your arousal more than if you're focusing on choreography or doing something 'right' or 'wrong'. Just live in the moment and enjoy."

Pep talk complete, I hit *Play* on the stereo and watch as the group of twenty-something, giggly girls turn into sexy women right before my eyes. Softly, I coach them.

"Long lines. Point your toes. Use your eyes to direct his gaze . . . that's it, Sarah."

The music gets bass-heavy, the lyrics more pointed, and every woman in here is feeling like she 'Earned It' as they work the floor, toss their hair, and let their hands trace their curves as their hips sway.

"Great job, ladies. Jason is one lucky man, Sarah."

She grins and the girls all high-five before grabbing drinks and sandwiches. Lesson's over. I don't mind if they toss back the tequila with abandon now. I let the music play, fiddling with the stereo so as not to intrude on their after-party.

I'm about to pull a fade and let them have their time when the maid of honor comes over.

"Hey, Allie? Do you think you could show us how it's *really* done? I mean, I feel like I'm definitely better at this than I was an hour ago, but maybe a bit of inspiration would help? It's not like I'm ever going to be dancer, but I'd like to seem . . . comparable?"

She says the word questioningly, like she's not sure if that's what she means, but I get it. Some women freak about their guys going to strip clubs, like the stripper has something they don't, and God knows, society encourages women to compare themselves enough.

"First," I tell her, "don't compare yourself to anyone else. You do you, and you'll be just fine. But if you want to see, I guess I can do a demonstration for you guys."

She nods, and I realize that the whole group was waiting to see if I'd agree. I really don't mind. I perform all the time and enjoy it. It's like my therapy, allowing me to live in the moment, creating a connection that threads from the music through my body to the audience.

It's a powerful rush, whether I'm dancing ballet or seduction or even working the pole. There's no pole here tonight, but that's okay too.

The women all crowd over, sitting on the floor and leaning back against the mirror with cupcakes in hand. I click into character, hitting *Play* on the stereo and striding to the middle of the floor as Imagine Dragons fills the room. It's not a routine I normally do, but I love it nonetheless.

Before my first hair flip, they're caught in my trap, cupcakes forgotten and mouths hanging open as I sway my hips, dropping to the floor in a slow plié and letting my knees splay wide. I stretch one leg out, letting my fingertips dance from my ankle to my hip before turning to plant my hands, lifting my hips in a sexier version of downward facing dog.

I dance and move, tease and tantalize until the final notes of the song ring out, and I let my eyes drop for a beat before looking up through my lashes at Sarah, making the bride feel extra-special as a way of saying thank you.

The women all clap, one hand popping against their other wrist so they don't drop their dick cakes.

"Wow," the maid of honor says. "I want to do *that!*"

I smile at the praise, but more importantly, seeing these women empowered and happy in their own sexiness and cheering on their fellow females is pretty amazing. It gets me through the cleanup, which actually isn't so bad as the designated driver makes sure all the garbage is hauled out.

I lock up the studio after the bachelorette party leaves, loving that not only did I make half the rental fee, but the maid of honor tipped me rather generously too.

It nearly made up for my missing one of my usual performances at Petals tonight. A piece of me wishes I could just go home, put on sweats, and curl up on the couch, but I promised Dominick, my boss at Petals, that I'd be in for my late-night performance. He'd been understanding about the missed time, and he probably would've given me the night off if I'd asked, but I need the money, so I can't skip the whole night even if I wanted to.

As I walk to my car, I scan the deserted lot. There are security lights so it's not dark, but the emptiness makes me feel vulnerable. I swear I can feel eyes watching me, following my every movement.

On stage, that's what I want. Here, alone in the parking lot, it feels spooky. It's been that way since that night, even if I've been able to get past most of it.

Still, I glance under my car and in the backseat, just like those Facebook warnings tell you to, and hop in, immediately locking the doors.

I pull out of the lot, laughing at myself a bit. I'd planned to stop for a Monster Zero on my way to the club, but with the way my heart is racing, I think I'll skip it and use the adrenaline pumping through my body to perk me up after the long day for my performance tonight.

CHAPTER

Two

DOMINICK

I WATCH her from my vantage point across the parking lot. Allie doesn't know it, but as soon as she started teaching classes at Encore Studio, I rented a second-floor apartment in the strip mall.

In theory, it could be a safe house. In reality, I know what it is. It's my blind, though I'm not hunting her, merely watching her to keep her safe. Sometimes, I come here to keep an eye on her myself. Other times, I delegate the task to one of my men, but tonight, I'd wanted to be here to make sure the bachelorette party hadn't gone astray. Judging by the smiles on everyone's faces when they left, it'd been fine.

She hurries to her car, looking around as though she can feel the weight of my gaze upon her. Perhaps she can.

The thought gives me pleasure.

I stand in the darkness, knowing my black suit and dark hair hide every trace of me through the tinted glass. I wait until she pulls away before heading to my own car.

I don't need the GPS tracker I had installed on her car to tell me where she's going, but I turn the app on anyway, letting the glowing green dot of her car soothe me as I start the car. It's not my usual Mercedes, but rather a nondescript black Lexus sedan, like so many others on the road in East Robinsville.

At least, until I touch the accelerator and the work that my boys at the chop shop did on it comes to life and I quickly leap out of the parking lot.

I easily catch up to her, maintaining a safe distance behind her so she doesn't notice me, and follow her straight to Petals from Heaven. I'm a little surprised. The other times I've guarded her like this, she usually stops for a quick energy drink and sometimes a bite to eat.

Tonight, though, I phone in to Logan, who's working the back door, and he wisely answers my call on the first ring.

"She's coming to the back parking lot. Escort her in," I tell him.

I pull over to the curb, my lights already turned off so that I blend into the night. I want to keep her safe, not creep her out. I know I'm walking that line. Shit, I'm probably over it, but I also know how to make sure she doesn't ever have to worry about her safety again.

Before she even turns her car off, Logan is at her door, his muscular frame properly contained within his suit, just like I insist. I can read his lips, greeting her politely and offering to accompany her inside to safety without a smile but also not hard. It's why I trust Logan to do this job more than the others. He walks that line perfectly.

I see the flash of lights as she locks her car before tossing her keys into her bag. Logan scans the lot, keeping his eyes open for any threats and off Allie.

Smart man.

He sees my car and gives the slightest lift of his chin. It's why he works for me. He's smart enough to know better than to touch what's mine but also skilled enough to protect it.

I wait until they're both inside and then move the Lexus to the front of the building, parking it in the far corner of the lot next door. I own it too, so no one will question the lengthy stay.

In my office, I check the crowd through the one-way glass that overlooks the floor. I have security monitors, of course, new ones that cover every inch of the club to make sure *nothing* ever happens again like what happened before.

But still, it's sometimes better to look out over the club this way. It gives me a better feeling for the atmosphere. I know that nothing is amiss, or else one of the security team would have alerted me, but I like to check for myself as well.

A man who depends solely on others is a man who is neither independent nor dependable.

Everything seems to be in order tonight though. There's a group of businessmen, more interested in their wheeling and dealing than the show, a bachelor party by the stage, a few couples, and multiple tables of single guys, both alone and in small groups.

Everyone is being respectful and behaving themselves, not that I'd have it any other way in my club. Some places may get rowdy, but not Petals. I won't allow it, and anyone who knows a damn thing about me wouldn't dare. I don't just run Petals with an iron fist. I run the whole damn city, though I prefer to keep that little tidbit quiet.

Let the local media think it's someone else. I don't need the adulation. I just want the power. Those who need to know, do, and those who don't should hope they never need to meet me or it's a sure sign their life insurance is about to come due.

The knock on the door is expected since I saw Logan climbing the stairs on the security monitor.

"Enter," I say simply.

Logan comes in, his bald head freshly shaved, his coat and slacks impeccable, and his respect obvious in his stance, feet apart and hands clutched behind him.

If I hadn't investigated him thoroughly myself, I'd think him a military man. But Logan's background isn't military. No, he grew up in strict fighting gyms, respect beaten into him by trainers who pushed him to be better with every landed punch and kick.

He's my best fighter, though I rarely need him to use his considerable skills. Why use a precision scalpel when a dirty axe does just as effective of a job? Logan seems to appreciate my respect for his abilities too, especially when he has a fight coming up and needs to stay fresh.

I like that about him too.

He has dreams and plans of his own and isn't dependent on me for some lifelong goal to be a made man in my crew. I don't play by the old-school rules like that anyway, though there are a few of my dad's old company men still running crews.

No, I prefer for everyone to know that today could be their last day and act accordingly, myself included. This isn't the old days. There are no gimmes, no free passes, nothing deserved. Only earned.

Logan waits for my eyes to land on him, the permission to speak silently given.

"Sir, the evening has been as expected. House's averaged eighty percent full, bar and waitresses running acceptable delivery times, and the second round of performances is well underway. Allie is in back, getting dressed, and she said she'd be ready for her stage time at midnight. Wilson is on the front door, Thomas on the private rooms, and Gavin and I are floating the crowd."

He pauses, knowing I'll double-check his report on the security monitor.

"Good. Anything else?"

Logan nods. "Pete came in early. Said to tell you that he knew your meeting wasn't until later, but he wanted to enjoy the evening before, if that was okay. He's ready whenever you are."

I turn back to the window, eyes searching, and then I see him sitting alone at a corner table, his back to the wall ensuring him a full view of the main floor. Pete is one of my captains, a holdover from my dad's days, though Pete was just a soldier then.

He's in his early sixties now, well past his prime, but he can still admire the view, he says. He runs the crew on the South Side, making sure product moves smoothly, the violence stays at a minimum, and the streets are safe for families. When he retires in a few years, it'll be tough to replace him.

"Very well. Send him a couple of fingers of Yamazaki in appreciation for his patience. Tell him I'll see him at one as arranged."

In the reflection of the glass, I see Logan dip his chin and leave, the door shutting softly behind him. Moments later, Sarah delivers a glass of the amber liquid to Pete. He holds it up aloft, toasting his thanks to the black windows he can see from his side, trusting that I'm watching.

But as the bass I know all too well begins, my eyes float to the stage.

At the press of a button, the speakers come to life, filling my office with the music. I sit in my desk chair, the black leather soft beneath me as I spin to watch the show.

She may be dancing for the fuckers down there on the floor, the ones laying twenties on the stage to tempt her into coming closer, but as her eyes glance up to the window where I'm sitting, I know who this show is *really* for.

She can't see me, but she's performing for me. There's a connection between us. It might be unspoken, but it's there, and in the months since I carried her away from the bloody shooting, it hasn't lessened. Even though we haven't acted on it . . . it's there.

I watch as she moves her lithe body from the back of the stage to the front, making eyes at every man along the rail.

One man has a stack of green sitting in front of him, and though I can't tell the denomination from here, it must be high-value because Allie chooses him as her mark. She drops down into a squat, her skirted ass resting on her heels and her knees spread wide.

I growl, knowing that even though her skirt hangs between her legs, the fucker is too damn close to her pussy. She runs a black fingertip along the jeweled strap of her tiny corset bra, leaning close as she pulls it out slightly.

The man takes the hint and slips a bill between her skin and the strap, thankfully for him, not touching her.

Watching her this way is somehow the sweetest torture, knowing that she enjoys being onstage and is getting what she needs, both personally and financially, but wanting to kill every asshole who so much as glances at her.

The demon on my shoulder reminds me that I like knowing that though they may watch, not a single one of them can lay a hand on her. No one ever does . . . because she's mine. Whether she acknowledges it or not doesn't change the fact that everyone else knows.

Allie slowly pulls her knees closed, waiting for the man to look up and meet her eyes. With a smile that could make an angel have lustful thoughts, she hair-flips around and drops to her hands and knees, her ass pressed back toward the rail. She glances over her shoulder, her eyes full of false heat, and pulls at her hip.

Forty dollars later, or hell, maybe it's two hundred, she crawls away, making sure her hips swing right and left with every inch closer to the pole she gets.

She's like a panther, all dark hair and honey skin in the warm light. She presses her shoulder to the pole, letting her head hang down, and with a kick, she's suddenly in a handstand, her ankles wrapped around the brass so quickly it seems like she floated there.

There's a collective gasp in the audience, and then Allie lets one ankle free, her leg stretching long before her foot comes to rest on the floor. With one leg on the pole and one on the floor, framed by her hands, she holds the splits position before she slowly, and with enviable control, lowers her leg from the pole to stand tall, as if what she just did was normal. She plays with the tie of her skirt, teasing it loose and then letting it drop to the stage at her feet.

Her costume tonight is one of my favorites, the thong framed in innocent pink satin even as the black see-through lace panel and jewels show her other side, a perfect blend of nice and naughty. The pink tone even gives me hints of the sweet ballerina inside her.

She stands proudly, letting everyone look their fill, though I suspect my eyes would never tire of her beauty, before beginning her show in earnest. It's worthy of the fucking Cirque de Soleil, trick after trick along the pole, spinning and climbing before inverting and dropping.

It's a show never seen in Petals before Allie arrived. She is somehow part gymnast, part dancer, and part goddess, elegance and grace woven through every athletic move as she seduces the audience.

And me.

Though she seduced me a long time ago, I find myself entranced once again by the siren song her body is singing to mine. Toward the end of her routine, she leans back against the pole, her knees bent in a sexy version of a plie with her legs spread wide.

Her hands trace her body, her breasts heaving in the corset cups, a sweet smile on her face. Her eyes look up, not at the crowd clapping and waving bills, but at the blacked-out windows to my office. I know she can't see me, but she must know that I'm watching her, my cock rock hard in my slacks and demanding attention.

I consider palming myself, knowing it'd only take a stroke or two before I'd cum all over my hand, likely saying her name as I did so, but I force myself to refrain.

I need to be clear-headed for the meeting with Pete, not in a post-orgasmic haze.

As Allie leaves the stage, I radio down to Logan.

"Go ahead and send Pete up."

Only a minute later, Pete sits across from me, my brain zeroing in on business, all thoughts of pleasure and Allie shutting off and getting locked down behind a wall. My cock's even mostly deflated, although it's not too happy about that particular situation.

My face is neutral as I greet him. "Pete. Good to see you."

He nods casually, well aware that his position and age do not get him any special privileges or allowances in my presence, though they may grant him some on his block.

"Dominick. Thank you for seeing me, and thank you for the drink. Truly a delicious treat. How'd you know I like Japanese whisky?"

I merely nod, already done with pleasantries and ready to get to the meat of the meeting.

Sensing this, Pete clears his throat and speaks again. "I've got a couple of new guys in my area I thought you'd want to know about."

"Soldiers?" I question. I don't like fresh heat in my town without preclearing it.

"Yes, but not in the way you mean," Pete says, choosing each word carefully. "Not Mob and not my guys. They're actual military, from what I can tell, out of uniform now, but they ride with a group out of Johnstown. The bikes are what caught my attention. Big, loud motherfuckers, running up and down my streets."

I choose not to correct his wording, both of us knowing that *all* the streets of this city are mine, not Pete's, even if he watches over a section for me. And perhaps a taste of ownership helps him take pride in his work, even if it's only an image of possession.

He shakes his head in annoyance and continues. "The two guys in my block are Robert Zallow and Anthony Chambers. One's a former Lieutenant, the other a Staff Sergeant, and the group they're riding with call themselves the Eagle Raiders. Not exactly a one-percenter group, but they get into enough shit that I wanted to mention it. Especially since these two fuckers are the first ones to set up home base in my area. I want to make sure they're not trying to expand territory, especially not into mine. I'm doing some looking, and I'll send you what I have, but it's not much. I figured you'd want to dig a bit deeper than I can, see what turns up. Hell, they might be useful, one way or another."

I nod, mentally recording the names and considering what I know about the local MC groups. East Robinsville is unclaimed by any biker group because it's claimed by me, but it's a prime thoroughfare to get from the docks to upstate and beyond. If the Eagle Raiders are trying to start a highway run through my city without seeking permission or paying their tolls, they've got another thing coming.

I won't allow it and would kill to prevent it . . . if I have to.

A knock on the door interrupts my dark thoughts.

"Enter," I say.

Logan's head pops around the door, not even fully entering. "Pardon me, sir. Just informing you of departure. Proceeding as scheduled."

I nod, and Logan closes the door behind him. I don't bother glancing at the monitors, knowing that he's got the situation handled. The situation being that Allie is done for the night and leaving the club. She's the headliner, and after that dance, she doesn't need to work again, especially after the long day she's had.

Either way, Gavin will follow standard operations and escort her to her car like he will every dancer when they leave tonight. Allie is parked in the back lot, where Logan will be waiting to follow her home and invisibly guard her until my arrival.

Pete grins as the door closes, unaware of the message that was sent.

"Your guys always tell you when they're headed home for the night? He tell you when he gets his dick wet too?"

He laughs, the lines at the corners of his eyes crinkling at his own joke, but I don't laugh because it isn't funny.

"He does whatever I tell him to. Simple as that, same as you," I say, reminding him that though he may be a high-ranking captain with a territory of his own to maintain, he's no better than any other man. "Now, give me the rest of your news."

It's not until hours later that I finally get to dismiss Logan and settle into my barebones apartment.

I neatly hang my jacket up in the front hall, untuck my shirt, and roll up my sleeves, sitting down with a nightcap of whisky.

I turn on the television, but it's not some late-night rerun that grabs my attention. No, it's the night-vision camera feed hidden in Allie's bedroom. She may be only one floor away from this secret apartment, but I'd needed more. More insight, more closeness, more of *her* to feed my obsession.

I know on some level it's wrong, intrusive, and a violation of her trust. At first, it had truly been for her safety. The threat back then was significant, and it was only with a bit of luck and the appearance of an unexpected ally that she never found out just how dangerous it was.

But she's no longer in danger. I dealt with the fallout from the shooting at Petals months ago. It was only recently that I've been forced to admit to myself that my surveillance wasn't for her.

It's always been for me.

CHAPTER

Three

ALLIE

"YOU WANT ME TO DO *WHAT*?" I screech in surprise, my eyes wide and my mouth hanging open.

Donna just smiles back, like she didn't just set my world atilt. "Look, I didn't know who she was either, but the publicity from your class is like a tidal wave that won't be stopped. You're seriously blowing up on Instagram and Facebook, and the studio's getting *lots* of attention."

I click my mouth closed and swallow.

When Eileen had said Donna wanted to talk to me today, it'd felt a little like getting called to the principal's office and was sure I was going to get in trouble. I figured some parent had found out about the private class and riled everyone up. By the time I knocked on Donna's door, I visualized parents pulling their kids from my classes in a mass-exodus of soccer mom hair flips and snarky comments. Maybe even a few *I'mma pray for yous* thrown in too.

What I didn't expect was . . . whatever this is. Donna sits before me in her small but tidy office, the walls covered top to bottom with pictures of her with students from the last thirty years. She still looks like a regal ballerina, thin and fit from dancing, with a harshly crisp traditional bun that's softened by the lines on her face that show how often she smiles.

"What do you mean? What attention?" I ask, scared of the answer. I can just see it now. *Tonight on Action News at Six, Dance Studio or Strip Club?*

"Allie?"

I blink, realizing Donna's talking. "Sorry, again?"

"It seems the maid of honor for that party—"

"Jenny. The maid of honor's name was Jenny."

Donna nods, snickering. "Yeah, do you know who Jenny Wartham is?"

I shake my head, utterly confused. "The maid of honor?"

Donna sighs, as if she'd hoped I knew. Sorry, Donna, I'm sort of too busy to keep up with celebrities outside of mainline sports and the dance world.

"Well, yeah. But she's also a bit of an internet celebrity, apparently. Now, I didn't know that when I booked the class. But she wrote this whole long Instagram post about your class and the great time they had."

My eyes shoot wide open in surprise. "She did?"

"Yeah, she didn't mention you by name, but she mentioned the studio and the amazing brunette who had her, and I quote, 'feeling like a Sex Kitten Goddess.' There were some pictures of cats and some various meows, which seemed crazy and weird to me, but the gist was that it was a raving review. And when I came in on Monday, my inbox was flooded, and Eileen has been answering calls requesting private classes and asking if we hold public classes too."

My breath escapes my chest in a whooshing sound as I slump, something I never do, but I'm so shocked that I can't even hold myself up for a moment.

"What? I thought it was just a one-time thing?" I say, though I'll admit to myself that now that I've done one, having another class would be fun. "I mean, Donna, I don't want to ruin the studio's rep as a ballet school because someone wants to do stripper-robics."

Donna locks her eyes on me, scoffing. "Not to put too fine a point on it, but this school is mine and I'll do what I want with it. I'm smart enough to know that people come here for ballet because of my reputation as a dancer and as a teacher. But as a businesswoman, I know how to use my resources, work the strengths, and play away from the weakness. And you are a strength, to me and to this studio. Allie, if you're up to it, I think it's time for your encore, my dear."

I nod like a bobblehead, encouraged. "Absolutely, I'm up to it. What are you thinking? Just private classes, or maybe do a public special event every once in a while? I'm open to whatever you think."

Donna claps in delight then points at me, grinning. "Good. Remember you said that, though, because I'm going to hold you to it."

I sit up straight again, feeling like this is Donna's big solo moment, what she was building up to for the whole rest of the conversation.

"All right, hit me. What are you thinking?"

"Well, like I said before, I want you to teach not just a class, but classes. I've been doing quite a bit of research and watched some rather steamy performances too. Everything from burlesque to striptease to pole fitness. And whew, let me tell you, I thought I'd seen some things, but no. *Now*, I've seen things."

She laughs, and I blush, thinking she'd probably faint at the tricks I pull on the pole at Petals. Thankfully, Donna has known about my other job since she hired me to teach a couple of adult beginner ballet classes, and she's okay with it. More than okay, considering she's given me several additional classes to teach. And she is the one who asked me to do the bachelorette party dance class in the first place.

She continues, "I think we've been given a golden opportunity here. It's no secret that profit margins for dance studios are low, but I think this is an untapped niche in East Robinsville. And to be honest, your name brings a certain clout with it."

Donna looks at me knowingly, and I wonder if maybe she has seen my performances before, though I'm careful to never post anything online. And recording is strictly forbidden at Petals. It's a rule heavily enforced by Dominick, so I'm almost 100 percent sure nobody would risk his wrath for a blurry, dark video. I don't even dance under the same name. At Petals, I'm Allie Angel, but here, I'm Allison Bancroft, and only my child students call me Allie.

"I guess."

Donna chuckles, reassuring me. "I want to begin offering classes a few days a week. Whatever you want to call it and whatever you want to do. We'd work the schedule around our current class offerings, and these would be yours, so we'd split the class fees fifty-fifty. The private classes . . . I doubled the charge for those, and nobody blinked an eye."

I stammer, shocked. "Doubled?"

Donna's smile is vibrant, infectious. "Yes, ma'am, doubled them and booked six already over the next three months alone, and we'd split those fifty-fifty like the bachelorette one. You with me so far?"

Holy shit. "Yeah, I'm with you. I'm *so* with you."

"Good, here's where the real fun starts. I want you to rent studio three from me, install some poles, and offer pole fitness classes. In return, I get the rent, low, of course, and ten percent of the class fees. You'd keep ninety percent. We'd be more like business partners."

Donna sits back in her chair, an expectant look on her face.

I'm stunned, shocked by everything she's saying. The opportunity, the possibilities astound me. It's definitely not what I ever saw myself doing, but honestly, I had to let go of that dream a long time ago.

Now I have the chance to not just instill a love of ballet in upcoming stars, but maybe help everyday women feel a little extra special too. It's heady. I mean, I can actually make a difference in the world, as small as it might be.

"Wow, that's a lot to take in. I'm definitely in for the private classes and a couple of weekly public ones too, as long as that's in addition to the ballet classes currently on my schedule."

Donna nods. "Of course. The company performance wouldn't be the same without you, and the kids respond well to your teaching."

I bite my lip, thinking quickly. "As for the pole classes, I'm definitely interested, but I'll need to do some research to see what the investment costs would be. Money's always an issue, and it sounds like this could be a big undertaking. But my answer's yes, if you'll let me do some homework."

Donna claps again, happy. "Whatever you need, but I'll say that we need to strike while the iron is hot. Let's get this rolling as fast as possible. Even if it's pole-less."

She offers me her hand, and I reach across the desk and shake it, the reality suddenly hitting me.

I can do this.

I *am* doing this.

I spend the rest of the day clicking around online, doing as much research as I can, from vendors to construction. I fall down the rabbit hole of watching videos of classes other studios offer to see what the competition is like too, but Donna's right.

There's nothing like what we're talking about doing within a hundred miles of East Robinsville. It's an untapped market, and we can be first to fill that need, even if it's a need people don't know exists . . . yet.

Hours later, I have what I think is a pretty good grip on what it'd cost to get started on paper. But it's admittedly a bit daunting and makes me question myself. I need backup. I move my laptop to the coffee table and flop onto the couch as I dial the one person who can talk me through this, my friend Maggie. She doesn't even answer with a hello but instead launches in full-on.

"Hey, girl! Long time no talk! What's up?"

That's Mags. Got me smiling before I even said a word. "Hey, Maggie. I know. It's been what, two weeks since we talked? I miss your face!"

That's not really that long, especially in the busy world she lives in these days, but I have missed her.

"Miss you too. But I've been out on assignment, and my new contract starts in two days. I'm just trying to decompress before I'm gone again."

"Wow, sounds intense."

That's putting it mildly, to say the least. Maggie works as a sort of 'researcher' for the FBI. Considering her past as an investigative journalist, she's good at her job. She's kind of the last person you'd suspect because she comes off as sweet and innocent, but beneath the surface lurks a whip-smart brain.

And her brain is what I need. I give her the short version of everything that's happened and what Donna proposed. Maggie hums in all the right places, tells me she's pulling up Jenny Wartham's Instagram, oohing and ahhing over the racy sections.

"Okay, this all sounds great, and your business plans seem sound, especially if you have the money. Invest in yourself, Allie."

I hum, waffling even though I know what I want to do. I'm just not sure it's the smart thing to do, especially when I have other debts that should probably take priority to my chasing a dream I never knew I had. But maybe this dream is the thing that could finally pay off those debts completely.

"You think so?"

She tsks through the line, as if I'm a naughty student. "You said the class went well, the women obviously felt like it did, and you made bank. You can duplicate that experience with no problem, and it sounds like people want you to. Expanding into pole classes sounds solid too, because Lord knows, you've got crazy skills on the pole. And it's a way for you to share that without . . ."

She pauses, and I know what she's going to say, so I finish the sentence for her. "Without getting naked on stage." I sigh, knowing she's right.

I certainly never thought I'd be a stripper, and while I don't get naked, only stripping down to a G-string and tiny bra tops, there's definitely something naughty about it.

Of course, I'll admit to myself that the little bit of exhibitionist in my makeup that makes me a performer is pretty okay with the taboo of stripping. It's different from ballet, of course, but I do enjoy it. Strutting the stage makes me feel powerful, in command of everyone in the room. Most people think it's about getting the audience's attention, but really, it's about making them hungry for my attention.

It's very much a symbiotic energy exchange and a total rush.

"You know I'm not judging you, Allie. You're a beautiful dancer, wherever you want to perform. I just have one question. Did you have fun teaching the class?"

I consider her question because it feels pivotal, maybe the most important part of our conversation.

"Absolutely. I got to witness that switch moment for those women, when they go from an everyday 'good girl' who does what's expected to a 'sexy siren' who feels powerful in her body and mind and can do whatever she feels honors that."

I blush at the intensity of my words but can't help but keep going. "Maybe that sounds silly. But it's empowering, usually in a way they don't expect, and it's inspiring to be a part of that."

Maggie's grin is evident in her voice as she replies, "I think you have your answer, girl. You didn't need me to tell you that. You just needed me to listen to you decide for yourself."

"You're right, as always. Thanks, girl. I appreciate the backup."

"Anytime and always. Well, except for the next two to three weeks. I've got a little . . . ah . . . work to do, and I'm incommunicado unless there's an emergency."

"And then we've got a coffee and mani-pedi date. Deal?"

She agrees, and we hang up. I lean back on the couch and stare up at the ceiling with a smile on my face. I can do this. I *am* doing this.

I'VE ALREADY BEEN ALERTED by the man on duty tonight that Allie is coming to the club. He's to give her the full respect and treatment she deserves. What I'm not sure of is . . . why is she here? It's not her night to work, though I'm happy to see her anytime I can.

But her choosing to come to me is rare. Though we play this game of cat and mouse, always orbiting each other, acutely aware of how close we come, I know she harbors some fear of me to counteract her attraction.

It's understandable. Allie's no fool, but she was thrown into the deep end of my world unwittingly and hasn't fully learned to swim. Before the shooting, my being a 'Mob boss' was just theoretical, a rumor she wondered about but didn't really give credence to.

She didn't break the rules I had in place, so she had no need to see or immerse herself in the reality of my life. But one shooting changed all that. Now, she's retreated into a gray zone where she pretends nothing's changed between us while we both know it has. I can see it in the way she looks at me the few times her eyes meet mine and when she looks up at my window as she dances. She might want to pretend that her life is normal . . . but her body and her eyes tell me something very different.

On my part, I know I've crossed a line. She's interfering with my business, and every time I step into one of the 'blinds' I've set up to keep an eye on her, I know I'm taking a risk. If she discovers me, she would be fully within reason to freak out, calling me a stalker and worse. But I swear, as much as I want to claim her as mine publicly, my number-one concern is seeing that she remains safe.

The knock on the door makes my heart stutter for a beat, and though I know my slacks and dress shirt are impeccable, I can't help but run my palms over my chest, smoothing my tie to make sure I look my best.

"Enter."

The door cracks open and Allie peeks in, looking unadorned compared to her usual stage makeup but so beautiful that she brings light into the club. I glance behind me, trying to calm myself and look at the relative plain appearance of Petals before opening hours. With normal lights on, the mystique of the club is killed, and it helps calm me a little bit.

"Hey, Dominick? Logan said I could come up?"

I grin at the question in her tone because all the guys know that Allie has a free pass to me, whether she knows it or not. I am hers, any time she wants me. I turn away from the club, away from the dullness awaiting magic and special effect to seem magical, and toward a creature, a woman who truly is magical.

"Of course. Come in. Sit."

I gesture to the leather chairs on the far side of my office and watch as she glides across the room. Allie never merely walks anywhere. She seems to float like an angel, but her hips naturally sway with the devil's seduction.

Her curves are covered in casual faded denim and a silky black tank top that almost looks like a chemise. It's simple and elegant, like she is. She perches on the edge of the chair, and I sink into the one across from her, relaxing back and letting my knees spread wide around her crossed legs even though there are two feet between us.

Her foot bounces, and I notice that she's wearing short-heeled boots, cute and nothing at all like what she wears on stage. She's anxious, and the rare sign of her nerves thrills me. Not that I want her to be uncomfortable around me. In fact, I want the exact opposite, but her jitters show that I have some effect on her, and it warms my icy heart.

Her full lips spread wide, but it's merely a polite smile, not reaching her eyes, which seem clouded with uncertainty.

"Thanks for seeing me. I, uh . . . I need to talk to you about my other job."

"I would love to see you anytime you'd like, Allison," I tell her with utter sincerity. It's refreshing, and I relish the luxury. "And please, tell me about the dance classes. I have been interested, and I'll admit, hoping that you have been successful. I'm proud of your courage in trying to expand your horizons."

The words are a rare honesty for me, no game or strategy, no ulterior motive, just truth. I would do anything for this woman, and she barely acknowledges my existence beyond my ownership of the club and a few longing looks, although the *longing* part may be just me. She is wholly unaware that she owns my heart, whatever there may be left of it.

She squirms in her seat, the leather creaking mellowly beneath her, and an impulsive bit of jealousy hits me that the chair gets to cup her ass the way I want to when I have to refrain.

"Oh, well . . . thank you," she says, blushing a little. "It's been going really well. In fact, I wanted to let you know that things have changed there. I know we originally talked about my teaching a couple of classes a week, and it's really grown a lot over the past few months. But one of the private party classes I did has taken on a life of it's own, and I feel like I need to give it a real shot. That means more nights there, more private classes, and I'm going to set up one of the studios to teach pole fitness classes."

Her words are one long run-on sentence, and at the end, she smiles like saying them aloud somehow makes her plans more real. I understand. Sometimes, reality is woven not from our thoughts but from our own speech which leads to the actions that make those words real.

Her excitement is infectious, bubbly, and light in the dark depths of my soul, an addicting brightness. I start to smile until a devastating thought occurs to me. I'm stricken, though I keep my voice coldly steady as my smile dims slightly.

"Are you giving notice? Do you want to stop dancing at Petals from Heaven, Allie?"

What I really mean is, 'Are you leaving me?' but I don't voice that question aloud. I can't say that anyway, because regardless of how I've claimed her in my mind and she's claimed my heart by her silent actions, the words have never been spoken. The reality has never been forged.

Still, when she shakes her head, my heart resumes beating.

"No!" she says, gasping before blushing. "I mean, not exactly. But I was hoping we might be able to rearrange my schedule some? Let me just do feature appearances once or twice each week instead of multiple slots several nights per week? I'm hoping that if my performances are rarer, people will flock to them like a headliner act and I'll still make enough money to supplement while I'm getting things off the ground at Encore."

It's an interesting idea, and I spin the family crest ring on my pinky finger, the one that denotes me as the head of the Angeline family, letting the idea turn, analyzing it from every angle as the silence stretches.

I normally wouldn't, especially for a girl who's just a dancer. Still, it's Allie. The word *just* doesn't apply to anything she does. She's never *just* anything, especially to me.

Our eyes are locked on one another, the tension between us palpable, at least to me. I wonder if she knows that I can see the racing flutter of her heartbeat at her neck. She unconsciously licks her lips, drawing my attention to the flash of her pink tongue, making me want to nip at her with soft kisses before biting her fuller bottom lip, leaving that sharp mark of possession I've dreamed of for months.

I let a victorious smirk take my face, and I decide on the best course of action. Though it does probably give me more benefits than she gets, it's not unfair by any means, and I do think she'll be agreeable to my terms.

Leaning forward, I clasp my hands between my legs, letting my elbows rest on my knees and closing the distance between us to so close that I could, if I wanted, pull her in to taste her forbidden sweetness.

"You are a delight, on and off the stage, Allie. I think you know that, which is why I'm certain your new venture will be a success. If there is anything I can do to assist with that, please let me know. It would be my honor."

She blushes, her eyes sparkling. "Dominick, thank you. I know . . . well, I know you're not the nicest man, but you're always good to me."

The compliment is somehow soothing and exciting, making me think just how *good* I could be to her. Or maybe how bad? But I lock those thoughts away, again denying myself and denying her the possibility of what we could be, and focus on what she's asking for now.

"As for your shifts here, instead of paying your house fee and tip-out and keeping the remainder of your tips as per usual, I propose something a bit different. Though not common, you do know we've done headliner feature acts before. Our standard contract in that respect is an eighty-twenty split of door cover charges. No house fee, but you would still tip-out for the DJ, waitstaff, and bartender. Tips would be yours after that. It's your idea about rarer performances being more in-demand but significantly amped up."

It's a good deal, one I've only offered a handful of times in my time as owner of Petals. With the proposal I'm presenting, Allie would receive a small portion of Petals's profits for the night, a flip of the norm and a hefty bump in her pay, and considering feature performers perform on-stage for much longer sets, the potential for tips is greater too.

It's an opportunity only given to the crème de la crème of dancers, ones I'm certain can fill the club and make both of us considerable bank.

Someone like Allie.

Her jaw drops open wide in shock, tempting me to fill her mouth with something I suspect we'd both like, but to my surprised delight, she's not mindlessly celebrating my offer.

Through her shock, her mind whirls around and lands on . . .

"Make it 75/25 and you have a deal."

The surprised chuckle escapes before I can stop it, but I recover, dipping my chin as I incline my head.

"Very well. 75/25. On one condition."

At my agreement, even with a caveat, she leans forward, bringing our lips within inches of each other, our breath mingling as she lifts one eyebrow in question. Though there is desire in her eyes, there's also a wariness, that hint of suspicion telling me that she's so much more than one of the typical girls downstairs who would trade their bodies to me in a heartbeat without so much as considering the cost. And as much as her body tempts me, it is this inner beauty that draws me in more, the innate goodness that remains inside her heart and the swift intellect behind the golden chocolate of her eyes.

"Dinner. That is the condition. Have dinner with me."

Her breath falters, and though she disguises it quickly, I see the quick flash of confusion in her eyes before she schools her features.

"Like a date? But that's like rule number one around here. Girls and staff don't mix."

She's not wrong. I have many rules, and one of the most steadfast ones is that there is no fraternization inside the club. Employees are strictly forbidden from dating, an offense punishable by many rather creative consequences, up to and including death, depending on the betrayal and rank of offenders.

Only one couple has ever violated that rule and gotten away with it, although I overlooked that because of the other benefits involved in that particular transaction. Having a marker with the FBI is a powerful token in my line of work.

I shrug my shoulders, smiling a little. "You are correct. And you know from personal experience that I don't break my own rules. How is Maggie, by the way?"

"Well, uhm . . . happy." Frustratingly, one half of that couple is one of Allie's best friends, but sometimes, you can't choose your friends. I couldn't deny Allie her friend in any case. "But you and I—"

"Would no longer be employer and employee," I finish for her reassuringly. "In this scenario, you become more contractor than employee, so a date is no different than if I saw the CEO of the beer distributing company I utilize but do not employ."

Her eyes narrow, her cheeks flushing in delightful jealousy. "And have you *dated* the beer CEO?"

I adore her reaction but keep my face neutral as I nod knowingly. "We have had dinner *many* times. Ron is a rather entertaining fellow, and his wife is delightful."

She chuckles, just the way I'd hoped she would, but then she sobers slightly, sarcasm teasing at the edges of her words.

"But you wouldn't be setting a very good example if you go around seemingly breaking your own rules. Some of your men could see it as your splitting hairs. You could be inciting mass-anarchy."

I lift my brows, thinking about my crew. "I sincerely doubt that. People are too fearful of me to risk my wrath over a bit of pussy or dick, as the case may be."

Instantly, I wish I hadn't phrased it so, because a weight falls between us. I take pride in speaking as an educated man, a man who might not have gone to Yale but still completed his MBA at a perfectly respectable university and who strives to make more of himself than the greaseball wise guy my grandfather was, no offense.

But my poor choice of words reminds Allie of who I am. *What* I am. The aftermath of the shooting tore the veil from her eyes more than anything else, and I had to reveal just how deep my connections ran. She knows that I'm in charge of East Robinsville, that I'm The Boss, the Don, though nobody uses that antiquated word anymore.

And though her eyes track me the same as they did before, full of restrained lust and a desire to know more about me, I can see that the questions beneath the surface of her attraction are scarier to ask, but they're ones she wants the answers to all the same.

She deserves those answers, and it's the other reason I've never pushed breaking my rule with her. Any woman who deserves to share my life with me to that level deserves to know. If we go there, she's going to know what I am, what I do, even if I don't want her involved.

I think Allie knows this, and she swallows, digging for her courage. My heart leaps as my brave girl finds it and graces me with another angelic smile.

"I would love to have dinner with you. Though not as a part of the agreement. Simply agree to the 75/25 split. You don't need to manipulate me with money to have dinner with you, Dominick. You . . . you never have."

My name on her lips is a heavenly hymn my sullied soul doesn't deserve, but I take it anyway, hoarding it like treasure while at the same time promising myself to make her scream it, sigh it, and sing it, again and again.

The fact that she is agreeing to dinner despite the agreement tells me everything I need to know. Allie wants me, maybe as much as I want her. We've been good, as good as we can be, which for me isn't much, but we've followed the rules.

And now it's time for something else. "Good. Then let's eat."

The lilting happy sound of her giggle delights me.

"I didn't realize you meant right now!" she argues. "I thought you meant you were going to pick me up for dinner sometime."

I shake my head, standing up reluctantly because I don't want to be an inch farther apart from her than I have to. I want to feel her breath on my skin forever . . . but I have to order dinner.

"I don't want to give you time to reconsider. So now it is."

That's the God's-honest truth because I know if I give her a moment to analyze this, she'll come out on the same side every time. The one where she doesn't go out with me at all.

So I'm pressing tonight, hoping that by keeping her slightly off balance, I can get more into her psyche, learn more about her, and maybe make her not so frightened of what I am.

Though I strongly suspect that's an exercise in futility. I pick up my phone, calling my favorite Italian restaurant, one of my own, of course.

"I want one large order of lasagna, salad for two, and a bowl of roasted tomato and basil soup." I nod as they repeat the order, promising to have it here as quickly as possible. I take the moment to let Thomas know since he's currently serving as front-door security.

"How'd you know I'd want soup?" Allie asks as I hang up.

Though I know her preferences in and out, I choose to tease her. "Just a lucky guess, I suppose. Though how do you know the soup isn't for me and the lasagna for you?"

Her smile is one that says she gets my humor, something most people would say I severely lack. "Well played, Dom."

Sitting back down, I frame her crossed legs with my spread ones again, though I pull her chair closer to mine, caging her in with my thighs.

"So, now that this is dinner," I say, intentionally not calling it a date because I know she's still a bit skittish, "tell me something about yourself I don't know."

I'm curious what she'll share, though I already know so much. I want to hear the stories of her past from her own lips.

"Hmm," she hums, obviously searching her mind as she glances off to the side. If I were a more artistic man, I would insist that she pose for a portrait because her profile is elegant, the slope of her nose giving way to her lush lips, and the graceful length of her neck begging me to nibble.

Instead, I stay in my seat, giving her time and space to adjust, patiently hooking her so as to reel her in without her even noticing. Finally, she turns back, eyes landing on mine.

"I always dreamed of being a dancer."

I tilt my head, amused. "And this is supposed to be new information? Allie, you *are* a dancer. I knew that the first moment I saw you perform."

She shakes her head like I don't get it. "No, not like this," she says, shaking her hand toward the wall of windows I currently have set to opaque so as not to allow the distractions of the club's pre-opening activities to invade this moment between us. "I mean, a *real* dancer. Ever since I was a little girl, it was all I ever wanted. To be up on stage, dancing and performing, creating those moments for the audience and sharing in their experience. And I worked my ass off for it too, hours of class and practice everyday, stretching until I cried, working until my toes bled and then bandaging them and continuing. It was all I thought about, dreamed about. It was *everything*."

This is nothing unknown to me, but it is fresh from her lips, so I let her continue. "And what happened to divert you from that dream?"

Allie raises an eyebrow, curious. "How do you know I didn't just give it up, that I didn't get so tired of the constant drive to be better that I just walked away?"

I give her a narrowed-eyed look, showing her a little bit of what I know of her past. "Because if you decided you didn't love it, you wouldn't be teaching ballet to the next generation. You wouldn't be performing in small community theater ballet productions. And you certainly wouldn't light up like a star just from talking about it. But you do all those things. Even as you talk about how hard it was, I can tell you miss it. So, what happened? Something to do with that scar on your ankle?"

She huffs out a woeful sigh, looking down at her leg, though her ankle is hidden by her jeans and boots. "Not quite. Or at least, not at first. The real problem was puberty."

I can't help the bark of laughter that escapes at the unexpected answer. "What?"

She smiles, though it's small and sad. "Well, several things, but that was the real trigger. Ballerinas are small, thin, light wisps of women, and I was until I turned sixteen. Luckily, or maybe unluckily, I was a late bloomer, but when I blossomed, I did so in a big way."

She holds her hands out in front of her chest like she's grasping huge melons, not the delectable full handfuls of breasts she actually possesses, which are in proportion to her curvy hips, giving her an hourglass shape.

"Almost overnight, I went from straight and thin to curvy, and no matter what I did to fight it, Mother Nature had other plans for my body. And I fought hard for years . . . diets, chest compression with elastic bandages, hours spent figuring out how to angle my hips so that I was never square to the directors, trying to mask it. I had to give up so much as the guys stopped wanting to do partner work with me. I knew I couldn't be the Prima, but I thought I could still at least be one of the cast, one of the ensemble."

I flush with anger. This precious being, not the center of attention? Insanity. Then again, the dance world has always been insane to me.

"Eventually, it caught up to me. I hadn't eaten anything significant in days. I'd been on a broth and celery cleanse before a performance, and I was weak but pushing through. I'd overstretched, but I'd been so pleased with my progress that I didn't consider that my body couldn't keep up. I did a move where I was supposed to land in a deep plié with my feet turned out, and I felt a pop. I collapsed to the stage and passed out from the pain."

My gut churns at her words, the story so very different from the dry words on paper I'd gotten in her background report. I can imagine a younger her, driven and hard-working, refusing to accept no for an answer from anyone, least of all herself.

She is still determined, but it's softened with a cynical acceptance that sometimes your best still isn't good enough, and perhaps now I understand why.

"And that was the ankle?"

She nods, rolling her right foot unconsciously. "Two ligaments, some space-age NASA stuff I can't pronounce . . . and that was the end of my *Sugar Plum Fairy* dreams."

Her voice is so heartbreaking, so sad, I want to gather her into my arms and reassure her that it doesn't matter. At least to me, it doesn't.

"I'm so very sorry, Allison. That sounds awful. Truly."

I don't try to temper the words with useless reassurances that she knows are untrue. I offer my true feeling of remorse that her dream was snatched from her.

She waves her hand, dismissing even the bare-boned words. "Like they say, the show must go on. I did months of physical therapy to make sure my ankle was strong and healthy again, but the real work was in here."

She touches her fingertip to her temple, and I give her a questioning look. "Three months of inpatient treatment at an eating disorder clinic and then years of therapy after, but I came out healthy. Better than I'd been in years, maybe ever."

A lightbulb goes off in my head, and I realize what brought her to Petals in the first place. It wasn't just dance.

"Your medical bills. You'd said when you began that you were paying off medical bills. You took them on yourself."

She nods, wounded but proud. "Of course. I didn't feel like my parents should have to pay for all that after paying top-dollar for my ballet for so many years. Dancing here has given me a way to pay off the hospital faster than I would've been able to with a desk job."

I nod, numbers whirling in my head, and though I know I could easily wipe her debt clean, I also know she would never allow it.

"But with a feature gig contract here plus your classes and private events at Encore, you should make considerable progress, right?"

She taps her nose and smiles as she points at me, grinning. "That's the plan. Taking over the world next week."

Her casual sass is enchanting, an uncommon behavior from most people when they sit alone with me. I'm accustomed to nerves or machismo, wolf tickets and bragging, fear and ego, and sometimes flat-out manipulative desire.

But Allie is none of those things. She's simply herself, and I want to bask in her authenticity and soak up the wholesome goodness of her soul that some might dismiss because of her job but is so readily obvious to anyone who takes the time to actually speak with her. I also like that while she may be deeply unsure about the ethics of what I do, at least on the surface, she is relaxing around me, talking and sharing with ease as we chat like two regular people, though the reality is that only one of us is 'normal'.

"What about your family? Do they know how you're paying the medical bills?"

She rolls her eyes like an exasperated teenager who just got asked a stupid question.

"Yes, and of course, they hate it. Which I understand, because who wants their kid to grow up to be a stripper? I definitely think they expected something a bit classier from me after all those hours at a ballet barre, but all things considered, they don't give me much of a hard time."

The thought of her parents criticizing her at all frustrates me, but I can understand their conflict, both wanting her to fly and satisfy her obvious need for the stage, while at the same time wanting to protect her and keep her selfishly to themselves.

"Class is not in what one chooses to do for a living, Allie," I reassure her, seeing the question hiding behind her eyes. After all, I've seen almost everything her body has to display. Many men would disrespect the woman inside at that point. But then again, I am not many men. "It is how you carry yourself, the way you stay true to your own compass. And you have done that beautifully, through both adversity and privilege, with a refined elegance that has shone through. In the end, you will shine like the star I've seen from the first moment we met."

The silence that follows is deafening, her cheeks pink with pleasure as the words sink in. I give her the moment to truly hear them, hoping she can feel the genuineness of them.

A knock on the door surprises me, which is a dangerous thing. I am always aware and alert of my surroundings, but while I've talked with Allie, listening to her story, I've been immersed completely in her.

It could have been a threat, though they likely wouldn't have knocked and would have to be ninjas to get past my outside security. Fortunately, it is merely our dinner delivery.

We move over to the casual seating area of my office, and I unpack the bag of food, setting each dish on the coffee table. Allie foregoes the couch in favor of sitting on the floor. I stare at her for a moment and then follow her lead.

I don't know that I've ever sat on the floor to eat, not even as a child, unless it was at a Japanese restaurant. My family was always more formal, more about rules and expectations of propriety. But sitting here this way feels oddly intimate, and I find that I enjoy being this casual with Allie, sharing a meal in my office at Petals, a place I rarely relax.

We're sitting close, just the small piece of glass holding our food between us, but the food delivery gave us a bit of a break, letting each of us reset from the deep conversation and the confidences Allie shared with me.

Dinner is delicious, with the anticipated lasagna and soup as mouthwatering and perfect as I could hope for. However, I pay little attention to the food, listening aptly instead as Allie gushes over her plans for Encore, going so far as to give me the breakdown of her business model for the pole dancing fitness classes.

The excitement and joy at the new undertaking is obvious as she speaks, lighting her from within with a warm glow that only serves to somehow make her that much more stunning.

"I mean, I know that fitness crazes come and go, but the big thing is striking when the iron's hot. If I can get the women in there for the sexy classes, they'll be happier and healthier. A bit of 'I am woman, hear me roar,' if you know what I mean. But most of all, I'm going to keep it fun for them, and then we'll . . ."

She's like a fountain of energy, words, and ideas, and as she rambles on, I find myself inordinately relaxed by the buzz she creates with her speech, her presence, with just . . . her.

CHAPTER

Five

ALLIE

"BEAUTIFUL, Isabella! Now reach through the top of your head and down through your toes. Find your length . . . yes," I encourage, seeing the already tall girl transform before my very eyes.

She'd already been a well-trained dancer when she joined my classes, but her progress has been rather phenomenal, if I do say so myself. She's at that awkward age where girls sometimes begin to try to hide away their inner light as their bodies become unfamiliar and seemingly strange. I'm bound and determined to make sure she lets her light shine like a beacon, so bright that others can't help but acknowledge her.

The music ends, and the whole group takes their curtseying bow, some graceful as swans and some still hatchlings finding their poise, but I applaud them, one and all.

"Great job today, ladies. I'll see you all on Wednesday, when we begin the next set of choreo. Make sure you do your home warmups in between now and then, and listen to the music."

There's a chorus of 'Thanks, Miss Allie!' and "Bye!' from the gaggle of girls, and they leave in a mass of buns, duffel bags, and booties. It's the flight of the tweeners, and I can't help but grin as I watch them go.

My next class is a bit easier, 'Baby Ballet,' which is mostly just jumping around and having fun to music with little kids between the ages of three and five. It's physically fun but mentally easy, which is a good thing since my mind begins to lose focus and wander back to my 'dinner' with Dominick.

He thought he was being so slick, but I know a date when I'm on it. There's been tension between us for months, going back to even before the shooting. And since that awful night? Even more sparks.

I think he honestly believes he is subtle, that I'm unaware of his eyes tracking me at the club. I know he's had people watching me as well, and while I haven't said anything to him about it, I do know that every time I go to Petals, I'm given a security detail on Secret Service levels going and coming out of the parking lot. He's protective of all the girls, but with me, there's just a little extra care.

Dom doesn't think I notice, but I do. I see everything. I watch him too . . . the way his broad shoulders sweep through the club and people move like parting seas before him, the way every word from his mouth is calculated and carefully considered, the dominant aura that surrounds him leaving no doubt of who's in charge.

I knew he was a boss long before I knew he was The Boss, and I was attracted to him then.

I'd held back from any flirtation for the longest time out of respect for his rule, though we'd made eyes at each other so many times I thought I'd combust just from the heat of his gaze.

It's part of who he is. I had enough pretty guys with bodies carved from stone and perfect faces when I was in the dance world. Dominick's handsome, yes, but it's in a dark, brooding, intellectual way. His body's not just strong but also stocky, his shoulders broad and thick, an intellectual savage, I would say.

For months, we circled each other, always wondering which of us was going to take that first step toward something more. Spoiler alert—it was never going to be me. I'm crazy, but not *that* crazy. And I think he was already close to giving in and making a move, but our little dance took a very abrupt ninety-degree turn when the shit hit the fan a few months ago and my world was sent flying totally off-kilter.

It forced me to recognize all the little signs that I overlooked, the hints that I didn't bother to add up because I was too busy crushing on my hot, slightly older, dominant boss. But now that I'm forced to acknowledge just who Dominick truly is, he honestly scares me a little bit. The fact that he's not *of* the Mob but actually *is* The Mob tears at me.

He's not someone to mess with, and I'm not sure I should involve myself with him. But with everything on the table, more or less, I can't help but admit that the twinge of danger he has only adds to his charms, attracting me more even as my mind wars with the stupidity of it.

He's the walking, talking, sexy epitome of the bad boy you know you should stay away from but want desperately anyway, even knowing it's going to end poorly. And even knowing the risk, I couldn't help but say yes to our dinner-not-date, despite the pretty blatant and cheesy segue.

Surprisingly, Dominick was easy to open up to about my past. I'd told him things I hadn't said aloud in years, and even then, only to a therapist. Perhaps even more shocking was the lighter conversation while we ate. He'd listened attentively to my gushing plans for the business with Encore, never once making me think he was bored of my excitement or thought my plans were silly.

If anything, he seemed quietly supportive, making insightful commentary and offering advice that actually helped my thoughts.

He also hadn't zeroed in on my eating after I'd dropped the eating disorder bombshell. It's not exactly top-secret or something I'm ashamed of, and I have told friends and boyfriends before, but there's always that adjustment period where they're suddenly hyper-aware of everything I eat.

Not Dominick. He was already hyper-aware of me, and that little factoid in my history didn't add or detract from his attentiveness.

But his willingness to move our orbiting interest in one another into a different path is both terrifying and thrilling. He's not a man to get involved with casually or thoughtlessly, but I guess on some complicated level, I've already been entangled with him.

Lord knows, I haven't dated, or dined, with anyone else in ages. It's not because I haven't been asked. I can barely go a shift at Petals without some guy dropping a note with his phone number or something on stage along with his money. Some have even had the guts to approach me in person. I'll give them credit, considering how protective Dominick's security is over me.

But I know where my heart lies and didn't want to disrespect Dominick by giving the guys more than a polite refusal, even if Dom was keeping his distance. That time seems to be over now, I think, and though my stomach has been doing little backflips that have nothing to do with the delicious food we shared, my heart races.

My thoughts are interrupted by a little voice at my side, and I look down to see Cindy, one of the five-year-olds, looking anxious and doing the pee-pee dance at the same time.

"Miss Allie? Isn't class over? The big hand is past the one again?"

I shake myself out of my reverie and glance at the clock, seeing that it's 7:08, eight minutes after class was supposed to end.

"Oh, thank you, Cindy. Yes, class dismissed. Thank you for the extra work tonight. Beautiful job, everyone."

They shuffle out, and luckily, I don't see any upset moms from keeping them over time. I clean up the studio quickly, making sure all the lights are off. The only other classes tonight are advanced classes that Donna's teaching to her students.

I give Donna a wave as I pass by her studio, where she's stretching out and preparing herself for teaching. Outside, the lot is well-lit, but there are still darker shadows where SUVs, trucks, or just the arrangement of poles mean the light doesn't quite reach.

I scan my surroundings like I'm supposed to, but I'm still surprised when I see Cindy's dad, Mr. Duncan, sitting on the trunk of his car, his head in his hands. He watched his daughter's class today, but . . . where is she?

"Mr. Duncan? Sir, are you okay?" His head pops up, and I see him sweep a quick finger under each eye, making me think he's crying or at least tearing up for some reason.

He stutters a bit and hops off the trunk, clearing his throat. "Oh, Allie! Sorry, I thought I was alone."

"No problem. You okay?"

He nods, but it seems more like he's trying to convince himself than telling the truth.

"Yeah . . . we're going through some stuff, and watching Cathy drive off with Cindy, knowing they're going home and I'm heading to one of those extended-stay studio hotels is rough. I just miss her."

Understanding dawns, and I feel my heart go out to him. I don't know what the issue is between him and his wife, but the man's obviously in pain. And those extended-stay places suck.

"I'm sorry to hear that. I had no idea. Do you miss Cindy or Cathy? Either way, you should tell them."

He smiles as he sniffles again, hooking his thumbs in his belt loops and looking bashful. "Cindy . . . I miss my little girl. Cathy can rot in hell, for all I care."

His words are spat out, coated in unexpected venom that makes me flinch. He sees the cringe and winces apologetically.

"Sorry, didn't mean to sound so mean. I found out she's been cheating on me. Lawyer said I should let her keep the house because it's best for Cindy, but then they get to home like nothing changed, and I'm alone. Ah, fuck, it's just a little raw right now, and I'm bitter as hell."

My eyebrows furrow at his pain, but I find I'm fresh out of encouraging responses and he doesn't seem to want the platitudes anyway. Mr. Duncan pushes off from the car and stretches his arms up and over his head, taking a long, shuddering breath before blowing it out as if to clear the painful thoughts.

"Enough of that drama. I really need to move on, I think."

Again, it seems like he's convincing himself more than me, so I shrug non-committedly. "If you're okay, Mr. Duncan . . ."

He nods and musters up a small smile. "Hey, I heard about your new classes. Congrats on that!"

His words are polite, the same ones several other parents have given me in response to the news, thankfully. Though there's something different about hearing them post-class from a mom with her child swirling around her legs than from a sad dad alone in a parking lot. A wiggle of concern blooms in my belly, though Mr. Duncan has always been nothing but nice to me.

"Thanks," I say as I reflexively scan the parking lot, wondering who Dom has following me tonight.

I don't feel the weight of Dom's gaze like I do sometimes, and my gut tells me that he would never let me talk to a man alone in a dark parking lot because he's way too powerful to let something like that slide. But there's no one around but me and Mr. Duncan.

But maybe Mr. Duncan's just trying to be nice. I mean, he hasn't said anything that—

"You should have the class do a recital like the girls do. I'm sure the husbands would love to come see that."

He just blew past the line of acceptable conversation, regardless of where we're standing, but out here, what he said somehow sounds even more skeevy. My nose crinkles in distaste, but he doesn't notice or doesn't care.

"You're really beautiful, you know that?"

I step back, gaining space between us, but before I can answer, there's a clanging noise as a metal bay door slams a few suites down from the dance studio. Both Mr. Duncan and me instinctually look over. Two big and broad silhouettes come into view, and then I can hear the guys' loud chatter and laughter as they joke around.

Whew, thank fuck. I was getting a bit nervous that Dom's guy, or guys in this case, I guess, were sleeping on the job. I don't think Mr. Duncan would really try anything, but you can never be too sure.

"Hey, guys, thanks for meeting me," I say, though I guess I wasn't really expecting anyone to show their face. Dom's guys are usually relatively discrete. *Relatively* being the operative word because how do you miss a big guy in an Italian suit following you down the sidewalk?

But they seem to read my discomfort and play along. The brunette who looks like he was carved from marble says, "Sure, no problem, baby."

His phrase throws me for a second, because at Petals, 'baby' is code for 'help me,' and it's ingrained in my head to hear 'danger' with the word. He should know that. Unless it's supposed to be some Jedi reverse mind trick, like he's telling me that he recognizes that I'm in danger? Convoluted, but as long as they're here, I'll take a little weirdness.

They give Mr. Duncan a careful look. He seems to catch up to the developing situation, realizing that he's on the losing side of the scale.

"Well, I guess I'd better get going. I'll leave you to your . . ." —he gestures at me and then to the two men— "evening. I'll see you next week when I drop off Cindy. Thanks for listening, Allie."

Mustering the most dignity he can, Mr. Duncan steps back and faux-casually goes over to his driver side door, getting inside. With a roar of the engine, he pulls out of the parking lot, gassing it down the street.

I turn back to my sorta-saviors, a bit wary since they're not my usual guys. "Thanks! You saved my bacon there. Mr. Duncan's probably safe, but you never can tell. I thought you weren't gonna come out for a minute there." They glance at each other, confusion written on their faces like they're still not sure what to say, and I try to fill in the quiet. "Sorry, I don't know if we've met yet. I'm Allie, but I guess you already know that. And you two are . . . ?"

I let the syllable hang, inviting them to answer, but there's a sudden slapping of shoes on the pavement to my right and I look over to see Logan running toward me. Talk about a welcome surprise.

The two guys go back on alert, though I think hear one mutter, "What the hell? Another one?"

I'm shocked as Logan growls as he gets closer, his hands balling into fists. "Get back."

I'm not sure if he's talking to me or the guys, but I step back anyway.

Logan puts himself between the guys and me, looking at the two guys. "Stay behind me."

"What's going on, Logan? How many guys are here tonight? Is something wrong?" I can feel my heart start racing in my chest, worry blooming that maybe something happened at Petals. Maybe something happened to Dominick. It's the only explanation for why I'd have three guards tonight.

Logan talks over his shoulder, eyes never leaving the two monsters in front of him. "They're not with us, Allie."

I gasp, realizing just how foolish I'd been. Hell, I'd jumped out of the frying pan and into the fire, a big ass bonfire that scared off the hurting dad I know and left me alone with two beasts I don't. All because I stupidly assumed they were Dominick's guys. But what else should I have thought when there's always some huge guy tailing me at Dom's instruction? This just seemed status quo.

"Oh, shit," I whisper, the curse coming out before I can stop it.

The brunette speaks again, apparently the spokesman for the pair as he tries to make eye contact with me and offers a friendly smile.

"Look, I don't know what's going on here. I'm Max, and this is my buddy, Dalton. We're opening an MMA gym right over there."

I back him up, telling Logan, "I know there's going to be some kind of gym opening soon. I've heard the occasional thumping metal and hip-hop coming from inside, but it didn't occur to me that they might be random guys. The timing was right, and I mean, look at them! I didn't care if they were Dom's guys, or powerlifters, or Crossfitters. Hell, I would've been happy if they were buff yoga dudes. Just someone to help me get a little distance."

Dalton smirks, and Max points behind him to the door they came out of and turns his attention back to Logan. "We came outside and . . . Allie, right? Seemed nervous with that guy, so we came to see if anything was going on."

Logan is still tense as he questions me. "That true? I missed some of it because I was coming down the stairs."

I nod, then realize he can't see me because his eyes haven't left Max and Dalton.

"Yeah, I just needed a little assist. I thought they were my guards for the night, and Mr. Duncan left. I don't even know if he meant anything, but he was weirding me out. No harm, no foul, Logan. Now, what the hell's going on?"

He snorts. "You know what's going on, Allie. You've had eyes on you all this time. You obviously know that."

His words shock me. Not that I didn't suspect—okay, I knew—but that he'd come out and say it. But if he's willing to not play shy with the truth, neither am I. "Okay, I knew that but have been choosing to ignore your lame attempts at 'reconnaissance'." I say the word with finger air-quotes because seriously, how am I supposed to miss Logan in a crowd? "But can we just pretend this never happened? That's what I want to do. Rewind ten minutes like zzzzzz." I make a whirring sound like my dad's old cassette tape player. "And maybe poof . . . none of this ever happened. Yeah?" I coat the request with sugary goodness, like it might entice him to agree with me.

Logan shakes his head. "You know I can't do that, Allie."

I knew that's what he'd say. Logan is a great guy, precise and intelligent in addition to being a badass in the ring. But he's not really a shades of grey kind of guy. To him, things are black or white, right or wrong, what he was told to do or not. And I'm sure Dominick has told him to report everything, judging by the way he confessed that Dom's keeping eyes on me.

Dalton, the blond with shaggy hair, finally speaks. "I feel like we're missing something here, but if everything's good, mind if we head on out? We had a long day and I'm wiped. Laying two thousand square feet of wrestling mat is a pain in the ass."

I've never laid wrestling mat, but I can imagine. "Yes, let's all do that. I'm ready to go home."

Max seems to be the more curious of my new neighbors, and he gives me another friendly but careful smile. "Before we go . . . Allie, are you okay with this guy?"

"Definitely safe with Logan. Only one guy I'd be safer with, and let's just say, it's probably good for all of us that he's not here." Just to be sure I'm correct that Dom's not lurking nearby, I give a pointed look around the parking lot.

Logan sighs and his head tilts back. I imagine he's saying a prayer of thanks that Dominick isn't here too. Ignoring him for a moment, I step around him and offer my hand to Max and Dalton.

"By the way, welcome to the neighborhood. Like I said, I'm Allie. I teach at Encore Studios."

I point over to the side, where our lit-up sign blazes brightly. They glance over and then back. "Yeah, we were going to go over soon, swap hellos and do a sound check so our music doesn't screw with your lessons and stuff . . ." Dalton says before his voice trails off and he looks back at Logan. "Not to make an already weird situation weirder, but aren't you Logan Hendricks? I follow your career, man."

Logan almost imperceptively nods, but Dalton catches it and gets excited. "Holy shit! You're like one of the best one-eighty-five guys around. What the hell are you doing out here?"

Logan's answer is deadpan sarcastic, but I can see the way his lips twitch in a small smirk. "Obviously, moonlighting."

Both Max and Dalton chuckle and then glance at me. I realize that my hand's still hanging out, and they both shake, their eyes naturally drifting down my body and back up. I'm used to it and almost don't give it a second thought, knowing that I'm fully covered in both dancewear and a top layer of sweats.

But Logan doesn't let it go so easily. "Careful. She's Dominick Angeline's."

Judging by the guys' reactions, that means something to them. I'm actually surprised, and it fills in a few blanks that Logan and I need to discuss. Having Dominick stake a claim on me is sexy as hell, but it's not actually him doing it, and I wonder what exactly Dominick has told Logan.

Max tilts his head slightly, and I can see his mind working as he quirks one brow, poking at Logan. "Angeline's what? His sister? Girlfriend? Cousin from a second marriage?"

Logan's grin is a feral baring of his teeth. "She is simply his."

And isn't that the absolute truth. But judging by what's happened and what Logan has said here tonight, Dom and I need to have a serious talk.

Dalton's humor breaks the tension as he laughs and says, "Okay, motion to move back to my action plan of leaving and going the fuck home. Seconded?" He doesn't wait for anyone to speak, continuing on. "Motion approved. We're out. But hey, man, anytime you're around, stop by. I'd love to pick your brain on your counters against a southpaw. You really picked that last guy apart with those."

Max and Dalton back up a few steps before hopping onto two gleaming motorcycles, starting them up to a huge bass rumble that echoes through the lot for a moment before lowering to a leonine purr. With two-fingered waves, they pull out. Logan turns to me, and I intercept him before he can pull a fade.

"Okay, you have about ten seconds to fill me in on what's going on before you find a ballet slipper shoved up your nose."

There's no way I can back up my threat, but Logan respects me, and he sighs, nodding.

"Fine. What do you already know?"

I shrug, surprised that he's willing to give me any information at all. "All of it. But I want to hear it from you, Stalker McStalkerson."

He laughs hollowly, shaking his head and muttering, "You have no idea." But then he looks at me. "How come you never said anything? Never called me out or asked Dominick outright?"

I bug my eyes out. "Seriously? Have you met him? I'm not scared of him, not one bit, but he's intimidating enough that I'm not really going to waltz into his office and start demanding answers, especially when there for a while, I really needed the security. Not because I was in danger, exactly, but the whole shooting thing was scary as fuck for someone like me, Logan. You guys' being around made me feel safer, and then I guess I just kind of got used to it. Maybe liked it a bit." I point a finger at him threateningly. "But if you tell him that, I'll tell him you play games on your phone when you're supposed to be on duty."

He sputters, "I do not!" But then he stops at my evil grin. "You'd do that, wouldn't you?" At my nod, he hooks a thumb over at a black sedan in the far corner of the parking lot. "All right, but not here. Your place?"

"I guess it's a given that you know where it is," I reply, annoyed. "You following me like usual?" I can't help but get in the dig. "And we talk there. Deal?"

"Deal."

At home, Logan walks me to my door, a new routine, apparently.

As I unlock the door, I stand aside, motioning him in. I'm not scared of Logan. In fact, he makes me feel safe, and it's probably easier for him to guard me from here than it is downstairs, or wherever it is he hides out.

I'm surprised, though, when he doesn't take a single step inside but instead crosses his arms, shaking his head once.

"He's coming to talk to you himself."

I can't decipher his tone, but he looks at me like this is bad news. Honestly, though, I don't care. Dom might be The Boss of East Robinsville, but he and I need to get some shit straight between us. Still, realizing that Dominick Angeline's coming to my apartment makes my heart flutter in my chest like a hummingbird after a Red Bull.

Dominick is coming here? Shit, I need to change and pick up a bit. I don't want him to think I'm a smelly mess, though that's probably more true than false on most days.

CHAPTER

Six

DOMINICK

"SAY THAT AGAIN, SLOWLY."

Logan's voice is filtering through the cabin of my car as he tells me again what happened after Allie left her classes tonight.

"And the MMA guys? Are they a problem?"

There's a beat of silence as Logan considers what I'm asking. "They're legit fighters, both heavyweights. No reputation for anything other than hard work and being tough sons of bitches. If anything, I'd say they might be good backup on-site if they agree to some terms."

I let that idea roll around in my head, nodding to myself. It would make keeping an eye on Allie easier now that my duck blind has apparently been discovered. I'm not upset with Logan about it. He did his job exactly as I requested, and I wouldn't have wanted him to lie. At least, not to her.

"I'll take that under advisement. I'll need full workups on them both . . . families, allegiances, strengths, and weaknesses."

"On it. You'll have it by tomorrow," Logan says, and knowing him, I'll probably have their grade-school report cards in there as well. He's that sort of thorough.

"And the rest? What exactly did she say?"

I listen as Logan explains that he had to break cover, and that Allie knew she'd been under observation, which was a surprise to me. I don't like surprises. Not at all. She says she knows *all of it*, which I seriously doubt, so I'll have to tease a bit at her to test the edges of her knowledge. I don't want to share too much, too soon.

I knew there'd come a time to reap what I've sown, even though I'll admit I'm a man who likes to control what goes on in my life. But I have crossed a line with Allie, and I need to deal with that.

I pull into my reserved spot and head upstairs. As I push the button for the third floor, my heart flutters a little as I realize I'm going to see her, to be in her space again, not by stealth and sneaking but by invitation.

It's an intriguing idea since this will be the first time she willingly lets me into her apartment. I've been here, of course, the first time when I took her home after the shooting, still shivering in my arms, and then again to carefully install the cameras.

But this will be a first of sorts.

Logan is in the hallway, giving me a respectful nod before pulling a fade and standing by the elevator door where he can keep his eye on the entire hallway without any issues.

At my knock, the door breezes open and she stands before me in a pair of short shorts and a strappy tank top that grazes her body. If I didn't know better, I'd think she dressed for me, but I know this is her usual nighttime attire. I understand. After a day of dance tights, she must want to be as comfortable as possible.

I step inside and turn as she closes the door.

"Allison," I greet her, my voice deep and intense. Until I saw her, I hadn't fully processed that tonight could have played out much differently. Forget the questions I'm going to have to answer, the explanations, and possibly her recriminations. The thought of something happening to her makes my blood run cold in my veins.

Her eyes drop for a moment, the picture of submission before she remembers herself and lifts her chocolate gaze to mine. There's fire in her eyes, an inferno I want to burn me, but also one that I want to tame and bring under my control . . . and she knows it, even if I've unknowingly stoked those particular embers tonight.

"Dominick," she mimics, holding a straight face for as long as she can before pointing toward her living room. "We have a lot to talk about."

Most people wouldn't dare speak to me in such a direct manner, not if they wanted to be sure of seeing next Christmas. But Allie's different, and she knows without a doubt that she's special to me now and that I'm likely going to let her have more leeway than most. I suspect she'll push and press my every button just to explore the reactions. But then, I tend to do the same thing, so I can't blame her for that.

"I'm not going to apologize," I tell her evenly. "I did what I did, and I'm willing to live with the consequences."

"Even if it means I don't want to see you again?" Allie asks, and I hope she's bluffing. "Face it, Dominick. We're not talking a legal line, although I know those don't mean anything to you and I'd never take that up anyway. But you crossed the lines of honor and respect, which I know you hold important."

I think about it, then nod. "I did. For that, you're right. I apologize."

I wait patiently to see if she'll give in, rewarded a moment later when she sighs and rolls her eyes.

"Come in. Want a drink?"

I follow her directive, sitting down on her plush couch. It's a bright red velvet piece with high, rolled arms and button tufting. It's bold and loud, especially with the mis-match of patterned pillows piled in the corners. It's as much Allie as my cold, sleek office is me.

"Do you have whiskey?"

She shakes her head. "Nope. Red wine, beer, and water are all I've got. Take it or leave it."

Sassy . . . and still a little pissed, but the apology seems to have taken the edge off the confrontation. I'm still going to tread carefully, though, because I don't want this to be my only visit to this particular domicile.

"Water would be fine. Thank you."

She pulls a jug from the fridge and fills two short glasses, bringing them over to set them on the coffee table. She sits down beside me, and I'm suddenly thankful for the abundance of pillows because they force her closer to me.

But she sits sideways, her legs crisscross folded between us, showing me a lot of very long and beautiful leg, but definitely not inviting.

"So, that's the polite hostess part. Let's hear it, Dom. All the nitty-gritty, all the yelling, all the everything. Let's get it out on the table."

My eyes narrow questioningly. "Have you ever heard me yell? At anyone, about anything?"

She tilts her head, thinking back. "Actually no, that's not your style. You're more Disappointed Dad with hard looks and calculated punishments. It's when you stop talking that you're scariest. But I was expecting *me* to be the one yelling. You know, since I'm the wronged party here and all."

Her rapid-fire speech slows as she finishes her thought with a dose of sarcasm on her tongue, and I set my glass back down from where I'd picked it up.

"You're very observant. How closely have you been watching *me*, Allie?" I ask as dark heat unfurls in my gut, and I'm far more interested in her answer than I have been in anything in a long time, though I suspect she won't let me get away with the stalling tactic for long.

She bites her lip nervously, the unconsciously coquettish gesture sending a line of heat down through my gut. I feel my cock stir in my slacks. While it isn't time for that yet, my cock seems to have a mind of its own. What it knows is that the woman who's captured my imagination and my heart is sitting just eighteen inches away from me, her chest rising and falling quickly as her heart hammers within.

"You know I have, Dominick. I've been watching you the same way you watch me." I sincerely doubt that's remotely true, which she concedes when a small smirk ghosts across my lips. "Okay, maybe not as closely as you, but still, I've been paying attention. But *my* watching isn't why we're here, is it?"

She looks me dead in the eye, demanding, "Who's following me, and more importantly, why?"

I lift an eyebrow, sipping my drink. "Logan said you assured him that you already knew everything. Perhaps I should ask you what you know, and we can go from there?"

It's a bit like cat and mouse, not showing my whole hand but throwing out the challenge to see if she accepts. And then pulling her this way and that, subtly closer to my reach with every move so that I can snare her and hold her close.

She growls, her voice hard, "What I know is that you have people following me. I know that you have an apartment by Encore. I know that you watch me sometimes and have security guys from work watch me too, usually Logan, but other people too. I know that I walked up to two big-ass motherfuckers thinking they were going to save me tonight, only to discover that they're just my new neighbors. What else is there?"

It's obvious she suspects that there is more and has likely even been looking for other signs of my shadowy observations. I stay silent and she adds more.

"A few times, I saw Logan down in the parking lot and waved, figuring he was seeing someone from the building. There's a cute girl who lives up on seven that I could see as his type. I figured he'd wave back, but he didn't, just kept his head buried in his phone."

A small giggle jiggles her chest, and I wonder what's funny about Logan and his phone. "I thought, for a busy guy, he seemed to sulk around me silently a lot."

I remind myself to both thank Logan and to advise him to work on his tailing skills. He's seen more of Allie than anyone else on my crew and more than once could have taken advantage. Thankfully, Logan is who he is and minds his business better than most lifelong men in my crew. It's too bad he doesn't want to be a permanent part of my team because he'd be an excellent asset, but I'll utilize him while he's available to me.

More important than my thoughts of Logan are that Allie didn't mention anything beyond the surveillance. She doesn't know about the apartment upstairs. I war with myself about telling her, but in the end, I can't imagine not being able to check in on her, so I stay mum about it for now, knowing it'll rightly be another log on the fire if she ever finds out.

"I'm impressed that you even caught what you did. It means you're observant of your surroundings and staying safe. Good girl."

The compliment comes naturally, but she beams at the praise for a split-second, or maybe it's the phrasing. I store that away in my mind for later and continue.

"You sure you want to know everything? If I remember right, you were pretty freaked out by what you learned last time you got a glimpse behind my curtain."

It's a polite way of reminding her just how ugly my world is. I've tried so damn hard to protect her from it, from me, but I just can't stay away any longer, even as I give her one last out to stop this madness.

"Tell me. I want to trust you. I know that's insane because of your job, but you've never given me a real reason not to trust you. Unless you lie to me right now. I'm going to give you a chance because you've earned it with me."

I take a deep breath and lay it out. She doesn't react when I confirm that I have a guy watch her at the studio and follow her to the club and home every day. However, when I tell her about the people watching her apartment, she colors.

"Dominick, what if I'd had someone over?"

"You always had freedom to choose your own . . . friends, even if I would not have approved," I force myself to admit. "I would not have liked it."

The dangerous confession hangs between us, the possessive tone of my words unmistakable.

"Tell me why. Why do you have your men following me? Why did Logan tell Max and Dalton that I'm yours? Like I belong to you," Allie says, and I can hear it in her voice. She's upset with me, but at the same time, she likes that I feel the way I do about her. She *wants* to be claimed, but only by someone who deserves it.

I'm not an emotional man. I'm a cold bastard who typically sees every angle of the game board and can strategize my way out of something unpleasant or into something desirable at will. But I'm not sure how to answer Allie's question without scaring the shit out of her.

I think she expects it'll be some light, superficial answer that she can romanticize, but this is not a fairy tale and I'm damn sure not some sweet prince.

I'm the Bastard King.

The honest truth is obsessive and possessive, even more than her own assumptions about the line she thinks I've crossed, and I know the edge I'm walking is fine.

But the thrill of any degree of openness with her is tempting.

"Both of those questions have the same answer," I reply, reaching out and putting my hand on top of hers. "From the moment I saw you in that corner, a blood-splattered angel, I felt it inside me. You are mine. We danced around it even before that, but that instant was the switch when you became the most important thing to me. And since then, I've been patient. Fuck, I've been so patient."

My voice goes quiet as I reach up to slip a tendril of hair behind her ear. Even with the majority locked in a tight ballerina bun, there are wisps of hair breaking free from the bonds she has them in. It feels a bit like Allie . . . easy and tight on the surface, but with a desire to be free.

At her core, Allie is a free spirit, tamed and tamped down by life and circumstance. Alternatively, I am cold at the surface, and the deeper one delves into my soul, there is only darkness. Perhaps that's why I'm so attracted to her light. I stroke my thumb along her jaw, and she tilts her chin, giving me greater access.

"Why did you wait? Why now?" she whispers.

I notice she doesn't ask what happens if she says no. She's giving herself to me, and somehow, I feel like I've both been granted a precious gift and sullied a flawless jewel. She doesn't deserve a bastard like me.

That doesn't stop me, though, as I grasp her chin in my fingers, bringing her eyes to mine.

"You weren't ready then. I wasn't sure if you would ever be able to deal with me and everything that comes with that. I'm still not sure, but with you no longer at the club, I couldn't hold myself back any longer. And while tonight might have been hurtful and my actions likely criminal, this feels like a karmic jumpstart, giving us a giant leap forward by exposing more than I ever thought I'd be able to. Every breath I take, I think of you. Every beat of my heart, I want you. Every thought in my mind is of you. And while some would call me a strong man, I could never, ever let you just leave my life without trying to at least come to this point, to look you in the eyes and tell you that whether you've known it or not, you are mine, marked eternally as such. Because you've marked me."

My words are intense, leaving no room for doubt at how serious I'm taking this with her. It's pedal to the metal, no coy dating with pecks on the cheek at the doorway. No will-he-won't-he. None of that shit. It's scary, it's frightening . . . it's jumping into the abyss without a parachute and praying your soul isn't consumed by it.

I only hope that she can find some dark romance in the honesty of them. Her breath hitches, her eyes jumping from my left to my right as she searches for . . . something. I don't bother to hide, wanting her to see me just this once.

All of me.

I might be an ugly monster that rules with an iron fist, a bastard that runs this town, but for her, I'm but a man whose heart is vulnerable to the one creature that can kill me with barely a thought . . . Allie Bancroft.

She lets the moment stretch, torturing me before mercifully placing her hand on my cheek and touching her forehead to mine.

"Okay. I'm ready—"

Before the words fully leave her lips, I'm on her, pressing her back against the pile of pillows and plundering her mouth. She has been in control for too long, leaving me dangling from a leash like a lovelorn puppy even though she was unaware of her power.

Even tonight, I submitted myself to her will and answered her questions. I apologized. That hasn't happened since, well, I can't remember. I have let her be the boss, but it's time I take the title back, show her who's in charge. Both here and everywhere.

I'm a force of nature. I'm thought, and will, and determination. I'm who took the world by the throat and am forcing it to bend to my plans.

I use a handful of her hair to hold her head in place, teasing and savoring her lips until she whines in need before giving her a deeper taste as our tongues twirl.

She tastes like cinnamon and coffee, a spicy combination much like her own fire. I press into her, needing every inch of her against me, even if there is a thin layer of fabric separating our skin.

Thinking of her skin, I reach down, running a rough hand up her thigh, enjoying the satin of the legs that have taunted me endlessly.

Going higher, I grasp a handful of her ass, kneading her soft tautness in my grip. She whimpers, and I remember something.

"I have watched for months, Allie. Every dance on stage, you do a special move. You do it on purpose to taunt me. You know it, don't you?" I ask, her eyes flaring in realization. She always does it, no matter the routine. She locks eyes on my window and lifts the right side of her skirt, rubbing her hand over her cheek before smacking it once, daring me as she gives me the private smile that has fueled my fantasies. "And I agree that you deserve a good spanking."

Without warning, I grab her around the waist, pulling her up from the couch and lifting her into my arms. She's light as a feather, and as she flies upward, she gasps at the weightless sensation.

"Whaaaa? What are you doing?"

I don't answer in words, instead turning and arranging her over my lap. Her head twists back, eyes glaring at me, but I can see the breathless anticipation underneath her argumentative nature.

Her eyes narrow, disagreement on her tongue, but I circumvent her with a good smack to her right cheek. She sputters incredulously, her eyes flaring.

"You actually *spanked* me?"

I give her a victorious smirk and do it again, this time to her left cheek before rubbing the fabric, wishing I could pull her shorts down and do it to her bare flesh. Later. My control of the world starts with my control of myself.

She doesn't say a word, but I can feel the slightest hint of vibration against my thighs and I realize that she moaned. I'm certain it was unintentional. This woman wouldn't give in so easily, but it's a sign that I'm moving in the right direction. I pop each cheek again and again in quick succession, her shorts riding up as she begins writhing in my lap. Soon, I can see at least half of each cheek, right at the dimpled part where her muscles pull the curve in slightly as she dances.

"I think you like your punishment, don't you, Allie?" I ask as I rub at the pinkening globes of her ass, soothing the ache as the warmth of her skin heats my palm. "Tell me."

Her moan is all the answer I need, and her hips buck, lifting her ass to my hand, begging for more. I grab the fabric of her shorts, pulling them up tight between her cheeks in a sexy version of a wedgie that shows me her ass but also lets her pussy rub against the seam of the shorts.

Unconsciously, she grinds against me, rubbing that seam up and down her slit, soaking herself so much I can feel the hot dampness through the leg of my slacks as my own cock rages against her side, thick and throbbing.

I give each cheek one more solid tap as she cries out, so close to coming I can feel the tension of the precipice she's riding. I bend down, laying one sweet kiss to each pained cheek and using my nose to nuzzle along her crack and close to her pussy, breathing her sweet arousal in, needing to take some piece of her into my soul.

Before she goes over, I carefully adjust her shorts, setting them back in place and helping her rise up from my legs. I place her in my lap, sitting on one thigh as if I'm Santa and she's going to tell me what she wants.

She hisses slightly at the pressure on her sore ass and wiggles as she searches for some release, but she eventually settles, releasing her breath in a shaky exhalation that tells me she's almost in pain from being denied her release.

I hold her wrists in the cage of my hands and all of her in the confines of my heart. She doesn't move, but I know she can feel the rock-hard throbbing pressing against the side of her thigh, my cock demanding that it be allowed to fill her sweet, cherished folds and release my passionate torrent inside her.

But not yet. Because Allie was right. I've violated the codes of honor. And as much as this means a new start between us, I haven't earned the right to that yet.

"Is that it?" she whispers softly, looking back at me in desire and confusion.

"Punishment and reward, sweetheart. For us both."

She murmurs again, seemingly understanding even as the words are unintelligible. She half turns, resting her head on my shoulder, and minutes later, she drifts off, my arms around her waist and her warmth telling me that I'm an undeserving bastard . . . but I hold on anyway.

CHAPTER
Seven

ALLIE

THE THOUGHT HITS me as I towel off in my bathroom the next morning, the steam swirling around me and my body still tingling from all that happened last night.

I think I'm dating Dominick Angeline, head of the Angeline crime family. Mob boss of all of East Robinsville.

How in the fuck did that happen?

How is this my life? I remember falling asleep last night . . . in his lap.

How embarrassing is that?

The hardest part was waking up in bed alone. I'd been oddly disappointed that he wasn't curled up around me in my small bed, fighting for space with my overabundance of pillows.

I'd even fantasized about what he might look like relaxed and vulnerable, all harshness softened from his features by a peaceful sleep. But over my morning coffee, I consider that he might've recognized that I'd need some space this morning to process everything and had left to be nice. Polite. Sweet, even.

I smile. These are not words I think most people would use to describe Dominick Angeline.

Maybe cold, indifferent, ruthless? And while I'm sure they're true in some sense, they're definitely a part of his work. You don't get to be The Boss by being polite and sweet. You get them by being a motherfucker.

But Dom's not that with me.

Not at all. And after our impromptu dinner and last night, whatever that was, I think we're . . . something?

Maybe dating isn't the word, but it's something more than this distant dance we've been doing, where all my attention is drawn to him the instant he enters a room. Where I search the shadows around me, hoping for a glimpse of him in some weird form of 'gotcha' like it's a game he doesn't know we're playing. Where he owns me without even truly acknowledging that he wants me.

I pause at that last thought, thinking it through.

That's not really true.

He may not acknowledge whatever we've had with grand gestures, but he's always had this way of looking at me like I'm his everything.

Until last night, I didn't realize the depth of emotion behind his protective measures. I didn't realize just how much of his everything I've been. He crossed the line, but still, that level of commitment makes me feel ten feet tall and bulletproof.

I've had men caught up in my stage persona beg to worship the ground I walk on, and others in my real life who started out normal but ultimately treated me like shit mentally. They didn't want the woman inside. They just wanted the package– my face, my tits, my ass. I can definitely put those to good advantage, as evidenced by my job, but it's left me more than a bit doubtful that any man would care what was underneath the pretty packaging.

But Dom is something else entirely. Dominick took control, unafraid to send lightning through my body, but in every motion, every word, every look, he truly does worship me, but it's balanced with the way he respects me. The real me, not some image he's created. He's actually taken the time to learn about me, albeit in an odd way.

But he sees me in a way no one else ever has. And that is the most powerful aphrodisiac, one that puts me under his spell, hungry for every morsel of his attention. His words. His touch.

He makes me feel beautiful on the inside. And outside of family, that's not something I've had.

With a smile, I scribble on a sticky note, *You are beautiful . . . on the inside.* I slap it on the floor-to-ceiling mirror in front of me, adding it to the mix of choreo notes and self-affirmations already in place there.

I continue practicing the routine I've created for this week's Diva Dance class. That's what I've decided to call my non-pole studio class, figuring that every woman wants to tap into her inner Sasha Fierce-slash-Beyoncé for a seductive performance now and again.

With a swish of my hips, I trace my curves, following the movements in the reflection, but the disarray of pillows on the couch behind me catches my eye, and I turn in place, my chest rising and falling as my heart continues to hammer in my chest.

Usually, having a dance space in my apartment is a good thing, even if it is my teeny-tiny dining room that's been converted with a full wall of mirrors and a ballet barre. The carpet's been covered with plywood and laminate until it's as smooth as a stage.

Yeah, I'm never getting the security deposit back, but it'd been a small price to pay for the comfort and release a 24/7 dance space allows.

Usually, I can tune everything else out when I practice, not seeing the dishes in the sink or the floor that needs to be vacuumed. But the disarrayed pillows draw me in like a moth to a flame, a visible reminder of what happened last night.

And specifically, what *didn't* happen.

After that spanking, I guess I'd expected him to press for more. Fuck, I wanted him to press me. I wanted him to tug my panties the rest of the way to the side, to mark me inside as well as out.

We've both been patient, but these months of prolonged foreplay have built an inferno inside me that's already on the edge of explosion. Even a small step like last night has me wanting to rush into his fire, arms wide open and eyes squeezed shut, leaping blindly into whatever may come.

Like that thick dick I felt pressed against my thigh last night. I can definitely see that coming for me.

Terrible puns aside, I haven't been with anyone in a long time. I was waiting for him, and it seems the time for waiting has finally come to fruition, if I can use his words last night as any indicator.

I'm not a shy woman, never been one to hem and haw about what I want, but I am a rule follower. There's a method to the madness in my mind, a progression from one step to the next that creates that beautiful flow of movement, and I've followed those steps precisely.

I've respected that Dominick wanted to keep me at arm's length while I was an employee. I've honored that he held himself back from me with an unspoken demand that I hold myself back from anyone but him, knowing that it sometimes left me lonely. And horny.

But the time for rules and games is over. He showed me his heart last night, with his words more than his body, but that's the true barometer of a man. And that's why after class tonight, I'm going to Petals.

I haven't been in over a week, and my first showcase feature isn't for another week and a half. I miss the other girls there, my friends and sisters in the sorority of skin, so a visit seems in order.

But the main reason is still to see Dominick.

I'm more than ready when I park in the back lot at Petals and wait for Gavin to park next to me.

After our chat last night, Dom had texted me this morning, saying that perhaps some openness was warranted, and then he gave me the schedule for my assigned detail for the week. It'd been a weirdly kind gift, like he was letting me in and dropping the curtain a bit more. Gavin's on 'Allie Patrol' tonight and followed me from the studio.

I'd asked if he would not tell Dom I'm on my way, wanting to surprise him, but he'd just laughed and said Dom knows where I am at all times anyway.

Cryptic, but I think he had already told Dom we were leaving the studio. Whatever. I'm just ready to see him, and if it's not quite a surprise, so be it.

The back door opens, and I rush inside, greeting Thomas. He's been here at Petals longer than I have, and I recognize he's someone within Dom's hierarchy now, but still, he's just a good guy to me, sometimes a bit off-color with his humor, but overall, a good guy.

Mostly, I beeline straight for the backstage dressing room. "Hey!" I call out as I burst through the door.

There's a chorus of high-pitched squeals from the girls, and then Tina, one of the other experienced girls, says, "Where the hell have you been, girl? I was gettin' ready to send you a thank-you card for the extra work!"

Her eyes are playful and teasing, belying her question and saying that she really just wants the details of what's been going on.

"Oh, you know, around. Been putting in a lot of hours at the studio. Amelia did fantastic today, by the way."

Tina smiles at the compliment about her little girl, who is the light of her existence. Tina supports both her daughter and her mother with her job at Petals, and her mother helps take care of Amelia in return, bringing her to Encore for weekly lessons.

"Yeah, well, guess she got something from me. Long as she don't have to do this shit too. I want my baby to put that brain she has to good use." She taps the side of her head.

I nod, giving Tina a warm look. "She's smart as a whip, Tina. You know that."

Tina smiles, then clears her throat. "I heard you added some sexy classes and are starting up some pole gig too. I plan on booking a private session to learn some of those tricks you've got. Time for you to teach us padawans."

We laugh at our jokes. She's an inner nerd at heart. "Seriously, though, good for you. As long as you keep teaching the babies, we're solid, because Amelia only goes to ballet for you."

Her words touch me. Maybe it's in the way Dom runs this place or maybe it's in how he hires us, but there's a real feeling of family. We really are a supportive group of girls, and I know they'd have my back in an instant if needed, the same way I would for them.

"Thanks, honey. I'm teaching the kids, but I'm still around here too," I assure Tina. "Actually, I've got a feature soon, and I'm keeping my fingers crossed that the finances work out on that idea. It's a bit counterintuitive to the usual *give them what they want*, more *only give them what they want every once in a while* and hope they pay extra for the rarity."

One of the other girls, a newbie named Sarah, chimes in. "Well, if they don't, I'm sure Boss Man will make up the difference for you."

She says it in a good-humored teasing way, but it stings a bit anyway. I try to laugh it off, not sounding all that convincing.

"Not really how that works." But at the five sets of eyes boring into me, I falter some more. "Uhm, so does everyone know?"

Tina laughs loudly. "Does everybody know?"

She looks at the other girls, her face telegraphing *Do you believe this shit?* When she turns back to me, she grins, but seeing my face, she gets up and talks to me in that mom voice that tells me she's going to make sure this is the last time anyone says anything about me and Dom.

"Hon, we've known there was something between the two of you for months. We knew you weren't breaking the rules. I woulda called your ass on that. But we could get high on the fumes of your chemistry just by walking by. What do you call those? Phera . . . phomo . . . pheromones?" She snaps her fingers. "Yeah, pheromones in spades. We had a pool going on for a while, betting on when you two would finally combust. Too bad Logan put a stop to that after his dates were all past. Sore loser, I think." She winks like that's funny, but I'm aghast.

"Whoa, I'm not really sure what to say to all that," I say quietly. "Tina, you—"

Tina pats my shoulder, ever the momma of the group, "Baby, nobody here is judging you for falling for Dominick. He's a good man, even with who he is, and it's not like any of us are jealous because we thought we had a chance with him. We've always known you've had that man on a string, for a lot longer than you've known it, and it's about damn time you yanked on that line."

She mimes jacking off, her hand pumping an invisible cock.

I laugh at her outrageous action as much as the thought that I have Dominick on a string. If anything, it's the exact opposite. I feel like he's not teasing me to him. He's just inserted himself into my life and expected that I'll accept that.

Funny thing is, I really want to. He's different than I'd thought, kinder and more respectful, and definitely hotter than the ice-cold image he projects. In fact, I can't believe I ever thought he was cold.

"Thanks, Tina," I reply, not hugging her simply because I don't want body glitter all over my black T-shirt. "All right, ladies, I think I'm gonna head upstairs to my man."

Claiming Dominick, even lightly to my friends, feels big, really big, but I think I like it.

It feels right.

There's a round of catcalls, but Tina's words are the most heartfelt. "Allie, go be happy. Go on, girl."

I swear she's looking at me with a hint of motherly pride as I leave the dressing room, which is extra-odd because Tina, for all her wisdom and life advice, isn't that much older than me. But the hand life dealt her made her pretty perceptive, and I'll keep her advice in mind.

Upstairs, I knock and go in at Dominick's called-out invitation.

I've gotta give him credit. He does a good job of pretending he hasn't known I've been downstairs for the past ten minutes as he crosses the room and kisses my cheek.

"A pleasant surprise. You couldn't wait to see me until later?"

I smirk at his cocky arrogance and assumptions, teasing back. "Maybe I came to see the girls, not you. I just wanted to toss you a bone before going and seeing how Sarah's new routine is working out."

His smile falls in increments, his eyes darkening at my insolence. If he were looking at anyone else this way, I'm sure they'd be shaking in terror. I'm shaking, but there's not a drop of fear in my blood.

No, for me, it's all adrenaline and arousal.

He smiles, calling my bluff. "Well then, by all means, let's get you a seat for the show." He takes my hand, leading me to the wall of glass windows.

He grabs his desk chair, a big black leather throne fit for a king.

No . . . fit for a Boss.

He sits down and pulls me into his lap. We face the windows, which are transparent right now, though I know that from the floor, they're blacked out.

I don't know what kind of one-way glass magic Dom invested in for this wall, but it's worth it. I feel like I'm floating above the crowd, with an unrestricted view of Sarah on stage as she twirls around the pole, one leg bent and one leg stretched long, her hair hanging down her back in a blonde sheet.

"Do you like what you see?" he whispers, his voice hot against my ear.

I squirm, trying to relieve the building pressure as my body responds to the warmth he's creating inside me already.

"She's good . . . knows how to play up her features and be sexy without being sleazy," I say, my eyes evaluating Sarah's technique. "You know, Tina said something about a private lesson to work on a trick or two. I hadn't thought of doing that too. I'm feeling a little like the Pied Piper of Stripperdom . . . women of all ages, stages, shapes, and sizes following me along to find their inner goddesses."

My voice is hushed, excitement tinged with the responsibility of helping these women grow in their own self-confidence and power. I gasp when Dominick's finger teases just above the waistband of my jeans, finding the sensitive skin of my back.

"I'd certainly follow you."

I smirk at the promise, glancing back to see him watching me, not looking at Sarah at all. "Dom, do you ever watch any of the dancers?"

"Of course," he says, still watching me. "Mostly the try-outs, and I try to catch each girl's performance every once in a while, strictly professionally to make sure they're fitting in well with the clientele. But I always watch your dances." He leans into me and teases my ear with hot breath. "Unprofessionally. I watch you just for myself."

His deep voice sends a thrill to me, and I turn back to watch Sarah just to keep myself under control. Still, Dom questions me. "Do you miss it? It's been a bit since you've been on stage."

I take my time before answering. I don't want to sound needy, but also, I want Dom to understand the nuance of what I want to say. I don't have the same skill with words that I do with my body. I can't express myself quite so clearly.

"Yes and no. I've always been on stage, performing in one way or another, and I enjoy that rush of connecting with the audience. But really, it's about me connecting with myself, with the shy insecurities, with the bold brashness, with the hopeful innocence and whatever else the piece requires of me. I get to experience and explore every facet of myself on stage."

The truth feels exposing, making me vulnerable, and I work to retreat to safer ground. "Plus, the applause is pretty sweet," I add with a grin, looking back over my shoulder. "I always thought you were clapping too."

Dominick doesn't smile back. Instead, he looks at me, looks into me like I'm a puzzle he's trying to solve, taking every word I say as a clue to some solution that ultimately explains me.

But I'm the simple one. He's the enigma blanketed in layers of questions. I feel like I'm just beginning to get to know him, and it's on his terms as he doles out tidbits of information like clues leading me deeper and deeper into his web.

It's on the tip of my tongue to ask, demand that he share a story with me, something, anything, just to learn about him. But before the words leave my tongue, he lifts me off his lap.

"Dance for me."

That is certainly not what I expected. "What?"

Dom pushes back and rolls himself back to his desk. "You miss the stage, miss exploring who you are. Do that for me, *with* me. Let me see who you are, right now, in this moment."

There's no request in any of his words, merely orders, soft as they may be. I walk to the center of his office, and he presses a button on the console on his desk, letting the speakers in his office come to life with the music from downstairs.

"I'm not dressed for this," I say awkwardly as I get a feel for the music.

Dominick's grin is feral but supportive. "I know. That's why this is sweeter. I don't want your stage persona, Allie. I just want to see *you*. I want to see you express yourself, how you feel, how you . . . exist. Tell me with your body what you want me to know."

I bend down, slipping my shoes off and setting them to the side, not in a sexy way, but just in a casual movement. Dom lifts an eyebrow but nods in encouragement.

"Good girl. Now dance . . . for me."

The music fills me, throbbing bass and drums that click inside me. I open my eyes, watching Dominick as I feel the tigress inside me begin to stalk her prey, the man she wants.

His gaze travels up and down my body, pausing at my tits and hips but also taking the time to appreciate every inch as I begin to move, sashaying across the floor before kicking my left leg up and coming up onto my right toes, thanking whatever genius came up with spandex denim. Dom's eyes widen as I hold the pose, bending my leg at the knee before lowering it while unbuttoning my jeans.

I tease them down my thighs, trying to accomplish the impossible . . . taking off fitted jeans without looking like a total doofus.

I do my best, a genuine smile crossing my face at the absurdity of wiggling the denim down and off.

I twirl, letting Dom see the curves of my ass peeking out from beneath my top before I slip it off too, turning to face him as I drop it to the floor. My curls flutter around my shoulders, and I shake my head, letting the length fall behind my shoulders so nothing is hidden. I reach behind my back and unhook my bra, pulsing my body to the beat slowly as I inch the lacy straps down my arms but hold the cups to my breasts.

The tease has Dominick panting, craning to see every inch of my body at once as his eyes dilate just from watching me. My nipples harden when I see the growing bulge in his slacks, knowing that I'm doing that to him. Me, Allison Bancroft, not Allie Angel.

I face away from him, letting him see the expanse of my back as I remove my bra and toss it overhead where it lands in his lap. He grabs it, fisting it like it's more than a slip of silky lace.

I swing my hips side to side, drawing his attention lower by running my hands down my curves to one of the two places I desperately want him to fill.

The other is my heart, but that seems dangerous to consider, so I let the dreamy thought drift away like my panties as they hit the floor and I step out of them.

Fully nude for him, I sway seductively.

"Stop," he says, softly but forcefully, his voice barely audible over the music from the speakers.

I freeze instantly, and Dom's eyes meet mine despite the enticement of my bared body.

"You have pretty words to explain your desire to dance, to be on stage, and they are true, but I think you haven't admitted the most obvious one."

I suddenly feel vulnerable again with nothing to hide behind, and the naughty fun of the moment squeezes in tight as I fear what he sees. He comes around the desk, and now I'm the one being stalked as he slips a hand around my neck. I don't resist but instead lift my chin defiantly in false bravado.

"What do you mean?"

He leans forward to whisper in my ear, holding me in place as if I'd try to get away. "You like to be watched. It feeds some beast in your core to not just explore those experiences but to have them watched by the audience."

He's not wrong, though the way he says it makes it seem dirtier than it is. I shrug, not giving him the satisfaction of my agreement nor the disappointment of a denial.

He growls, turning me around and pushing me forward until I'm pressed up against the glass. I know that we can see out, but the people below can't see us.

"Look down there, Allison. See all those people in the audience? Do you want them to watch you dance, watch you seduce me with your smile and your sexy body? Do you want them to watch while I fuck your sweet pussy?"

With his last question, he moves his free hand down my back to cup me, hissing as he discovers how wet I am.

Not willing to admit it, I sass back as a last-ditch effort of rebellion. "If I'm the exhibitionist, you're the voyeur, always watching from your perch above everyone else. You like to watch and manipulate people like chess pieces for your game."

He's not nearly as shy about the admission as I am, chuckling proudly. "I do like to watch . . . but only you. And I'm going to watch you give yourself fully to me, right here, overlooking that entire audience. Perhaps I'll make the glass transparent? Would you like that?"

I bite my lip, shaking my head. "No, not them. Just you."

His grin is full of victorious pride as my words betray me, confirming the exhibitionist tendencies I'd never really given a second thought. He rewards the honesty by slipping his fingers through my folds, gathering my juices and spreading them over my clit.

His touch is teasing, never staying exactly where I want him, not out of lack of skill but simply because he can since he's in control.

He presses me firmly against the window, the cool glass against my cheek and breasts in contrast to the heat he's building at my core as he tugs my hips back, forcing me to arch for him.

He smacks my ass, and I whimper in need. "Good girl," he praises me, and I can't help but circle my hips, wanting more, *needing* more. "Tell me. Who do you need?"

"You," I whimper, and at the first thrust of his finger inside me, I involuntarily clench down, wanting to feel every inch, even if it's not his cock.

His groan is guttural from beside me, and his finger slips deeper, curling and making my fingers claw against the glass.

"So fucking tight, Allie. I don't know if you can even take my cock in your tiny pussy. It's going to be a stretch, that's for damn sure."

He's dirty, his normally formal tones forgotten as I drive him as wild as he's driving me. And his words are enough to bring me closer to coming, imagining how full I'll feel when he finally gives in to what we both want.

A gush of wetness eases his way as he adds a second finger before beginning to fingerfuck me in earnest. My eyes flutter closed at the overwhelming sensation, but Dominick slaps my ass, his voice harsh and commanding.

"No, keep your eyes open and on the crowd below you, so clueless to your getting filled with my fingers right above them. So close, but they don't deserve your exhibition. Only I do, so give me one, Allie. I'm watching, and I want to see you come for me."

Instantly, I'm on the edge, ready to shatter at the slightest stimulation, and Dominick does what I don't expect. He shoves another thick finger inside me, and the stretch verges on pain, but the pleasure is so overwhelming that I come hard, crying out his name and steaming the glass with my panting breaths.

Ignoring his order to keep my eyes on the audience, I focus on Dominick, whose eyes are burning with something bigger, deeper, darker than lust as he watches me. I can feel my juices leaking over his fingers, and the weight of his gaze sends me spiraling again, an aftershock orgasm riding the wave of the first.

His fingers still deep inside me, he growls into my ear, "Tell me, Allie. In this moment, whose are you?"

I don't even think about my answer, the word quietly falling from my lips unbidden and honest. "Yours."

I see the flash in the depths of his eyes though his expression doesn't change, and then he presses a gentle kiss to my neck before whispering in my ear, so soft I almost miss it, the breath of absolution upon his soul. "Mine."

CHAPTER

Eight

DOMINICK

LOOKING at the front door of the duplex I'm standing in front of, I'm struck by how often my business is conducted in the most innocuous of settings. The door's painted bright blue, like sunny skies and happiness. The house itself is a bright white, seemingly freshly painted.

I can appreciate that someone is caring for the home, and even their color palette. Nothing garish, but also nothing beige and boring. It's tasteful, and that's something I can give credit for. Though who's doing the caring leaves a bitter taste in my mouth.

I glance once at Gavin, who stands by the car at the curb.

At his nod that everything is clear, I lift my fist and knock twice. There's a screeching cry from inside and a hushed voice whispering, both sounds getting closer to the door.

When it creaks open, I see a tiny woman with a bundle of blanket in her arms. I can't see the baby cradled there, but as most people aren't in the habit of caring for baby banshees, I make the obvious assumption.

The woman looks confused but continues her bouncing attempt to soothe the baby.

"Can I help you?" Her voice is high-pitched, not unpleasant, but it adds to the youthful effect of her threadbare cutoff shorts and tank top. The only major signs that she's not a high school babysitter are the tattoos trailing down her left arm and the possessive way she's holding the baby, obviously her own and not a paid charge.

I can understand her feeling of protectiveness, though her first mistake was in opening the door at all to a stranger she doesn't know. She might be experienced, but she's not that wise.

"Myra Cole?"

I remind myself to say it as though it's a question, though I already know exactly who she is.

"Yes," she replies warily. "Who're you?"

"I'm Dominick Angeline. May I come in?"

My name means nothing to her, a pleasant surprise. Myra's blue eyes scan me head to toe as the door inches closed ever so slightly.

Smart woman.

"What's this about?" she asks, bouncing the babe and stealthily moving the door another two inches closed with her hip. The baby, sensing the tension in her mother, stops caterwauling, and I get a glimpse of a round, if still mostly bald, head.

My lips tilt up in the slightest smile, not altogether fake, designed to put her at ease. "I'm here to see Robert Zallow."

She's good, not flinching at all at the name, no increased breathing, not a single tell. The lack of reaction is what tells me that it's a practiced response. Most people, when they're confronted with a strange request, will at least narrow their eyes a little in confusion.

Myra doesn't. "Don't know anybody by that name. If you'll excuse me . . . have a good day."

She makes no attempt to hide her movement to close the door this time, but there's no way she's getting the door closed past my shoulder. I lower my voice, dropping the soft tones.

"Let's not play coy. I'm here to see Mr. Zallow. I'm willing to sit on your couch like a proper guest while he comes home, or I can meet him in a less . . . *pleasant* situation."

I let her imagination fill in the gaps. I find that people are much more creative than I am with threats. Myra's no exception, coming up with ones specific to her own fears. It's a twisted joy of mine, watching her eyes flicker as her own worst-case scenario filters through her mind, wondering if I can make it come true.

I wait as she swallows once and then opens the door and gestures with her chin toward what looks like a living room. "Won't you come in, Mr. Angeline? Would you like a drink?"

Her voice is pure saccharin, fake politeness with an undercurrent of fear. I step inside, taking in the small home with a glance. A couch and single chair take up the living room space, likely once fluffy, but now the lumps are apparent. There's a tear in the fabric, but someone's already mended it with secure if ugly stitching.

The television sits on a wooden cabinet, locks already in place on the doors though the baby likely can't even sit up yet.

It shows care, forethought, and attention to detail, along with an intention to stay here long-term.

I go over and settle into the chair, unwilling to offer the entry my back, and resume pleasantries.

"Thank you, Miss Cole. Water would be lovely."

She disappears into the kitchen for a moment, and I hear the faucet turn on and off before she reappears, handing me a plastic cup emblazoned with a BBQ joint's name on it.

Her hand is steady, though her eyes are twitchy, watching for any threatening movement.

I feign taking a small sip, though I doubt she has poison handy. Still, I didn't get to where I am by being careless. Resting the drink on the arm of the chair, I gesture to the phone on the couch, a small smile on my lips.

"Feel free to call Robert when you're ready."

She bends down to grab the phone, choosing to stand rather than sit, keeping herself close to the back-door exit. Smart lady.

It's a pity she's running with an Eagle Raider, though a woman like her being with Zallow is already perhaps a more valuable recommendation than I'd previously received on his character.

She picks up the phone and dials quickly, whispering harshly when the call's picked up. "Sorry to bother you at work, but there's someone here to see you." She pauses a second, and I presume he repeats her words because she says again, "Yes, here. Sitting in your chair in the living room. Says his name is Dominick Angeline."

I see the moment the questions in her eyes turn to terror and watch as she takes two steps back, getting closer to the back door.

"Miss Cole," I say, raising my voice simply to make sure that it comes through clearly on the other end of the phone call, "if I'd wanted to harm you, I would have already. I merely wish to speak to him."

I hear the yell as the phone slips from her ear, and on the other end, a deep voice promises, "I'm on my way, baby."

There's a soft buzzing tone as the line disconnects, and I imagine that right now, Robert Zallow is probably setting a personal best sprint time out of whatever job he's working at, rushing home to come in like a saving knight in shining armor to rescue his woman from the big, bad dragon.

That's me.

But not now.

Though I can be monstrous, dangerous, and threatening, today is merely about setting boundaries and expectations. If Robert Zallow can behave like a gentleman, this should be nothing more than a polite but professional conversation.

Five silent, frozen minutes later, the loud rumble of a Harley being driven to its limits breaks the tension. I can feel Myra's relief at the return of her man. Apparently she's just as entwined in this apparent fairy tale where he's rushing in to save her.

Odd how those childhood stories are so deeply ingrained in our psyches. I suspect that it steers more of our behavior than most people are willing to admit.

But if anything, the man rushing through the door and shoving Myra and her baby behind him is no prince. Instead, he's a big bad wolf, a mess of shaggy blond hair windblown from the frantic ride, cheeks rough with weeks of growth, and an oil-stained tank top and jeans atop black engineer boots.

He doesn't look at Myra, his eyes fixed on me.

"You okay?" he says over his shoulder.

Her response has just a touch of vinegar, but she's quiet at least. "I'm fine. Mr. Angeline has been polite . . . mostly."

I lift my eyebrows at that, considering I've been more than polite under the circumstances. Her man's defensively hard look would be scary if I were anyone other than who I am. Behind Robert, I can see Gavin coming up the walkway, but I shake my head once, stopping him. No need for that yet.

"Please sit," I say, choosing to let the steam out of the pot before the situation boils over needlessly, though ordering a man around in his own home is rather cocky of me. I lean back, taking a small delight that my chair is apparently 'his chair', watching as he sinks to the couch.

"Go on and take the baby to the bedroom, Myra," he says.

She takes a step toward the hall, following his instructions wordlessly, but I hold up a hand, stopping her. "That won't be necessary. I believe you both should hear this . . . since it concerns the entire family. Please sit."

She pulls the baby tighter to her body, her eyes flashing to Zallow, and he scoots to the side, keeping himself between me and her as she sits beside him.

I take a deep breath, letting a long sigh out into the room.

"There are times when melodrama takes over the world. This is one of those times, I suspect. This feels like a rather significant build-up to what is really just a mere conversation. Mr. Zallow, I am Dominick Angeline. I suspect that means something to you. I simply wanted to stop by and introduce myself, seeing as how you've moved into East Robinsville so suddenly. And without my permission."

His eyes narrow as he takes me in, still trying to decide whether I'm here to harm his blossoming family. Still, he sees that I haven't moved in any threatening way.

"My apologies, Sir. My move-in was unexpected." He glances at the baby and then back at me. "And unrelated to any work or affiliations I may have."

His words are careful and crisp, like the military man I know him to be, but also ones of intelligence and manners. I re-evaluate him as he speaks. He might look a little wild, but there are brains behind that outer mask. I wonder if the discrepancy is intentional, meant to confuse others and lead them to underestimate him.

I won't make that mistake. I can see the cunning light in his eyes and recognize a man who could be either a valuable ally or a deadly opponent.

I rub at my chin as though I'm thinking, but I already know my play here, what will give me the upper hand. "Perhaps you'll let me tell you a story?"

He swallows once, an involuntary tell, but nods his chin. I lean forward, uncrossing my legs and planting my elbows on my knees, looking Zallow directly in his eyes.

"Once upon a time, there was a king. He was known as the Bastard King, not because of his birth but because he ruled his kingdom with an unyielding grip. He kept his subjects safe from threats outside their borders." I glance pointedly out the window and then back to the family before me. "But also from dangers within. To do so, he kept a tight rein on everything and everyone who lived in his kingdom. He knows all. Names, addresses, familial ties, allegiances, strengths, weaknesses . . . everything that made even those who loved him admit privately that yes, he was a bit of a bastard. He didn't like engaging in violence but knew it was a tool, a necessary evil, if you will. But more commonly, his showing up for a friendly chat to someone's home would be considered a sign of respect or a warning if they had mis-stepped in some way. Only after ignoring a warning would he lose his . . . patient nature."

"Some, I'm sure, have tried to take advantage of that king," Zallow says in reply, and I nod. "Yet he stayed solidly on the throne."

"Because he only warned once," I reply. "Then he crushed his opponents mercilessly. I'm sure you understand. If someone from East Robinsville, say, one of Pete's boys, decided to set up shop next to your clubhouse in Johnstown, you'd have something to say about that. Correct?"

Zallow scoffs lightly. "Damn straight, we would."

Myra gives him a harsh glare, and he clears his throat, continuing. "I'm not setting up shop here, Mr. Angeline. Just trying to make a home."

I nod. "I'm aware of that, or this conversation would be rather different. I'll admit I don't always hold true to the fairy tale and give warnings. Sometimes, harsher engagement is necessary from the get-go. Something I'm sure you understand. You also understand rank and protocol from both your time in the service and your time with the Eagle Raiders. Yet, you chose to skirt both in this instance, which begs the question . . . *why*?"

His face clouds, and his gaze turns inward, as though he's deciding something important. After a few moments, he looks up, his eyes full of concern.

"Mr. Angeline, do you have someone? A woman? A best friend? A dog, for fuck's sake? Someone really important?"

Allie flashes to mind, but I'm certainly not telling this man about my love life. Instead, I hum an agreement, which he seems to accept because he continues.

"Then you understand loving someone so much that you want to shout it from the fucking rooftops, tattoo their name on your skin, claim them proudly everywhere you go, but knowing that would be dangerous for them. So you bottle that up and keep how special they are private to protect them from the bad parts of your life. And you know they deserve better, and you wish that you could give it to them, but you're giving them all you have and just hanging on for dear life, hoping that it's enough. To keep them with you and to keep them safe, always walking that line."

His words are honest and hit with a sharp sting, more accurate than he could've guessed. And with his simple declaration, the pieces fall into place. These two MC soldiers aren't living here as any means of moving into my city. They're merely watching each other's backs as one of their own tries to find whatever version of a 'happily ever after' he can.

It's poetic in a way, a tiny dandelion whisper of hope to even a monster like me. I nod my head several times and let the corners of my mouth tilt up in a hint of a smile.

"I can understand that, even appreciate it. But rules are rules. What exactly are you willing to do to stay on the proper side of that line?"

Zallow's off the couch in an instant flash of anger, his words spat with the venom he has yet to show. "I'm not one of your guys, Angeline. I've already pledged allegiance and that's not fucking changing."

I didn't move when he stood and I don't now either, simply sitting back and letting my sigh of disappointment wash over them both. Myra grabs at his hand, pulling him back to the couch beside her. She holds his hand tightly, her thumb running a soothing path along his skin. It's a fascinating thing to behold, the way he relaxes in increments from her mere touch.

She's obviously somewhat submissive to him, she'd have to be to be his Old Lady, but she has such power in their dynamic. It reminds me of Allie and myself, though Allie has yet to recognize the power she holds over me.

Once she has calmed the beast, I give him a genuine smile. "I never asked you to. In fact, I respect that more than you'd know. But that wasn't what I was implying when I said rules are rules."

His eyebrows furrow together, and then he gets it. He growls under his breath, frustrated and searching for a way out of doing this. Such a simple thing, a small ask, really, but it's the point of the matter between men like us. Of course, he's not on my level, but he is a proud man, and I'm asking him to castrate himself, in front of his woman, no less.

He looks to Myra and then to the babe I've yet to glimpse in the bundle of blankets, his eyes soft, but when he turns back to me, his gaze hardens.

The words are forced out of his throat, but they come. "Mr. Angeline, may I live inside your city with my family? I intend no ill will toward you and yours. I merely wish to live a simple, happy life, knowing we are safe here."

I know he can see the sparkling light of triumph in my eyes, though the win is small now that I know he's not a scout looking for a way into my town.

"You and your family are more than welcome in East Robinsville, Mr.

Zallow . . . provided you maintain a household, not a stronghold. No more than your immediate family plus one at any time. I will make Pete aware of our arrangements, and I trust that you will do the same for Mr. Chambers as his VP."

Robert nods, and then he realizes what I said a heartbeat later. "How did you—" he starts to ask.

I tsk a bit, giving him a knowing smirk. "Did you forget what I told you about the king? He maintains his throne because he knows everything, even those things that others think are hidden from his sight. Please tell Silas hello for me."

I pause, waiting for it to sink in that I'm acquainted with his MC President. He pales for a moment before reddening, his jaw clenching as I turn to Myra.

"Miss Cole, my condolences on the unexpected loss of your mother. It seems you've done her memory a great service with the way you've maintained her home." I turn toward Robert. "Take good care of them."

Confident that I've dropped enough information to assure his continued easy homesteading and lack of violence in my town, I make my way to the door.

I glance back once, taking in the family. The love is obvious, even through the fear of the moment. He would die to protect them. He loves them that much. The vision is oddly sentimental to me, making me wistful for happier times with my own father and mother, before I knew what the family business really was and I'd thought my father simply a businessman who would regale us with silly stories over Sunday dinners.

The door swings shut behind me, and I climb into the back of my Mercedes, letting Gavin drive us to the club as I text Pete.

Eagle Raiders secure. Zallows + one allowed safe passage. Be watchful.

I know that Zallows prostrated himself today, but if a future situation requires him to break his vow to me, he will readily do so because his allegiance lies elsewhere.

I'll let sleeping dogs lie, but I won't turn my back.

"HEY ALLIE, can you come here for a minute, please?" I hear Donna ask from the front lobby. I finish wiping down the mirror and toss the rag and spray bottle of cleaner back in the cabinet in the corner.

"Coming!" I holler and fast-walk down the hallway. I can see Donna and Eileen at her desk, looking back and forth between me and something in the lobby. Confusion is written all over their faces, which makes my steps slow and my eyebrows pull together. "What's up, guys?"

Eileen's face breaks into a huge grin, her eyes open wide, and she points a finger to something I can't see, licking her upper lip like a giant chocolate gummy bear's in the lobby . . . or Chris Pine. She's got a thing for him.

I take a few more steps and I see what has them all buzzy. Standing in the lobby of Encore is Dominick. He's dressed as he always is, in a custom-tailored suit that emphasizes his broad shoulders, a silk tie and pocket square . . . yet somehow, he looks oddly at ease, considering there are gym bags and kids sprawled out on the floor around him and a group of three moms in the corner openly ogling him.

When he sees me, his eyes light up for a moment before going dark as he takes me in. I'm not dressed inappropriately for the studio, but the dance shorts and sports bra seem to make him . . . angry?

Or is that desire making his eyes stormy?

Maybe an equal measure of both, I decide, but whatever it is, it's heated and fiery, making me want to twirl around a bit to give him a better view.

"Allison," he says, his voice seeming deeper than usual in the space that usually only holds teenage girl screeches and classical music with the occasional burst of pop. As far as greetings go, it's light on the words but feels heavy, powerful.

"Dominick," I reply, trying to sound as casual and as normal as he does, if anything, to screw with Donna's and Eileen's heads. It's a total fail, as my voice comes out breathy and fizzy. I want to shout, 'He came to see me at work!' and then I want to tell the moms in the corner to back the fuck up because he's mine.

Instead, my eyes stay locked with his, which seems to amuse him for some reason, and I wonder if he can read my mind. He steps forward, placing a chaste kiss to my cheek, and I'm surrounded by his spicy, masculine scent. I fight to hold myself back from climbing him like a spider monkey and burying my nose in his neck for another hit. Instead, I step back as he turns and picks something up from the small table next to him.

I'm shocked and blushing furiously when he holds out a small bouquet. "These are for you."

I take the wrapped flowers, burying my nose in them, but honestly, he smells better.

"Thank you," I tell him politely, trying to maintain my dignity in the lobby as best I can. "Wildflowers? You seem like a roses kind of guy."

He smirks, the cocky one that lets me know he's about to say something he knows I'll like, and then twists a lock of my hair around his finger before stroking the back of my neck.

"I do prefer roses, but you're more like a wildflower. A bit untamed and unruly, but beautiful not in spite of the wildness but because of it."

His words are quiet, meant for me, but I can hear every woman in the room sigh. A few of the older girls, just at that age when boys stop being icky and start being interesting, even gawk openly. I laugh and give him a saucy wink and kiss him on the cheek.

"Well played, Mr. Angeline."

His lips twitch like he's fighting back a grin himself.

"What are you doing here?" I ask, surprised to see him. I lead him off to the side of the room, where we can have at least a modicum of privacy, and lower my voice. "Is everything okay? I saw Logan's car in the lot already, and he's supposed to be my shadow home today."

Dominick looks pleased. I think it's because I've been inordinately agreeable to the whole chaperone thing. It was weird at first, no lie, but I've already gotten so used to it that having it in the open seems natural.

"He was. But I've asked him to check out the gym next door. They're friendly now, apparently, and he's over there working on jiu-jitsu techniques in his off time."

I grin, glad to hear it. "I'm glad Logan made friends with Max and Dalton."

His eyes narrow when I say their names, obviously not liking that on my lips, so I correct it immediately but with enough sass to let him know I saw his flash of jealousy.

"So, *Dominick*, if Logan's busy now, who's escorting me home tonight?"

I play coy as if I don't know that's why he's here, and at the sound of his name on my lips, he chuckles, rolling his eyes.

"Me. Get your bag."

I offer him a soft smile and consider arguing back just for fun, but he knows as well as I do that I want this. I want him to show up, bring me flowers, take me home . . . or just take me wherever he is.

So I don't bother with the façade, instead looking back toward reception, where everyone's still trying to do their best to pretend they're not listening. It makes me grin.

"Hey, Donna. I'm all done with classes and Studio Two is clean. Mind if I knock off a little early today?"

From behind her, I can hear Eileen snicker, but Donna tosses me a thumbs-up. "Honestly, I don't know why you're still here. I'd already be halfway down the interstate if a man like that showed up with flowers for me."

I squeak a bit, trying my best not to jump up and down like a teenager. "Good point! Here, hold these, please." I set the flowers back in Dominick's hands and still can't help breaking out into a *chasse* down the hallway to get my things.

He must make a move to follow me because I hear Donna clear her throat. "Nuh-uh. You stay right there, Mister. She said she just cleaned Studio Two, and I'm not redoing it because you two made a mess in it. Don't bother denying it. I can read that you're a split-second away from doing things I won't say in front of the teenagers."

I laugh, but the fact that she can see that in the tension between us is sweet and sexy. I pull loose sweats on over my shorts, a V-neck T-shirt over my bra, and slipper boots on my feet.

It's not a sexy look by any stretch of the imagination. It's more ragamuffin college girl than anything refined, but it's standard dance cover-up gear and all I have with me.

Doesn't matter, though. When I step back into the lobby, Dominick looks at me like I'm dressed to the nines for a night on the town.

"Ready, beautiful?"

I realize it's probably one of the only times he's asked me a question, not given me orders or leading statements, and I can't help but blush again. It feels important, like he's letting me decide for myself whether I'm ready, not just to go, but to go with him.

Obviously, this isn't just a casual ride home. But nothing with Dominick is ever casual, I suspect.

Still, he's letting me decide.

"I'm absolutely ready," I tell him and hope he hears the deeper meaning in my words too. Judging by the approval I see in his eyes as he hands me back the bouquet, he heard it loud and clear.

He escorts me to the door on his elbow, oohs and ahhs echoing behind us, but it's not the usual romantic gesture I'd expect. Instead, when he opens the studio door, he steps outside and scans before he lets me exit. He crosses the lot to his car, but he doesn't hold my hand and walk beside me, rather staying one step in front of me, his head on a swivel the whole time.

He does open the car door for me and lets me get comfortably situated before closing it behind me, but never once does he peek down my T-shirt.

It's somehow gentlemanly and tactical all at the same time, and I can't decide how that makes me feel. I'm definitely not used to caring who's in the parking lot, other than the usual female safety measures, which I've been much more cautious about since Mr. Duncan's little scene.

But Dominick's eye is practiced and actively seeking out threats. It's strange, like I'm suddenly Whitney Houston in *The Bodyguard*, my lover going all Secret Service on me, and I wonder if there's a gun underneath Dom's suit jacket. It's a reminder that I am just a regular average woman and he's . . . *him*.

I'm not putting myself down. I know I'm the shit, but there's something *more* to Dominick. It's nothing you can put a finger on, just an importance, a weight, a responsibility he bears that I can't imagine. Not when the most important thing I do is pay my bills on time, and I have a bad habit of leaving a trail of dirty coffee cups in my wake. He's just . . . extra.

He comes around, getting in, and I don't even have to ask what'll happen to my car. If I need it before tomorrow, it'll be there, perhaps even washed, waxed, and last week's Starbucks cups cleaned out of the passenger seat.

I am surprised when he pulls out of the lot and goes right instead of left as I expect. "Hey, I live that way," I say, pointing behind us.

"I know," he says simply.

I raise an eyebrow, looking at him, but he doesn't turn his eyes off the road, handling the Mercedes with the respect it deserves.

"I thought you said you were taking me home?"

"I am," he replies. "To *my* home."

There's no hint of a smile, no sign he's joking. His words broach no argument, not that I would, but at the stoplight, he looks to see my reaction. That look tells me more than any words could.

He's used to getting his way, people jumping when he says to, and though he likes to order me around, he cares whether I want to do what he's demanding. He's domineering, but with good intentions, at least where I'm concerned. He's a man who may never ask my permission for anything, but I have no doubt that if I said to take me to my apartment, he would.

But I don't want to go there. I want to see where Dominick lives, what his space looks like, feels like.

My answer is a smile, and I place my hand on top of his big right hand until the light changes, and I wiggle back, enjoying the luxury of leather seats and ready to see where this ride takes me.

His home is beautiful, a huge house on the outskirts of town, with vaguely Italian décor with statues on pedestals and fancy paintings like a museum, poufy leather couches with tufting, and perfectly-placed pillows and throws.

It feels warm and inviting, but nothing like the man.

It's like a decorator version of what a mansion should look like.

I settle down on the couch, running my hand over the pillow as Dom watches me curiously. "What do you think?"

I war with whether to be polite or honest and decide that he'd see through any falseness anyway, so why not go for broke?

"It's pretty, but completely *not* you. You hired someone to decorate and gave them free reign. It's them, not you."

His lips draw down until they're nearly invisible, and for a second, I think I overstepped big-time, but then he chuckles, nodding. "You are very observant, Allison. What would you have expected if it was 'me'?"

Now that's a dangerous question, but I stick with honesty as the best policy and jump into the deep end.

I let the words rush out before I'm even aware of thinking them, "Modern. Sleek lines, nothing extraneous or fluffy. Keep the leather seating, but it'd be a different style. More metal accents, bare-boned but with each item being one of luxury. Something you appreciate, not merely fancy because of the price tag on it. Like . . . your office?"

He seems surprised, and his smile widens a little more as he comes over and sits next to me. "Good read. And you? What does your space speak about you?"

I consider the question, thinking about my apartment and what I thought of as I decorated it. "Brightness. Dance. Comfort. Layered. In that order."

He nods, taking my chin and turning my face to look into my soul. "I agree. Your home is a good representation of your own vibrancy. It's light and exotic. It feels like your inner chaos exploded all around you."

My burgeoning smile falls, and I'm struck by a sudden bout of insecurity. Dom's so buttoned up, every I dotted, every T crossed. But me . . .

"Is that a good thing? You don't exactly seem like the chaos type, if you know what I mean?"

I let my eyes drift down his pristine shirt and slacks, his black shoes buffed to a military shine with a fresh wax, and back up to his carefully combed dark hair. Everything about him screams power, control, and dominance. In contrast, I'm wild, sloppy, and weak.

Dominick lets me scan him, then he leans closer, invading my space but not touching me. I mindlessly arch my back, yearning for contact, wanting more, impossibly aware of the heat of his skin just beyond the borders of mine.

"My entire life depends on predictability, knowing others' moves before they do themselves, and analyzing every factor in my life from every angle."

Disappointment blooms in my gut, the voice in my head chastising me for thinking I could be more than a fuck for a man like Dominick. But the ever-hopeful pixie in my heart whispers that if he wanted a quick fuck, he wouldn't have shown up to my new work and brought me to his home. He wouldn't follow me and protect me, even when it's not needed.

He certainly doesn't do that for the other dancers at Petals. Maybe . . . maybe I do have a place in his life, the crazy loop-di-loop straw that stirs his quiet drink into a tornado and brings a bit of chaos to his perfect order?

The thought gives me the strength to meet his eyes equally. "And what is my place in that life of order, Dominick?"

Dominick takes my hand, his voice strong and sure. "You are impossible to predict. The things you say, the way you behave, the paths your mind takes, I never quite know with you. I find it invigorating and refreshing. Your chaos disturbs me, but I daresay, I secretly find it beautiful in a messy way. As if your being is livelier simply because you don't try to cage it into submission."

His words wash over me, silkily working their way into every dark crevice where doubts and insecurities lie, filling me with breath. Before I can consider the consequences, I attack him, pressing my full lips to his with abandon and letting my body finally press against his completely.

Every hard plane of his chest and abdomen meets my softness, my breasts and belly conforming around him to maximize every bit of contact as I climb into his lap, straddling him and pinning him to the couch temporarily.

He tastes of coffee and mint, energizing and powerful. His hands catch on my hips, an automatic response to my weight being thrown on him, but then he grasps my flesh, dimpling my skin under his fingers.

I can feel the thoughts swirling in his head, the buzz of whether we should do this, or maybe it's whether we should do this now. But I've wanted it, wanted him as I tracked him as much as he watched me. The rules may have changed mere days ago, but this has been months coming and I'm not willing to wait any longer.

I nibble at his bottom lip, demanding his presence in this moment, here with me, not in his thoughts. For this instant, I'm the boss, and the sharp edge of my teeth seems to do the trick. He growls into me and I swallow the sound.

"Allison—" he starts, and I can hear his question in the singular word. I don't want his hesitation, so I cut him off, something I know he'd never allow someone else, but I take the liberty anyway, taking him at his word that he appreciates my challenging personality.

"Fuck me, Dominick," I growl, grinding down onto the hard bulge that's appeared in his trousers, rubbing it against the heat between my legs. "Fill me and make me yours."

There's the briefest flash of surprise at my words, and then he takes control, his hands tightening around my ass cheeks and cupping me roughly.

"You have no idea what you're asking for, but very well, love. Remember, you asked for this." His words are a dark promise, one I want to hold him to and that I have every belief he can deliver on.

Sitting forward, he surges off the couch and lifts me like I'm as light as a feather, his strength thrilling me as my legs wrap around his torso naturally. He strides down the hall and up a flight of marble stairs, carrying me easily before tossing me onto a bed.

I want to look around, take in his space here, but my eyes refuse to leave his. His fingers dig into the waistband of my sweats, taking them and the shorts underneath off in one fell swoop while I pull my shirt and bra over my head.

Bared to him, I pose like I'm gracing the cover of a naughty calendar, not a single doubt in my head as to how sexy he finds me when he looks at me the way he is.

His jacket seems to evaporate he has it off so quickly, his fingers flying as they undo his shirt, virtually throwing it and his undershirt off.

It's the first time I've seen this much of his skin, and I want to touch every inch of his chest, to trace the other tattoos I didn't even know he had. They're not overly done, but they're there, and my mouth waters as I think about outlining each and every one of them with my tongue.

I lift to my elbows to make sure I don't miss a thing as he keeps going. As many times as he's watched me strip down to next to nothing, it feels sexy to watch him remove his clothes for me, though there's no slow seduction. It's all rushed need.

His hands work at his belt, and his slacks fall before he lowers the front of his boxer-briefs, letting his cock out.

My breath stutters, failing me. It's like the rest of him, thick and powerful, the wide tip standing proudly from his body. He wraps a hand around the length, and as he gives himself a stroke, a bead of precum pearls at the tip.

His voice is deep, smooth as silk as he sees my hungry reaction, but there's an undercurrent of arrogance. "Like what you see?"

I like that it sounds like something I'd say, like maybe my sass is rubbing off on him just a little bit. I bite my lip, looking up at him through my lashes, and nod, not sure exactly what I'm begging for.

"Please."

He climbs onto the bed, looming over me as he lays me back, and I spread my legs, welcoming him. He grinds his hips against mine, rubbing his cock along my folds, coating himself in my wetness. I can feel my legs trembling, my hips lifting to encourage him where I need him.

Dominick pins me between his arms, his eyes burning with an inner light, their depths gleaming with lust and . . . more, just for me.

"You have no idea how long I've waited for this, how many times I've dreamed of you this way," he rasps, his body vibrating from the restraint as he looks at me, his hips paused momentarily. "In my bed, begging for my cock, ready to take everything I can give you."

I can hear the promise in the dirty words, and I want it all. I wrap my arms around his back, and my breathy moan seems to be the tipping point. He thrusts into me in one sharp movement, sheathing himself fully, driving the breath out of my body. He's huge, and even with the fingering he gave me a few days ago, my body is shocked, galvanized as if I'm a newly-broken virgin, opening for the first time.

He pauses balls-deep, filling me until I'm riding that edge of pleasure and pain. I can feel my inner walls quivering, gripping him greedily, so I wrap my legs around his, tangling with him to hold him inside me. My nails score his back, and I growl, demanding more.

"Yes," I cry out softly as he rolls his hips, making the pain melt away. He lies on me, pressing me into the soft bedding with his weight and slipping his hands under my shoulders to clasp me to him, pinning me helpless to the foam as he kisses me hard.

I arch, both loving and hating the restraint. I want to perform for him, to show him how much he pleases me, how he makes my soul cry out for his completion, but instead, I'm forced to take what he offers me.

His strokes are sharp and short as he rapidly spears into me, hitting a spot deep inside me that drives me wild.

"Oh, my God, Dominick," I cry out, already dangerously close to coming.

His eyes seek out mine, the room's bright light leaving nowhere to hide. He can see me, the reckless abandon he's driven me to as I beg and plead for more, shamelessly wanting him to take me to the edge. But I can see him too, see the depth of his desire. I can see the joy at finally being right where we've both wanted him to be, inside me, making us into one, if only for a moment.

Our breath mingles in the small space between us, creating a world all our own. Dominick presses his forehead against mine, his hips slapping roughly against me and shaking my body all the way up my spine.

"Look at me, Allison. Say my name when you come."

It's a demand, but one I happily obey, not wanting to look away from him for even a second. He slams into me, hard enough that I know I'll feel his mark tomorrow, and his name escapes with every thrust, over and over again, like a mantra. I leap into the abyss this time, unafraid as he holds me tightly, knowing that he's got me, and I'm awash in the pleasure.

"Dominick . . . Dominick . . ."

And though my eyes try to roll in pleasure, his fierce look holds me steady, and I stay connected to him as the tidal wave washes through me. He grimaces, his cock growing impossibly harder inside me as I squeeze against his thickness. I can feel him holding back, but I need him to give in to this moment, so I boldly entice him.

"Come inside me, Dominick. Please."

I think the pleading note does it, and he stills, holding himself deep inside me as he roars. I feel the throbbing heat as he fills me, but as full as I feel, both with his cock and his cum, what fills me the most is my name on his lips, breathy and weak, as though it takes everything he has to get the three syllables past his lips.

"Allison."

CHAPTER

Ten

DOMINICK

"HERE. EAT THIS," I say, placing a small plate of cheese and crackers on the island in front of Allie.

She's mussed and soft, wearing my undershirt and nothing else. Her hair seems to be held up in a bun by magic because she just did some fancy twist with practiced ease and it stayed.

It's one of the multitudes of secrets I want to know about her.

"Yes, sir," she says sassily, one eyebrow quirked and a smirk taking her lips. She tosses me a sarcastic salute and then reaches out to pick up a cracker and a small slice of cheese, stacking them and popping the whole thing in her mouth.

A win for us both. I set a glass of water in front of her too and watch raptly as she stacks another slice of cheese onto a cracker before holding it out to me.

It's such a small gesture, but the sweet offering has multiple layers of meaning, and I eat from her hand, making sure to nibble her fingertips slightly.

Her giggle brings a full smile unbidden to my face. It feels both odd and somehow natural, like something I've forgotten how to do. I try to remember the last time I smiled without having some ulterior motive behind it, the last time I laughed with true humor.

It's been a depressingly long time. The realization makes me frown, and Allie's eyebrows lift in worry.

"Hey, where'd you go?" she asks around a mouthful of crumbly cracker.

I wipe a crumb from her lip with my thumb, shaking my head. "Just thinking."

As my silence draws out a bit longer, she sighs, giving me a *Come on, buddy* look. "Normally, people say, 'penny for your thoughts,' but I'm thinking you couldn't give a rat's ass about a penny, so how about a kiss for your thoughts?"

She grins, flirtatious and happy at the brilliance of her idea. She's not wrong. It's a good negotiation point for our current situation and she knows it.

"Okay, but I'll take the kiss first."

I lean in toward her, forcing my way between her legs as she sits on the barstool. She lifts her chin, her lips pursing slightly. I pause for a moment to marvel at her absolute beauty, cupping her chin and forcing her to lift higher to meet me as I bend down.

With one last look into her eyes, I kiss her, enjoying the moment her lashes flutter as she closes her eyes to enjoy the contact. Only then do I close my eyes too, and I let myself plunge, lost in her wild brambles and the overwhelming emotions she draws out of me so easily.

Breathlessly, she breaks the kiss, another angelic smile on her face. "Wow. That was . . . wow. But don't think I forgot our deal. What were you thinking about that took your smile and turned it upside down?"

She reaches up, pushing at the corners of my mouth with her fingers like I'm a frowning toddler. It's irreverent madness and I love that she feels comfortable enough to do it.

I let her tease a small smile out once again before confessing. "You make me smile so easily, and I was trying to remember the last time I truly smiled or laughed in happiness. It was painfully long ago, I'm afraid."

Her mouth opens in surprise. "That's . . ." she says before pausing and shaking her head and starting over.

"Tell me something that made you smile. From a long time ago or from recently, whatever you want. Just tell me something that made you happy."

I lift my eyebrow and giving a pointed look down the hallway toward my bedroom. "Well . . ."

She laughs but puts a finger to my mouth before I can say more. "Not that, although I'll give you a bonus as incentive to spill your guts." She pauses to let her meaning sink in, then points down the hall and stage-whispers like her words are a secret, "*That* was awesome, maybe more missionary than I expected from you, but also so much more . . . intensely intimate than I've ever had."

She blushes as she says it, like she rethought her confession halfway through but completed the thought anyway. Her guts impress me, make me want to give as much as she is, which is the point, I suppose.

I sit on the barstool next to her, trying to decide what to divulge.

"First, I'll agree *that* was something different. You are different." I run my hand along her bare thigh, wishing I could avoid the rest of the conversation and just throw her on the island and fuck her again. Maybe a little less missionary this time, perhaps with her cheek pressed to the granite and her apple ass in the air for me. I have a suspicion I'll always want to be inside her. Every moment I'm not feels like I'm missing an integral part of my being. She's the one person I've ever felt totally at ease with, and being inside her . . . it's heaven.

But I owe her something beyond the physical, at least for a moment. "Something that made me smile? Once upon a time, I was a little boy."

She feigns shock, teasing me with a hand on her cheek. "You? A little boy? That's hard to imagine. You seem like the type that just sprang forth, fully-grown and serious, with the weight of the world on his shoulders. You were probably born with an Armani suit on. Tell me I'm wrong."

I laugh, shaking my head. "I wasn't that bad."

"Well then, tell me about Little Dominick. Paint me a picture of that first."

I think back, nodding to myself as I recall the memories. "Actually, I guess I was a bit like a mini-me even then, a serious child who mostly read, played chess, and excelled at school. I didn't really have many friends, at first because I was quiet and studious, not really the gregarious kid who drew people in."

Allie hums, and I continue. "Later, some who were in the know became afraid of me because of my dad. But as I grew up, I learned to use that to my advantage, and I spent most of my teen years as a bit of a hellion, confident that no one could or would dare touch me. I was, I'm sorry to say, a bit of an entitled jerk. Ironically, I'd become what I thought I didn't want to be. That changed on my sixteenth birthday though."

In my mind, I can see my mother holding up my favorite chocolate cake, a sad smile on her face illuminated by the single candle. I hadn't understood it then, but she'd known that when I blew out that candle, my world would change and I would become an apprentice for my father.

"That was when I started working for my father as his right hand . . . good, bad, or ugly, and there was plenty of each. It shaped me, changed me. I'd already gone from a quiet, nerdy kid into a rowdy street urchin too cocky for his own good, but after that I became . . . The Boss."

It's the first time we've acknowledged the elephant in the room since she first found out exactly who I am. It's been mentioned in conversations, but it's the first time those words have crossed my lips about myself in her presence. I gird myself for her reaction, ready for the judgment and the disgust to cross her face.

But there isn't any. Instead, she studies me silently for a heartbeat, then another. "You've heard the expression 'rough around the edges'?"

I nod, unsure where she's going with this. "Yeah?"

She continues. "I think that once upon a time, you were rough around the edges. I've heard stories. Hell, I've seen you have to handle business in the club a time or two. You're street smart, willing to cheat, get dirty, do what's needed. But also, like a sword, you've honed your edges through years of work, experience, and knowledge, and now, you're more like the sharpest blade, gleaming and dangerous on the surface. But still with that roughness at the core. You are The Boss, with all that entails, but you're also still that quiet boy too. You've spent so long trying to hide it . . . but I see it. And to me, I think it's the best part about you, Dom. You know what I've noticed?"

"What's that?" I ask, and she gives me a smile that stops my heart again.

"You almost never curse in your work. You don't need to because you let your intelligence help you get your point across with a fierce elegance. But when we're together, you do curse, and I think it's because you relax around me, let your rough edges show. Side note—it's hot when you talk dirty, so don't be using fancy language for that shit or I'll cover your mouth so you don't distract me with some thees and thous. A well-timed 'Fuck, Allie' can sometimes say more than a whole Shakespearean sonnet, know what I mean?"

She winks at me, then grins. "You could do with a bit of crazy to shake up your controlled, precise existence and force you to let loose and enjoy life. I know you're The Boss, but spend some time as the hellion and the quiet kid too. I'd like to get to know all three characters you have hiding in there." She lays a hand on my chest and then pats me like that's a done deal.

Her words soothe something in me I didn't even know was ruffled, a question I didn't know I had. "That sounds oddly accurate."

The quiet descends and stretches out between us, but it's comfortable, our eyes locked on one another as the weight of my confession and her analysis sinks in. The fact that she's so insightful but somehow not running honestly surprises me.

It forces me to think about myself some. She's right. I have hidden a lot of myself behind my mask as The Boss. But that's part of me as well. I'm not some melodramatic character from a movie, itching to let go of my position in order to retire to a quiet life. But I do want to be able to do . . . *more*.

She smiles. "Okay, let's rewind to where we started. Tell me something that made you smile."

She's giving me an opportunity for lightness, recognizing that I'm uncomfortable with the unusual plumbing of the depths of my soul, my past, and my psyche. But telling her things doesn't feel like exposing a weakness. It feels like bringing her into my mind, my heart, my past, present, and future.

I purposefully frown, screwing my face up like I'm thinking hard to even remember. "Ah, I did smile the time I put Don Rivaldi in his place for trying to start a coup in my town. That was entertaining."

She laughs, semi-familiar with the incidents surrounding Don Rivaldi since it involved her bestie, Maggie. "An evil genius grin isn't the same thing as a smile. Try again."

I think back further, looking in my mental archives for what she's asking, and then I remember. "When I beat my father at chess for the first time."

"Ooh, that's better," Allie says. "Tell me!" she squeals, wiggling in her seat a bit like an excited puppy.

The echo of the smile from my youth ghosts across my face as I tell her the story. "My dad and I used to play chess after dinner every chance we could. It was our thing. He'd talk and impart wisdom. I didn't realize at the time that he was grooming me to take over. I just thought he was sharing about his day with me. Edited versions, but sharing nonetheless."

I think back to those nights in my father's study. He had a classic study, all leather and oak, and the chess board had its own special table. The pieces were carved stone, obsidian and marble, the board inlaid with gold. It felt like a special board, a magic talisman to teach me wisdom. Maybe it did.

"We'd play, and he always won. I read books about chess strategies from the masters, learned different plays to counter his moves, all so I could be better. It felt like if I could win against the greatest man I knew, then I'd have really accomplished something. But whatever I did, I couldn't beat him.

"One night when I was fourteen, I finally did it. I was so stupidly arrogant about it too, downright cocky as I strutted around with a big smile on my face and told Mom all about my win.

"But when I looked at Father, that was when I really smiled. He was so proud of me, not mad that he'd lost to a kid but proud that we'd both played our best and I'd come out on top. It took me a long time to realize how prophetic that was. I try to make sure he would always still be proud of me."

She reaches up to run her fingers through my hair, her nails scratching my scalp deliciously. "I'm sure he would be. You're quite a man, Dominick Angeline."

Her words elicit a truly genuine smile from me, wide and as unrestrained as she is. "Do you play chess?"

Her laugh is infectious. "Normally, I'd say yes, but I'm afraid you're gonna wipe the board with me in five moves."

I chuckle, standing up. "I'll take it easy on you," I vow, taking her hand and leading her to my office, where my father's chess board rests on a side table between two chairs. It's just as it always has been, right down to the chipped bishop on the obsidian side, a product of my over-eagerness when I was seven. "It's a game of kings . . . and their queens."

She settles in the plush armchair, crossing her legs in front of her like a child, but there is nothing innocent in the way she looks up at me, her voice sultry and her intent clear.

"Maybe I like it when you *don't* go easy on me."

She's not talking about chess anymore. I let a bit of growl into my voice, challenging her. "Maybe we'll make this a win in three moves then, so we can see just how *not-easy* you like it."

She rises to the bait, planting her feet cutely on the floor. "Challenge accepted."

I settle down behind the board, looking across at her. "Ladies first."

Allie grins, resting her chin in her palm "Mmm, giving me the advantage? Rather sure of yourself, aren't you? What if I'm actually sandbagging you?"

"I'll take the risk," I reply, getting into the game as we each make our opening moves. I'll admit that my competitiveness almost immediately kicks in, but I'm enjoying playing the game with her.

She's good, but it's an uneven match. Still, I find myself making moves to prolong the game, but she calls me on it the second time I pass up a chance at checkmate.

"If I didn't know better, I'd think you were trying to let me win. But that can't be. So maybe it's that you want to play longer?" She lifts one eyebrow teasingly, and I hum, but Allie isn't having any of that. "Too bad. I had other thoughts on ways we could play, ones that don't involve chess."

Her voice promises all types of heat, and it's a distraction move that I've never had used on me before. I sit back in my chair, deciding on my strategy for her more than the game as I eye her.

Ever the impulsive one, she reaches for the hem of her shirt and pulls it over her head, unceremoniously exposing her body to me, perfection in the flesh. With a smirk, she leans back, her breasts rising proudly from her chest.

"Your move."

I force myself to wait one second, not letting her have the upper hand before I stand, lifting the board and table out of the way in one smooth movement, and then I'm on her, her chair scooting back a few inches from my power. I shove her legs open, her knees resting over the arms of the chair and her pussy spread wide for me.

So pretty, so pink, so . . . mine.

Slowly, I sink to my knees in front of her, making her wait and watch every inch that I get closer to her center. I can see the pulse at her throat fluttering, giving away her façade of patience, but that's okay because I'm not patient anymore either.

I need her again, her taste on my tongue, my name on her lips, her wild abandon as she comes for me. I nibble at her inner thigh, drawing a groan of desire from her throat.

I've resisted tasting her, waiting for this moment when she would be spread out, offered to me without hesitation. I want to look in her eyes as we see each other's reaction to the first touch, and it's magic as I lick along her pussy, so sweet and feminine. Immediately, I suck on her bud, fluttering my tongue over it, and her hands weave into my hair, holding me there in a silent demand for more.

I tease her, savoring her lips and sipping on her sweet, tangy wine before sliding two fingers inside her, rubbing along her front wall and finding the rough spot that I know drives her wild when I coordinate strokes of it and flicks of my tongue on her clit.

"Oh, fuck, Dominick, right there, yes," she moans with each breathy exhale.

I give her a few strokes, watching as she takes my fingers over and over inside her and enjoying the glistening evidence of her arousal.

"So perfect, Allison. You said you didn't want me to go easy on you. Is that still true?" I ask, knowing that my 'soft' tongue is harder for her to handle than even the fiercest assault on her pussy.

She cries out, begging for me, and I lift up on my knees, getting a better angle to dominate her. I slide my free hand up to cup her neck, not putting choking pressure but letting her know that I'm there and that she shouldn't move or fight back.

She bites her lip, but I can see the pleading agreement in her eyes. I fingerfuck her hard, slamming into her with power and using my thumb along her clit when I have the opportunity.

"That's it, take it hard, love. You can handle it, handle me. I want this pussy to know who it belongs to with every step you take tomorrow."

She's getting close, I can feel her walls swelling and clenching, and her eyes flutter closed. I pause, my thumb resting on her pulsing clit but not moving at all, drawing it out until she opens her eyes to look at me in silent pleading.

"Say it, Allie. Whose pussy is this? Tell me as you come all over my fingers."

She groans a guttural sound, more primal than I've ever heard from her before, and that I pulled that noise from her makes my cock throb in my sweats. She whispers, her voice almost lost from her repeated pleas.

"Yours . . . it's yours, Dominick."

I stroke her clit once more, and her back arches so hard I can hear her spine crackle like fireworks, her breath catching as shudders grip her muscles, her pussy quivering. I ride her through every wave, drawing every last drop of pleasure from her with softening strokes until she can't breathe, and I tenderly squeeze her throat.

"Stay just like that."

She freezes as I withdraw and pull my sweats down, my rock-hard cock already weeping a joyous stream of precum. I swipe my fingers through her messy pussy, gathering her orgasm, and rub the sticky slickness on my shaft quickly. I jack myself with long strokes, pumping hard and fast into my fist. My tip bumps along her clit, edging her toward overstimulation, but I like the way she flinches every time I touch her.

Allie's eyes track my every move, like she's memorizing the way I enjoy being touched, like she's getting off on watching me get off.

"Fuck, Dom . . . that's so hot. Come on me."

I'm shaking, my thighs tight with impending release, and I'm already on the edge. "I'm going to mark you outside like I marked you inside."

She nods, though I don't think she's aware she does it. And with three more strokes, I grunt, my cum splashing across her mound as I come hard. A thrill rolls through me when as soon as Allie feels the heat of it, she slips a fingertip into the puddle, spreading it and rubbing it into her skin, tracing something in silent letters that I can't quite make out. Lifting her finger, she slides it into her mouth, moaning at the flavor of me, which triggers one more jerky spasm from me that lands like an exclamation point at the top of her cleft.

Spent, I fold over her, kissing her fully, my heart pounding at the combination of our flavors on our tongues. Her lips tilt up into a smile even as we kiss, and when I pull back to look at her, I can see the devil in her eyes.

"I think we both won that game."

She looks so damn proud of her joke, but I tell her seriously, "Love, make no mistake. You might've had a good game, but I certainly came out on top."

Her laugh is all the answer I need to know I'm right.

CHAPTER
Eleven

ALLIE

"I SWEAR, Gavin, I'm fine. I don't need you in here crowding the guys while they're working," I tell him, exasperated by his forced all-up-in-my-business jokes. At least Donna's gotten used to him. Actually, I think she sort of thinks he's cute in a *Let me introduce you to my granddaughter* kind of way.

He flashes me a wide, white smile that I'm sure gets him plenty of pussy, especially when it's partnered with his wide, strong body and lighthearted personality.

But the gleam of his grin just annoys me even more. He shakes his head, leaning down to keep his voice quiet enough that not *everyone* in East Robinsville knows who I'm seeing.

"Allie, it's cute that you think I'm leaving while you have strange men in the studio talking to you and looking you up and down. Maybe you don't give a shit about my balls, but I'm rather attached to them and don't want your man chopping them off anytime soon."

I roll my eyes, laughing. "What if I promise to ask Dom to leave your balls alone? Then will you let me get some work done?"

He pales. "For fuck's sake, do not mention my name and balls in the same sentence ever, but especially not to him unless you're a heartless bitch. Which, to be clear, I don't think you are."

He sounds hopeful and not altogether sure of whether that's true or not. I relieve his tension with a wink and pat him on the shoulder.

"Fine, but as soon as the workers are out of here, so are you. I'm here for the long haul today, deep-cleaning for my first class next week. So my evening detail can take over when I head home. Deal?"

Gavin smirks, probably relieved. "You drive a hard bargain, but deal."

He takes my offered hand, shaking it firmly before saying, "You know

I'm not agreeing to that because you said it but because that was already my assignment for the day, right?"

I growl. "Ugh. Men."

He laughs at my pseudo-frustration, because really, I'm not all that upset about it. Gavin's a good guy, and I don't mind the chaperoning, but I had hopes to get the poles installed before lunch. And it's creeping up on late afternoon now. The hours just seemed to get nibbled away this entire morning.

First it was the contractors showing up fifteen minutes late, then parts not being in the boxes, which required a trip to the hardware store . . . just one thing after another.

We could've just used what we had, and if I were at home, I probably would've. But here, everything should be up to code. Still, it's taken forever for the contractors to install the poles.

Instead of getting frustrated, I go back to doing prep work around the room, setting up a small area in the corner with hooks where clients can store their jackets and coverups and a bench where they can sit down to change out of street shoes. Eventually, I figure some of the girls will be rocking the stage stilettos, but it might take a little while for some of them to really get into the flow.

I add a throw pillow with big tassels that says *You are Amazing* in gold lamé lettering on a soft pink background to the bench. It's perfect, a motto for every woman, every class, every day.

I'm just making sure I've got my playlist ready when I hear a voice behind me. "Ma'am?"

I look up to see the head crewman, Mr. Bayer, looking at me. He's middle-aged, with a bit of a beer gut that's mostly hidden by the stained Eagles T-shirt he's wearing. He's got his assistant with him, a younger guy who's probably learning the ropes.

"Yes? You all done?"

He nods, but I can see the gleam in his eyes as he looks me up and down. "Yeah, but the poles need a, uh, uhm . . . test run. Just to be on the safe side."

He says it with a hint of sleaze to his tone. It's one I've heard before. I lift one eyebrow, my eyes narrowing as he makes me feel dirty, like I should just hop up on the pole and put on a show for him. As if it's only natural because he did me a favor by installing the poles.

Except it's not a favor. I fucking hired him to do a job and he did it. Nothing more, nothing less.

Planting my hands on my hips, I glare at him until he starts to fidget, and only then do I speak.

"Then I'd guess you'd better hop on up there and try those poles out since that's what I'm paying you to do. Make sure they're all nice and secure. I'd hate for someone to get hurt after your company did the installation, catch an insurance claim or something."

He shrinks a bit and walks off, but under his breath, I can hear him mutter, "Not like I can't see it any time I want to at the club."

I take a breath, balling my indignation into a missile and taking aim. "Hey, Mr. Bayer?"

He turns around, a sour look on his face. "Not anymore. Consider yourself banned, from here and from Petals. Drop off your invoice at the front desk on your way out."

The raised voices get Gavin's attention, and a few seconds later, he's in the doorway, filling the whole thing as his shoulders brush from wood to wood.

"What's going on, Allie?"

There's a moment of anticipation where I wonder if this is about to get ugly. Gavin's pretty easygoing, but he's one of Dom's guys for a reason. And even if these two contractors have hammers in their tool belts, things probably wouldn't go very well for them.

Bayer looks over, realizing that yes, he just fucked up. He quivers, and I decide to let him off the hook, but my voice is hard.

"Everything's fine. Mr. Bayer was just packing up his things. Please make sure that he leaves safely . . . and that he understands he's *persona non grata* here and at the club."

Gavin's eyes narrow and his chest puffs a bit, making him look even broader, and his rumbling growl could make a lion piss his fur. "That sounds like a problem to me."

Mr. Bayer turns to Gavin, looking outraged that someone's violating the 'bro code' or something. "You just gonna let a whore like that make rules for the best titty bar in town? Bitch is just a piece of ass, showing off for money."

I suppose I should have a thick skin after the length of time I've been dancing. I get it, my performances are about sexual fantasy. And I'd love to say that his words wash over me like they're nothing, but *whore* is just one insult that I don't think I'll ever get used to. There's a line for me, one that maybe some people don't recognize or don't respect, but it's there, big and bold. Why do some people think that just because I'm a dancer, I'm hopping on every dick that walks by?

But I do gasp, just a little, as my jaw drops in fury. Bayer's assistant even has the good sense to look chagrined at his boss's gross assessment, and he backs up a step. It maybe saves him a beating as Gavin steps forward, his patience gone.

"Time to go, asshole," he says, grabbing Bayer by the collar and jerking him forward. "And if she says you're out, you're out. If she decides to not be so fucking graciously nice and says you're dead, you won't live to see another sunrise. So I'd suggest you get the fuck out before I start asking her for permission. Hell, another minute and I might even ask for forgiveness instead of permission."

Bayer stumbles forward, looking desperately at me in some pathetic plea for help as Gavin half-drags him toward the door. I have no pity on him, though. It's what he deserves for thinking that I would happily put on a private thank-you show for a skeevy, gross misogynist like him.

His assistant gulps down his fear and grabs the tool box, casting nervous glances at me as he scrambles out the door, almost bowing as he leaves.

"Thank you!"

I sort of feel bad for the kid. He didn't do anything wrong today. In fact, he was almost Boy Scout polite the whole time.

A moment later, I hear applause from the reception area, and Gavin comes back in, his eyes ignoring the ruckus behind him as he checks on me. "You okay?"

I nod, realizing that it's probably Donna cheering him on. "Don't worry, guy was just a dick. Nothing I haven't dealt with before."

Gavin shakes his head, rubbing at his neck. "Yeah, that part sucks about my job. My opinion, you girls shouldn't have to deal with shit like that. Hey, uh . . . so you're here for the rest of the day, right? Cleaning and prepping?"

"Yeah . . . why?" I ask suspiciously.

Gavin grins, shaking his head furiously. "Oh, no reason. Like you said . . . I was here until the crew left, then you'd be on your own until your go-home detail comes. That's good, right? I mean, this place is busy enough and you'll stay inside?"

He's talking to me but taking baby steps toward the door and glancing behind him like he needs to go all of a sudden. I put my hands on my hips, trying to look intimidating, but I suspect that Gavin is a lot harder to scare than I'd first thought.

He is a big badass underneath his affable exterior, apparently, and I have a feeling about what he's about to go do. He's about to go teach Mr. Bayer a lesson.

"Go ahead and go. But do me a favor. If you *have* to do it, just scare him, maybe give him a little lesson in appropriate customer service. Make sure he knows the proper way to treat a lady next time. Can we stop it there though?"

He's taken aback at first by my knowing what he's up to, then he breaks out into a disarmingly boyish grin, and he flashes me a thumbs-up.

"Gotcha. Although I don't know what you're talking about, Allie. I just have some errands to run this afternoon. Nothing to be concerned about."

With a wink, he's out the door.

Donna's already got her next class in warmups, so I avoid any ribbing from her as I retreat to my studio, locking the door and grinning to myself. Assholes like Bayer will always exist, but good guys like Gavin do too, and hopefully, the balance will always tip that way.

An hour flashes by as I do my last-chance cleaning. Slowly but surely, the space is coming together, I think with a smile. Warmth bubbles up inside me. It feels like . . . pride.

I'm doing something scary, something that takes some major courage, but I'm chasing those damn butterflies in my gut like they're going to lead me someplace awesome. Because I think this whole setup really could change my life for the better in so many ways.

Actually, I feel like I'm on the precipice of a lot of changes. Professionally, personally, it's like everything is right on the verge of falling into place. With just a little nudge here and a little hip bump there, I'll be better than I ever would've thought possible just a few short years ago when everything seemed so bleak.

Excited at the prospect and at my excellent use of cleaning time, I decide to get started on polishing the chrome finish of the newly-installed poles. Each one will take me hours to get ready for class, removing the greasy ick of the factory and the installation, and especially Mr. Bayer's bad juju vibes on them.

I head to the front, pausing for a moment to remember that I'm supposed to stay inside like Gavin said. But the special cleaner I need is in my car.

Screw it. I'm grown-ass woman who can sure as fuck walk across the parking lot without permission. It's something I've done thousands of times. No biggie.

Feeling my sass, even at such a little thing, feels good, a tiny bit of wild rebellion, but a small piece of me realizes how crazy that sounds.

I'm halfway down the sidewalk when I hear a deep voice behind me.

"Allie?"

I turn, recognizing the voice instantly, but seeing him standing here in front of me is an unexpected surprise. I'm sure a few birds are startled at my high-pitched squeal of delight as I run toward him, launching myself into his arms with the full trust that he'll catch me.

"Oh, my God!" I exclaim. He spins us once with the momentum of my leap and then sets me on my feet, engulfing me in a big hug. Once upon a time, he was the same height I was, but now he's easily a foot taller and twice as wide as I am. Still buried in the hug, I whisper into his chest, "TJ! Holy shit! What are you doing here?"

He sighs, patting my back, and sets me down on the sidewalk. "Long story, Allie-Gator. Wanna go to dinner and I'll tell you all about it?"

"Of course!" I say with a laugh and a grin. He drops down in front of me, and like so many times before, I hop on piggy-back style.

"Do you need to lock up?" he asks.

I stare at him, thinking I'll wake up and this will be a dream any second, but I shake my head. "No, the owner's got another class going."

Without another question, he gallops down the sidewalk, me laughing at his silly antics. Just like before. Just like always. Unceremoniously, he plops me in the seat of his truck, and we roar out of the lot.

Max

"Keep going, kids. Hold for eight, seven, six . . ." I say, when suddenly, the parking lot quiet is broken by a scream.

Screams aren't really standard fare around here, not like the neighborhood back home. Around here, it's all proper manners and nice neighbors, and my last class is usually just us and the crickets chirping as the sun goes down.

But I've got responsibilities and duties now, so I turn, instantly on alert and ready to protect my charges against whatever incoming assault may be going down.

I realize as I look out the gym's open bay door that it's more squeal than scream, a happy, exuberant sound. Hell, if this were an adult class with my normal assortment of death metal blaring, I probably wouldn't have heard it at all. I scan the lot and see Allie running down the sidewalk toward a tall guy with a big smile on her face.

My brows knit together as I watch her jump into his arms, her legs wrapping around his torso and their arms encircling each other. One spin later, she's back on solid ground but they're still hugging it out.

They're too far away for me to hear them, but she seems happy to see the guy, whoever he is. Even from here, I can see he's a big motherfucker, not like Dalton and me, but a tall, broad guy who carries himself with a sense that he could take care of business.

I turn back to my students, who have decided that I'm done counting. They're sitting on the ground, their squat positions given up. Kids . . . they'll work their asses off on the fun stuff, but champions aren't made of the fun stuff.

"All right, guys," I announce, going over to the boxing timer on the wall and flipping the switches. "Good job. One more cycle and we'll call it a night. Burpees, pushups, and sprawls. One minute each."

They groan a bit but get to work. That's the good thing about the youngsters . . . nearly endless energy. As the timer goes, I watch their burpees but hear laughter from behind me.

I turn, keeping an eye on the kids but watching as the guy deposits Allie into a truck and they go speeding out of the lot. It's not until the kids are halfway through their one-minute sprawls that I put it together that he looked nothing like Dominick's usual guys.

I've met Logan, and he's even been hanging out in the gym with us a bit. He's a monster of a guy, and I've seen another guy escorting Allie out sometimes too. And both of them, when they're on chaperone detail, are respectfully distant, dressed in fancy clothes, and on guard as they give her coverage similar to the Secret Service.

Allie seemed comfortable, but something is uneasy in my gut. That guy just isn't the usual, and it feels off for some reason.

Logan casually asked Dalton and me to keep an eye out for her, nothing official, but just a friendly request. Thing is . . . Logan isn't going to just make a friendly request like that for no reason. I know who he works for, who Allie belongs to, and the fight game isn't so far from its old Mafia roots that you don't get to know a few names around the streets. This feels like something I should call about.

Getting all up in Dominick Angeline's business is the absolute last thing I want to do. But not calling him when I see something out of the norm sounds like a sure-fire way to get my ass kicked. Or worse.

I let the kids finish their drills and give them a quick dismissal before heading for my desk, where my cellphone sits like a package of dynamite waiting to make the call I'm dreading.

CHAPTER

Twelve

DOMINICK

"SAY THAT AGAIN, SLOWLY," I tell Logan, my knuckles rapping on my steering wheel in a measured beat to try and calm myself down. I heard every word he said the first time. I just don't want to believe it.

What is she doing? What is she thinking, leaving the studio off schedule with an unvetted man?

"Max called. Said he saw Allie run toward a guy, hopped into his arms with a smile on her face. They hugged and then he carried her to a truck and they left."

His report is objective, no judgments, no emotion, just the facts.

"I'm already in the car, heading back. Stay close and make sure she's safe, but do not engage. Understood?"

Logan accepts the order evenly, even though I'm probably interrupting his evening off. "Of course, Sir. I'll be in touch."

As soon as the call disconnects, I press the accelerator on my Mercedes, speeding up a little. I open the tracking app and see the green dot that tells me where she is. Frustratingly, it doesn't tell me if she's okay, but knowing her location gives me the tiniest sliver of reassurance. But it still doesn't answer the questions I have.

My mind races to every possible scenario . . . has she been kidnapped because of her importance to me? If someone thinks to use her as a pawn against me, I would readily slash, burn, and destroy everyone and everything involved. I would tear this city to pieces before anything truly damaging could happen to her.

The thought of what could be happening to Allie makes a knot of dread form in my gut.

The timing seems oddly convenient as well. The majority of my time is spent in East Robinsville, never more than a half hour from her side.

Today is the rare break from my routine as I left town on a short road trip to pay my old friend Silas a visit. It's too opportunistic to be coincidence, and I wonder if perhaps his Eagle Raiders had something to do with this.

But for what purpose? To what end? I seriously doubt they want a war.

I evaluate everything I know about Silas and his Eagle Raiders, and I can't find a path that makes sense for that case. Silas is much more straight-forward, a product of the open road. When he comes for someone, he's about as subtle as one of his unmuffled Harleys rolling down the street at full-throttle.

So, if not Silas, then who? I think through what little I know.

It seems she knew the man and that her leaving wasn't against her will. Could the man be an old lover? If it's something more mundane like an ex, I'll have to handle her messy emotions. Because her leaving me is no longer an option. She is mine, body, mind, and soul. I won't allow any other possibility.

My Mercedes purrs in contrast to the loud thoughts in my head, a techno-logical ghost gliding over the miles of asphalt, relatively silent death coming, if need be. I still don't know what I'm going to do except that I'll try to remain calm. But if someone has taken my Allie, whether they be an ex who needs a lesson by castration, an enemy who needs a lesson in death, or . . .

There is another possibility.

Sure. There's a chance she just went willingly with a friend, although the blatant disregard for the reasonable protocol we've established would certainly warrant another discussion. And maybe a spanking.

One that she would not enjoy quite as much as the last. I'll never lay a hand on her in anger, but she needs to understand that her safety is of utmost importance to me. If a bit of pinkened skin and a sore ass get that message into her beautiful brain, then so be it.

But I have to hope that she is smarter than that, that she understands how dangerous the city can be for her and wouldn't go traipsing around unescorted after we'd agreed to chaperones for her safety.

My phone rings again, and I have a moment of hope that it is her, but the name flashing on the screen isn't hers.

"Yes."

Logan's voice comes through the speakers. "Sir, I've got eyes on her in a food truck park. Currently, she's sitting on the tailgate with the unknown male. They purchased some smoothies and a burrito and have been talking ever since. She does not appear to be in distress."

Cold fury runs through my body, every muscle tensing. She's sitting, happy as a lark, with another man while I consider the awful things that might be happening to her if she'd been kidnapped.

Every bit of my being demands that I swoop into that food truck lot and grab her up, take her home, and demand an explanation. But a lightning-fast analysis tells me that without a doubt, it's the wrong move.

First, by showing Allie just how much of a possessive asshole I am. I'm already walking a fine line with that, I know. I need her to understand that she's as precious as diamonds and as necessary as air to me without coming off as a suffocating tyrant.

Secondly, there could be implications within my work. A public showing of her power over me, her disregard for basic rules, and that she is valuable to me would paint our relationship in a light there would be no recovering from. Word would spread, and she would be a constant weakness in my stronghold, an ever-present target for those who wish me harm.

As disappointed as I am, Allie is who she is . . . unpredictable, uncaged, and prone to flights of fancy. It both draws me to her and disturbs me. She is okay, totally safe with Logan observing her, and under no duress with her current company.

No, I'm the only one under strain in this situation, apparently, but I can withstand it.

I make a decision, one that will be the best move on both fronts. "Stay on her but out of sight. I'm going to her apartment."

"Understood," Logan says before clearing his throat. "And sir, I'm sorry."

The line goes dead, him hanging up on me this time, something that I normally would not be pleased with, but I'm too caught up in Allie to care. His words give me more of an answer as to his assessment than anything else has tonight.

I get to Allie's apartment and use my key, the one that I had copied months ago. Sitting in the dark of her living room, surrounded by the spicy floral scent of her perfume, I wait.

Logan sends me a photo he surreptitiously took of the two of them. The man does appear tall and broad, as Max reported, his hair shaggily grown out and in need of a trim, his skin sun-bronzed and faintly lined, putting his age close to Allie's but his life significantly harder than hers.

They look cozy, familiar in the picture. It angers me anew, and I trace her smile thoughtfully.

Could I let her go? If she truly doesn't care for me other than for sex, could I just let her walk out of my life?

No. I can never hurt her, but Allie's leaving my life would be worse than having my heart ripped out.

Logan sends me a text message. It seems she's coming straight here, with him. My eyes glare at the green dot on my screen, watching it move closer and closer.

It's not long before I hear the shuffle of footsteps on the hall tile outside and take a deep breath.

Showtime.

The door opens, the hallway light silhouetting the two of them for a brief moment before she flicks on the light.

"Allison," I say simply.

My voice is a harsh rumble.

Faster than I would've given the man credit for, he shoves Allie behind him, pulling a gun from his waistband. A tiny seed of approval at his protectiveness tries to take root, but I can't accept that he is protecting her from me.

From me?

From the man who has protected her for months, even at the detriment to my own sanity?

She gasps in alarmed surprise, but when she realizes who's sitting in her living room, the fire in her eyes is half relief and half anger.

"What the fuck, Dominick? What in the . . . you scared the shit out of me!"

The man's appraising gaze never leaves me, his hand steady on the gun. "You know this guy, Allie?"

She rolls her eyes, carefully putting a hand on his wrist. "Yeah, he's my . . . Dominick. Put the gun down, TJ. Why the hell do you even have that?"

But he doesn't lower the gun, smartly still reading me as a threat regardless of Allie's placating touch. "You gave this fucker a key?"

Allie's eyes whip to mine, and I take the chance of looking away from the armed man to give her a look, silently asking, *Really?* She presses her lips together in defeat and pushes harder on his wrist.

"Seriously, just put the gun down, TJ."

He slowly lowers the piece, and I rise from the couch just as slowly, stepping closer to Allie. "You missed your detail. Seems you've been running around town with an unknown male, Allison."

Her eyes flare, and in my use of her full name and formal tone, she realizes just how much she's scared me and pissed me off. In a tumble, her apology rushes out in one long breath.

"Oh, fuck! I didn't think. I just got so excited about TJ being here. I'm so sorry. Oh, introductions would probably help now that we're not shooting anyone or scaring the shit out of them. TJ, this is Dominick. Dominick, this is TJ."

I pause, my eyes flickering back and forth from Allie to TJ. He doesn't move, and while he's lowered his piece, this close, I can see it's a decent little Smith & Wesson.

"So I've surmised. What I don't know is who TJ is to you, Allie."

She flushes and rubs behind her ear as she glances at him, and he lifts a brow slightly in a way that I've seen across from me at breakfast for the past few days, telling me the answer even before the words come out.

"TJ's my brother."

In an instant, my world is set right once again.

Not kidnapped.

Not *with another man.*

Just willfully and knowingly putting herself in danger as if she's not my fucking heart, walking around at risk. My relief swirls with frustrated anger at her lackadaisical attitude.

No, not *her* attitude. I'm angry with myself, for not using my head and realizing that Allie has people in her life. Decent people whom I have yet to meet. I need to leave, get myself under control.

How ironic is that?

The man of utmost control almost spinning out because his woman went out for an impromptu dinner with her brother?

My jaw muscles nearly cramp as I gnash my teeth, trying to force out some words that might explain my actions without making too much of an idiot of myself.

"I thought you'd been kidnapped, Allie," I say quietly, her eyes softening when she sees the emotion underneath my voice. "I feared I would be painting the streets red with the blood of whoever dared to lay a finger on you. While you were out having fun and sipping smoothies, I was trying to determine whether I would have to save you or avenge you."

Her chin drops and her eyes go to the floor. "I'm sorry. I just didn't think. I'm not used to all this yet."

I nod my head and clear my throat. "Look at me."

She looks up at me, and I realize . . . there's no reason to apologize. The fault is mine and mine alone, and it's my responsibility to educate her about my life. Something I've been woefully inadequate with if she didn't understand the possible ramifications of her actions. A simple phone call is all it would've taken, from either of us, and this whole mess could've been avoided.

"We'll talk about this later, but you did nothing wrong. I'm sorry. Logan will be downstairs tonight. Enjoy your visit with your brother."

I take the few steps toward her, laying a kiss to her temple as I hold her hand for a brief moment. I can feel the tension through TJ, and his grip on the gun tightens ever so slightly, though his finger is off the trigger. He's still uncertain whether I pose a threat to his sister.

There are times to answer a question with words . . . but I believe TJ needs a more visceral demonstration. Before my lips even lose contact with Allie's skin, I make a grab for the gun, quickly and easily twisting it from his hand, a maneuver I learned years ago and still have the occasion to use from time to time.

"Motherfuck—" he stutters loudly. Instead of turning his gun around on him, though, I take a step back, dropping the clip and clearing the chamber before I offer it back to him, grip-first.

"A hint. In my line of work, if you pull a gun, you'd better be prepared to use it without hesitation. If you don't, you could end up having it taken from you, or worse."

His face flushes with indignation at being disarmed, but he reaches his hand out and takes it. "I look forward to our next meeting," I tell him.

In the silence of the moment, I leave, not sure what to make of everything that just happened. It's an uncomfortable feeling, not one I commonly feel. Simply put, Allie has me on such a tight rope, so readily able to pull me this way and that. It's discomforting.

But at the same time, I want nothing more than to be on her string, and her on mine, endlessly tied up in one another. I stride to the elevator, getting on, and though I have every intention of hitting *One*, my finger hovers and I press *Four*, admitting to myself at least that I can't leave her tonight.

Not after all the ugly images my fear played through my head, like a horror movie I couldn't escape. Before I call Logan and inform him of my change of plans, I place a call to another old friend.

"Yeah, it's me. I need everything you can get me on a TJ Bancroft. Tonight."

CHAPTER

Thirteen

ALLIE

DOM CLOSES the door behind himself with a soft snick. The silence is painful. It would have been easier if he'd slammed it or yelled at me, storming out of here. At least then, I could get a read on how angry he must be.

Instead, he walked out almost like a phantom, his presence here but at the same time, I don't even have anything to lash back against. He somehow makes the quiet sound of the door shutting behind him sound like a gunshot to my heart.

I know I'm not wrong. I'm just not used to the transparency of a detail and somehow needing to report my whereabouts to someone.

He's not wrong either though. If I'm to accept him as part of my life, I need to recognize that he has enemies, enemies who would use me as a weapon against him if they had a chance. What's that old saying? It's not paranoia if they're actually out to get you?

That's Dominick's life every day.

From beside me, TJ kneels, picking up the clip from his gun before hunting for the single ejected round and replacing them before turning to me.

"What the fuck was that, Allie?"

I sigh, looking at him and wondering when I get to ask him why my big brother's carrying a gun like he's a gangster himself. "Let me get you a beer. It's kind of a long story."

TJ says nothing for a minute, casually plopping down on the couch and making himself at home while I grab him a beer from the fridge and pour myself a hearty glass of red wine. I'm pretty sure I'm going to need it.

Handing TJ his beer, I sit down on the floor, a cushion under my butt.

"I don't know where to start," I say, truthfully not sure how to explain the dance I've been doing with Dominick for months, nor who he is, exactly, both to me and to East Robinsville. "How about you start with why you're carrying a gun?"

TJ shakes his head. "Nice attempt at diversion, but remember, I taught you those tricks. So we'll talk about that later, *maybe*. Right now, I'm worried about my sister, who just had some guy chilling in her apartment when she got home. So let's start with who the fuck that guy is to you. Then tell me why you have a fucking guard detail. And wrap it up with how some slick asshole in a custom-tailored suit just disarmed me like I'm a damn noob. My old Top Sergeant would have kicked my ass if he'd seen that."

His voice is nearly a yell, but I know he's worried about me. My brother . . . still my protector, in his mind.

It takes me a little while, a full glass of wine for me, and TJ's three-quarters of the way through his beer while I give him an edited version, explaining that Dom's my boss at the club, and how we'd flirted and made eyes for months before anything actually happened. That recently, we've become more.

"So anyway, we sort of have a thing going."

"Are you telling me that your strip-club-owner boss is now your *boyfriend*?" TJ growls, disbelief and anger mixing in equal parts in his voice. "Are you shitting me, Allie-gator?"

I smile a bit at the label, even though TJ's obviously not happy about it. "You just saw him. Would you say he's a boy-*anything*? Yes, we're dating. Although, he's not really the casual type. Neither am I, I guess. It's gotten very serious, very fast. And before you ask, he isn't taking advantage of me because of work. He stayed away from me because of his being my boss. Not until my work contract changed did he even approach me."

TJ swallows back his frustration and finishes off his beer. "Okay, so you've got a boyfriend. I'm not done with that, but let's move on to question two. Why do you have a protective detail? Are you in trouble?"

I shake my head, standing up to get us both refills. "No, not really. He's just being careful. He's a powerful man in this city, and that comes with risks, Teej. They're real, and Dom's well-equipped to handle them. I'm not, and I'm certainly not used to *being* a risk. I just didn't think about it when I saw you. I know better."

TJ looks incredulous, accepting his beer only by reflex. "*You know better?* Are you serious right now? Do you hear yourself? Is that why you suddenly went from laughing and giggly girl-out-with-her-brother to shrinking-violet-apologetic when you saw him? If that's what he does to you, I should have pulled the fucking trigger."

I shift, pulling my legs underneath me and taking a big gulp of wine.

"It's not like that. It's just his . . . life requires that I accept limitations. Limitations that he places upon himself just as much as he asks me to do the same. He's sweet in his own way, protective and caring, and he encourages me to become all I can be. But what I did tonight is like . . ." I search my mind for something to make him understand. "Being protective is like his love language or something, and I just shit all over that. Imagine if you'd bought Janine a dozen red roses and instead of saying thank you and putting them in a vase, she just ignored them and forgot, let them rot on the counter without a care. It's a piss-poor analogy, but pretty much spot-on."

He flinches and runs his hands over his face, his eyes downcast. "Well, I won't be bringing Janine roses any damn time soon anymore. That's for fucking sure."

His voice breaks at the end, and suddenly, I realize why my bro's turned up out of the blue. All evening, we've been chatting, reminiscing about the good old days, and it hadn't occurred to me that he's been intentionally directing the conversation to the past so that he didn't have to talk about the present.

I'd been so caught up in my own head, not sure how to explain everything going on in my own life, that I'd readily let him keep us in the carefree days of our youth.

But now I can see that was a mistake. Regardless of my relationship with Dominick, and TJ's questions about how Dom can be overprotective, my brother's in pain, and he has issues that we need to discuss. I'm okay, but he suddenly looks like he's truly not.

"Spill the beans, TJ. What's going on with Janine?"

He sits silently, his jaw opening from time to time as he tries to start, but each time, he closes it. I noticed the habit the last time we were together, something he picked up in his time in the military. Before then, he'd talk first, think later. Now my brother's a lot more thoughtful.

"She's been distant when I'd get to call home," TJ finally says quietly, rubbing at his cheeks. "I thought the deployment was wearing on her. Shit, I understand. It was wearing on me too."

He huffs a laugh full of pain, and I reach over to take his hand. He squeezes back, holding on for dear life.

"I wanted to surprise her, thought it'd be like one of the fucking viral videos with her running into my arms and hugging me tight when I came home early. Hell, I even put in for a transfer so I could stay stateside for a bit, be home for dinner and shit."

I see the tear run down his cheek, but he swipes it away angrily. He's quiet for a solid minute, lost in the video playing out in his head.

"What happened when you got home?" I ask, forcing him back to this moment.

"I took a buddy with me. He'd used his hazard pay to buy one of those really good camcorders. Like the dude could have filmed for Channel 7 with the fucking thing. I wanted it captured for eternity, you understand? I walked in the house, grinning like a fucking fool at the load of laundry waiting to be folded on the couch and the dishes in the sink. It felt real, ya know? Like she hadn't spit-shined up for some big homecoming. I remember smelling vanilla cupcakes, best damn smell ever."

He pauses, shaking his head miserably. "Janine doesn't cook, not a lick. But she likes the house to smell like she's been baking so she burns these candles all the time."

I nod, and he disappears back into his story.

"So I'm walking down the hall, my buddy following me, recording. But when I opened the bedroom door, thinking she was going to be so happy to see me, she was . . . she was . . ."

He chokes, growling out in frustration.

"She was what, TJ?"

He takes a fortifying breath, spitting the words out like they burn his tongue. "She was getting railed by some guy. I caught her red-handed, Allie. Fucking some guy in our bed while I was on deployment."

I wince, pain and shock rolling through me. I've met Janine a bunch of times and always liked her. She was a bit distant while TJ was on deployment, having her own circle of support, but she'd been nothing but good to him.

Until now.

"Oh, my God! I'm so sorry!" I whisper, squeezing his hand. "What'd you do? Please tell me you didn't kill the guy, or if you did, let me call Dominick to see if he can hide the body."

It's just an attempt at humor, something he and I have done at inappropriate times since we were little kids, but TJ's eyes flash dangerously, and I wince.

"Too soon?"

He coughs and shakes his head. "No, and no, I didn't kill him. Dude saw me and bolted out of there like his ass was on fire, yelling he didn't know she was married. Didn't even put his clothes on, just scooped up his pants like a fumbled football. He's not the one I was mad at anyway."

His voice gets hard, bitterness seeping in at the edges, "She's the one that stood up there in a white fucking dress, promising me forever, in front of everyone we knew and cared about. We talked about my deployments, had a plan so she wouldn't be left alone. She just changed her mind? Or fell out of love? Or fucking got bored? I don't know what the fuck she was thinking, but I know it's over. I packed my shit and got the hell outta there."

I nod in understanding. "I'm so sorry. I don't know what to say other than that sucks and I'm sorry. Anything you need, I'm here for you, brother. TJ—" I stop myself. "Fuck, I want to kick her ass for you!"

The corners of his mouth tilt up just a tiny bit, and he lets out a watery sigh that tells me the worst of the storm is past.

"No, don't do that, even though it might be fun to watch, and the thought that you would means a lot."

We hug, and when we lean, back I punch TJ lightly in the chest. "Don't forget, I fought Susannah Brighton for you in the fourth grade when she stole your lunch money. I can sure lay a beatdown on Janine now if need be. You'd just have to hold my earrings because something tells me that bitch would fight dirtier than old Susannah."

It's a weak attempt at humor, but it seems to break him out of the dark pit he's circling. I'm still shocked she'd be that cruel, and if I were anywhere near where she is, I'd be smacking that bitch up right properly.

"Seriously TJ, I'm sorry. You deserve better than that."

His brave shrug is half-hearted, but his broken heart is painfully obvious on his face. "I know that, but there are nights I blame myself too. Lot of what-ifs, like what if I'd made her my number-one and not the uniform. I made my move to be here for her, but I guess it was too little, too late."

I grab the shaggy sides of his hair, forcing him to look at me. "You listen and you listen good, Mister. This is her screw-up. She made those promises, and she's the one who went back on her word. You did exactly what you said you'd do, and she didn't. This is not on you. You're one of the best people I know, and you deserve better than her."

"Thanks, Allie-Gator."

Slowly, our conversation starts up again, returning to the safe zone of banal chatter about his buddies overseas and all the things he's seen and done. I think the distraction is good for him, at least for a bit, and we studiously avoid discussing Janine or Dominick for the rest of the night. As the clock hits midnight, he staggers up, weaving a little before walking toward my bathroom.

"I think I'm gonna need to crash on your couch tonight, Sis. That is, if your boytoy isn't coming back for a midnight booty call?"

"It's so not like that, assface."

He smirks, planting a hand on the doorframe of my bathroom. "Too soon?"

That's it. I grab a pillow and toss it at him, hitting him squarely in the nose, a trick I probably couldn't repeat if I wanted to.

"Keep it up, GI Joe. You're welcome to the couch, and if Dom does show back up, I'll make sure to keep the moans and screams to an *uncomfortable* level. 'Oh, Daddy, just like that!' "

TJ blinks before pretending to gag, reminding me of when we were kids and I was asked out for my first date. He'd somehow just watched *The Girl Next Door* and told me Robbie Jenkins was going to shove his tongue in my mouth. I'd thought he was kidding, going on and on about how gross that was until he was rolling on the floor, laughing at my innocence.

"You're welcome to my couch for as many nights as you want, TJ. You know that, right?"

His voice filters through the bathroom door, where I'm glad he's at least learned to close it behind him. As a kid, I had to listen to too much. "It's just tonight. I've got a room while I'm in town."

"Fuck that!" I argue. "No, you'll stay here. That's what family is for."

There's silence from the bathroom until the toilet flushes and TJ comes out, wiping at his mouth like he always does after he's used mouthwash.

"Allie, I'm doing good right now, especially considering our night. But it hits me sometimes, and I don't want to have a breakdown in front of my sister again. I just need some space. But thanks for tonight."

I understand but wish he would just stay here and let me take care of him a bit. Getting up, I nab him a blanket and pillow from the linen closet and help him set up the couch into a makeshift bed.

"Here you go . . . hope you don't mind the pink fuzziness."

TJ's sleepy but still waves his hands in mock protest. "Allie, stop. I've slept sitting upright, on the ground in the freezing cold and the sweltering heat, and with a light shining in my eyes. A cushy couch with a pillow and a blanket is already a luxury I appreciate."

I pat his arm, nodding. "Okay, holler if you need anything. We'll do breakfast in the morning, 'kay?"

He grunts as he rolls onto his side, and I choose to take that as agreement. Before I even make it down the hallway, I can hear his even breathing. Guess he really can fall asleep anywhere, anytime.

Lucky him, because I don't think I'll sleep at all tonight.

Heading back to my bedroom, I pick up my phone. I want to call Dominick, needing to hear his voice, but I'm not sure if this is something we should do on the phone. I can't imagine how terrified he must've been. He's not a man with friends, family, and definitely not one with lovers he cares about. I suspect he's let me in closer than anyone in a long time.

I hit speed dial, waiting for Logan to pick up instead.

"Yes?" His voice is stone-cold.

"Um, hey, Logan. I am so sorry for any problem I might've caused. Did you or the guys get in trouble?"

Logan chuckles darkly, and I can hear him shift around, probably sitting in his car or something. "Trouble? No, although Gavin feels like crap right now, even though he did exactly what he was supposed to do." His words are double-edged, hitting home the point that I didn't hold up my end of the deal. "Allie, gonna be honest. You scared us shitless."

That's Logan, always straight to the point. "I know. And I'll fix it, I promise. But I need you to do something for me tonight."

His scoff is pretty obvious, even through my phone. "You're asking me for a favor, at midnight, after giving up my night off to chase you all over town? You got some big brass ones, Allie."

I startle, realization dawning. "How did you track me down? You didn't follow me from the studio, and Dom said something about smoothies. How'd he know that?"

I can't see him, but I can almost hear the shrug in his words. "You need to discuss that with him. Some of it's just that I've got skills. So, what did you want?"

He's back to all-business, his voice crisp and distant, not the sometimes slightly friendlier guy he's been with me lately. I guess I deserve it after what I've put him through.

"Can you watch him for me, Logan? When he left, he was cold, and I know it sounds crazy, but he's not that man with me. Ever. And I'm scared for him tonight. Can you just make sure he's okay?"

He sighs, the sound staticky in the phone. "He's fine. He's tucked in for the night. Safe and sound. I promise."

His words reassure me and give me the tiniest sliver of hope that I might actually sleep.

CHAPTER
Fourteen

DOMINICK

SETTLING into the rich leather chair behind my home office desk, I pick up the file folder that Logan hand-delivered an hour ago. I twist my head first one way, then the other, the pops satisfying as the crackles ripple down my spine, relaxing me.

Before opening the file, I look at the picture. It's strange, how the eyes are so similar, and there's a hint of shared lineage in the jawline that I can see now. His deep brown eyes stare back at me from the matte paper, full of neutral apathy. No smile, no anger, just one of roughly a million soldiers, but this one is different, special. Not because of anything he's done but because of who he is.

Specialist Tyler David Bancroft, Junior. Also known as TJ . . . Tyler Junior.

I reach over and pick up my tumbler of scotch, sipping at it as I study TJ's file. He's probably the apple of his daddy's eye, I'd wager. More importantly, he's the brother of my Allie.

Last night did not go well. I was too angry, too hurt. As real as possible threats are, paranoia had let ugly possibilities brew in my mind. Though I think her brother might be the type to find some degree of respect in my actions, judging by the way he instantly protected her. He wasn't quite as ruthless as he should have been. He did make a mistake . . . but he was willing to pull a gun on a stranger.

It could have been worse. He could've been a weakling, one of the sheep that make up so many of the common man. Maybe throw out some bluster and then squeal in the corner when he's pushed. The kind of man I couldn't possibly respect.

No, TJ is someone worthy of my attention, though the idea of going toe-to-toe with him over Allie should give me pause. But strangely enough, I find the idea of testing myself against him invigorating, as if I can prove myself worthy and earn her affection.

I sigh at the fanciful ideology and return to studying my target. TJ is currently on leave from the Army for three months pending a transfer. Seems TJ somehow timed his rotation just right and figured out a way to get himself three months of time off before going off to be a chopper pilot. Smart boy.

Looking over his service record, all his reports show him to be an excellent soldier, intelligent and well-equipped to both do what he's told and think on his feet. The letter from his platoon leader said he was only recommending TJ because he knew he'd lose him one way or another. Either to Warrant Officer school or to his being snatched away to be a Sergeant in another unit. So professionally, he's stellar.

Personally, though, his life seems to be falling apart. While no papers have been filed, it seems his wife spent his year overseas getting frisky.

After finding out, TJ waited for his unit to get back from the 'Stan before going on leave, and he's currently got a room in a hotel across town on the South Side, Pete's territory.

Everything in his backstory corresponds with the matching report I have on Allison. Father and mother happily married, well-educated, and live in the suburbs two states away.

But the things I really need to know aren't on these pages, though I'm going to give my people credit. It's a good start. There are so many intangibles about someone, like how Allie's pre-employment report didn't speak to her inappropriate sense of humor, her work ethic . . . her ability to make a desolate man feel alive again. I suspect there are key factors missing from TJ's report too.

And I don't like missing information.

My entire empire is built on knowing things before others and reading people better than anyone else. It's what allows me to be in place before my opponents know what happened. It gives me strength.

While this file tells me a lot, it doesn't tell me everything. And until I know, I'm going to have to consider TJ a problem.

A worthy adversary, perhaps . . . but regardless of the matter, he's a danger to what I'm building with Allie.

I close his file and set it on the side of my desk, thinking for a moment until the sound of feet thundering down the hall to my office catches my attention. I'm reaching for the pistol I keep under my lap drawer when the door opens, and my hand relaxes as I see Allie burst through like the world's cutest rhino charge.

"Dominick!" Allie says loudly.

At the same time, one of the cleaning staff pushes past and says at the same time, "I'm sorry, sir." Fiona's saucy accent blares over Allie's words, cutting her off. "I told Miss Bancroft she was welcome but to please wait for someone to announce her."

Allie's glare captures my attention and I wave Fiona off. She's new. She doesn't know Allie has free reign to come and go as she pleases. Fiona nods, shutting the door quietly behind her, leaving me alone with Allie.

She's fuming, her hands planted on her hips and looking so adorable that I have to grin at her gall before remembering that I'm supposed to be mad at her too. Quickly, I rearrange my features into the coolly collected sneer I typically use to show disappointment.

Allie, of course, is my opposite, and since she's riled up too, her madness comes out in a flurry of energetic pacing, her skirt flexing and thigh muscles bunching in ways that leave my cock tingling in my pants.

"So, I spent the night thinking, and some of breakfast too . . . TJ says hi, by the way."

Sarcasm coats her last words, and she tosses her hair. I want to pull it to my nose and see if it smells as heavenly as it gleams in the light of my office.

Instead, I lift one eyebrow warily. "I see."

"Well, okay, he didn't say that exactly, but he didn't stop me when I told him where I was going, so considering the Mexican standoff we had rolling last night, I'm choosing to call that a win, Mister. Anyway, that can't happen again. Not the gun pulling, not the scary drama where you think something bad happened just because I went for a smoothie, and not the stomping off angry deal. Okay, that one was a bit exaggerated. You definitely didn't stomp off, but you get my point."

Honestly, I have virtually no idea what she's talking about. All I can think about is the way her frenetic energy envelops me, the flush on her cheeks making me want to cup her face, the rapid-fire pace of her words making me want to kiss her to shut her up.

She stops, her word salad finally coming to a stop as she stares at me, and after a moment, I decipher enough to respond. "And what do you propose to do about this?"

I'm genuinely curious what she thinks is the appropriate response to everything that's gone on. To me, the best-case scenario would be for her to do as she's told and allow my guards to be with her at all times, for my sanity and her safety. For her to submit to being mine completely.

Not tamed. She's too wild, too beautifully unique to ever be tamed, and that would dim her gloriousness. But a little . . . domestication? Constraint? Maybe.

My lips tilt up at the idea of a tame Allie, not even able to picture what such a creature would look like. She's like a lioness. Sure, you can stick one in a cage, but that's cruel. If you are going to have one, let it have safety barriers but plenty of area to roam.

The question is . . . will Allie be willing to live within the barriers I've built for myself as well? Because if she's a lioness, I'm a lion, the pride leader.

"I propose transparency," she replies. "Again, I'm willing to admit that I was wrong. You were too," she says, getting a hit in, but I don't stop her roll. "And yes, I realize this is eerily similar to my guard issue before, though that one was accidental, a reasonable assumption on my part, and this one was thoughtlessly intentional. But I'll come back to that."

She holds up one finger, her eyes flashing and her head shaking back and forth. "Wait, Dom. Let's put our cards on the table, shall we?"

"I don't play poker, but I do own an underground casino, so why not?"

My unusual half-joke gets a small smile from Allie, who twists and sits down on the edge of my desk, which is amazingly cute.

"Fine. Here goes . . . I like you a whole fucking lot. And I don't say that lightly or to many people. I'm excited to get to know you more. So, I am sorry. Truly sorry for scaring you."

I inhale deeply through my nose, surprised at how soothing her words are to my soul. "Apology accepted."

She quirks her eyebrow, planting a hand on my desk blotter and leaning down, staring into my eyes.

"And?"

I lean forward. "And what?"

Allie sighs dramatically, not seeing my subtle sarcasm, and hops off my desk, taking two paces before turning and throwing her hands in the air. "And this is the part where you apologize for sitting in my apartment like a creeper. It's also where you explain how you got in my apartment in the first place and how you knew I'd been 'sipping smoothies' when I didn't have anyone with me when I left the studio."

I drum my fingers on the desk, not wanting to lie to her but afraid to tell her the full truth.

My hesitation is apparent, and she comes back around to sit on my desk again, looking into my eyes. "Transparency, Dominick. You want it from me, you need to give it back."

She's throwing down a gauntlet, and I know that I could lose her in this moment if I don't share some hard truths.

"I can't give you that in all things, nor would you want it, Allie," I tell her with a shake of my head. "There are things that if you knew them, they could put you in danger. But I will say that putting a tracker in someone's phone is rather easy. Logan followed it and watched you for me until I could get back to town."

"And getting in my apartment?"

That one's easy. "Your doorknob was replaced a few months back, remember? The locksmith gave me a copy of the key."

"He just gave you a key?" she asks, looking horrified. "What the hell? You could've been a fucking serial killer, for all he knew!"

I clear my throat, realizing again just how . . . innocent Allie is. Secrets of bad men aren't something she's used to. The biggest one, of course, is sitting in this very chair.

"I'm quite certain he knew exactly who I was."

"Oh," she says quietly, nodding. "Okay, so to surmise, the locksmith gave the friendly local Mob boss a key to my apartment, you're tracking my phone, and you have guards following me everywhere."

She stops, then looks up like she's not believing the words that are coming out of her mouth. "You know that's crazy, right? It's like some tier-one stalker shit, Dominick. You're freaking me out."

There is honesty in her voice, but I can tell that she's only saying it because she thinks she should be nervous about it. Her heart is racing, but it's not in fear.

Or at least, not totally in fear.

I reach up, tracing the flutter in her neck, enjoying the satin of her skin beneath my palm. Unconsciously, she tilts her head, giving me more access and proving me right. She's not scared of me. She simply thinks she should be.

"Transparency," I whisper, my voice hushed, barely audible in my soundproofed office. "I like you a lot too, Allison. More than like, though I won't say it now and scare you away. Because I can see that all that I've done scares you, but the words I could say scare us both."

She nods, but in her eyes, I see the same hunger for them that I have. "Dom—"

"But my life comes with a certain degree of violence and unpleasantness, and the idea that you might get caught up in that terrifies and saddens me," I continue softly, stroking her cheek. "The night of the shooting, you were given a small taste of the world I live with every day. So for doing what I've done, I won't apologize. For not telling you, yes, I do apologize. But for us to take this further, to explore this . . ."

I let my hand slip down her neck, a finger tracing along her collarbone, and delight at the goosebumps that rise against my touch. Her eyes flutter closed, and she lets out a soft sigh.

I wait until her eyes open again, this time dark with desire, but I have to hold back a little. She must know.

"There will be rules, and you need to follow them."

Her eyes flash, and she pulls back, breaking our contact as she looks at me warily. "Rules? I don't think I like the sound of that."

I chuckle and lean back in my chair. "I'm sure you don't, but you must follow them or . . . you must leave. For your own safety."

She doesn't like the ultimatum one bit. But I can't waver on this. I can't allow any negotiation.

"Perhaps you'd like to hear the rules before you decide?"

She nods once, crossing her arms over her chest.

"Rule number one. You need to stay where you're supposed to be at all times. If there is a change in plans, you notify me or the guard watching you. I'm not trying to stop you from going anywhere you want, but someone will know where you are at all times.

"Rule number two. Your phone is to be turned on, charged, and with you at all times so that you can be tracked.

"Rule number three. Trust that I have your wellbeing in mind, and if there is a time where I ask you to go somewhere or do something that sounds wrong, you do as I instruct you to. I can't have you questioning me in the moment if there's a security risk. I can explain later, but in the moment, go without question."

It's basically things we've already discussed, just laid much barer with no pretty words and devoid of modifiers like *please* and *thank you*. These are non-negotiable and she must understand that.

She looks at me with sass in her eyes. "And if I agree to these terms, do they hold true for you as well? Are you going to tell me your whereabouts every hour of the day and let me track your phone and such?"

She already knows the answer to her questions, but I still lay it out. "No. I'll be as open and honest with you as I can be, but knowing everything would be dangerous information. But you can trust that I'm being as safe as possible while doing my job."

"Can I trust that you're not out fucking some woman in every corner of the city?" she asks, her words pouty with disappointment at turnabout not being fair play. I force her legs to spread open for me, her knees laid back against the edge of my desk, and harshly knead her honeyed thighs, dimpling the skin with my rough handling.

She gasps, but she lets me hold her there, not fighting to close her thighs against me. "You can trust that the only woman I have any interest in—have had interest in—is right here in front of me."

I lean in, inhaling her spicy floral scent before nuzzling against the silk covering her mound. Allie gasps, running her hand through my hair, urging me closer.

"This pretty pussy of yours is all I want . . . to eat, to fuck, to own."

She groans above me, my dirty words igniting her passion as much as my closeness. Her hips roll, desperate to get closer to my mouth. Running my thumb down the inside of her leg, I rub her through the flimsy fabric, enjoying the slickness as her panties become drenched. "So sweet, so *mine*."

Suddenly, she sits up, palm to my shoulder, pushing me away and panting, "Wait, wait."

I growl at her like a toddler throwing a tantrum after having his favorite toy taken away and hold myself steady, not letting her move me from the cradle of her legs.

"Dom . . . remember I said I'd come back to my messing up again?"

I barely nod, knowing that this is important but at the same time not wanting to handle it right this moment.

My words vibrate against her skin. "Do you want to remind me of that now, Allison?"

I lick a long line up the crease where her leg meets her body, nibbling along the edge of her panties, and Allie whimpers but keeps her voice steady and slightly stronger than before.

"Yes, I do. Do you remember what you did when I was bad then?"

I freeze, my eyes meeting hers and seeing the meaning in their depths. She's asking for it, not in so many words, but she's giving me the opening to spank her ass.

The power in that is not in the actual contact of my hand on her skin but in the trust she places in me to allow it. The gift of what she's offering floors me.

In this instant, I can see a future where this woman will give me everything I demand, to be my one and true queen, equal, partner, Yin to my Yang . . . and still somehow surprise me.

I push back from her and get up, my cock straining my pants to her delighted notice as I remove my tie, letting my voice drop lower.

"Turn around and bend over, Allison."

She hops from the desk, spinning around and bending forward. My flexible girl grabs her ankles, her ass presented high in the air.

I push her skirt up to encircle her waist and rip the silky panties down her legs, leaving them bunched around her knees. I stay back, enjoying the view for a moment before touching her, running my fingertips over her outer hip, my cock throbbing as she shivers.

"Dominick . . ."

I place a steadying hand on her lower back. "Allison. Rule number one."

I smack her right cheek hard, instantly pinking it before caressing it, the heat mixed with the soothing gentleness that makes her cry out in want and desire.

"Be where I'm supposed to be. Check in if it changes."

I pause and whisper roughly, "Why?"

She turns to look at me, her eyes flashing with acceptance. "To keep me safe."

It's good enough, a superficial understanding of the deeper truth. I spank her twice more before caressing her again, my fingers brushing lower to the wet dampness of her center.

"Rule number two. Tell me."

Her answer is instant, eager this time. "Keep my phone with me."

My hand stills and I repeat my question. "Why?"

She sobs ever so softly, her voice ragged as I trace her pussy lips. "Care . . . because you care."

Ah, closer to the truth. My girl is insightful.

I give her three smacks. Each blow is exciting, demanding, and painful. I never, ever will cause her real pain, but at the same time, this mock pain is electric to us both.

"Rule number three."

She pauses, and I can see her mind working, making me wonder what her concern is with the rule.

Finally, she simply says, "Trust you."

My breath is taken away at the honesty in her words. I'd expected her to robotically quote back what I'd said, but she boiled it down to the real meaning behind the words.

She's right.

Rule three is simply . . . trust.

I lean down, laying a gentle kiss to her heated skin, and she shivers as I ask once more, "Why?"

"Because I'm yours," she whispers, trembling.

And that's it, the deepest truth we have revealed yet. I know there will be more, both ugly and pretty, but I have to hold back, even as I demand her all.

She's not ready for me, not entirely, but she will be.

I can't allow myself to even entertain any other possibility.

Her knees give out, and she sinks down to the carpet, coyly looking over her shoulder at me.

"Do you remember what else you said that night?" Her flirty smile doesn't let me search for the words she wants, so she answers her own question. "Reward and punishment."

I bite my lip to stop from smirking, knowing exactly what she wants, and instead, I have to force venom into my words. "And do you think you deserve a reward after scaring the fuck out of me?"

She shakes her head, her ass moving hypnotically in time with her swishing hair. "No, but I think you deserve one."

I can't hold back my smirk any longer as I nod, unbuckling my pants and letting them fall before pulling my hard cock from my boxer briefs. She turns and crawls two steps to get closer, her ass settling on her heels and her eyes locked on mine as she takes me in her hand.

I'm throbbing, aching to feel her touch as her silky soft palm grips me surely, stroking up and down. She leans in, pressing a kiss to my crown and then swirling her tongue around my slit to taste my precum.

"Mmm . . . you're delicious, Dominick."

"Go ahead, Allie," I whisper, watching her. "Suck me down your throat. Give me my reward."

Her lips stretch wide around my girth, and I know she's having a hard time taking all of me, but she works at it, coating me in saliva and relaxing into the up and down bobbing of her head.

Deeper and deeper with every thrust, I let her lead until she guides me to her throat, gagging ever so slightly. She seems to take it as a personal failure and doubles down, going faster and deeper, fighting the impulse to stop for breath.

She's driving me mad, but I want even more of her. "Do you trust me, Allison?"

The look in her eyes tells me more than any words ever could, but she still tries, humming her answer against my skin. I spread my legs wider, taking a solid stance, and twist my fingers into her hair, forcing her head still and holding her under my control.

I pull back, letting her breathe, and she gasps and puts her hands behind her back. "Take me."

I growl lightly as I start to fuck her mouth, pounding hard and fast, much rougher than she was able to suck me. She gags as I press into her throat, her eyes watering, and I watch carefully to see if she's had enough. But she bravely takes it all as lust shines in her eyes, increasing even as tears start to trickle down her cheeks. I know not to stop though, as her tongue doesn't try to push me out but instead swirls and takes me, pulling me in deeper.

And she's never looked lovelier.

Amid the symphony of her moans and choking, I grunt, talking her through it all. "That's a good girl, Allie. Take me and I'll give you a reward too. You're going to swallow every drop of my cum."

Her eyes beg, as hungry for her reward as I am to give it. I tilt her head back slightly, letting her throat open more, and use my grip on her head to help move her against me, taking her for my own pleasure.

I see her hips squirm, and I know she wants to have release, but she's such a good girl, her hands still clenched behind her back.

"Hmm, so good of you. If I were cruel, I'd leave you on the edge so you remember the rules. Should I?"

She whimpers against me, and I shake my head, smiling down at her. "I want you to come, Allie. Come with my cock down your throat and your fingers buried in your pussy. Reward us both."

Permission granted, her hand almost flies between her legs as she buries her fingers deep in her pussy. Her moans become more desperate as I slam into her mouth, my balls resting on her chin as she swallows. The caress of her throat sends me over, and I hold her there, nose buried against me as I give her jet after jet of my cum.

She swallows it all down before she moans helplessly around her mouthful of my creamy cock, her orgasm ripping through her so quickly it startles us both, her body jerking and shuddering against me.

I pull back slowly, letting her lick every droplet from my skin, sucking and nuzzling my softening cockhead before she withdraws her hand from her pussy.

"Give it to me," I command, holding out my hand for her fingers. She rises to her knees, reaching up as I bend down slightly, sucking her slick fingers into my mouth and cleaning her until there's nothing but her normal sublime taste on my tongue.

Letting her go, I help her up before we readjust our clothes. Sitting down in my chair, I gather her in my arms, holding her and somehow feeling like we just survived our first gauntlet. The bit I've revealed could've easily been too much for her.

She'd be well within her rights, and her right mind, to run screaming from me now, while there's still a small chance I'd let her go. Instead, she presses her cheek to my chest, holding me tightly.

"So, about rule one."

I can't help it. I can hear her teasing tone, but I still growl. "Non-negotiable."

I can feel her smile against me, and she runs a hand through my hair. "Chill out, I'm not arguing. I'm giving notice. TJ is coming over for dinner tonight. You're coming too. You are two of the most important men in my life, and you definitely got off to a bad start, so I'm calling a do-over. Tonight."

I have work tonight, nothing special, just schmoozing around the club and keeping an eye on things. But that can wait until later.

"Fine. What time?"

She hops out of my lap, making me regret it for a moment, but she's so excited that I smile along with her as she squeals. "Really? I thought that was going to be a harder sell! I mean . . . yeah, you're coming to dinner. It's *non-optional*."

She dropped her voice there at the end in an imitation of my normal gravely growl. "I'm not that bad."

"So you say," she taunts before humming. "How about seven thirty?"

I kiss her forehead, pleased. More than enough time. "And this afternoon? Do you need an escort anywhere?"

She starts to shake her head no and then reconsiders and sighs. "Yes, I'm going to the grocery store and then home. This is going to take some getting used to. What if I just want to run out and get ice cream at midnight? Am I going to have to wait for Logan or Gavin or whoever to get there just so I can go to the store?"

I smirk, shaking my head. "First, you don't like ice cream. Second, you could call a delivery service. Third, if you must get out, then yes, you'd wait for an escort. Most of the time, though, someone would be there within five minutes. Clear?"

She doesn't like it, but I can tell she's trying her best. "Yeah, yeah . . . understood. But it's weird. And overkill. Do *you* get escorted everywhere?"

"When I need it, yes."

We agreed on transparency, but I'm already holding back from her. Baby steps, I tell myself. She thinks an escort is too much, though she didn't balk at the tracking that much.

But the sheer depth of my obsession? Cameras and the apartments?

Weird? More like criminal.

But that's who I am. That's my life.

She'll adjust, little by little, one baby step at a time.

Fifteen

ALLIE

DINNER IS NOT GOING WELL. I'd planned everything as well as I could, setting the coffee table with a tablecloth and candles, even giving the floor pillows a fresh fluff so we'd be comfortable sitting on them.

Not the usual dinner party set-up, but when my dining room is more dance studio, it's what I've got.

Maybe I'd been stupid to think getting the two of them together under better circumstances would make the introductions friendlier, the conversation politer, the air more welcoming.

Nope. Not with these two, apparently. I guess maybe it's asking for a bit too much, too fast, considering the start.

It's been a tense hour of interrogation-style questions, dismissive answers, and barely-contained dick measuring as TJ tries to intimidate Dominick with some version of big brother protectiveness. It might work with another man, but not with Dom.

I try to stop my near-constant eye rolls. I'm no expert, but TJ's antics are clearly telling more about himself than anything he's gleaning from Dominick. I could have told him it was a waste of time. Dom's spent years hiding himself behind a mask.

And we've barely started the main course. I take a bite of my chicken parmigiana, thinking for the third time that I should've made something less time-intensive that I could just shove in their mouths to keep them quiet.

Speaking of . . . "More bread?" I ask, offering the breadsticks and crossing my fingers under the table that TJ might eat a whole stick of garlicky goodness in one go. Because if he keeps this up, I'm going to be stuffing one in his ear. "Teej?"

His crooked eyebrow tells me he knows what I'm trying to do, but he takes one anyway, taking a bite and talking around the mouthful with a look that tells me, *Take that.*

"So, you own a strip club?" TJ somehow manages to sneer the words without losing a crumb of breadstick.

Dom's eyes flick to me, wondering how much I've told him.

I glare back, telling him wordlessly, *Of course, I didn't tell him. I'm not stupid.* That's not my story to tell, and not one I'd share without permission. And a shot of something strong to give me courage.

Dominick's attention returns to TJ. "Yes, I own several businesses, one of which is a club."

"A strip club," TJ says with scorn. TJ is trying to make the club sound seedy and disgusting, and by his ownership, painting Dominick with the same brush. But his disdain for the club stabs at me like a knife, hot betrayal burning through me. I set my fork down with a clatter.

Both men turn to me at the sharp sound, and TJ immediately reads the anger in my eyes. He grimaces, and his shoulders slump a little. "Shit. Alliegator, I didn't mean it like that."

Once upon a time, I would've wilted and just forgiven him, but this is something I've had to deal with over and over again, finding strength I didn't know I had, to handle other people's misconceptions. I swing my legs around, getting up onto my knees and squaring my shoulders, strong and proud as I stare at my brother.

"Bullshit. You meant it just like that, trying to say that Dom's some sleazy guy who owns a sketchy club full of whores. That's what you implied. But while you were busy insulting him, you forgot . . . I fucking work there."

He cringes at my words, but also my volume, which has increased as I verbally slay him. "Allie—"

"I'm not defending Dominick—he doesn't need me to do that—but defending myself and my friends. The girls there at Petals, they're good people who work hard. I don't need you sitting at my dinner table insulting them or me."

TJ reaches for my hand. "I'm sorry. I didn't mean it like that, truly. I know you're an amazing dancer and a good person. I just . . ." He shakes his head, trying to put his thoughts together. Finally, he speaks, his voice quiet. "I just didn't think this was where you were headed. You're a stripper, dating your boss. You've gotta see how I could want more than that for you."

I squeeze his hand, understanding that he's coming from a place of good intentions but going about it all wrong. He doesn't understand . . . yet. But that doesn't mean his verbal barbs hurt any less. Part of me wants to rage back. *How dare he insult me like that?* "The truth is, you're right. I am a stripper, dating my boss. It just doesn't mean what you think it does. It's so much more than you realize. And *I* am more than you think I am . . . stronger, happier, healthier than you've probably ever known me to be. You just can't see it. And that makes me sad, not angry."

Dominick has been quiet during our exchange. I appreciate that he let me handle it on my own, seeing that this was something I needed to do myself.

But I know he's analyzing every word and expression and takes his time before he finally speaks. "TJ, when was the last time you saw Allison dance?"

TJ flushes nearly a deep purple, in either embarrassment or anger or some combination of the two, I can't really tell. "I don't want to see her like that."

Dominick sighs slightly, and I'm glad he's patient. "Not at my club. That I can understand. But anywhere. What about watching her do ballet?"

TJ's mouth snaps closed, and I don't think Dominick realizes just how much of a 'punch' he just landed on TJ. "Oh, it's been a while, I guess. I've been gone and it was always kind of her thing."

He looks at me, both of us thinking back through the years and various recitals my family came to. TJ would whine about it beforehand, like brothers do, I suppose, but he was always the loudest clapper, cheering me with enthusiasm.

"Probably three or four years ago. Right before I joined the service."

Dominick hums and looks at me with so much intensity in his eyes that I feel my pulse start to race with each passing second. "She is beauty in motion on the stage, both at the club, where she brings more grace and elegance than the clientele probably deserves, and in her ballet performances. The public performance she had of The Nutcracker . . . she brought the house down. She is still your little sister, the sweet ballerina who needed her brother's protection and support. But she is also a fierce woman who stakes her territory on the Petals stage, needs permission from no one to be her best self, and quite frankly, I'm honored to call her my woman."

His sweetly expressive words turn hard, challenging as he stares at TJ, who's shrinking by the second. "Allison also happens to work her ass off on the pole, on the barre, and in life. She deserves a family who supports her in that, not one that makes her feel 'less than' because of the choices she's made."

TJ nods, suitably chastised, but my heart's soaring in my chest at Dominick's words. I've seen him be rough, handling business like a monster, and dirty, bending me over his knee, but this is my favorite Dominick. The one who wields his usage of words even better than his control over the city.

That's his true power, the brilliance of his mind. And it's sexy as fuck. I grin, both at the irony of my foul language compared to Dom's and from the joy springing from inside to shine on my face.

"I didn't know you came to see my Nutcracker performance."

Dominick's look is pure smoldering desire, devotion, and a demonstration of the man he is. "An opportunity to see you do what you love is a gift I would not waste."

Swoon. I think I literally wobble a bit, lightheadedly giddy and on the verge of jumping into his lap. But we're not alone, and the air is only recently cleared, so I somehow restrain myself. But it's hard. So fucking hard. I wonder if he is?

For a moment, I have a mental flash of him ripping the pink leotard I like to wear for personal practice off my body and slamming into me as I stretch, one leg up and the other out, fully open to his vicious hammering. I know one thing . . . I'd love every second of it.

At the sound of a throat clearing, I mentally return to the present moment to see Dominick looking rather amused and TJ rolling his eyes, although mostly good-naturedly now.

"Oh, uh, thank you," I tell Dominick.

"Of course."

We have a moment of eye-fucking, the connection heating up though we both hold our positions on our floor pillows.

TJ decides to break in. "So, Prima Ballerina, tell me all about your new studio work then."

Eager to keep some positive momentum going, I launch into telling him all about the ballet classes I teach, the upcoming kids' performance, making sure to also include how successful my Diva Dance classes have been and that I'm leading pole classes at Encore too.

"I'm not going to pretend that what I do is common, but it's something I'm good at and that I enjoy. And it's paying off my medical bills faster than any other job I could have so that Mom and Dad don't have to worry about them."

TJ frowns. "You know Mom and Dad, hell, even I, would take on those bills in a second if it meant you weren't a stripper. They worried so much and wanted you to be healthy for so long, and now that you are, you're an—"

He stops himself, but I want to hear the words. I need to know what my brother thinks of me. "Finish your sentence, TJ. I'm a what?"

He shakes his head, like he knows he shouldn't say it, but I'm not letting him off that easily. It feels like this fight has been a long time coming, and we need to clear the air, even if it gets worse before it gets better. We're family, have pressed each other's buttons for so long and so well, that I know him like I know the back of my hand. So I poke at him, picking at just the right scab to force his hand.

"Don't wuss out now. You obviously have an opinion, so speak up or shut up. And I've never known you to be a pussy."

He growls. "Fine, you want to hear it? An embarrassment, Allie. You're an embarrassment. You think Mom and Dad are sitting around bragging about their stripper daughter to their friends over dinner?"

Fury runs through me at his audacity. "Oh, but they're bragging about their soldier son? Because you're doing *so* well right now?"

He recoils as if I slapped him, and I instantly regret throwing that in his face, the shame of my cruelty making me feel small inside. I truly didn't think about what I was saying, didn't realize that it would sound like I was blaming him for Janine's actions until the words were already out.

"I'm sorry, TJ. I didn't mean it like that, and I shouldn't have said it anyway."

But he shakes my apology off, turning his ire on Dominick once again. "You think you're good enough for my sister, huh? Because what I see is you turning her into a bitch."

He gets up, shoving the table slightly and stomping to the kitchen, where I can hear him breathing raggedly. My heart is in my throat as I wonder how everything went so wrong. TJ and I have always been so close, two peas in a pod. Sure, we've had fights, even some real doozies back in high school, but not like this. I'm horrified, embarrassed by our behavior with each other, but it's even worse that it happened in front of Dominick. I let my eyes drift toward him, afraid of the judgment and disappointment I'll see.

Dominick looks to me, his eyes full of so much that I can't even decipher everything swirling in their icy depths. He takes a steadying breath and looks at me with eyes full of . . . something.

"I don't, you know."

I lift my eyebrows questioningly, so caught up in TJ's outburst and my shame that I've totally lost the train of the conversation.

"Huh?"

"Think I'm good enough for you. Your brother's right. My world is dark and ugly, I'm violent and possessive, and you are light and beauty, strong and wild. But my heart has chosen you, and whether you want it or not, it's yours. And your heart is mine. *You* are mine, Allison. I'm choosing to be transparent with you as we agreed, but know that it's an unfamiliar territory for me. This is only for you."

I sit quietly, not sure what to say. It's powerful, more than anyone has ever spoken to me, certainly more than a man has shared. It feels good, but the intensity of his emotions is a lot to bear, and the dark depths both scare me and excite me equally.

He doesn't wait for my response, instead leaning over and weaving his fingers into my hair, holding my face lifted toward him to plant a soft kiss to my cheek. I fade into the supportive hold he has on me, needing the crutch for a moment.

The soft and hard, the brush of his lips and the grip on my head, are everything with him, driving me mad. I want him more than I even know . . . and at the same time, I'm afraid that I'm going to explode if I do.

I still can't turn away, and as I lay my head on his chest, he kisses my head one more time, his breath warm in my ear.

"Talk to your brother. He loves you and is hurting, drowning in a world of misery, and his only way to deal with it is to lash out at the one person he feels safest with . . . you. I know it's an impossible task, but don't take it personally. The harsh judgments he had are more telling of what he feels about himself right now, not you. He feels worthless, embarrassed, lost to someone else's decisions."

"You know about his wife?" I murmur, unsurprised somehow. "What she did?"

I can feel Dom's chin press into the top of my head once as he nods. "Yes."

I hear the challenge, daring me to ask how he knows, why he knows . . . because TJ sure as fuck didn't tell him. But I know Dominick and have no doubt that he had a full background check on TJ as soon as I introduced them.

It's not right, it's invasive and hostile, but it's who Dominick is. I sigh, sad and angry that Janine is putting TJ through the wringer but not able to forgive him so readily for the gut punches he's delivered to me tonight.

"Talk to him, Allison."

I nod. "I will."

"I need you to know, it took everything in me to restrain myself from coming to your defense tonight. I hate that he spoke to you that way, and if it were anyone else, I would've destroyed them. But you are a force, Allison. Mouthy, strong, with big brass balls and a sensitive heart. Tonight, you didn't need protection. Even though it hurt and was hard, maybe even ugly, you protected yourself. And it was glorious."

He lays a chaste kiss to my lips, and I breathe him in, letting the smoky wood smell of his cologne and faint hints of garlic and tomato surround me, buoy me for the upcoming storm.

TJ

I can still hear them. My fingernails scour at my scalp, pulling at the strands that feel so foreign atop my head, looking for any distraction. But their voices still register. He admits to her that he's unworthy of her, flat-out telling her that his world is violent and dangerous. But even that he couches in fancy words.

He's a slick fucker, I'll give him that.

And Allie seems totally enamored with his bullshit, not hearing through the pretty to the gritty reality. When he says, 'you are mine', I have to crouch down to stop myself from rushing in and punching the fuck out of him.

She isn't his.

She isn't anyone's.

She's my baby sister. She deserves better than this, better than him, for damn sure. She should have a good life, teaching kids ballet, performing in city performances if that's what makes her happy, maybe having a couple of kids of her own.

She deserves a good man who treats her right, not like a possession to claim. His assessment that I'm lashing out is spot-on, and though I refuse to admit it, the painful weight sits heavily on my shoulders.

I'm a loser . . . failed at my marriage, though I was willing to give her fucking everything. I hurt my sister, though she's the one person who's always been by my side, and I'm a disappointment to my parents, who loved Janine and were ecstatically pressing for grandchildren.

Yeah, sorry guys, definitely not happening now. It's all just so fucked up. I hear the door open and close, signaling that Dominick has left, and know my time is up. Allie is gonna be gunning for me, as well she should. But I can't deal with that right now.

I need to get out of here, get my shit straight or just get shit-faced, I'm not sure which.

But I know that I can't be here with Allie's sad eyes and encouragement to talk about my feelings.

I stride back into the living room, making a bee-line for the door, but Allie's words stop me for a moment.

"TJ, wait. We need to talk."

She doesn't sound angry, and it's tempting, but I shake my head and don't stop walking until my hand is on the doorknob. "Look, I'm sorry for the hurtful shit I said. Really, I am, Allie. But this shit show tonight? That guy? With his obsessive 'you're mine' shit? The club dancing? You deserve a hell of a lot better than that. You should get the whole picket fence, two-point-five kids, and a dog type of life. Fuck knows, you've earned it. And I can't sit back and watch while you toss it all away, working for a guy like that who'll only hurt you in the long run."

I don't let her respond, slamming the door behind me on my way out.

Way to go, asshole. Two seconds after the devil whispers pretty words in her ear, you're the one who cuts her feet out from underneath her. Who looks like the devil now?

I shake my head, angry at myself, at her, at him. Down the hall, I start to hit the button for the elevator and realize with a vague unease that the elevator is going up, not down.

I'm literally seconds behind Dominick and he should've taken the elevator down to the first floor to get to his car, but he went up to the fourth floor?

Something is off here.

I already don't like this guy, but this is . . . wrong. I turn and quietly enter the stairwell at the end of the hall, adjacent to the elevator, going up a floor. I wish I had my gun with me, but out of respect for Allie, I left it in my truck tonight. No time at the moment, although I can bet money that Dominick's carrying.

Slowly and quietly, I crack the door open to peek into the fourth-floor hallway. I see Dominick's back, his broad shoulders encased in a steel-grey dress shirt unmistakable. Silently, I watch as he pulls a keyring from his pocket and unlocks a door on the other end. He enters and the door clicks closed behind him.

I wait one heartbeat and then close the stairwell door, pausing as I try to think about the ramifications.

Dominick has an apartment in Allie's building.

I search my brain. *Did I know that? Did Allie say anything about them both working together and living in the same building?*

But I can't come up with any instance where she's said anything of the sort. And Dominick screams wealth and privilege, from his fancy clothes to the ridiculous ring on his pinky finger.

This building's nice enough, a damn sight better than the barracks, but this isn't his sort of place.

I almost go back to Allie and demand that she follow me up here and bang on Dominick's door. I imagine his smug face falling at being found out, but at the last moment, I stop myself, thinking.

What have I found, exactly?

If this is something innocent, or worse yet, that Allie knows about, I'm going to look like a goddamn fool. The imaginary image in my head shifts to one where he sweet-talks his way out of whatever this is and Allie believes him, making me even more of an ass.

I need to play this smart. I think she's safe, well, safe enough, for the night.

Turning as casually as I can, I make my exit, discreetly peeking in on every floor for anything unusual, but I see nothing until I hit the parking lot. Outside, I see a black Lexus across the street, a bald guy sitting in the driver's seat not even trying to avoid giving me an eye fuck as I come outside. Obviously, that's Dominick's guard he has stationed on Allie, which strangely doesn't make me feel any better.

I head to my truck and take my pistol out as soon as I have the doors locked and sit there for a full five minutes to see if the bald guy follows me, but all's quiet.

Driving back toward the hotel, I decide to stop at the bar down the street. A beer and some crappy tunes are just what I need to think this thing through.

Leaving my gun in the truck again, because guns and alcohol do not mix, I head inside. The bar is like one of a million others all around the world, dark and dingy, with buzzing neon and a ball game on the television.

Behind the bar, the tender's a woman, not too bad looking, honestly, but right now, it wouldn't fucking matter who it was, and I wouldn't give them a second glance.

"What can I get ya?"

"Draft, please."

She leaves, and I'm able to disappear into my thoughts for a bit.

For once, they're not about Janine and what I'm going to do alone, but about my sister and how I'm going to help her.

Missions . . . I know how to handle those.

CHAPTER
Sixteen

DOMINICK

SITTING BACK IN MY CHAIR, I take the time to let options play out in my head. It's the same whether I'm in business mode or personal mode. I saw it firsthand on the chess board, learning that it wasn't just about my next move but about what happens ten moves from now.

And I'm doing that now as I steeple my fingers, considering every play, every angle, every possibility.

What are the pieces of the game that I know?

I know TJ dislikes me for frankly valid reasons. He's taking out his anger with his own situation on Allison. Still, he was aware enough that he followed me upstairs and saw me enter my apartment. And he made Logan sitting outside.

Those last two facts are what give me pause. It makes me wonder . . . what could he be up to? And is he thinking clearly?

He's a smart man, military trained and experienced. Despite the future military career opportunities, he's a man who might feel he has nothing left to lose except for the one person he holds closest, my Allison.

I wished I'd realized he was behind me, but I have to give him credit that he was rather stealthy in that. Only the building security system, which I'm hacked into, of course, alerted me that the stairwell had been breached.

What surprised me, however, was that he didn't immediately return to Allie to sell me out.

That has my internal alarm bells beeping. He's up to something.

We've already established that he thinks I'm unworthy of her, but perhaps with this ammunition, he thinks Allie would see the logic of his argument. Perhaps he's right, that he could spin this in such a way that it would be the tipping point for her.

I don't think so, but I can't be totally sure.

My phone rings on the desk, the buzzing vibrating it across the surface.

Seeing Gavin's name, I purse my lips. He's on pickup duty tonight, making the rounds to trusted locations, and it should be an easy evening for him. Nothing worthy of a call.

"Yes?"

"Uh, hey, Boss. Sorry to bother you, but I'm out doing pickups. I was doing my check-ins with Logan per protocol, and I saw something he said you'd be interested in."

There's a pause I don't bother filling. Gavin's a good man, and there are times when his garrulous nature and easygoing talk are helpful. He can put people at ease a lot easier than Logan or myself. Still, I value words like they are nuggets of gold and find that Gavin spends his far too easily, so I sit back, waiting.

When he receives no response, he continues. "Yeah, or maybe not something so much as someone. I'm on the South Side, at Harry's place. Allie's brother is sitting on a barstool, nursing his second beer and staring vacantly at the wrestling. Shit show tonight, by the way."

"That's it?" I ask, blinking.

Gavin clears his throat. "Yes, sir. Logan said you'd want to know."

"Thank you, Gavin. That'll be all. Continue as scheduled for the night."

"Sure thing, Boss," Gavin says, hanging up quickly.

I set my phone down and lean back, another move on the chessboard becoming visible. I doubt TJ is drinking his worries away. He's not the type.

He's plotting.

Two can play that game, and I'm a Grand Master of it. The question, of course, is which piece I should use to counter him? Never do I consider whether what I'm doing is the right thing, whether it makes me more of a lowlife, or perhaps if I'm doing him a favor. No, I just decide . . . who do I use?

I pick my phone back up, dialing a number. The fact that the phone is picked up before the second ring and that a soft voice answers the phone tells me the baby is asleep.

"Hello?"

"Miss Cole, how are you and Violet this evening?"

The way her breath stops for a moment tells me that she recognizes my voice and knows exactly who I am this time.

"Mr. Angeline!" she says, and I can hear her moving before her voice picks up again, this time louder. "How . . . I mean, uhm . . . how are you?"

"Shh," I reassure her, "No need to wake the baby. I'm just checking in."

"Oh, we're fine," Miss Cole says, relieved but still suspicious. "Although I'm wondering why you're calling. Robbie's been good. We're all good here."

Her words are stilted, coming bit by bit, but she's centering herself as the strong woman I know her to be with every syllable, protective of her blossoming family.

"Good, good. Speaking of which, is Mr. Zallow available presently?"

"I . . ."

I know she's going to tell me no, so I cut her off, letting a threat enter my tone. "Put him on the phone."

She sighs, and I hear more footsteps, a door open, and then she says in a background voice, "For you. It's Angeline."

There's a rustle and then a deep voice comes on the line. "Yeah?"

I'm not accustomed to being greeted so casually, but this man owes me no respect beyond basic civility. In some ways, it's refreshing, even if it is something I will need to curtail in the future.

And good form requires me to demand it anyway. "Mr. Zallow. I have an assignment for you."

He huffs a small laugh. "Polite decline. We've gone over this already. My allegiance isn't to you, and it never will be."

"Oh, but you do have a previous allegiance," I remind him, revealing my trump card. "To your military brethren."

I know he's a good man at heart and I'm happy to exploit that. That I would invoke his military experience will surely irk him but pique his interest as well.

He growls so softly he probably thinks I didn't hear him. "I'm listening."

Victory. So sweet sometimes. "I know of a man, a fellow soldier, who has recently come to town."

"Yeah, so? Lots of vets in town."

I hum, nodding to myself. "True . . . but this one, like you, has seen the horrors of a wartime environment. And when he came back, he was hit with another deep wound. His woman was unfaithful and there's the resulting emotional turmoil from that. While your emotional scars are not the same, I believe you can commiserate."

Zallow sighs. "And you're telling me this why?"

"He's at Harry's, down the street from you," I explain. "And I believe he may be contemplating . . . an unwise course of action. One that I do not want to see him undertake. If it were up to me, I would be happiest if this man were to finish his leave and next month report for duty. And so I thought that perhaps you and Mr. Chambers would like to have a beer with a fellow soldier in his time of need. Keep him busy so that no harm befalls him."

"What are you, the soldier suicide prevention hotline now?" Zallow asks, his gallows sarcasm oddly endearing.

But I don't let on. "Have a friendly drink with him. That's all I ask, though I may check in to see how the friendship is progressing to make sure he is okay. I would truly hate for my hand to be forced in this matter."

I let the implied threat dangle, knowing that I wouldn't hurt TJ, but Rob

Zallow knows nothing of the sort. Whatever bonds of *esprit de corps* that remain in his heart tip the scales for him, and he relents.

"Fine. I'm feeling like a beer anyway. But it's on your tab."

His little jab does make me chuckle. It is too bad the man doesn't work for me. He's entertaining. "Very well, Mr. Zallow. That can easily be arranged."

I click *End* on the call, placing one more. The crackle of the open line sounds for a moment before I hear an old, nicotine-roughened voice.

"Harry's."

"Hello, Harry. This is Dominick Angeline. I have a couple of friends coming in soon, most likely on motorcycles. If they are respectful, please quietly let their drinks be on my tab."

Harry's been wise to the game for decades and is unflappable. "Sure thing."

I spend the next few hours watching Allie putter around her apartment. She cleaned up the mess left from our dinner, placing the leftovers into her refrigerator, though I suspect she won't eat the heavy pasta again since she barely picked at it.

I wonder if it's TJ's favorite? Or perhaps because she wanted to find a happy medium between my heritage and her cooking skills? TJ didn't say much, but he'd dug in with gusto until things had started to verbally go awry.

She'd done her usual nightly routine of stretching in her converted dining space. The first time I'd seen her stretching that way, I'd thought she was preparing to dance, but she'd merely worked through every muscle, getting long and loose, and then retiring to the shower before falling into bed. It seems to be meditative for her, and it's become a comforting routine for me as well, giving me time to appreciate the work she puts into her craft but also letting me study the long lines of her sexy body. And now she's sleeping in the mess of blankets and pillows on her bed.

Knowing she's safe, I decide to get some work done and head to Petals to check in for the night.

Things are well at the club, a quiet evening with no complaints from anyone. I'm halfway through my paperwork when I look up and see it's nearly two in the morning and time for Harry's last call. Pulling out my phone, I make another call, this time waiting three rings before it's picked up.

"Hello?" the deep voice says, relaxed but not drunkenly slurred.

"How was your evening?"

Zallow sighs, pissed. "If you know my damn number, why'd you call the house and get Myra all freaked out?"

I don't answer him because he already knows the weight his woman's word carries with him, and now he's even more aware that I know it too.

Finally, he answers my question. "My evening was fine. Met your guy,

TJ. We talked tours and shit mostly. Seemed well enough. Not suicidal or any shit like that, just down about his wife. So why the drama and ruse?"

I choose to ignore the inquiry. I may know my opponent's moves, but revealing my own is not a habit I engage in often.

"And your next engagement?"

Robert clicks his tongue. "Tony made plans with him to grab a bite to eat later this week. Tony thought it'd be good for TJ to see some fresh ass even if it was just in fun."

"Very good."

"Look, it's none of my business, and I probably don't want it to be, but what's up with this guy?" Zallow asks me. "He doesn't seem like your business type."

"Perhaps I'm just looking out for him," I reply. "Like a guardian angel."

Zallow chuckles darkly. "You're no angel. You're the fucking devil incarnate, Angeline."

"Indeed."

I hang up before Zallow can question me any further.

CHAPTER

Seventeen

ALLIE

"OH, my gosh, you're the worst, Eileen! I'm trying to convince my brother that I'm an upstanding, moral woman with discriminating taste. You are not helping my cause!" I say laughingly as Eileen tells TJ the story of how I'd once suggested an open bar at the parents' recital as a fundraiser.

Donna had been aghast at the impropriety, Eileen had outright laughed, and I still don't see what the big deal is. People might balk at first, but by the time the third group of beginner ballet starts and you've already seen endless renditions of *Zippidy Doo Dah* or *Waltz of the Flowers*, half of the parents are ready to run for the nearest bottle of whatever they can find. And with the premium prices we could charge for some pinot noir, I'm pretty sure the studio would have made a serious, serious profit.

TJ laughs, though, unsurprised. "That's my sis, the *immoral* majority."

I like that he's teasing me and hanging out without too much weirdness. After dinner with Dom, I was worried. "Come on, Teej, help me get ready for tonight. I'm putting you to work, and not just your mouth."

"Haven't had any complaints yet," he says, a joke we've had since all the way back to his high school days, but before I can toss back the standard reply of *That's what she said*, his face sours.

Shit, he just remembered Janine. I'm sure like a lot of trauma, it hits him at odd times. I'm worried about TJ, especially after the whole drama of dinner the other night.

But we had a good talk, and we both apologized a bunch of times, explaining ourselves a bit more rationally and calmly. There were hugs and tears, mostly on my part, though I'd swear I saw some shininess to his tough-guy eyes too. Now he seems to be trying to move on, so I am too. He's my brother and he's hurting, so I'm going to cut him some slack.

He has done the same for me, putting up with some serious shit when I wasn't in a good head space before, angry about my lost ballet career and my body's betrayal. But he took it and loved me through it, letting the sharp barbs I'd thrown bounce off because he knew it wasn't really about him. It'd been about my pain back then. And now, it seems it's my turn to return the favor and be the unflinching support he needs.

That's what you do for family.

So we hang out together in Studio Three, me getting some ripped-up T-shirts before we start cleaning the poles like I'd intended the day TJ showed up. It's even a good time as I work a little bit of fun into my cleaning, buffing each brass pole to a gleaming shine, climbing higher and higher to get the top section before taking one long drop to the floor for a final buff.

TJ, who's been cleaning a pole in a much more traditional fashion, turns as he sees me in the mirror, his jaw dropping. "What the hell, Allie? I didn't know you could do that!"

I spin on the floor before rolling to my feet and grinning. I love drops. "What? Slide down the pole? We have talked about what I do, you know."

He shakes his head, rubbing at his cheek. "I know, I just didn't realize . . . I mean, it's not like I've ever pictured you doing that."

I smile, understanding that because the thought of my brother doing anything sexual is a mental peanut butter and Drano sandwich to me. I just don't do it. I'm well aware he's a grown man and has a sex life, but I don't need to know anything about it.

"You wanna see?" I ask, looking at the pole next to me. "Not the whole stage routine, but I can show you some of my tricks."

He's unsure, terror and discomfort written all over his face.

I laugh. "Seriously, it's not gonna be bad. Watch."

Before TJ can answer, I walk around the pole, skipping the hip sway to just gather momentum. With a thrilling whoosh, I flip upside down, letting my legs stretch tall along the pole and my arms splaying wide in a T as I spin.

I laugh at my upside-down vantage of TJ's open-mouthed surprise. He plops down, leaning back against the mirror while I do a few more tricks before finishing in my favorite head-first hands-free death drop into a back walk-over off the pole, finishing with the splits.

"Ta-da" I say, grinning and waving jazz hands out wide.

TJ claps, at first in total awe before speeding up. He was always my biggest fan, at least before when it was ballet. "Wow, Allie-gator. That was . . . you are . . . wow."

Getting up, I do a silly curtsy, holding out an imaginary skirt and smiling. "Thank you."

We both laugh as I sink to the floor beside him, and it feels right between us again for a moment, like we're still those same kids who stayed up late watching movies and annoying Dad with our feigned confusion when he'd tell bad jokes.

"So, what'd you think?"

TJ shakes his head. "I about lost my lunch when you took a dive toward the floor. I thought for sure I was gonna be mopping up your brains and having to tell Mom that I watched while you fell on your head. Not that I haven't done that before."

I mime holding a phone up to my ear, "Hey, Mom, TJ just let me plummet to my death and didn't even try to stop me." I let all the child-like whine I can muster into my voice to sell it.

He grins, a genuine happy smile, and it feels good to have this moment with him, no Janine, no Dominick, no awkwardness after the fight.

He sobers slightly, "Allie, you're really good. I didn't realize you could do all that." He bites his lip like he's looking for words. "I don't want to see you dressed for work, but I could watch you do that all day. It's like you took all your ballet, added some gymnastics to it, and then went vertical. Oh, and decided to add spins just for shits and giggles because why the hell not?"

I glance at the pole, agreeing. "That's pretty much the theory."

He clears his throat and strokes at his chin. "Will you tell me about the club? I want to understand."

I look into his eyes, searching for any ill intent, but it seems like he's almost trying to be supportive, accepting. "I've been there for a while now. It'll sound weird, but it's a good place. Dominick makes sure it's clean and safe, and the staff there are good people. I've made friends, almost a family of sorts there. We look out for each other. It's just lingerie, although the outfits are . . . you're right, you don't want to watch. But it's okay. I'm comfortable with it now, just another costume, you know? And I make really good money. I've already paid off over half of my treatment center bills. You know there's no other way I could've done that, and Mom and Dad shouldn't have to."

"It really does seem like you love it, but I can't help but feel like I failed you or something. I didn't realize back then how dire things had gotten for you, and you're still dealing with the fallout of that financially. I feel like I should've given you my enlistment bonus or been sending you my deployment bonuses to make it easier for you to move on. It's not like Janine needed it."

We're in dangerous territory again, and I hurry to steer the subject back to safe territory, not wanting to test the tenuous truce we've called.

"Just that you're making the offer says a lot about you, TJ. You supported me through all my years of dance and all my years of recovery. I'm at a good place now, healthy and financially independent. And dancing. I thought I would never get to dance again, but I get to dance every day. Here," I say, gesturing around us at the studio, "and at the club. I won't be there forever.

I'm already stepping back and doing just features instead of weekly shows. But I get to *dance*, TJ. Maybe it's not how I always dreamed, but I get to dance."

He nods, but I can see there's still hesitation in his eyes. But he's trying and that means a lot to me.

He's known about my job at Petals, but it was always sort of surface, cerebral but not in his face. I think being here, it's gotten a lot more real, and it's hitting him harder than either of us expected.

I can understand that because I can't say I was ecstatic about his joining the Army when he told me he was enlisting. I wanted him to go to college, maybe find a frat he could act like an idiot with some before landing a six-figure job. Kind of the stereotypical high-school senior dream. But nope, he just decided to do his own thing, and I was terrified he was never going to come home again, or even if he did, that he'd be so different that I wouldn't recognize him.

But I've mostly gotten over myself and my fears and supported the hell out of him while he was serving, sending care packages and letters every chance I could. That's what family is supposed to do, support you the best they can even when they don't necessarily agree with what you're choosing. And he is different, but not in the way I'd feared. He's harder, stronger, and more cynical, but he's still my Teej under the tough shell.

"Okay, Allie-gator. I'm gonna do my best to support you, just like I always have. But from afar. I'm not coming to the club to cheer for you like a recital."

I feign shock, letting my jaw drop dramatically. "You'd better not. I remember how you were! Clapping the loudest and the longest like it was an audience participation competition. It'd be hella awkward for you to do that at Petals. Though some of the girls would probably love to meet you."

His smile falters, and I realize it sounded like I was going to set him up with one of my friends. "I didn't mean . . ."

"I . . . can't," TJ says, babbling a little over me. He takes a deep breath and looks at me carefully. "Look, I don't want to talk about her and all that shit right now. How about you tell me more about Dominick instead?"

He's trying to sound casual, but a warning siren starts going off after the disaster we had at dinner. I try to think positive, though, because TJ is asking, maybe open to understanding from my point of view, even if he and Dom are never going to be best buddies.

Even still, I double-check. "You sure?"

He lets out a dramatic sigh and shrugs. "If you're hanging out with him, I want to know more. I didn't think you'd be with . . . a guy like *that*."

Okay, so not exactly open-minded, but baby steps. I try to gather my thoughts. "We met at Petals. He owns the club and a bunch of other businesses."

I choose my words carefully because as far as I know, TJ doesn't know the full story of who Dominick is. And if he's struggling to accept the little things like his owning a club, the bigger stuff like his being The Boss is a definite no-go.

"He said that at dinner too," TJ says warily. "How many businesses? Which ones?"

"I don't know," I reply evenly. "We don't really talk business."

TJ raises a brow but nods, letting it go for the moment, and I continue. "We made eyes at each other for months, so much that the other girls would tease me about it. But he was a total professional until I came in and asked to stop being an employee because of my stuff here."

"Then he asked you out?"

I think back and laugh. "Well, not exactly, but we did have dinner that night. It was the start of something more for us."

TJ hums darkly. "Is that when the guard dogs start following you around?"

I see where he's going, and I set my hand on TJ's shoulder, trying to relieve his worries. "It's not like that. The guys had been following me for a while before then. There was some drama at the club a while back, nothing to do with me, but I got caught up in it and Dom started having his guys check in on me. It was a bit awkward when I realized what was going on, but while Dom's not a classical romantic. His heart was in the right place. He wanted me safe. They tried to stay invisible, but when I found out, we decided to just be open about the whole thing. So now I know which guy is my detail for the day and we're friends. It's just a nice thing he does, and it gives him peace of mind to know I'm protected."

"But they're his employees, his guys, so their loyalty is to him," TJ says carefully. "You have no privacy, no say-so, and you're just giving that up willingly?"

"Sounds like your life in the military," I counter but then answer him honestly. "I'm not doing anything sneaky, so I don't see the big deal." I shrug. "Really, who cares?"

"Do you know where he is every second of every day?" TJ asks a little more forcefully. "Do you have a team of guards reporting to you about his whereabouts? Or is that just one-sided?"

I blink, remembering when Dom had said that'd be potentially dangerous information for me. "I don't know where he is 24/7, but I don't need to. I trust him. He's good to me, TJ."

TJ snorts derisively. "Sugar daddies usually are. Are you sure he's not sleeping with the other girls at the club too?"

His words are venomous, poison, and my palms itch to slap the shit out of him. Instead, I settle for smacking him in the shoulder and getting up to pace. "Fuck you, TJ. Dom's not that kind. He understands fucking loyalty."

Ouch, perhaps there was venom in my words too, but they get through, and he reaches out, grabbing my wrist. "I'm sorry, Allie. I was over the line."

But the damage is done and I'm mad at TJ's continued dismissal of how good Dom and I are together.

"Do I think he was a monk before we started dating?" I ask, turning on him. "Of fucking course not, TJ. But what I know is that we laugh and play chess, he challenges me, and I challenge him, and I like that I'm the only person he's let past his ice-cold mask to see the warm, caring man inside. Yeah, he's intense. Yeah, he's possessive, but I've fallen for him and I need you to back me up on this."

"Do you hear yourself? Words *you* just used to describe your boyfriend—cold, intense, possessive. Does that sound like your dream guy, Allie?" TJ scoffs. "What would you tell me if I introduced you to a woman like that? He just bosses you around and you do his bidding like a damn puppy! That's not you, or at least not the Allie I knew. And who knows what all he's hiding. This is the honeymoon period. Does it feel like everything's roses and champagne? I can tell you what it looks like from the outside, and it sure ain't a 'happily ever after'. What happens the next time you find out he's hiding shit from you? What happens when—"

He tries to say more, I can see the words on the tip of his tongue, but I cut him off. "Don't make this about you and Janine!" I beg. "She hid stuff from you, admittedly really shitty stuff that I wish hadn't happened to you, but that doesn't mean Dominick is hiding things from me. Maybe it's not the relationship you imagined for me, maybe it's not what you would want for yourself, but it's mine, and I want it just like it is."

"You want me to just stand back and watch while you shrink yourself to fit into his world," TJ growls, getting up and right in my face. "But you don't even know what the fuck that world really is." His voice softens as he holds my arms, not letting me escape his eyes. "I remember you . . . Allie who wanted to be a ballerina, who dreamed of dancing her life away and then retiring to live a happy life with a husband and kids. I just don't see you having that with a man like Dominick. But the important thing is, do *you* see yourself having a life like that with him? Is that something you're willing to give up for him? Because I've seen you around this studio, the way you bend down to talk to the kids, the way you light up when they share something with you or finally get a move right. That life you used to dream about? You still want it. And do you think *Cold Monster* is going to be the daddy you always wanted for your kids?"

I'm silent, shocked by his hard words and how they stick painfully in my heart. They hurt because they're true to some degree. Dominick and I are still new, so intensely powerful, like nothing I've ever imagined, but new.

Is this a path I want to go down?

What does the future look like with him? It's really hard to visualize Dominick burping a baby, changing its diapers, teaching a child to play chess, loving and caring for them as they grow up. I can't see Dom teaching a little boy how to play catch.

It's harder than I'd like to admit, but maybe that's because I've never seen him in that role.

I do know deep down in my gut that he'd move heaven and earth to see me and our children happy. And that is worth more than all the dirty diapers in the world.

TJ softens, his hands relaxing a little on my arms. "Allie-gator, my life is FUBARed. I thought I was making a good choice with Janine, and I ignored some warning flags that I should've paid attention to. Now I'm paying the price and it fucking sucks. I'm just trying to do for you what I wish someone had done for me. I love you, Sis."

I sigh, hugging him. He's my brother, after all. We're going to disagree, fight, and nitpick at old wounds, but at the end of the day, I know he's always got my back, hell or high water.

And I love him for it. He's hurting and trying to protect me. I just don't want or need the protection right now.

I'm fine.

Dominick is fine.

Together, we are so much better than fine.

I'm on the verge of a pivotal point in my life, I can feel it. The connection with Dominick feels steady, pulsing with not just heat but possibility, with the harmony that I've sensed a few times in dance when you click with a partner and you just *know*.

The opportunities at the studio are exciting and will give me some financial stability and let me grow as a dancer, but also as a businesswoman.

I feel strong, comfortable in my skin, and like I'm growing in a good way. If Dom were trying to really hem me in, to put me on a leash, he wouldn't be so encouraging.

I just wish TJ could see that.

I look around the room, seeing my future here at the studio, and it gives me a warm, bubbly feeling until I see the clock on the wall. "Oh, shit, it's late. Come on."

TJ follows me to the front door, not quite as comfortable as before, but still okay-ish as I throw my bag over my shoulder and look outside. "What's up?"

"Logan is following me home tonight. He works out at the gym over there, and I told him I'd be done twenty minutes ago. He must've gotten caught up though. He's usually on time."

TJ follows my line of sight, noticing the newly-installed glowing sign for Mat Madness. "Well, let's go meet him."

I take a step toward the door and freeze, shaking my head. "No, I'm supposed to wait here for him. Let me just text him."

TJ's anger is instant and hot, undercut with worry. "Seriously? Do you hear yourself right now? You think you're not a trained puppy? You won't even walk out of your fucking cage without permission to go four doors down a fucking strip mall to meet the guy assigned to you. You do hear how fucked up that is, right?"

"I made a promise and I'm keeping it," I reply, refusing to get baited into another argument. "Something you should understand and appreciate."

TJ shakes his head. "A promise to have a guard, right? What the hell am I? A trained fucking soldier, Allie. Let's go."

He has a point. I agreed to a guard, and TJ definitely qualifies. "Fine. Come on then, GI Joe."

The studio door closes behind us and we walk across the lot, just a few doors down, but it does feel oddly like a rebellion. I may be Dominick's, and the thought of being his does make my heart and my body thump just a little bit faster, a little bit hotter, but I'm still me.

A good girl through and through, but with a dash of crazy to keep things interesting.

We go into Mat Madness and see Logan tussling with a blond guy on the matted floor. Max and Dalton stand on opposing sides, yelling out instructions. Max calls time, and Logan and the guy separate, knocking knuckles and trading grins.

Logan looks up, seeing me, and his face falls. "Fuck. What time is it?"

"It's good," I reassure him, waving it off as Max helps the blond guy up and gives him some quiet words of advice on the other side of the mat. "TJ walked me over."

Logan takes an appraising look up and down TJ. TJ takes the initiative, offering his hand. "Tyler Bancroft. Call me TJ."

"Logan Hendricks. Good to meet you. Sorry I lost track of time."

"No problem. I've been taking care of Allie-gator my whole life. Not stopping now," TJ says with a hint of a threat in his tone, though the words are sweet.

While I introduce TJ to Max and Dalton, Logan grabs his bag, changing in what has to be World-Record time. It's funny. It's the first time I've ever seen him so casual, a T-shirt and loose sweatpants along with a pair of Nike running shoes.

"You ready?" he asks.

I glance over at TJ, who's looking at one of the heavy bags and tapping it with his fist while chatting with Dalton. "Yeah, just heading home tonight, right, TJ?"

TJ turns, tossing me a little wave. "I think I'm gonna take off, actually, since you're in good hands now. Got dinner plans, and I think you've probably had enough of my ugly mug for one day."

I'm surprised he's leaving but glad to hear that he has dinner plans. After the back and forth of the day, a little time apart to settle might do us both good.

"Okay," I say, coming over. "But call me tomorrow? That's an order."

TJ grins, giving me a mock-salute before wrapping his arms around me in a hug. "I love you, Sis," he says quietly in my ear. "Just want you to be happy."

CHAPTER

Eighteen

DOMINICK

STANDING AT HER DOOR, I have that moment of unease. Is this the day she's had enough and leaves me? Or am I to be granted one more day of reprieve, of fizzy sunshine and burbling happiness instead of the chill and cold deadness my heart normally feels?

The moment of truth comes as her door opens, and my soul leaps when I see her face light up. I take a moment to bask in her glorious brilliance, letting her joy at seeing me on her doorstep nourish the seeds of hope deep within me. And though I'm not a religious man, I pray that those seeds take root and blossom into tall, sturdy trees befitting the strength of our love.

"Hey!" Allie says, letting me in before giving me a quick hug. "You're early! I thought you might be the delivery guy."

"I know what I want for dinner," I say salaciously, letting my eyes rove down her curves as my body tingles from the quick press of her against me. She's dressed in yoga pants and a soft sweater that slips off one shoulder, a hint of a lacy strap peeking out. I can't help myself. I lean in to kiss her, intending to be soft and slow, but the scent of her perfume hits me and the kiss turns passionate and needy.

It's been days since I've had her beneath me, barely able to find stolen moments together over the last week while she rushes around with work and her brother. But in this moment, she is here with me, mine and mine alone. The depth of my desire for her hits me full-force and she seems to be suffering from the same degree of need. Her full lips meld to mine, and when her tongue slips out to taste along my bottom lip, I growl and open for her, forcing her to do the same for me.

We're still standing in the open doorway, but I give real consideration to hiking her up my body, pressing her back against the door, and filling her right here. Let all of East Robinsville hear as she screams my name. She'd be a gift to me with every moan.

I need this woman soon, need to feel her walls clench around me as she's left boneless from the pleasure I'm giving her. I need to see her give in to me, give everything to me and take all of me in return.

We're this close, my hand sliding down her back to her waistband, when the long buzz of my phone in my pocket stops me, both of us chuckling at the tickling sensation. I step back from the kiss reluctantly, placing a line of sweet kisses down her neck to her exposed shoulder as I pull my phone out to silence the alert.

"Dinner is here," I say.

Her eyebrows pull together. "How do you know that?" I give her a hard look, judging her openness. For once in my life, I can't read her, and my instincts scream at me to dodge the question until I can foresee the outcome of sharing.

A tiny angel on my shoulder, one that must've been placed there by Allie because I've certainly never had a conscience before, whispers in my mind . . . *tell her. Remember, trust?*

Still not sure if it's the right play, I decide to jump with the voice. Turning my phone around, I open an app, showing her the screen. "Remember, I told you I can ping your phone? I'm also hacked into this building's security. I get an alert whenever your code is used."

"You're . . ."

"I know a guy," I reply, trying to keep my voice light to ease the shock. "You said you thought I was the delivery guy so I'm assuming the usage of your code a moment ago is our dinner being dropped off."

I can see the gates drop down in her mind, closing her off from me. I hate it. I want to shake her and make her understand that it has to be this way. Before I can do anything foolish, however, the elevator dings.

"I'll get dinner. Can you take this?" I say instead, holding out the gift bag I brought for her. I'd almost dropped it in favor of holding her in my arms while we kissed, but I'm glad I kept my head enough to keep it in my grip. It's too fragile, too important to risk breaking.

"Yeah, what is it?" Allie asks cautiously, her eyes on the bag.

"A present for you," I say simply, signing the charge slip. I'm about to slip the guy a folded twenty as his tip when I see the way he's looking at my Allie and instead shut the door in his face.

Bag of food in hand, I stride into the kitchen, making myself at home. In some ways, though, this place already feels more like home than my own house does. It's like being wrapped up in all things Allie . . . things she has chosen on every surface, her subtly spicy floral scent in the air, her dancewear crumpled in the corner, waiting for her to do laundry.

It's oddly both comforting and exciting to have to nudge them out of the way in order to be in her space. I take plates from the cabinet and fill them with her order, Chinese chicken and vegetables.

It smells delicious, and I set the plates on the coffee table, along with silverware and glasses of water.

Looking up from my seat, I notice she hasn't moved, her gift bag still hanging from her right hand and a suspicious look on her face. Trying to be encouraging, I pat the cushion next to me.

"Come, sit. Open your present."

She does so robotically, sinking to sit on the floor pillow by the table. "How'd you know where everything is in my cabinets?"

"I've eaten dinner here several times now. I'm observant by nature and have seen you pull dishes from the cabinets, from the dishwasher, and even from the sink where you fake-whined about having to wash them by hand and threatened to switch to only paper plates and plastic forks. I'm sure if we were at my house, you'd know which cabinet the plates are in too."

Allie pauses and then a tiny smile curls her lips. "Cabinet right of the stove. I remember thinking it was weird because they should be in the left cabinet."

I grin as she sees my point. "I actually agree with you, but my chef is left-handed. She set it up so she can spatula with her left hand, grab dishes out of the rack in there with her right, and plate dinner without even having to take her eyes off the pan. I suspect that if she had to do it in reverse, there'd be a higher chance of her dropping my dinner, so I let her put the plates wherever the hell she wants to. As long as I get to eat."

She laughs at my joke, and I move to put the awkwardness behind us. "Please, open your gift. I've been burning with curiosity about whether you'd like it."

Allie lifts an eyebrow but nods and begins tossing tissue paper around like confetti with a smile already on her face. "You know, if you got me diamonds—"

"I thought about it, but no. They're not precious enough."

Her curiosity piqued, she reaches deeper, pulling out a heavy wooden box wrapped with a silk bow. "What is it?"

It's a rhetorical question as her hands are already tugging at the bow, a delighted gasp coming from her lips as she opens the box. "Oh, my gosh, they're beautiful!" she exclaims, lifting out the first piece, an ornately carved piece of white ash. Appropriately enough, it's the Queen. "Are these hand-carved?"

"Yes, each chess piece is done by hand," I tell her, letting her explore each piece. "The board's walnut and beech, and the pieces are ash and black oak. I thought about getting a stone board, but I decided a folding board so that you can store it or take it with us wherever we go would be more appropriate."

It's an important gift for me, both in the actual chessboard and in the admission that I want to go wherever this woman is. It's sort of a connection, from the fond memories I've had with my father, and now after a few games with Allie, it's something I want to share with her, too.

I'm sure my father is looking down on me, approving of the continuation of our tradition. Allie caresses each piece before closing the case and looking up at me through those beautiful mile-long lashes of hers.

"Thank you, Dominick. I know this means a lot to you. I want you to know it means a lot to me too." Her lips lift in a soft little smile and she moves closer to me, tilting her chin up. "Thank you."

She leans in and kisses me, but almost instantly, the passion from our earlier greeting reignites anew.

Dinner forgotten, she crawls into my lap, straddling me, her pussy hot against my cock. I grab her hips, pulling her fiercely against me so she feels how hard she makes me, how even just a few touches of her lips against mine leave me iron-hard and throbbing for her.

She whimpers, grinding against me. "Dom . . . be dirty," she begs. "Show me."

"Fuck, Allie," I growl, letting her past my outer shell to the deep, feral, filthy part of me. "I need to be inside you."

I climb to my feet, pulling her up with me before hoisting her in my arms, her legs wrapping around my waist as I stride down the hallway to her bedroom. I lay her gently down, stripping her clothes off and placing a pillow under her head. I like her like this, nude and in the nest of blankets and pillows on her bed, waiting for me to fill her, to fuck her, to make her mine.

She stretches artistically, showing off for me before reaching out with a soft hand. "You have on too many clothes. Take them off." Her grin is pure wickedness, a dare if ever I saw one.

"Then you show me something too. Touch yourself. Let me watch you."

She blushes, and I think for one second that she might refuse, but then the dirty girl I know she has inside wins over. She's pretty in pink, she's dirty in denim, and she's naughty in nude . . . and watching her is like a fantasy come to life.

Her finger traces along her sternum, the burgundy of her nail dark against her honey skin, and I watch the path she takes, letting her lead me along to wherever she wants to direct my gaze.

"Like this?" she teases.

"Beautiful. But not enough to get my shirt off. More."

Her pupils dilate at the challenge, and she brings her hands up her body, taking a breast in each one. She uses her thumbs to tease at her nipples, my fingers undoing my tie as they harden into diamond points that beg for my tongue.

I press my lips together, denying myself her taste so that I can watch her.

Instead, I begin unbuttoning my shirt slowly, rewarding her continued movements.

"Yes, keep doing that, Allison," I growl, shrugging my shirt off and then tracing my rough palms over my chest as her eyes devour my skin. "Spread your legs."

She obeys, placing her feet flat on the bed and letting her knees splay open to give me an unobstructed view of her pink pussy.

"Like this?"

I nod, groaning. "Good girl. So pretty. Now feel how wet you already are."

Allie's right hand moves like it has a mind of its own, down her belly to her core, cupping herself and moaning as her head falls to the side and her eyes flutter closed. She strokes, the warmth burning against her fingers I'm sure, but she doesn't dip inside . . . she wants permission.

"Please," she begs. She's so naturally obedient, strong but right now so turned on and wanting to make me happy. I'm ecstatic.

"No need to beg. Touch yourself," I encourage her, undoing my belt and then the clasp on my pants. "Give yourself what you need."

She whines, knowing that I have what she really needs, but she begins sliding a finger along her slit, spreading her honey up over her clit. It's one of the sexiest things I've ever seen. I ease my zipper down, the soft click of the metal teeth pulling apart bringing her eyes back to me.

"Take it out, Dominick. Let me see you too."

My eyes flick between hers, dark with lust, and her fingers, which disappear inside her and reappear, shiny with her arousal. I'm torn, needing to grip myself, needing to taste her, needing to fuck her. The war rages inside me, filling me with lust.

But I know that my thirst for her requires sating first, and I drop to my knees at her bedside. "Let me taste you. Rub your clit."

She cries out but does it. Her hips buck into her hand as my tongue licks along her pussy, drinking her down. I reach up, laying my forearm across her hips, holding her in place.

"Faster, Allison," I order, my words muffled by her wet lips against my mouth. "Let me see you make yourself come all over my face. I want to taste your cum. Then I'll fuck you deep and hard, just the way you want."

I can feel her eyes as she looks down her body at me, but my gaze is locked on her hand, watching her fingers blur across her clit and timing my licks with her pace. I add my thumb, teasing in circles at her asshole, and I feel her clench and relax against me.

And then every muscle in her body freezes, tight and coiled in anticipation of the moment, and then she suddenly unfurls beneath me, free in her explosion. It's exactly what I want for her, both here in this bed and in life, for her to find her freedom wrapped in the cocoon of my love.

I flip her over, placing the pillow under her hips to arch her back. Kicking my pants and shoes off, I crawl up on my knees, lifting her hips until my cock is ready, pressed against her. She looks back over her shoulder, and my heart stops for an instant as I freeze. She gives me the slightest of nods, and I sheathe myself inside her deeply with one powerful stroke.

Instantly, my heart resumes beating, my soul is cleansed of the sin I inflict upon it everyday, and my mind quiets in peace. I am here, no future to consider, no plans to manipulate, no concerns weighing my shoulders down. I'm where I'm supposed to be, with the woman I'm meant to be with. Forever.

Allie sighs, and I tell myself it's because she feels complete with me inside her as well, but I don't dare ask, not sure I could withstand an unexpected answer when all my defenses are down.

"Ohh, Dom . . . move. I need you to move."

I squeeze her ass, loving the way it clenches under my hand as I lean in and kiss her shoulder softly, growling when I pull back.

"When I'm ready. Right now, I'm enjoying the way your velvet walls grip me, kissing along my cock, like your greedy pussy has been waiting just for me."

She moans, writhing back against me, fucking herself on my cock. I let her for a few strokes, giving her just enough leeway to let her punish herself, teasing and tantalizing herself but unable to get what she really needs.

"Such a naughty girl, using my cock like that. You need me to give you more?"

She mumbles incoherently, but she nods, tremors rolling up her spine as I pull back and thrust in slowly, torturing both of us and making her eyes flutter closed.

"Then give me your hands, Allison."

She reaches her hands behind her, elbows bent and holding one another. I place a strong hand over her forearms, pinning them to her back before gathering her chocolate tresses in my other hand. I pull back gently, forcing her back to arch, opening her pussy even more as I thrust in deeper and find where that edge of pleasure and pain is for her, knowing I'm going to push her limits.

"Remember you asked for this, Allison."

It's both a promise and a warning, and I slam into her, her body quaking with the force of my thrust. She cries out sharply, and I thrust again and again, picking up speed until I'm fucking her hard and rough, deep and fast.

We're a single body, the sharing of our fluids only making this more savage, and we both strive for more.

"Oh, my God, Dominick!"

I grin ferally, my inner beast unleashed as my hips smack her ass. "You like that, don't you, Allison? You want me to fuck your pussy hard so you know who it belongs to, isn't that right?"

"Yes!" she screams senselessly. "Yes!"

I'm not sure if she's answering my questions or just begging me to keep going. I lean forward, my whisper harsh in her ear. "Who do you belong to? Say my name when you come, Allison."

She shudders, the words more breath than sound, but she says it, sanctifying this and blessing me with her words. "Dominick. I'm yours, Dominick."

I can feel her pussy quivering around me, hungrily milking my cock as it demands my cum. I can't hold back anymore, physically or emotionally, as she repeats the words I so desperately need to hear, the ones that give me the relief that she is mine. My hands tighten, my arms going rock-hard to keep her still, and I pound into her with deep, hard thrusts, each one emphasized with a word.

"I. Love. You. Allison. You. Are. Mine."

The words and thoughts ratchet into a roar as everything releases, and I fill her with rope after rope of my hot cum, filling her to overflowing as it leaks out around me.

When I can breathe again, I stay pressed against Allie, releasing her arms and hair but wrapping my arms around her waist, grinding inside her as I look down. I marvel at the sight of her puffy lips still gripping me. If I could, I would never leave the warmth of Allie's pussy, the shiny slick juices all over both of us. It's the sexiest thing I've ever seen.

Evidence of our fucking. Proof of our love.

I slip out of her and crawl up next to her, lying on my back and pulling her to my side, where she lays her head on my chest.

"Are you lying in the wet spot?" she asks after a hushed few moments. "I think we made a *bit* of a mess."

I smile lazily, my fingers tracing the soft skin at her shoulder. "I would happily lay in our wet spot if it meant cuddling with you after fucking you like that."

She lifts up onto her elbows, a syrupy grin washing over face. "You say the sweetest things, always sounding like you're quoting poetry or some famous literature guy, when they're just your own words. But I think *that* is probably the sweetest thing you've ever said to me because I know what a sacrifice lying in the wet spot is. Especially for a guy like you."

I grin and roll, putting her under me.

She squeals, laughing at the same time. "What are you doing? You said you'd lie in the wet spot but you're getting me all in it now."

"Not willing to sacrifice for me?" I say with a straight face.

She giggles and agrees. "Okay, maybe a little."

It's quiet for a moment, both of us just enjoying sharing space, sharing breath.

"I heard you, you know."

Her eyes lift to mine, almost shy with the admission, and I can see she thinks I spoke the words in the heat of the moment, that I didn't mean them. I brush a lock of hair back from her cheek, tracing her cheekbone with my thumb.

"I meant every word. I love you, Allison. And you are mine. Today, tomorrow, forever."

CHAPTER

Nineteen

ALLIE

THERE'S A MOMENT OF SILENCE, and my brain resonates with the intensity of his words. It's seemingly so sudden, but my heart and soul leave no doubt that he's telling me the truth. He loves me. And in that instant, the truth strikes me hard. I love him too.

I take a big breath and an even bigger leap into the abyss that is Dominick Angeline's world. "I love you, too."

The wide, bright smile and the utter happiness in his eyes tell me that he was scared . . . that nobody's ever told him that before and meant it like I do. I feel like he's opening a window to his soul, letting me in, and I can see through the cracks in his armor to the real man beneath the persona.

He pulls me to him and kisses me sweetly, our tongues tangling together like we can taste the words we've spoken, savor them like candy. When we part, we snuggle back together, both of us on our sides, our arms and legs knotted in one another, drifting off into totally blissful slumber.

I awaken minutes or hours later, I don't really know. At first, I wonder if everything was just a crazy dream, but when I feel his weight on me, I know it was real.

I'm in love with Dominick Angeline and he's in love with me.

Boom. Mic drop.

But I really need to get up and pee. I wiggle, and he pulls me tighter at first, not letting me go, and I laughingly press on his shoulder.

"Let me up or the wet spot on the bed isn't going to be nearly as sexy."

Dom's lips twitch in a sleepy laugh, and he lets go. "Okay, okay."

I get to the door, looking back when I hear him turn over. "Hey . . . when I get back, wanna play strip chess?"

"You're already naked," he says, stating the obvious.

"Oh, guess we'll have to figure out something other than clothes to bet with," I tease.

He smirks, getting up on an elbow. "Dirty girl. I like it."

After a quick potty break, I wash my hands and try to clean myself up a bit in the bathroom mirror. Wiping under my eyes to remove the mascara streaks and pulling my hair back up into its messy bun, I call it good and grab the chessboard and pieces from the living room.

I expect to see Dominick still lazing in bed when I get back, maybe asleep, maybe lying on his back with his cock saying he's woke as fuck. What I don't expect is to see him messing with the smoke detector in the corner, his naked butt and legs stretched long as he stands on tiptoe to mess around with the device on my ceiling.

"What are you doing?" I ask.

"I thought I saw the light flash red and wanted to make sure the batteries are okay," he says, pointing. "You know, every six months and all."

But there's something about the frozen neutral look on his face, like his usual expressiveness with me has disappeared. It's his business face, I realize. The words are pretty smooth too, slipping off his tongue easily. But it's in that silky smoothness I can tell there's something more. And though I can't explain it, somehow, I can tell he's lying. Mere moments after being inside me and saying 'I love you' for the first time, he's being untruthful.

The disparity breaks my heart, and I feel as naïve as TJ made me out to be.

I take a step backward, hurt and confused over why he'd lie about something so unimportant as my smoke detector. I stumble ever so slightly and grab at the door frame, realizing a moment too late that the chess set's slipping, and the heavy weight falls at my feet, an inch from my toes as pieces scatter.

"Allie? Are you okay?" Dominick says, rushing for me, but I'm already on balance again, holding my hand up as I put space between us.

"No. You just lied to me, Dom. Your fucking hands-on privileges are revoked when you're doing that. Don't touch me."

He flinches like I'm the one who just cracked his heart and he pulls up, his face fraught with concern. "Allie, what's wrong? I was just checking the battery. Everything's fine."

He says it like I'm crazy, like he's coddling a child who just found out there's no Santa, but I can see the tension in the lines at the corners of his eyes and his chest rising and falling just a bit too fast. Shit, he's good, but he's got a tell. He's hiding something, maybe not lying that time, but deceiving me all the same.

"You're lying to me. Don't do it, Dominick. Don't you fucking lie after you just told me you love me and fucked my brains out. Trans-fucking-parency, remember? If you want it, you need to give it." My voice rises as I point a finger at him. He crowds into me until I'm digging a very nice mani-cure into his chest.

To his credit, he doesn't step back from my anger, though I can see each word lash him like a whip. Instead, he looks steadily into my eyes, keeping his voice low and calm.

"Allie, I told you there would be things I can't share with you, that it would be dangerous. I'll be as open as I can, and I am more open with you than I have been with anyone, but you're not ready for it all."

Though this man would never beg, I can hear the plea in his words, asking me to let this go. But while I can let go of a lot of things, this is *my home*. If he wants some arm candy that'll bend to his every whim like a willow tree, he needs a reminder that I'm not that girl. I have been to hell and fought my way to get back to where I am today. I am strong, not a weak willow but a fucking oak tree rising up to the sky, and I will not let him come in and slowly chop me away. He's never tried to do that before, but I can feel the sharp edge of the axe's blade in this moment. I'm not backing down.

"Let me decide that for myself," I demand. "Tell me what the fuck is going on, what you're doing. The truth. Or you're going to find yourself outside buck-ass naked with Logan giving you a ride home."

I'm not sure how something so seemingly minor has become something so gargantuan, but it has. And it feels like I'm doing the right thing. What-ever he was doing, it's just the tip of an iceberg that can sink us if we don't course-correct right the fuck now.

Dominick's eyes glare at me, sharp as flint, analyzing even as their depths implore me again to let this go. Finally, he sighs and looks to the ceil-ing, and I'd swear he's praying, though he doesn't seem the type.

"Forgive me. I want you to remember that I love you. More than life itself, I love you. And I didn't want to share this yet, but I knew I'd have to eventually."

"Share what?" I demand, my patience gone.

"Here," he says, grabbing my robe off the hook behind the door and holding it out for me. "I think it might be best to show you."

The words are sarcastic, biting, and unlike him, which makes me curious, so I slip my arms into the robe, tying it at my waist as he pulls on his slacks. Bare-chested and barefoot, he holds his hand out to me.

"Come, Allison."

He already seems resigned that this is going to be bad, and I fight the urge to rewind the last few minutes, to go back and have never seen him messing with the smoke detector, for him to have never lied to me.

But I need the truth.

This man holds my heart and is this close to having the keys to my soul as well. If I'm to give him all of me, I need all of him. So I step back, mindlessly slipping my feet into my fuzzy bunny slippers I keep by the door for late-night trash runs and follow him into the hallway.

"What is this? Is this rule three? Where I just go wherever you say without question?" I awkwardly joke, the pain in my voice evident even to my own ears.

Dominick frowns thoughtfully. "Perhaps rule three, but not the no-questions-asked aspect. More about the trust we have established."

That sounds dire, and the foreshadowing of what I'm about to see sits heavy in my gut, bile threatening to rise up in rebellion.

We walk down the hallway silently, though I look at him with a raised eyebrow when we get on the elevator and he presses the *Four* button. We walk down a hallway very much like the one we just left, and when Dominick stops at the door directly above my own, an eerie sense of déjà vu sweeps through me.

I'm shocked as Dominick pulls a key out of his pocket, glancing at me as he unlocks the door. He pushes it open and gestures for me to enter with a sweeping hand.

"What is this?" I say, stepping inside.

It's laid out identically to my place, but bare-boned, just a couch in the living room and a folding table in the dining area. I can see a coffee pot on the kitchen counter. It's devoid of personality, cold and barren. I can't see the bedroom, but as Dom closes the door behind us, he seems comfortable here.

Looking around again, I can see a hook on the wall, and my mind flashes an image of him casually hanging his suit jacket there. But . . . why? He's got a place, a much nicer place than this.

"This way," he says, his voice deep and pained. Whatever this is, he's . . . ashamed of it.

Whether it's at what he's done or at getting caught, I don't know. I follow him down the hall to the bedroom, and when he turns on the light, I'm greeted with an unexpected sight.

There's a small bed, barely larger than a cot, really, but most of the back wall is dominated by a wide folding table, and on top of it are four computer monitors, all of them flat and dark.

The meaning flashes in my mind and I gasp. No . . . no way. I turn to him, furious. "Are you fucking kidding me, Dom? Are you spying on me?"

A cold shiver runs through my body as I pray that I'm wrong. *Let this not be anything like that. Please.*

Instead of answering, Dominick clicks a switch on a central box and the screens flash to life, each one showing . . . my apartment. The screens are split, my parking space and car in the garage, my front door, and more.

I gasp, horrified at the invasion of my privacy, and reach out to touch the screen showing my bed, the sheets and pillows still mussed from where we just fucked.

Dominick stands tall, his hands behind his back, almost like he's awaiting my judgment, like he knows this is beyond the pale. He'd told me it was too soon, and maybe I should've believed him. But I don't think I would've ever been ready for *this*.

"What is this, Dominick?" I whisper, not able to find all the right words.

His eyes cut to mine, cold and fierce. "I protect what is mine, Allison. And you've been mine for a long time. We both know that. I love you, and you love me too."

The words hit hard, more steel than silk this time, and for the first time, I can really see the man that others see in Dominick. The monster.

It's what he's shown the rest of the world but never me. Now, though, he has slipped into that persona, so distant and unfeeling, when this is the moment I need him most. It infuriates me.

I rage at him, pressing on his chest, the muscles hard and unyielding under my pounding fists. "How long, Dominick? How long have you been watching me like this? Do you sit up here in your little hidey-hole, watching me eat dinner, dance, clean? Do you watch me fucking myself and jack off like a perv? This is wrong! It's a violation of everything we have, do you get that? Or *had*, because I can't live like this. You're not my boyfriend. You're a fucking stalker whose dream is finally coming true, isn't it? I guess you pulled one over on me."

I collapse, the tears bursting free, burning like acid down my cheeks as I bury my face in my hands, muttering to myself. "So fucking stupid, Allison. Should've known . . . just a stripper. He's a monster."

He roars, grabbing my shoulders and shaking me lightly to get my attention. If it were anyone else, I'd be afraid, but even in this pit of hell, I don't think he'll hurt me, not physically, anyway. But considering he just smashed my heart to pieces, maybe my faith in him is just another sign of how stupid I am, how naïve I am for believing he could love me and that I knew him.

Dom's voice is angry, fury dripping from every word, but it's not directed at me . . . it's directed at himself. "You are too good for the pity party woe is me shit. Stop it. You've worked too hard to let those thoughts have purchase in your mind again. You are a beautiful, strong, brilliant light. And I'm the one who's the darkness. I should have stayed away, pushed you away, but I just wanted a bit of your sun. You're right, I'm a monster, and I never told you otherwise. I will be until the day I die. But I do love you, and you have given me more happiness than I possibly deserve. But I'm a selfish bastard, Allison, and I want more. I want you. Forever. I love you. But I live in this world where I have to be The Boss . . . or I die."

I'm a tornado of thoughts and emotions, not sure which way is left or right or what to make of his words, so I latch on to the last thing he said.

"I know you're The Boss, but this is so much more than that!" I cry out, pushing all four monitors from the desk in a destructive warpath. "I could have accepted that! But I wanted US!" I snatch the laptop I think controls all of it and hurl it across the room where it smashes against the wall. The crashing sound as it hits the floor seems to break open a damn inside him.

"Do you? Do you really get that I'm the boss for the whole damn town?" he thunders, his voice shaking as he gestures toward the front of the apartment and the rest of town. "I know the rules because I make them. I know the expectations because I set them. And then here you come, not fitting into any of that. It drives me crazy, so fucking crazy. But I love it. I'm a cold machine, dead inside while I do the things I know have to be done, what I was raised to do. But you put life back into my existence. With you, I don't feel dead. I don't feel alone. I feel like I can be myself, not The Boss, not Dominick Angeline . . . but just me." He thumps his chest, reiterating his words.

He slumps, his shoulders sagging slightly, and he swallows. "And the thought that I could lose that, lose you, kills me. When you're out there, walking around and doing whatever crazy shit you're getting into for the day, you take my heart with you. And I'm that man again, empty and icy. It's not until you're back by my side, when I can see that you're okay, that I can breathe again, that my heart stars to beat again. How can I apologize for that? To protect an angel, I'll gladly be the devil."

It's honest. It's bare. It's Dominick.

It feels like the biggest share of our time together, or maybe the biggest share he's ever given anyone, judging by the ragged way he's breathing. The heaviness of his truth hangs in the air between us.

But I'm not sure it's enough.

"So what am I supposed to do?" I ask, lowering my voice. "Just go along with this because your life is scary? This is *crazy*, Dominick. It's too much. I don't know if this is the life I want," I say, shaking my head. "What do I get? Cameras, guards, danger, and not knowing where you are or what you're doing for my own good? How is that a partnership?"

He huffs, maybe because he doesn't understand . . . or maybe more because he does. "You get me. And I get you. That's all we need. Each other. The rest of it is outside us. Just the things that allow us to *be us*. I love you, Allison."

"You keep saying that," I whisper sadly. "And I know you do. I truly believe that. And I understand that this is how you love. But just because this is the only way you can love, it doesn't mean it's the way I need to be loved. It may be your all, but that doesn't mean it's enough. I need more than protection. I need respect."

The words are almost poignant, and Dom's shoulders slump as the reality hits him. The little devil on my shoulder echoes TJ's words from before, asking me if this is the life I want, the life I dream of.

And this time, I don't brush it off. I listen.

"I need some time," I add after a moment. "I need to think this through. I think you should go. When you're here, it's all messed up in my head, because yes, I do love you. But you're talking about a whole life like this, living in a sanitized bubble because you think I can't handle the dark side of your life. Well, maybe I can't, but I need to decide that for myself. And you need to decide whether you're strong enough to let me not be that perfect angel you think I am."

Dominick holds my upper arms in his hands, gripping me tightly but not hurting me, and I almost wish he would hurt me, smack my ass and take control so I don't have to decide our fate, our future.

But he doesn't. Though he wants me in this gilded cage, he wants me to come freely to it, to him.

His words are quiet, his emotions back on lockdown, but even now, when he's trying so hard to erect his shields, I can see the open honesty in his eyes.

"I understand. It's a lot. But you are it for me, Allison. Choose me or don't, but you will always be mine and I will always be yours. Logan will be downstairs if you need anything."

I shake my head, tightening my belt. "No. I need to be alone. *Truly* alone. No guards, no you. I need space."

He nods, kisses my forehead, and leaves.

I sag to my knees, tears burning my cheeks as the weight of everything pulls me down.

Everything in my head tells me this is crazy, to run far and wide to get away from the pressure of his rules and expectations, an inherent need to rebel against any restraint forcing its way through my soul.

But my heart thuds dully, just wanting him to come back and hold me.

I force myself up, needing to see if he does what I asked, like it's a litmus test that will tell me I did the right thing. I walk over to the window, peeking out the blinds.

Through blurry tears, I see Logan's car pull away, then Dom's black Mercedes leave the garage and do the same. I feel alone without him here.

For the first time in a long time, I am alone.

CHAPTER

Twenty

ALLIE

I TAKE a few minutes to get back to my apartment. Luckily but stupidly, I left my front door unlocked. I stay under control pretty well until the door closes and I slump onto my bed, the tears flowing freely as my heart shatters.

I bury my face in a pillow for a moment before realizing it smells like him, and I angrily snatch its velvet softness and hurl it across the room.

Out of the corner of my eye, I see a blinking light and look up at my smoke detector. The small green light taunts me. "Did you see that? Yeah? Fuck you!"

I'm not sure who I'm talking to. I pretty much destroyed the surveillance setup upstairs. But I need to rage at someone or something so the obvious culprit of crashing my happy moment is the inanimate device on the ceiling. I know that's stupid and that this is all on Dominick, but I have to do something.

Swiping the salty tears from my cheeks, I jump up and rush to the kitchen to grab my little 'one-step' and hurry back to my bedroom. It's a tough reach. I'm on tiptoe as my fingers scrabble to find that spot on the edge of the cover to get it off. With every passing second, my rage at the stupid chunk of cheap shit plastic rises, and I yank hard.

No dice, but in my anger, a piece of plastic slices my finger. It's not serious, but the sight of the blood shocks me enough to tamp down my anger and give me pause. Sticking my thumb in my mouth, I climb down, heading to the bathroom to run cool water on my finger.

A tight Band-Aid later, and it's fine.

If only my life were so easily cared for. I chance looking at myself in the mirror and am shocked by the haunted-looking specter staring back.

Is that me? How did I end up here, of all places?

Not able to meet my own eyes any longer, in the mirror, I see the reflection of the hallway behind me and distantly, my living room couch.

And paranoia sets in. Although is it really paranoia if you know someone really has been watching you?

For the next hour, I examine every corner, nook, cranny, and crack in my apartment, looking for something that looks out of place. I examine every smoke detector, even though I know they've been compromised.

This is bullshit. What he did is a violation I would've never imagined. I'm angry, hurt, and embarrassed. Your home is supposed to be your haven, your sanctuary, and now I feel vulnerable. Not knowing what to do, I reach out to the one person I trust to help me.

"Hello?" His voice is tight, as if he's preparing for a fight from me like last time. But I've got no fight left in me.

"TJ?" I greet him, my scratchy throat and the ghost of my tears making my voice hoarse. "I need help."

God bless my brother. His reply is immediate and heartfelt. "What's wrong, Allie? Are you hurt?"

A humorless laugh escapes, and yeah, I sound just a little crazy. "Yes, but not like that. He . . . oh, God, listen, can you . . . can you just come over?"

I can already hear him shuffling around on his side of the line. "I'm coming, Sis. Whatever that motherfucker did, I'm coming. I've got you."

I hang up, letting the phone drop and hanging my head. I let the tears take over again, sobbing silently. I need to get them out because as much as I need TJ right now, I know he's going to come in like a steamroller. If he sees me in tears, he's going to go postal, and that I don't want or need.

I just need his strength. That's why I called him, because he's always been there for me, and I don't think I can do this alone.

I manage to get halfway cleaned up and decently dressed before his booming knocks threaten to break my door in off its hinges, and as I shuffle to the front door in some old yoga pants and a T-shirt, I wish I'd showered before calling him.

I feel a little squelch inside me, and I remember that I'm still holding his mark. But . . . I think I might forever. He's in my pussy, in my heart, and apparently, all over my damn apartment.

TJ rushes in when I open the door, like he's looking for terrorists or something in here with me. Finally, when he sees I'm alone, he turns and gathers me up in a fierce embrace.

"What happened? What's going on?"

I can't answer at first, not without losing control of my emotions, and he leads me over to the couch, where I sit.

Through hiccups, I tell him, "Everything was fine. We had sex, but . . ."

I feel TJ tense beside me, thinking the worst, and I reassure him. "No, it was fine, it was better than fine. It was everything. He told me he loved me."

The words force me into morose silence, trembling on the edge of tears again, and through his hug, I feel TJ's patience wearing thin. "I need you to talk to me here. What's going on? Because I'm about to go find that piece of shit and fucking kill him, and I don't even know what for."

I hold him tighter, not letting him go. "After, I went to the kitchen, and when I came back, he was messing with the smoke detector. I didn't know."

"Know what, Allie?" TJ says through clenched teeth.

"He's been spying on me!" I rasp. "Cameras outside, in the smoke detectors, you name it."

"The fucker was watching you without consent?"

His voice is eerily calm and steady, and I wonder if this is him in soldier mode.

I nod. "I caught him messing around with the smoke detector. I demanded to know what he was doing. He took me . . . oh, God, he took me upstairs. He's got an apartment up there with monitors. TJ, who does something like that?"

TJ pets my hair, trying to comfort me. "Someone real fucked up, Alliegator. Someone who doesn't deserve you."

He's quiet for a moment, and when he speaks again, there's guilt in his voice. "Allie, I knew he had an apartment upstairs. I followed him after dinner, saw him go in. I wasn't sure what was going on, so I didn't say anything. I couldn't prove anything, and you didn't seem open to hearing anything negative about him. I wasn't sure whether you knew or not."

I push away from him, pissed. "You knew?"

"I tried to tell you he was bad news!" he exclaims before forcing himself to lower his voice. "I tried to tell myself that it was just a place for the guards to stay on patrol. You know, a place someone could grab some Zs or something. Since they were following you, I figured they had to have a home base. But I didn't think . . . this. Who the fuck is this guy, Allie? What are you messed up in?"

Even now, I defend him with my silence, keeping his secrets. I shake my head, not answering TJ's questions.

"You know what? It doesn't fucking matter. You are a grown-ass woman and you know what needs to happen. Say it."

I know TJ's looking for some big clarity moment where I denounce anything and everything Dominick and tell him that he was right all along.

But I'm not there yet.

If anything, therapy taught me that I can't leapfrog ahead. I have to be right where I am, and that's okay. I feel betrayed, angry, and hurt, yes.

But I also love him. And no matter what people like to claim, you can't just turn off love. I would if I could, and I know I don't have to act on it, but it's there, still burning like embers, ridiculing my stupidity. But the pain itself serves as a lesson I won't soon forget.

"Just help me," I finally say. "I want this place bug-free."

TJ nods, but I can see the disappointment in his eyes. I can almost see him telling himself . . . *one step at a time*. It used to be *one bite at a time* but though I've been eating healthy for years now, those urges, ugly and mean, still have roots in my psyche.

The insecurities never really go away. I've just gotten better at shutting them up. But now they whisper to me. *Stupid girl. Never good enough. You thought a man like that would want you. He just wanted to use you.*

TJ takes my hand, likely knowing that my inner monologue has gone dark, but he's a man of action.

He pulls me into my bedroom, and after a moment of taking the scene in, he snatches all the sheets off my bed and balls them up, carting them into the bathroom and coming back a moment later, a false smile on his face.

"Well, I made sure the hamper lid still works. The dust bunnies at the bottom are pissed though."

I smile wanly, and he climbs up on the stool I'd abandoned, already reaching for something in his back pocket. Pulling out a knife, he studies the cover for a moment before opening up the blade and using it as a screwdriver to take the whole thing down.

"It looks like . . . yeah, got it."

TJ takes me with him, room to room, as he takes down each smoke detector so I can bear witness to each painful betrayal. An hour later, I have a box full of evidence of Dominick's sick obsession.

TJ sets me on the couch and then goes through an exhaustive search of my apartment, looking for bugs and other cameras, though he admits he's not an expert. It feels like a fresh violation all over again, even though I told him to do it. Seriously, having my brother go through my lingerie drawer to make sure there's nothing we missed wasn't cool.

He's thorough though, not saying anything as he opens every cabinet, pulls out every drawer, lifts everything to see if there's anything attached to wooden frames or in crevices. Finally, he brushes his hands off and puts the knife away.

He takes a quick trip to the building's dumpster and returns, using our childhood secret clubhouse knock. It's a small thing, but it's reassuring somehow.

He fills a glass with water and downs it. "Okay, pack a bag and you can come back to the hotel with me."

I shake my head, curling deeper into the pile of pillows on my couch and pulling the blanket that's on the back tightly around me, like a security blanket. "No. This is my home. You checked everything, Dom and Logan are gone. I'm not leaving."

I know I sound petulant and whiny, but I'm hoping TJ will cut me some slack after my night. He's not quite willing to give it up though. Turning to me, he leans against the kitchen counter, his voice quiet and softly pleading.

"Come on, Allie. I've got two double beds in my room, comfy and warm, safe and . . . not here."

"Nope," I reply, shaking my head. "I won't be chased from my home."

Funny. I never felt in danger until Dom, and now he's the one I'm in the most danger from. He's the only one with access to hurt my heart, my body, my soul.

TJ looks around, and I understand the feeling. Even though he's searched, there's still that little niggling feeling that we've missed something, that we've got a big hi-def camera or something pointed right at us and it's streaming video of me right now.

"Listen, Allie, I can't leave. I just don't feel like you're in a safe place. But I won't force you. Can I stay the night?"

His question unknots a giant ball of tension from my chest, and I nod. TJ drops down on the couch beside me, relieved.

"Yeah, I'd like that."

"I got you, Sis," TJ says quietly, looking down between his knees.

After a few minutes, he speaks up again. "How'd everything get so fucked up, Allie-gator? What happened?"

I don't answer because he seems to be leading himself somewhere, processing something in his own mind. His head falls back to the couch and he stares at the ceiling.

"When I was in high school, I had this whole picture, you know? You were gonna be this famous dancer, living in Manhattan or LA or Paris or some shit, and I was going to be the soldier boy. Yeah, I was thinking about it even then. Blame Dad with all those old fucking John Wayne movies, I guess. Then, well, I had Janine, dreaming of happily ever afters and all that romantic shit. I thought I was gonna come home, surprise Janine with being back, and we'd be *happy*. I mean, I was going to surprise her with damn-near a guaranteed year at the base stateside. We'd get the family started, have a couple of kids, dinner at home. And somehow, it all got shot to hell. Now I'm stuck here, without her, without the dream, without the happily ever after. I filed for divorce, did I tell you that?"

"No, you didn't," I reply, but I'm really not that surprised after what he told me. "I'm so sorry, TJ. If you need anything, please just say the word and I'm there."

The offer is real, but I know he won't call on me. That's not how he operates. He's always been the caregiver, not the care-receiver. He's always taken care of me, patiently and with his whole heart. It's one of the things I love most about him and an example I've always tried to live up to myself. Still, he nods, his head rolling over to look at me.

"Thanks, Allie."

I sit forward, putting a hand on his knee. "It's her loss, you know? You're an amazing man, TJ, and if she couldn't see that, didn't appreciate that, it's her loss."

He picks his head up and looks me dead in the eye. "His loss too. You're better than this, better than him. You deserve more than to be questioned and followed, kept in a cage. You are one of the strongest people I know, Allie. You've fought and reinvented yourself so many times, and you're so close to getting out of the tunnel you've been in for so long that I swear . . . looking at you, it hurts because your light is so bright. You can leave your debts behind, this life behind, and get all the things you've always wanted. Don't let him keep you in the dark."

Twenty-One

DOMINICK

EVERY MORNING when I wake up, I look at the calendar, each blank square stabbing in my heart as I look back at that night.

Two weeks. Two weeks, and tomorrow, the calendar changes over, taking that night off the page. And not a single word.

I've felt myself retreating day by day as my mind starts to fray before crystalizing back into the ice-cold, manipulative fucker I was before Allie. I hadn't realized how much she'd changed me, melting my frozen heart in a watershed of rebirth, shaping me into something better. But now, without her light, her sun, her warmth, every thawed drop has refrozen into sharp edges, making me ready to gut anyone who so much as looks at me sideways.

It's only by sheer force of will that I haven't gone on a rampage of violence, slashing and burning the city so it hurts as much as I do. Even before, I never felt this insane. Never felt this primal desire to destroy things.

Ironically, the more of a bastard I become, the busier Petals has been. In a twisted sense of irony, every night has more patrons, more people wanting a front-row seat for Armageddon, like I'm some daytime soap opera villain they want to see destroyed by his own weakness. But even as the darkness inside me grows, I keep my façade, stoic and impassive, not giving an ounce of show to the vultures.

I still make the required appearances for formality's sake, shaking hands here and there around the floor because it's expected and it would show weakness on my part if I didn't. That's something I'm unwilling the bear. I've been conditioned since birth to never, ever show weakness.

Instead of letting that happen, I take a few moments to have a seat at a table near the stage with a group of influential local businessmen, offering them a round of Jack on the house.

Nothing fancy—they don't deserve the fine imported stuff—but they're so enamored to watch Trish's turn on the pole that it doesn't matter.

I lift my glass in silent salute and hold it there as each man lifts his in kind. I wait, not saying anything but giving each of them a hard look of expectation. These pampered princes haven't tipped Trish at all during her performance and they're taking up one of the prime tables. Unacceptable and downright rude.

Still holding my drink aloft, I watch as they set theirs down, quickly grabbing twenties from their wallets and holding them up. Trish sashays over, giving me a look of appreciation, but I don't acknowledge her in any way. She plucks the bill from each man and blows them all a kiss as she moves on.

I finally take the Jack in one gulp, not even feeling the burn of the whisky down my throat. A sense of relief washes through the men, and they follow suit, taking their shots at once too.

The ritual completed, I rise, laying a heavy hand on the shoulder of the leader of the little group, wishing them a good rest of their evening before continuing my way upstairs.

I can hear Logan coming up the stairs behind me as I enter my office, the weight of the crown weighing heavily on my head. I know he wouldn't dare approach without a reason, but I wish he would just leave me to sink into the darkness of my soul alone.

No such luck. He's a professional. I could order him to leave me alone for the rest of the night unless it's an emergency, but I've been doing that too often over the past two weeks.

Besides, he's my only source of intel, and even if it's a bitter, vile pill that I have to take each day as he shares his news with me, I swallow it eagerly. I know Logan's hoping that it'll soothe the beast I've become before my state of mind starts threatening everyone's well-being.

"Sir?" Logan says, asking for permission to come into my office and begin.

I wave him inside, holding up a hand as I sit down in my chair, pinching the bridge of my nose, trying to prepare myself. He must sense permission because he begins his report.

"Allie had routine classes today for Thursdays, two children's classes and her Diva class. Her Diva Dance class was full this week, three new attendees, all married females, nothing amiss. She had her first Pole Fitness class last night, also full, seemed to be majority of dance moms from Encore."

As hurt as I've been, I'm glad for her. She deserves every success in her dance dreams, and I hum, signaling for Logan to keep going. I need to get this over with, but I also want every morsel of insight to savor.

"After work, TJ met her. They went for dinner at a Mexican restaurant, then back to her apartment. He stayed until just before midnight. Allie stayed in the rest of the evening. Wilson is on duty tonight."

"Wilson?" I bark, suddenly angry. That's a change in schedule, something I can question and reasonably expect an answer on, something I can be angry at without seeming like a heartbroken, lovelorn puppy. I make a plan, and it should be followed to the letter.

To his credit, Logan doesn't so much as flinch at my outburst. At least, for me, it's an outburst.

"Yes sir. There was an incident before TJ arrived."

"What happened?" I growl, reining in my anger. "Is Allie okay?"

Logan holds up a hand, unruffled. "She is, though she almost took my head off." He says it with an amused tone, like whatever happened was funny to him.

"Logan."

My single word cuts through his attempt at lightness and refocuses him back to business.

"Of course, sir. I was at Mat Madness, not for duty but because Max and Dalton let me use their stuff in exchange for pointers on their amateur fighters. I've been helping them coach one of the up-and-coming kids."

He pauses like he's waiting for me have something to say about that, but I don't have patience for that right now. "Continue."

"She must have seen my car in the parking lot, assumed I was there to watch her," Logan says, turning slightly red. "She stormed in, and before I could even greet her, she ripped me a new one, the gist of which was to *leave her the fuck alone*, and then she stomped out. Whole thing took maybe a minute? Max and Dalton were rather amused at seeing her hand me my ass while I stood there like a gaping fish."

I have a flash of pride in my girl. It's good to imagine her unafraid of someone as athletic and dangerous as Logan. Not that Logan would touch Allie. He's a good man and has strict orders not to unless it's for her own safety.

But her ire at being watched means she's still fighting with herself over what we are, what I mean to her. I swallow the painful thought down, not willing to let Logan see my hurt at her dismissal of what we have.

"So what does that have to do with Wilson being on duty tonight?" I ask.

Logan rubs at his jaw. "You want us to stay invisible, Boss. Allie knows Gavin and me, knows our cars, knows our builds well enough to spot us in a crowd. Wilson might not be the best, but he's . . . invisible because she doesn't know him that well. I also told him to dress casually when he's on patrol, just one more way to be inconspicuous. Because she's obviously looking, testing to see if you've really left her alone."

I growl to let Logan know he's walking a fine edge.

After our fight, I'd had to tell him and Gavin to step back in their chaperoning, to be invisible once again. Logan, who sort of knows what happened, hadn't liked it, but he'd done it when I reminded him that though Allie might not want to be guarded, she damn well needs the bare minimum because the whole town knows she is mine.

And though there may be suspicions as to why I've been such an asshole lately, no one really knows that there is trouble in our fucked-up version of paradise, so she's very much at risk.

"Wilson?" I muse. "He's a good asset here at the club, but this assignment is more important. Do you trust him to do his job, keep her safe, not be seen, and not touch her if he is?"

Logan nods immediately. "I do. I stressed the importance of the matter to him . . . personally."

With a sigh, I acquiesce. "Very well."

He turns to go but stops with one hand on the doorknob. He looks up and then turns to face me fully, his hands crossed in front of him.

"Sir, may I speak freely?"

It's a big thing to ask me in my current mood, and he knows it. To be honest, I'm not sure I want to hear what he has to say, but his proximity to Allison teases at me, wanting any tidbit of intel he might have on her.

I have done my best and haven't contacted her, haven't spied on her or knocked on her door to beg entry, but it's been hard. Without the insights from Logan and Gavin, I'm not sure I could've withstood the last two weeks.

I nod, not saying a word so he knows to be cautious.

Logan clears his throat. "Dominick, she looks like hell. She's holding it together, putting on a smile for the kids and the ladies in her classes, but it's fake. She's fraying around the edges. Her eyes are puffy like she's been crying a lot, and I think she's even lost weight. The light through the window says she's got her TV on into the early hours of the morning, so either she's not sleeping or she's sleeping in the living room. I think she's falling apart."

In an instant, I'm out of my chair, pacing back and forth. I run my fingers through my hair, grabbing handfuls and pulling hard to punish myself for doing this to her. I hate that she is in pain. I can withstand anything but that. I need to go, need to hold her in my arms and tell her that everything will be okay. Reassure her and myself. She will come around. She has to.

I make a move toward the door and Logan bravely steps in front of me, halting my progress. "Sir. Stop. I wasn't finished, and I can read it all over your face, but you can't go to her. She's working it out. It's hurting her, but you're in no condition to go to her either. As much as she looks like shit, you're just as bad."

He knows his words piss me off, and I narrow my eyes at him, pressing my shoulders back and standing upright. A king demanding reverence. "Excuse me?"

Logan doesn't back down as I expected and continues. "You don't wear it on your sleeve like she does, but you're just as unraveled. I get it, she's special. Everyone who's spent five minutes with her knows that. She brought you to life, like the miracle worker she is. Now she's gone, and you're five different kinds of fucked up because of it. Just as much as she needs to figure shit out, so do you. Don't go fuck her up more than she already is because you can't handle your shit."

It's probably the longest string of words I've ever heard from Logan, which sucks because he's one hundred percent right and we both know it. Still, his words sting, and my hand clenches in desire to punch him for the liberties he's taking speaking to me, even if I gave him permission to do so.

Instead, after a moment, my hand relaxes and I reach up, patting him on the shoulder. "Perhaps you're right, Logan."

He nods. "You're a good man, Dominick. As much as you can be. But what you're asking her to do, to be, is a lot for someone who has no frame of reference for the world you live in. She doesn't understand. But I think she *could*. You can't keep her compartmentalized like you have been. Either she's in all the way or out all the way." He pauses, letting that sink in. "I think you need to bring her in, or at least give her the option. Be clear on it, none of this cloak and dagger shit that you're good at. But just . . . give the girl a minute to miss you."

A tiny smile of encouragement flashes on his lips, gone so fast I almost think I imagined it, but it was there. "You think she does? Miss me?"

The rare moment of weakness escapes with the hopeful question before I can stop it, but Logan doesn't take advantage. "I know she does."

It helps, and I take a deep breath, going back to my office chair and sitting down to gather my thoughts. "What was she wearing for her first pole fitness class last night?"

It's an odd segue, and though he looks confused, Logan takes a moment before answering. "I don't know, sir. The classroom has no windows, you know, and when she came out, she was in her normal sweats, like I said. Same pair she was wearing when she chewed me out. But earlier, when she greeted the ladies in the lobby, she had on black shorts and a baby pink tank top. Why?"

I take a moment to savor the image in my mind. "Thank you, Logan. That'll be all."

He doesn't question me further, hearing that our moment of friendly chatter has ended. But I know without a doubt that my Allison misses me now.

I sent her the package of dancewear with an encouraging note about her first class. Maybe it hadn't been the smartest play, to push myself into her life when she'd so adamantly forced me out.

But she'd worn the outfit, which means she read the note I sent.

Maybe there is a chance I can earn my way back into her life.

But the last time I tried to do a delicate dance, it ended in spectacular flames and nine thousand dollars' worth of broken surveillance equipment.

And my gut tells me that if I go in like a bull in a china shop, demanding and pressuring with expectations of obedience, Allie would rebel like the hellcat she is. While I enjoy her moments of wildness, I need it to be within reason.

There's got to be a way to keep her safe, to keep her by my side, and to keep her mine.

Twenty-Two

ALLIE

"OH, my goodness, girl. You look like . . ." Maggie says as I open the door before her voice stalls.

She just looks at me, her mouth pursing as she tries to find a nice way to put it.

Finally, I just wave her inside. "Helluva greeting after not seeing me for so long. And you can say it, I look like shit. Believe me, I'm well aware because I feel even worse."

Maggie shakes her head, her newly-dyed platinum curls bouncing. "No, I mean you look fine, just . . ."

She doesn't finish the thought, just grabs me in a big hug, squeezing me tight. She's surprisingly strong for a little thing. I'd forgotten just how much.

"Grr, I could just shoot that man for what he's doing to you," she says when she lets me go, and though my lips tilt up slightly, it's far from my usual beaming smile. "I can do it, you know. I think the law's on my side."

"Thanks. It's the thought that counts, though I'd never want that. Even the thought of you brandishing a weapon kinda freaks me out. Like a Killer Kewpie Doll," I reply, watching her plop down on my couch.

She grins, a full showing of her teeth like it's a really funny joke. "You know me, I'm just your everyday FBI consultant Barbie doll. I'll shoot you full of holes, infiltrate your organization, and discover all your dirty secrets. Then I'll make cupcakes, paint my nails, and break your eardrums with my karaoke. Gotta have balance, you know?"

The sarcasm is a newer development in Maggie's personality, and I like it. She used to be exceedingly sweet and innocent, but her man Shane has apparently changed that a little.

She still doesn't curse, which of course means I'm even dirtier in my talk around her, trying to get her to let an F-bomb drop. So far, I've succeeded exactly once, an effort that took a lot of wine after a customer at Petals grabbed her ass, but today might be number two.

"You wanna drink?" I ask. "Oh, you can toss the jacket anywhere." I vaguely gesture to the hooks by the front door, which are so overloaded that there's a pile of hoodies on the floor too. At least they're in the general vicinity of where they're supposed to be.

Maggie looks around for the first time, seeing the mess I've created over the past two weeks. I'm not exactly a neat freak to begin with, and two weeks of going to work and then crashing on my couch haven't done a thing for my cleanliness, though some of it's been TJ. He went through here with a stick and some doohickey, checking every wall I've got. And then he moved stuff out of the way to install new camera-less smoke detectors. Only problem is, he didn't put everything back.

"Why don't we just head out?" Maggie finally offers. "Our appointment's in thirty minutes anyway."

Foregoing the idea of a drink, I nod and follow Maggie out, making sure to lock my door behind me. Her car's in the parking lot, a nice, new, very bland-looking Suburban.

"You planning on killing the planet one-handed?"

"Bureau issue . . . I gotta return it on Monday," Maggie says.

We get to the salon, and it's not until we sit in the big vibrating chairs with our feet soaking in the tubs that she finally looks over, her eyes piercing.

"Okay, what happened? Hit me with the whole sordid story."

This is us, what we have done countless times before. We've been through a weird tumblypants change in our friendship, but through it all, we've just become closer. And this is how we do our thing.

I give her an edited version, leaving out names because you never know who is listening. "And then after agreeing to transparency and telling me about some of it, he leaves out the biggest fucking part."

"What?"

"The spying! He had cameras all in my apartment. And he didn't tell me! When I caught him, he was fiddling with the smoke detector!"

Maggie cringes, biting her lip worriedly. "Yeah, that's awful. I mean, we have cameras at our place for security, I get that. But we know about them."

I shake my head, my deep sadness of the last days replaced again by fresh anger.

Maggie eyeballs me. "Okay, so let me just say something and have you not bite my head off, deal?"

I don't like the sound of this, but I nod.

"So if you were dating a celebrity or a politician or something, would you mind the guards, the trackers, the reporting of your whereabouts, the cameras? Because, not that Shane is any of those things, but that sounds oddly familiar to my life."

I open my mouth to answer, but before I can, she reaches into her purse, pulling out her phone. "See? Tracker. Cameras at home—want to see my bedroom right now?"

She clicks a few times on the screen, and her made-up bed, complete with pink floral pillows, pops into view. "And while I may not have a guard right now, I do partner up when I go into the field. When it's not with Shane, he gets so nervous I swear he pees his jockeys if I don't check in with him."

"But you know about all that stuff, and knew it going in," I argue.

Maggie holds up her hand, and I sit back, holding back my frustration. It's not her, it's this whole shitty mess. "I know," she says after I'm fully in my seat again. "I'm just trying to figure out what the exact problem is. Is it the monitoring or is it that he didn't tell you, because those are very different problems with potentially different solutions."

"I'm not sure," I admit. "I just know I'm mad. And sad. And just grr!" I finish with a growl of . . . confusion? Frustration? I'm not quite sure.

"Well, you're fully allowed to be pissed off," Maggie says, "and let's be honest. By your own words, you didn't have a problem with the guards. You knew who" —she raises a brow pointedly— "and *what* he is, and that his job would mean some additional precautions."

"I know," I admit. "I'm still shocked you're not shitting kittens over it."

Maggie shrugs. "I did at first, but I've learned nothing is black or white, good or bad. There are evil people on the right side of the law and good people on the wrong side. I'd like to think Dom's one of those. But without a doubt, it is a different life. If you can't handle that, definitely get out now because he can't change that part of his world. My opinion, though . . . what's got your tutu in a twist are the secrets, which I totally understand. I'd be pissed too."

"I am pissed," I agree. "But—"

She cuts me off, shaking her head. "I'm not done. Buckle up, because things are about to get bumpy. What about sad?" Maggie asks. "The million-dollar question. Do you miss him?"

I think about it, not saying anything as the foot bath finishes and the techs come to start messing with our toenails. Finally, I nod. "I do. But then I feel stupid for missing him. I shouldn't want him, not after this."

"Should, would, could," Maggie sing-songs dismissively. "Doesn't mean a thing. Just labels people put on expectations. Don't box yourself in based on what someone else would do or thinks you should do. If you love him, make your peace with who he is and who you have to be to stay with him. It'll require some give and take from both of you, but it's doable. If you don't love him, let him go and move on. It'll hurt, but you'll both be okay eventually."

The casual way she says it is like a sharp knife in my gut, forcing me to picture my future without Dominick at my side, and more painfully, to picture his without me there.

Maggie's comments make me think . . . would Dom ever open up to another person, let down his façade and be real, play chess with them and talk to them? I'm not sure I want it to be me by his side, but I sure as fuck don't want anyone else there either. Still, the thought of him alone breaks my heart.

At the same time, I try to picture myself with the happy husband and two kids behind a white picket fence, like TJ keeps talking about, both for him and for me. The all-American dream, I guess. And while it is what I've always wanted, the picture blurs and the only face I can see beside me is Dominick's. It's ridiculous because he's definitely not that guy, but a tiny voice in my head whispers . . . *maybe he could be?*

And that's just it. There's so much I know about him but so much I don't. And I can't go through the rest of my life only getting a portion of him while he demands all of me. I need to know both sides of his life, personal and professional, to see if I can handle it, to see if I can accept it.

The manicurist holds up a book of swatches, asking me what color I want. I don't even think. I just point to the bloodiest red I see. It matches my feeling. I'm just bleeding out from the inside.

Maybe the lacquer will be a reminder, a visible shield to protect me tonight. Protect me from him.

———

This is impossible. I'm a strong badass bitch, but I can't do this. Okay, I'm not really a badass bitch, but I am strong. I have fought my way through auditions where I was rejected on sight for my hair color, I have worked my body to its limits to master leaps and spins, and I have battled mental demons that still try to seduce me into their darkness with ugly thoughts about my worthiness.

I've done all that. But warming up at home, I'm not sure I can step on the stage at Petals tonight, knowing that Dominick will be in his office, watching me.

I snort at the thought. I'd always known he watched me dance, even though I couldn't see through the blackout windows. I'd imagined him there on the other side of the glass, our connection pulsing through the din and sin of the club long before we'd actually touched.

It would fuel me, and I delighted in the show I was putting on for him, because even as the crowd watched, it was for him. But it was knowingly and willingly.

After talking to Maggie today, I had hoped to feel some clarity on the situation, but I'm still waffling. Option one, smack him stupid for doing that without telling me, getting a promise of honesty henceforth, and then forgiving him in a blaze of makeup sex glory. Option two, just walk away, however painful that may be.

I'm on the verge of talking myself out of going when my phone rings. I consider not answering, just hiding away in my room, nestled in the covers. No . . . one way or another, that's not who I want to be. Instead, I look at the name flashing on my phone. I don't want to admit, even to myself, that there's a small part of me that's disappointed it's not Dominick.

Other than that one gift with a tasteful card that simply said *My heart is with you. I know you can soar like the beautiful creature you have always been,* he hasn't contacted me in two weeks, honoring the time and space I said I needed.

The note had been signed with a scratchy capital D as if I'd have thought the gift had come from anyone else. It was a painfully reminding prick that he'd encouraged me to do the pole classes in the first place, and the simple and elegant wording had brought tears to my eyes.

But this isn't Dom. "Hey, Trish."

Trish isn't one to mince words, especially when she's gone into Mom-mode. Tonight's no exception. "Do not 'hey, Trish' me. Where the hell are you, woman? You should've been here thirty minutes ago to claim your spot in the dressing room. As it is, I'm fighting the vultures off because with you not here every night, it's technically not 'yours' anymore. I'm about ready to get my damn pepper spray. Hey, I said hands off!" she says, and I can't help but smile as I hear her continuing to rant on the other end to someone in the dressing room. "You'd better back that ass up. This station is Allie's tonight, so tonight is the night you learn to share a mirror with someone else. Shoo . . . that's right, there ya go."

Ah, Trish. Bubbly but fierce as fuck. God, I love her. "Thanks for looking out, girl. But I don't know if I'm coming."

Trish's laughter rings out in my ear. "What the fuck ever! If you don't get down here ASAP, there's going to be a riot, backstage and front of stage too. Fuckin' house is damn-near chanting your name. So if you're bailing, you'd better give a girl a head start to get outta dodge. There won't be a sequin left standing if this place pops."

The crowd doesn't bother me, but it doesn't excite me like usual either. I take a deep breath, shaking my head. "I don't know if I can, Trish. I know he's there."

Trish clucks her tongue, lowering her voice. "Look, honey, I don't know what's going on with you and Dom. I just know that he's been a beast for the last couple of weeks. But you've both promoed this appearance like mad, and I'm pretty sure you need the money. I'm not shitting you. This place is packed wall to wall. Me and a few of the girls, we dropped hints with the right people. You know, the gossipy folks. Told them you've been working on a new trick or two and were gonna knock some socks off, theirs, not yours, obviously, because nobody's working the pole in ugly ass socks." She waits for me to laugh at the bad joke, but at my silence, she keeps going. "Bottom line, you're a dancer, right? Don't let drama steal your bankroll. Drama is gonna pass, but those greenbacks will too, so you'd better get 'em while the getting's good."

She's right. I do need the money. But it's not enough motivation to face him.

"Plus, don't let Boss Man keep you down. You get up there and do your job like a pro and show him that whatever he did, he fucked up the best thing he's ever gonna have. Because you sure as hell are, Allie. Show him that you can handle yourself, with or without his nonsense. Don't let him take this from you too."

That lights a fire under my ass, and I reach down, snagging my bag. "You're right. I'm on my way."

Trish's grin is audible over the phone line, and she hums happily. "That's my girl. I'll meet you at the back door. One thing. Don't you dare tell that man that I said one ugly word about him. I got a family to support, Allie."

It's a joke, but also there's a healthy dose of fear in her words and I'm reminded that while I'm lost in relationship drama with Dominick, he truly is a man most people are scared of.

I'm not scared of him, though. I'm pissed at him. The thought somehow gives me an extra boost of power, and I strut to my car.

"Trish, I hundred percent promise you, it stays you-me-God. That's it."

Twenty minutes later, I park in Petals's lot and head to the back door, the same as I have so many times before, but I'm different inside. Gavin, who's on door security, doesn't even have a chance to open it for me when the door bursts open and Trish barrels through, sweeping me up in a big glitter-fueled hug.

"Holy shit, I've missed you! Come on, let's get you ready before the floor goes wild."

I grin, following her in the door. "I'm sure it's not that busy."

Gavin holds the door open for us both but fails to stifle a chuckle. "You gotta be blind, Allie. Did you see the front lot? It's so damn busy we had to bring in two valets because even the overflow lot next door is full, and we stopped letting people in about thirty minutes ago because the fire marshal decided tonight was a good night to check the place out."

He rolls his eyes, and I realize that I've missed him and Logan, had gotten used to hanging out with them everyday. I reach up and hug his neck. "How you doing, Gavin?"

He hugs me back briefly but brotherly and smiles down, a hint of sadness in his eyes. "Me? Fine. *Him*, not so much."

I bite my lip and sidestep the question I want to ask. "And Logan?"

Gavin grimaces, then forces a smile. "I think he's catching the brunt of the upstairs heat, but he seems to be getting his frustrations out on the mat. He's training a kid over at that MMA place by you."

I nod, feeling like hell. After going off on Logan, Max came by the dance studio to talk with me and told me about Logan helping out.

"Yeah, I might owe him an apology."

"Fuck it, he's cool. He understands."

Trish, eager to get things going, drags me away, pulling me into the dressing room. "We can all play Twenty Questions and shit later. Right now, though, you need to get glammed and get right in your head. Give me your phone so I can play your music for you."

This is why I love this girl. She could be mad that I'm taking the spotlight tonight, could be apathetic about whatever shit's going on in my life, could be gossipy about me and Dominick.

Nope, she's running stuff like a boss herself. In the middle of this chaos, she's the one keeping her head and issuing orders, making sure things get done. She's the girl you want by your side when stuff is going well because she'll celebrate right, but also the one you want by your side when it's all wrong because she'll hold you up when your knees give out. My music starts, and I give Trish a nod.

"Thanks, girl. You're a good egg."

She smirks. "I know." And then she's off, mothering the other girls and helping them get ready for their performances. Securing garters, pulling corsets tight, and adding an extra touch of glitter. And then another. Man, she *loves* glitter.

I start applying my makeup, going with a heavy smoky eye and red lips to go with my red costume for the evening. I needed something hard, something fierce to give me a bit of armor to do this, not because of the dancing. That, I enjoy and could do in my sleep.

This armor's to protect me from Dominick. I know he prefers me in pink, softer, more real, and that's exactly why I'm going full-vixen tonight.

Putting a wall between us, rebelling against him while flipping him the finger metaphorically, and making my own stand, my own way.

Listening to my headphones as Beyoncé belts out about running the world, it seems Trish was right. I am getting into the right headspace for this. I've got enough time to wrap it all up, do a full double-check of my costume, my hair and makeup, and every speck of glitter—yeah, Trish added some extra—and then it's go time.

I head to the 'gorilla position' behind the curtain, and moments later, I hear the DJ announcing me, getting the already worked-up crowd whipped into a frenzy.

It's weirdly . . . fun. I might not be a rock star, but I can understand the thrill, the rush as it hits me harder than ever before.

I remember that this is why I enjoy performing, that connection between me and the audience, sharing the experience of the moment.

My music starts, the intro long and sultry so I have time to make my entrance and walk the rail. I have a moment of falling out of character, so shocked by the sheer volume of people in the room.

Gavin wasn't lying. This place is packed, but they've made sure it's not sleazy. There's no concert vibe with horndogs packed five-deep around the stage in a standing-room-only leer fest.

Instead, they've moved in additional tables and chairs to fit as many people in the space as possible.

My mind whirls with the unexpected number of people, but my music reaches its first bridge into a crescendo that signals me to approach the pole.

It jolts me, and I adjust, dropping back into performer mode.

Immersed in the music, the throbbing erotic beat fuels me. My body spins and twirls, moving with a routine so memorized I don't even think about it. It just flows as an extension of my soul.

Time passes without my even realizing it as I dance, making eyes at the audience before swaying into my next move.

Fifteen minutes. Two extended-version songs with a short break that isn't silent but gives me a chance to catch my breath, work the crowd, and reposition on the stage.

The second song's the challenge, the pole routine that has me working my body hard. The stage lighting lowers to a deep red as I do my final tricks, glad that my new pole class has at least given me plenty of practice time to perfect my new favorites.

Of course, whatever new thing I'm doing is always my favorite. I climb up high, locking my left leg on the pole and arching my back. Lifting my right leg behind me, I arabesque and let the spin ensure everyone's eyes are on me.

Stopping the slow turn, I arch even further, reaching back to grab my right foot and lift it even higher behind me, the arabesque becoming a vertical split known as the Eagle. I hold the pose, feeling the stretch in my legs as there's a round of applause.

Without warning, I release and let my leg and head fall simultaneously, giving the impression that I'm out of control, but it's a planned part of my choreography to get upside down on the pole.

I switch positions, letting my legs free to spread wide as my right elbow locks around the chrome, my left elbow goes around my leg, and I clasp my hands for support.

It's a yoga pose called Bird of Paradise that's been adapted for the pole, and it's the perfect complement to my sexy ballet-inspired set. I hold the position, letting the slow spin show off the lines of my legs before I gain momentum, doing a fast flip so I'm upright once again, my legs on one side of the pole as I bicycle along on invisible pedals, getting closer to the floor with every rotation around the pole.

Finally, I touch down on pointed feet, and I flip my dark curtain of hair, resting back on the pole as I lower to the floor to gather the piles of bills.

My outro music plays as I crawl along, smiling and flirting with the people at the rail.

In this moment, I feel accomplished. I'm successful at the studio, the classes are going phenomenally well, even better than Donna and I had thought, and the feature here is an obvious hit.

But as I reach the edge of the curtain and look back, I feel fucking empty. I didn't dance for the money in my hand, though my bills will appreciate it. I danced for another reason, one I'm only willing to admit to myself. The thought triggers me to look up to the windows, something I'd purposefully avoided doing during the routine. But I can't help it now.

To my surprise, the windows are not all blacked out. Instead, on the far left, there's one transparent window, framing Dominick as he stands tall and proud, stoically watching me.

Our eyes meet, gasoline on the fire inside me, but I'm not sure if it's anger or want. Seeing him so close, but so far, brings back the times we both knew what we wanted but stayed away.

It seems pointless and stupid that we wasted so much time then. But what am I doing now? Am I making a stand, protecting myself from the fallout of a life where he takes my wild freedom and I allow him to put me in a cage?

Or am I wasting time, time I could be with him?

I can see it in his eyes, feel him holding back from me even across the rowdy space between us. Finally, he lifts his whiskey in salute and swallows the whole shot in one go, then turns away.

An instant later, the window is black.

CHAPTER

Twenty~Three

DOMINICK

I HADN'T EVEN PRETENDED that I wasn't going to watch, didn't lie to myself that way.

I've been starving, desperate for even a hint of her, a whisper of her scent, her passion, her fire. It's worn me down and nearly broken me.

But tonight, I am going to feed the dark part inside of me that wants her, needs her, owns her. She struts the stage, made up in sultry paint and red lingerie that her natural beauty doesn't need, and I know she did that for one reason only.

To fight me.

To show me that she can be whoever she pleases.

But it pleases me too.

I want her to embrace every facet of her personality . . . the sweet and the sultry, the submissive and the sassy, the bold and the brash, and the bared and the buttoned-up.

I don't want a two-dimensional figure, a shadow of a woman. I want her to explore every interest she has. I just want her to explore them with me.

I will admit that I want her protected, but not in a cage. Or at least not a restricting one. I want her to realize that the cage I want to offer her is the same wildlife preserve that I live in, a place where she can be all she dreams of, safely free in her wild chaos.

I want her to soar and test her limits. I want her to be my queen.

An image of the chess set I gifted her falling to the floor at her feet flashes through my mind, a lance of pain in its wake. I've wondered too often if any of the pieces were broken, and if they were, what it means to my heart.

With a forced breath, I return to the moment, here and now, watching my

Allison dance. I could do this all day, every day. Her grace and elegance astound me and make me see beauty in function, light in the dark.

But Logan is correct. Allie has lost weight, which concerns me. The shadows under her eyes are well-disguised with stage makeup, but I can see the weariness on her.

She hasn't looked up yet. I know because I purposefully left one window clear so that she could see me watching, a symbol of the transparency she wishes for between us. It's a small gesture, but she'll understand.

It's not until the end, as she's almost off-stage, that she looks up and our eyes meet. My heart stops at the pain I see in her expression. I hate that I put it there and wish that she would let me soothe it away and take care of her.

But I don't know how to compromise on this, balancing the risks to her life over her discomfort with being kept safe. And as much as I hate to admit it, she wasn't able to handle the truth of my life and how pervasive my love for her has become. I'd known she wasn't ready, but I'd truly hoped that we'd get there one day soon. But fate had forced my hand.

I lift the tumbler of scotch and swallow my drink in one gulp, the taste smooth on the jagged shards inside me, before turning away. I hit a switch, and the windows blacken to their normal matte exterior finish, leaving me in nearly soundproofed privacy.

I sit in contemplation, knowing she's in the building, so close but unattainable, at least for now. I want to rush down there, to throw everyone out my way and reclaim her, remind her that she's mine. But I don't move a muscle, forcing myself to stay in my chair, gripping the low armrests to ground myself.

When my phone buzzes, I almost jump, lost in my own thoughts of how to right things with Allison, to get her to return to my side. Glancing down at the lit screen, I see Logan's name and just two words, but my heart stops.

She's coming.

I glance up to the security displays and see Allie on the stairs, coming to my office. I consider whether I should turn the monitors off, not wanting to put salt in the wound, but I decide against it. She must know that this is the truth of me, of my life.

Even my own home is bugged. If she is to share this life with me, she must accept that reality. It's a big nature park, but it's still restricted.

Her knock is soft and tentative, which hurts, ironically. Part of me wishes she would have just kicked in the door and started kicking ass. That she is hesitant, maybe even fearful of me, is a jolt to my soul.

"Come in," I reply, my voice steady even as my heart races. I have sat at the table with the biggest, baddest men in the underworld, have killed in cold blood for nothing more than my family name, and am by all accounts a scarily icy opponent in any conflict, but this woman is my complete undoing.

She has reduced me to weakness, pierced all my defenses, and left me teetering on the edge of oblivion even as she's worn herself down the same way.

Shakespeare's infamous quote skitters across my mind. *Though she be but little, she is fierce.*

And my Allison is fierce, strong enough to stand at my side but also strong enough to stand against me and bring me to my knees. A worthier opponent I could never find, but also a more brilliant ally does not exist.

She closes the door behind her, coming to stand before me with her shoulders back, prepared for battle. She still has on the somewhat smeared remains of her makeup. Even stage makeup cannot withstand the amount of hard work she's been doing, and her mussed hair flows over her shoulders in battle snarls. If I were a betting man, I'd wager her sexy red lingerie is underneath the oversized black sweats she's currently wearing.

She's trying to get out of here as fast as she can. Trying to get away from me.

She lifts her chin, challenging me. "I'm not here to discuss personal matters, only business. We need to go over receipts for the night so I can get my share."

Though my every instinct is to rush her, press her into a chair, and beg for forgiveness with my tongue buried in her pussy, I know it's not the right move. Not for her, not for me, and not for us. Not now.

"If that's what you wish," I say, feigning acquiescence. "Please, sit."

I gesture to the chairs in the sitting area of my office, not wanting my desk between us. If this is the only taste I have of her at this instant, then I don't want even a scrap of paper between us.

She sits primly on the chair's edge, not relaxing even an inch. "So, fifty dollars a person entry tonight times . . . do you have a head count from the door yet?"

I eye her, keeping my face neutral. "The fire marshal said our capacity is maxed at 350. Logan will have exact figures after closing, but I'm certain we hit it, maybe exceeded ever so slightly."

She does some quick math in her head, ticking off things on her fingers to help out. "So the door take is at least $17,500, and my share at twenty-five percent is . . ."

I already ran the numbers on a calculator earlier. "About forty-four hundred minus tip share. Not a bad night."

"Says you," she huffs before looking to the side, whispering quietly to herself, "Took everything I had to walk in here tonight."

Finally, I'm getting to her, ruffling her feathers and pulling her away from her desire to stay all-business. I lean forward, wanting to use this moment of honesty not as a weakness but to show her that I'm just as broken by what's happened between us.

"Allison, I've had to near-physically restrain myself from breaking down your door for the last two weeks to force you to listen to me. It took everything I have to let you walk on that stage tonight without being marked by me. And it's taking every drop of control I possess to remain in this chair and not drop at your feet to worship you like the queen that you are."

I clasp my hands between my spread knees to watch her eyes come to me, her lips trembling as she realizes what I've said.

"Dom, don't," she finally gasps, shaking her head. "I can't."

"Don't what?" I challenge her, my voice thick with emotion. "Want you, need you? Because I know one thing, Allison."

I get up slowly, not wanting to startle or frighten her, and close the small gap between us. Bending forward, I place my hands on the armrests on either side of her and lean down to whisper hotly in her ear.

"You have damned me. I am yours. And you are mine."

She turns her head away, and though I suspect it's more to keep her lips from mine and create some space between us, she only succeeds in giving me greater access to her neck.

I lay soft kisses and licks along the tendon stretched tight there, letting her ragged breath be my guide. She whimpers as I get close to the juncture of her neck and shoulder, so I bite gently, not breaking the skin, but so that she feels the gentle tug of my teeth. I taste her sweat, drawing her flesh into my mouth and sucking to pull blood to the surface, wanting her to see that I am with her even when she's alone later.

Because I know that she will leave me again.

It will take time. She is fighting herself as much as anything else, but she is still mine.

"You already know that you hold my heart, and though a part of you wants to rip your heart from me, I can't let you go. I love you, Allison. Always," I whisper, and a tear slips down her cheek. I chase it with my tongue, catching its saltiness and savoring it, though I don't want her to cry.

She turns to look at me, her chocolate eyes pleading with me to stop this madness, but I can't. With her bright red lips so close, I can't stop myself from tasting them.

She cries out against my lips, her hands going to my shirt, and though I think she initially intended to push me away, instead, she pulls me closer and kisses me back. Between kisses, she speaks in stilted utterances, foregoing breath. "I shouldn't. It's wrong. I can't be . . . who you want me to be."

Confusion races through me, and I pull back from her, searching her face. Her eyes meet mine again, and then she breaks, the tears wrecking the last of her makeup as sobs shake her body.

Reaching down, I gather her into my arms, holding her like a child in my lap as she shudders, her face hidden in her hands as I inhale the clean heat of her heavenly scent. When she can breathe again, I tilt her chin to look me in the eye.

"Allison, what are you talking about? You are already exactly who I want you to be. I'm not trying to change you." I rub her back, trying to comfort her, but she's still looking at me uncertainly. "I love you, Allison Bancroft, just as you are."

She shakes her head, taking a deep breath before answering. "But you are trying to change me. I'm not some kept woman, Dominick. I don't need guards and trackers and cameras. And *secrets*."

The last word is hissed like a cobra's venom on her tongue. It strikes home, lashing me like a whip, and I fall back, the chair the only thing holding me up.

"Allie, for two weeks, I've thought of nothing but that word. My life, it needs secrets. My empire is built on them, a foundation of knowing every-thing about everything. When I'm with you, I feel different, but the truth is I am not a good man, Allie. But you make me want to be. You make me wish that I were some regular Joe with a nine-to-five job, a minivan, khakis, and a golden retriever or something that could offer you an easy life. But I can't give you that. All I can give you is me. And I am a cold, cruel, manipulative bastard who is in charge of a corrupt city."

She looks at me, but I'm rolling. I can't let her interrupt me. I don't have the strength to do this again.

"My life, every moment is filled with risks. I am not trying to make you a 'kept woman'. I am trying to make you *my* woman, which means keeping you safe. I know my world isn't yours, and I wanted to introduce it to you slowly so that exactly *this* didn't happen. All the security isn't because of you. It's because of me, and it tears at my black, black heart that I'm respon-sible for doing this to you. But I need them so that nothing happens to you. Because I couldn't bear that."

She watches me as I shudder, completely unfazed by my anguish and not scared of the monster that I am. "But what if it was the opposite? What if I tried to get you to leave your world, get that 9-to-5 and be a regular guy like you said? You couldn't do it. You're not willing to change for me, but you want me to change for you."

I look at her incredulously. "You really think that?"

I stand up, holding her in my arms, but turn to set her back in the chair so I can pace. I don't like it, the way she's studying me, but I need the move-ment to organize the chaos of thoughts in my head.

I don't like chaos. I am orderly and methodical, but in this moment, I am the tempest incarnate, swirling and uncontrolled. My steps echo in the quiet room, my eyes bouncing from her to the floor and back to her.

"I am a monster, Allie. Can you not see that? Ask anyone and they'll tell you the worst mistake of your life was to look at me the first time we met and see something other than the truth. I don't smile, I don't feel. I just rule like the calculating manipulator I am, whether I want the responsibility or not. Except with you. With you, I'm not a monster. I'm just a man, so quickly buoyed or crumbled by your every word. Weak, vulnerable . . . afraid. And in love. With you."

I chance looking at her and hate the way she's staring at me. Like she doesn't know me at all. Walking closer, I get down on my knees, bowing my head to the floor in total and complete subjugation to her.

"I am sorry I didn't tell you everything about the surveillance. Truly sorry. Please, that's everything. I swear it is. But you have to know that if you want me the way I want you, you will have to endure those things, and you'll have to trust me."

I hear her whisper softly in the silence, piercing my heart with every word. "Rule three. Trust."

Before I can ask her whether that means she does or doesn't trust me, the door bursts open and Logan appears. Quickly, I leap to my feet, but he looks on unfazed, all-business.

"Sorry, sir. Emergency. We need to go. Now."

I'm instantly back in The Boss mode, though I step in front of Allie, putting myself between her and Logan so that she can pull herself together.

"What's wrong?"

Logan glances to Allie and replies *sotto voce*. "Pete called. There's trouble. *He's* involved."

Allie doesn't see it, but I catch the way he jerks his chin toward Allie. There's only one 'he' Logan would mention in relation to Allie other than me. TJ. I turn to Allie. "Stay here. Please. The guys are downstairs to keep you safe, but I need to deal with this."

She doesn't agree or disagree before Logan interrupts. "Sir, it might be best to bring her."

I look to him, eyes narrowed as I analyze his motive for wanting to bring Allie close to anything that might be construed as trouble. He doesn't back down, though, his voice still low and calm but unafraid.

He grins, though it is grim. "Sir, that *minute* we talked about giving her . . . it's up. Decision time for both of you."

Logan is a smart man. It's why I've entrusted so much to him, and even without the full picture of what I'm walking into, I have faith that he has my back and my best interests at heart.

Turning to Allie, I hold out my hand. "Let's go, Allison."

CHAPTER

Twenty~Four

ALLIE

IT FEELS STRANGE, riding in the back of a car while Logan and Dom sit up front. We're riding toward something, although they've been super-light on details.

Logan looks at me in the rearview mirror. I can't decide whether he's begging me to be onboard with whatever is happening or warning me off. Maybe both?

Still, until he gets the word from Dominick, he insists on talking in roundabout terms that remind me of when my parents would talk about 'adult things' with me and TJ in the room. Like when Grandma Ellie got cancer. It's infuriating and confusing all at the same time because I'm definitely listening closely, trying to figure out what the fuck is going on.

"Pete called. Unauthorized transport through the South Side."

Dominick's eyes are on the passing landscape out the window, seeing something in the darkness I can't, or maybe he's just using the white noise of the passing vista to help his mind focus. Either way, I can see his reflection, and the hard clench of his jaw and the way his face has gone from the expressive vulnerability of his office to a cold Terminator-like sternness is frightening.

"Involvement?" he asks crisply.

Only because my eyes are ping-ponging this entire trip do I catch Logan's slight wince, his mouth twisting down at the corners before he answers. "Chambers . . . plus one."

None of this means anything to me, except the word 'unauthorized'. That obviously means that something is going down in Dom's town without his permission, and I can't imagine that's a good thing.

Who would be stupid enough, brazen enough to do something under

Dom's nose without his go-ahead? And why did Logan want to bring me? It seems like a risk Dom wouldn't usually take.

Dominick doesn't give me answers or explanations though, just picks up his phone and dials a number by memory.

I can only hear his side of the conversation. "Silas? It's Angeline."

There's a slight pause, and Dom speaks again. "Chambers was making a run."

Another pause, and this time, I hear a deep but tiny voice shout 'fuck' loud enough that it's audible from Dom's phone.

"Am I to take it by that response that you did not authorize it?"

While Dom listens to whoever Silas is, he traces patterns on the window of the car, almost all of them geometrically perfect.

"Very well. There may be other complications, but I leave Chambers to your discretion."

Another pause, and I wonder . . . did Dom just give permission for someone to die?

"Acceptable. Consider this a gracious gift, Silas. Tonight could've ended much differently for you."

Dom doesn't wait for a response, hanging up as Logan pulls into a totally darkened parking lot. I've had plenty of time in the car to let my eyes adjust, so I can see the shadowy shape of what looks like a fifteen-foot moving truck.

A moment later, the moon comes out from behind the clouds and I see more shadows and realize there are two men on the ground, with another small group of men surrounding them.

Suddenly, I really don't want to get out of the car. I'm terrified of what is about to happen, knowing I'm going to see the true Dominick Angeline. The monster. The boogie man people of East Robinsville fear.

It's time to meet The Boss.

Though he may not be those things with me, I've been fooling myself that he isn't that. I realize I've been living a fantasy, pretending that Dom's some 'villain with a heart of gold' who only pretends to be a ruthless bastard in order to stay alive. And I don't want my pretty fantasy shattered.

"No. No . . . uh-uh," I moan wildly, shaking my head. "I don't want to do this. I don't need to see this."

Dominick turns around in the shotgun seat, reaching back to lay a hand on my knee, looking back at me. "Allison, this is my world. This is who I am, what I am. Evil, perhaps, but a necessary one. You need to see, and you need to know."

I want one more moment of innocence, one more taste of who he is right now before my image of him is forever tarnished. I lean forward and he meets me. I kiss him softly, and it feels like a goodbye. In a way, it is. A goodbye to the delusion I've been allowing myself. His lips move against mine for a moment, soft and sweet, but all too soon, he pulls away, and I can see the mask come back on, his eyes going ice-cold and hard.

Undoing his seatbelt, he looks at Logan, his voice hard. "Stay with her, Logan. No matter what."

Logan dips his chin once and Dominick gets out. I can't hear, but I see him greet and shake hands with an older guy in a suit and give a nod of greeting to the three other men holding guns on the guys on the ground.

But when Dominick says something to the two guys on the dirty asphalt, they both look up.

One of them I don't know. The other is . . . TJ.

Before Logan can say anything or do anything to stop me, I'm out the back door of the car, running to him. "TJ! Oh, my God. What the hell is going on?"

TJ looks at me, obviously surprised at seeing me here. "Allie? What the fuck? Get out of here!"

I should do what he says, but in that moment, my eyes involuntarily turn to Dominick, looking for his guidance. I'm in way over my head here, and I don't know what's happening, but on some level, I trust that Dominick isn't going to hurt me.

The next instant, Logan is at my side, holding me back from TJ. Pulling me away, he growls lightly in my ear, "Settle down, Allie. Watch, learn, and understand."

Logan's the sort of man who always sounds hard. It's part of what makes him a good bouncer, but in the time I've known him, I've learned to read his rumbles. This time, there's no bullshit, no compromise. He's as intense as he can be, and I know if he has to, he'll pick me up like a child and drag me away.

I stop fighting him so that I can stay, though I'm not sure if it's for TJ or for Dominick. Maybe both, to some degree. I stand on my own quietly, and he slowly lets go. Logan and Dominick have a quick, silent conversation with their eyes, and whatever else is passed, I know that from this moment on, Logan is personally responsible for my safety. Knowing Logan, that means he'd lay his life down in the process and not even think twice about it.

My interruption settled, Dominick returns his attention to the man in the suit, though TJ is still begging me with his eyes to run like hell.

"Pete, this is Allie. Allie, this is Pete. He's the man on the South Side. A good boss."

Something in the way he says it makes me hear the lower-case 'boss' instead of the upper-case Boss I've heard others whisper when they talk about Dom. He doesn't tell Pete who I am, and I wonder if that's because Pete already knows or if that particular piece of information is something he doesn't need to know.

Usually, I'd shake hands with an introduction, but my gut tells me to stay where I am. Dominick is on edge, and while the signs of his stress are very well-disguised, they're there. His right hand is half-clenched, and the little wisp of hair just above his right temple is out of place.

I'm probably the only person in the world who would notice that, though. Instead, everyone else would likely see that his shoulders are down and tension-free, his breathing is slow and even, and by all accounts, we could just be having a casual meeting with friends about helping out with apartment moving tomorrow.

Except for the guns and the guys on the ground.

TJ on the ground.

I look down at him again, hating that he's in this position and not understanding why. He's still screaming at me with his eyes, anguish and apology in their depths.

I want to jump in and demand answers, but Logan's words flash in my mind and I wait. Dominick glances at me, and though he doesn't say it, I can see the gleam in his eye, telling me I'm doing the right thing. Telling me to trust him.

The kind flicker is gone when he looks back to Pete. "Pete, as you were saying?"

Pete swallows, eyeing my presence carefully, but he clears his throat and continues. "Yeah, so I got word a shipment was coming through. Knew you hadn't authorized it or you would've let me know, and it would've been my guys, not these assholes. So I had my guys stop the truck, and here we are."

He seems kinda smarmy and talks to Dominick like they're old pals, even making it seem like he's a big shot. Maybe he is, but Dom doesn't seem impressed.

"And you found out about the shipment when?"

Pete flushes a little but answers. "Got word about a bit of trouble earlier today, but wasn't sure it was real until we actually saw the truck."

Dominick purses his lips, pinching his left shirt cuff to pluck off an invisible piece of lint, and when he answers, his voice is emotionless.

"I see. So you had intel but didn't feel the need to tell me. Instead, you decided to choose your own course of action, also without authorization. Have you forgotten that there's a proper way to do things? Seems you're taking a lot of liberties. Just like these guys."

Without warning, Dominick's right foot pistons out, kicking who I'm guessing is Chambers dead in his chest. He's knocked back, rolling over, but Dom's foot meets him in the gut, driving the wind out of him. Though it's Chambers on the ground coughing and moaning, the threat is obviously to Pete and everyone knows it.

"I was watching my South Side, like I'm supposed to," Pete says defensively, still trying to sound strong but wilting by the word. "My guys stopped the truck, like I told them to."

He's emphasizing everything about this seeming like his territory . . . me, my, I'm, which feels dangerous. East Robinsville's Dominick's, not his. He's just the store manager.

"Dom, I knew it was a big night at the club and I didn't want to interrupt your night of dancing," he says, more than a little disrespect in his eyes as he glances at me. In that moment, it's apparent that he knows exactly who I am by the way he leers at me.

Though I'm fully dressed in sweats, I've never felt more naked, which pisses me off. I glare back, my fists bunching at my sides, telling him with my eyes to fuck off and hoping Dominick tells him out loud because I'm not real sure of the rules here.

Not that I've ever been one for rule following.

"Fuck you, Pete," I say, disrespect and dismissal dripping from the words.

There's a tiny piece of me that acknowledges it's a stupid thing to do, but I'm secretly curious how Dom is going to respond.

My heart leaps as I see the slightest uptick of his lips, not a smile, but enough of one that I know he approves of my outburst and might even be a little amused.

But when he turns back to Pete, there is no smile and his neutrally impassive expression has given way to a clenched jaw and stormy eyes.

"It seems that you're getting a false sense of your importance, your power," Dominick says, pulling everyone's attention back to him. "That's something I can't have. I have given you some slack because of your experience, but let me be clear. You are a pawn trying to claim a crown that doesn't fit. I let you 'run' the South Side as my eyes and ears, but in doing so, you are to share that insight so that I can actually do something with it. Perhaps stop us from having an evening like this at all. Something avoidable with a single phone call."

Dominick tsks as he steps closer to Pete, who's watching with true fear in his eyes now. In a blur of movement, Dominick backhands him across the face, his ring popping the skin open at the point of contact as a thin line of blood instantly appears.

I gasp, my hands covering my mouth as my eyes shoot wide open.

I feel Logan place one staying hand on my shoulder, lightly but enough to remind me that this is a test, as much for me as it is for Dominick.

Pete wipes his cheek, and though he's cowering slightly, I can see the fury in his eyes. Dominick leans into Pete, forcing him to tilt back and putting him at a disadvantage. His voice is cold and sharp, cutting through the night air like a laser.

"Do not fool yourself, Pete. We are not friends. This is not *your* territory, and these are not *your* men. Everything you see, everything you eat, everything you touch . . . it's *mine*."

Pete starts to say something but freezes when Dominick cuts his eyes over to the three guys with guns. Instantly, they point their weapons at Pete.

To his credit, Pete stands tall in the face of the threat, head held high, but his retreat is complete as he takes a step back and adjusts his jacket lapels.

"My apologies, sir. Won't happen again, Mr. Angeline."

The moment stretches, and I'm holding my breath, waiting for the sharp cracking pop from my nightmares, the sound of a pistol going off and someone suddenly blooming red from some part of their body. But the silence holds as Dominick stares Pete down, searching his face for something, and whatever it is, he must see it because he relaxes incrementally and the tension in the small group lowers.

Looking around, I realize these men are just as scared as I am. Even Logan, who can dish out violence with his bare hands in the octagon like it's nothing, is relieved too.

Still, while the guns lower, nobody moves.

Dominick sighs like a disappointed parent and turns back to Chambers, who's gotten himself together enough to be sitting on the ground.

"What's in the truck?" Dominick asks.

Before Chambers can answer, a loud rumble fills the quiet night and everyone turns to look at the approaching headlights.

"Who the hell is that?" Pete growls, confused.

Dominick smiles. It's full of teeth, but instead of looking happy, he looks feral. But also, he looks a little pleased?

What could make him that cocky in the midst of all this? The sound gets closer, and I see a big motorcycle and a muscle car approach. Half the guys turn their eyes away, but I forget and am immediately plunged back into night blindness as the engines turn off.

In those few moments of silence, Dom speaks.

"You may go now, Pete."

It's an order couched in pleasantness.

"I will be watching for any further signs of *trouble*."

Everyone hears the implication. Pete steps back, waving 'his' guys back with him, and they all retreat slowly, none of them stupid or courageous enough to give Dom their backs.

Instead, as bootheels crunch on the blacktop and two newcomers approach, their eyes flick back and forth worriedly. As I look at them, I understand. It feels like everything just got worse. I had no doubt that Dom could handle whatever sniveling shit Pete was up to.

But these two new guys look rough.

They're tall, hulking men, one with a beard and long blond hair making him look like a Viking, the other an older man with salt-and-pepper hair and eyes that even in the darkness burn with a hellish fire that says he's seen some shit and come out the other side.

Nobody says anything until Pete and his men get into their cars and pull out of the lot. In the deep silence that follows, there are three groups, the rough biker-looking men, TJ and Chambers in the middle, and Dom, Logan, and myself on the other side. It's like some weird sandwich, and I wonder if I'm the mayo or the pickle. No, not the pickle for sure, considering the swinging dicks around me right now as the men all take each other's measure.

Finally, the Viking looks at Chambers and TJ, then up at Dom. "Well, ain't this some shit we got here, Angeline?"

My eyebrows raise at his lazy tone, not disrespectful but just zero fear. Either he knows something I don't, which is probably likely, or he's fucking clueless about Dom.

CHAPTER

Twenty~Five

DOMINICK

OUT OF THE corner of my eye, I see Logan subtly move in front of Allie, not cutting her off but making sure that if something kicks off, she's covered. Good man.

On the ground, Chambers starts to get up. "Fucking hell, Robbie. Where've you been, man?"

He's suddenly laughing and jovial, like he thinks Robert Zallow is here to save him, but one look at Robbie's eyes and I know that's not the case at all.

"Get on the ground, Chambers," I growl as he gets to a knee, but he knows who he answers to. Instead of following my order, he looks at Robbie and gets to his feet, but I don't give him another warning, sweeping his feet out from underneath him and sending him crashing back to the cracked asphalt.

"As I was saying, what's in the truck?"

Chambers looks to Robbie again, but I plant my foot on his chest, pressing down on his ribs. I don't lean my full weight into him, showing a glimmer of mercy mostly because Allie is here, but when I withdraw my shoe, his full attention is on me.

"*Fuck* . . . fine. Open and see for yourself, asshole."

Chambers is digging his hole deeper and deeper, and I suspect he'll need a literal one before the night is through.

I nod to Zallow, who nods to Victor. I've never met him before, but I know all the players in Silas's crew because you never know when the insight might come in handy.

Like tonight.

Victor is Silas's Sergeant at Arms, a former Marine Scout Sniper and a weapons expert, and it makes me wonder if Silas suspects the unauthorized shipment contains guns.

Victor goes over to the truck, unlocking the door and pushing it up, the rollaway door rattling on its frame.

Suddenly, Victor steps back as a chorus of cries fills the night air, and Zallow flashes a flashlight over the interior of the truck box, spitting out a harsh echo of my own thoughts.

"Fucking hell."

Not guns, not drugs. Instead, a small group of perhaps a dozen or so women and children huddle against the back wall of the moving van, fear and confusion written boldly on their faces.

Victor recovers quickly, holding his hands out, showing he doesn't have anything in his hands, and rattles off clear, if badly accented, Spanish.

"No problema, estais seguro. You're safe, okay?"

He turns to Robbie, his look telling me what I need to know. Silas didn't know about this. His guys didn't know about this. And they're furious, judging by the glares they send Chambers's way.

The scared women are Allie's breaking point, and she rushes forward, dodging around Logan. "Oh, my God, help them! TJ, what the fuck are you doing?"

Victor stops Allie from climbing into the truck, but at my unintentional growl, he sets her down gently.

"You are not getting in there right now. It's not safe until we know what's going on. Now, how about you don't get me killed for stopping you, 'kay?" Victor says gruffly.

TJ's eyes dart from Allie to me, and he clears his throat. "Tony said he needed help with a coyote trip. They've got their menfolk north already, working up in the Midwest on cattle ranches and farms. They're meeting them there."

Suddenly, Chambers laughs heartily. "Can you believe the fucking choir boy savior complex on this one? Hero for his country soldier shit. Just told him it was a rescue mission and he was right on board. Yes, sir," he mimics, sloppily saluting, though I know he's a soldier himself.

It's an intentional slight.

TJ turns to Chambers, his anger growing before my very eyes, which tells me that Chambers did mislead him. "You're trafficking them, aren't you? I fucking asked you that. You lied to me, you son of a bitch."

I don't move as TJ launches himself at Chambers, tackling him to the ground and proceeding to pound him into the pavement. It's not a fair fight, not after what I've already done to Chambers, but I don't interfere as TJ caves in his nose, the crack audible even through the sound of fists meeting flesh. TJ doesn't stop, landing shot after shot to Tony's face and body.

"Enough," Zallow calls out finally, or maybe it's too soon. Chambers deserves worse than a beatdown for what he was planning to do to these women and children.

When TJ doesn't stop, he grabs him by the arm and pulls him off. "Goddammit, at ease! He's still my brother. Get the fuck off, TJ."

"*Uno momento,*" Victor says, holding up a finger to the whimpering women before closing the back of the truck. They cry out, but he throws the latch anyway. Allie lays her palm to the door, whispering something I can't hear.

For now, Zallow faces me squarely, his arms crossed over his chest and his feet spread, trying to look dominant. I'm sure it works for him more often than not, but posturing and feathers are for peacocks. I don't need some anthropologic dominance posture to be in charge because I actually am.

"Angeline, Silas said Tony was ours to handle. TJ, yours. Agreed?"

I look at the two men sitting on the ground, one beaten and broken and the other only restrained by his training.

I dip my chin once in agreement, but as Victor begins to move to Zallow's side, I call out, stopping them. "Allie, come here."

She doesn't want to leave the truck. I can see it in her eyes, the glitter of tears pooling in the corners. But she obeys without complaint, and I take her hand, holding it tightly. Through my touch, I give her all the strength I can, all the encouragement, and the silent message that she's been amazing so far. It's far less than I wish I could give her.

Perhaps this is a mistake. Maybe I should shuffle her off to the car with Logan and hide this from her.

But she wants no secrets.

She wants transparency.

And as painful as it is for both of us, she'll get it. No matter how ugly. No matter the stains it will leave on her soul.

It's a fraction of the ones I bear, but she is innocent, more than I ever was, considering the family I grew up in.

Victor raises his gun and Chambers sobers, the realization dawning that he's in far deeper shit than he thought.

"What . . . wait? Vic! You're my brother. You can't do this. Silas won't—"

Perhaps in his former life, Chambers was a man who could give orders. His file said that he served his country with courage and honor during two tours, one in Iraq, another in Afghanistan. And maybe he's served Silas courageously afterward, I don't know. But now he's at the end of his road, and like most men, he pleads for his life, all notions of honor or toughness forgotten.

Some would look down on him, but I don't. I've seen too many strong men do the same thing and too few truly face it with dignity. Death comes for us all, and when it does . . .

Victor's voice is stone-cold, devoid of all emotion. "Silas's orders."

The words stop Chambers's pleas, and though he is reluctant, he moves to swing his legs beneath him so that he's in a kneeling position. I'm surprised, and I tilt my head a little as he looks up at Victor, clearing his throat.

"Tell him . . . tell him thank you for everything he's done for me. And that I'm sorry for fucking up so badly."

Though I wish we were not here, not in this position tonight, there is some small amount of honor in the way Chambers faces the consequences for his choices, and I offer him a silent, respectful salute.

Victor nods once and then pulls the trigger.

Allie doesn't scream, but her knees unhinge, and I catch her as she looks wildly from Chambers's body to her brother, and finally, to me.

"No," she whispers pleadingly. "Please, Dominick, no."

I growl in her ear, forcing her to listen. "He brought this on himself, and he got what he deserved. You do not even want to have a glimpse of the hell those women and children in that truck would have been heartlessly sold into. At his hands, Allie. The world is better, and we are all safer without him."

She cries, the tears flowing as she sobs silently into her hands, but she nods so I think she heard me. TJ clears his throat, turning to me with as much dignity as he can.

"Just let us go, me and Allie. We'll go and you'll never see us again. We won't say a word. Please."

I know the last word was a fight for him, and yes, he'll plead, not for himself but for his sister. There is strength in him, more than men in my line of work often have.

"There's no need. She's not going anywhere. She's mine."

TJ nods, seemingly understanding that I'm not killing him on the spot. He's lucky. If he'd been knowingly trafficking those in the truck, I would've meted out harsher punishment than even Chambers received. His blood connection to Allie would not have saved him.

I would've made it hurt, sent a message to the city about what I allow and what I do not.

But TJ was deceived and thought he was doing something good.

Besides, I was the one who called Zallow and set all this in motion, hooking TJ up with Tony. It was not intended to lead to this, but regardless, I must bear a drop of the onus for beginning this mess with that small action.

Eventually, Zallow breaks the silence of our staredown, pulling out his phone and making a call, most likely to Silas.

"Vic's driving the truck. It's a mess. Tony was making a traffic run. Need a cleanup and someone for Vic's ride."

"Send Mac," Victor whines to Robbie. "I don't want nobody else driving Suzanne."

Victor turns to me, shrugging. "Suzanne's my baby. 1970 Plymouth

Roadrunner. 325 horsepower, but the clutch is still a bit finicky. Mac's the only one I trust to get her home without stripping out my gearbox."

That he can talk about his car when his fallen brother is at his feet tells more about him than I think he realizes. Zallow relays the information and hangs up.

"Okay, it's covered."

"Where are you taking the truck? The women and children?" I ask.

Zallow looks to the closed door, haunted as if he can see inside. "We've got a place where they'll be safe, and some connections. No harm will come to them."

With a mental checklist complete, I turn to Logan, silently telling him that it's time to go. There will be more to deal with tonight, so much more, but what we can do here is done. Silas's Eagle Raiders will take care of their own and the victims, so it is best if I am no longer here.

As TJ climbs in the front seat next to Logan, I open the door for Allie, ushering her inside. As she ducks her head, Zallow's voice makes her freeze. "Hey, Angeline!"

I turn, lifting an eyebrow in question. "Two things. One, Myra says thank you for all the baby shit and told me to invite you to dinner or she'd have my nuts in a vice. So consider yourself invited."

I smirk at that, knowing that inviting the devil into your home must be hard for him, but he's more scared of making his woman unhappy than he is of me. It's oddly sweet. But by his tone, he doesn't truly want me to come over. Smart man.

"And two. Quit sending shit to my Old Lady, asshole."

His face and voice remain that lightly threatening growl, which is his normal tone of voice. But a moment later, he breaks into a laughing grin, and though it is maudlin under the circumstances, I smile back and give him an unusual gift. Honesty.

"As you wish. I merely wanted to make their life a little more comfortable. I find your family . . . inspiring."

He looks taken aback, then remembers himself. "Well, don't be looking at us as your hashtag-couples goals. We've got our own troubles. Read a fucking romance book or something if that's your kink, Angeline."

His wave is dismissive, but I can hear the notes in his voice, the pride on his face. He recognizes how special his relationship is, a woman strong enough to withstand the life he leads. The thought burns in my mind, and I turn back to Allie to find her staring at me like she's never seen me before, like something confusing just clicked in her mind.

The ride to my house is quiet, each of us lost in thought. Even TJ is quiet, perhaps assisted by occasional glances from Logan. I'm analyzing the events of the evening, making a note to call Silas for follow-up on the trafficking victims. I trust him or I wouldn't have let them take the truck, but a call to ensure they are cared for sends the appropriate message.

I'm focusing on the business side because I'm not sure what's going on in Allie's head, and that, quite honestly, terrifies me. I glance down at our joined hands and rub a soothing circle on the back of her hand, hoping she can feel the depth of my feelings in the bare touch.

We pull up to my place, and Logan looks to me for orders. "Head back to the club to check in. Call me with a report."

He nods, and I help Allie out of the car and lead her to the front door while TJ trails along behind us. As soon as we get inside, it all hits her, and I can see the weariness weighing on her. She slumps, and I hold her close. She buries her head in my chest and I rub her back in calming strokes. She sniffles a bit and then stands tall, still trying to be strong.

"I'm going to go clean up."

She walks down the hall to the bathroom, and I think she needs this moment alone more than she needs to clean up the few shadows of makeup still on her face.

TJ watches her go too, and as the door closes, he turns to me, his hands down by his sides but the tension coiled in his body telling me he's more than ready to fight if that's what it comes to.

"Is this where you try to take me out, tell Allie that I left, and create some cover story about how I died in service?"

It's not a bad idea. It would solve a lot of my problems, take the devil who tells her to run from me off Allison's shoulder.

Instead, I chuckle and casually wipe at my ring with my handkerchief. "You said 'try,' but if I wanted you dead, you would be already. I have not killed you, nor do I intend to, because it would hurt her. And that is the last thing I want."

"Why?"

I look into TJ's eyes, deadly serious. "I love her."

He huffs a humorless laugh, shaking his head in rejection of my words. "Love her? And this is how you show her?"

I shrug, turning my back to him and walking away. "It's what she asked for. Transparency. No secrets. Follow me."

I can feel TJ's confusion at my apparent disregard for his posture or his words, but after a moment, he follows me into the living room, where he stops, looking around.

"Nice place."

I don't say a word as I walk over to my wet bar and hold up a decanter. "Drink?"

He nods, and I pour three tumblers of scotch. Allie comes in, looking freshly scrubbed with her hair piled on top of her head. She has on one of my long-sleeved T-shirts, so big it's almost a dress on her, and a pair of my gym socks. If her brother weren't here and things weren't so questionable, I'd snatch her up and carry her to my bed.

I like her in my space, in my clothes, raw and bare-faced with no walls between us. But looking into her eyes, I can see there is still a wall. It's not brick. It's made of the questions, the doubts, the fear she has of me. And I have perhaps this one and only chance to knock it down before the foundations settle and it becomes permanent.

I offer her the crystal tumbler, helping to steady her hand for a moment when she shakes. "Drink, Allison. It'll settle you."

She nods and tosses back the scotch like a shot. I take the tumbler, rinsing it out and setting it aside as she sits on the couch. TJ takes the spot next to her, pointedly looking at me, daring me to move him or her.

Unwilling to risk action that could further hurt the situation, I offer TJ his drink before reluctantly taking the chair on the corner of the sofa. Settling down, I take a sip of my own scotch before setting the glass on the coffee table.

Allie pulls her feet up, curling her legs underneath her, and I can't help but read into the fact that she leans away from TJ and toward me.

"Dominick?"

There is so much in the single word, every emotion rushing through her blood buried in its soft plea. I can't look away, needing to see her, needing her to see me. Instead, I lean forward, placing my elbows on my splayed knees.

"You said no secrets, Allison. Is that still what you want?"

She bites her lip, and I can see her uncertainty, but this is the biggest crux of her concerns. What I do with her brother might be at the top of her mind, but this is the actual key point. She'll either accept me as I am or not, but I can't have her halfway.

She's better than that. She doesn't say yes, but I see the choice in her eyes.

I clear my throat and lay it all out for her.

"I am Dominick Angeline, head of the Angeline family, The Boss of East Robinsville. I take my job seriously and do everything in my power to make it a safe place. I work methodically to ensure everyone under my rule is provided for. It's not a pretty job, and there is often ugliness. But it is a responsibility I've been groomed for, a weight I bear by virtue of the last name given to me by my father, a future I hold by sheer force and the will to do what is necessary."

Allie's heard all these things before, in snippets and snatches, but for TJ, the whole truth hits him like a juggernaut's charge, and when I finish, he shakes his head slightly.

"Son of a bitch! You really are a fucking Mob boss? I fucking knew it had to be something like that."

"No TJ, I'm not *a* boss. I'm *The* Boss. At least, around here."

"This is why you had guards on her and were spying on her," TJ replies, anger coloring his words as he puts the whole picture together. "Because by being with you, she's in true danger."

"Yes and no," I reply honestly. "Months ago, your sister was an innocent bystander when someone tried to wage war with me. It was dealt with, but there was bloodshed, and I vowed that Allie would never come to harm if I could help it. So the guards are for her safety, protection from those who might wish to do me harm by hurting the one person I care most about."

I look to Allie, who's holding her breath. "But yes, some of the surveillance was for me. Because long before you knew it, and forever, you are mine."

TJ jeers, "I think you believe that sounds sweet or some shit, but it's creepy as fuck. I took down the cameras from her living room, her kitchen, her bedroom. That's not love. It's control. It's obsession."

Though he argues, the connection between Allie and me never falters. Her eyes never stray from mine. "It is all of those. Love, control, obsession. And insanity. But you enjoy that, don't you, Allison?"

TJ can sense he's losing her the same way I can feel her body yearning to come to mine, so he tries a different tact.

"So you had Tony killed? Shot right in the forehead by his own club?"

"No. I merely allowed them to do what they saw fit. Mr. Chambers's punishment was decided by them and then carried out," I reply. "He nearly instigated a war between his Eagle Raiders and me tonight, and it was only luck and that you've also been on my radar that prevented it, TJ. Do you think he could've returned to the fold, having betrayed his President? You know better than that, Specialist Bancroft. Disobeying orders is simply not allowed, not by me and certainly not by Silas. Tony knew that."

"And what about me? How come I'm not lying dead in a dirty parking lot?"

I sigh, knowing that this might be a decided matter to me, but it's of paramount importance to him. And through him, Allie.

"As I've already told you, firstly, because by hurting you, it would hurt Allie. I would sacrifice anything, anyone, including myself, to prevent that. Though I may not deserve her, my goal is to spend every day for the rest of my life striving to be worthy of her and making her happy. Secondly, your involvement tonight, while your own doing, may have been instigated by my own action."

"What? The truck was yours?" TJ asks, thinking he's found a chink in my armor, and I narrow my eyes.

"Absolutely not," I reply, a hint of anger in my voice. "I do not traffic people. Ever. But your involvement . . . the first ripple in the pond was at my encouragement. That night we first met, you left after dinner, upset. I knew why, and it wasn't just me. So I reached out to Zallow, asking him to have a drink with a fellow soldier. My desire was to keep you busy, admittedly, to lessen your influence over Allie, but also for you to truly have support in your time of need. It appears that your friendship with Mr. Chambers developed from there. Though I may have thrown the stone, may even be responsible for the first wave, your choices from there were your own."

I can see that he's searching for a way out of this, but he's a true man, and in the end, he sags, accepting the blame for his actions and at the same time, accepting that he may not be able to rescue Allie from me, though it is only in his mind that she needs a savior.

He's a good brother. He wants to simply grab Allie and leave, but he knows as well as I do that she won't stand for that. She won't leave with him any more than she'll stay with me simply because we want that.

I just wish I knew which way she was leaning, but her expression gives nothing away, her beautiful face a mask as she processes tonight's events and fills in blanks on the past couple of weeks that have now become clear.

My phone rings, and I know I need to answer it. I don't want to leave them alone, don't want to give TJ the advantage of free influence with Allie's mind, but if she can be so easily swayed, then perhaps it's for the best.

"Excuse me. I need to take this."

I stand, giving TJ a glance, and despite his obvious fury at my liberties, I lean down to press a kiss to Allison's temple, breathing her in. She sighs softly at my touch, relaxing even as she presses up to me.

I'd wager she's unaware she's done so, but both TJ and I realize it and recognize what it means.

She is mine.

CHAPTER

Twenty-Six

ALLIE

AS SOON AS Dominick is out of the room, TJ turns to me, struggling to keep his voice down. "What the fuck, Allie? Did you know he was the leader of the Mob?"

The unbridled anger in his voice makes me cringe a little, but arguing with TJ is the most familiar thing I've had happen to me tonight, and the steel at my core springs quickly to life.

"What the fuck to *you*, TJ?"

He looks at me like I've lost my mind, so I reform what I'm saying and try again. "I'm serious, what the fuck? What part of this is where you get to give me a hard time for who I'm dating after what you got your dumb ass mixed up in? He's the one who rescued you from some really shady shit tonight, TJ."

"I—"

I growl, popping him in the chest. "You're fucked mentally from what Janine did, I get that. But you told me you've still got a career in the Army. What happened tonight was your *best*-case scenario! Option one was that you'd get caught by some patrol car and end up dishonorably discharged and in prison for human trafficking. Option two was that you actually delivered those women and children into hell. But no, thanks to Dominick, those people are safe, you're not in prison, and you're also not dead. So wipe that look off your face. I think I'm the one who gets to ask you 'What the fuck?' this time."

TJ jumps up from the couch, pacing and tugging at his hair in frustration. "I didn't know! I met Tony and Robbie at the bar, and yeah, I hung out with Tony a bit. He said he understood. He got Jodie'd by his girl while he was in Iraq himself. So we talked about tours and shit. At dinner a couple of weeks ago, he told me he was working with an underground group, running missions to smuggle people to safety. He knew a couple of guys from Central America, and he said that whatever you see on the news, the reality is even worse. So I thought I was helping. I thought maybe, just maybe, I could do something good, *be* something good."

My voice softens at the vehemence of his confession, and I get up, still pissed but understanding that he'd acted with good intentions.

"But you ended up almost getting those people sold into God knows what! TJ, you are good. A good man, a good soldier, a good brother, but this is messed up."

He can't hear me over the thoughts in his own head, a trait that seems to run in the family. He mutters to himself, "Not a good man if I almost fucked those people over like that. Not a good brother if I've let you get tangled up with whatever Mob boss shit Dominick is doing! Sure as hell not a good husband, judging by the way Janine tossed me away."

I'm not sure he even meant to say that aloud, but his words make me realize just how much he's hurting. I don't know the mental steps he went through that led him to all of this, but somehow, his heartbreak over Janine ended with his actions tonight. I suspect it was a combination of his desire to focus on the mission, have an impact, maybe even a bit of a confidence boost after she destroyed him.

I grab him, hugging him tightly, trying a therapy trick I learned to quiet my own demons. "Tell those voices in your head to shut up. That's my brother they're talking about, and I love him. I love you, Teej."

He wraps his arms around me too, then lays his head on top of mine, squeezing me back. "How did everything get so fucked, Allie-gator?"

I don't answer for awhile, wishing I could freeze time and figure everything out and then hit *Play* again. But I can't. I pull back.

"TJ, listen to me. You are a great brother, the best I could ever wish for. Nothing will ever, ever make me stop loving you. And I am so sorry about Janine, but you're going to move on."

"How?" he asks, and I sigh in relief because at least this one's easy.

"One day at a time. They taught me that, and even though it's cliché, it's true. But tonight, we live with it. Not forget, but forgive ourselves and live with it. You're going to report for duty and enjoy the new assignment or put in for another one. Eventually, you'll date again. But no matter what, you're going to be okay. Tonight, what might've happened will be lesson, a reminder to find what you need inside you, not in some mission."

His smile is grim. "You sound like a therapist."

My lips tilt up a little, and I shrug. "Well, I've spent enough time with them. Speaking of which, if you need one, get one. And if you don't wanna talk to them, I'll be here."

He steps back, his eyes still full of worry. "But I can't leave you here, not with him. Don't ask me to do that, or I'm going to throw you over my shoulder and run you out of here. It's hard enough knowing that I couldn't protect my sister the last time she needed me, and that was saving you from yourself. I can't leave you with him now." He shakes his head, remembering what Dom said. "And what's this about a shooting?"

I shrug. I never gave TJ or my parents the details, not wanting to scare them. "Bad shit by bad men. But Dom protected me then. And in a weird way, he still is."

TJ growls, still upset. "He's a bad guy, Allie. You deserve better."

I frown, putting my hands on TJ's chest. "I don't know what the future holds with Dominick, but I'm going to figure it out. He loves me, in his twisted way. But it's a good twisty, like curly fries. He'll never hurt me, I know that. More importantly, I love him, and I owe it to myself to give that a chance."

"Do you hear the disclaimers you're spewing?" TJ asks, still upset. "He loves me in a 'twisted way'. It shouldn't be like that."

I sigh, knowing he doesn't get it, and truthfully, may never get it. "Maybe. But it is what it is. We spend all our lives growing up with this image of what life is supposed to be. We draw it in our minds from tv shows, books, our parents, just the whole world around us. But the reality isn't always like that. We don't get to order it up like a burger made our way. So what about just saying fuck it and taking life as it comes to us?"

"Sounds like a recipe for madness," TJ grumbles. "I don't understand, Allie."

"You don't have to understand it to support me. Just like I supported your enlisting, even though it was the last thing I wanted for you and I didn't understand it at the time. But Dom makes me happy, and I know you want that. And if a day comes that I'm done, that I can't or won't accept Dom and his life, I'll need my brother to swoop in to help me pick up the pieces of my heart. But right now, even with all the shit from tonight, the only thing I want is for him to hold me."

His shock is obvious. And if you'd told me that this is how tonight was going to go, I never would've believed it. I started out painfully separated from Dom due to his betrayal, and the violence of tonight was vicious, both things that should have me making my escape. Knowing Dom is The Boss and seeing him in action are two very different things.

I'm probably in shock too, from the stark reality of what could've happened to those women, and definitely from seeing Tony shot right in front of me. I don't forgive him, not Tony, not Victor, and not Dominick. But I can see the grey like Maggie said. I can understand that there are good guys on the wrong side, and sometimes even they have to do awful things for the greater good. It's a harsh justice, but it is righteous in a dark way.

And in this moment, I know it. I'm his, no matter what. The curtain is down, the magic is gone, and he's still all I want.

"Even after all this?" he asks. "I feel like the devil is holding your hand,

and you're asking me to just let you go because he's nice to you and said some pretty words. But he is a monster, make no mistake."

I take a big breath, trying to put into words what I'm feeling, trying to make him understand. "TJ, once upon a time, you told me that ballet wasn't worth what it had done to me. It fucked up my body and fucked up my mind. You told me to walk away from it, and I could've done that. But I knew that ballet was my soul, and no substitute would fulfill me the way dance did. But I knew, so I worked my ass off, healed my body, which was the easy part, and eventually, I got my head right, which was so much harder. And then I found a way to dance again. A way that is healthy for me. Not the way I imagined as a child, but at Petals, and now at the studio too. Something that had been bad for me in a lot of ways, dance . . . I've made it into my sanctuary again, like it should've always been. Dominick may be bad for a lot of reasons, and to a lot of people. But he's good for me and good to me. And that's enough. He's my sanctuary. Not the life I envisioned, not the one you keep telling me to chase, but one I want to live if it's by his side."

TJ frowns. "But if that analogy is true, what if he's what ballet was for you back then? The thing that fucks you up again, maybe worse than before?"

It's a thought that's run around in my head, and I smile softly because I already have the answer. "Then I'll have you to help me. If I could go back in time, knowing all the hell I went through, I would still start ballet. I would still want that first tutu when I was three, would want to push myself to begin pointe classes at nine, would still go on every audition that turned me down. Because it made me who I am. And TJ . . . I *like* who I am. If Dominick ends up being like that, something that gives me purpose, gives me joy, and then at some point destroys me, I will burn knowing that I chose it. That I wanted every moment of happiness, knowing that the devastation might come. Would you give up every happy memory you have with Janine because of how it ended? Would you trade the inside jokes, the joy you felt when you fell in love with her, the beauty of how you came together if you didn't have to feel the pain you're in now? Or is the loss of that happiness what makes you angry?"

I can see the shine of tears in his eyes. I hate that I'm prying at a scab that is so sensitive, but I need him to support me, even if he doesn't understand.

"I don't feel like I'm doing the right thing here, but I need to go and let you figure this out, don't I?" he says, resigned to my choice.

I lift to my toes, planting a kiss to his cheek. "I'm okay, TJ. I promise."

He sighs heavily but steps back, nodding. "Okay, I'll trust you. I'm gonna go for a walk, call an Uber or something to go back to the hotel. I need to think some shit through. It's been a weird night."

I give him one more hug and he pats my back. "No matter what, I've got you, Allie-gator. Love you, Sis."

I smile, my eyes puffy and burning with held-back tears, but these are happy ones. It's not a perfect parting, but considering all the drama of the night, it's pretty damn good.

"Love you too. And I've got you. And remember, my offer to beat the shit outta Janine still stands anytime you wanna take me up on it."

"Same offer to you. Anytime you need me to, I'll kick his ass," he says, smiling, but the look in his eyes says he means it.

Suddenly, it feels like old times, the two of us against the world, though maybe a little wiser, a little more jaded, but at each other's back even when we're at each other's throats. We've had some pretty major blowouts, both as kids and more recently, but in the end, we're family and that's all that matters. I'd kill for him, I'd die for him, I'd bring the shovel to the body-burying party, no questions asked for him, though hopefully, it never comes to any of that. Point being, he's my brother.

He gives me a little two-fingered wave and disappears into the foyer, the door clicking quietly before closing softly.

I take a deep breath after he's gone. I know that I figured some things out through my conversation with TJ, truly worked my way through a mental labyrinth of who I am, who I'm supposed to be, and maybe most enlightening of all, who I want to be. As to my heart, it knows exactly what it wants. But tonight was a test for me too. And honestly, I'm not sure I passed.

I walk down the hall toward Dom's office, listening to see if he's still on the phone but only hearing silence. The door is open and the room is deserted, so I take soft steps toward his bedroom.

When I stand in the doorway, the sight breaks my heart. Dominick, the cold, unfeeling monster that everyone fears, sits on the edge of the bed, utterly broken. His shoulders are rounded, his head hanging, agony pouring off him in waves.

"Dom?" I whisper, worried.

His head jerks up, his eyebrows lifting as he sees me, a hopeful gleam coming into his eyes. "Allison? You stayed? I thought I heard the door. I was sure you'd left."

Now his misery makes sense and hope blooms in my heart. He thought I left him, went with TJ. I shake my head, stepping tentatively toward him. I sink to my knees before him but don't touch him. I'm not sure if I should.

"That was TJ. I . . . I don't want to leave. Do you want me to?"

He cups my face in his palm, and I lean into him, wanting his touch so much that I raise my hand to hold him there and close my eyes, savoring the slight rasp of the calluses on his fingertips against my cheek.

"No," he says, his voice jagged and rough. "I don't want you to leave. Ever. Allie, I'm yours."

I know we have so much to talk about, and it'll be hard, but I can face it with him. "Dom—"

Whatever I was going to say is swept away as he leans forward and steals the words with a kiss, his mouth devouring mine as he holds me in place.

I give it all to him, all words, all power, all control. With this kiss, I let him know the truth. Yes, he owns me.

The difference is that I'm giving him everything knowingly and willingly this time. No secrets, nothing held back. I want him, want his cage, however gilded or rusty it may be. As long as he lives inside it with me. We'll have to talk, hammer out the details soon, but his kiss vows to me that we will do it together, and that's enough for the moment.

He grabs under my arms, suddenly yanking me onto the bed and rolling, pinning me beneath his weight as his mouth consumes me even more deeply. As his mouth works at my neck, his hand creeps lower, pulling the long T-shirt up by the fistful until my panties are exposed.

I'd needed to change out of my sweats earlier, wishing I could shed the memory of the scene at the truck as easily as the clothes. I'd wanted the comfort of Dom's scent surrounding me, but going into the living room for a difficult discussion had not seemed like the time to go commando, so I 'd left my red panties from my stage costume on underneath his shirt. And now as he looks at me, I'm so glad I did.

Dominick groans painfully as he traces the line of them at my hip, bringing goosebumps to the surface.

"My Allison . . . so beautiful. When I saw these on your honey skin tonight, all I wanted to do was rip them off and claim you. Make sure every man in there knew exactly who you belong to."

I bite my lip, permission given in my eyes, but while I expect him to roughly tear them, I'm thrilled as he gently slips them down my legs, tossing them to the floor before tenderly caressing my calves, kissing the sole of my left foot as he does.

The control he has not just over me but over himself is magnificent. I'd trust him either way, rough and brutal or sweet and soft, but I know that we're on the precipice of something here that there is no coming back from.

He kisses up my leg, soft tickles and arousing sparks alternating until he's between my legs, his fingertips soft on my pussy as he spreads my lips. His eyes never waver as he smiles cockily.

I think to tease him about his smugness, if for no other reason than to entice him, challenge him, but he moves in too fast, his tongue tracing a wet line from my opening to my clit.

I cry out, my hands grabbing at his head to hold him there, wanting every drop of pleasure he can give me, needing that connection as I'm under his control.

He licks and sucks as I buck against him, not fighting him but fighting for more, until he smacks at my hip before pinning me with a hard grip.

I let him hold me down, let him take me higher and higher, knowing I'm going to be sent flying to heaven. He nibbles at my clit, and the sharp pain followed by the flutter of his tongue pushes me over, and I scream, my legs clamped tightly against the sides of his head. I can't take any more and I know I'm smothering him, but I don't care. I pull him closer even as I overload, and Dominick senses it, laying one lingering kiss to my clit like he knows it's just on the verge of too much.

Gasping, my chest heaving, I look down at him between my thighs. He's beautiful, his dark hair mussed from my hands, his eyes bright with depraved desires, and his mouth shiny with my juices.

He's a monster. My monster, obsessed with me in a way that should terrify me. But as he prowls up my body, I'm not scared. I'm hungry for more.

He kisses me, and I moan at the taste of myself on his tongue. But he takes it away from me as he lifts to his knees, pulling my legs onto his shoulders. We both look between us, his cock thick and hard and already leaking precum onto me as he rubs his head along my sensitive clit.

"Please," I beg, needing him inside me, needing him to tell me with his body that we're going to be okay. That he believes I am strong enough to be what he needs by his side.

He's my king. I'm his queen.

Whatever that means, whatever it takes, I'll learn, not because I want to please him but because I want to. For me. For us.

His gaze meets mine, like he wants to watch my face as he enters me, his eyes burning with unspoken soulful release, and he slams balls-deep into me in one stroke, driving my breath out of me in one sharp, glorious explosion.

"Yes!" I cry, fighting to keep my eyes open, wanting to see him too as my walls quiver around him, teetering on edge again from the way he stretches me. It's an overload, from tonight's dance, to the terror of the parking lot, to the conversations here in Dom's house. And now this. I'm in need of release, again and again, and Dom knows it.

He pounds into me, giving me no mercy. But I neither want nor need it. I simply need *him*, however he comes to me.

He leans forward, bending me in half easily, thanks to my flexibility, and grabs my hands, holding them to the bed with our fingers interlaced. His hips piston against my ass as he fills me and retreats, pulling all the way out and leaving me desperately empty and wanting his next stroke. He thrusts in deeply, taking me over and over until everything from before, everything outside this moment is washed away in our passion. And it is just us. Now.

We are reborn, exposed and vulnerable, with no secrets from one another, just the way it should be. "I love you, Dominick Angeline."

I say his full name intentionally, communicating as best I can that I accept him, all of him, just as he is. Not the monster, not the man, but both and everything in between.

He hears me and roars, the orgasm crashing through him at my words, and he rides me hard as he fills me with his hot cum, sending me off on another wave of bliss too. It's huge, powerful and monstrous, and that's just what I want. It's what I need.

As the tremors slow for both of us, he lets go of my hands and lowers my legs to the bed before lying on top of me, his legs splayed enough to not crush me, but instead, he's a warm, large, powerful security blanket. One with soulful eyes that search my face and hands that brush a lock of hair away to make sure there's nothing between us.

"Allie, are you sure? I can't let you go, but that doesn't mean you have to accept me."

I notice he hasn't said it back, but I know why. He's trying to raise his shields, to prevent himself from being hurt, but I know he loves me. Looking up into the scruffy face, the steel eyes, the face of my king, I know what he needs. He needs *my* strength, and in that sharing of our strength, we're more than the sum of our individual abilities.

So I give it to him, unconditionally. "I love you, Dominick. Yeah, there are some things we'll have to talk about and some fights we're probably going to have—fair warning, I fight dirty—but I'll let you in on a little secret . . ."

He lifts his eyebrows, waiting, and I can't help but grin. "My secret plan to always get my way is to annoy the fuck out of you until you give in." I smile like it's a genius idea. It actually really is. He just doesn't realize how annoying I can be when I put my mind to it.

He smirks. "Ah, but if you misbehave, you already know there will be consequences."

He says it like he's already imagining some dirty punishments he could mete out, and though I have a quick mental flash of blood blooming on Tony's forehead as the punishment he received, I willfully choose to let that go, knowing that though Dom might be a dangerous man, he would move heaven and earth for me and would never hurt me.

I tap his nose. "Silly man. If I like it, is it really a punishment? It's a win-win for me either way. I get my way, or I get a good punishment that'll leave us both sweaty and satisfied. And I'm betting that I could get you to agree to just about anything if I pouted enough or had you gag-deep in my throat. Or maybe . . . well, there are things I could tease you with that *nobody's* had before."

He swallows, then laughs fully at my sexy tease, and it's like beautiful music to my soul. I want to record it and dance around to the sound of his chest-rumbling baritone.

I smile, just taking it in.

He smiles too, but when it's over, he sighs, sounding a little sad. "I don't remember the last time I laughed that hard. You bring out good things in me, woman. Though they may be few and far between and buried beneath layers of mud and muck in my soul."

I smile big enough for the both of us. "I'll find them, but you only get to share them with me. I'm a greedy, possessive girl like that."

His face is serious. "And I'm an obsessive, overprotective asshole. But I love you, Allison Bancroft."

And finally, the dark question in my core dissolves.

CHAPTER

Twenty-Seven

DOMINICK

SHE SLEEPS PEACEFULLY, and I dread waking her, but know it's inevitable. We made our peace last night, but there are still landmines to traverse that could blow the whole accord to smithereens.

But I need to know. I need to make sure she understands what I'm giving her, what I'm offering, and that I want to take those steps to have her fully at my side without a barrier between us.

So I'm ripping my mask the rest of the way off, exposing it all to see if she truly wants no secrets between us. To see if she truly wants me.

Placing my hand on her shoulder, I shake her gently, my voice soft but firm. "Allison."

She stirs but moans softly before wiggling in place and drifting back into sleep. I set the hot cup of coffee I've prepared for her on the nightstand and run a hand through her hair, rubbing my fingertip along the curve of her earlobe where I know she's slightly ticklish.

"Wake up, Allie."

She does so in stages, almost putting on a show with it as her long legs stretch under the blankets and she twists her body this way and that before her arms stretch overhead, almost in a caricature of wakefulness. Finally, her eyes open and a smile breaks across her face.

"Rule one. If you're waking me up, there'd better be coffee or sex involved."

I can't stop the curl of my lips, and I have to tease back. "Do you have a preference?"

She looks me up and down, eyes tracing the tattoos on my broad chest and down to where my hips disappear into my sweatpants. Her gaze leaves a trail of heat in its wake, and I suddenly feel a small dose of what she must experience when she performs, that sexy sway of power I hold knowing she wants me.

I play with her, picking up the coffee mug and taking a sip of the bitter roast, moaning softly as the hot liquid rolls down my throat. As soon as the cup's clear of my mouth, she lurches for me, sheets falling to her waist and giving me quite the morning view.

"Gimme! That's my coffee."

I'm tempted to pull it back until her body is pressed against me and I get a moment of bliss from feeling her breasts pressed against my skin, but I relent, handing it to her carefully. She takes it with a smile, her eyes closing, and a moan works its way free as she takes a sip.

"Not sure how I feel about being second-string to your daily dose of caffeine."

She shrugs and winks. "Well, at least now you know how to bribe me." She rises to her knees, wiggling her hips again. "Coffee, dick, or both."

She takes another sip but raises a pointed brow as she notices that her little dance has certainly woken up another part of my body, smirking as she sees my cock thickening unrestrained, tenting against my pants.

"While I would love nothing more than to bury any part of me I could inside anything you'd let me have access to, I think we might have some pressing matters to attend to."

She wrinkles her nose, setting the cup aside. "Ew, Dominick. I mean, it's bad enough you're hitting me up with the 'we need to talk' speech right after we wake up, but do you have to make it sound like a business meeting? I tell you what, why don't you go get the chessboard? I think you promised me a game of strip chess with some dirty side-bets. We can talk while we play."

I think she's fucking brilliant, coming up with a distraction to get us through what is bound to be an awkward conversation, though the memory of the fight after we'd initially made that plan stings.

"Don't move," I order her, and go get my board from my office, carefully carrying it back. I set it on the bed and climb in across from her. She sits on top of the blankets now, wearing only my T-shirt.

"Seems like the strip part of these bets will be over rather quickly," I say as I look her over, noting silently that I only have a pair of sweatpants on myself. "Hope you have some valuable bets to make."

Her look is pure seduction, and she rolls her shoulders back, showing exactly what she can distract me with if she wants to.

"You know I do."

We set up the pieces and I let her go first. We play a couple of moves each, both of us moving our pawns but making no real progress. I'm not really trying to push her, and besides, neither of us is truly focused on the game. It's just busy work for our hands.

Allie breaks first. "So last night was fucking awful. How often is it . . . that?"

Right to the point, no beating around the bush from her, which I appreciate.

"I feel like the answer to that question might be bigger than you think," I reply as I counter her move, placing a pawn in a position where either she takes it and I take her bishop with my rook, or she retreats. "You're asking for complete honesty, which I will give you. This house, this room, can be a place for that. If you want it."

She nods, as I knew she would, and pulls her bishop back. Even if she doubts her ability to accept my world, she wants all the information to make that call.

"Go ahead."

"I run a tight ship in East Robinsville," I reply, taking my time as I ponder my next move, "and everything dark passes through only on my approval after the transporter pays a percentage to the family. I do my best to keep the city as safe as possible. That means controlling the influx of drugs, weapons, and people."

Allie looks at me sharply. "You said you don't traffic people."

"I don't, nor do I allow it," I clarify for her. "But by giving my disapproval, I must then enforce that ruling. Like last night. My life is not like some made-for-TV movie, full of drama and shootouts. Most days are boring, checking in with businesses, meeting with Captains and Lieutenants, and monitoring all the moving parts that make East Robinsville what it is. Having said that, there is danger, real threats to me and to you. Those who are not in power always imagine it is some glorious feeling of control, like an ultimate ego boost, and they'll do anything to experience it, not realizing that it is more like . . ."

I pause, searching my mind for the right words, and finally land on a funny phrasing I heard recently.

"It's like trying to herd kittens, but they're tiger kittens, not housecats. They will scratch and bite the hand that feeds them merely to be difficult because they do not know any better."

She laughs at my explanation and makes her next move. "That sounds oddly accurate. But if it's so hard, such a heavy responsibility, why do it? Why not let someone else do it or let everyone do their own thing?"

I move a pawn forward, sacrificing it but not mentioning that I should remove my pants, letting the bets go for now in favor of the raw nakedness of our souls.

"An anarchist, are you?" I ask with a smirk. She shakes her head and I continue. "I will not let my city fall into the hands of someone who would ruin it with their narcissistic need for power. It is mine by birthright, but it remains mine because I am willing to do whatever is necessary for it, not for me."

She runs a red fingertip along her King piece, my words turning in her head. "I think I can understand that. You couch it in pretty words like you always do, but every kingdom has war, insurgents, and instabilities. I need to know, though, Dominick. If I'm going to do this with you, I will not be set aside like some pretty woman without a brain in her head, kept in the dark as you do shady or dangerous things. Look at this board. A player who hides their Queen away is going to lose every game."

"True, but real life isn't chess."

Allie smirks, trying a different route. "You'll have to tell me everything, all of it, even the parts you know I won't like. One, because I won't stand for it any other way, and two, because I think you need that. Somewhere you can filter all the ugliness, a soft place to land, someone who doesn't give a shit about the city but cares for you. Let me be that for you?"

I look at her in surprise, sitting up to my knees to lean over the board and kiss her. She leans into me, our kiss warm, smoldering, but not naughty . . . yet.

I whisper against her lips, letting her taste the truth. "You already are."

She smacks her lips against mine and pulls back slightly. I watch as the smile grows from a small hint to a wide, full exuberance. She's happy, and I marvel that I can be the cause of that for her, something I rarely give to anyone, but she seems to take it from me easily.

I can see she's aroused too, but when my eyes flicker down to her stiffening nipples, she holds up a hand. "Whoa, cowboy. We're not done with Serious Talk. But remind me to return to that."

She winks at me, but a moment later, the roller coaster of emotion drops in freefall and her face is washed in a sense of sadness as doubt takes her.

"I'm scared, Dominick. Seeing what happened last night, I don't know if I can really be the right woman for all *that* out there." She waves a hand at the window, indicating the city outside. "But I'm damn sure I can be the one for you, if you'll let me."

I can see her demons chasing her, whispering in her ear that she's weak, not good enough, can't handle this, but I am fierce enough to fight her demons. More importantly, though, she can fight them herself and has done so many times over, beating them into a box in her mind. I just need to be the backup sometimes, give her the right words to remind her. She's the true Rocky Balboa. I'm just Mick, though thankfully, younger and better-looking.

"Allison, I know you are strong enough. Last night was the deep end, and you got tossed in without warning to a near worst-case scenario with it being your family, but I can be your water wings until you're comfortable swimming. Because yes, I'd appreciate your opinion, your insight, and your tendency to make things a little chaotic. We balance each other, I think." I take her hands in mine, vowing, "You are the only one I would want to be by my side, here or anywhere. You're mine, Allison. Before you even knew it, you were mine. And before you'd even asked for it, you had my heart. And it is the same today as it will be tomorrow."

Allie takes a deep breath, and I hope she's letting the promise of my words fill her, leaving no room for doubts. Finally, she lets the air out slowly through her nose and looks me squarely in the eyes.

"So that means trackers, guards, and all that again? Cameras?"

Part of me feels like things have come full-circle, and we're right back where we were weeks ago. Even as readily as she seems to have accepted the ugly parts of my role as The Boss and the cold machinations I'm known for, I'm hesitant to subject her to the constant watchfulness again.

But it simply can't be any other way.

"Yes, though we can ensure full transparency. You'll know everything. I need that from you or I'll go mad with worry, Allie. But," I say, holding up a hand before she can object, "I offer something in return."

"What's that?" she asks, tapping her fingers together.

"Reciprocation. If you ask, I will tell you. If it is something I do not think you'd wish to hear, I will warn you. But if you insist, I will tell you. You will be the only person in the world with such access to my whereabouts, but more importantly, to my body, my heart, and my mind."

She moves a pawn on the board, stalling, and my heart ceases beating as I wait for her verdict. Finally, she looks at me, steady and sure. "I can do that."

It feels like a negotiation, but she's giving me everything, and I'm more than happy to take all of her, hoard it for myself if I can, and then yearn for more. I'm greedy, I know that.

She bites her lip and then I see it.

She's set me up. Somehow, someway, she had already reached that determination in her mind. She might have been willing to fight me for my giving in on my transparency, but she had made up her mind sometime during the night, maybe in her sleep, that she was mine.

I'm not mad. If anything, it just proves to me just how special Allie is. She's going to keep me on my toes, keep my mind sharp and my heart full.

But there is something more.

"Dom?"

I give her my full attention, the chessboard all but forgotten as we move to the endgame of the real contest we've been having over this bed.

"When Robbie said you were sending stuff to his Old Lady, you called his family interesting. What did you mean?"

The tension in her shoulders seems heavy compared to the question, and I analyze it, looking for hidden subtext or something she would deem important because she doesn't seem the least bit jealous. She's . . . curious.

"As part of Zallow entering my territory without clearing it with me, I went to his house," I explain carefully. "I met Myra, his woman, and their daughter, Violet. They're a good match. He is a rough man and has seen and done awful things, and though Myra is small, she is strong enough to be there for him. In return, he worships the ground she walks on. After he and I smoothed over our differences, I sent them a few baby goods as congratulations, to make their life easier. I take it that he didn't appreciate the gift as much as I'd hoped."

I grin, knowing that he had appreciated them in his own way, but he's a prideful man who wants to provide for his child himself, something I can respect.

Judging by the way Allie has moved from biting to full-on chewing her bottom lip, there's still something bothering her. I reach out, placing my hand on my King and tilting it over, surrendering to her.

"Just ask it, Allie. No secrets."

"Do you want kids?" she blurts without hesitation. "I mean—"

Though I know she is on birth control, my first illogical thought is that she's pregnant and my heart soars. "Are you . . . ?" I say, eyes jumping to her belly.

She places her hands there, blocking my sight, gasping. "Oh! No! I just mean . . . ever?"

I beat back the swarm of butterflies that had taken flight at her words, knowing that they will have their time, but it is not yet. Instead, I reach across the board and lay my hands on top of hers.

"Allison, it would be my pleasure to see your belly swell with our child, to hold a baby created from our love."

Her eyes tear even as her lips smile. "Really? But how? With all this?"

I shrug. "My childhood was seemingly normal, with private schools, bodyguards, reading, and chess games with my father."

Allie bursts out laughing. "None of that is normal, you goofball. Not by a mile. But I guess it can be done. Part of me was just worried that you didn't want that."

Her words get quieter, and I can feel that this is the root of her worries, the thing that has held her back.

"Why would you think that, Allison?" I ask gently. "Do you want children?"

She nods, and my heart leaps in my chest. "I do. Not now, but I really do want that husband, wife, two-point-five kids and a dog family. But I want it with you, so maybe we'll have to make it a guard dog and the kids can call the bodyguard Uncle Joe?"

She looks at me hopefully. And I know in this moment that I will do anything this woman wants me to.

"I think that's reasonable."

Her smile emerges from the depths of her soul, so bright that it dazzles the sun as she beams, just freed from darkness. We can do this. She is willing to stand at my side, perhaps not in spite of what I am but because of it.

She finds romance in my obsession, beauty in my icy heart, and worthiness in my dirty soul. With a small smile, I pluck her Queen and place it next to my now upright King in the middle of the board.

"It seems we have a winner."

Allie nods, biting her lip. "I'm not sure, but I think that was an illegal move there."

"You get used to those with me," I deadpan. "Now take that shirt off and lie down. I think that ass needs a good spanking."

She laughs and flips over, sending the other pieces of the set tumbling off the board and onto the comforter.

"Sounds to me like *I'm* the winner."

In moments, my shirt she's wearing goes flying across the room to land haphazardly on a chair and her ass wiggles in the air before me. I take the time to set the chess pieces aside, mostly because I don't want a piece of marble to roll underneath my knee in the middle of our passion but also in deference to the sentimental value of my father's chessboard.

He taught me so much in those hours on either side of the board. Patience, strategy, sacrifice.

And I think I'll need every one of those lessons with my Allison.

Twenty~Eight

ALLIE

A few months later . . .

"AND STEP, two, three, and lift. Let the spin build, extend your leg, and then your arms," I say, coaching the class through a basic move on the pole.

The women beam, proud of themselves, feeling powerful in their bodies. And they should be. They're amazing. Clapping, I give them a celebratory yell, embracing the woohoo girl inside me for a moment.

"Yes! And land it, dropping that booty to your heels, open your knees wide into a Hello Kitty, and close that peekaboo tease. Lead up with your ass, letting your head stay low . . . and pow!"

The ladies scissor their knees *Single Ladies* style and then drag their hands up their thighs to finish in their closing poses. If their men were here, there'd be some babies getting made tonight.

Excited, I run around the room in my heels, high-fiving each woman as they break pose and the room goes bubbly and giggly with laughter.

"Great job, everyone! Beautiful and fierce!"

I can see the praise warming their spirits, but more importantly, they're feeling it from within, having been transformed from busy women rushing around, focusing on everyone else, into goddesses, unlocking their own inner sexy.

Their faces remind me again why I have the best job ever. My mission is literally to make women feel good about themselves and love the body they have, and I'm rewarded every time I see someone go from tentative newbie to stomping pole queen over the course of a few classes.

As everyone waves goodbye, I do my daily cleanup, running a cleansing towel up and down each pole. Tomorrow, I'll use my 'pole polisher,' as Donna laughingly calls it, which makes sure every inch of brass remains gleaming.

I'm just finishing up when I hear a soft knock on the doorframe, and Donna asks, "Good class?"

"Yeah, great one!" I reply, tossing my cleaning rag behind my back and catching it.

Donna hums. "Well, receipts look great, and we're getting enough interest that you might need to open another class."

I've considered it because my pole classes, private lessons, and Diva Dance classes are almost always fully booked, so there's definitely a demand for it. But between those, the private bachelorette parties, ballet classes, and the once-a-month feature at Petals, I'm doing everything I can.

Although some of that dancing isn't *just* for me. Dominick has been putting my body to work every morning and night, and while I love it, something's got to give. I don't want it to be my body, so I'm carefully weighing each commitment before signing on.

I finally respond, "I'm going to leave my schedule as it is so I have time to practice for myself. I need that too."

Donna nods, her smile one of motherly approval. Before she can say anything, Eileen sticks her head in, grinning lewdly.

"Hey, Allie, your chunka escort is here for the night."

I grin, knowing that she's taken to giving Logan a good-natured hard time about his weight. He's simultaneously bulking up and leaning out, something about weight classes. I don't understand the reasoning behind it, but he can go on for hours on end about his macros.

Luckily, I don't understand a word, or I would've had to tell him to shut up about it, and I don't want to do that because I like Logan and our guard-slash-friend relationship. Though I have years under my belt with healthy eating, one of the key components of lifelong recovery is to not overanalyze and focus on what I put in my mouth, which is basically what he's doing in a healthy way. Making healthy choices and *not* obsessing is how I know I'm doing well.

And I am doing very well.

A couple of feature appearances at Petals paid off what was left of my medical bills, and with the classes doing so well and my partnership with Donna, I'm truly a successful businesswoman. I've even drawn up a tentative five-year plan to buy in with Donna on the ballet side of the business and be full co-owners. She's told me that she'd like to retire one day, maybe travel and see all the top ballet company performances, and that she'd be honored to metaphorically hand her pointe shoes to me. One day, that'd be a great honor.

For now, though, I'm happy.

"Thanks, Eileen! I'll see you tomorrow. Remind Sydney to stretch her feet tonight. She's this close to pointe." I hold up my finger and thumb an inch apart.

"Trust me, I know," Eileen says with a laugh. "It's all she talks about, and I won't have to remind her to stretch. I'll have to tell her to stop stretching. I've had to resist telling her that there are much more disappointing 'few inches' she'll have to deal with later."

I laugh, loving that Sydney is so dedicated but also that Eileen doesn't let her go too far and still wants her to be a kid. Picking up my practice heels, I change out, laying them carefully into my duffel bag and pulling on sweats and Nikes.

"Hey Logan, how was your practice today?" I ask as I enter the lobby. He's grinning, his hair still wet from his shower after MMA practice and wearing a fresh set of athletic clothes.

Honestly, workout stuff is almost all I ever see him in now. He's stepped back from doing shift work at Petals, focusing on an upcoming fight. He laid out his normal training day for me, up at five in the morning and down by nine thirty, and I'll admit, he's got dedication.

He's thanked me and Dom for the shift in his duties, which mostly consist of escorting me from home to Encore and back again, with a midday gap where we run errands.

I think it's a routine that works well for both of us.

"Feeling good," Logan says, sipping at some nuclear green drink that supposedly has a bunch of protein. "How was your class?"

"Excellent," I reply, adjusting my bag. "I even met someone I think you'd be interested in."

It's a common tease between us. I don't understand why he's single when he's such a kind-hearted badass. But like always, he shakes his head.

"Nope. No matchmaking here. I've got an evil, cold-hearted mistress already . . . the ring. It's all I have time for right now. If you're itching to play matchmaker, work on Max or Dalton."

He throws them under the bus easily, my mind already scheming. Now that I'm in love, I guess I want to share the happiness and let everyone experience the joy. Admittedly, my relationship with Dom might not be most folks' ideal, but it works for us.

Even TJ is slowly coming around, now that his divorce is final and he's let go of most of the bitterness, starting to realize that he's going to be okay. I think it's that he is truly enjoying his new life, though it's different than he pictured. His new job is awesome, and he made some good friends immediately with the guys he flies with. He's got something new to focus on and it's good for him.

I do think he still wishes I had an easy, Hallmark movie-type love story, but he'll at least sit down to dinner with Dominick and me now. He even jokes around a bit, once telling Dom that if he's in charge of the city, could he please do something about the potholes on 8th Street? So he accepts the situation somewhat, but at the same time, he hugs me goodbye every time we see each other and offers to whisk me away anytime I'm ready. It's a tricky balance but a tightrope we're walking together.

It'll take time, but we'll get there.

We have to, because I love them both, and they both love me.

"So," Logan says, interrupting my thoughts. "The usual tonight?"

"Yeah, I want to rinse off and then head home."

'Home' is, of course, Dominick's house. Well, *our* house. It took us about two seconds to agree to move in together after we completed a very vigorous, very angst-filled, very sweaty, and very *complete* weekend of negotiations. We kept my third- and his fourth-floor apartments as safehouses, but I moved all my things into the apartment across the parking lot from the studio.

It's been a godsend to be able to have a place this close to work when I need to clean up before going home.

We walk across the lot in silence as I let Logan work, his eyes diligently scanning though there has never been a single threat toward me. Only once was there even a hint of something wrong, but it turned out to be a back-firing pickup truck. It was good to know that Logan's not all for show, though, because he'd had me on the ground and covered to make sure I stayed safe in an instant. Once we'd realized it was safe, I'd jokingly started counting and called it a TKO. I'd declared him the winner and did a fairly decent imitation of a cheerleader right there in the parking lot, much to his chagrin.

At the top of the stairs, Logan stops, glancing at the phone buzzing in his hand. "Hey, I need to make a couple of calls. You okay if I stay in the hall while you do your thing?"

"Everything okay?" I ask, worried.

He smiles, something dancing in his eyes. "Yeah, nothing to worry about. Just gonna wait out here."

He sits down in a chair and shoos me down the hall where I let myself in. The door closes behind me and I feel the chill in the air instantly. Every light is off except for one, a spotlight over the pole I had installed in the dining room here.

Dominick had laughingly asked me if I even knew what dining rooms were for, and I'd felt like it was an accomplishment to be able to joke like that after my love-hate history with food.

I'm still working on getting one put in at home, mostly because all the ceilings are so damn tall, but for now, the light shining on this shiny pole calls to me. I can feel his presence, know he's sitting in the shadows of the living room, can smell the faint hint of his favorite scotch.

And though I'm not in our house, I am home. With him. Wherever he is, that's where I want to be. We've found our own routine as well, learning how to click our seemingly odd puzzle shapes together, softening here, growing there until it's a seamless fit. He laughs at my crazy impulsiveness and smiles at my messes. I take delight in his detailed plans and perfectly-arranged sock drawer, though I did buy him some checkerboard ones emblazoned with chess pieces and a bright font proclaiming, *Don't Fuck with the King!* He's even worn them . . . around the house. Baby steps, I guess, but I'm determined to get him to do a little hip-wiggling strip-tease for me and get down to nothing but those socks. Hashtag-dream it and make it happen!

But for now, it seems like it's my turn to put on a show, even if I don't have any cool or even sexy socks. Silently, I set my bag down, kicking off my Nikes and sweats, slipping my heels back on, and stand tall. At the last minute, I pull my tank over my head too. In my sports bra and yoga shorts, I approach the pole, smiling to myself as the music begins.

The song he chooses isn't a song I have choreography to, it's just a slow-driving bass line that resonates through my body. There aren't any words even, just the throb and the music, and so I dance for him. I dance for *me*. Swaying my hips and tracing my curves, I work my way up to spinning around the pole. I don't do the fancy death-defying tricks, the showy moves meant to shock the audience into tipping more.

This isn't about that. Instead, I seduce him, my eyes boring into the darkness, willing him to see me, to watch me. And though I can't see him, I can feel the heat of his gaze on my skin, can almost taste his need in the air around me.

I need more, need him.

I take slow steps toward the mirrored wall, pulling my sports bra over my head and freeing everything for him. In the reflection, I watch myself palm my breasts, their fullness almost painful.

In the darkness, I can see a shadow move, and he's on his feet silently, slowly moving closer. I push my shorts down, stepping out of them too, to stand in only my heels as he becomes visible in the light, his dress slacks perfect and his white dress shirt already halfway unbuttoned.

His heat licks at my skin as he presses himself to my back, one arm slipped around my waist and the other at my throat, turning my head to meet his eyes.

"I've dismissed Logan for the night. You have a new escort home."

I can see the darkness in their icy depths, can read that he wants me rough tonight, and I gratefully oblige, pressing my hips back into his hardness. I never know exactly what I will get with him. Sometimes slow and sweet, taking hours to worship every inch of me, letting me 'boss' him around. Other times, he's a beast, rough and hard, brutally using my body in ways I never knew I'd love.

But always, he's in control.

Even when I tempt him too much, begging him to lose control, he never falters, his control absolute. Always. It's become the stabilizing foundation for my chaotic ways, the cage for the black swan I can be, and the freedom for the woman I never knew I could be.

His coarse growl into my ear sends shivers down my spine. "Mine."

I nod, the movement putting the slightest bit of pressure on my neck where his hand lies. "Yours."

His hand releases my waist, and I hear the slip of the leather as he undoes his belt and slacks. I push back, knowing what's coming and loving it. After all, this is the secret reason I bought these heels. They're just the right height.

I whimper as his cock pushes into me, filling me and completing that connection we always need with one another. I look back in the mirror, watching the ecstasy on his face that leaves my heart filled with warmth, even as my pussy throbs with another type of welcome heat.

Dom uses his body to press me against the glass, my nipples hardening at the cold even as I buck back to take him deeper. Gripping my hips, he holds me steady as he starts viciously pounding my tight pussy, sending shockwaves up my spine almost in beat with the music that's still playing. Cries pour from my mouth like I'm singing, adding my own creative lyrics, but it is just his name over and over against the throbbing bass and electric strings.

"Look in the mirror, Allison," Dominick grunts, pulling me back enough to actually see. "Watch me claim your pussy, mark it as mine. Watch . . . us."

I do as he says, enjoying the way the spotlight creates shadows and high-lights along our skin, the way his muscles flex and my ass jiggles with every stroke. My eyes are drawn to the shaded spot where he disappears inside me, anticipation building, amplifying the feeling of him filling me.

Still, I'm drawn upward, until my eyes meet his and that's all I need. I see the love there, raw and vulnerable, and his joy that he has found it with me.

He is a monster, but he is my monster.

And I love him.

His cock swells, impossibly harder inside me a moment before he comes, and his pleasure triggers my own, a sharp cracking sound filling my ears as I scream his name. He pumps his cum deep inside me making my pussy spasm, milking everything from him hungrily.

As our breathing returns to a more normal pace, he holds me tight, biting at my earlobe and then his hot breath is there as he whispers, "I love you, Allison."

There is no doubt, no question in my heart when I look to him and whisper the same words back, "I love you, Dominick."

We step back, and I realize what the cracking sound is. That last thrust accidentally made us break one of the mirror panels. "Uhm . . . seven years' bad luck?"

Dominick grins. "I make my own luck."

We both do.

Epilogue

One year

I HATE that I had to take care of some work today, knowing that she's been looking forward to our anniversary dinner. But I have something to tell her, and I'm not one for surprises.

But this one can't be avoided any longer. Pausing, I pull up her phone GPS, seeing that she's at home, and a small knot of stress loosens in my belly.

She's fine to come and go as she pleases, especially since she's quite good about staying with her guard now. So much so that I've had to find other misbehaviors to 'punish' her for, but I rather think she enjoys coming up with new, creative ways to get me to spank her ass. It's become a game for us, one we both enjoy.

Knowing she's home safe, getting ready for our date, comforts me. I don't even hesitate about opening the home security app. She knows about the cameras. Besides, the only two phones in the world with access are mine and hers.

It's become a game she plays with me from time to time. Lots of things you can do with a security camera and a naughty girl.

Scanning the camera feeds, I find her.

Perched on the bathroom counter in a sexy bra and panties set, she's applying her makeup with her hair up in curlers. I watch her, tracing the line of her body on the small screen and wishing I could do so for real.

Her mascara complete, she leans back, and I can see her contemplating something for a moment.

She glances up to the camera in the corner of the room, and I can see the smirk on her face. She knows I'm watching, can feel my eyes even when I'm not there, and will often text me just as my eyes are on her. Or sometimes, she delights in torturing me with a show that makes me race home. One of those inventive misbehaviors she's discovered because there are lots of things you can do with a security camera and a naughty bad girl.

Today, she seemingly ignores her instinct that she's being watched and picks up the towel from the counter, dropping it casually over the little plastic stick sitting there. So she finally knows. My 'surprise' is ruined.

I'm not disappointed. I have waited for her to realize it, for her to tell me.

I knew weeks ago, could taste the difference in her honey, could feel the ripeness of her breasts, and I knew she was late. It seems my anniversary surprise is a great one, the best one. Allison is mine, and our child will be mine as well.

Somehow, a monster like me found his happy ending. I've gotten my obsession. My love. My Allie. And now she is creating life where before there was nothing, the same as she did for my heart.

She looks back to the camera and gives a little two-fingered wave as she grins.

I'm instantly out of my chair and headed home to take care of what is mine.

Always.

The End. Thank you for reading!

If you enjoyed this book, want to see where they are in the future? Is it a boy or a girl? **Just go here** to get a bonus short story of Allie, Dom, and their little one, three years later!

Also, make sure to check out Dirty Deeds. Allie & Dom are secondary characters, with Allie's friend Maggie as the heroine, and Shane, one of Dom's former men, as the Hero. Read on for a preview!

Extended Epilogue

ALLIE

THE LATE SPRING sun is warm on my shoulders, and I know I shouldn't be just lounging on a bench like this, but it feels too good not to. After a mild winter, East Robinsville got hit with a St. Patrick's Week cold snap that had me under enough layers to make feel like I was turning into a snowgirl.

So when I woke up this morning and the sun was out, I felt the light soaking into my soul and I just couldn't help running to the park. Literally, actually, as my jogging top and leggings got a workout that they haven't since I bought them.

I'm not much of a jogger, I tend to 'prance' too much as I run. But it feels good to stretch out, arching my shoulders and posing a little, my arms planted behind me, my chest opening up to the sky.

Feeling just a little naughty, I bring my legs up, knowing I probably look like the infamous girl on a million truckers' mudflaps but I'm only thinking of one man in particular. It's been awhile since I put on a private show for Dom... maybe-

"Mommy! Mommy! Look! Whee!"

My eyes snap open, and while I know it's only a two foot slide down a pole to a padded playground surface, my heart drops into my stomach as my now three year old daughter Isabella wraps her little legs around the metal and throws her arms out wide, using just her thighs to control her descent. She's having fun, but I can't help but worry she's a hair's breadth from tumbling headfirst into the ground and breaking her neck.

Nothing has taught me the power of some of my moves more than watching Isabella do little kid versions of them. Before I can even open my mouth though she's safely on the ground, running towards me.

"You see?!" she exclaims.

"I saw," I reply, but Isabella ignores me to run past the bench to go pelting into Logan, who's looking like the world's most badass jogging buddy in his Under Armor shirt, long shorts, and pushing my jogging stroller in front of him. Normally I'd be the one pushing it to take Bella out on excursions like this, but he said that after his latest win, he's had enough 'detraining' and is ready to start getting back into fight shape. Not too sure what that is, the man looks like he can't get into any better shape if you ask me.

"Uncle Logan, you saw?" Bella demands, grabbing his leg and not letting go until he answers. "I did the Fairy Spiral!"

"You sure did, Chipmunk," Logan says, sweeping her up into a hug. "You did great. I'm gonna let you down now though, you're getting so big!"

"But Uncle Logan, I barely come up to your knee! And you wrestle biiiiig guys!" She puts her hand up as high as she can.

Logan just smiles and sits her down. "And you're sprouting up bigger every day. Say, how about the swings? Go get started and I'll be there in a minute," Logan offers, and Bella giggles, tousling his hair before he sets her down and she goes sprinting for the playset again.

Logan comes over, reaching into the stroller bag and taking out a bottle of water for me and raising an eyebrow. "How does she know?"

I shrug, smiling. "After you spent three weeks not coming around while you were training, she just had to know what her favorite Uncle Logan was up to, and why he couldn't be there for her half birthday party. And no, don't get me started. As you know, she can be quite . . . strong-willed."

"That she is," Logan says, sitting down on the bench and taking out another bottle. "Takes after her mother."

I laugh, touched. Logan's still my bodyguard, but I'd say he's more Isabella's bodyguard than mine.

His protective instincts are so strong. The first time Baby Bella grabbed onto his finger with a chubby little fist and smiled up at him with the puffy baby cheeks that's earned her his nickname of Chipmunk, I swear his heart melted. He's loved her as intensely as if she were his own ever since, and while certain politics have meant that he's not officially her godfather... he's Uncle Logan, which is all that counts.

Still, he's always professional about certain things. It's more than a job for him I think, he does it to honor both Isabella, myself, and Dom. It's the only 'duty' he still does for Dominick, unless you count the money Dom has made betting on Logan's fights.

Thinking of his latest fight, I glance out of the side of my eye at him. "So how's the ring card girl? What's her name... Brittany?"

Logan snorts, shaking his head. "Sorry Allie, that's not me. Besides, I've got a girl. She's over there on the teeter totter, and likes talking about that new She-Ra remake."

"Come on Logan," I tease, knowing my obsession with him finding a woman good enough for him is a little weird, but he's almost like a second brother to me. And now that I've found happiness, I want to spread it around. And Logan's just too good a guy for him to keep playing the single game. "Bella's three. It's not like she's going to get upset and kick your ass if you have an actual girlfriend."

Logan chuckles, shaking his head. "You want to bet? Bella might get her hair and daredevil attitude from her mother, but her... possessiveness? That's pure Dominick there. I get a girlfriend, and Bella's going to be paying me a visit along with her friends Louisville and Slugger, and there goes my fight career."

I laugh, Logan's so funny at times.

Logan nods, and stretches out his calf. "Seriously though. Not my type."

I hum, a skill I've picked up from Dom, watching my daughter tire of the teeter totter. She goes over to another child, and they strike up that sort of easy instant friendship that three year olds seem to find better than adults ever do.

Isabella and her new friend get up and run over to the swings, but before they can get there Bella trips and falls, bumping her elbows on the ground. I'm up, but before I can even get halfway there, Bella's favorite superhero in a custom-fit black suit appears out of nowhere, scooping her up even before she can cry.

"Daddy!"

Dominick hugs her, kissing her elbows one after another as she holds them up, making her giggle. Setting her down, he smiles as she runs off, turning towards us.

"How was the run?" he asks me.

"You should have joined us on more than just a cell phone tracker," I tease, hugging him. "How's work?"

"Good... although there are a few things I'd like to talk over with you if you don't mind," Dom says. "Logan, would you mind taking the stroller back to the house?"

"Of course sir," Logan says. "By the way, I've got a new kid down at the gym who's been working hard. Looking to make his pro debut soon."

"Oh really?" Dominick asks. "It wouldn't happen to be that lightweight that I saw at the amateur championships, would it?"

"Same kid. We've been working hard, he's ready for the prime time. Think I could interest you in tickets? Undercard, but still."

Dom nods and Logan nods back, turning to me and waving. "See you tomorrow, Allie."

"Eight AM, Logan," I confirm. "I've got to get down to the studio for my own workout, can't let this mommy weight stick!"

I turn to Dom, who's smirking. "What?"

"I happen to think motherhood looks amazing on my wife," Dominick growls, pulling me close and kissing me tenderly. "Any curves you've added just make you even more beautiful."

I laugh, patting his chest. "Down boy. There's children present."

Speaking of children, before we can continue Bella comes running up, grinning. "Daddy, I want to ride the swings!"

"Come oooon, Daddy," Bella says, grabbing her father's hand and dragging him towards her target. Dom looks back at me with that look of genuine enamored helplessness that our daughter pulls of out everyone around her. Yeah, he might still be East Robinsville's Boss… but we both know who the *real* Boss is around here, and her favorite color's pink.

As we push Isabella, in between commands of 'Higher!' and 'Too High!' we talk.

"So things are going well?" I ask.

Dom nods, smiling. "As well as can be expected. There is a situation I'd like your opinion on."

It's probably the greatest gift that he's ever given me. I've dealt with the constraints on our lives, to the point that it's almost second nature. Vacation plans involve a lot more than buying plane tickets, going out to dinner means we have to limit ourselves. I shop only at certain stores, and if I want to do something that's outside of the routine, I need to clear it with Dom, who'll have Logan or one of the other men he trusts go check it out.

But it's never been a big deal. I rarely have to wait. And ordering from Amazon through the dance studio isn't a problem, it's actually a convenient way to keep birthday gifts hidden from a little girl who loves sticking her nose into *everything*.

And I've adopted it all. In return, Dom's let me in more, as much as I want. Transparency, and as I've learned more, he's come to trust my judgement. One day, he started asking my advice, saying that I understand 'soft power' better than he does. It's stuck for both of us.

I wouldn't say I'm a *mafiosa*, but I know things.

"What's going on?" I ask, taking a turn pushing Isabella while Dom collects his thoughts.

"We've been invited to a wedding," Dom says, "and the families involved are… like ours."

"Is that so? What's the issue?"

"The issue is… the groom's father is an ally, a good friend in the business sense," Dom says. "The bride however is from a family that we have had tensions with. I would like to take advantage of this event to gain an ally."

"That's easy. We go, we enjoy ourselves, and we wish the bride and groom a happy marriage."

Dom nods. "Yes. That, of course. But it is the idea of a wedding gift that I could use your help."

It's a good question, and one that I can understand. If Dom goes too inexpensive, the bride's family could see it as an insult. On the other hand, if he goes too far the other way, it could be seen as a backhanded sort of compliment.

"Two things then," I say in between pushing Isabella. "First, when we get home we can sit down tonight after someone goes to bed and we can do some shopping, and you can tell me everything about both sides. Second, at the wedding, let me give the gift to the bride personally."

"Why's that?" Dom asks, and I grin.

"We can be extravagant, and err on that side, but since it came from me rather than from you, you'll have a buffer. The bride's family will see me, the bride herself will be happy another woman offered her the gift, and nobody would be able to think that you were trying to curry favor with either the family or, god forbid, with the bride herself. And if they do, the bride will be the one to set them straight."

Dom grins, liking my thinking.

"Mommy!" Isabella says, pulling my attention back to her. "I'm gonna jump!"

Dom and I are one voice in our reply. "NO!"

———

The moon's high in the sky, and I nurse the glass of red wine in my hand, relaxing as I sit out on the back porch, enjoying the night air. It's not something I would have expected, getting to enjoy evenings again. For too long, the sun going down meant I was just getting started with my day, and the nighttime was work time. Even being a ballet teacher, not too much has changed there other than my shift ends earlier, but it's not like I can give lessons at one in the afternoon.

When I learned I was pregnant, Dom and I knew there'd be adjustments, that our family life would be different from what other people have. After all, most of Dom's major work happens between the hours of eight at night and two in the morning. Even with him trying to frontload as much of his daily dealings as he can, most evenings were spent working.

But Dom's put some rules in place... and they've made life wonderful. First of all, three nights a week, is family time. Unless something's burning down, he's not to be disturbed. Instead, he reads with Isabella, helps tuck her into bed, and cuddles her to sleep before he and I have our time.

Because of some things related to his work, it's been five days since Dom's been able to do that, but tonight is family night, and sitting back, humming a little Rita Ora tune that my teen group is doing an interpretive ballet to. It's a catchy tune, although part of me's starting to wonder if I'm getting old, because I had never heard it before when the girls came in all giggly over it.

He doesn't make any attempt to hide his approach, and his feet click as he crosses the flagstones and settles onto the outdoor loveseat next to me, putting an arm around my shoulders.

"I promised our daughter that the first thing I'd tell you is that she loves you very much."

I chuckle and set my wine aside before curling up against my husband and laying my head on his shoulder. "I'll take it. Before we know it she's going to say she hates us and refuses to be seen in public with us at all."

Dominick hums. "I hope not. At least, I hope she understands that we love her."

"She will… but I have a feeling she's gonna have her rebellious period. She's an Angeline through and through."

"And a Bancroft," Dom reminds me, kissing the top of my head before adopting a falsetto. "Look Mommy, I'm going to jump!"

"I really have to ask Logan what he's letting her do when they go on playdates by themselves," I murmur, running my hand over Dom's chest. I love exploring the thick muscles there, even as I feel some new ridges. "My love, what have you been up to?"

Dom lifts an eyebrow. "Like what you feel?"

"You know I do. So what have you been doing?"

Dom hums, and gives my shoulders a squeeze. "I asked Logan to do a favor for me. That apartment near the studio… it has a complete home gym in it now."

I laugh, he's always surprising me. "You told me it was under renovation, that's why I couldn't use it for awhile!"

"I wasn't lying. Not exactly," Dom chuckles defensively. "I was having the floor reinforced and the equipment installed. I didn't tell you because you're so… you don't need it."

"Why thank you. And what's that in your left hand?"

Dom looks at the small bag in his left hand, lifting an eyebrow. "Why?"

"Because it's got a bow on top, and I can tell by the twinkle in your eye that you've got an idea in your head. What?" I ask, reaching for it. Dom pulls it away playfully, making me crawl into his lap to try and reach it, straddling him on the loveseat as he teases me back and forth before wrapping his arms around me and I stop, looking into his eyes.

"I love you," he says with that quiet intensity that thrills me to the very core. "I love you more than I can ever put into words."

I ignore his present and put my arms around his neck, looking into his face. The dim light from inside caresses his face in a softly golden light. He's so real. Every flaw, from the slight crook to his nose to the way his forehead hoods his eyebrows makes him more than handsome… he's my husband, my heart, and my life mate.

"I love you. It was fate we came together, and while that journey hasn't always been pain free, I wouldn't trade it for a fairytale princess story."

I lower my lips to his, and our kiss is soft, deep, exploring the years we've been together and finding our joining. When we part, I smile, then giggle. "So do I get my present now?"

Dom laughs, nodding, and hands me the bag. "Although I'm not sure it's a present for you, or for me."

"Is that so?" I ask, opening the bag and grinning. "A set of clothes?"

Dom shrugs, and I look inside more closely. The bra and panty set are beautiful, matched silk that doesn't have a label but is clearly high quality, every inch feels like a cloud under my fingertips. It's royal purple, and along the edge of the cups are stones that I'm afraid to ask if they're real diamonds or just Swarovski... because knowing Dom, it could be either. The lingerie is elegant, sexy, and I grin as I see the white blouse and black skirt underneath.

"Someone's got plans."

"I want you to dance for me," Dom says, reaching around and cupping my ass. "It's been too long since I've seen the most beautiful dancer in the world perform just for me."

I purse my lips, thinking. It has been a long time, and I know part of it was my own insecurities. Isabella blew up my hips and belly like a hot air balloon, and in the postpartum period there were plenty of times I had to remind myself that I was fine just as I was.

Even now, when I dance it's hard not to think of it as a workout, and to find the joy of just the movement. "You know I can't do the spinning death drop anymore."

"I don't care. Never did," Dom admits. "What makes you sexy isn't in pulling off acrobatics. It's in your heart, your soul, and in the way you can reach through the space between us and grab my heart, my soul, and yes, my balls all at once... and set all three of them on fire."

I nod, and give him a smile. "Then give me ten minutes to get ready. Don't be wearing anything too difficult to undo."

"Why's that?" Dom asks, and I grin, leaning in to kiss his ear.

"Because after this dance, I want to make love with my husband."

I get up, and as I enter the house again I hear Dominick chuckle under his breath, his words soft in the spring air. "I can't fucking wait."

About the Author

Big Fat Fake Series:
My Big Fat Fake Wedding | | My Big Fat Fake Engagement | | My Big Fat Fake Honeymoon

Standalones:
Drop Dead Gorgeous | | The Dare | | The Blind Date

Bennett Boys Ranch:
Buck Wild | | Riding Hard | | Racing Hearts

The Tannen Boys:
Rough Love | | Rough Edge | | Rough Country

Dirty Fairy Tales:
Beauty and the Billionaire | | Not So Prince Charming | | Happily Never After

www.ingramcontent.com/pod-product-compliance
Lightning Source LLC
Chambersburg PA
CBHW031227310726
48971CB00004B/915